Note from the author:

The Chronothon is part of a book series that includes *In Times Like These,* however, either book can be enjoyed independently. Some of the time travel terms and methods used in *The Chronothon* are explained more thoroughly in *In Times Like These,* but in the interest of the story, I have opted to not spend as much time on explanations in this novel. Instead, I have included a glossary located at the end of this book to aid readers whenever the twists and turns of temporal travel threaten to send brain cells into revolt. Use it at your leisure, or simply hold on and enjoy the ride. Thanks for reading.

THE CHRONOTHON

Nathan Van Coops

Skylighter
Press
St. Petersburg, Florida

"Time travel is hard. Let's get that straight first thing. If you think any part of this will be simple, you can stop now and have a safe, happy, life. Of course, if you're reading this, you're likely not content with safe."-Journal of Dr. Harold Quickly, 2037

Chapter 1

I feel very alive considering I haven't been born yet. Across the expanse of grasses and water stretching to the distant shoreline, the rumbling of rocket engines is causing the wild birds to take to the air in droves. As they stream past my perch on top of the abandoned radio tower, their cries are lost in the roar of the machine beyond them. I have a clear view of the amber glow from the Saturn V rocket. Apollo 11 is hoisting humanity's dreams toward the heavens in a historic panorama in front of me, but I can't stop looking at the girl.

This is the third day I've woken up and existed as an affront to the laws of nature. I've bent them before of course, but this is the first time I've journeyed beyond my own lifetime—what should have been my lifetime in any case—and she's the one who got me into this.

Mym's arms are draped on the lower railing while her legs swing gently as they dangle over the edge. Her chin is propped on her arms and her blue eyes are on the rocket streaming its way skyward. After a moment they narrow slightly. "You know, Ben, I may stop taking you awesome places if you aren't even going to pay attention." Her voice is scolding, but when she turns her head, her eyes are playful. She tries to hold her mouth tight in an expression of aggravation, but as I glower back at her, her cheeks start creeping upward until she's grinning uncontrollably.

My legs are crossed below me, a safe distance back from the edge of the platform. A month ago, I wouldn't have dreamed of being this high up. A lot of things have changed about me in a month. For one, I used to stay in my own time. The chronometer on my wrist changed that. Mym's dad let me keep it. I did save his life, but I don't believe that was his reason for letting me have it. I think he wanted to let me into this world of his—the world where time is no longer about straight lines, but about paths not taken, a secret world where consecutive events in your life don't have to be consecutive at all.

Last night, we caught the Beatles in their last concert at Candlestick Park. This morning, I ate my breakfast a table away from Salvador Dali at a café in Spain, and still made it here to Florida in time for the launch. Not a moment was wasted in airport security or waiting for a calendar page to turn.

Mym leans back onto her hands and watches the twisting trail of rocket smoke dissipate in the wind. She looks happy.

"Do you just wake up amazed every day?" I ask.

She tilts her gaze toward me. "Don't you?"

"I do now. This is incredible. It's like every day is your birthday, or Christmas."

"I know a guy who does that." She smiles. "He only does birthdays and holidays. I think every day should be a good day though, if you're doing it right."

"Well, this certainly makes that a lot easier." I twist the dials on my chronometer. "You get to pick out the really good days."

Mym studies me briefly then turns skyward again. "It's easier to have good days now." She closes her eyes, soaking in the sunshine. I nod, though I know she can't see me. In the excitement of our traveling the past couple of days, I sometimes forget that she spent the last few years trying to find a way to keep her father from being murdered. It hasn't been all good days. But she doesn't seem to be thinking about that now. Her face is relaxed, her skin lit by the sun. She looks young. I wonder again how old she is. *Early twenties? Does she even know?* If I hadn't spent the last quarter century with my days encapsulated in sequential boxes, if Thursday could come after Sunday or spring follow fall, would I know my age? Would I feel it somehow? Would I care?

Mym is still an enigma to me. As I watch her chest slowly rising and falling with each breath, I wonder—not for the first time—why she picked me to come with her on this adventure. She's the type of girl who doesn't seem to realize the effect she has on people. I'm the opposite. I feel like I've always known where I stand. I get a few glances from the girls, maybe not all of them, but the ones who don't mind a guy who gets his hands dirty for a living—the ones who don't run off if I occasionally let a long swim at the beach pass for a shower, or pick them up for a date on my old motorcycle. I used to know where I stood anyway until I met her—a petite, blonde time traveler with a taste for adventure. Now it's like starting over.

I let my gaze drift back to the now vacant sky. "So where's the next stop?"

THE CHRONOTHON

She opens her eyes. "Hmm. We're still in the sixties. Anything else you want to catch while you're here, or do you want to head to the seventies?"

"You're the pro at this. I'm totally at your mercy."

"Ooh. Totally?"

"Um, maybe I'm going to regret that."

"Nope. You said totally. I know exactly where I'm taking you." She swings her legs up, tucking one underneath her, and faces me.

"Oh God. That smirk on your face is scaring me. Where are we going?"

"You just dial the settings." She rifles through her messenger bag and hands me a long silver tube and a hard rubber wheel. It takes me a moment to identify the wheel without the rest of its parts, but then it dawns on me.

"We're going roller skating?"

"Better. It's roller disco!" She beams. "Degravitize that."

"Oh Lord. Disco?" I roll my eyes, but set to work with the silver degravitizer, scanning it across the roller skate wheel like Mym taught me, removing the gravitite particles inside that enabled it to follow us through time. I consider objecting to the idea, but I have to be honest with myself, I'd probably follow her anywhere.

"So where does one go to roller disco in the seventies?"

"The beginning." Mym rummages around and removes more items.

"And where is the beginning?"

"Brooklyn." She's intent on something in her hands. "I'm taking you to The Empire."

She's studying a photo of a shelf with an iron, a bowl of whisks, and a pair of purple suede roller skates on it.

"Is that at the roller rink?"

"No. We can't make it to The Empire straight from here. It's too far to jump with these chronometers. That's okay, we need to stop and pick up my skates anyway." She stands and adjusts her satchel, then sticks her hand out for the wheel. I toss it to her, and she sets it precariously on the railing. "Okay. Don't shake the tower."

I step cautiously toward her. "What's the date?"

"May 18th, 1973. 1600 Zulu."

I dial the time into my chronometer and reach for the top of the roller skate wheel. "We good on elevation?"

Mym extends a tape measure to the platform at our feet and checks the height of the railing. "Perfect."

My right hand is poised atop my chronometer, the fingertips of my chronometer hand pressed to the wheel, keeping firm contact to our anchor in real time.

"Wait. Hang on." Mym squints at the photo and then rotates the wheel 180 degrees. "We don't want to end up in the floor." She grins up at me. "Ready?"

"Ready as I'm going to be." I eye the long drop from the platform, then quickly bring my attention back to the wheel. Once we're gone, the wheel will likely tumble to the ground, but we'll be years away.

"Three . . . two . . . one . . . push."

I press the pin on the side of my chronometer and blink.

The room smells like dust and potpourri. I take my fingers off the roller skate on the shelf in front of me and eye my surroundings. Old women are picking through clothing racks and bric-a-brac as dim light filters through dingy subterranean windows. In the corner, the cash register drawer dings as it shuts. The chime blends with the muffled sounds of car horns and traffic.

"You keep your skates in a thrift store?"

"It's not easy to find purple suede skates in my size." Mym picks up the skates and holds them to her cheek. "And they have rainbow laces. You have to snatch treasure up when you find it."

"I guess so." I smile and follow her toward the counter. I almost collide with her as she stops at a rack of sunglasses and plucks a pair of men's aviators from among them. She turns and slips them on.

"What do you think?"

"Um, I think they're a little big for your face."

She considers me briefly. "I feel bad for you."

"What? Why?"

"Because you're going to have to keep looking at them. I love them." She grins and spins back toward the counter. A bell rings as the door to the basement shop opens and a gust of wind follows a middle-aged woman inside. It brings the smell of truck exhaust and hot dogs. I step toward the door and grab it before it closes. Outside, the concrete steps lead upward to a sidewalk full of foot traffic, and beyond the road, a six-story apartment building. I glance back briefly at Mym paying for her skates and then climb upward into the urban noise.

Cabs and trucks clog the street as pedestrians stream past me, a fashionable mix of wide collars and ties, plaid bellbottoms, paisley shirts, and a smattering of turtlenecks and sweater vests. I stand on the top step of the thrift store entrance and breathe in 1973 New York. Despite the exhaust and a faint odor of trash, there is a tang of salt breeze in the air and a pleasant mix of ethnic foods. After a few moments, Mym joins me. "It's great, right?"

"Sure is busy."

"Well, it's the middle of the day in Manhattan."

"Where's this place we're going skating?"

"It's in Brooklyn, but that's not for a couple of years yet. Come on, you want to grab lunch?"

"Yeah, I could eat."

"There's this little Italian place called Angelina's on Mulberry Street that has the most amazing calzones. It's a bit of a walk, but it's worth it."

"I'm in."

It's cool in the shade of the buildings, and I relish the brief moments of sun on my bare arms as we traverse the corner crosswalk. I dodge pedestrians while trying to keep up with Mym's brisk pace as she plunges into the shadow of the next building. She moves with the confidence of someone at home in her surroundings, flitting among the foot traffic with fluid ease, her purple skates hung casually over one shoulder. I narrowly miss being run down by a bicycle and stuff my hands into my jeans pockets to make myself a little thinner. As I skirt past a pair of rabbis, I find Mym waiting for me near a streetlight.

"Come on, pokey. I want to beat the lunch rush."

"Hey, I take up a lot more space than you do. I think these people treat that as a sin."

"People here live fast." She observes me over the rim of her new sunglasses. "Better learn to keep up." She winks before leading the way on. I appreciate her figure as she walks away, watching the curves that my hands have yet to touch. I entertain the thought for just a moment, then jog to catch up.

"You come to New York a lot?" I fall into step beside her.

"I try to. There are some great people here."

"There's certainly enough to choose from."

Mym slows to look at me. "You've never been to New York?"

"I passed through once as a kid with my parents, but I've never explored it as an adult."

"Then today is your lucky day. After lunch I can give you the tour."

"You going to show me the constructing of the Empire State Building?"

"Hmm, that would be a long way back," she muses. "Although I've always wanted to get a picture of me like one of those guys eating lunch up on the girders over the city. We might have to add that to the extended tour."

"Ha. You'll have to have one of the workers snap that shot. No way you're getting me out there on one of those."

"You just wait, Ben. A few weeks of traveling with me, and we'll have those heights issues vanquished."

My heartbeat quickens. I haven't asked how long she plans on traveling around with me. The idea of getting weeks with her makes me feel happy enough that I imagine I might be coaxed onto a few girders after all. I try not to show the eagerness on my face. "I guess we'll see."

An opening shop door halts me in my tracks as a group of women spills out onto the sidewalk from a boutique. A pretty young mother snags a wheel of her stroller on the doorstop, bringing the ladies behind her to a halt. I grab the door handle and open the door farther to help her extricate it.

"Thanks so much." The woman smiles, and another half dozen ladies thank me as I hold the door for their exit. The press of women moves onward along the sidewalk and I stretch to peer over their heads.

Mym is three shops down, shaking her head, but smiling. As I close the door behind the last straggler, another figure lurches up from the next shop entrance. In a tattered corduroy coat and porous straw fedora, he ricochets off a planter near the doorway and staggers toward the women. The group parts like a flock of swallows, reconvening beyond him with titters of consternation and a few hands held to noses.

The vagrant ignores the slight and tips his fedora in delayed cordiality, but stays his stumbling course toward me. I step to the side, but he sways with me, reaching out to my arms, raised to avert our collision. His right hand wraps around my wrist and clamps it with a near painful strength.

"Whoa, buddy. You doing okay?" I plant my other hand against his chest, to keep him at a distance and prop him up. His lean face is lined and dirty, but his stark, gray eyes have a sharp clarity despite his unbalanced state. I recoil from the scent of stale beer and halitosis, but before I can free my wrist from his grasp, he teeters and falls, dragging my arm across my body and down to the ground. Pain shoots up my wrist as my palm strikes the concrete and my vision suddenly goes dark. I've landed partially atop the vagrant, my other hand outstretched to the sidewalk beyond his head. I jerk my left arm out of his grip and jolt back to my feet. The world is changed.

Shaded sunlight has been replaced with an ink black sky. Streetlights illuminate sidewalks only populated by a few restaurant patrons retreating into the night. Mym is gone. I spin around and search the way I've come. I've been displaced. I check my chronometer. It still reads the settings I had from my last jump. *How is that possible? Shouldn't I have ended up on this sidewalk in daylight?*

The vagrant is struggling to get back to his feet. His left hand is crushing his straw hat as he tries to get his legs under him. He stretches a hand out to me for assistance. I sigh and grab his wrist, pulling a little more firmly than necessary. On his feet, the man gives me a scowl. "You didn't have to knock me down!" This is followed by a jerk as he pulls his arm from my grip and staggers toward the wall, a trail of slurred curses in his wake.

I look back to my surroundings and rub my wrist. My pulse throbs against the band of my chronometer. I gingerly remove it and hold it in my hand. This is the second time I've injured my wrist in a week. It was only just beginning to heal from the first fall. On that occasion, I plummeted out a window trying to save my friend. I considered myself lucky to have walked away with just a sprain. Getting knocked down by a random homeless man seems far less worthwhile.

I recheck my chronometer settings. Still set to 1600 Zulu. *So how is it nighttime? Did the jolt from the fall break it?* I study the different concentric rings, seeing if anything is amiss. Nothing is wrong externally. I give it a shake and listen for anything loose inside. Nothing.

Shit. What am I supposed to do now? I look around, hoping that at any moment Mym will suddenly appear to scold me for being careless and take us along our way. There is no one except a cab driver sitting outside a bar at the end of the block, his hazard lights pulsing their warning to the night. At a loss for what to do, I walk back the way I've come. The streets are less inviting in the darkness. The towering buildings no longer look inspiring, but loom overhead on the fringe of night, lifeless hulks obliterating the stars.

I slip my chronometer onto my other wrist and fidget with the dials. I consider trying to jump back to the time I left. *Will it still work? I don't even know how far I've gone. Will I have enough power to get back?* My mind goes back to Dr. Quickly's lessons, and the varied tales he told of ways time travelers could meet their demise. They involved everything from fusing into walls to flinging yourself off the planet into the void of space. *Those were things that could happen with a working chronometer. What about if it's broken? Am I going to blink myself out of existence?* I've heard stories of time travelers not anchoring themselves properly for a jump and vanishing completely. Some say there is a place you go that exists outside of time, but there the line between science and urban legend starts to blur. Every time traveler learns early on to avoid that scenario.

Those lessons feel as though they're a long time ago, though for me it's only been a matter of weeks. History would say it hasn't happened yet. It will be nearly a decade till I'm even born, farther still when I'll first be sent through time. But this is time travel. Middles can come before beginnings, and it's anyone's guess where the end might be.

As I cross to the next block, I glance down the side street and note a cluster of young men loitering on the stoop of an apartment building. A dozen eyes follow my progress. Without my usual method of escape, I feel suddenly vulnerable under their gaze. I check myself to keep from walking faster. I continue with feigned ease for another half block until I'm well out of sight, and then stop.

Get yourself together, Ben. You're fine. You're just in New York . . . in 1973. I glance back at the vacant street behind me and then force myself to think. *What now?* I do a mental inventory of my belongings. Besides a possibly broken chronometer, my possessions are down to a wallet, pen, Swiss Army knife, and Mym's degravitizer that I forgot to put back in her backpack. I also have Dr. Quickly's worn leather journal stuck in my back pants pocket. I pull that out and walk a few steps toward the nearest streetlamp to read it. I flip through the handwritten scribbles and drawings, searching for the section on the workings of the chronometer. The book had been a gift, but a utilitarian one, filled with the carefully depicted details of a lifetime of research.

I stop on a page showing a partially disassembled chronometer. Staring at the drawing of the component parts, I immediately realize I'm out of my depth. *Even if I had the tools, there's no way I would even be able to recognize what was broken.* I slap the journal shut. A murmur alerts me that the men from the stoop have moved to the corner behind me. The tallest of the bunch is eyeing me from under a disheveled mop of hair, one hand conspicuously lingering in the pocket of his sweatshirt. The expressions on the young men's faces range from frigid to glacial. I break my eyes away and continue walking. A subtle shuffling indicates that I won't be alone.

They've just got somewhere to go this direction. Nothing to worry about.

A bus rumbles past but doesn't slow. A single old man is staring into the night from the illuminated interior, lost in a daydream or his own reflection. I'm nearly at the corner and, other than my skulking shadows, all pedestrians seem to have evaporated. *Isn't this supposed to be the city that never sleeps?*

I'm just considering breaking into a run when a smoke-black Cadillac materializes from the side street. It oozes to the curb at the corner ahead of me and, as I approach, hearty chuckles trickle from the darkness of the open rear window. "Benjamin, Benjamin, Benjamin. We've been looking all over for you. You had us worried, my friend."

The door swings open and the dome light illuminates the plush interior and the lounging figure of a substantial, well-dressed man in his forties. His glossy hair matches his Burt Reynolds mustache. I've never seen him before. "You shouldn't just go wandering off around here, Ben. The locals can get territorial in the wee hours."

I stoop to peer into the car. The driver is a hulk in a suit coat. The man in the back pats the seat next to him. "Get in."

"I don't know you."

The man's eyes narrow, but then his face lightens and he gives me a cheek-stretching grin. "I forget how young you still are, Ben. Of course! This is your first time meeting me." He extends a hand. "Gioachino Amadeus. But call me Geo." I let his hand linger in midair. Finally, he pats the seat next to him. "Come on. We'll get you out of here."

I glance back down the sidewalk. My flock of followers has stalled out mid-block and is idling near a barred grocer's shop. A few of them are involved in subtle conversation, but the tall one is still just staring at me.

"How did you know where to find me?"

Geo stretches his arm along the back of the seat with a knowing smile. "We time travelers have to stick together, Benjamin."

"Mym sent you?"

"You don't think she'd just leave you out here on your own do you? You can trust me, Ben. We're destined to be great friends."

"Most of my friends drive themselves."

"Well then, it looks like you're moving up in the world. Now hop in. We've got places to be."

I take one last look at the city skyline, blending vaguely into a motor oil sky, and climb in. The Cadillac ebbs back into the street, and as the dome light fades, we are swallowed by the ocean of night.

"To time travel, you will need: a body and clothing embedded with gravitites, a chronometer, a suitable anchor, and a willingness to change everything about your life as you know it. The last item tends to be the stickler."–Journal of Dr. Harold Quickly, 1998

Chapter 2

Past the bulging veins in the driver's neck, the clock on the dash reads 03:28. I settle into my seat and find the seatbelt. Geo is watching me with an amused, crooked smile.

"What's the date today?" I ask.

"It's May 19th. But not for much longer."

"Are we headed back to yesterday? I'm supposed to be going to lunch."

"And that is exactly where we'll take you, but we have a stop to make first."

"Where's Mym?"

"She's waiting right where you left her. Why did you leave her, by the way? What're you doing on the streets in the middle of the night?"

"I don't know. I got knocked down and just ended up here. I think there may be an issue with my chronometer."

"That sounds serious. You should probably let me have someone look at that for you." Geo's eyes stay fixed on my chronometer until I slip my arm to my side. "I have some great people for that sort of thing."

The car makes a series of turns and suddenly plunges down an alley. The driver veers past a set of dumpsters, and the headlights wash over a pair of men with shoulder holsters standing sentry near a metal service door. The car continues past without slowing, and I twist in my seat to take another look at the guards out the back window.

"They're with me," Geo says. "We take security very seriously."

As we near the end of the alley, the way is blocked by a shipping container that occupies the entire space between the buildings. Two more sentries are standing at its doors with automatic weapons. A third guard appears on the left and the driver rolls his window down and slows for him. The guard nods in recognition and signals to the other two. We are close enough to hear the clank of the handle being thrown on the cargo container doors, and they swing wide ahead of us. The driver accelerates and aims the Cadillac up two wheel-width ramps, plunging us into the blackness of the container. I clamp down on the door handle when I realize he isn't braking, and tense my muscles, expecting any second to crash into the back of the container. Instead, the car is suddenly bathed in daylight as we exit the other side. A rat darts out of the way as we descend the ramps. I bounce once as the rear wheels hit the pavement. I pivot in my seat and see two more guards swinging the container doors shut behind us.

"Holy shit! That was crazy." I tilt my head to see the sun beyond the top of the alley's buildings. The driver pulls back into midday traffic and rolls his window up to shut out the blaring noise and exhaust fumes.

"First trip through a time gate?" Geo is watching my face.

"That's what that was?"

"I told you, Benjamin. You're moving up in the world."

The car snakes its way through the arteries of Manhattan and flows out through an ornate colonnade onto a suspension bridge over the river. Another bridge parallels it to the right. I lean forward and address the driver. "Is this the Brooklyn Bridge?"

It's Geo who responds. "No. That one is. This is the Manhattan Bridge."

The driver continues as though I'd never existed. I lean back in my seat, then address Geo. "Is he not allowed to talk or something?"

"Tonio is not much for small talk, but he has other admirable qualities. He finds talking less useful." I note scarred knuckles on the meaty hands resting on the steering wheel and realize that I don't want to know his other hobbies. As if sensing my unease, Geo smiles at me. "Don't worry, Ben. You're in good hands. It helps to have versatile friends in the world these days. It can be a dangerous place out there. You're safe now."

"Where are we going?"

"We're going to get you back, but first I need to drop in on my mother."

"Your mother?"

"Mothers love it when you visit, Ben. It's the sunshine of their days. And a man who doesn't respect his mother is not a man. Wouldn't you agree?"

"Mmm. Yeah."

"She'll be elated to meet you. You have quite the reputation in time traveling circles."

"Your mother is a time traveler, too?"

"Well, not in a very active capacity. She mostly prefers to stay at home, but she won't say no to the occasional trip to Sicily or Sardinia, and she hates to fly."

"How does she know who I am?"

"Most time travelers have heard of you, Ben. I don't know that most would know you on sight, but your name, that's common knowledge. Anyone who has studied the life of Harold Quickly has to come across your story. I don't think I'd be far off to suggest that many view you as a hero."

"A hero?"

"Of course! You saved Dr. Quickly from the jaws of death! How could you not be?"

"I guess I never really thought about it like that."

"I think you'll find that the name Benjamin Travers will earn you more than a few drinks from the guys, and as for the ladies ..." He gives me a conspiratorial wink.

"Well, I guess that's good news." My mind shuffles through the memories of my time with Dr. Quickly and the fight to save him. For me it was less than a week ago, but time is irrelevant in this new crowd. The story may have been passed on for years, decades, centuries. *Hero. There are definitely worse titles.*

As I muse out the window on my newfound reputation, the driver wends his way to a residential neighborhood labeled Dyker Heights. We pull up to a palatial manor house surrounded by a low brick wall, crammed amidst other more modest homes. A sliding metal gate parts for our arrival. Three dark-haired children are playing tag on the front lawn. They pause as the Cadillac enters the gate and then sprint for the car. The trio gives the driver a wide birth as he exits, but when Geo opens his door, they clamor about him eagerly, vying for his attention.

I climb out of the car and watch as Geo picks up the little girl and tosses her in the air. She shrieks and giggles until he puts her down. The two boys likewise beam with affection when Geo musses their hair. He gestures for me to follow and mounts the steps to the door, the children bobbing in his wake.

The front door opens before we reach it, and we're met by a grinning man in a blazer. His neck has overrun his collar, and his jacket is unbuttoned to ease the strain on its already stressed proportions. The man greets Geo with an embrace and a kiss on both cheeks. Geo slaps him on the shoulder and says something I don't catch. He then turns to me. "Benjamin, I'd like you to meet Don Bartholomew Amadeus, my cousin."

The man reaches out and swallows my hand in his. His vigorous handshake threatens to dislocate my shoulder, but his beaming smile is infectious. "It's an honor."

"The pleasure's mine, I'm sure." I try to equal his enthusiasm.

How does Mym know these people?

Passing the foyer, we enter a din of conversation set over a clattering backdrop of forks and dishes. The large dining room hosts a table to seat a dozen diners. Half are in position over platters and cups, while a spare dozen mill about the room, leaning on mantles or rotating out of the kitchen bearing plates and smiles.

Geo's arrival is met with more kisses and embraces. He is thronged with grinning adults and leg-clinging children. The doters part for a heavyset woman with a broad face and a mole on her lip, who hands off a plate to a miscellaneous relative, and spreads her arms wide for Geo.

"Hello, Mama."

The woman claps her hands to Geo's face and kisses him, speaking Italian salutations I don't understand. The two commune rapidly, and finally my presence is addressed. Geo's mother turns to me and squints a smile that could be confused with a grimace. She steps past Geo and slaps a thick hand to my face. For a moment I fear I may get kissed as well, but she contents herself with patting my face twice, then returns her attention to her son. After a few more rapid exchanges, the mother gestures us toward the table and wades back through the relatives to the kitchen.

"Have a seat, Benjamin." Geo points to the open positions around the table. "Mama is going to fix you a plate."

"Oh, thank you. I was actually on my way to eat lunch with Mym, so I'm not sure I should wreck my appetite."

"Consider this your appetizer." Geo smiles. "I doubt Mama is going to let you out the door without sampling her Meatball Parmesan."

The diners at the table vary in ages. I find an open seat near a grandfatherly man in a suit coat who is engrossed in shredding bits of bread on his plate. He doesn't pay me any attention as I sit down. A man half his age, with oversized eyebrows, sits across from him. The second man watches me get settled and then hands me the breadbasket.

"You a time traveler?" he asks.

"Yes." I take the basket from him. "Are you?"

The man shakes his head vigorously. "No, no. You wouldn't catch me doing that. I like to keep my feet right here and now. What's your gimmick, though? How did you get to be one?"

"That's a bit of a long story. You probably don't want to hear it all, but have you heard of Dr. Harold Quickly?"

"That scientist guy? The one that discovered the whatchamacallit particles—the gravities?"

"Gravi-tites," I enunciate. "But, yeah. He's the one that taught me."

"He turned you into a time traveler?"

"No. That part was accidental. Some colleagues of his tried to duplicate his work in my hometown. They had an accident and a few of my friends and I were affected. Dr. Quickly taught us how to survive, taught us the technical stuff."

The man holds his hands up. "It's all beyond me. Geo don't talk about it much, if you know what I mean. Tends to keep to his own friends." He laughs but glances around. I get the sense he doesn't want his complaints heard by our host.

Geo is conversing with an attractive twenty-something woman in the corner of the room. She's taller than Geo by an inch or so, with black hair that reaches the middle of her back. I'm about to ask the man how old Geo is, but he gets up from the table abruptly and heads for the kitchen.

The old man with the suit coat has finished shredding his bread and is using the fragments to sop up sauce on his plate. Despite his best efforts, much of it is ending up in his shaggy white mustache. The man with the beetling eyebrows doesn't return, so I fidget with my silverware and glance around at my other companions, wondering how long this detour will take. To the right of the vacated seat is a boy of perhaps fifteen. He hasn't looked directly at me yet, but I wait until he gets done loading his fork and wave at him.

"Hey."

He raises his eyes to mine.

"Do you know who that woman is? The one Geo is talking to?"

The boy glances at the pair and looks back to me, still chewing his pasta. "That's Ariella."

"Is that his wife?"

The boy shakes his head. "Geo's not married."

"So what's her story?"

The boy shrugs and goes back to his food. I watch the conversation between Geo and Ariella with curiosity. She looks unhappy, but even in her unhappiness, her face is strikingly beautiful. She's listening to Geo with lips tight, a thin line of resistance to speech, while her eyes flash with unspoken responses.

Her silence seems to be all that is required, because Geo breaks away and grabs the arm of another passing male relative and the two retire through the double glass doors to the deck overlooking the back lawn. Ariella stays standing, her mind still engaged with the things that have just been said. Her stillness is statuesque until, as if sensing my attention, her eyes lock on mine. Anger simmers beneath green shaded lashes. I retreat to the breadbasket, fiddling with a dinner roll and regretting my intrusion.

THE CHRONOTHON

Geo's mother appears at my elbow with a heaping plate of pasta and meatballs trimmed with garlic bread and steamed asparagus. She slides the mountain of food in front of me with a symphony of Italian, of which I comprehend not a single word. My cheek gets pinched and my head is patted firmly, then I'm left with a fork in hand and stared at by half a dozen matronly faces. Mrs. Amadeus has been joined by what I gather are aunts or female cousins, all of whom share her ample proportions and intense gaze of expectation.

"Eat! Eat!" Mrs. Amadeus pokes my shoulder with a thick finger.

"Thank you. It looks delicious."

I dutifully stab my fork into the pile of noodles and, after an awkwardly long attempt to wrangle the errant strands onto the tines, manage to stuff them into my mouth. I make some muffled noises of enjoyment that seem to satisfy the women. They disperse back to the kitchen with murmured comments that I can't help but suspect are about my need for a bib. As I grab my knife and try to hack the noodles down to a more manageable size, Don Bartholomew deposits himself in the chair next to me.

"You look like a healthy young man, Benjamin. Healthy appetite."

"Well, I don't always eat this much. . . ."

"As a young man, I was the same way. I would put away three plates at a sitting." He pats his protruding belly. "Not that you could ever tell, eh?"

"I can see why. This is really good."

"When I was your age, I was an athlete. I could wrestle and box. I was amateur champion in my division. The medals are at home on my mantel."

"That's cool."

"Have you ever boxed?"

"No. Just messing around as a kid in friends' garages and whatnot. I've never been in a ring for real."

"It's an exhilarating feeling. Pitting yourself against another man in competition is a way to know your worth. Did you compete in school? You look like an athlete."

"I played baseball growing up. Ran a little track in high school."

"Ah, a runner. My son Horacio is a runner. He races in all kinds of competitions. I'll introduce you."

I nod as I carve off a section of meatball and fork it into my mouth.

"Horacio!" Don Bartholomew bellows toward the foyer. I nearly choke on the meatball in surprise. Two young men near the door are likewise startled by the yell and turn to see the cause of the commotion. Don Bartholomew waves his oversized paw at them. "Go find my son!"

The two men look at each other and one shrugs. They slip dutifully through the doorway on their new errand. "Time to put these fellows to work," Don Bartholomew says, as he tears into a dinner roll. "Friends of my son, but the two of them together aren't equal to a quarter of my boy. You'll like Horacio. He's very talented. Takes after his old man." He nudges me with his elbow.

Geo returns from the deck and pauses to put his hand on my shoulder. "Everything to your liking, Benjamin?"

"Yes, the food is great, but I'm not sure I can eat all this. What time are you thinking of heading out?"

"Soon enough. Enjoy the company for a bit longer. We'll have you back on your way shortly. I see you and Barty here have gotten to know each other."

"Did you know the boy is an athlete, Geo?" Don Bartholomew thumps me on the shoulder with his fist for emphasis. I do my best not to groan from the impact.

"Is he now?" Geo looks down at me with new curiosity.

"Runner," Don Bartholomew adds. "I'm going to introduce him to Horacio. It's about time Horacio had another man around who knows a thing or two about competition. These ninnies he hangs around with don't know anything about proving themselves as men."

"I didn't know you were a competitive runner, Benjamin," Geo says. "That is news."

"Um, Don Bartholomew is being overly generous."

"You don't run races?" Geo cocks his head.

"Well I guess I still run some 5Ks from time to time. We have a Turkey Trot at Thanksgiving that gets a little intense . . ."

"What is a Turkey Trot?" Don Bartholomew moves his head closer to me. I shrink back under his inspection.

"Um, it's a charity race. You run to support local charitable organizations and . . . cure diseases and stuff."

Don Bartholomew surveys my face skeptically for a few moments, but then bobs his head in increasingly larger nods. Finally he slaps me on the shoulder again. "Good. Racing with a purpose. It is good for a man to have a purpose. And to win. Do you win this turkey race?"

"Uh, I do all right. Competition is pretty fierce, but sure. I hold my own." I get distracted from the conversation momentarily when I notice Ariella taking a seat diagonally from me. Her face is still serious, but I note her taking an interest in what Don Bartholomew is saying. I realize he's still speaking to me, and try to pay attention.

" . . . and we once chased greased pigs as part of our boxing training. How fast is this turkey that you race?"

"Oh. There's not actually a real turkey that I know of." My explanation is mercifully interrupted by the return of the two men from the doorway. Striding ahead of them is a well-built man of perhaps thirty, whose muscled arms and abundant body hair are straining the confines of his T-shirt. He surveys the room with an air of boredom before snatching up the chair next to Ariella and spinning it around. He straddles the seat and leans his elbows across the back. I note with a twinge of appreciation that Ariella is not paying him any attention.

"You wanted me, Pop?"

"Horacio, I want you to meet Benjamin."

Horacio considers me apathetically from across the table.

"Benjamin Travers," Geo adds.

This addition registers on Horacio's face. He rises from his chair and extends his hand across the table, clamping down on mine like a vise. "I've heard about you."

"Something good hopefully," I reply.

He releases my hand and settles back into his chair. I notice that his handshake has dipped my elbow into my pasta sauce. I attempt to remove it discreetly with my napkin, but I catch a smirk on Ariella's face.

"I was just telling Benjamin about your competitions," Don Bartholomew beams. "He is also a competitor."

"Which races have you won?" Horacio asks.

"Just some distance races in high school. I haven't won anything recently."

"Ah. So no real competitions then." Horacio leans back and crosses his arms.

"What types of races do you run?" I try to keep my voice polite.

"The kind that matter."

"Are you training for the Olympics or something?"

Horacio smirks at the suggestion. "I race chronothons."

"Oh."

"Horacio is speaking of a race for time travelers," Geo explains. "It's a rather unique event."

"What you meant to say is that you get disqualified from chronothons, don't you, Horacio?" Ariella's voice is smooth and subtle. "You haven't actually completed one yet, isn't that correct?"

Horacio scowls at her, but Ariella's expression is unrepentant.

"That was horseshit and you know it. This time will be different."

Geo leans past me and casually snatches up a dinner roll. "You know, Ben, you should try entering a chronothon. You'd be quite the hit."

"What does it involve?"

"It's a lot like your charity 5Ks, really. A bunch of time travelers get together and have a race. Only it jumps through different time periods. It's a lot of fun. The proceeds go toward some philanthropic organizations. I'm sure the race committee would love to have someone with your reputation in the running. It would be great for publicity."

"It sounds pretty cool. I'll have to check one out sometime."

"I believe the next one coming up has some new elements. You are signed up already aren't you, Horacio?" Geo asks. "Don't you get to go to the Mediterranean this race?"

"I'm not sure he can handle it," Horacio says, eyeing me from across the table. "He hasn't been training."

I consider throwing a dinner roll at his face, but repress the urge. "Yeah, I'll probably just observe. Sounds like a good show."

"You should not let my son discourage you with his appearance," Don Bartholomew interjects. "He is an excellent athlete, but many other less talented people also compete. Even our Ariella is in competition this round. Aren't you?"

Ariella narrows her eyes, but she smiles as she responds, "Yes, actually. I figure one of us ought to make the finish line for a change."

Horacio snorts in derision. "You think you're going to beat me?"

"I think your previous record suggests a pretty good window of opportunity for that, yeah."

"You're fooling yourself, woman."

"We'll just have to see."

"I've been training every day." He rises from his chair and plants his right foot on the seat. He yanks back the length of his already meager athletic shorts, almost to his groin, and slaps his thigh. "Have you seen these legs? Have you?"

Ariella averts her face from the view of his crotch, and shakes her head. She looks at me and rolls her eyes. Horacio is flexing the muscles in his thigh and strokes his calf with his hand. "You think you can handle this?"

God, this guy's a tool.

"You know what? Maybe I will enter after all." I smile at Don Bartholomew. "Your son is pretty inspiring."

Horacio glares at me, noting the sarcasm in my voice. Don Bartholomew is oblivious to it however, and slaps me on the back. "He is inspiring! I knew you two would hit it off!"

Horacio spins his chair around and shoves it back under the table. He glares at me and I hold his gaze until he tosses his hair out of his eyes and walks away. I note Ariella watching me, and as my eyes meet hers, she gives me a nod and the hint of a smile.

Geo gets distracted by another passing relative, so I return my attention to Don Bartholomew, who is eager to regale me with more stories of his youth. I nod in the appropriate places and mumble occasional polite admiration between mouthfuls of pasta. My response does not seem especially required to maintain the large man's momentum. I cast occasional glances at Ariella, but she's involved in conversation with a young woman behind her. After a few minutes, she rises, and the pair disappears into the foyer.

Don Bartholomew is describing the play by play of a fight between himself and what was apparently the strongest, largest boxer in the history of New York, when I finally concede defeat and push my plate away. The old man with the shaggy mustache has nodded off and is beginning to snore. Most of the other diners have departed, and other than Don Bartholomew laughing at his own clever stories, the noisy chaos has died down to a murmur. I find what could conceivably be considered an ending to one of the boxing feats and slide my chair back.

"That is really fascinating. Do you happen to know where the restroom is?"

Geo suddenly appears behind me. "I can point the way for you."

"Oh, hey. There you are. I was thinking I should probably be heading back ..."

"We're leaving now. I had Tonio pull the car up. What did you think of the family?"

"They're all really nice."

"Headed out so soon, Geo?" Don Bartholomew rises from his chair with all the speed of a hippopotamus in mud. He steadies himself with the back of the chair and puts his other hand on Geo's shoulder.

Geo pats him on the back. "Places to be, cousin. The clock never stops."

Don Bartholomew shakes my hand again. "You're going to do great things, Benjamin. I can tell."

"Thank you. You're very kind."

His sudden slap on my back helps propel me forward as I make for the door.

Out in the hallway, Geo points to a flight of stairs. "You'll find a bathroom just upstairs to the right. I'll be out in the car when you're ready."

"Okay, thanks." I climb the stairs, turn a corner, and find myself face to face with Ariella. "Oh, hey," I manage.

"Hello."

I'm suddenly stupefied by her proximity and beauty, and stumble for something else to say. "Um, I was just headed for the, uh . . ."

She pushes the door open behind her, revealing the white-tiled floor and marble-topped sink of the bathroom.

"Yeah, that'd be the one." I move toward the door, but she doesn't step aside, forcing me into even closer proximity to try to make it around her.

"I'm glad you'll be in the race." Her voice is soft and almost vulnerable.

"What? Oh, yeah. It sounds like fun."

"Horacio is . . ."

"A jerk?" I offer.

"Worse than that. It will be nice having someone worthwhile to compete with."

She smells like vanilla.

"Well, I'm sure it will be a good time. When is it actually? I was kind of fuzzy on the specifics."

She takes ahold of my hand. I'm startled by her sudden touch and almost retract it involuntarily. She turns my palm upward and strokes the lines on it with her thumb. I get a tingling chill up my neck. "Here." She pulls something from her pocket with her other hand, and lays it across my fingertips. A thin translucent boomerang in shape, it makes my fingertips look purple when looking through it. She gently moves my thumb to the top surface and sandwiches my hand and the device between hers. Her hands are warm and firm. Her body is even closer to mine now and I can't help staring at her lips as she lifts her face to me. "You sure you want to do this?"

"I love an adventure," I reply.

"So that's a yes?" She tilts her head coyly to the side and smiles.

"That's a yes."

"Good."

I feel a tingling from the device against my fingertips and it beeps. It's back in her pocket in an instant, and she slips past me into the center of the hall. "I guess I'll be seeing you soon." She stares into my eyes and backs toward the stairs.

I falter for words again and just watch her go.

"Someone will be in touch about the details. Don't let me hold you up. Looks like you have some business to attend to." She smiles playfully and nods toward the bathroom door.

"Oh, uh yeah. So I guess I'll see you later." I push open the door a little farther and when I look back, she's descending the stairs, her raven hair wafting behind her.

Damn. Way to be smooth, Ben.

When I reemerge from the bathroom and make it downstairs, the house has gone quiet. I poke my head into the dining room, thinking I may catch another glimpse of Ariella, but the room is vacant. Even the clattering sound of dishes from the kitchen has ceased. I walk onto the front porch and find the Cadillac idling in the driveway. The back door is open, so I climb in.

Geo is looking out the window on the opposite side and doesn't speak, so I simply shut my door and the car starts rolling. After a few blocks of awkward silence I can't take it anymore. "You'll have to thank your mother for me. I didn't get a chance to say goodbye."

Geo returns to me as if from a daydream, and smiles, though the smile seems slow in coming. "I'm very happy you were able to visit. I know all my relatives enjoyed your company. Most especially Don Bartholomew. I haven't seen him take to someone like that in quite some time."

"They were all really nice."

"I spoke to someone about the glitch in your chronometer. He gave me a few common things to look for. Let me take a look." He holds out his hand.

I reluctantly slide my chronometer off my wrist and drop it into his hand. He pulls what looks like a miniature stethoscope out of his pocket and installs the earpieces. He then puts the cupped end to the back of my chronometer and listens as he moves a few of the dials and concentric rings. I can't quite make out what he's doing, but after a moment he hands the chronometer back.

"There you go. Just a quick reset was all it needed. He said it's not at all uncommon on those models."

I examine my chronometer cautiously, but seeing no discrepancies, slip it back onto my wrist. "Thanks."

Geo lapses into silence again and I resign myself to staring out the window as we make our way back to Manhattan. When we arrive, Tonio pulls up to the same boutique where I had my collision with the homeless man. Geo gets out of the car with me and guides me to the sidewalk.

"Let me help you out with those calculations." He reaches for my arm and takes it firmly in his. He takes longer than I would to find the right settings, but makes the movements with confidence.

"What time are you sending me back to?"

"Just a moment after you left."

"How do you know when that was?"

"I know because Mym knows. You'll want to use that bit of pavement right there." Geo points to a spot on the sidewalk.

"Thank you for your help. I'm not sure how I can repay you."

"You don't need to thank me, Ben." Geo's face is serious and sterile.

"And you've already repaid me."

"Will I be seeing you again?"

This time Geo smiles. "Of that you can be certain." He turns on his heel and climbs into the car. Just before he shuts the door, he pauses mid-motion. "Be sure to give the Quicklys my regards." The car door slams and the Cadillac eases back into traffic.

After I watch the car disappear into the congestion, I dodge a couple of pedestrians and locate the specified spot on the sidewalk for my jump. I look down at my chronometer settings and double-check what Geo has selected.

Seems logical.

I wait till the immediate area is clear, and squat, pretending to tie my shoe. I slip my chronometer hand to the concrete and reach for the pin. I've never made a jump before where I didn't get my data from my own research or from one of the Quicklys. The thought gives me a moment's pause. *I guess I just need to be trusting.*

I push the pin and blink.

"You can't just think about jump locations as physical spaces. They are also windows of time. Successful time traveling means aligning both—ideally when there is nothing there to impale you."—Journal of Dr. Harold Quickly, 2102

Chapter 3

The expressions on the faces around me are all various stages of surprise or fear. One of the women from the group in the boutique is gaping at me with eyes and mouth both open wide. Murmurs emanate from the other pedestrians.

"Did you see what he just did?"

"What happened to the old man?"

"He just made that guy vanish!"

The couple nearest me retreats against the wall as I get to my feet. The young man steps in front of the woman defensively. Suddenly, Mym is at my elbow. Her face is serious and her eyes questioning. "What are you doing, Ben? Come on!" She yanks on my arm and drags me into the street. The crowd on the sidewalk watches me get towed between the cluttered cars to the far side. Mym releases my arm at the sidewalk but doesn't stop moving until we are another half a block down. Finally she steps into the corner of a shop selling tourist souvenirs and spins to face me. "What was that, Ben? What were you thinking?"

I'm not used to the anger in her voice. "I don't know. It wasn't me."

"What do you mean, it wasn't you?" Her eyes search my face.

"I got knocked down. I thought you knew. I think it was something wrong with my chronometer."

"You thought I knew? How would I know?"

"You sent Geo. You sent him to pick me up!"

"Geo? What Geo?" Her forehead is wrinkled in confusion.

"Geo Amadeus. He picked me up in his car . . ."

"Gioachino Amadeus? You were just with Gioachino Amadeus?" Her hand goes to her head in alarm.

I'm taken aback by her response. "You didn't send him?"

"No! Why would I send a gangster to get you?"

"Gangster?"

"That's putting it lightly, Ben. Gioachino Amadeus is about the last possible person you want to meet, and if he knows we're here, we need to go." She sets her skates down, removes her messenger bag, and begins rooting through it.

My mind races through my encounter with the Italian. "He seemed pretty nice to me. . . ."

Mym stops moving and looks back up at me. "Nice?" She considers my face as if checking to see if I've lost my mind. "What exactly did he want from you, Ben?"

"Nothing. He said he was just bringing me back. He helped me fix my chronometer."

"What's wrong with it?"

"I don't know. When that homeless guy knocked me down, we jumped forward to tomorrow night, but the settings never changed."

"How? How would you go anywhere?"

"I don't know. That's what I thought. Geo said it just needed to be reset."

Mym looks at my chronometer skeptically, then continues rummaging around in her bag until she pulls out a brass compass and an accompanying photo. She degravitizes the compass, then hands it to me. "Here. You're going to put your finger on south and hold on to me."

"We're not using my chronometer?"

"No. I don't trust that thing right now. We'll go with mine."

I pause as an Asian woman with an armful of "I love New York" T-shirts and a miniature Statue of Liberty squeezes between us. Mym pulls at the chain around her neck and removes her ball-shaped chronometer from under her shirt. She dials in the settings from the back of the photo and then takes the compass from my hand and sets it on a low shelf next to us.

"We'll have to drop a couple feet on the other end, but there's not much we can do about it."

"Okay." I grab onto her arm just above her elbow. Mym uses the arm I'm holding for her chronometer and extends her other hand to the compass.

"Here we go." She pushes the pin and we blink.

Rough dirt crunches under my sneakers when I land. We've appeared outdoors at the end of a rough-hewn wooden table. A steady breeze is rustling a pair of maps that are weighed down by the compass at our fingertips. Mym yanks on my arm and pulls me behind a canvas tent held up with wooden poles. Crouching behind the tent, I take in the lush greenery around the clearing.

"Are we in the jungle?"

"Shhh! Be quiet! I'll hear us." She gestures beyond the tent to a blonde little girl holding a camera, walking away toward the grassy bank of a stream.

"Holy crap. That's you? How old are you there?"

"Eight," she whispers.

"Where are we?"

"Ecuador."

The little Mym scuttles down the bank of the stream and disappears from view.

"Come on." Mym turns and heads the other direction. I follow her as she plunges into the jungle.

The dense foliage resonates with the hum of insects and a continual chorus of bird calls. I duck beneath an enormous fern frond and push through a mess of flowering vines. As we clamber up a mossy embankment onto a thin animal trail, Mym follows it uphill, moving onward without hesitation. I follow as fast as I can, attempting to find sure footing among the loose stones.

The dense air conspires with the vegetation to slow my progress. The damp heat gives me the impression of swimming as much as hiking, pushing onward through the wall of humidity. "Where are we going?" I'm scrambling to keep up with Mym's pace.

"I'm taking you to see my dad. He'll know what to do."

We jump a gully with a trickling stream and then climb the roots of a banyan tree to mount the opposite bank. When we finally arrive at the top of the hill, we enter a clearing populated with high grasses and, at the far side, a trio of fluttering canvas tents. Before we reach the tents, the sound of laughter turns Mym to the right. The tall grasses shield the owners of the laughing voices until we're almost upon them. Mym parts the grass at the edge of another small stream to reveal two middle-aged men seated on buckets, ankle deep in the water. The legs of their cargo pants are rolled up to their knees and both are holding wood-framed sifting screens.

I recognize Dr. Quickly, though he's younger than I'm used to. His hair is only streaked with gray and his movements are vigorous as he sloshes water and sand about in the screen. The man next to Dr. Quickly is the first to notice us. His deep black skin is contrasted by the radiant smile that spreads across his face upon seeing Mym. He leans back on his bucket and tosses his screen to the muddy embankment.

"All your ruckus has attracted visitors, Harry." His voice is deep, with a hint of an accent.

Dr. Quickly turns our direction and smiles. "This is a nice surprise. I just got through telling Abe how I was looking forward to the days when you'd stop filling the cooking pots with your frog collections every trip to the rainforest. I didn't expect you to grow up quite this fast though. . . ."

"You leave a girl alone in a jungle, she's bound to make herself some friends, Dad."

"It seems you have moved on from frogs." The man named Abe is looking at me now. "Or have you taken to kissing them, and this is your new prince?"

"Frogs are less trouble," Mym says, looking at me. "This is Ben."

Abe rises from his bucket and wades through the stream to shake my hand.

"Abraham." His grip is firm, though still soggy.

"It's nice to meet you."

"I was wondering when I would see you again." Dr. Quickly rises also and gives me a nod.

"I wasn't sure you'd remember me." The only time I had previously encountered the younger version of Dr. Quickly was mere minutes before his laboratory burned down in 1986. With no chronological order to our meetings, and the constantly diverging streams of time, it was nearly impossible for me to predict if this was the same man. "It's good to see you again," I add.

"So, to what do we owe the pleasure?" Dr. Quickly asks. "I know you probably didn't come for the amphibians this trip."

Mym shakes her head. "I need your advice, Dad. Abraham's, too, since he's here."

"We're all ears. I'd offer you a bucket to sit on but we seem to be fresh out. Should we take this conversation over to the dry site?"

"That's probably better," Mym replies.

We file through the grass to the area where we spotted the tents, and rearrange some of the tool crates and the two collapsible wooden chairs for seating. "Is it something serious?" Dr. Quickly is watching Mym's face. It occurs to me what an odd sensation he must feel, viewing the older version of the child he is raising now.

"I'm not really sure yet. Ben ran into Gioachino Amadeus. There was an incident in New York."

I notice an immediate change in expression in Abraham's face at this comment, but he stays silent. Dr. Quickly's expression also grows somber. "That's rarely a good event. How did he locate you?"

Mym nods in my direction. "Ben got displaced. He says he just picked him up and brought him back, but Ben's chronometer never changed settings. Something odd happened."

Dr. Quickly looks at my arm and scrunches up his eyebrows. "You mind if I see?" I slip the chronometer off my wrist and hand it to him. He turns it over in his palm and inspects it carefully. After a few moments he hands it to Abraham. "What do you make of it?"

"Abraham is the one who designed these models," Mym explains. "If anyone can find a defect in it, he will."

Abraham studies the chronometer carefully but doesn't move any of the dials. "I would need to open it up to inspect it properly. Do you mind, Benjamin?"

"No. Of course not. I'd like to know what happened."

"How did this event occur?" Dr. Quickly asks. "How did you get displaced?"

I tell him about the homeless man and our fall to the concrete. "Is it possible I broke something?"

"That's not likely." Abraham has gotten up and extracted a fabric wrapped tool kit from one of the backpacks, and is laying out tools on top of a crate. "A simple fall shouldn't have been capable of damaging any of the workings."

"And you're sure you didn't involuntarily trigger the device yourself?" Dr. Quickly is paying close attention to my face as I respond.

"I didn't have a hand on it at the time. The guy had grabbed that arm when we tipped over. I suppose he might have pushed the pin. My settings never moved though, so wouldn't I have gone back to the time I arrived there?"

"Was the directional slider on the side selected to forward or backward?" Abraham asks.

"It was still on forward. We had just jumped from 1969."

"Then it couldn't have taken you back to the time you arrived."

"Yeah, that makes sense. So how could I end up a day ahead?"

"What did this homeless person look like?" Dr. Quickly leans forward with his elbows on his knees.

"I guess he was middle-aged maybe. It was hard to tell. Scruffy, kind of hawkish face, dirty clothes. He had a straw hat."

"Anything unique, like tattoos?"

"No. not that I could see. The only thing that stuck out to me was that he had these creepy gray eyes. Kind of an unnerving stare. It happened fast, but I remember noticing that about him. That and he stunk quite a lot."

"Well, it's not much to go on, but it could be something." Dr. Quickly scratches his chin.

"You think he was involved somehow?"

Mym chimes in. "If he was a time traveler, that would explain why Ben's chronometer settings never moved. He could have caused the jump himself."

"Tell me this, Benjamin, when you fell, what happened to the homeless man? Did he stay in the time you left, or go forward with you?"

"Oh. He came with me. I don't know why I didn't think about that before. So that means he had to be a time traveler or he wouldn't have gone anywhere."

"Why go through all that trouble just to bring Benjamin right back?" Abraham says. "Unless they planted something on him. Perhaps to track him."

"You think they would want to follow me?" I try to remember anyone putting anything on me.

"Did they give you anything?" Dr. Quickly asks. "Anything at all?"

"No. They fed me lunch." I glance at Mym. "I told him I was headed to eat with Mym, but he wanted me to try his mother's Meatball Parmesan."

"It would be pretty unlikely to smuggle a tracking device into food." Abraham sets the back of my chronometer aside and begins examining the interior parts with a magnifying glass. "Not if you intended to track him more than a couple days."

"Is there any chance he really was just being nice and taking me home?" The suggestion seems feeble coming out of my mouth.

"I suppose there's good in everyone," Dr. Quickly says. "But it would certainly be a bit out of character. And it wouldn't explain why they went through the effort of picking you up in the first place."

"What's so bad about him?"

"I don't know if 'bad' is the exact word I would use, but he's certainly disreputable." Dr. Quickly stands up and walks behind Abraham to view over his shoulder.

"Amadeus is known for being all about money," Mym explains. "He has an army of loan sharks and bookies. He's made his fortune as a time traveler by winning bets, but now he's moved on."

"Moved on to what?"

"Organizing." Dr. Quickly says. He puts his hands in his pockets and looks at me. "He's a promoter for all kinds of high profile events that are attractive to time travelers. Successful time travelers usually have more money than they know what to do with after a while. At least the greedy ones do. But once they acquire their wealth, many of them get bored and want more diverting activities."

"Like what?"

"Oh, the things wealthy elite like to pride themselves on, safaris, visiting exotic time streams, hunting now extinct animals, that sort of thing. That and competitions."

I get a sudden sinking feeling in my stomach. "What sort of

competitions?"

"Barbaric ones usually," Mym says.

"Like what?"

"Like things that would be far too illegal for anyone other than a time traveler to dream of getting away with. He sets up these events and then his bookies bring in his revenue. I'm sure he's worth billions by now, but I don't think it's the money that motivates him. I think he enjoys the reputation." She pauses when she sees my face. "What's wrong, Ben?"

"Are you all right?" Dr. Quickly steps toward me. "You look like you've gone ill."

I hold my hand to my head, remembering the device in Ariella's pocket. "I think I know why they grabbed me."

"Sure, all parenting is tough, but you think you've got it bad? Try enforcing a curfew on a teenage daughter who can time travel."–Journal of Dr. Harold Quickly, 1997

Chapter 4

"You entered a chronothon? What's wrong with you?" Mym's voice has reached a level of intensity that I've never encountered.

"I didn't know it was a big deal . . ."

"You're going to get yourself killed!" Her accusing glare makes me want to flee for the jungle, but I stay fixed to my crate. "Don't you have any idea what these people are like?"

"Mym, let's give the boy some slack. It may not be that bad." Dr. Quickly rises from his chair.

"Dad! You're gonna defend this?" Mym gestures to what I assume to be all the most disappointing aspects of me, simultaneously.

"Ben obviously made a mistake, but let's not get out the tar and feathers just yet." Dr. Quickly puts a hand on my shoulder. "Benjamin, what inspired this sudden interest in racing a chronothon?"

I think about Ariella's lips a few inches from mine, and Horacio's derisive smirk as he mocked the idea of me competing, but think better of sharing those moments. "They made it out to be a charity event. They didn't say when it was or anything. I'm sure I can get out of it."

"Hm. It seems unusual that they would go to all this effort just to sign you up for a charity event," Quickly muses.

"So I take it that it's something else?" I glance at Mym. Her forehead is crinkled in aggravation. "I'm a little vague on what the big deal is."

Abraham has stopped investigating my chronometer for the moment and has leaned back in his chair. "Chronothons themselves aren't necessarily a terrible thing, but I don't know that I would ever call them a 'charity event.' I believe a lot of people make a great deal of money from them. But the race is not likely the problem. I imagine young Mym here is merely looking out for your safety."

"Gioachino Amadeus being involved does worry me," Dr. Quickly adds. "He's not typically the most generous of souls from what I've gathered. I haven't had too many personal dealings with him, but I also know that I don't plan to." He glances at Mym, as if fact-checking himself, to see if a future version of him might have other ideas. Mym stays silent. Her arms are crossed and she's not looking at me.

"So what do I do? Do I need to go back and tell him I don't want to join the race?" I glance from face to face.

"I would certainly suggest you try," Dr. Quickly says. "Did he say when you are supposed to compete in this race?"

"She just said someone would be in touch."

"She?" Dr. Quickly asks. Mym turns to look at me now, her eyes probing my face.

"Uh, yeah. This woman who was there at dinner."

"What was her name?" Mym's voice is emotionless.

"They said her name was Ariella." The name has no effect on Dr. Quickly or Abraham, but I think I see a flicker of recognition on Mym's.

"Do you know her?" Dr. Quickly questions his daughter. Mym doesn't answer. Instead she drops her arms and turns away from me.

"I need a minute." She backs up a step and spins around, pushes her way into the tall grass and disappears. I stand up and debate going after her, but pause under Dr. Quickly's gaze.

"Is there anything I should know about?" he asks.

"No. Not that I know of." *I have no idea what's going on right now, so why should anyone else?*

Abraham's attention is back to my chronometer. He studies it with a magnifying glass, then sets it back on the crate in front of him. "I certainly don't see anything wrong with this, Benjamin. Nothing that could explain your involuntary displacement." He checks the latch on the band and strokes his chin. "I can give you a tamper-proof latch for this. I have a new design that will keep anyone but you from getting it off your wrist."

"That might be good." I walk behind him and look over his shoulder at the inner workings of my chronometer, the intricate pieces are a shining puzzle of gears and diodes. "How do you know what you're looking at?"

"It's not so complex when you take it piece by piece."

"How did you learn to make these?"

Abraham hands me the magnifying glass so I can inspect it more closely. "I used to be a watch maker before I met Harry. He made time machines. It sounded much more exciting."

"Don't let Abraham sell himself short. He made exquisite watches," Dr. Quickly says. "That's how I found him."

I examine the workings of the chronometer with curiosity, then set it back down. "Any chance you could teach me a little about it? I've never taken apart a watch before, but I was a boat mechanic back home. I like knowing how things work when I use them, and how to fix them when they break."

Abraham looks at Dr. Quickly and the scientist shrugs. "The older me already gave the boy a chronometer to keep. I suppose I must have known what I was doing. May as well teach him how to fix it."

Abraham nods and looks me over. "If you have some technical skill, you might do all right. But you won't be starting with this." He holds up the chronometer. He sets it back down and rises from his chair. He pulls the flap of the nearest tent open and disappears inside. When he reemerges, he places a brass, mechanical alarm clock on the crate in front of me. "Here. You can use my tools. Disassemble this completely. If you can get it back together and working, we'll consider letting you touch a chronometer."

Dr. Quickly rises from his chair and collects the sifting pans. Abraham joins him. "We'll be back in a bit. You can find us in the creek if you need us." As they vanish back into the grasses, I hear Dr. Quickly's voice again. "Why'd you have to give him *my* alarm clock?"

I can't hear Abraham's response, but I can hear their laughter slowly fading into the distance. I smile, but my smile slowly wanes as I turn toward the side of camp where Mym disappeared. *That's what you need to be fixing.* I unroll the tools on the crate and set to work on the alarm clock.

The casing comes apart easily enough, and I set the small screws carefully on a rag to keep track of them. The inside of the clock looks surprisingly complex, with at least a dozen gears on a frame and a large coiled spring. I examine it from all sides. *Now what?*

I work a steel keeper off the front of the frame, and suddenly the spring comes uncoiled. Something flies off and strikes the grass ahead of me, and I try unsuccessfully to dodge a gear that ricochets off my forehead. *Shit.* I twist on my crate. The gear is lying in the dirt behind me, so I snatch it up. I glance over to the grass where the other object disappeared, then consider the clock innards in my hand, trying to recognize what's missing. *Damn it.*

I set the clock down and walk over to the grass where I think the object could have landed. Squatting down, I begin parting the stems to inspect between them. After a minute or two of fruitless searching, I'm interrupted by a sudden sneeze to my right. Tracing the source of the noise through the grasses, I spy a pair of blue eyes peering at me from under a mess of dirty blonde hair. The little girl's knee length pants are muddied and grass-stained, but she is holding her camera securely in both hands, as if nothing in the world will be allowed to harm it.

"Hey there."

The little girl considers me quietly for a moment, then steps closer. "What are you looking for?"

I scratch my head. "You know, I'm not really sure."

The girl advances a little farther and looks at the ground where I've been searching. "Then how are you going to know when you find it?"

I study the little Mym before me. Her forearms are tan and there are sun freckles on her nose. Her dirty nails and scratched hands match the roughed-up appearance of her clothes. Her pockets are stretched full of something lumpy.

"You a jungle adventurer?" I smile at her.

"I'm a photo journalist. What are you?"

"Right now I'm a doodad locator."

"A doodad?"

"Could've been a thingamajiggy, or possibly a whosie-whatsit. I'm still not quite sure."

The girl grins. "Can I help?"

"Definitely."

The little Mym gets closer and squats next to me. I go back to parting the grass stems, and she follows my example. After a few minutes, I spot the steel pin with a tiny knob on the end, resting close to Mym's foot.

"I feel like we're sooo close." I put my hand to my forehead and close my eyes. "It's almost like I can *feel* it nearby. It's here somewhere, I just can't put my foot on it."

"Don't you mean finger? Isn't it supposed to be 'put my finger on it?'" Mym says.

I sneak a peek through my nearly closed eyelids at Mym's questioning face. "Nope. Definitely feeling a foot."

Mym scours the ground some more. "I found it!"

"Nice!" I open my eyes and take the steel pin she offers to me. "Yep, that's my doodad."

"You knew it was there, didn't you?"

"You don't believe in my psychic powers?" I stand up and try to look offended.

Mym tilts her head as she considers me. "Do you have any other powers?"

"Doodad locating is pretty much it. Though I do know how to make a really good Key lime pie."

"That's not a psychic power."

"No? I guess not then."

Mym follows me back to the crate where my clock is lying, partially disassembled. She watches me sit down and start fiddling with the gears.

"What are you doing to it?"

"Abraham wants me to take it all apart, and then put it back together again."

"Oh." She watches me unscrew another knob. "You should take a picture of it. That way you know what it's supposed to look like."

"Hmm. That's actually a really good idea. You don't happen to know anybody with a camera do you?"

Mym grins and steps to my side of the crate. She holds her camera to her eye and takes her time adjusting the lens. Her hands are steady. Finally she clicks the shutter and holds the camera away from her face to see the image on the back of the digital display. The camera looks very similar to the ASP time traveling camera Dr. Quickly taught me to use in 1986.

"Did you get a good one?"

"Yeah."

"Here, I'll let you shoot the other sides." I hold the clock at different angles while she takes more photos. When we're done, she checks the images.

"Do you want me to print them out for you?"

"Can you do that here?"

"Yes." Mym smiles.

That smile hasn't changed. Still enchanting, even at eight.

She disappears into one of the camp tents. About fifteen minutes later, she reemerges with six small photos of the different angles of the clock. By now I've got most of the clock in pieces.

"These turned out great," I say as I examine her shots.

"That one is fuzzy on the edge." She points to a corner.

"Wouldn't have noticed if you hadn't pointed it out. You're a pretty great photo journalist."

Mym nods slowly, acknowledging this to be true, then plants herself in the camp chair opposite me. "How did you get here? Did I bring you?"

"Were you wishing real hard for a whosie-whatsit locator?"

Mym shakes her head. "No. I saw me. Down by the river."

"Oh." I consider what that might mean. *Is Mym going to be upset that her younger self saw her?* "Did you talk to . . . you?"

"No. I just looked." Mym fiddles with a leaf. "I've met me before, from when I'm older, but Dad says it's not good to interact with yourself very much. He says 'creating temporal paradoxes is universally irresponsible.'"

"Well, he probably knows best."

She drops the leaf. "I looked sad. Why was I sad?"

"I don't know. I'm hoping it's not for too long, though. Hey, you want to get a shot of this thing all in pieces so I can prove to Abraham that I had it apart? Don't want him to think I was cheating when I get it back together."

Mym nods and hops up to take some more photos.

My fear of Abraham not knowing I had it apart proves unfounded, as when he returns an hour later, I'm still not finished reassembling it. When he looks over my shoulder at my progress, I'm still trying to match up pieces. "These two gears look almost identical, but I can't figure out which one goes where." I finger the two troublesome parts in my palm.

"Looks like you had some assistance." Abraham picks up one of Mym's photos and examines it.

"Yeah." I wonder if he's going to be upset that I had help, but his smile is reassuring. "A second set of eyes is always a good idea. So is very careful examination." He nods toward my hand. I hold the two gears up close to my face. On closer inspection, I notice one has a small spacer under the gear that the other one lacks.

"Oh. That makes sense why it wasn't fitting." I slide the gear into place and set it with a lock pin.

"Attention to detail is essential in clock work," Abraham says.

Abraham and Dr. Quickly set about preparing some food for dinner as I continue my assignment. Mym helps her dad stoke a fire and chop an onion. I try to concentrate on my task but am soon distracted by the smell of sizzling meat and vegetables. Mym prods the frying pan with a long wooden spoon. She catches my eye and gives me a shy smile.

My mouth is watering when Abraham walks over to me with a steaming plate in his hands. "Oh, thanks, that smells amazing."

"Hmm?" Abraham raises an eyebrow. "Oh, no. This one is for me." He picks up a dripping piece of shredded beef with his fingertips and puts it in his mouth. "Dinner is only for folks who have finished their chores. Isn't that right, Mym?"

"Whoa, seriously?" I look over to Quickly and Mym seated on the other side of the fire. Mym pauses in chewing her mouthful of veggies and shrugs. "Dude, that's cold."

"Actually it's really hot and delicious." Abraham licks his fingers. "Might still be that way, if you hurry up." He savors his next bite with a little more gusto than I think is necessary and goes to join the others.

I grumble internally for a few minutes, but once I concentrate on the clock, the last few parts go back on without much trouble. I double-check Mym's photos one last time before reinstalling the back cover. I turn the key and feel a wave of relief as the ticking begins. Rising from my crate, I cross to the other side of the fire where the others have made a table out of the other gear. Abraham leans back in his chair and extends a hand. I relinquish the clock, feeling like I'm in grade school, handing in arithmetic homework.

Abraham holds the clock to his ear momentarily, then examines the outside of the housing. "Not bad. Clock works. Now for the real test." He flips the alarm lever and turns the setting knob. He sets the clock on the table between us. "A minute ought to do it."

Abraham and Dr. Quickly resume eating, but Mym has stalled, and looks from the clock to my face in curiosity. I'm left standing awkwardly at attention, watching the slow progress of the second hand. I inadvertently begin counting the seconds, going over the clock parts in my mind. *Did I get that alarm stop reinstalled the right direction?* Time seems to have slowed as the second hand creeps onward. My eyes are glued to the clock face as it ticks the last five seconds. *Three, two, one...* A clunk issues from the clock. Then silence. My heart sinks. Abraham glances up and raises an eyebrow. He fixes me with a disappointed glare.

Shit. What did I forg—

The bells erupt into a raucous cacophony of sound. It's accompanied by Abraham and Dr. Quickly's laughter.

"You should have seen your face," Abraham points at me and releases a jovial belly laugh that shakes his whole torso.

Dr. Quickly is chuckling, too. "The '68 Penguin always has a delay on the bell hammer."

Abraham is still laughing gleefully. He gives a sudden snort as he doubles over. Mym is grinning, too, though I suspect it's just from watching Abraham's mirth.

Clock maker practical jokes. Now I've seen it all. I smile in spite of myself. The big man's continuing laughter is contagious.

Dr. Quickly hands me a plate. "Sit. Eat."

Abraham finally settles down but has to wipe tears from his eyes between his still intermittent chuckles.

The camp food tastes like the best thing I've ever eaten. I mow through the juicy beef shreds and grilled corn in a matter of minutes. I try to take my time with the other vegetables, but find it challenging.

"So what are you guys looking for in that stream?" I pause between bites to get the question out.

Dr. Quickly leans back in his chair and works a toothpick through his teeth. "Evidence. We think we might be onto some naturally occurring forms of gravitite particles. There have been suggestions of naturally occurring wormholes that could exist in various parts of the universe. This site is one of our more promising locations on the planet."

"That's cool."

"Very cool," Dr. Quickly replies. "Nature constantly presents us with new surprises. Somewhere in these mountains, we suspect there may have been some kind of temporal anomaly. We're slowing homing in on it."

"You do this sort of thing often?"

"We're discovering an entirely new area of science, it's hard not to be consumed with the sheer excitement of it all."

"You're a time traveler, though. Couldn't you just jump forward to a time when all of this has already been discovered?"

"That's the exciting part. I'm the one discovering it, so in order to reach those future timestreams, at some point I have to get down to the nitty gritty of actual discovery. I love it, so I wouldn't have it any other way."

"And you get to raise your daughter in a jungle, so I guess that's a perk." I smile at Mym. "Speaking of your daughter . . ."

"I know what you're going to ask. You'll just have to be patient. She'll be back."

We clean up the remnants of dinner, and Abraham points me back to my crate. He sets a lantern and a chronometer in front of me. Next, he hands me a magnifying lens of the type you wear in your eye. "Here. You'll need a loupe and some of the precision tools for this."

"Now?"

"Tempus Fugit, Benjamin. And the hour of our death draws nearer with each ticking second."

"Well gee, if you're going to put it so cheerfully . . ."

Abraham smiles. "Ignoring reality does not make it any less persistent. And you've got work to do."

"Fair enough." I seat the magnifying loupe in my eye, pick up the tools, and set to work.

"Gravitites are particles that exist free of time. Once they become a part of you, time is forced to release its hold on your destiny. What you do with that freedom is up to you. Try to show some originality."–Journal of Dr. Harold Quickly, 1885

Chapter 5

The stars are out, and the jungle is pulsing with the sounds of mating insects, but my world has shrunk to the confines of the lantern light. Abraham guides me through the components of the chronometer, step-by-step. The gears and movements are microscopic compared to the alarm clock, but I do my best to keep up with Abe's descriptions.

"... and the color of the diodes is another good indicator of the capabilities of the main capacitor." I scribble occasional notes and drawings on a blank page of Quickly's journal. I've noticed Dr. Quickly casting occasional glances at the book. I can't fault his curiosity, considering that it holds entries from a future version of him, events he has yet to experience. I imagine there is a less complete edition of the journal somewhere among his belongings in the camp. I admire his composure. I'm not sure I would be able to resist knowing my own future.

Dr. Quickly instead exerts his energy toward prompting his daughter to bed.

"But Dad, I'm not tired!" Mym casts furtive glances my way, perhaps hoping for a champion to defend later bed times. "You let me stay up for the meteor shower!"

"There are no meteors tonight, Mym. No more stalling. You can say goodnight to Mr. Abraham and Mr. Benjamin if you like."

Mym walks over to our makeshift table and hugs Abraham, "Goodnight, Mr. Abraham."

"Good night, child." Abraham pats Mym's back with affection. She pauses in front of me, seemingly unsure of how to proceed.

"Goodnight, Mym." I extend my hand. "It was a pleasure to meet you."

She shakes my hand lightly. "Nice to meet you, too." She smiles and flees for her tent. Dr. Quickly follows to make sure she's settled.

"Good kid. Easy to see why she turned out so well."

Abraham nods. "There has never been a time I haven't enjoyed her company."

When Dr. Quickly reemerges from Mym's tent, he retrieves a flashlight from the table and walks to the edge of the camp. I observe with curiosity as he flashes the light to the west in three long bursts, followed by one long, one short, and a final long. Thirty seconds later, the older Mym emerges from the tree line.

Abraham is still instructing me, so I try to pay attention, but I sneak peeks at Mym as she gets closer. *What was she doing this whole time? Is she really that mad?*

" . . . and don't forget to double-check the wiring diagram after each component installation. You can't change the overlap pattern."

Mym only looks at me briefly as she passes by. Our eyes meet momentarily, and I wave, but her closed-lipped smile barely registers on her face, never showing in her eyes. *Damn. I'm worse off than I thought.*

Mym joins Dr. Quickly on the other side of the dwindling fire, keeping their conversation inaudible from my position. I focus on my chore at hand.

"Get that all back together and then you can try it," Abraham says.

"Whoa, try it? On myself?"

"You have to have confidence in your own work if you're going to do this regularly. I do sometimes perform my initial prototype tests on the lab animals, but only the new designs. I didn't bring any along in any case. I suppose you could try to capture a squirrel . . ."

"Will you at least look it over for me, before I put the back on?"

Abraham smiles. "I have been, Benjamin. But yes, I'll check it again. Like I said before, another pair of eyes is always a good idea."

Abraham surveys the results of my tinkering with his magnifying glass, then hands it back to me. "Your work shows promise. You'll have to visit my shop in Berne sometime. You'd like getting to work on some of the new models." I nod and accept the chronometer, then start reassembling the back.

"Do you make a lot of them?"

"Just what we need, for the most part. Sometimes I do special orders for people, but it's a selective process. Can't be giving out chronometers to just anyone."

When I finish my assembly, I slip the chronometer back onto my left wrist and flex it. It's still a little sore, but feels better. I latch the band with the new lock mechanism Abraham has helped me install, and tug on it to make sure it's secure.

"Why don't you take a quick hop, and test it out." Abraham gestures toward the coffee can on the crate next to us. "Couple seconds or so."

My heart begins to beat faster, but I get up and take a position near the can. I set my chronometer for a three second jump and glance over to where Mym and Dr. Quickly are sitting. They are facing away from us, unmindful of our activities. *No worries guys, might accidentally be fusing myself into the center of the earth over here, but no problem. No need to look up.* I take my position near my anchor, stretching the fingertips of my chronometer hand to touch the rippled metal can. Abraham is looking on casually. I touch my other hand to the chronometer, trying not to think about every boat motor I've ever made mistakes on. *Don't you die, Ben. Don't you even think about it.* I take one last glance at Mym and push the pin.

The fire is still smoldering, insects still chirruping, earth spinning away on its axis, and I'm still properly fixed to its surface. The three seconds I've miraculously skipped over have hardly seemed to make a difference. *Oh thank you, God.*

I step back to my crate and slump onto it. Abraham is smiling. "Well done, Benjamin."

"I don't know how you guys do it, man. I've done a fair amount of jumps now, but I can never be blasé about it. I feel like every one is a minor heart attack."

"Good. Keep that fear. The fear will keep you sharp. It'll keep you alive, so long as it doesn't stop you from doing what needs to be done."

"So you still get scared of it, too?"

"I'd be a fool not to. We're tampering with the very structure of reality, using it to navigate space and time in ways human beings have never imagined. But the excitement of that discovery tempers the fear, so that certainly helps."

Dr. Quickly and Mym rise from their seats and walk our way. I stand back up.

"Well, Benjamin, how did it go?" Dr. Quickly inquires.

"Not bad. Got it apart and back together again anyway. That's a start, I guess."

"Replacing components is about all I can usually manage myself." He smiles. "I leave my major repairs to more accomplished hands." Abraham bows slightly at the compliment. "Mym and I have been discussing your situation, and we feel it's best if she gets you home."

"Home?" My apartment in 2009 is about the last place I feel like being right now. "Shouldn't I be going back to Geo and getting out of this somehow?"

"We discussed that. Your own time and place are where they are likely to try to contact you, so we think it's best if we get you back there. The sooner you get in touch, the more likely you'll be able to decline this." Dr. Quickly lays a hand on my shoulder. "You seem like a good man,

Benjamin, and I understand from Mym that I owe you quite a lot, but I'd be inclined to help you anyway, so I'm sure others will also find you reasonable in your request. I don't know much about chronothons, but I know some acquaintances that have been involved with them, and I don't think the race committee is comprised of bad folks. I'm sure they're open to reason."

Mym steps to my side. "We should get going."

Abraham has disappeared inside his tent briefly, but when he reappears, he extends his hand to me. He puts a tin into my outstretched palm. "These might come in handy. I keep a few spare parts and tools in here and a couple of diagrams. Nothing comprehensive, but good enough for roadside repair."

"Thank you." I slip the tin into my pocket and shake his hand. Dr. Quickly extends his as well.

"Good luck, Benjamin. I'm sure you'll get things sorted out." I'm not sure if he's referring to my prospects with the race or with his daughter, but I thank him anyway. *I need all the luck I can get with both.*

Mym and I walk to the edge of the clearing before she extracts our next anchor from her pack. The chrome door handle seems sterile and clean. Most likely it belongs somewhere just as boring. I wait while she uses the degravitizer on it.

"No roller disco?"

Mym avoids eye contact with me as she selects the settings from the back of the photo and hands it to me. "No. Not right now." I set my chronometer and return the photo. She stuffs it into the bag and starts the countdown, "Three, two, one." We blink.

We traverse the next few destinations in near silence. It isn't until we're stopped at a diner in the mid-eighties to charge our chronometers that we get a chance to talk. We've taken to a booth with a pair of milkshakes, the charging chronometers hidden from view on the seats beside us, looking for all the world like a pair of contented lovers. The inaccuracy of the situation irks me.

"Mym, I know that I obviously upset you. It wasn't on purpose."

She finally looks me in the eye and nods. Her expression isn't angry. It's more an air of resignation. "I know, Ben. I shouldn't be so hard on you. You didn't know. You're new at this. But couldn't you see what was happening? With Geo?"

"He seemed nice. I guess I was just happy to be out of the situation on the street. I was a little lost."

"I know. But Ben, you have to understand. We spend most of our lives having to avoid people like him. There are so many people who would love to get their hands on my dad, rarely for good reasons. You saw his lab before it burned, how he had to hide it, the tunnels . . ."

"I guess I never really thought about how hard that must be."

"It's not just the hiding. We're used to that. Things are going to be different now . . . since he died."

"But we saved him."

"We shouldn't have."

I cock my head in confusion. "What do you mean?"

Mym frowns. "I wasn't strong enough. I wasn't ready to lose him. But in some ways I will anyway. I already have."

"I don't understand."

"What I did was wrong. Changing things, changing the past. He told me I shouldn't. I knew I was supposed to let him go. You can't change the past. My dad died back there. Maybe I would have stopped trying to save him, but I met you, and you told me that you saved him. I knew it had been done already and I just needed to make it happen. So I did." Mym considers my face. "And I'm grateful. I wasn't ready to live in a world without him. It's just been him and me this whole time. But I messed up. I didn't get it right the first try. So now there are other timestreams. Other times where Mym Quickly lost her dad."

"How many are there?" I try to grasp the idea of more Mym's traveling around the universe.

"At least three."

"Oh. So how will I know the difference between them and you, if . . . if I meet one?"

"They wouldn't know about all of this recent stuff. The other versions of me were gone when Dad died, still in Italy. So when you finally saved him, I had to stay behind to tell them."

"That's why you didn't come forward with us?"

Mym nods. "I had to keep them from doing what I did: going back and trying to save him and making even more timestreams."

"Did it work?"

"Yes, but it's still going to be hard. There are four of me now from different timestreams, with one Dad between us. It's not really fair to not let them see him, since I'm the one who caused this."

"I'd never really thought about that." I consider the Mym before me. Her eyebrows are furrowed in frustration.

Her voice gets softer as she speaks again, "You'd think with all these people around, you'd never get lonely. It's the opposite. You can't keep any of them for yourself." She looks up to my eyes. "When I saw you again and knew we would succeed, I didn't really know what was going to happen, but I knew—I knew I didn't want to share you."

I get a flutter in my stomach and resist the urge to grin. Mym's face is still serious. I reach my hand across the table toward hers, but she draws it away.

"But now you signed yourself up for a chronothon; a race that can take you thousands of years away. You'll be so far, I could never find you, no matter how hard I tried."

"Mym, I didn't think about that—"

"No. You didn't." She reaches under the table and yanks her chronometer charger out of the socket. She bundles the cord into her bag and slides out of the booth.

"Mym—"

"We should go." She turns her back on me and heads for the door.

I fumble through my pockets for some tip money and stuff it under my milkshake glass before chasing her out of the diner. Mym is across the street by the time I catch up. I reach out and grab her arm. "Mym, wait."

She turns and looks at my face, her blue eyes locked on mine, expectant, maybe even hopeful, that I'll have something to say that will erase the predicament we're in. I falter. "Look . . . I'll fix it. Somehow." Her eyes drop to my chest. She stretches her hand out till just her fingertips are pressed over my heart. I'm suddenly more aware of my heartbeat.

"It's okay." She withdraws her hand. "Some things just aren't meant to be." She turns away again.

I can think of nothing else to say as we make our final jumps to 2009. We arrive in my neighborhood at a mailbox a few blocks from my apartment. Mym immediately starts degravitizing her next anchor. I can't see the photo, but the anchor is a glass ball like I used in my initial training. Hers looks much older, the interior a whirl of purples and blues. I wonder how many places it could take her. She adjusts the settings on her chronometer pendant and holds the anchor out to me.

"Would you mind holding it for me?"

I let her lay it in my left palm and orient it correctly. She touches my hand only briefly as she raises it to the correct height. She's careful not to touch me again as she places her hand over the anchor. It occurs to me that it would only take a touch, a stretch of my fingertips to make contact with her, and I could go along for the ride. I keep my hand straight, and watch her face. Her eyes finally meet mine when she has her other hand to the pin of her chronometer. I struggle with what to say, but the words won't come.

Her expression is impassive. "Goodbye, B—"

My other arm shoots out and I grasp the hair behind her head, pulling her face toward mine as I press my lips abruptly to hers. I can feel her breath catch, then the movement of her lips on mine. Accepting, responding. Then they pull away. I open my eyes to find Mym staring into them, searching. Her expression is no longer impassive but, what? *Surprised? Excited?* I only have time to register the faintest of smile lines crinkling the corners of her eyes, when I notice her hand still on the pin of her chronometer. She vanishes.

The image of her face lingers in my vision as if my brain refuses to acknowledge her absence. Finally I look down to the glass anchor in my hand, her innocuous, unassuming exit, to when? *Where did you go, Mym?* I attempt to stop my train of thought before it reaches the real question I want answered. *Is she ever coming back?* I'm too late. I can think of nothing else as I trudge the couple of blocks to my apartment.

I'm still in a daze when I get the door open. I stare at my hallway and then the coffee table in total disinterest. Finally I register the blinking light on the end of my cell phone. I pick it up and flip it open. Three missed calls and two voicemails, all from my job. I check the calendar date on the phone. *Shit. I've missed two days of work.* I consider the fact that I'm most likely fired as my thumb hovers over the "return call" button. I realize I don't care, and toss the phone at the couch. I move into the kitchen and reach for the refrigerator, contemplating the memory of my boss's face turning red whenever she'd chew someone out. The fridge is bare.

"God, Benjamin. You can bend space and time, but you can't keep groceries in your refrigerator?" I shut the door in frustration.

"Those were my thoughts exactly."

My heart jolts in my chest. I search for the source of the voice and freeze at the sight of the man sitting at my kitchen table. Everything about him is dark. Black eyes are shadowed by greasy black hair. His dark skin and even his leather trench coat and military boots seem to be dimming the natural light in my usually sunny dining room. The only things light about him are the scar running through his left eyebrow, and the gleam of sunlight off the gun at his fingertips. His hand is resting gently atop the stainless barrel that's lying casually pointed in my direction.

"There were bets on how long it would take you to come home. Some thought we'd never find you here." His voice is gravel. His fingertip gently strokes the length of the gun before he returns his hand to his lap. "Luckily I gave you credit for more guts than most. Looks like I'll be the winner."

"Where else would I be?" I try to sound calm.

"Running for your life. Trying to get lost. Going somewhere I could never find you."

"You didn't want to bet on that?"

The man gives me something close to a smile. "I know there's no such place."

I take a step toward him. "You don't need to chase me because I'm resigning. I don't want to race."

"Is that so?"

"Yes."

"I disagree. I think you're going to decide it's in your best interest to participate in this event." His eyes fall on the gun in front of him. He considers it with curiosity as if it's some exotic foreign specimen newly arrived on my kitchen table.

"So you're the authority on who resigns from chronothons?"

His gaze shifts to me. "I suppose I am. I act on behalf of your authorities. Some of them in any case. The ones that apply to you, for sure."

"I want to speak to them myself. I'm going to tell them that Geo coerced me into this dishonestly."

"Coerced? That's a strong accusation. Let me clarify this situation for you, since you are having trouble grasping it." He gestures with his right hand and a holographic image springs from the floor between us. It's a scene of Geo's dining room. "You recognize the diners?"

I see myself at the table, contending with the plate of Meatball Parmesan. I remain silent.

"The man sitting next to you is Judge Ciril Heperly. I'd say he's been on the race council for, oh, about thirty years. Mr. Gioachino Amadeus has a written statement from him, that he witnessed you volunteering for the race of your own free will. In fact, he says you jumped at the chance."

"The old mustached guy? He was asleep for half the night!"

"That's not what he says. He claims he was awake the whole time."

"He's asleep right now!" I point to the holographic image of the old man, but the hologram vanishes. I'm left staring at the man in black, my finger pointing at his chest.

"Your word against his. Who's the committee likely to believe?"

I drop my hand back to my side. "So what do you want? Are you just here to intimidate me?"

He reaches into the pocket of his jacket and extracts a rectangular container. "I'm here to set your timer." He places the container on the table and flips open the lid. Scooping inside the box, he lifts out a metallic bracelet and lets it dangle at the tip of his finger.

"Timer for what?"

"You're a racer. Racers get timed."

He grips the bracelet and stands up. He's tall, at least even with my height. His proportions are angular and lean, and I would guess I outweigh him, but his manner as he shoves a chair aside suggests a hardness of temperament that I'm not ready to tangle with. And there's the gun. I inch my other hand closer to my chronometer.

"Uh-uh." He wags a finger at me. "You're not going to make me chase you now are you? After we just had this discussion?" He appraises me from a few feet away. "You're going to end up tagged with this bracelet one way or the other. You might run for a while. Hell, you might be fifty and living under some rock in the negative primes by the time I catch you, but make no mistake, you'll be attending this race. Wouldn't you rather compete while you're young enough to have a chance at winning?" He picks his gun up from the table and holsters it. I put my hands to my hips. He smirks. "Good decision."

The man slides a section of the bracelet apart and presses a number of buttons on a miniature keypad. The bracelet springs open.

"Who are you?"

"That's irrelevant."

"Too irrelevant for you to have a name?"

"Names get overused when everyone knows them. I prefer to not have my name sullied by the mouths of the undeserving. Hold out your arm."

"At least I don't have to worry about you flattering my ego, to rope me into some event I shouldn't be involved in. Oh, wait. That was your buddies' jobs. And that already happened." I extend my right arm.

"Gioachino Amadeus has one job. To make money. His methods simply vary."

"And your job?"

"I make sure people keep their promises." He snaps the bracelet onto my wrist and closes the control panel. "My methods also vary." He reaches into his jacket again and extracts an enormous syringe. "Roll up your sleeve."

"Whoa!" I step away. "What the hell is that?"

"Your vaccine."

"Vaccine against what? Elephantitus?"

The man considers the length of the needle as he removes its protective wrapper. "Maybe. I just give the shots, I don't ask what's in them."

"Even more reason. You've got to be crazy if you think I'm getting stuck with that."

"Your prerogative, I guess. You want to retch your guts out with the Spanish Flu in some outdated hospital, I guess you can." He moves the syringe back to the container.

"Spanish Flu? They'll send me somewhere with Spanish Flu?"

"Could be Ebola for all I know. No one knows the course prior to the race. So they can't very well tell you what you're being vaccinated against, can they? It would ruin the suspense."

"Son of a bitch," I mutter as I roll up my sleeve. "If I do get Ebola, I'm coming back and infecting you."

"Just think of this as a free health care perk." The man slides the needle into my shoulder. "The side effects are usually mild anyway. A little blurry vision, maybe a nose bleed or two. Involuntary time travel . . ."

"What?"

"I'm kidding." The man extracts the needle and tosses me a piece of gauze. "Or who knows? Maybe I'm not. Either way, just tell yourself you had no choice."

"I thought you said it was my prerogative."

"Yeah, you could take it in the arm, like a man, or I could have beaten you unconscious and stabbed it into your ass. Those were your options. Now don't you feel like you've made wise decisions so far? Cheer up." He smacks me in the shoulder where he injected me. I wince from the pain.

I look at my wrist and note the display on my new arm ornament. "This looks like a countdown."

The man pulls a degravitizer and a matchbook from his pocket. "It is. You're going to be at the start line of the chronothon by the time that reaches zero."

"Or else?"

"Or else it turns into a different kind of race. You don't want to sign up for that one, either." He hands me a slip of paper and a pencil, then sets to work degravitizing his matchbook.

"What do you need me to write?"

"Nothing. That pencil is your anchor. It will get you in front of the registration committee. They can fill you in on the rest. The jump coordinates and elevations are on the paper." He sets the matchbook on the edge of my kitchen counter and applies his index finger to it.

I turn the slip of paper over. "Ireland?"

"Yeah, but pack light. You won't be staying long."

He disappears.

"Anchor yourself. Firmly. Never make a jump without solid contact with your anchor. The ether of time is littered with involuntary travelers who couldn't grasp the concept of holding on."–Journal of Dr. Harold Quickly, 2125

Chapter 6

The phone rings five times before Francesca picks up. "Hey, Ben. What's up?" She sounds out of breath.

"I'm pretty sure I'm fired, and that's not even remotely the bad news."

She pauses. "You want me to come over?"

"Actually, I was hoping we could go grab some food. I'm starving. Did you eat yet?"

"I ate, but I'll come get you. Be there in a few minutes."

Of all my friends, only a few know about my recent experience with time travel. Those few only know because they were with me the day it happened. Our experience caused us to spend weeks in the past but I haven't even had the chance to attempt to tell anyone else. Not that anyone would be likely to believe me anyway.

I snag the matchbook off the counter and take it outside with me to the sidewalk. I've watched about half the matches burn their way toward my fingertips by the time Francesca arrives. She turns down the radio as I climb into her Camry. She's still in her workout clothes, her dark hair pulled back into a ponytail.

"Hey," she says.

"Hey, Fresca. I appreciate you doing this."

"Sure. We've missed you the last couple days. Carson and I came by your place yesterday and left a note on your car. Did you get it?"

"You guys hanging out again?"

"Something like that. Everything's different now, you know? It's nice being around someone who knows what I'm talking about. And you've been MIA. What've you been doing?"

"I took a trip."

"Like a trip, trip, or . . ." She nods toward my chronometer. " . . . you know, a trip?"

"The latter." I fill her in as briefly as I can about my excursion with Mym, as she exits my neighborhood.

"Spain? Really? Where did you sleep at night? Did anything happen? I need details."

"Nothing like that. Money's not really an issue for her, so we could afford separate rooms."

"That's no fun. So no romantic progress?" She alternates between watching my face and the road.

"Kind of. I kissed her."

"Ooh, yeah? How did it happen? Tell me, tell me!"

"It was kind of weird timing. She was leaving, and I wasn't sure she was coming back. I'm still not sure."

"What? Why?" Francesca pulls into the Chipotle parking lot and shuts off the ignition.

I hold my wrist up and jiggle the bracelet. "I got myself into some trouble."

"For wearing man jewelry?"

"It's a little worse than that." I wait till I'm through the ordering line and seated across a booth from Francesca before continuing the story. Francesca tears the top off the bag of chips while watching my face expectantly.

"I'm going to be in a race. A race for time travelers."

Francesca cocks her head. "Okay. Go on . . ."

"Only it's not just a race. I think these guys might be some kind of mafia. They're big time, whoever they are. Powerful. Influential."

"What do they want with you?" She dunks a chip into the salsa.

"I don't really know. I just know they tricked me into signing up for this thing and they aren't going to let me out of it."

"Did you tell Dr. Quickly? What did Mym say?"

"They thought I should try to beg out from the race committee, tell them I got conned. I planned on trying that, but when I got home, a guy was waiting in my kitchen with this." I finger the bracelet, watching the seconds ticking down. "He wasn't messing around. He made it pretty clear that I'm not getting out of it."

"He was from the race?"

"I don't even know. I feel so far over my head on this I can't even tell you. I just know somebody wants me involved in this thing, and they're not going to let up. Until I have more pieces of the puzzle, I just have to keep going. I wanted to tell you, though. I don't know why they picked me, but they may target you guys, too. If you or Blake or Carson see anybody suspicious lurking around, you should blink out of there first and ask questions later. And watch out for anyone peddling flattering bullshit, though I'm probably the only one who falls for that."

"What are you going to do?" Francesca stretches a hand out to mine.

"I need to find some help. I'm tired of feeling clueless. And I need to figure out how to race a chronothon, apparently."

"Are you going to find Dr. Quickly again?"

"If I can. He's the only ally I've got, unless Mym turns back up."

"She will." Francesca pats my hand. "She has to recognize a good thing when she sees it."

After lunch, Francesca pulls up to the curb in front of the Saint Petersburg Temporal Studies Society and lets the engine idle. The low industrial building where Dr. Quickly began his research is nestled in an otherwise residential neighborhood. A chain link fence has been left open for a team of electrical workers who are making adjustments to a transformer from the top of their bucket truck. A few other workers are replacing glass on some of the windows. I'm puzzled by the activity until I realize it's only been a couple days in 'regular time' since the accident that originally sent my friends and me back in time. They are still recovering from the damage.

"You want me to come in with you?" Francesca asks.

"I'll just see if he's in there and come back out. He may still not want us showing our faces in there." I consider the glass doors of the building, remembering the last time we visited.

"That was twenty-three years ago." Francesca says. "And in a different timestream. There's no way he would remember that conversation."

"I'm going to err on the side of caution anyway." I climb out of the car and survey the building windows. Dr. Quickly vanished from this facility in the 1990s, but if I'm correct, there is still one man left inside who can help me.

The young receptionist at the desk smiles at me as I enter the lobby.

"Good afternoon, sir. How can we help you?" Her fingers are still poised over her keyboard.

"I'm looking for Malcolm Longines. Is he in today?"

The woman spins in her chair and snatches up the phone receiver. "Let me page him. May I tell him who's inquiring?"

"Benjamin Travers."

I linger near an aquarium and watch a sea snail inch itself along the glass until I hear the double-doors swing open behind me. The man standing in the doorway is dark-skinned and in his mid-fifties. His curved nose and serious expression haven't changed since I saw him last, despite the aging. Dr. Quickly's longtime assistant shows no sign of recognition.

"Mr. Travers. It's a pleasure to meet you. Please follow me."

I trail him through the doors into an empty conference room just off the main hallway. He closes the door gently behind us and gestures me to a seat. He takes a seat opposite me, folding his hands over a manila envelope on the table.

"Malcolm, I know you won't remember me . . ." I begin. I look into his eyes, remembering the last day I saw him, police lights flashing in the street after I pulled him from a burning building.

"I won't," he interrupts, holding up a hand. "And please don't feel the necessity of telling me the circumstances. That is not the role of a 'constant.'"

Constant Malcolm.

"But while I may not be a time traveler, I am aware of who you are, and I've been advised to pass along this information." He slides the manila envelope across the table.

"You were? By whom?" I pick up the envelope, curious about what it may contain.

"Please don't open it here. It would be best if I didn't know the contents. Miss Quickly left the package for you, and my instructions were to ask no further questions."

Mym. She did come back. I'm tempted to ignore him and tear into the package immediately, but I resist the urge. "Thank you, Malcolm. Now I owe you one."

Malcolm stands and holds open the door for me. "I'm sure I don't know to what you are referring, but you are welcome." A hint of a smile threatens to show itself on his face.

I pause in the hallway. "If you see Mym again, will you pass a message along for me?"

"Of course, sir."

"Tell her that I'll be back, and I want to pick up where we left off."

Malcolm nods. "Is there any specific time period of Miss Quickly's life that this message should be addressed to?"

"All of it," I say. "Tell her that applies to always."

Francesca eyes the package as I climb into the passenger seat. I shut the door and tear the end open, shaking the contents into my palm.

"Somebody got you a watch?"

The wristwatch in my hand is gold with a leather band. The accompanying photo shows it resting on a wooden table.

"Somebody got me an anchor." I hold up the photo. "Looks like I get to hang out with Abraham again."

"Again?"

"Yeah. I got to meet him in the early seventies. You'd like him."

Francesca pulls into the street and navigates her way back to my apartment. I fiddle with the watch in my hand. "Hey, Fresca?"

"Yeah?"

"Can you do me a favor?"

"Sure. What's that?"

"You know where I keep the spare key to my place, right?
She nods.

"Good. If anything happens, and I'm not saying it's going to, but if anything does, will you let my folks know and, you know, my other friends? I've got all their numbers in my address book and my phone."

Francesca considers my face. "Is it going to be that dangerous?"

I chew my cheek a little before responding. "No. I mean, I hope not. But it's time travel, you know? I don't know what the hell I'm doing half the time . . . and this time, shit, I really have no clue."

"Then you pay attention to the people that do, and you stick with them, okay?" She pulls over outside my apartment and directs her attention to me. "Ben, in the last few weeks I've seen you do all kinds of things. None of which you could do the week before. I don't know how we would have gotten home without you. I'm so glad we're back, and it sucks that you aren't able to be done yet, but let's be honest, how long were you going to stick around with a chronometer on your wrist anyway? I know you, and going back to fixing boats wasn't going to cut it anymore."

"Not like I have much of a choice now."

"I saw the way you looked at her, Ben. No marina job was going to keep you from running off the first time she winked at you."

"And look where that got me." I shake the timer bracelet at her.

"Then you know what? You go win that damn race. Bring Mym back a shiny medal. You know us girls, we love things that sparkle." She smirks at me.

I let myself smile back. "You ought to be a motivational speaker."

"Shut up."

"No, I'm being serious. That helped. Really."

Francesca smiles. "Good. Because I meant it."

I reach across the armrest and give her a hug. "Tell Carson and the others I said hey. I'll come hang with you as soon as I get back."

"You'd better."

I stand on the sidewalk till she pulls away, then wave.

I take the steps to my apartment two at a time. There are no more surprise guests inside, though I check every room just to be sure. I collect every piece of clothing I own that has gravitites imbedded, since only those items will be able to make the trip, and realize I don't have much to pack. Then I figure out I have no way to transport it anyway. I end up layering a couple of shirts underneath my leather jacket and add an extra pair of athletic shorts under my pants, before stuffing my pockets with my pocketknife, pen, Quickly's journal, and Abe's tool kit. I use Mym's degravitizer to check the pencil that my visitor left me for gravitites. It still hasn't been purged, so I stuff that and its location notes into my pocket as well. Next I check the watch. The green light on the degravitizer shines brightly, letting me know the anchor is gravitite-free and ready for use. *Let's see what you've got for me this time, Abe.* I dial in my chronometer and touch my fingertips to the watch-face. The timer on my bracelet blinks forty-eight hours. *Guess I'd better be a fast learner.*

I push the pin.

The watch now lies on a table in a dining room, the like of which I've never seen. The wall behind the table is entirely glass and the view is an expansive valley rimmed with snowcapped mountains. I step toward the window. The few trees near the house strain for footing as the ground plummets away from them. I can see at least a thousand feet down the rocky mountainside before the forest repopulates the slope. My stomach turns and I return my gaze to the inside of the house. The sound of a shutting cupboard guides me around the corner into a kitchen where I find Abraham watching a teakettle. He looks comfortably dressed for the cold in a thick knit sweater and hiking boots. I notice he has two mugs on the counter.

"You were expecting company?" I lean against the doorpost.

Abraham grins as he faces me. "Anchors make for precise arrival times. Tea?"

"Sure. That sounds great. Some place you've got here."

"It's an old ski cabin that's been significantly updated. You like it?"

"If you don't mind teetering on a precipice all day. Not sure I'd have had the courage to build it. I probably would have put mine in the valley."

"I enjoy the solitude. Eight months of the year the roads are impassable. Makes for a cozy retreat for an old watch-maker like me." He pours a cup of hot water and hands it to me.

"You guys are big on privacy." I think about what Mym said regarding Dr. Quickly's tunnels.

"Perhaps if the world were a kinder place, we wouldn't need to be." He slides a plate with a selection of teas across the countertop. His smile is warm. He doesn't look any older than the last time I saw him. He considers my face a moment. "When did you sleep last, Benjamin?"

"Um, the 1960s, I guess." I tear open a tea packet and dunk the bag into my water.

"Hmm. You may want to look into that. You're looking a bit ragged." He hands me a spoon.

"It's been a long day. And I don't seem to have much time." I hold up my arm with the bracelet on it.

"Yes. I had a suspicion you might not be getting out of that. We're going to need to get you on your way shortly if we're going to have any chance of getting you some training."

"You can train me?"

Abraham shakes his head. "I'm not very knowledgeable about chronothons, but we've had some contact with someone who has."

"Really?"

"Mym had Harry look up one of his buddies for you, Charlie Barnes. Charlie's been through more than his share of adventures, including a few chronothons."

"You talked to Mym?" *Everybody gets to talk to her but me.*

"She called earlier to let me know you'd be coming."

"Where is she?"

"Hard to say. She called in on the T.P.T. so she could be anywhere."

"What's a tee pee tee?" I blow across the top of my mug.

"Tachyon Pulse Transmitter. It's like a telephone for time travelers. I keep one here at the lodge. There are only a few in the world during this century, but the Quickly's have one of the others. Comes in handy."

"Sounds like it."

Abraham appears to be studying me. Finally he cocks his head to the side. "Are you wearing all of your clothes simultaneously?"

"Yup." I sip my tea and smile.

"Thought so. Come on. Let's get you fixed up."

He leads the way out of the kitchen and into a back den. The wooden bookshelves stuffed with knickknacks remind me of Quickly's lab. Photos and anchors share space with what looks like a sizeable collection of classic literature. Many of the names on the spines are foreign to me, but reside next to titans like Twain and Tolkien and Kipling, making me wonder if they could be the revered authors of the future. An oak desk bathed in lamplight is cluttered with items I recognize: flashlight, canteen, compass, matches, and fishhooks. A coil of wire lies atop a battered copy of the Boy Scout Handbook.

"I wasn't sure what you'd need so I tried to cover the basics." Abraham surveys the desk. "One thing mountain cabins are good for, is being equipped for survival."

"Thank you. That's awesome, but I didn't bring anything to carry it all in."

"Got you covered." Abraham reaches behind the desk, picks up a canvas messenger bag, and tosses it to me. "Go ahead and load up. You might be able to fit a few of your extra layers in there, too."

"Thanks."

"I'm supposed to get you to Charlie. From there, he should be able to sort the rest of the plan out. You should try to get some rest. I'm guessing you're going to need it."

"Is Charlie nearby?"

"No. I was told to take you to Ireland in 2016."

"Oh. That makes sense. That's where it's supposed to start." I extract the slip of paper my visitor gave me and hand it to Abe. He considers the time coordinates.

"This is right near the start. We're going to get you there a little early and try to buy you some time." He hands the paper back to me. "These folks don't seem to want you to have much opportunity for preparation. Hardly seems sporting."

"I didn't get the impression they were looking for me to succeed."

"Well, I guess we'll have to change their minds for them. Help me with this other gear." Abe points me to another set of canvas army duffels on the floor. One has a bunch of poles sticking out one end.

"What's all this?"

"These are our accommodations for the evening. Hope you like camping."

We use a piece of stone Abe got from Charlie as the anchor for our jump. We arrive just after sundown on a flat boulder at the edge of a clearing. I shift the duffel strap on my shoulder and breathe in the fresh, damp air of the country. Abraham steps into the knee-high grass and strides toward the forest's edge. He considers the trees, then takes in the view the opposite direction, a downward slope of pasture, and beyond a fieldstone wall, a small, quiet lake.

"Right here will do." The duffel falls from his shoulder with a thump. "Let's get the tent set up and we can still enjoy some of this evening."

I help unload the duffels and am surprised to find how much Abraham has managed to pack. Besides the tent that looks big enough to walk around in, we have two aluminum and canvas cots, sleeping bags, lantern, portable cookware and camp chairs. There is even a pair of marshmallow skewers and a bag of marshmallows. Abraham grins when I hold up the bag.

"I figured there's no use wasting a night of perfectly good campfire weather."

By the time I have the tent and our cots situated, Abraham has a decent blaze going. I help him gather more wood from the forest edge to pile near the fire, then settle into a camp chair beside him. The stars are out, and a steady croaking chorus is coming from the lake. The serenity of the scene seems a stark contrast to the pace of my past day and the relentless countdown occurring on my wrist. I turn the bracelet's display away from my eye line and concentrate on Abraham stacking marshmallows onto his skewer. His puffs of gooey dessert are a toasty brown by the time he speaks.

"I sometimes feel that this is where we find the meaning of the universe." He holds the skewer up for inspection and watches the trio of marshmallows slide into one another.

"At the end of a marshmallow poker?"

"Seems as likely a place as any." He slips one off the end and blows on it before popping it into his mouth.

"I suppose it's a reasonable analogy." I pierce one of my own and dangle it over the fire. "Sometimes you get a treat, sometimes all your hopes go up in flames."

Abraham holds his remaining marshmallows lower in the fire and deliberately sets them ablaze before extracting them and blowing them out. "And sometimes what seems like disaster is actually the best treat of all."

We sit in the quiet for a while, soaking up the calm. I try my best to repress a yawn, but it gets the better of me and I let it out.

"You should get some sleep, Ben." Abraham brandishes his now empty marshmallow skewer. "I'll defend us from the leprechauns."

"Probably a good idea." I take a sip from my water bottle and retreat to the tent. I kick off my shoes but don't bother to undress. I simply crash on top of my sleeping bag in a heap.

Footprints disappear into the desert. A mustached man is holding a stuffed shrimp surrounded by elegant women. The Labrador wearing saddlebags keeps barking toward a doorway. I turn to look and an astronaut gets torn limb from limb by a dead-eyed, salivating mob. They're snarling at me. I'm hovering just above the horde of savages as they claw and leap below. *How long till they reach me*? A voice is lingering in the background of my mind, calling out softly at first, then louder and louder. It's calling my name, but I can't answer. I try to choke out a response, but nothing comes. Something inside me has withered. My hands in front of me are pale, cold, stiff. I realize I'm dead, but there is something beyond that, a dread of something worse, lingering just out of sight. The something wants to hurt me. No, not hurt me; consume me. The voice yells louder. It's my voice.

I jolt awake on my cot. My heart is pounding under my ribs and I put a hand to my chest in silent appreciation of my still functioning body. *What kind of nightmare was that?* The silhouette of the dark shape on the cot across from me rises and falls gently with each breath. I roll onto my back and contemplate the ceiling of the tent, listening to Abraham's light snoring. Eventually, my heartbeat slows and my eyelids drift closed. This time I find only black, dreamless sleep.

"Gravitites must be removed from your anchors prior to use. Can't jump to an object's future if it comes with you. Good news is, you'll see it again on the other side. Keep careful track of your jump photos and anchors that you've used. A single note can save your life."–Journal of Dr. Harold Quickly, 2080

Chapter 7

The sounds of the morning are boots scuffing dirt and the occasional shouts of men giving orders. Someone has a hammer. The metallic ringing of steel being pounded rhythmically into the ground drives the last hope of sleep from my mind. I roll over on my cot and open my eyes.

Abraham is in his camp chair, sipping a steaming mug of coffee and reading the newspaper as if nothing in the world could disturb his calm. I stretch my arms, then let them fall limp to my sides. Abraham sets the paper in his lap and appraises me.

"Sleep well?"

"I'm not sure how I slept at all. I can't decide if they designed these things for sleeping or for just torturing your back." I twist and struggle my way off the canvas cot.

The lantern is still on, but the tent is now lit well enough with the dawning sun to see without it.

"Perhaps you will find more comfortable accommodations during your race." Abraham's eyes are kind, but I can tell his comment holds more hope than truth.

"Have you had any word from the trainer?" I pour a little of my bottled water on my towel and use it to dab my face.

"Yes, actually. Charlie should be here any time now. He said he'll want to get started immediately, so I'm to have you ready."

"Hmm," I mumble, before succumbing to a yawn.

"So. Are you ready?" Abraham examines me over his reading glasses.

"Yeah, sure. Ready."

"Splendid," he replies, and goes back to reading the paper.

I consider the man as I'm pulling on a clean shirt and can't help but wonder if his state of ease is partly affected to keep me calm. I grab my socks and shoes and have a seat on the edge of the cot to put them on. *Then again, he can be as calm as he likes, he's not the one who has to compete in this thing.*

I've just finished tying my sneakers when the flap of the tent is flung open by a broad-chested man in cargo pants. His ruddy complexion and freckled skin suggest decades of life spent outdoors. He reminds me of my high school baseball coach. He looks from Abraham to me and back to Abraham in the matter of a second.

"Right then! Should we get started?"

I push off from the cot and stand, offering a hand to the man. "I'm Benjamin."

"Of course you are." He takes my hand. "Charlie Barnes." Charlie looks back to Abraham, who hasn't moved from his position. "Abe. Good to see you."

Abraham nods cordially and goes back to reading his paper.

"Okay! Let's get to it." Charlie spins and disappears back outside. I snatch up my water bottle and follow him into the sunlight.

During the night, the landscape has transformed. The pasture is filled with tents and portable dwellings of every shape and color. Any direction I turn, I see people erecting poles, hammering tent stakes or offloading supplies from vehicles. There are more than a few RV's and, more shockingly, one large boat parked nowhere near the water but beached at a slight list to starboard in the high grass near the fence line.

I feel like I've awoken inside a traveling circus. The people we pass interest me just as much. The new tent city is teeming with citizens of all ages and shapes. I spy a lanky man in a silver cape, directing a pair of teenagers who are unloading luggage from the back of a van. A dog wearing saddlebags trots past me and disappears into a tent decorated with rainbow streamers. *Why does that seem familiar?*

Charlie leads the way through the sprouting abodes with determined strides. He comes to a dark-green canvas tent roughly the same size as Abraham's, and plunges directly inside. The interior couldn't be more different. Where Abraham's tent was spacious and outfitted with amenities for comfort, Charlie's is clearly meant for utility. It's packed full of storage cases with sturdy locks, and in the center, a portable table that's already buried in timestream charts.

"Did you list your inventory yet?" Charlie begins unlocking one of the crates.

"Uh, no. I didn't write it all down."

"Okay, no problem. I've got a checklist we can use." He pulls a laminated, spiral ringed manual from the crate and flips it open. Next he pops the cap off a dry erase marker and sits down at the table. "Let's hit the basics first." He gestures toward the other camp chair, and I sit.

"All right. I assume you have most of this stuff covered but we'll go over it anyway. You have a pup tent?"

"Um, actually no. I've got a sleeping bag."

"Going to rough it, eh? I've known guys to try that. I always preferred the tent, though. You never know what's going to try to crawl into that sack with you. You got bug spray?"

"No. I forgot that."

"No problem. I think I've got spares. Okay, running shoes."

"Yes."

"Firearms and spare ammunition."

"No . . ."

"You didn't bring a gun?"

"Didn't know I'd need one."

"You bring any kind of weapons?"

"I have a pocket knife."

Charlie leans back in his chair and appraises me. "Okay, well that's your call I guess, but I would go in with a bit more than that."

"What would I be shooting? I thought this was a race."

"Yeah, it is. But it's a race that could take us through some pretty dangerous territory. There're snakes to think about, sometimes bears, mountain lions, regular lions . . ."

"They're going to make us race with lions?"

"You're not racing the lions, but you're sure gonna wanna get away if you see some. This race can take you damn near anywhere. That means you ought to be ready for anything. It's a lot easier to feel ready for anything when you've got a twelve-gauge in your hands."

"That makes sense."

Charlie strokes his chin. "I guess we can make do with my gun. Okay. First aid kit."

I shake my head.

"Canteen, water purification tablets, and desalinization capsules."

"I have the canteen."

Charlie checks off the box for canteen. I'm beginning to feel like a disappointment as he rattles off another list of items I don't possess from his checklist. At the end of it, he lays the list down on the table and studies me.

"Harry said you were green at this, but did he fill you in on what this race is like at all?"

"Not really. I got the impression that chronothons weren't really something he paid much attention to."

"That's true enough. Scientists of his sort don't really spend much time with this crowd, but I would have thought maybe Mym could have filled you in. She's pretty knowledgeable about most anything to do with time traveling."

"Yeah, well, she and I aren't at an all time high on the communication front right now."

"No?" Charlie's jaw works, then he leans back in his chair. He lays his palms flat on the table and looks at me. "I hate to have to ask you this, but I need to know we've got the basics covered. You do know how this works, right? Time travel? In general?" He glances at the chronometer on my wrist. "You can use that thing, right?"

"Yeah. I've only been doing it a few weeks really, but I have the basics."

Charlie nods but raises a palm toward me. "Do me a favor and elaborate a bit. Explain to me what you know, just so we're on the same page."

"Okay." I shift in my seat, trying to pick a place to start. "So basically, time isn't linear. We can jump forward or backward and navigate to the same or different time streams if we use anchors from the time and place we want to go." I lay my fingertips on the edge of the table to indicate touching an anchor, then simulate moving the dials on my chronometer. "You select the increment of time you want to jump, stay in firm contact with your anchor, and the chronometer moves you forward or backward to the point in time where the anchor will be. You end up in the same position relative to the anchor as when you left, only in a different time."

Charlie chews his cheek a little. "All right. You know about getting the gravitites out of the anchors, right?"

"Yeah." I pull Mym's silver degravitizer out and set it on the table for his inspection. "Stuff with gravities in it can time travel and stuff without gravitites won't, so if you're carrying your own anchors and decide you want to use one, you have to get the gravitites out first so the anchor won't try to come along for the ride when you activate your chronometer."

"What about paradoxes, and creating new timestreams? How do you avoid those?"

"Well, you can't do something you never did, or . . . not do something that you know you will do. Dr. Quickly would say 'What happened has happened.' We can't change our own past, just choose to live somewhere different."

"And why don't we want to create paradoxes?"

I contemplate my answer before responding. "Because it's universally irresponsible?"

One of Charlie's eyebrows rises slightly but he nods. "That's one way to put it, I suppose. Harry doesn't spend much time in centuries beyond the twenty-first so he doesn't deal with this too much, but the powers-that-be get to be real sticklers about time travelers making new timestreams or causing paradoxes. Harry was always damn careful just by his nature. He's not the type to get into trouble with a race committee or anybody else, and it's not likely that he would care about their mutterings anyway, but it will definitely get you disqualified from this race. Possibly worse. Not to mention the personal harm you can cause by making new versions of your life, or trying to get your brain right after a bad paradox."

I do my best to look attentive. "No paradoxes. No problem."

Charlie stands and scratches the back of his head. "Well, okay. Sounds like you've got the gist of it. Would've liked if they could've set you up better race-wise, but no matter. We'll get things sorted out. I told Harry I'd help you, and that's what I'm going to do. I have a lot of my gear from my races. Wasn't sure what we'd need, so I brought most of it. Looks like that was a good choice. I'll get your help unpacking it." He scans the crates. He picks up a paperback with the trophy race logo on it and tosses it into my lap. "You'll want to brush up on the rules."

I thumb through the couple hundred pages of lawyer-speak. "Is there a Cliff's Notes version of this thing? This looks pretty technical."

"There's really only a couple basic rules. Race has to stay linear, so like we said, no creating paradoxes or new timestreams. You also aren't allowed to jump back in time more than a designated amount before the gate deposited you in the level. It's not often you'd want to, but people used that to cause disruptions in the past."

"How?"

"Well, in the very first chronothon, before they made that rule, a guy named Dorchester was first through the gate. He immediately jumped back two years and started constructing a thirty-foot stone dome around the gate exit. By the time the next racer came through, he had the thing all wired with trap doors and everything. Oh, that's the other main rule. No inflicting grievous harm on other racers. Come to think of it, Dorchester was responsible for all three of those rules . . . There's a fair bit of other stuff in there too, of course, but I guess that can wait. We ought to go check the roster. They should've posted it by now."

"The roster?"

"Yeah. Let's go check out our competition." Charlie locks the crate and pushes his way out of the tent again.

I trail behind him as we weave around more tent lines and dodge people bustling about the camp. We pause at the main thoroughfare for a lifted sport utility vehicle that rumbles past blaring music. A trio of young guys, and an attractive blonde woman are inside. The tires are as tall as my chin.

We pass a much larger tent that's open on all sides with rows of tables and benches set parallel to one another. A food truck is parked at the far end and servers are dishing out plates to a line of patrons.

"Looks like that'll be the mess tent. We can stop in there on the way back and see what they're serving."

My stomach growls as if triggered by proximity, but we continue toward the stone arch at the end of the pasture. A small crowd is standing near the right pillar, discussing the contents of a sheet of paper secured to the stones.

Charlie elbows his way through, getting occasional nods from people who recognize him. I slide up behind him and look over his shoulder as he runs his finger down the column of racer names. I count about twenty in the racer column. I recognize Horacio and Ariella's names on the list. My own name is near the bottom, and Charlie's is directly next to it in the guides column.

"Looks like Cliff is back as guide for one of the Marsh kids." Charlie snaps a photo of the list with his phone. "They could be allies for us."

"We can have allies?"

"Yeah, it never hurts to have help. It's a competition, but it doesn't mean you can't be sporting about it."

We make our way back to the mess tent and get in line at the cafeteria-style buffet. Charlie is intently scanning the other people in line, and the diners at the tables.

"See anybody else you recognize?" I ask. I glance about also, but see no one I know.

"A few. Not many. Lots of rookies this round. There were a couple veterans on the racer list and a half dozen former racers on the guides list. The rest were pro guides or rookie racers."

"What's a pro guide?"

"Most of the time, guides fall into two categories: former competitors who have enough experience to qualify as guides, or people who have been through the guide training course and been certified as pro guides."

"Is there an advantage to one versus the other?"

"I'd like to think race experience is an invaluable asset, but I'm obviously a bit biased. I have to admit, some of the pro guides are pretty talented. They get a lot of language training, and a more structured training regimen than we race veterans have. We all take the same exam to get certified, so you have to pass that either way, but they do usually score higher."

"Sounds like being a guide is harder than being a racer." I pick up a tray and some utensils.

"Good. It is. Glad to know I'll be appreciated. Racers get all the glory, but guide work has its benefits, too. And the pay is great in most cases."

"Oh yeah. We never talked about how much I'm going to need to pay you for this."

Charlie pats me on the shoulder. "Don't worry, we'll work something out. I promised Harry I'd help you, so that's the main thing. I'm sure we can manage some kind of payment after."

"What's a usual rate for a guide?"

"Eh, two or three mil I guess."

"Mil? Like million? Dollars?"

Charlie smiles reassuringly, "Don't worry. Like I said, we'll work something out. We win this thing, there'll be plenty of cash floating around."

"Okay." *Three million . . . I guess I may need to win after all.*

The women at the buffet serve us scrambled eggs and sausages with cheese grits and pancakes. I get a double portion of sausage links just for good measure.

A fifty-something man with a rough stubble beard spots Charlie from outside the tent and ducks under the side-flap to greet us.

"Barnes! I thought you knew better than to show your face around here."

"Cliff! I saw your name on the guide list, but couldn't imagine you'd really be that stupid."

Cliff grins and grabs Charlie's hand, clapping him on the back with his other hand and making Charlie's juice slosh over on his tray. Charlie doesn't notice. He sails into more insults of Cliff's spreading middle and general ineptitude and Cliff laughs, a deep guttural chuckle that wells up and overflows with gusto. Finally Cliff looks over Charlie's shoulder to me. I smile in greeting.

"This your protégé?"

Charlie turns to me. "Benjamin Travers, meet Cliff Sutherland." I extend a hand. "Cliff's one of the most veteran guides you can find in this game. Won the fifth Chronothon as a racer and had multiple second place finishes."

"An honorable place to finish, too," Cliff says, taking my hand and nodding at Charlie.

"Don't rub it in, you old bastard," Charlie growls.

Cliff grins. "Well, if he wants an education in how to finish second, there could be no finer teacher than you, Barnes. How many was it? Four?"

"You know the record. Get out of the way, you pompous ass. Let us eat in peace." Charlie climbs over a bench and settles in at a table. I join him and Cliff slides in on the other side.

"Maybe you've got greatness in you as a guide, Barnes."

"We'll see. I saw you're guiding one of the Marshes."

"Yeah, Jettison Marsh. He's a good kid, pretty sharp. His sister is racing, too. Their father asked me to keep an eye on them. They've been training pretty hard so they should be in good shape for whatever this race throws at them, but their father thought I'd better be along anyway."

"Who's guiding the girl?"

"Mayra Summers."

"She's not bad. I remember her races." Charlie shoves a forkful of eggs into his mouth.

"So are there obstacles in this race?" I say.

"Did you not tell him anything yet?" Cliff asks.

Charlie is still chewing but he mumbles a response. "We're getting there."

Cliff addresses me. "Chronothons are all about obstacles. It's not just point A to point B stuff. You're gonna have to hit checkpoints of course, but you've also got a task at each level. The task boxes are specific for each racer. You'll get an objective you have to meet before clearing the level."

"What kind of objectives?"

"Oh, it varies a lot. Mostly you have to collect something unique from that time period. We've had to collect goblets, civil war bullets, paintings . . . Charlie, what was it you had to get off that Indian tribe?"

"War bonnet."

"Ha. That's right." Cliff slaps his leg. "You should have seen Charlie here come streaking up to the time gate. I'd just gotten there myself, when he comes galloping up on this ragged looking Palomino. His guide was on the back wearing the war bonnet, feathers flying everywhere. The look on his face! What was his name? Morton? Murphy?"

"Marvin." Charlie smiles.

"Ha. That's right. Marvin. What ever happened to that guy?"

"He quit. The stress got to him. I heard he stopped time traveling all together. Lives in Iowa now, some time in the twenty-first century I think."

"Poor ol' Marvin. Nothing like getting a few arrows shot at you to let you know what you're made of." Cliff grins at me.

"Do you get shot at a lot in this sort of thing?" My sausages have suddenly become less appetizing.

"Nah, that's pretty rare." Cliff shakes his head reassuringly. "Charlie here just took more risks than average in his youth. I'm sure he's mellowed by now."

Charlie looks at me. "I have no intentions of getting us shot this round, Ben. Don't worry. Most levels are pretty benign."

"So you complete your task, get to the next time gate, and then what?" I ask.

"Do it all over again," Cliff says. "Usually there're eight or ten levels depending on complexity. First one through them all, with all their tasks completed, wins."

"Seems simple enough."

"It's a good time," Cliff says. "Nothing quite like it. You'll get people who say it's just thrill seeking, and too dangerous, but there's much more to it than that. Strategy and planning, and all kinds of skills make up a winning run. It's the best challenge out there if you ask me. Nothing else will give you that edge, 'cept maybe fightin' in a war. But this way has better scenery and better looking women." Cliff pushes up from the table and adjusts his pants under his slightly sagging belly. "But you'll get to see it all firsthand. I'd best be getting back to my own brood of up-and-comers. They'll be wondering where I've wandered off to. Good meeting you, kid. Barnes, I'll catch up with you later."

Charlie salutes with his fork and mumbles something unintelligible through a mouthful of grits.

"He seems pretty cool," I say when Cliff has left.

Charlie swallows and dabs at his mouth with a paper towel. "Cliff's a good man. We'll be able to count on him during the race if we need him. The Marshes aren't a bad bunch, either. Their father used to be on the race design committee, so they grew up with chronothons. They'll be tough competition, but they'll be allies, too."

"This sounds like a lot of fun. The Quicklys kind of made it sound like I was on a suicide mission doing this. It doesn't seem like anything sinister that I need to be scared of."

"Sinister? Nah. I mean, don't get me wrong, there's plenty of danger, and we've had a few accidents and fatalities over the years, but most folks who have their heads on straight come through just fine. The race committee usually does a pretty good job of balancing 'interesting' with 'safe' when it comes to their race designs." Charlie gets up from the table and tosses his trash into a bin.

"Do you really think we have a chance of winning it?"

Charlie considers me thoughtfully. "I'll be honest. You with no race experience and us with scarcely any training time together, we're definitely going to be considered a long shot. But this ain't my first rodeo, and if you have half the guts Harry says you do, we should do all right. Now, come on. We've got work to do."

We spend the rest of the morning unloading crates of supplies in Charlie's tent and organizing the things we'll need. Charlie trades out my shoulder bag for one of his packs. Besides having substantially more room, the new pack boasts the ability to keep its compartments watertight and has a number of straps and clips for attaching accessories. I stuff it with whatever Charlie instructs me to. The vitals include: flashlights, matches and a flint, first aid supplies, rope, and drinking water tablets. I manage to cram my leather jacket in there, along with the few other items I brought from home. I also end up rolling Abe's shoulder bag into it, in case I need another bag later. Charlie pores over the variety of maps and timestream charts, before settling on two detailed maps of the world and some blank paper and pencils. He rolls them into a waterproof tube and tosses it to me. "Each chronothon can take you to entirely new places, so we'll most likely have to figure it out as we go."

"So you don't have any idea where they're sending us?"

"The game designers are limited by only being able to send us to locations where they've installed time gates, but they've been working pretty hard at developing new ones from what I've heard. I wouldn't be surprised if they really push the limits this round."

"Who are the game designers?" I work on shoving the tube into my pack.

"They're a combination of engineers and other creative types, usually. Most of them have science backgrounds or previous game management experience. They coordinate the installation of the gates for each race, and design the challenges for the levels.

"There's a larger race committee that the designers for each round are chosen from. The race design is kept secret, even from other committee members, so as to keep the competition fair. There've been occasional information leaks, but they usually keep a pretty tight lid on things. This round, the security has been extra tight. When we go for dinner tonight, we'll see if anyone has any new details, but I doubt anybody will know much."

"When do we get to know our order for the race?"

"They should post it in the morning. We'll have a few hours to strategize depending on our position, and then we'll be through the gate and running."

"How will we know what we need to do?"

"We'll find our task box and go from there. Usually it's somewhere near the outlet of the gate. First priority will be figuring out where we are, based on our environment. The designers love to throw curveballs at you right in the beginning. One time I came out of a gate into an underwater tube and hadn't the foggiest clue which way was up. The tube filled with water quick when I tried to get out of it, and I had to think fast. Luckily I had an inflatable vest with me. I deployed that and it hauled me to the surface."

"Are we going to have those?"

"Oh. Good point, we should probably pack some. Check the crate in the back."

The afternoon sun is already well into its descent by the time I get a break. I wander back through the camp, looking for Abraham's tent among the cluttered new arrivals. I find him out front in his camp chair, much as I left him, ensconced in a book, with little attention spent on the myriad passersby.

"Having a good day?"

He looks up at the sound of my voice. "Splendid. Just finishing an account of castaways in the South Pacific. Fascinating tales."

"Going to pay them a visit?"

Abraham considers the cover of the book. "Hmm. I suppose I could. But I don't imagine their solitude would have been as meaningful then." He flicks a bug off the cover and sets the book on the ground.

"Charlie wants to know if you want to join us for dinner. Apparently there's going to be some kind of presentation. He says the food will be good."

"That sounds like a marvelous idea." Abraham eases himself out of the camp chair. "And how about you? You adjusting all right?"

"Yeah, I guess so. It's a lot to take in. I'm definitely in way over my head, but Charlie seems really knowledgeable. He's pretty nice, too, so I think I'll be okay."

"I'm glad you two are getting along well. I figured you would. You both have adventurer's souls. I'm sure you gentlemen are going to have a lot of planning and strategizing for your start tomorrow, so if you are settled okay, I think I may depart after dinner."

"You aren't going to stick around for the start?" I feel a twinge of disappointment.

"I think it's going to be a tumultuous affair, and you'll have plenty to keep your attention. I'll do my best to be at the finish line, however, to see you come through victorious."

"I'm just shooting for coming through, period."

"That will be a victory in itself then." Abraham smiles.

The camp has been filled to capacity now, and as Abraham and I make our way back to Charlie, we're forced to navigate through more and more people. I recognize a few as racers from the mess tent this morning, but the newer arrivals have a different attitude about them. Excitable. Frenzied even. A teenage girl in a turquoise skirt snaps a picture of me as I walk by. *They're race fans.*

"Hey, Abraham?"

"Yes, Ben."

"Am I a celebrity? Among time travelers, I mean." I check Abraham's face for any kind of surprise or derision. I see neither. He surveys a group of young twenty-somethings sharing beers from a cooler. Most of the group are wearing red shirts with the letters ATS on them and a shield emblem with an hour glass. One shirt says ATS Prep.

His manner is unchanged when he replies. "I would imagine in this sport, you might be a candidate for some celebrity by the end."

"But I wasn't a celebrity before, right?"

"Not that I'm aware of. Did you do something noteworthy?"

I won the dunce award for getting suckered into this. "No. I guess not."

When we arrive at Charlie's tent, he's standing out front wearing a clean polo shirt. A tiny square of tissue is stuck to his skin just above his collar, remedying a mishap from his latest encounter with a razor. He has an electronic tablet in his hand and gestures for us to hurry. We follow him into his tent and as soon as we're inside, he holds up the tablet. "Did you know you were under contract with Bellini & Phillips for this race?"

"Who?" I try to read his expression. *Is he upset or excited?*

"Bellini & Phillips! The bank! What made you sign a contract with a mob bank?"

Okay. Upset.

"I didn't sign a contract with anybody." I try my best to look innocent.

Charlie waves the image on the tablet. "This is a fingerprint authenticated contract with Bellini & Phillips, with your name on it! I went to check with the committee about financing the race fees, and they gave me this. Your fees have been covered. My fee as well. Very well covered. You must have some kind of confidence in winning this thing to want to take out a contract with B&P. Talk about some sharks."

"I didn't mean to sign up for anything. This was all a setup." I give Charlie an abbreviated account of my time in Geo's house, doing my best to avoid the embarrassing parts, but with limited success.

"You let some girl swipe your fingerprints, and you didn't even ask what you were signing?" Charlie appears dumbfounded.

"Yeah. Sort of," I mumble.

"Why? What could compel you to do that?"

"I don't know exactly, this guy was being a jerk, and she was really pretty . . ."

Charlie's other hand comes out of nowhere and thumps me in the head.

"Ow." I straighten back up from the blow, on guard for any more surprises.

"I ought to give you about fifty more of those," Charlie grumbles. "B&P . . . you really are green. Worst-case scenario, if we come in last, I probably have enough cash around to cover my end, as long as their interest isn't too outrageous, but you'd better hope to place somewhere pretty decent if you're going to pay off those goons and still keep your fingers and toes."

"I didn't do this on purpose."

Charlie's expression softens. "I know you didn't, kid. But it's time you learn, this world isn't full of sunshine and daisies. These people mean business, and sometimes that business means running over the folks who aren't paying attention. If you're going to play in their game, you'd better start learning how to either keep up or steer clear."

Abraham rests a hand on my shoulder. "We have established that Benjamin was persuaded into this arrangement by less than honorable means, but what we don't have an explanation for, is why. Gioacchino Amadeus is not likely to go to this much effort simply so a bank can make a few grand in interest payments. I think we need to assume there is more going on."

Charlie frowns. "Geo made his money as a bookie, so I'd bet my last Cohiba that he's got a fix in somewhere."

I slump onto a crate. "Well I don't get the impression he's banking on me winning, so I guess we can rule that out."

"No. That's a given." Charlie tosses his tablet onto his cot. "But we need to see if we can't find out more specifics. I'll poke around and see if any of the other guides know anything. For now, let's get over to the mess tent for the opening and see what's going on. We have a lot of work to do yet and I'd like to get a good look at our competition."

Abraham and I trail Charlie to the mess tent, only slowing for the periodic greetings Charlie receives from other racers headed the same direction. The mess tent has been transformed since breakfast. The area has been roped off with a perimeter of about fifty feet on every side, where stern-faced men in suits are keeping rows of oglers at bay. Some race staff volunteers are checking bracelets and keeping out curious race fans at the entrance, but they allow Abraham through after a nod from Charlie. A man in a fedora along the rope line nudges his teenage son and begins snapping photos of Charlie. The crowd murmurs and more cameras begin to flash. Charlie ushers us into the front antechamber of the tent to get us out of sight. Through the opening in the next set of canvas flaps I can make out diners at long tables with floor length tablecloths and sparkling silverware. Most are wearing ties or dresses.

THE CHRONOTHON

The ambient buzz of conversation is interspersed with the clink of glassware and what sounds like live instrumental music.

"I didn't know this was going to be dressy." I lean in toward Charlie's ear. "Should I go put on a nicer shirt or something?"

Charlie considers my T-shirt and jeans before responding. "Did you bring a nicer shirt?"

"No. Not really . . ."

"Don't worry about it then."

"But I feel pretty underdressed. Am I going to be laughed at or anything?" A woman in a sequined top slips past us, followed by a man in a sport coat.

Charlie peeks through the flap at the seated diners, then turns his attention back to me. "Listen, kid. We may not have much going for us right now in this competition, what with you being greener than hell, and us with no time to train together, but none of these jokers know that. For all they know you could be the most promising racer in chronothon history. They'll all know me, and more than a few will recognize 'ol Abe here. You walk in between the two of us and that'll get a little attention. You may not have much in the way of credentials or style just yet, but you've got mystery on your side." He slaps me on the shoulder. "Ben Travers. Man of Mystery. Who's going to know any better? So just stand up straight and walk in there like you have all the confidence in the world. I'll take care of the rest."

"Okay."

I try to straighten out a crease in my shirt as Charlie pushes open the flap to the dining room. Abraham smiles and gestures me forward. The sea of faces turns to see who's entering.

Mystery man. Mystery man. No problem. I got this.

I step inside.

"Time travelers have experience with racism and sexism and all manner of social ills from their journeys through the centuries. You would think it would make them more tolerant of other people's freedoms. Hasn't seemed to stop them from criticizing my taste in ties . . ."–Journal of Dr. Harold Quickly, 1968

Chapter 8

The creature staring at me from the back table isn't human. I'm pretty sure of that. For one thing, he's forest green. Then there are the horns to consider, little nubby horns that run in parallel ridges from his brow to the back of his head. More ridges adorn his cheekbones under his pitch-black eyes. But even with the horns, I'm not sure he's the most intimidating face in the room.

Charlie leads us past dozens of diverse faces that show varying levels of interest in our arrival. Horacio is lounging at a table near the main aisle in an expensive, three-piece suit. The top three buttons of his dress shirt are unbuttoned, exposing the two gold chains around his neck. He looks away with a smirk when I catch his eye, returning his attention to the two women on either side of him. *Did he bring dates to this thing?* Ariella is seated at the far end of his table also. I try to contort my face into some expression that will convey my displeasure with her—let her know that tonight I'll be immune to her even more dramatic beauty—but she's absorbed in conversation with a frigid-looking woman beside her and never looks up.

The Academy of Temporal Sciences logo adorns a tablecloth to my left. I recognize the three guys and the blonde from the lifted truck seated around it. The bulky fair-haired guy facing me makes a comment I don't hear and the other three snicker. He grins, flashing brilliant white teeth and casually holding his pint glass aloft at my passing.

The only face that seems legitimately excited to see me is a sandy-colored Labrador retriever that wags its tail as I pass by. Its owner is a boy of nine or ten, seated by himself and wearing a colorful helmet in the shape of a snail. The boy doesn't look up as we pass, but stays engrossed in the menu in his lap.

The far end of the tent has been altered to include a raised platform. A head table has been erected and a dozen well-dressed officials are seated at both sides of a man in a distinctly more elaborate chair. His silvered hair adds an air of authority, though he's not distinguished enough to avoid needing a name badge like his contemporaries. I'm too far away to read it, however, and Charlie gestures me toward a seat before we get any closer.

We've been given a spot at the same table as Cliff. He shakes Charlie's hand and introduces the guy and girl sitting next to him. "Charlie, I think you've met Jettison and Genesis Marsh?"

Charlie extends his hand to the girl first. "Good to see you again, Genesis. You've both grown up since I saw you last. I think you might have only been waist high the last time."

Genesis smiles and accepts his handshake.

"You know Abraham as well, I believe," Charlie continues.

I watch Genesis shake Abe's hand. Her dirty blonde hair is tied back in a ponytail. She's athletically built, and I'm happy that she and her brother seem to have missed the dressing up memo too. They're both wearing Adidas tracksuits. Even so, they somehow seem to fit in better than I do. Jettison stands to shake Charlie's hand. He's likewise broad-shouldered and fit. His light blue eyes match his sister's, but his expression is more serious. When Charlie introduces me next, Jettison's handshake is solid but brief. Genesis invites me to take the chair next to her.

My curiosity won't wait any longer. I stoop toward her.

"What is that green dude back there? Is he . . . an alien?"

Genesis casts a casual look toward the back of the tent, making me wonder if she could have thought I meant a different horned creature. "Yeah, looks like an Anya Morey. Kind of unusual to see one alone. Usually you see them in gangs."

"Gangs?"

"Yeah, groups or family clusters at least." She turns back to me. "First time seeing an off-worlder?"

"Is it that obvious?"

"Unless your eyes always pop out of your head like that."

I frown and take my seat. Jettison leans across the table toward us. "I heard he's good. Fast. Adaptable. Super-tough skin. He'll have an advantage against the elements."

"He'll need it," Cliff chimes in. "With a face like that he'll have plenty of disadvantages, too. This race isn't all about being fast. It's about completing missions. And that takes all kinds of skills. People skills."

"No one wants to hear about your brothel expeditions," Charlie quips.

"Hey, they can hide your objective anywhere." Cliff grins. "Can't blame me for searching the most fun places first."

Our chatter is cut short by a brunette woman at the head table standing and tapping a microphone.

"Ladies and gentlemen, if I could have your attention please, our honorable chairman will now say a few words."

The silver-haired man rises slowly and casually waves to acknowledge the smattering of applause.

"Thank you. Thank you." He waits longer than necessary for the applause to die off. "I'm pleased to be in the company of so many esteemed colleagues, and accomplished athletes." He holds a hand to his chest. "And humbled to be selected as your chairman for what is, beyond a doubt, the most exquisite and fascinating chronothon that has ever been designed. This race committee—" He gestures to the others at the table, "—as well as many members of ASCOTT, have really outdone themselves, and are to be commended." He initiates another round of applause himself this time, and the other heads at the table bob and nod at each other.

I catch a shared look between Jettison and Genesis. Jettison rolls his eyes and Genesis smiles.

I lean toward her. "What's ASCOTT?"

"It stands for Allied Scientific Coalition of Time Travelers. They're what you might call the leadership of the time travel community, but we aren't very impressed with their methods."

"Coalition of ass clowns," Jet mumbles, and Genesis snickers into her sleeve.

The chairman continues his speech, holding his arms wide to the audience. "All of you racers and accomplished guides will be experiencing the collective work of dozens of committed volunteers, who have journeyed into the far reaches of time to set up the levels and time gates for this competition. The scale and grandeur of this course far exceeds that of any prior chronothon. We owe a great debt of gratitude to our generous sponsors, especially Digi-Com, United Machine, and Ambrose Cybergenics, for funding this venture. And of course a big thank you to Doctor Pia Chopra for organizing our sponsors again this year." An Indian woman at the right side of the table pops to her feet for the next round of applause.

Charlie has been scanning the tables of competitors and nudges me with an elbow, pointing toward a table at the front. "You see the man in the silver cape? That's Admiral Silas McGovern. Usually just goes by 'The Admiral.' He's competed in every chronothon since the beginning. Doesn't always place very high these days, but he's got experience out the ying yang. We'll be keeping an eye on him out on the course. Guy next to him is Harrison Wabash. He has his pro guide credentials and at least three chronothons as a racer under his belt. He was always a contender as a racer, so together they make quite the team."

Both the men are older than Charlie by as much as a decade, but they look to be in great shape. They are dressed in slacks and sport coats that would easily escape attention if it weren't for the shimmering silver cape hung from the Admiral's shoulders. The Admiral's white hair is smoothed back from his prominent forehead. He is listening attentively to the chairman's ongoing litany of gratitude. The man identified as Wabash has struck a more relaxed pose, stretched back from the table with legs crossed and his hands resting atop his knee. His posture is attentive to the speaker, but I notice him casually sizing up the other tables also.

My gaze drifts back over the tables behind him. The Academy of Temporal Sciences group seems to have rapidly lost interest in the speaker. They have their heads leaned close together, and the bulky one who saluted me earlier is pointing at the table next to them, where the kid in the snail helmet is facing away toward the chairman. The other two guys grin, and the black-skinned one, who looks to be the youngest, stretches out a hand to the breadbasket and slides a roll into his lap. He casts a couple of surreptitious glances at the neighboring tables, then lobs the roll, bouncing it perfectly off the boy's helmet.

The group immediately goes back to affected attention to the speaker. The blonde girl has a slightly scolding frown, but the guys are barely containing their mirth. The boy in the helmet turns his head just slightly after the impact, but goes back to listening to the speech without facing their table. The dog, having seen the roll become a projectile, apparently deems it to now be fair game, and stretches up to the table to snag it. This causes the guys at the ATS table to contort their faces in even more silent laughter.

"Hey, is there an age limit to this race?" I ask Charlie. "That kid over there seems awfully young to be a competitor."

Charlie glances toward that side of the tent then returns his gaze to the speaker's table. "Don't even get me started on that mess. The kid obviously met the committee's qualifications, but how they let him enter his dog as his guide is beyond me."

"The pooch probably has keener senses than you, Barnes," Cliff says. "He'd definitely know to stay clear of that temple in Goa you barged into. What did they throw at you? Tiger urine?"

Charlie's eyes narrow, but he can't hold his expression of irritation against Cliff's euphoric smile. He wags a finger in Cliff's direction. "I probably still smelled better than you that round." He turns to me. "Ask him about the best way to cross a Palestinian pig farm some time."

The chairman has finally concluded his thank-you speech and is scrolling down an electronic display under the microphone. "All of you have been registered at this point and have been entered into the lottery for starting position. The results will be posted in the morning. We will synchronize the race bands at noon, and the first team will be through the gate at 12:30. You'll be staggered in five-minute intervals, per usual for the first level. Pole positions and intervals will vary after that according to rank. Remember that no individual time traveling is authorized from now until entering the start gate. Violations will result in disqualification and heavy fines." He pauses and smiles. "Celebrate with anticipation tonight, because tomorrow will bring wonders. Good luck racers, and may time be on your side."

The rest of the head table stands to applaud the chairman. A few racers and guides do as well, but the majority of us keep our seats. The musicians in the corner strike up their song again as a rotating hologram of a trophy appears over the head table, peppering the tent with light beams like a prism. A small army of servers appears, bearing trays and dispersing entrees. The tent quickly fills with the clamoring of excited voices and the clatter of forks and knives.

"So where are you from, Benjamin Travers?" Genesis tears open a roll and gestures to her brother for the butter.

"Florida. Saint Petersburg."

"Oh yeah? Which timestream?"

"Oh." I think back to my lessons in timestream navigation. "I'm from the November Prime."

"A prime, huh?" She jerks her head toward her brother. "We're from a prime, too. Victor Prime. Hopefully that name works to our advantage." She grins.

The servers deposit platters of food along the center of the table, and we each get little plates to use, tapas style. I pack mine full of little pasta shells stuffed with cheese, a kabob of roasted meats and veggies, and a handful of fresh berries. My plate runs out of room fast, but I try to wrangle some grilled corn on the cob along the edge anyway. Charlie has finished a brief survey of the other tables and turns his attention back to me.

"Lots of new faces in here. It will be hard to know who the toughest competition is going to be till we're through the first stage. They usually space rendezvous locations every couple levels in the beginning. They call everything up to that first rendezvous a stage. First ones to arrive will get the most time to rest up. That can be crucial toward the end, when everybody is wearing down. The rendezvous get shorter and farther apart. By then we'll definitely know who's who."

"How important is the pole position lottery?" I get the words out between mouthfuls.

"It gets more relevant later on. The first level usually takes place over a large area. Plenty of room to get lost and lose time. If they stick to that model, it leaves a lot of possibility for position changes. We just need to get our mission objective and make sure we get our orientation right. People love to go dashing around right out of the gate before they really know where they're headed. A few minutes spent on good navigation can save hours of backtracking later." He reaches into his pocket and extracts a tarnished brass compass, laying it on the table between us. "You want to know your best tool? It's that right there." He forks a chunk of ham into his mouth and stares into space while chewing on it. "Well . . . that and the shotgun."

Cliff chimes in. "And the matches, and the water, and the flashlight . . ."

"Okay ,fine," Charlie replies. "There are a lot of things. But that one," he stabs a finger at the compass again, "that one is going to save us time. And that's what it's all about."

Charlie and Cliff continue to regale us with stories of past exploits throughout the rest of dinner. Genesis and I laugh loudly at their jokes. Jettison smiles, too, but there are moments where his reaction to some of Cliff's tales makes me wonder if he's worried about his choice in guides. Genesis's guide shows up midway through the meal and takes the seat on the opposite side of her. She introduces herself as Mayra and nods to Charlie and Cliff. She's in her early forties, fit and attractive, with short auburn hair, and delicate features. Her face bears a serious edge, and before long, she and Genesis are caught up talking about the race. Mayra seems a bit uncomfortable with me in such close proximity, but I'm happy to see that Genesis gives no indication she's concerned that I might be spying on their strategy.

By the time we've finished dessert, tiny plates litter the table in teetering stacks, despite the servers' best efforts to clear them. Charlie leans back from the table, balancing his chair on two legs, and holds out the beer in his hand. "Here's to the last good meal this side of who-knows-when. From here on out it's liable to be dried seaweed and charred dog."

"To charred dog!" Cliff holds his mug aloft as well.

I clink my beer against Charlie's, hoping the Labrador across the aisle isn't somehow smart enough to be offended, and take a swig.

The post-dinner festivities include a massive bonfire at the edge of the lake and live music from multiple bands. While the dinner music had been instrumental and soothing, the bands at the lakeshore range everywhere from folky banjo and guitar ballads to alternative grunge rock. Jettison and Genesis name off some of the artists for me from our VIP section on the elevated hilltop next to the lake. The race fans have been allowed right up next to the stage and are a mass of jumping, cheering applause with the introduction of each new song or artist.

"This is one of my favorite parts of being a time traveler," Genesis says, leaning closer to me so I can hear her. "You don't have to wait for all the best bands to come up with their good stuff. You can go straight for the 'Best of' albums and only fill your music library with the cream of the crop."

"You're always ahead of the trends, huh?"

Genesis smiles. "Oh yeah, time travelers are the worst kind of hipsters."

Jettison pauses his beer on the way to his lips. "You want to hear what a collaboration of Regina Spektor, Billie Holiday and Johann Sebastian Bach would sound like? Gen's probably found a timestream that has that album."

Genesis nods slowly. "Yeah, I think I actually have that already. They got Clapton to play guitar."

I find myself smiling irrepressibly. I open another beer and take in the view of the sky. Flashing stage lights mix with moonlight and the orange glow of the bonfire, casting bizarre moving shadows on the backdrop of forest around us. The sounds are all music and laughter and applause.

"Are these fans all time travelers? I never realized there were this many."

Jettison finishes a swallow of his beer and nods. He gestures to the crowd with the bottle. "This is a pretty good sized group, but you're looking at travelers from two or three centuries and probably fifty different timestreams. They aren't all fulltime, licensed travelers; most are probably here on waivers, but they didn't want to miss an event like this."

"How many time travelers are there?"

"Hard to say. You don't have many in your timestream. Time travel won't go public there for a while. In other streams there are at least a few thousand with licenses, then there are the off-grid folks, and old-school travelers that got grandfathered in."

"What am I considered?"

"Oh, you're definitely old-school." Jettison raises the bottle to his lips again.

I turn away from the spectacle the musicians are making and see Cliff, Charlie, and Abraham chatting at the rear of the VIP section, as far as possible from the speakers. Abraham notices me and gestures for me to join them. I work my way through the other racers till I can face them.

"It's about that time, Benjamin," Abraham says. "Charlie and I moved the few belongings you had in my tent over to his. You'll be able to sleep there tonight."

"If I'm capable of sleeping." I smile. "Excitement is going to have to wear down a bit first."

Abraham shakes my hand. "It's good to be excited. This will be quite an adventure. I'll be looking forward to your retelling of it when I see you on the other side."

"I don't know how to thank you, Abraham. You've been amazing."

"Thank me by paying attention to Charlie here. He's got plenty of experience to guide you through this. You listen to him and keep yourself safe."

"I will."

Charlie looks at me. "My first bit of guidance for you to heed, since Abe is here as a witness, is to not stay up too late. Go have your fun with Jet and Gen, but get to bed at a decent hour. We've got plenty to do yet in the morning before the starting gun."

"Yes, sir." I nod.

"All right. I'll see you back at the tent. Abe, I'll walk you back."

Cliff pauses before following them. "Tell those two that the same goes for them." He jerks his head in the Marsh siblings' direction. "Especially Gen. Mayra looks like a sweet woman, but she's a holy terror when she's angry. Ain't none of us needs that with our cornflakes."

"Got it."

I linger, watching the three men working their way down the other side of the hill to the camp. It makes me wonder what it must be like to have contemporaries to share a lifetime of adventures with.

First you have to live that long, Ben.

I work my way back through the crowd to Jettison and Genesis. Jettison salutes me with his beer. "How are our fearless leaders?"

"Headed to bed. They told us we're expected at breakfast, bright and early."

"Well, it's all the same to the ones sleeping. They won't know the difference."

"Mayra will," Genesis says. "She's probably pacing the tent right now, waiting for me."

"How did you pick her as a guide?" I ask.

"Dad knows her. She's been in a couple of chronothons, and he thought she'd be a good mentor for me. She knows her stuff, that's for sure. She's just wound a little tighter than most."

"Well Mayra can wait up for another beer." Jettison pops the top on a bottle and hands it to his sister. He holds his own drink aloft. "Here's to tomorrows. And lots more of 'em." The three of us clink our beers together.

"Maybe some more yesterdays, too." Genesis says.

Charlie is snoring lightly when I eventually make it back to the tent. Our packs are organized and ready to go near the door. Charlie's other crates and containers have disappeared. It makes me wonder where his home is and whether he was just there for a visit. *I guess he can get away with it. No bracelet on his wrist.* I look down at mine. The countdown is less than twelve hours now. I watch a few more seconds blink away, then kick off my shoes and crawl onto my cot. I pull my shirt off, then give it a cursory sniff. It smells like bonfire. Or the rest of me does. *I need to find where they're hiding the showers in the morning.*

I lie back and stare at the ceiling of the tent. I can still hear the distant sounds of the concert crowd dispersing. A woman's laugh stands out among a backdrop of slowly fading chatter. It makes me wonder where Mym is tonight. *Someday after this race, I'll just have to go find out.* The thought gives me pause. *Would that work? Could some future version of me be out there with her right now?* I think about the possibility and realize it could be true. *I just need to live long enough to make it happen.* I drift off to thoughts of finding her after being victorious in the race. *No more rookie time traveler. Chronothon veteran. Maybe that would bring her back . . .*

My dreams are blackness and sound. I feel like I'm drowning. Rushing water is pounding over me, and I can't find which direction is up, but I can hear someone calling my name. Then I'm staring at an open plateau that stretches as far as the eye can see. In the center is a cluster of circus tents, all stripes and fluttering canvas. A warm breeze is making the illustrated banners on top snap and pop. The wind has kicked up a dust devil that's whirling toward me across the cracked earth. I turn to walk away, but stumble and fall. The image changes and I'm in a field of grass in darkness, slumped to my knees, my hands outstretched on my lap. They are dripping blood. I'm transfixed by a droplet jiggling on the end of a blade of grass. I don't want to breathe because the droplet will fall. Most of all, I don't want to move my eyes because I don't want to see what's lying in the grass. The gravitational pull is too strong. My neck muscles betray me and my gaze lifts. Mere inches, but far enough to see the bloody fingerprint on the glass lens of a tarnished brass compass.

My eyes fly open and I find I'm clenching the rails of my cot. *Holy shit that was vivid.* I stare at the ceiling of the tent again, trying to breathe reality in gulps and dispel the paralyzing fear. I prop myself on my elbow and attempt to focus on Charlie's cot, trying to make out his sleeping form. The tent is silent. No sounds of snoring. The blackness around Charlie's cot refuses to reveal him. My feet hit the floor while my mind is still in protest. *Go back to sleep. It's just bad dreams.* I rise anyway and stumble forward into the blackness. My eyes finally focus enough to tell me the truth. The cot is empty.

I throw open the flap of the tent and step into the moonlight. The moon is lingering just over the tree line, sinking slowly for the horizon. My immediate surroundings are silent, but off in the distance the sounds of the race-fan camp trickle through the darkness. Some must be outlasting the night, not wanting to waste any of their experience on sleeping. I move the other direction, away from the noise, silent on bare feet. The grass is wet with dew. I consider the droplets on the blades and start moving faster.

It was just a dream, Ben.

But my mind won't let it go. I break into a trot, skirting past tent ropes and vehicles and out into the open meadow. I follow the path toward the lake, worn in now from the night's traffic. The ground is littered with the paraphernalia of revelers, empty beer bottles and a few lost articles of clothing. I start running in earnest now. Not knowing why, just compelled, needing to know that my mind has not come unhinged.

Once I'm past the lake, my pace slows. I'm close now. I've trotted down a hillside that I know I've never traveled before, but my feet have found the way with no trouble, even dodging the rocks and fallen limbs that emerge from the darkness. I reach the bottom of the hill and stop. I don't want to go any farther. I don't want to walk down to the stream that has cut its way through the hills, but I do. And there in the tall grass is the shape I've been avoiding, the prostrate figment of my imagination. I stare at it, willing it to disappear, but it refuses. I creep forward. The dark mass takes shape. I avert my eyes to the trees beyond the hill, but my heart jolts in my chest again. A trick of the moonlight or blonde curly hair on the receding silhouette of a young woman? I try to focus again. *No. There's no one there.*

The figment on the ground refuses to vanish. I step closer and go to my knees beside it. Beside him. My hands reach his chest and shake him. *You have to wake up. This all depends on you.* Darkness spreads under my hands as I press the shirt against the still warm flesh. Wet, warm darkness wicks its way through the fibers of the cotton, seeping up through my fingers. I pull my hands away and stare at them in horror, dripping slowly into the grass.

My eyes finally find the compass resting in Charlie's outstretched hand.

"You can't change the past, not really. You just create a new version of it. Sometimes it's for the better; usually you've just multiplied your problems."–Journal of Dr. Harold Quickly, 1977

Chapter 9

The flickering lights are bouncing up and down the hill like a caravan of miners, or technologically advanced ants. There are voices and vehicles at the top of the hill. The glowing ants have brought a stretcher. Then one is in front of me, his eyes still illuminated faintly from his walk down the hill. He's asking me questions, wants to know if I can understand him. Can I say something? I should be able to, but my throat hurts. I've been yelling. *When did I stop yelling?*

The body has been covered up. I'm standing now, still shirtless and barefoot in the dewy grass. The moon has set and the predawn darkness seems poised to swallow us up. But people are awake now, a sea of strangers swarming over the hillside, some bearing flashlights, others have the same glowing eyes as the emergency responders. I would find the image disturbing if I wasn't already so deeply disturbed. Another EMT tries to ask me questions, but I ignore him and stare toward the tree line, probing the shadows between the trees. There are no more apparitions, blonde or otherwise.

The crowd on the hillside suddenly parts like sheep from a sheepdog as an oversized man bellows at them. Cliff steams through the crowd to the nearest emergency responder and wrenches her away from the conversation she was in. "What in the hell's going on? Where is he?"

Cliff spots me and abandons the EMT in the middle of her response. He strides toward me but stops short when he catches sight of the covered body. He alters course and heads for it immediately.

"Sir, you need to keep back." A young man in a police uniform barely steps into Cliff's path before being summarily shoved aside, tripping over his feet and collapsing onto his back in the grass.

Cliff pays no attention and snatches the blanket off the body. It hangs in his hand like a deflated ghost as he takes in the pale, bloodless countenance of his friend. He stares at the body in silence for only a second, then reaches down and tears open Charlie's shirt, exposing the two wounds in his chest.

"Sir, you can't touch that!" Another uniformed man lunges toward him. "There needs to be an investigation."

"Damn right there'll be an investigation!" Cliff bellows. He tosses the sheet at the officer and spins on his heel. He walks straight to me and stares me in the face. "What happened?"

Nothing comes out. I feel my mouth opening but there's no sound. Cliff slaps me, hard enough that a glob of spit escapes my lips and trickles out the corner of my mouth. "Snap out of it, Travers! I need some answers."

The officer that Cliff knocked over is back on his feet and fingering a taser on his belt, perhaps deciding if Cliff's behavior has warranted its use, or perhaps wondering if it would even do any good against him. My eyes focus back to Cliff's face. The slap helped. I feel more awake to my surroundings.

"He was missing," I manage. "I went looking for him."

"How'd you know he'd be all the way out here?"

"I don't know."

Cliff grabs my arm. "What was he doing out here?" His eyes bore into mine, as if trying to extract what I've seen.

"I don't know. I don't. I thought I was still dreaming."

"Did you see what happened?"

"No." I think about the apparition in the trees. "No, nothing."

Cliff frowns and points up the hill. "Come on. Let's get out of here. Maybe something'll come to you."

The walk to the camp seems to take twice as long. Whispers multiply among the passersby as we make our way through. News has traveled fast, and people part for us with eyes wide at my condition. I imagine I must look a mess, half-naked and smeared with blood. When we arrive at Charlie's tent, a group of people is muttering outside. They grow silent as we approach, disbanding in different directions, but still following our progress with their eyes.

Cliff yanks open the flap and thrusts me inside. I expected privacy, but I get none. Four men in gray official's suits are waiting inside. I recognize the silver-haired chairman in the center. He turns to us and stretches a hand out to Cliff as soon as he enters. "Mr. Sutherland, I'm sorry for your loss. I know you and Mr. Barnes were good friends."

Cliff accepts the handshake grudgingly, and mutters a thank you, his rage suddenly muted by the unexpected politeness of the conversation. The chairman continues without looking at me. "We have already dispatched an investigator to the time of the incident to observe what occurred and we have provided the information to the authorities, so they can issue arrest warrants for the parties involved."

"Who did it?" Cliff snarls. "Give me the name."

The chairman contorts his face into a mask of sympathy, and stretches a hand to the air between us, as if to smooth away the difficulty. "I'm unfortunately not at liberty to discuss the details of the incident at this time. And I must caution you that the authorities have warned against anyone else tampering with the investigation." He looks at me now, his eyes running from my face to my grass-stained jeans and dirty feet before returning his attention to Cliff. "But you can be assured, justice will be done."

Cliff steps forward, dwarfing the chairman by his proximity, and stares him in the face. "I'll be knowing that name. Sooner or later. And when you have them in custody, you can tell them that's their last day breathing. That's all the justice they'll get."

The chairman shrinks under Cliff's glare and finds an exit by addressing me again. "Mr. Travers, I understand this is a big upset in your plans for the race today, but we have made arrangements for you regarding a guide so that you may stay entered in the competition, should you so choose."

My voice is rough when it comes out. "You still expect me to compete?"

"We expect nothing. If you would like to resign from the race, that will of course be your option. If you are able to settle the issue with your financial sponsors, then you are perfectly capable of doing as you wish. You will be considered a forfeit and will still be responsible for your entrance and course fees, since we are past the term of cancellation stated in the official rules." He frowns sympathetically. "We would like to be able to make exceptions in extreme cases like this, but the rules are the rules. Unfortunately I don't have the authority to change them. I'm sure you understand."

The other men around the chairman have been mimicking his informal body language, but as he straightens up, they do also.

"I wanted to make sure we personally expressed the race committee's deepest sympathies, but it's time we get back to our duties." The chairman gives a stiff bow and navigates around the rigid form of Cliff, making his way for the exit. "Good day to you, gentlemen." His clones follow him out in single file.

Cliff stands still for another moment, then turns to consider me. His eyes stop briefly on my bloodstained hands, then he moves toward the end of Charlie's cot. He snatches up a tin basin from the floor and Charlie's towel hanging off the end of the cot. He shoves them both into my hands. Next he stoops to retrieve Charlie's water jug and sets that in the basin as well. "Get yourself cleaned up." Without another word, he ducks, and shoves his way out of the tent.

I stare at the items in my arms with apathy and sink to the floor with them. My clothes are still scattered around my cot, one sneaker still laced and lying on its side where I kicked it off. My jeans are dirty around the bottom of the pant legs and have green stains on the knees, but my eye catches a dot of dark red on the front of my right pocket. A solitary drip of human blood. It bothers me. The red on my hands bothers me, too. I snatch up the container of water and pour some of it over my hands, alternating them and letting the excess fall into the basin. I scrub at them frantically with the towel, transferring the red into the fibers as fast as I can.

Next, I wet a corner of the towel and dab at the spot on my pocket. I press into the denim but feel something rigid behind it. I set the towel aside and reach into my pocket. When I pull my hand out and turn it over, it reveals the tarnished brass of Charlie's compass. I stare at it for a few moments, then pick up the towel and begin wiping it off, taking care to get all the blood from the lips and crevasses around the glass. I wipe my finger along the glass, carefully removing the smudges. When I'm satisfied with its condition, I lay it on the cot. Next, I strip off my pants and scrub at the red dot on the pocket till that side of my jeans is a giant wet spot. Wet, but no blood. I lay them on the cot, too. Turning away, I reach for my pack to find a change of clothes, but my eye catches a shadow on the other side of the tent. I look up to find the man from my apartment standing in the corner. I'm too irritated to be startled.

"Shit, man. Haven't you people ever heard of privacy?" I straighten up, still vaguely aware that I'm only in my boxer shorts, but not concerned enough to care.

The man is still dressed in all black, his expression as cold as it was at our last meeting. He takes a step forward, his boots leaving indents in the canvas floor of the tent.

"I thought it might be time for a reminder visit. You seem to be having difficulty following instructions."

"What are you talking about? I'm here, aren't I?"

"You're here early. I gave you coordinates to be at the registration building this morning. You've been here for over a day." He picks up a chart that had been leaning on Charlie's cot and casually glances at the contents before tossing it aside.

"You're mad that I didn't show up as completely unprepared as you wanted me to be? You're mad that I tried to give myself some kind of fighting chance?"

"What you did was involve people who shouldn't have been involved." He kicks one of Charlie's boots out of the way and makes his way closer.

His disregard for Charlie's things immediately gets under my skin.

I feel my expression harden. "You've got your friends. I've got mine. How I got here should be none of your concern."

"It's my concern when you go off script and add players to this game that are not meant to be part of this. And now look what's happened."

I lunge toward him. "It was you, wasn't it?" My hands reach for his throat. They don't make it. In a blur, the man catches my bad wrist and twists it, contorting my arm and making me wince in pain. His other hand shoots out to my neck and shoves me backward into the center tent pole. The top of the tent quivers as he slams my head against the aluminum. He keeps his grip on my throat and hisses at me. "Listen, you little ingrate. This is not about you. Everyone has their part to play. If you want to live to see the end game, you'll start remembering your role."

He squeezes my neck tighter. "You are in this. To the end. You keep trying to change the rules, more people are going to get hurt. Got that?" He releases his grip on my throat and drops his arm.

I rub my hand across my neck and glare at him. "What's your role? Besides being an asshole?"

He ignores me and moves to the opening of the tent. He pauses with the flap half open. "Just be at that registration building or we'll be having another meeting. The next one won't be as pleasant." He ducks out of the tent and disappears.

The sun has risen enough for me to douse the lantern. I open my pack and rummage through it until I find the pencil and the scrap of paper the man gave me in my apartment. I consider the time on the note and check the alarm clock next to Charlie's cot. *Shit. That's soon.* I locate a clean shirt and settle for putting on my still soggy jeans since I didn't bring any other pants. Once my shoes are on, I make for the exit, but pause near Charlie's pack. I don't know how much time I'll have to come back for things. *Probably none if these people have any say in it.*

I stoop and look into Charlie's pack. I realize I don't know which items he put into which packs. I try to do a quick inventory of mine to compare, but there isn't enough time to do it well. His leather gun belt is lying near his cot. I pick it up and feel the weight of the revolver. I think of Charlie lying dead in the grass without it and then try to shake the visual from my head. I shove the revolver and holster into my pack and retrieve Charlie's extra rounds from the side pocket of his equipment, trading space with the tube of timestream charts, since I don't really know how to read them. I sling my pack onto my back and pick up my canteen and Charlie's compass from my cot. One more look around the tent yields nothing I feel I need, so I step into the morning sun.

The camp is still mostly quiet. A few porters are loading supplies onto hand trucks or golf carts for transport to the starting line. I extract the slip of paper with the registration coordinates from my pocket, trying to ascertain its physical location. The jump coordinates don't help me. I walk across the main path to a burly man in a parka who is loading water jugs into the back of a pickup truck.

"Excuse me. Can you point me to main registration?"

He sizes me up from under bushy black eyebrows before pointing to the woods. "There's a road cut through the trees a couple hundred yards down. Registration building's along that road, about halfway to the start gate."

"Thanks."

The porter nods and goes back to his work. I make my way to the tree line and follow it down the hill, tromping through the tall grass at the forest's edge. I imagine there is a better-worn path somewhere that people have been using but I appreciate the momentary solitude. As I crest the next hill, I pause at the top to admire the view. The morning sun is shining through a layer of mist coming off the lake. Birds are chirping to each other in the trees behind me. I cinch my pack a little tighter. *Always wanted to see Ireland. Never thought it would be like this.*

At the bottom of the next hill I find the dirt road and follow it into the woods. The registration building is a single story structure with a wide, wooden, wrap-around porch. Some race volunteers are lingering on the porch drinking coffee from paper cups, and they watch me as I clomp up the steps. The double doors lead into a large, wood-floored hall with a stage at the far end. Tables have been set up at the foot of the stage and a banner hangs behind them with a trophy logo and the names of sponsors on either side. A few volunteers are chatting in the corner near a snack machine, leaving only a couple seated at the registration table.

A young woman in a red T-shirt seated at the center of the table looks up from her electronic tablet and greets me cheerily. "Hello, sir. How can we help you today?"

I adjust my pack on my shoulders and step forward. "I'm Benjamin Travers. I'm racing today."

"Okay, fantastic. Let me look you up." She brushes a strand of strawberry blonde hair behind her ear and swipes at the tablet with her other hand. "Okay, here we go. Travers. It says here . . . you lost your guide and need a new one?"

I can feel the anger rising in my voice. "I didn't lose him. He got—" I pause, considering her attentive, curious expression. *She doesn't know. It's not her fault.* I start over. "Yes. I need a guide."

"Okay, no problem. It looks like we still have plenty of qualified candidates available in the alternates pool. All of them have outstanding credentials. Did you have someone in particular in mind?" Her eyes are bright and she beams at me as she waits expectantly for my answer.

"I really don't know any of them. Can you just pick me the best available?" *For whatever it's worth. This thing is clearly rigged against me anyway.*

The girl seems delighted at this prospect. "Oh absolutely! We have some great options here for you, lots of good candidates. Do you have a preference of men or women? Are you concerned about that? Some racers are married or in relationships, and their spouses don't want them racing with members of the opposite sex . . . or same sex, depending on their, you know, orientation." She watches my face. "So are you, um, married? Or . . ."

"No, I'm not married."

"Great! I mean, right, that's good to know. Any relationships that are, you know, complicating anything?"

"Uh, no. I guess not."

"Okay." The corners of her mouth turn up slightly as she searches the screen. "Well, our top ranked alternate is a man. Young man. Viznir Najjar. He had the highest marks this round on the guide exam. He's a graduate of the ATS field program, and fluent in five languages. It also says here he made the Turkish National Jai Alai team at the age of fourteen." The girl's eyebrows rise at this. "So I guess that's good, huh?" She looks back up at me.

I shrug. "I've never seen anybody play Jai Alai. I'm not really sure what that is."

"Haha. Actually, I'm not really sure either," she laughs nervously. "But it has to mean he's athletic, right? Isn't it like lacrosse, kind of?"

"I really couldn't tell you."

She looks at the screen and back to me again. "Okay, the automatic profile match has him as your best choice but do you want me to go over some more?"

"No, he sounds fine. Let's just go with him. I don't really care." *Not like any of them are going to be able to help me much anyway.*

"Okay, great!" She grins up at me. "If you can just press your finger here—" she turns the tablet toward me and indicates an empty box. "— you can confirm your selection."

I hesitate over the pad. "This is all I'm authorizing, right? I'm not being contracted into anything else, or signing something that gives away all my internal organs or something . . ."

"Oh no! Just this." She looks concerned that I could suspect her tablet of something malicious.

"I've just had some bad experiences with that lately."

"Someone's trying to take your organs?" She holds a hand to her mouth, barely concealing her expression of horror.

"No. Not literally that. Just some other things." I take the tablet from her.

"Oh, good, because I've heard about things like that. Urban legends you know, about people coming back from the future to try to harvest organs. Trying to get younger parts to keep themselves alive..." She looks away at the windows, as if worried someone may be looking to steal her organs at any moment.

"Really?" I follow her gaze to the windows. "That happens?"

"Um. Well, I don't know. My dad is always telling me to be careful and watch out for stuff like that. I think he's just concerned, you know? Like normal parent stuff."

"Yeah, definitely." I press my thumb to the square and it blinks green. I hand the tablet back. The girl is looking into my eyes as she accepts it.

"I'll have someone go and get him." She glances at the tablet again. "Get Viznir. You are welcome to wait in here or out on the porch. It shouldn't take long."

"Okay, thanks. I appreciate it."

"It's totally no problem . . . Ben." She smiles again. "I'm Carly, by the way."

"Ben," I say. "But you just said that, so yeah. Nice to meet you."

She averts her eyes but looks back again as I turn away. I can feel her stare on my back as I push through the double doors. *Way to go, Ben. Another random girl with your fingerprint. You probably just signed up for the next ten chronothons.*

There are still a handful of volunteers to my left, lingering around the railing of the porch. I go right instead, following the wooden decking around the corner to the side of the building facing the woods. The porch is vacant on that side, but at the far end, facing the rear of the building, I spot a wicker rocking chair. I make my way over to it and have just walked past the corner when I realize it is not the only one. A trio of chairs is spaced a few feet from one another and the third chair is occupied. The occupant has the skin color of a Pacific islander. His black hair is styled in a short afro and he's dressed casually in khaki shorts and a rugby shirt. He seems to be just staring into the woods through thin-framed glasses. I follow his eye line but can't make out what he's looking at.

"Hey, you mind if I sit here?" I swing my pack off and set it next to the closest rocking chair. The young man makes no response, but continues staring into the woods. His fingers are making occasional taps on the armrests of his chair. I'm about to speak again, but notice a device connected from his glasses to his ear. *Is he listening to music?* I take my seat and get settled. After a moment, I check the woods again, trying to make out what he is so concentrated on. I see nothing but trees and shrubs. His fingers continue their incessant tapping in fits and spurts. It makes me wonder if he is perhaps mentally ill or obsessive compulsive.

I lean back in the Adirondack style rocker and rock back and forth a couple of times, trying to let the calm of the scenery keep the chaos of my morning at bay. But the more I stare at the woods, the more thoughts of my blonde apparition reoccur. *It couldn't have been her. Your mind was just playing tricks because you want to see her.* I wrestle with the thought. *Did I really want to see her badly enough to see her there? Would I want to see her at the scene of Charlie's murder?* I try to shake the thought from my head. The young man next to me is still tapping away at his armrests.

"Hey, man. You okay?" I lean forward in my chair to be farther into his eye line. This time he notices me. He pulls his glasses from his face and sits up straighter.

"Oh, hey. Sorry. I was kind of getting in the zone there. Didn't see you."

"Yeah, I could tell. What were you staring at?" I jerk my head toward the woods.

"What? Oh. No, I wasn't staring. It was these." He holds the glasses up, angling the interior of the lenses toward me. "Just getting some work done."

The interior of the lenses shimmers with an internal glow and I can just make out an image of some photos and a block of text.

"Oh. Cool. Is that a computer screen?"

"Yeah, they're digi-lenses. Old tech, but they work. I didn't want to bring my good stuff in case I lost them."

"Seems pretty fancy to me."

The young man considers me. His eyes are friendly and have a sharpness about them that hints at intelligence. "What time are you from?"

"2009, I guess. That's the most recent place I'd call home anyway."

"Ah, a local. You been back here in the twenty-first century for a while?"

"Actually I'm from here. Well not here, here. Not 2016. I'm really from 2009."

"Oh shit. Really? What's your name?" He leans forward in his chair.

"Benjamin. Benjamin Travers." We're too far away from each other for a handshake so I stay seated.

"I'm Milo." He gives me a nod. "You don't meet many people from the early years. Tourists of course, checking out the scene, or maybe in events like this when they set them in the past to add color, but I've never met a time traveler who was actually from here. Are you an analog? What do you use for hardware?"

"Uh, I guess I am. I've got a chronometer." I hold my wrist aloft.

He lets out a low whistle. "Dang. You really are old school. So no grid contact at all? No traces?"

"What's a trace?"

"Tracing is the tracking method. How you keep track of your timestream history so you don't accidentally overlap yourself."

"Oh. Like a logbook?"

"Yeah, logbooks are the original way. Some of the old timers still do that, and people that want to live off the Grid. Or people living in pre-Grid times."

"I've heard of the Grid. Somebody mentioned that to me one time."

"Just heard of it? It's a pretty big deal. You must not have been very far forward yet."

"No, not yet. What's the Grid for?"

Milo taps a button on his glasses to turn off the display and slides them back onto his face. "Well, if you're registered with the Grid, it keeps you from running into other time travelers or yourself by jumping to the same time and location simultaneously. It was a huge advancement in time travel technology from your day. The rate of involuntary fusions dropped by over seventy percent when it was implemented. Pretty much everybody after the 2160s is registered with it. They made it mandatory that any new travelers being infused with gravitites be automatically registered."

"So it can track everybody?"

"Well, it can track all the registered people. There's still a few out there who run analog, like you I guess. But like I said, that's the old school way. Pretty much everybody's had a trace done at some point. The results are private. They give you the only copy of your file, so no one else can use it to track you. That way you have the option to destroy it if you want to."

"What does it involve?"

"They inject this probe into your skin temporarily, and it reads your timestream signature from the gravitites in your body." He pauses to see if I'm getting it. "So you know how you have a baseline, right? That's the place you're originally from. You aim any old degravitizer at someone and take a reading and it will show you their home timestream frequency, because that's where the molecules of you were originally made. All the parts of you that aren't gravitites still resonate with your home frequency. But when you became a time traveler you had the gravitites infused into you. Those let you move to different timestreams, and this probe can read them. They can study the gravitites and tell which timestreams you've been to and when. It saves you having to write it all down. Most people just leave the probe in, that way they can check their trace history anytime they need to."

"But people can use that to track you?"

"Yeah, potentially. So you don't want to go giving your trace history to anyone who hates you or let them get access to your probe's data. They could go to any point in your past and screw with your life. But like I said, that's why they keep all the results confidential. There are privacy laws about that stuff. Some people don't care. They like to show people their traces. Kind of like a passport full of visas. You can brag about all the timestreams you've visited."

"Who came up with all this tracing?"

"A few companies do traces. Ambrose Cybergenics is the big one. They hold the original patent."

"I feel like I've heard that name before."

"Of course you have. They're one of the sponsors of this race."

"Oh, right. So when are you from?" I lean forward, curious to have someone so knowledgeable to talk to.

"I grew up in the 2140s. Like a lot of these academy kids."

"Did you go to the Academy?"

"No. I mostly studied on my own. I took the exams with an ASCOTT facility and got infused there. Been mostly traveling with my own crowd since."

"How far have you been? In time, I mean?"

Milo contemplates the horizon momentarily before turning back to me. "Pretty far, I guess. Forward anyway. Made it up to the edge of the twenty-fifth century. That was a long haul, though. My unit will only do seven and a half years at a pop usually. Maybe eight if I get it tuned just right. What's yours do?"

I look at my chronometer. "Mine only goes to five. Used to need external power even for that but I had a mod done recently. Now it can do about five unplugged."

Milo nods. "That's pretty good for an analog device. Actually that's good, period. Can I see it?'" He begins to get up.

"Um, I'd rather not. No offense."

"Oh, no problem." He settles back in his chair. "I've just never seen one before."

"Yeah, It's pretty cool." I fiddle with the dials on my chronometer. "I'd show it to you, but I haven't had the best experiences with people lately. Sorry."

"No worries. I get that. Plus with a race coming up, it's probably not great to go showing the competition what you're working with."

"So what about the past?" I try to change the topic. "How far have you been that way?"

Milo stares off into the woods for real now. "Not far. That's why I wanted to race a chronothon. It's tough to go very far into the past without the time gate technology. Chronothons are special events so they waive a lot of rules, but usually they make you get permits to come back to timestreams like this one where time travel isn't public knowledge yet. It was a long hike to get back here for this. Trying to find safe anchors to get back to anywhere pre-photography times gets super hard. And the lack of electrical power is a huge factor. Most people from my century barely make it back this far, let alone earlier. And then there are all the environmental factors to consider."

"Like what?"

"Language barriers, transportation issues, getting lost, slavery, diseases. You name it. I've heard half the recon travelers for these chronothon gates never make it back."

"It's that bad?"

"Oh yeah. Time gates are ridiculously expensive to set up, so they have to be really selective of where they send their building crews. Getting a crew back a thousand years is a huge undertaking. ASCOTT lost tons of scientists and money that way, back when they were trying to keep the expeditions for scientific purposes only. I know they lost at least four expedition teams trying to find Jesus."

"What happened to them?"

"Who knows? Some say they never made it past the Dark Ages. A lot of experts suspect they got lost or killed by the Romans. A few figure that Jesus might have just been exactly who he said he was and raptured up the lot of them as soon as they arrived. It's anybody's guess really. ASCOTT ran out of money in any case, and had to team up with the entertainment industry to get better funding for time gates. Chronothons bring in a lot more sponsorship dollars than purely scientific excursions, apparently."

"Sounds about right. People in my time love stuff like this. That's how we lost MTV to reality TV shows."

Milo nods knowingly and smiles. "I guess some things never change." He glances at the bracelet on his wrist. "Hey, I gotta get going so I can get ready. Good talking to you." He pushes himself out of his rocking chair.

"Yeah. Good talking to you."

"See you at the starting line. Hopefully we can chat more later."

"Sounds great."

He gives me a quick salute and heads the other way around the building.

I watch him disappear around the corner, then go back to contemplating the woods and wondering what it might feel like to get involuntarily raptured.

"Of all the messy ends available to time travelers, fusing oneself into another object is perhaps the most gruesome. We are a fragile species when it comes down to it. Our bodies don't appreciate being combined with the furniture."–Journal of Dr. Harold Quickly, 1880

Chapter 10

"Are you Benjamin Travers?"

I twist in my chair to see who's speaking. The olive-skinned young man is standing at a distance, considering me. His right hand rests on a pistol at his hip. His eyes flit from me to my bag and back. I stand up to greet him.

"Are you Viznir?" I walk the couple of paces to him and extend my hand. He removes his hand from his gun and shakes mine lightly, still sizing me up.

"I understand you lost your guide under unusual circumstances." His dark eyes are reading my face attentively.

"Yes. He was murdered this morning." I put my hands back in my pockets, wondering how much he has heard, and hoping he won't ask me to relive it. Chatting with Milo has been a good distraction, and I'm not eager to let my mind go back to that bloody scene.

"I see. I'm sorry for your loss."

"Thanks. I appreciate it. So I guess we don't have much time before this thing gets going. What's the next step?"

"I think we should discuss our general strategy and make sure we understand each other."

"Okay, that sounds good. So far my strategy has just been to get through it, but I'm open to raising the bar a little."

Viznir nods. "I've been hoping to be involved in a chronothon for many years. I've studied many strategies, so I believe I can help us achieve more. You should collect your things. We'll make our way to the starting line."

I pick up my pack and follow him along the porch to the front of the building. Viznir is dressed in cargo pants that look like they could be military issue. Besides the pistol, he has a flashlight and a hard black leather pouch attached to his belt. At the front of the building he picks up a pack of his own and hefts it onto his back. He's shorter than me but seems fit and strong for his size. He leads the way up the road away from the registration building.

"You have friends here? Anybody come to see you off?" I ask.

Viznir hitches his pack higher on his back and keeps his eyes ahead. "I'm paid to be here per our contract, so I plan to be as professional as possible. I didn't feel it was something I should invite friends to."

"Oh. Gotcha. Well it wouldn't have bothered me. If you wanted to you could."

"I'll see my family when this is over, but I have a job to do first."

"Right. First things first." I lapse into silence.

The road has acquired more activity. Porters still relay belongings in carts and trucks, but most of the traffic is pedestrians—race fans laughing and smiling as they make their way to the starting gate. It takes only a few minutes of walking until we reach a clearing. The time gate itself dominates the landscape. Two stone pillars rise from the ground approximately thirty feet, spaced about a car length apart. The pillars are cordoned off with a chain link fence attended by guards. Around the perimeter of the fence, bleachers have been erected and are more than halfway filled.

"We're this way." Viznir gestures toward a staging area to the right where racers are checking their equipment. Guards allow us passage through a gap in the fence when I show them my bracelet.

I spot the academy kids loading their supplies into the back of their SUV. Today the vehicle has doors and a top, and I recognize it as a not-too-distant-future Humvee. I turn to Viznir. "They're allowed to take a vehicle?"

"Yes. That is permitted. Whatever will fit through the time gate is allowed, but not all the time gates will be this large." He gestures to the pillars. "They'll see."

The ATS kids are not the only teams with a mode of transportation. The Admiral and his guide, Harrison Wabash, have their supplies attached to the saddles of horses. Ariella and her guide are likewise on horseback and are walking the animals slowly around the interior of the fence. The kid with the snail helmet has his supplies and his dog loaded into the back of an undersized dune buggy. The dog is lying comfortably atop a pile of supplies just forward of the engine and panting happily at his surroundings.

I'm happy to see that I'm not the only one on foot. Many of the other teams, including Horacio, are milling around small piles of belongings. The irritated expression on Horacio's face as Ariella passes on her horse makes me wonder if he's regretting not having thought of that himself. She catches my eye briefly as she trots by, but immediately looks away.

Her advantage of being on horseback doesn't bother me. *I wouldn't have the foggiest idea how to gravitize a horse.*

Viznir points to some numbered stakes near the front of the time gate. "Those will be our starting positions. Wait here and I'll go check the list to see where we start." I give him a nod and he makes a beeline toward an official's tent near the fence.

A pair of jumbo projector screens are mounted at either side of the time gate, angled at opposing sets of bleachers. The view on the screens alternates between advertisements from sponsors and shots of the racers and their guides. I try to locate the cameras, but can't see any cameramen. A voice behind me distracts me from my search.

"They let you have another guide, Travers? I'd have disqualified you on the spot." Horacio is attended by a man I vaguely recognize from Geo's house. He's a hair shorter than Horacio, but also muscular in an equally too-tight T-shirt. The pair of them size me up from a few feet away. "You know, Donny, I hear they found Travers here right next to his guide's body, with blood all over him. How long you think it will be till they come lock him up?"

My temper flares but I deliberately keep from clenching my fists. I adjust my pack and look back to the projector screens.

Donny's voice is higher pitched than I expect from his appearance. "I don't know, Rock, I'm not sure he'd last long in prison. He probably ought to run now, don't you think?"

Horacio has stepped closer and is now speaking behind my ear. "Yeah, I think he should, Donny. If he knows what's good for him."

I make a point of continuing to look at the screens and keeping my voice calm. "You make your friends call you 'Rock,' Horacio? Was that the only thing that matched your IQ?"

Donny's mouth draws into a tight line as he steps in front of me. He swells for a confrontation. I'm deliberately not looking at Horacio but I feel his hand grab my shoulder and he tries to jerk me backward. I brace myself on my back heel and don't move as he hisses in my ear. "I'm a rock like the kind you don't want to be up against. Donny here is the hard place."

I shrug out from under Horacio's hand and take a step to the side so I can face both of them. "I really appreciate the flattery, guys. But I'm not sure you should be telling me how 'hard' you get around me. You're not really my type."

Donny's face reddens as he grabs at the straps of my pack. "You're gonna be in a world of hurt when you step through that gate, smartass. You've got nobody to watch your back." His grip tightens and I get a nose full of his cologne.

"You've got about a thousand watching yours, Donny." I give him a grin and nod toward the projector screens. He stares at me in confusion before he turns and sees the image of us in high definition on both screens. Laughter erupts from the bleachers as he tries to compose himself for the cameras. He releases his grip on me and steps back with Horacio.

"Laugh it up, Travers," Horacio scowls. "You'll be lucky if you finish last in this race."

"Lucky if you finish at all," Donny adds, before they turn back toward their possessions. I watch them wave to the cameras a few times until Viznir suddenly reappears at my side.

"Everything okay?" He follows my eyes to where Horacio and Donny are standing.

"Yeah, you know. Just making friends."

He holds up a paper card. "We're number four. That's a pretty good position to start with."

"Cool." I consider the card with the bold number four on it and our names printed neatly below it. "Hey, Viznir?"

"Yeah?"

"Are people saying that I killed Charlie?"

Viznir hesitates before responding. "People are saying a lot of things, but that doesn't really mean anything. There are rumors, but that's all."

I contemplate the grass at my feet. "I didn't kill him, you know."

He sniffs once and looks away. "I didn't think so." He pulls his pack from his back and begins looking through it. He selects an electronic pad from a front pocket and presses a power button. "We'll need to keep track of our time on the course. Your bracelet is going to keep a record of your time spent in each level but I like to have a backup. Not to sound cliché, but time is obviously of the essence in this race. The victor can be decided from a matter of seconds. We'll need to be diligent about our time keeping and take advantage of every opportunity to take a lead." He looks at my wrist. "Is that thing reliable?"

I finger my chronometer. "Yeah. Definitely. What are you using?"

He lifts the shirtsleeve on his left arm and reveals a black band around his bicep. I see a sort of flexible screen on the band. It's hard to tell what its functions are without it being powered on, but it looks to be a touchscreen interface.

"It's a Temprovibe 5," Viznir explains. "It's got much faster grid link times than the previous models, but it functions gridless as well, for this type of environment."

I try not to look as lost as I feel. "Looks cool, man."

"It has a built-in spectrometer for reading the timestream you're in and it will auto-lock if you're not making good contact with your anchor. Keeps you from involuntarily jumping yourself into the Neverwhere."

"I've heard of that," I say. "That's supposedly where you end up if you make a jump without an anchor, right? You believe in that?"

Viznir tugs his shirtsleeve back over his Temprovibe. "That's what some say. Most think you just die, or vanish. I've heard enough stories about the Neverwhere, though, to think it might be true. The Temprovibe has me covered in any case. I don't plan to find out."

I check my chronometer again. "I guess I'll just have to keep making sure to hold on tight."

Viznir swipes through some images on his tablet. "I've collected as much data as I could on our competition. First team through is going to be Tad Masterson and Blaine Savage. They won first position in the lottery."

"Which ones are they?" I take my pack off my shoulder and let it slump to the ground. *That thing's gotta weigh twenty pounds.*

Viznir points to the Humvee. "Those two. The younger, black guy is Blaine. The big, blonde guy is Tad. They have a close affiliation with another team here apparently, Deanna Simpson and Preston Marquez. They're probably over there somewhere, too."

"Yeah, I saw them all sitting together last night." I think about the incident with the dinner roll. "Hey, who's the kid with the snail helmet on his head? What's his story?" I look over to the miniature dune buggy, where the boy is systematically checking all the compartments on his vehicle.

"Jonah Sprocket." Viznir doesn't look up from his tablet. "His dad is Ebenezer Sprocket, the inventor. Although that's apparently not the original family name. Ebenezer changed it. He used to be called Spunkhorn."

"Not sure I'd want to stay a Spunkhorn for long either," I say. "What did the dad invent?"

"Used to work for Ambrose Cybergenics. He left and started tinkering around on his own, apparently." Viznir flips through images on his screen. "He has a forum online for selling anti-infusion devices, whatever those are. I'll have to look into it."

"And the dog?"

"Barley. Nothing much here about him, other than he's officially registered as a guide."

"And that's legal? Wasn't there some kind of test you had to take to be a guide? Charlie made it sound like it was pretty hard."

Viznir drops his eyes back to his screen. "It was hard. You have to go before a panel of judges and face their questions. They can ask you about anything. You have to demonstrate your abilities."

"Well the dog must have exhibited something." I consider the animal lying across the packs in the back of the dune buggy. He doesn't look especially intelligent.

"I guess we'll just have to see. Let's go get into place. We don't have long now till the synchronization."

I pick up my pack and follow Viznir to the post in the ground that's labeled #4.

As I dump the pack at the base of the stake, my stomach makes an audible growl. I take a swig from my canteen to quiet it. "Hey, what's the food situation like during this race? I kinda skipped breakfast today."

Viznir eyes me skeptically. "You didn't pack any food?"

"Was I supposed to?"

"I certainly did. God knows what the local food is going to be like. We could be anywhere. I don't plan on eating bugs."

"What did you pack?"

"Trail mix, protein bars, vitamin supplements, beef jerky—" My stomach makes another even louder grumble and Viznir eyes me suspiciously. "But I'm saving all of that for the trip. Maybe you can snag something from the committee tent." He gestures toward the entrance. "I'll watch your stuff if you want."

"All right. Maybe I will." I glance toward the crowd around the fence, wondering if there are vendors in the bleachers. "I'll check it out and be right back." I walk back the way we came, making my way toward the entrance gate. The bleachers are completely filled now and other race fans that didn't manage to get seats have begun congregating around the chest-high fence that surrounds the time gate. I spot a man selling sausages and hot dogs from a cart to a line of people near the bleachers and make my way toward the gate to get to him. As I approach the fence, a group of middle-aged couples watches my progress with expressions that seem to grow more sour with every step I take. I recognize the man in the fedora who took photos of Charlie last night. I'm almost close enough to hear their conversation when something impacts me in the head. I stagger sideways from the blow.

"Murderer!" The shout comes from somewhere to my left. I look to the ground and find the projectile I've been hit with is a fist-sized apple. I rub the side of my head, more from surprise than pain, but now more faces are glaring at me from the crowd. Others are merely looking around in curiosity, wondering what the ruckus is about. The mutters seem to spread through the group in waves as people in-the-know point at me and chatter to the people around them. Another cluster of hostile faces begins making its way slowly toward the entrance gate. One woman pauses to yell at me. "You should be in prison! You're a disgrace!" A few more insults emanate from vague regions of the crowd. My path to the hot dog vendor seems suddenly more hazardous.

I stoop and pick up the apple. One side has been bruised from where it struck me, but the skin hasn't broken. I rub it on a clean portion of my shirt and keep it. I take one more look at the scowling couples near the fence before turning around and making my way back through the other racers. Once I'm far enough away from the fence line, I pause and take a bite of the apple.

Ahead of me, near a post labeled #19, a pair of men are arranging items into hard-sided cases attached to an ATV. The man facing me has a rough stubble beard and is outfitted in a heavy coat that looks like it may have been military issue. He has a pistol in a shoulder holster partially concealed under his coat. The man helping him has his back to me at first, but as he makes his way around the front of the ATV, I realize he's an identical twin of the other man. He is likewise wearing a jacket and shoulder holster and has his facial hair trimmed to the same length. He helps his brother add the last couple of items to the case and latches it, then leans over and kisses him quickly on the mouth before returning to the other side of the ATV.

My hand with the apple is frozen halfway to my lips as I try to understand what I just saw happen. I'm still standing that way when I hear someone call my name. I turn around and find Milo striding toward me.

"Hey, thought that was you." He smiles and gives a quick wave as he walks the last few steps toward me. The expression on my face must still be irregular, because he pauses and his brow furrows. "Is everything all right?"

"What? Yeah, totally. Good to see you. I just saw something kind of weird."

"Oh yeah?" Milo perks up.

"You see these two guys up there with the ATV?" I point with the free fingers of my apple hand. "They look like twin brothers, but they just kissed each other. That seems kind of strange, right? I mean, I have plenty of gay friends, but I've never heard of someone being gay for their own sibling. Is that legal in the future?"

Milo studies the men, then his face registers recognition. "Oh! Those guys. Yeah, those are the Ivans. They're not twin brothers."

"Oh. Good. That seemed a little creepy. They sure look alike, though."

"Oh they are. That's because they're the same guy. They're not twins. It's two versions of the same person. They're just also a couple."

I try to wrap my head around this new information. "It's the same guy? And he's just gay . . . with himself?"

"Yeah." Milo nods. "He's a narcissist in the most literal sense of the word. He's actually in love with himself. That happens sometimes. Kind of frowned upon socially, but I don't think anyone can really make a case for it being illegal. You can pretty much do what you want with yourself, because it's you."

I take another bite of my apple and chew it slowly, taking another look at the two men and trying to decide if that explanation is more or less creepy than when I thought they were brothers. "Okay, I guess I'm going to learn a few more things than I thought in this race." I smile at Milo, then spit an apple seed into the grass.

"You all set to go? I saw you got the number four spot. That's pretty sweet." Milo gestures toward the post where Viznir is watching over our things.

"Yeah. We got pretty lucky, I guess. Where did you end up?"

Milo points to the left. "We're right here at fourteen."

I identify the post he's referring to and note the girl leaning against it. She's checking the barrel of a weapon I've never seen before. It looks to be some sort of handgun but it's got a scope and a bunch of dials on it. Her outfit is likewise nothing I've seen before. She's predominantly dressed in linen and leather, but with a liberal interspersing of metal rings and gadgetry. She has a pair of old aviator goggles around her neck and a bandana looped under a floppy cap. Her auburn hair has tumbled out from under the cap in wavy tangles. Despite the unusual clothing, she clearly has an attractive figure. She catches me looking at her and immediately moves toward me, latching her weapon closed as she strides up.

"What's your problem, wide-eyes? You got something you need to say?" She keeps her eyes locked on mine as she stops in front of me.

"Benjamin Travers, meet Kara LaCuesta." Milo gestures toward her politely.

I extend my hand, but she merely raises her weapon and leans it against her shoulder.

"Did you murder your guide this morning, Travers?" Her words come out like bullets.

"No."

"You a wiztard asshole like everybody says?"

"Everybody who?" I ask, frowning. "I just got here."

"You stay out of our way, got it?" She points a finger at me with her other hand. I notice her fingerless glove has some sort of chronometer built into it. "I don't like your face. So don't put it anywhere where it's going to get smashed, because I won't hesitate to be the one to do it. And you'd better learn to keep your eyeballs to yourself or you're gonna lose 'em." She wheels about and marches back to her belongings.

I watch her go with my mouth hanging slightly open before turning back to Milo. "Well that conversation went exactly how I imagined it."

Milo laughs. "She's something, huh?"

"What's a 'wiztard?'"

"Beats me. Must be lingo from her century. Doesn't sound flattering though, does it?"

"She's your guide?"

"Yeah." He grins. "She's really nice to me, since we're a team, but she's like a junkyard dog with everybody else. It's kinda sweet if you think about it." He looks toward Kara with the smile still on his face.

"Oh yeah. Charming." I turn my attention back to my apple. "How did you end up with her?"

"Ah. Well . . . she was the top scoring girl in the guide pool. I kind of figured she'd be an intellectual bookish type with the high marks she had on all her exams. Never expected to get a blaster-toting badass. But I'm pretty happy about it. We've been having a good time training together. I'm just excited she's on my team and not someone else's."

"Yeah, lucky you, I guess." The jumbo screens switch to a view of the official's podium. "Speaking of guides, I should probably get back to mine. Looks like they're getting ready to start this thing."

"Good luck out there," Milo says. "See you at the rendezvous."

"Good luck to you, too." I give Milo a casual salute and make my way back to Viznir, who is watching the screens attentively. He glances at me as I walk up.

"You found something?"

"Yeah, more or less." I take the last bite from my apple core and toss it into the grass.

The audio for the Jumbotrons switches to the microphone at the official's podium. I recognize the Indian woman from last night on the screen. She smiles and raises her hands amid cheers from the spectators.

"Ladies and gentlemen, it's my honor to welcome you to the starting line!"

The crowd erupts into another round of cheering. The woman smiles pleasantly and lets the noise settle before continuing. "Today you will see these competitors embark on stage one of what will undoubtedly be the most spectacular chronothon ever arranged. Our time gate building teams have made excursions farther into the depths of time than ever before, scouring timestreams previously untouched by time travelers, in a quest to bring you the most exotic, exciting, and fascinating events in competition history. Through the generosity of our sponsors, especially

Digi-com, United Machine, and Ambrose Cybergenics, we are able to broadcast key scenes of this race from more in-level cameras than ever before, and bring the finest in entertainment to all of our viewers, both here in person, and linked into our broadcast from home."

The woman pauses for dramatic effect. "Without further ado, I would like to present to you, our chairman for this committee, who will announce our race positions. Please put your hands together for Dr. Florian Schnyder!"

The chairman rises from his chair and waves to the crowd. He rests his palms on the edge of the podium until the crowd quiets. "Racers, your race bands are now being synched with the time gate for your departure to level one."

The timer countdown on my bracelet has been erased. A green light and the number four are now flashing on the display.

"Your race bands will be your key to survival, as they are your ticket out of each level. Guard them well." He gestures to the monoliths. "These ancient stones, in this unassuming corner of the universe, have been outfitted with the finest in transverse time gate technology. This blend of past and future is representative of all of you gathered here today. You take your knowledge of a broader world into the distant reaches of time, and through your experience, will bring back elements of past and future. You link together a larger universe into one family of time travelers. As competitors, you represent all of us. Do us proud!"

The crowd erupts into applause again. The chairman raises his hand. "In position number one, we have two students from The Academy of Temporal Sciences, Tad Masterson and Blaine Savage." A section of the bleachers full of fans in red erupts into applause. "They will have a five minute head start on the other side. Let's get you gentlemen into position."

Blaine waves to the crowd as Tad climbs into the driver's seat of the Humvee. He revs the engine and pulls up to the two standing stones. It looks like the vehicle will only narrowly fit through.

Viznir drops his eyes to his tablet. "They'll only have about a fifteen minute lead on us through the gate. That's not bad at all. We should be able to take advantage of our position. We'll have almost an hour lead on the last team."

"Even though lots of them have transportation?" Deanna, the blonde from the Academy, and her guide Preston, are mounting dirt bikes behind us. Like Tad and Blaine, they are both wearing their red Academy shirts. From a distance, the black hourglass logo reminds me of the markings on a black widow.

"It will just depend on the terrain. Transportation may not help them in a swamp, or in a dense urban setting."

A flash of light brings my attention back to the time gate. A shimmering wall has appeared between the stones, and the sight is met with more cheering from the stands. Tad revs the engine again, and as the Indian woman on the Jumbo-tron waves her flag, the Humvee accelerates through the opening. I watch in amazement as it vanishes into the space between the stones.

"That's really cool."

Viznir stuffs his tablet into a waterproof pocket on his pack and swings the pack onto his back. "Get ready. They'll move us through quickly."

"Aren't they doing five minute intervals?"

"It's programmed for that exiting the gate, yes, but that doesn't mean they have to keep that spacing going in. The entrance spacing is irrelevant. They have the exits timed so we won't get fused into one another coming out."

"Oh. That makes sense." I pick up my pack and get myself ready to go. My heart rate has gone up. Despite the horror of my morning, the excitement of the crowd is contagious. I can feel the adrenaline starting to build.

The next team to line up is an overweight man and a petite Asian woman. Both are wearing wide-brimmed straw hats and are dressed in lightweight, flowing clothing. They don't have transportation, but do have their extra belongings aboard some type of sleigh. The sleigh is rigged to a harness over the man's shoulders and glides along behind him as he steps toward the shimmering wall. The chairman waves them through after announcing their names, and they likewise disappear.

The team ahead of us I vaguely recognize from the dinner, a pair of black men wearing camouflage, carrying automatic weapons, and sporting some sort of military insignia on their packs.

"Marco Thomas and Andre Watts!" The chairman has no sooner announced their names than the duo sprints forward through the opening, their combat boots tromping blades of grass in time with one another.

The massive stones now loom over us as Viznir and I take our places before the gate. Upon closer inspection, I can see the monoliths have symbols carved into them and it makes me wonder what Celtic meaning they might have had before they were elected for use by the chronothon committee.

"Benjamin Travers and Viznir Najjar!"

The crowd reaction is mostly polite clapping, but a few boos come from the fence line. Viznir's eyes are fixed on the chairman as he watches for the signal. I take a deep breath.

Here we go.

"Now!" Viznir exclaims, and we trot quickly toward the iridescent wall. I can still make out the watery image of the clearing edge and the far fence through the gate, but with another step, both of us are swallowed by the multicolored light.

"We are a race of explorers and adventurers. Once we have expanded into the vast reaches of space, time will remain our greatest frontier." —
Journal of Dr. Harold Quickly, 1996

Chapter 11

My eyes are slow to adjust after the brilliance of the crossing. I wonder for a moment if I'm still stuck inside the gate somehow, but as the darkness around me comes into focus, I realize I'm not in a tunnel of time. I'm in a real tunnel. Bright sunlight is pouring through an opening fifty yards ahead, but it doesn't reach where we're standing. I turn to look at what we just passed through, but see only a limestone wall. I'm about to touch it, but Viznir's voice stops me. "Leave it alone. We need to find our objective."

I can't see much of anything other than the sunlight at the distant end of the tunnel. The walls around us are still shrouded in darkness.

"I have a flashlight somewhere." I begin to take my pack off, but Viznir is faster. A beam of light flicks on from his hand and he immediately scans it around the walls.

"There they are." He aims the beam at a long row of silver rings anchored into the wall. Each one has a metal box hanging from it. He strides forward and points to one in particular. "This one's ours."

I stand next to him and look at the box. It has my name stamped on an ID plate on the outside. The box is secured to the ring with a metal loop that's at least half an inch thick.

"How are we supposed to get it down?"

Viznir contemplates the problem momentarily, then grabs my shoulder and pushes me toward it. "It must be your bracelet. Use that."

I lift my right wrist to the box, and sure enough, the attachment ring springs open. I catch the box before it can fall to the ground.

"Cool. Let's get out into the light where we can see what's in it." I clutch the metal box tightly and make my way toward the exit of the tunnel. As we near the sunlight, I get a better sense of the tunnel. It's made up of limestone bricks neatly set together to form the arch. The floor is likewise stone, but covered with more and more fine grains of sand as we reach the end. When we step into the direct sunlight, I can see exactly why. All around us are nothing but sand dunes. At my feet, two tire tracks are plainly visible exiting the tunnel and then veering sharply to the right. They disappear over a dune that's at least twenty feet high.

"So much for a dense urban environment, huh?" I look to Viznir. He already has his tablet out and is using it to scan the sky and the sand dunes. He points it at the only cloud in the sky and shakes his head.

"No satellites. We're definitely in the past. Not getting a good reading here though. I'll check the spectrometer." He rolls up his shirtsleeve and begins fiddling with the electronic pad on his arm.

I inspect the box in my hands, turning it over and considering its nondescript sides. Other than the nameplate riveted to the side, there appears to be nothing significant about it and no obvious means of getting it open. I turn it over a couple of times, checking each side, then finally do the only thing I can think of. I wave my bracelet at it again. There is an immediate click, and the side I'm looking at pops loose at one edge. I smile at my success and pry it open the rest of the way. Inside is a folded piece of thick brown paper.

"This timestream is nothing I've seen on the charts. We must be in a very remote fringe right now." Viznir has removed a device about the size of a TV remote from his pack and is busy aiming it at the sand in various locations. "This signature is a frequency that my spectrometer doesn't recognize. We might be in a negative branch. It's hard to know." He tilts his head to the sky again. "Still appears to be Planet Earth from what I can tell. No atmospheric issues so far. We'll just need a way to figure out where on the planet we might be." He looks back to his electronic tablet and starts moving things around. "I think I can coordinate a sextant reading with this."

"I'm pretty sure we're in Egypt," I say.

He looks up from his tablet and furrows his brow. "How did you make that calculation?"

"I didn't. They gave us a map." I hold it out to him. "There's a drawing of a sphinx on it. Only one of those around that I know of." I glance up at the sun, then point over a dune to our left. "I think it's that way, but I'll double-check." Viznir takes the map from my hand and I reach into my pocket for Charlie's compass. I flip it open and line up the needle with north. "Yep. Sphinx is that way." I point again.

"It looks like we're headed to something else, though," Viznir says. He tilts his head to read the writing down the side of the map. "This picture on the side is what we're after." He lifts the map so I can see. "Looks like some sort of vase. It shows the symbols we need to identify. I'll scan it and see what the research turns up."

When he's done scanning it, I take the map back. "Nice. Okay, so I see the next time gate here. What's this other symbol next to it?"

"That's the repository for our items. They never use items with gravitites installed so you can't cheat by jumping back to an earlier moment than when you arrived in the level. Well, you can, I suppose, but your bracelet will still keep a record and you won't be able to transport your item to earlier than when you discovered it. The clock doesn't stop until the item is in the repository and the time gate has been opened."

I look at my bracelet. The display has indeed changed to a clock again and is counting up by seconds and tenths of a second. The rapidly changing numbers give me a sense of urgency. "Okay, then I guess we'd better get moving."

Viznir's response is cut off by the sound of engines echoing in the tunnel. A moment later, Preston and Deanna come blasting into the sunlight on their dirt bikes. Preston sprays an arc of sand as he makes a turn at the base of the first dune. His shaggy hair is partially covering one eye. He guns the throttle and launches himself up the dune, disappearing immediately over the other side. Deanna is a second behind and pauses briefly when she sees us. She gives me a quick nod, then likewise guns her dirt bike over the dune and disappears.

"I guess they're not going our way." I check the map in my hands and note their direction was west. "We need to go northeast for our vase thingy."

Viznir puts his spectrometer away and cinches his pack, but keeps his tablet out. "Okay, let's get going."

For the first few dips and rises we see nothing, but merely trudge our way up and down the gritty sand dunes. I do my best to keep sand out of my shoes, but have limited success.

"If the Sphinx is here, that narrows our timeline for where we might be. If we could get a look at its level of completion or erosion, we could date it further. We shouldn't be farther back than 2500 BC in any event."

"2500 BC?" I stop moving. "You think we're that far back? That's four and a half thousand years!"

Viznir nods. "There's no telling just yet." He fiddles with his tablet some more and keeps walking.

I observe the sky and sand with a new sense of awe, wondering what the world might be like over two thousand years before Christ.

As we struggle our way up a significantly bigger sand dune, I call out to Viznir ahead of me, "If we get over this hill and it turns out we're in 2005, I'm going to kick you for getting my hopes up."

Viznir reaches the crest of the dune and pauses, then extends a hand toward the horizon. "See for yourself."

I ascend the last couple of feet to the top of the dune and assess the desert in the direction he's pointing. Only it's no longer just desert. A short distance farther on, the barren dunes turn to level ground, and as it nears the banks of the river, lush vegetation takes control. The riverbank is teeming with activity. Rafts and barges float their way northward along the water, carrying goods and passengers. Farther along the river, the irrigated farmlands turn to an urban metropolis like I've never seen. Stone walls and enormous columns surround elaborate temple structures. Lower class homes dot the landscape in clusters of reed-thatched roofs and clay walls.

I consult my map again. "It looks like our vase is somewhere near the river, but the exit gate is near the outskirts of the city."

"We'll need to hurry," Viznir says. "The more teams get spotted entering the city, the more chaos it will create. If we can get in and out quickly, we can avoid trouble."

"Sounds good to me."

We slide our way down the dune to the hard-packed earth below, and after cutting though a farmer's field, we hit a road. We've only made it about a quarter mile before we come upon the outer limits of the city. A couple of men pushing a cart give us a wide berth on the road, trying to avoid staring at us, but having a difficult time.

"The social class system here may be to our advantage," Viznir says. "If they don't know whether or not we are upper class citizens, they may steer clear."

"I just hiked out of the desert in blue jeans and sneakers. You really think we can pass for upper class?"

"Perhaps we should aim for a lower class. However, somewhere above slaves would be good."

"Yeah. That sounds more reasonable, but these guys are all wearing tunics or no shirts at all. We stand out right now either way."

As we reach dwellings along the road, a group of curious children discovers us. They have none of their elders' discretion and mill around us babbling in a tongue I can't begin to decipher.

"Do you speak ancient Egyptian, Viznir?" I wave at the children and smile.

"No, but I may be able to translate a bit if we need to." He's cradling his tablet in the crook of his arm, keeping it well out of reach of the children. I pat one of the littlest kids on the head before Viznir scolds me. "Don't encourage them or we'll never be rid of them."

The gaggle of kids has drawn the attention of more adults as well. Both men and women slow their activities to watch our passing, not sure what to make of our clothing and belongings. The road gets gradually more populated as we get closer to the city, and we attract more and more attention. Nearing an intersection, I spot a man with an open air shop selling woven goods from under a canopy attached to his house. Among the mats and blankets, there are also a number of tunics in varying styles. I grab Viznir's elbow and steer him that direction.

"We should see if we can blend in better."

The weaver seems very unsure about us as we approach, but as it becomes clear that we are coming to his establishment, he begins bowing to us, keeping his eyes averted and bobbing up and down behind his table of goods. He's short and seems like he could use a few extra meals.

"Hi there." I wave and smile, my greeting utterly useless as he isn't looking and can't understand me. I realize I have nothing else I can say so I just continue to smile, hoping he will pay attention and stop staring at the ground. After a few moments, he finally raises his eyes. My continued grinning seems to have an effect and he finally stops bowing.

I point toward the tunics he has neatly hanging from a rope and he follows my gesture but doesn't move.

"Viznir, do we have any money?"

"I have some, but nothing from this era."

The weaver has used his new ability to look up to survey us and our belongings, seeming unsure how to proceed. I swing my pack off my shoulders, trying to think if there is anything I'd be willing to part with for the purposes of bartering. Finally my eyes fall on the silver box I received my map in that I've been carrying attached to my pack. I unhook it and cradle it in my hands.

"Any reason why we'd still need this?"

Viznir shakes his head. "But these people won't be able to open and close it without electronic arm bands."

"Yeah, but it's super lightweight metal, like maybe some kind of aluminum. They probably don't have anything like this yet. He ought to be able to sell it to somebody for something."

"It's worth a shot, I guess."

I stand up and hold the box out to the man, thrusting it forward a few times to indicate he should take it. The man doesn't move. He simply stares at me and stays near his doorway.

"He's scared of us," Viznir says.

I set the box on the inside edge of the table, next to a pile of woven bags.

"Hey man, I'm just gonna leave this here for you." I make my way around the table and begin unhooking two tunics from the rope. I watch the weaver out of the corner of my eye, wondering if he's going to start yelling or grabbing at me, but he just stands there watching. When I've got the tunics unhooked, I hand one to Viznir, and we slip them on over our clothes. I pick up my pack and turn back to the weaver. He still says nothing but seems to be somewhat more relaxed now that we're leaving. I give him a bow and he gives a short bow and smile in return.

"Okay. Ancient Egyptian shopping, check." I smile at Viznir. "Now we're getting somewhere."

We still draw plenty of attention as we continue down the road because of the children, and what I guess to be our hairstyles the way people keep staring at my head, but the clothing does help somewhat. We continue to be a source of surreptitious stares and comments until the locals' attention is distracted by the sound of hooves on the road. Viznir and I join the adults who are clearing out of the way amid shouts from behind us as two riders gallop up the road. Ariella and her guide streak by, leaned forward and egging their horses toward the city. Ariella spots us and smiles as she hurls past, her hair flowing behind her in the wind.

The crowd of pedestrians rapidly loses interest in Viznir and me as they convene to discuss this latest spectacle of two women on horseback, dressed in men's clothing. The instantaneous chatter consumes the street, and many of the children who had been tagging along with us race ahead to try to follow the horses.

The roadway gets more and more congested as we get closer to the city walls, and now everyone is paying attention in the wake of Ariella's passing. Her strategy of blazing through the streets before anyone can realize she's coming seems to have worked out for her but has definitely drawn attention to the road. Ahead, a quartet of bare-chested men with spears and shields are working their way through the crowd and yelling. Citizens point and gesture toward the walls and the men break into pairs. One set stays on the road while the other two break into a jog toward the city.

"We'd better hurry if we're going to get through," Viznir says. We duck off the road behind some houses and jog past the soldiers' position. We cut through a few alleys full of garbage before coming back onto the road.

"This place we're going is some kind of temple, right? The symbol has a guy with an alligator head."

Viznir nods and considers his tablet. "The symbols are for a Nile river god named Sobek. He's the crocodile god. Also a fertility god associated with impregnating people, and with semen."

"That's gross, dude. Why would they make a crocodile-man a god of fertility?"

"Beats me, but that's where our temple will be, or the shrine at least. This says the main temple was in Kom Ombo in the south, but there is a sect here in Cairo that keeps a shrine, too."

"I'm guessing a crocodile shrine would be along the waterfront. Let's head that way." I point downhill, toward the bustling streets near the river.

The shrine is not difficult to find. It dominates the other buildings with tall columns and a raised stone stairway that elevates the building from the street level. Viznir and I pause in the neighboring gardens to consider the building. The steps on one side of the shrine run all the way into the river where people are dabbling in the water. Among them are a group of men wearing elaborate wigs and eye make-up. They are gesturing and speaking loudly toward the water. Two boats in the river are rowing upstream and seem to be making for the group. A few dozen commoners are watching them, casting frequent glances toward the river and standing back a respectful distance from the guards around the men in wigs.

"Those men are part of the priestly class," Viznir explains.

"Well let's hope whatever ceremony they're performing is going to take a while, because they did a nice job of leaving the door open." I point to the top of the stairs. Viznir's eyes follow my hand to the entrance of the shrine. The crowd and guards have all joined the priests at the water's edge, leaving the gate to the shrine wide open.

"Come on, we need to hurry!" I crouch low behind a hedge of jasmine and sprint through the garden, keeping one hand on my canteen and trying not to let my belongings clatter too much.

The garden directly borders the broad steps that wrap around the shrine, but the gate lies in the middle of a wall at the top of the steps. I pause at the extreme edge of the garden, realizing that no matter what we do, we will have to be in the open the rest of the way. The crowd still seems fixated on the activities of the priests. I hear splashing and a few shouts of approval about whatever they're doing.

Viznir assesses the situation. "We're almost there. We just need to appear like we fit in."

"How do we do that?"

"I don't know. Just walk casual."

"Walk . . . like an Egyptian?" I smile broadly.

Viznir stares at me, perplexed. "Yeah, I suppose. Why are you laughing?"

"Oh come on, seriously? You don't get that joke? What did they teach you in that guide school?" I leave Viznir frowning at me in confusion and step into the open, climbing the dozen steps one by one to the outer wall. Viznir hurries to catch up. We reach the top and slowly make our way toward the center gate. I point one of my palms in front of me and one behind, slowly alternating them as I creep along the wall.

"What are you doing?" Viznir whispers, agitation in his voice. "You're going to attract more attention!"

I keep my eyes on the backs of the crowd around the priests and go back to walking normally, but can't resist smiling. "Hey, Viznir. What did all the kids in the marketplace say?"

"How should I know? They said all kinds of things."

"Nope. They said, 'Way-oh-way-ohh!'" I grin uncontrollably as I slip around the inside of the gate and out of sight from the river.

"Glad to see you're taking this all seriously." Viznir scowls, but he looks relieved to be inside.

The shrine's massive bronze doors are closed, but I spy some other options along the edges. "Come on, Vizzy. Let's find our vase!" I run through the small courtyard and duck into an open side door at the corner of the building. The hallway I find myself in is cool and dim after the direct sunlight. My eyes slowly adjust to the change. We're in a long corridor of alcoves lit by torches and a little ambient sunlight from somewhere above us. The wall to the right is broken up with curtained doorways. As I pass one, I glimpse the open space in the middle of the shrine through a gap in the curtains and note the glimmering reflection of water.

"The most important relics are usually kept in the back, but keep an eye out anyway," Viznir says. "We don't know what this vase was used for."

We scan the alcoves we pass and check each statuary for an item that resembles our drawing. The alcoves seem to be dedicated to the various sexual exploits of Sobek, the half man, half crocodile. Drawings along the walls show him conquering mortals and being generally adored by women. He is frequently sporting a headdress that features what look like a pair of squared off ears of corn. I don't get long to puzzle over them because we're forced to duck out of sight when a pair of guards rounds the corner. Viznir and I scramble to opposite sides of the hallway. He ensconces himself behind an altar in the alcove, while I'm left with my pack squeezed against the wall in a curtained doorway, feeling terribly exposed. As the footsteps of the guards grow nearer, I take a cautious peek beyond the curtain. Seeing no one, I duck behind it.

I'm now in the central room of the shrine. Square columns around the perimeter of the room block much of my view, but at the center of the room, about fifty feet away in a patch of direct sunlight, a table is standing with a variety of ceramic items on it. One of the items is a vase. I reach into my pocket and quietly retrieve my map, checking the markings. It's too difficult to tell from a distance if the markings match exactly, but the shape is definitely right.

When the footsteps of the guards have passed, I pull the curtain aside and gesture to Viznir, who is poking his head up behind the altar. "I think I found it," I whisper. Viznir scans the hallway and dashes across to join me. I point to the patch of sunlight. "Look!"

Viznir gets out his tablet and checks the expanded image on his screen before nodding. "We need to figure out how to get to it."

I step through the doorway and move left, trying to locate a way around the pool. Viznir and I scurry from column to column till I see the bridge. The center of the room is completely surrounded by water with the exception of a narrow walkway that runs longitudinally from the front entrance to the back of the building. It's divided by the stone island in the center of the pool. I peer around the corner of the last column toward the backside of the bridge and eye the table with the vase. It stands just past a massive stone slab that has been erected in the center of the island.

"It's right there. I'm just going to run up and grab it."

Viznir checks the perimeter of the room for any sign of the guards and nods. I step from the safety of the column and walk briskly across the stone walkway, trying not to think about getting diced by blades in the floor or poison darted, or any other grisly end I remember from a childhood of watching Indiana Jones movies.

I reach the island without incident and step up to the table. There are a variety of bowls and utensils, including one particularly elaborate looking knife, but nothing under the vase seems to resemble a pressure switch that could bring the temple down around my ears. I confirm that the markings are the same as the ones on my map, then tuck my map away and grasp the vase with both hands. It's heavy, and something sloshes inside as I lift it. I turn slowly to show it to Viznir but then almost lose my grip in shock when I see what's behind me.

"Holy sh—" I bobble the vase.

Tied to the front side of the stone slab is a young girl. Her hands are attached with silken ropes to metal rings. She's wearing a dress of pure white cotton and has some kind of ceremonial makeup on her face. She's been gagged with the same material as her dress and she stares at me with wide eyes. Even with the makeup, I can tell she can't be older than fifteen.

"You scared the crap out of me."

The girl's wide eyes watch me with fear and confusion.

Viznir has only made it halfway over the bridge and appears confused about my reaction to the stone. A massive creaking comes from the front of the shrine. I watch in horror as the great doors are thrust open by a quartet of muscled guards. I'm frozen in place still holding the vase as a procession led by a priest with a reptilian headdress makes its way through the doors. The men behind the head priest are heaving on ropes, half guiding, half dragging an enormous, still-dripping crocodile.

The procession makes it half a dozen steps inside before the head priest looks up and sees me. His sudden stop brings the whole group to a halt and more eyes find Viznir and me staring back at them. No one moves. The expression on the head priest's face slowly changes from shock to anger.

"Ben! We need to run!" Viznir whispers through his teeth.

"Viznir, I need you to come grab this! RIGHT NOW!" I dump the contents of the vase onto the floor. Red fluid and chunks of something soft splatter the stone. I pause long enough to recognize the foot of a chicken in the mix, but don't have time to be disgusted. I spin and toss the vase to Viznir. His eyes go wide and he goes to one knee as he cradle-catches it. I pull my Swiss Army knife from my pants pocket and open the blade. He stares at me with irritation, still not able to see what's on my side of the stone slab.

I start cutting through the silken rope at the girl's right wrist and cast a quick glance to the front of the shrine. The priest has recovered his wits and shouts orders at the guards who pushed open the doors. The two who had been roaming the corridor also appear near the hallway where Viznir and I entered. A sudden commotion behind the priest distracts them, as the crocodile, perhaps sensing a moment of weakness, whips its tail and sends a half dozen of its captors sprawling to the floor. The men at the front blanch as the animal propels itself forward, creating more slack in the ropes and scattering the men around its head. It thrashes back and forth, loosening the ropes around its snout, and lets out a tremendous hiss.

I work my way to the girl's second wrist. Realizing that I'm helping her and not planning to cut her, the girl's eyes flit from the crowd back to my knife and she uses her free hand to keep tension on the rope so I can cut through it faster. As my blade severs the last strand around her wrist, I drop to her left ankle and she works the knot at her right ankle with her fingers.

"What the hell?" Viznir appears at the front of the stone, still carrying the vase and a frightened expression on his face. He takes a hasty look at the girl and yells at me. "What are you doing? We need to go! Now!"

"Distract them!" I yell back. "Just a few more seconds!"

The guards from the corridor are the only ones who have heeded the head priest's frantic gesturing and have now set foot on the front of the bridge, drawing their swords and advancing toward us. Viznir draws the pistol from his hip and manages to flip off the safety with a finger from his hand that's cradling the vase. He holds it up and fires two shots into the ceiling. The crowd and the guards freeze in position, except for the few still trying to dodge the crocodile. The crocodile makes a final bid for freedom and plunges forward through its remaining captors and into the pool, dragging two men into the water with it.

The girl gets her foot free at the same time I finish cutting the ties on my side. She wastes no time in pulling herself around the stone slab and sprinting away across the bridge. Viznir and I scramble to follow her. When I reach the pillars at the end of the bridge, I glance back and see that the priests have ordered guards around the sides to cut us off, but we have a good head start. I dash as fast as I can to keep up with the girl who is dodging between columns and making toward the opposite corner of the building from where we entered. We streak past a pair of guards who have arrived from the back, but not having been in the room for our discovery, they merely stare at us in shock as we race by. We escape into an open courtyard followed by shouts from behind us in the shrine. A few moments later, the guards realize their mistake and pursue us.

The girl vaults lightly over a low, stone wall and Viznir and I throw ourselves forcefully over it to follow her. She leads us along a narrow path between two tall buildings before we suddenly emerge into a public street. Commoners are busy trading or haggling in the open-air marketplace, but stop what they're doing when they see the barefoot girl in her snow-white dress apparently fleeing from two men in unusual shoes. We don't slow down to wait for their next reaction. Instead we follow the girl between buildings again as she plunges through alleyways that seem to twist and turn in all directions. Finally, after switching back on what must be the tenth filth-littered alley, she pauses and waits for us to catch up. She stands near the intersection of two pathways, eyeing us cautiously as we pant our way closer. I lean over with my hands on my knees to catch my breath.

When I straighten up, I pull the map from my pocket and unfold it. I show it to the girl and point to the time gate. "We need to go here." I jab my finger at the spot a few times for emphasis.

She nods and studies the map briefly before taking the alley to the right and gesturing for us to follow. Her pace has thankfully slowed and we're able to keep up this time. I try not to keep looking back, but it's hard not to worry about our pursuers. Viznir pulls a T-shirt from his pack and uses it to wrap the vase in an effort to conceal it. I don't bother to remind him what had been in the vase. *He's doing that laundry.*

We've begun to climb a hill, and when we pass through intersections,

I can make out the tops of roofs at the waterside. The girl steers us into an alley that appears to have no exit, and at first I think she's made a mistake, but she pivots and points to a rough-hewn ladder that leads to the roof of the adjacent building. She gestures for me to climb it. I pause, not having any way to tell her that I'm not a fan of climbing things, least of all rickety, four thousand year old ladders, but she looks expectantly at me and I put my foot on the bottom rung. Luckily the ladder only reaches up one story. I climb dutifully onto the flat rooftop, making a point not to look down, and move away from the edge. Viznir and the girl follow me up. She walks to the opposite side of the house and looks toward the river. Something she sees in the street attracts her attention. Viznir joins her at the edge and follows her gaze. "Well, I'll be damned. Never thought I'd see that . . ."

Curiosity gets the better of me, and despite my nervousness, I inch my way closer. Looking over Viznir's shoulder, I can view the crowd in the street. They are all fixated in one direction, but instead of growing excited, they're lapsing into silence, and people farther along the street begin falling to their faces, prostrate on the ground. I stretch to see, expecting to spot some sort of lord, or even the Pharaoh, but instead, to my amazement, I see the green-skinned alien from the race banquet. He's striding confidently along the street carrying an ornate walking staff. He's followed by a group of soldiers who keep their heads bowed and won't look directly at him. The people in the street likewise don't look up, but keep their faces low in submission as he passes.

"They don't even seem scared." Viznir frowns. "You'd think they'd be out of their minds about him, especially seeing how they reacted to us. It's almost like they've seen someone like him before."

"Maybe they have." I feel the smile growing on my face. "You ever see that TV show, *Ancient Aliens?*"

Viznir shakes his head.

"My friend Megan used to make me watch it with her. If I had a camera right now, I could take a photo that would vindicate one of her favorite conspiracy theories. All we'd need to do then is capture Bigfoot on the way home and we'd really be in the club." I smile at the memory.

"Look at those horns on his head. Who would have thought he'd have it that easy?" Viznir shakes his head.

Apparently finished watching the spectacle below us, the girl walks to the other side of the house and casually leaps over the gap to the veranda of a house next door. She turns and gestures for us to follow. My stomach sinks. Viznir is about to follow her over when he sees my face.

"What's the matter?"

"I don't do heights very well."

Viznir laughs as if I'm joking. "Seriously? After a run-in with a giant crocodile? You're scared of falling? We're doing really well on time. If this girl can get us to the time gate quickly, we may even advance in the rankings."

I nod and exhale forcefully, trying not to think about what comes next. I step to the edge of the building but keep my eyes straight ahead to where the girl is standing. *If she can do it, I can do it.*

I stall for a moment and swing my pack off my back. I toss it over the gap to lighten myself for the leap. I use one hand to steady my canteen and force myself forward. I clear the distance easily, but my heart is hammering in my chest after my landing. I don't look back as I pick up my pack. A moment later, Viznir is standing next to me. The girl says something and Viznir responds, but for some reason I can't hear what he's saying.

"Benjamin!" The voice is sudden and loud but it doesn't sound like Viznir. I turn around and glance behind me, but see no one.

"What?" I say to Viznir.

He looks at me in confusion. His mouth is moving, but I still can't hear him.

"Benjamin Travers!" This time I recognize the voice, but there's no need to look for its source. I drop to my knees and topple over to my side, my vision of Viznir's ankles slowly diminishing to black.

"Chronometers were my greatest invention, but they can change your life in unexpected ways. Like, another-self-steals-your-wife unexpected. Be ready for that."–Journal of Dr. Harold Quickly, 1958

Chapter 12

When I open my eyes, a wrinkled Egyptian woman is peering down at me. Viznir slowly comes into focus as well. While the expression on the woman's face seems like concern, Viznir just looks annoyed.

"What happened?" I mutter.

"That's what I was going to ask you." He frowns. "You just keeled over for no reason."

The old woman is dabbing a wet cloth on my forehead and muttering things. She doesn't seem to have any of her teeth left. I slowly prop myself up to my elbow. I'm lying on a reed mat on the floor. It's cushioned slightly by a blanket and someone has put a lumpy, linen pillow under my head.

"Where's the girl?" I survey the room, checking for anyone else I'm missing.

"She's gone. Wouldn't stay any longer. She apparently told this old woman to look after you, then took off."

"Where are we?"

"Still on the roof. We just dragged you in from the veranda to this upper room. This woman lives here. You've been out for over two hours." He says the last sentence with obvious irritation.

"Two hours?" I check the timer on my wrist. It's ticking into the fourth hour of the level. "Damn it."

"Yeah. Exactly. We were doing so well, too. We would have had a shot at the lead. Now the city is in chaos from all the other racers coming through. It's going to be a mess. We need to get out of here. If we're lucky we still won't be dead last. What the hell happened to you?"

I think about the voice I heard before I blacked out. The same voice as my dreams. *My voice.* I think better of disclosing that information. "It was probably just the heat, or maybe I got lightheaded. Kind of been running on empty in the food department today."

Viznir frowns again, but rummages in his pack and hands me a granola bar.

"Thanks." I unwrap the end and take a bite, then get to my feet. I bow to the old woman and she smiles at me. I feel around in my pockets but realize I have nothing to offer her in payment. I opt to just give her a hug instead. She laughs like a little girl at this and smiles another toothless grin at me. Viznir bows to her and we step back onto the veranda. I check the rooftops around us. "Which way did the girl go?"

"I don't know, but she told me we needed to go that way." Viznir points north along the street. "As best I can tell from the map, the time gate shouldn't be far from here. The rooftops will still be the best way to avoid the guards."

I nod in resignation as I finish the last of my granola bar. I look for somewhere to put the wrapper, but finally just stuff it into a pocket of my pack. *Didn't travel four thousand years to start littering future garbage.* I straighten the pack on my shoulders and follow Viznir to the next rooftop. Fortunately, most of the houses are so close together that I can step easily from one to the next. I do my best not to look down and utter a silent prayer of thanks for being born of tall parents.

We make it a couple hundred yards until we finally arrive at a plaza at the intersection of four streets. In the center of the plaza is a stone-rimmed well. A wooden pulley system has been arranged near it, but there are no Egyptians around. The plaza is instead littered with vehicles from the future. The Humvee is parked next to a stone extension to the cistern that has a hinged metal lid on it. I recognize the other racers' vehicles also. Dirt bikes and ATVs and Jonah's dune buggy are all parked chaotically around the well. One of the vehicles must still be running, because I can hear the distinct sound of an engine and smell a whiff of exhaust.

"Where are all the people?" I scan the plaza from our position on the rooftop.

"Hiding." Viznir points to a doorway on the far side. I can just make out a few faces peering around the edges of the frame. They appear to be watching something in the plaza. After a moment, I see a large man stumble from behind the Humvee. His hands keep going to his head and he's looking around the plaza frantically. I recognize him as one of the racers who went through the gate ahead of me. He's lost his hat, but his sled is pulled up next to the metal lid to the side of the cistern.

Viznir watches the man scrambling around for a few seconds, then looks for a way off the roof. "We need to get down there. I don't know why the place isn't crawling with palace guards, but we'd better hurry if we want it to stay that way." He slides over the edge of the house and drops to the back of a wooden cart parked adjacent to the wall. From there he jumps easily to the ground. I toss my pack down and follow him over.

Once we're on the ground, we trot quickly through the plaza. I keep scanning the buildings, on lookout for soldiers. I see more commoners clustered into corners and peeking out windows, but no one seems anxious to stop us.

The overweight man in the flowing clothes is dripping with sweat. He jerks on the metal lid of the repository in frustration, but gives up and runs to look down the well again. He curses and is turning to repeat the process when he spots us. He staggers toward us with his arms open and panic on his face. "You! You have to open it! You have to get me through!"

Viznir and I approach him slowly.

"What's wrong?" I ask.

"The gate won't open for me! I deposited my item but the gate won't activate."

"Where's your guide?" Viznir looks around the plaza at the scattered vehicles.

"She's hiding with a group of women in the market." He points to one of the doorways. "We've been here for half an hour but the gate won't open!"

"You put your object in the repository? What was it?" Viznir gestures for me to join him by the lid of the repository.

"It was just a rock. A big, black rock. I had to retrieve it from the limestone quarry."

"You sure you got the right one?" I ask.

"Yes! Yes, it was right where the map said it would be, but I put it inside and now it's gone. It just vanished! Look for yourself!" The man points to the lid of the repository. "I tried to get back in again but it locked me out!"

I place my bracelet hand on the handle of the lid and hear a clunk. I pull it open and reveal the contents. The repository has been divided into various compartments that match the shapes of the objects they hold. The compartments are labeled with our names. I recognize the ornate staff the alien was carrying in the longest compartment. The nametag reads 'Mooruvio Bozzlestitch'. My name is written in a compartment just large enough for our vase.

"Mine was right there!" The sweaty man points to an empty hole that says 'Dennis Perry.'

Viznir leans over and places the vase gently in the repository, then motions for me to close the lid.

"See, I did it just like that!" The man's eyes are wide. "Just the same, but the gate didn't activate."

I step to the well and look into the hole. The sunlight penetrates the depths and reflects off water at the bottom, but after a moment, the view begins to change. Halfway down, the light begins to take on different colors.

"Is it working?" Dennis asks. "Did it open?"

I'm about to answer when Viznir steps between us. He has his pistol drawn and aims it toward Dennis.

The oversized man shrinks at the sight. "No! Please. You have to let us through with you. You can't leave us like this."

"The gate only opens for two." Viznir says. "You know how the system works."

I try to calm the man down. "When we get through we can let the officials know you're having trouble. They'll be able to send someone to help you." I look to Viznir. "Right? We can do that, can't we?"

"Yes." Viznir hasn't taken his eyes off Dennis. "Now back away."

The expression on Dennis's face begins to change from anxiety to anger. His cheeks redden and he clenches his fists. A sudden noise from behind me makes me turn. The rear door of the Humvee flies open and the Asian woman erupts from inside. She launches through the air with a knife clenched in one hand.

"Oh shit!" I duck and dive sideways. Her knife catches the corner of my pack and she lands on all fours. I clamber back to my feet and scramble toward Viznir. He's kept his pistol aimed at Dennis. I fumble through my pack and yank the revolver out with the holster still attached. I pull the gun loose and point it at the Asian woman.

"We're going!" There's anger in Viznir's voice now and he backs toward the well. "Ben, I have to be the first through. It will close behind you. Hold them back."

It takes me a moment to realize I still need to cock the gun. I pull back the hammer and aim again. The Asian woman scowls at me but backs up a step. Behind her I see commotion in the street. A line of soldiers is filing into the plaza. They are no longer disorganized as they were in the shrine. Someone has given them orders and they begin to encircle our position in an unbroken but expanding line.

Fear has crept back into Dennis's eyes. He looks imploringly at Viznir, but Viznir steps onto the edge of the well with his gun still pointed at Dennis's midsection. "Get out of here. Someone will be back for you." He looks at me. "Ben, it's time to go."

As I keep the pistol aimed at the woman with the knife, my eyes drift to the display on my bracelet. The number 19 is beginning to flash rapidly. Viznir holsters his gun and secures the strap over it. "Don't think this stunt will be forgotten." He gives Dennis one last venomous glare and steps into the well. He vanishes soundlessly into the depths.

I exhale slowly and step onto the edge, still keeping the pistol aimed towards the couple, but I realize I don't want to be taking any kind of fall with a cocked weapon. I aim the gun at the sky and pull the trigger. The noise sends a flock of pigeons fluttering from one of the buildings. The constricting ring of soldiers falters in their movement in sudden insecurity. Dennis uses the momentary confusion to grab the hand of the Asian woman and direct her toward the Humvee. She clambers inside and he follows her, slamming the door and locking it. I peer into the void below me and take a step, my heartbeat thudding in protest. I hold the pistol pressed to my chest and drop.

The flash of color heralds a change in scenery, but to my horror I'm now plummeting even farther than I would have been in the well. Fortunately my destination is still water. I have just enough time to see Viznir swimming toward the edge of the underground lake before my feet hit the surface. The water is frigid after the heat of the plaza, and darkness engulfs me as I'm submerged into the depths. Underwater, my pack is now an anchor, resisting my efforts to claw my way back to the surface. Not willing to let it go, I stuff the pistol into the waist of my pants and use my one free hand to struggle upward.

My face barely breaks the surface long enough for a gulp of air before I'm pulled under again. Struggling to keep near the surface, and encumbered by jeans and sneakers, I have a sudden recollection of Charlie and fumble for the side pocket of my pack. I unfasten the flap and tug at the yellow nylon life vest stashed inside. The plastic buckle for the vest is in my hand; I clip it through a strap of my pack so I don't lose it. In the darkness of the water I can see next to nothing, but my fingers find the pull cord and I yank it forcefully, hoping I'm pulling it the right direction. The CO_2 canister deploys the vest and gives my pack enough buoyancy to start rising. I resurface into the dim light of the cave, splashing and sputtering.

Viznir has crawled out of the water onto a rock ledge. The open mouth of the cave lets enough sunlight in for me to see my way to him. The sound of crashing water at the cave mouth clues me in to the presence of the falls on the other side and I kick harder to steer well clear, dragging my pack behind me. Once I reach the rocks, Viznir wades in to give me a hand. His tunic is gone. Like mine, it's now floating at the bottom of an Egyptian well, unable to pass through the gate with us.

I emerge dripping and waterlogged and throw my pack onto the rocks. "I guess that's one way to keep up the excitement."

Viznir rings out the front of his shirt and gestures with his head toward the wall of the cave. "All for the entertainment of the fans." I look up and see a rigid metal cage bolted to the cave wall with a camera inside.

"So how does that work? They can stream that somehow?"

"Someone here has to send the footage back. They play it to the crowd to make it seem like it's live, but they have the footage beforehand."

"Before? So when we left Ireland for Egypt, they already had the footage of what was going to happen, even though for us it hadn't happened yet?"

"Yeah."

"That's bizarre. What if we had done something different than what was on the recording?"

"We couldn't have, or it wouldn't have been recorded. The committee is very strict about the timestream staying linear in this race."

I pour water out of my pistol barrel as I think this over, then stuff it back inside my pack. "So if the race committee has footage of what happened in a level thousands of years before we entered it, does that mean they already know how it ends?"

Viznir rummages around in his pack. "They might. I don't know. The committee keeps all of that info highly classified."

I detach the inflated life vest from my pack, and after scanning the cave, set it on the ground. "They must send someone to clean up all this stuff, right? We just left a bunch of vehicles from the future lying around ancient Egypt. Some archeologist isn't going to dig that up in a pharaoh's tomb now, are they?"

Viznir shrugs. "I don't know. They never taught us how that works."

"Won't that screw up history if they don't?"

"Nobody's history that we know." He aims his spectrometer at the rocks. "We're still way out on the fringe. I'm getting a reading that the spectrometer recognizes, but it's nowhere near the central streams. This is probably a timestream the committee got a permit to use for the race. Nobody cares if it gets screwed up. Could be that no time travelers have ever been here before."

I shoulder my pack and squish my way toward the cave mouth. "I guess we'd better see where we are then." I step up to the cave wall, where two metal boxes still hang among the row of hooks, and wave my bracelet at the one with my name, catching the box as it detaches.

I carefully navigate the wet rocks at the cave mouth and emerge into midday sun. Outside, the river plunges downhill. A footpath has been worn along the edge of the bank and twists its way into the woods. The path has been recently trod by a couple dozen feet and at least one set of paws. Some of the tracks are still muddy. Downriver, the view opens up to green fields and hills, and a patch of smoke hangs over a distant city.

"It's beautiful here." I pull my eyes away from the view long enough to open my objective box. Inside, my instructions have been rolled into a scroll. Viznir steps up next to me with his tablet as I unroll it. The drawings are in multicolored inks, interspersed with numerals and writing.

I hand it to Viznir to scan. "Do you read Latin?"

Viznir inspects the scroll with curiosity. "Actually, I do."

As he scans the scroll, I take time to ponder our surroundings. Just to the other side of the river, a stone wall juts into the falls at an angle and divides the flow, sending a large portion along its other side where a two-story tower has been erected. The water passes into the base of the tower. On the far side of the structure, a thick wall protrudes into the woods, disappearing downhill at an angle away from the river.

Viznir puts the scroll back in my hands and begins zooming into images on his tablet. "We're after a ring. Looks like some type of family seal on it. Probably the type used to authenticate correspondence. It's Roman, ancient Roman from the looks of it. We'll need to figure out how to narrow that timeframe. The empire lasted for centuries in most timestreams." He looks up from the tablet and gestures downhill. "We need to get moving. It's a long walk to the bridge."

I've been studying the map on the scroll and look back across the river to the stone tower and the wall headed into the woods. Viznir has already started down the path when I call to him. "Hey, hold on a minute."

He pauses, but looks irritated. "We're already behind as it is."

I ignore his dirty looks, remembering what Charlie said about a few minutes spent on orientation being able to save hours later. "Look at that stone wall over there. You know what that is?"

Viznir shakes his head.

"That's the start of an aqueduct. And it's on the map." I hold up the scroll. "Look, this is the road down the hill, right? There's the bridge, and the road that leads into the city. It's all on the other side of the river. But look how far out of the way the river bends before we get to the bridge. Then we have to walk all the way back west again to get to the city. This line goes directly there."

"That's not a road." Viznir frowns.

"No. That's the aqueduct. But it's plenty wide enough to walk on top of. It has to be downhill the whole way in order to work. If we take that, instead of the road, we'll save at least an hour of walking."

"But the aqueduct is on the other side of the river. We aren't. We can't cross that." He points to the falls coming out of the cave. "We'll get washed away."

"It wasn't that bad inside. The lake was pretty calm till the opening.

If we can make it out that side, we'll already be on the correct side of the river. We won't need that bridge."

Viznir points to the tracks on the path. "Everyone else clearly went this way."

"I know." I smile. "Everyone else did."

He pauses to consider what that might mean for us. "We might be able to overtake a few positions . . ."

"We're already last. Can't hurt, right?"

Finally he takes a few steps back up the path. "Okay. We can try it."

I climb carefully along the rocks and back into the cave. At its narrowest, the cave mouth is only about ten yards wide, but there is no convenient landing on the far side, only a thin jagged edge of a foothold before the water plummets over the falls. When I'm back inside near the objective hooks, I open my pack and find the coil of rope Charlie had me pack. I uncoil the length of it and tie one end around my waist. I toss the middle section to Viznir. "Here. Hold that. If I start to go over the falls, I'm counting on you to drag me back."

Without my pack, I have a much easier time swimming, though shoes and jeans are still far from ideal. I kick hard to stay away from the pull of the current going over the falls and make the other side without incident. Once I've climbed the narrow ledge at the opening of the cave, I tie the two loose ends of rope together and drape the loop over my shoulder. Viznir does the same on his side of the opening, and using this homemade pulley system, we relay both packs across.

As Viznir wades into the water, I realize that I'm in a much worse position to try to help him stay away from the pull of the falls than he was for me. The slack in the rope from him swimming toward me is nothing but a hindrance to him so I scramble to reel it in as fast as I can. Viznir swims hard, but as he nears my side he struggles to keep out of the current. It doesn't work.

Son of a bitch.

He lets out a gurgling cry as the water rushes around him and forces him over the edge. He has a hand stretched toward me but I don't risk losing my footing to reach for it. I heave on the rope instead, throwing my weight back against the rock wall and digging in my heels. His flailing body tumbles over the falls but swings out of the current and slams rather roughly against the sloping wall to the side of the downpour. I grip the rope as tight as I can. I can no longer see him but I can hear him cursing on the other side of the ledge. After a moment I feel the rope go slack.

"Hey! You all right?" I get to my hands and knees and peer over the edge.

Viznir is clinging to a rock ledge and giving me an icy glare. "Just pull me up."

I pull overhand on the rope until Viznir is able to gain the ledge I'm standing on. "Sorry, dude."

"You were supposed to keep me from going over."

"I did. You're not at the bottom of the falls." I smile.

"Barely."

"Maybe you should have swum harder."

Viznir picks up his pack and stalks into the woods. I heft my pack over my shoulder before following him. I find him on the stone stairs of the tower appraising the length of aqueduct. He climbs to the second level and watches the water flowing into the opening. When I join him, he's staring along the length of wall into the woods. "If you really want to improve your time to the bottom of the hill, you should just climb in there."

I stare at the aqueduct and consider the rushing water swirling around in the reservoir. "Is there a way back out?"

"I was kidding."

"Oh."

Viznir clomps up to the top of the aqueduct and begins trudging down it, leaving wet footprints with every step. I follow, marveling at the beauty of the woods around us. "It's pretty nice here, huh? The air is super clean."

"Enjoy it. It won't smell that way in a city full of sweaty Romans and their commodes."

"Ah, I hadn't thought about that. At least we smell better now. I needed a good rinsing off."

The walk along the top of the aqueduct is easy with the exception of a few trees that have grown too close and oblige us to climb through their boughs to continue. About every fifty yards, we pass metal plates in the stonework. I eye each one until finally the curiosity makes me stop and lift one up. The plate moves easily and reveals an access shaft into the aqueduct's piping. The water is flowing smoothly through the ceramic lined pipe and splashes a little at the opening.

"What are you doing?" Viznir glowers back at me in irritation again.

"Just seeing how this thing works. It's pretty impressive." I slide the plate back over the hole and continue on. "I'm amazed they did all this with their technology. Obviously they didn't have pumps and such to keep this flowing. They must have to access these maintenance hatches when they do repairs or clean out clogs. I wonder what they used for levels to get the angles right. They must have invented some kind of bubble level."

Viznir stays quiet and walks on, apparently uninterested in the workings of ancient engineering. I trot to catch up, then slow again as we pass over a gulley between two hills. The aqueduct stays its course, but the ground drops away beneath it. I shy away from the edges and keep my eyes on the next hill, a hundred or so yards ahead of us.

Just don't look down, Ben.

I try to lose myself in the sounds of the woods and the clomping of our feet. *Keep walking. Don't look down. Keep walking. Don't look down.* After a few minutes, the rhythmic stomping of our steps seems to take on a new depth of sound. I'm watching Viznir's feet ahead of me, wondering what has changed, when he suddenly stops. I stop too, but the stomping continues. I look up to find Viznir staring into the woods to the right. Below us, on the slope of the hill, a dirt road cuts at an angle to the aqueduct and meets a footbridge that spans a narrow stream in the gulley. The tromping is coming from the cadenced steps of a group of soldiers with spears emerging from the woods. The leader of the group is on horseback. A few more riders flank the soldiers as well. One of the men to the right of the column has paused in the brush, his horse stamping its front hoof in eagerness to continue. The rider looks up and spots us atop the aqueduct. He shouts something in Latin and urges his horse forward. The leader of the column twists in his saddle and follows the man's eye line to us.

"Are they going to be mad we're up here?" I step closer to Viznir.

He puts his hand to his pistol. "I don't think they're pleased."

The leader of the column of soldiers rapidly splits his men. He sends the first group scrambling up the hill to cut us off. One of the horsemen leaps his horse over the stream and is followed by a dozen foot soldiers who file across the bridge and begin scaling the hill behind us. To my dismay, the men in the next group the leader gestures to are all carrying bows and quivers of arrows. They disperse at his command and take positions in the trees.

One of the horsemen yells something and gestures for us to get down. Viznir pulls his tablet from his pack and begins scanning rapidly through it. I step up next to him to see what he's doing. "What's our plan here, man? You have something in here about this?"

"I need to remember how to express this." He looks up from his tablet and shouts toward the soldier. "Venimus in pace!"

The commander doesn't seem to notice. He merely assigns more soldiers from the column up the hill. The column has not ended. To the contrary, more keep arriving every moment. A half dozen more on horseback have arrived also and have taken up positions near the commander.

The first horseman yells at us again, "Tu transgrediendi! Festina descendi!"

"What was that one?" I ask.

Viznir looks at me and frowns. "We're in trouble. We don't have time for this." He slides his tablet into his pack and draws his pistol. "Get your gun ready. We may have to shoot our way out."

"These guys have bows and arrows and swords. It doesn't seem like a fair fight."

"You might think differently when they start shooting." He levels his pistol at the far end of the aqueduct and walks forward. Soldiers have taken up positions in the woods at both sides now and some are beginning to scale the sides of the aqueduct. Behind us, the same strategy is unfolding on the hill we came from. As I follow Viznir forward, my foot strikes one of the metal maintenance covers and the hollow sound reverberates faintly. I look past Viznir and note that there are no more covers between us and the soldiers.

"Hey, Viznir."

He turns.

"I may have our way out of this mess." I tap the toe of my shoe against the cover. "Actually it was your idea."

Viznir shakes his head. "We'd drown."

"Not if we can make it to the next maintenance hatch faster than they can."

"No way." He faces forward again. "We shoot our way through."

"I didn't come two thousand years to commit mass murder. How many people are you going to have to kill to get through?"

"They might run once we take out a couple of them. "

I point to the archers in the trees. "These guys conquered most of Europe, Viznir. I don't think they're trained to run." I squat to slide the maintenance cover away, hoping the soldiers won't catch on until it's too late. My still soggy rope is coiled on the side of my pack. I cut a piece and use it to attach the pack to my ankle. Looking past Viznir's legs I can see the first soldier has made it to the top of the aqueduct and is advancing toward us with his spear lowered and shield up. Viznir still has his gun aimed that direction, but his resolve appears to be wavering.

"Hurry up then. These guys are going to see you soon and start shooting."

I secure my pack's waterproof flaps before dropping it down the hole. The water splashes and churns as it tugs on it. The pressure threatens to pull me in forcefully but I resist and ease myself in slowly. "Just when we were starting to dry off, huh?" I smile at Viznir and drop the rest of the way. As I do, the soldier shouts. My pack vanishes into the ceramic piping and I squeeze myself after it, laying flat on my back and keeping my arms above my head. As the water surges over my shoulders, I hold the edge of the shaft and take a last deep breath. Viznir's feet land to either side of my head with a splash. "Go! Go! They're shooting!" I let the water pressure push me forward.

The angle of the aqueduct is not very steep, so once the initial thrust of the water propels me forward, I don't continue very fast. The discomfort in my lungs increases as each snag and spot of friction slows me down. *Am I going to get stuck in here?* The pressure of the river stays sufficient however and keeps me bumping along through the darkness. I keep one of my hands along the top of the pipe, feeling for the next maintenance opening. I realize after a few moments that my hand is no longer wet. The volume of the water in the pipe, while high, is not completely filling it.

Well I don't mind if I do. I stretch my face up into the air pocket and take a gulp, scraping my nose just slightly, but happy to ease the pressure in my lungs. While I'm enjoying my new supply of oxygen, a thin ring of sunlight passes overhead. *Shit!* I reach for the edge of the maintenance shaft and my fingertips just brush the corner before I'm pushed past it. I try to brace myself against the walls to arrest my momentum like a stubborn kid in a playground slide, but the water pressure builds too quickly and I can't hold on. I relax and let it carry me onward. I steal a couple more gulps of air from the surface but stay vigilant this time, and when the next shaft comes, I'm ready. I thrust both arms upward and grasp at the stony interior of the hole, pulling my torso clear of the water and scrambling to find purchase with my feet. The pack around my ankle is working against me but I manage to jam my heel into a joint just as Viznir collides with me.

"Ow!" I struggle to maintain my grip on the wall. Luckily Viznir's feet only grazed my back, but he's now wedged beneath me. His face emerges from the water in the half-light below me, sputtering and cursing.

"What are you doing?" He finally spits out the words.

"Trying to get out. You want out, or do you want to keep going? There's air in here. It's not that bad!"

He pushes off from me in an effort to get his head higher. The water level is rising in the shaft from our sudden obstruction of the pipe.

"Whatever you're doing, just do it faster!" he garbles at me.

"Okay, I'm going to take this a bit farther and get us away from those soldiers. Breathe from the surface!"

He nods just before the water climbs over his face again. I release my grip on the wall and let the pressure pull me back into the pipe. For a while I can hear Viznir's feet clumping through the pipe near my head, but as we travel on, we gain some separation. I let the water move us along smoothly, taking periodic breaths and watching for exits. We pass a half dozen more before I feel myself slowing down. It seems to be taking longer than normal to reach the next maintenance hatch. Then, all of a sudden, my motion stops completely. The water is flowing fluidly past me, but the pressure is no longer strong enough to force my weight forward. I lift my head and find I'm in an even larger air pocket. I twist my head because I can hear noises behind me.

"Viznir?"

"Yeah!" His voice echoes in the confined space.

"You stuck?"

"Yeah!"

"Me too. I'm gonna keep working my way down."

"Fine."

I kick at my pack and get it to slide ahead of me as I wriggle my way onward. A dozen yards farther, I reach the maintenance shaft. The reduced water pressure makes it easier to climb up this time. I push the cover away from the hole and squint as the bright sunlight greets me. I wrangle my pack out of the water and untie it, shoving it out of the hole, then climb out after it. When I'm up, I lean over to help Viznir. Once he's flopped his upper half out of the hole, I stand to look around.

We're no longer in the woods. Instead, the aqueduct has leveled out as it crosses irrigated fields of crops. Looking down to my right, I notice a pair of slave farmers staring transfixed with tools in their hands, watching me. I wave, but stay away from the edge of the aqueduct, as we are still alarmingly high up. Along the left side, the scene is much more urban. Buildings have sprung up everywhere and the atmosphere is active. Ahead, even at a distance, the city walls seem massive. Fortunately for us, prior to the aqueduct reaching the walls, it crosses through a tower, not unlike the one we entered at the source, though this one is significantly taller.

"That thing ought to have some stairs in it, wouldn't you think?" I point it out to Viznir.

"It'd better. I don't think they'll let us through the city walls on this. That part's bound to be guarded."

It turns out the tower we reach is guarded too, but judging from the feminine giggling I hear through the window, no one is expecting visitors to climb in from the top of the aqueduct. I look down at my soaking wet pants, wondering how much of a mess I'll make climbing through the window. Every bit of me squishes, and my jeans have already begun to chafe against my thighs. I brush some droplets off the face of my chronometer and have a sudden epiphany. "Hey, Viznir, back up and give me two seconds." Viznir frowns but steps back. I dial my chronometer for a two second jump and touch my fingertips to the wall of the tower. I smile at Viznir and press the pin. When I reappear, all the water in my clothes and pack has dutifully stayed behind and splashed all over the top of the aqueduct. I run a hand over my dry clothing with satisfaction.

"That's a brilliant idea." Viznir pushes the sleeve up on his shirt and fiddles with his Temprovibe. I exchange places with him so he can use the tower wall as an anchor, too. When he activates his Temprovibe, all the non-gravitite infused droplets in his hair and clothing seem to hover for an instant, outlining the man who formerly occupied that space, before plummeting to the surface of the aqueduct. Two seconds later, he's back.

"We should have thought of that sooner," I say. "I don't know what I was thinking going around soggy. I'm going to use that every time I get out of the shower. I'll save hours of laundering towels."

Viznir stands on tiptoe to peer over the stone window ledge. "I can see the stairs. If we can get past the guard, it's an easy exit. Boost me up."

I cradle my hands and give Viznir a foothold. He uses it to climb through and disappear inside. I hop up and grasp the inside ledge of the window. Viznir is creeping across the wood floor toward a heavy, drawn curtain at the far side. The laughter and giggling is coming from the other side of the room. He peeks around the corner of the curtain, pauses a moment, then gestures for me to follow. I ease myself through the window on all fours and am about to get to my feet when my canteen slips out of a pocket of my pack and clatters to the floor.

Shit.

I snatch up the container and creep toward Viznir at the stairway door. The curtain flings open, revealing a partially clad Roman soldier and two mostly undressed women companions behind him on a thick wooden table. The soldier freezes at the sight of us, his expression full of confusion. He seems unsure whether to be upset about the intrusion or repentant for getting caught off guard.

"Viznir, how do you say 'dereliction of duty' in Latin?" I whisper. "You should yell at him."

Viznir considers the muscled man before us and the spear leaned against the archway. "Nope. We're running." He spins and darts for the stairs.

"Whoa, wait!" I straighten up and face the soldier. His expression has gone from surprise to anger in an instant. He reaches for the spear and I make a break for the exit. Through the doorway, the stairs ascend and descend from the landing. Viznir is already halfway to the landing below. I pause momentarily, then take the stairs going up.

He shouts at me, "What are you doing?"

"Buying us some time!" I take the steps two at a time as the soldier enters the stairwell.

The diversionary tactic stops him short as he considers which of us to pursue, then apparently deciding I'll be the easiest to trap, begins climbing after me. I listen to the thudding of his footsteps on the wooden planks as I climb, and do a quick calculation of how long it will take him to close the gap between us. Glancing up to ensure there are enough stairs above me to make my plan worthwhile, I ascend just out of sight, spin the dial on my chronometer, press my palm to the stairwell wall, and push the pin.

When I reappear, the seven seconds I skipped over have given the soldier ample time to pass my position. I listen to his angry snorting as he stomps his way upward, then gingerly work my way down, slowly increasing speed as I put more distance between us. As I'm passing the guardroom, one of the women peeks her head around the corner to see what's happening. I smile and wave as I sprint by, before racing down the rest of the stairs.

Viznir is at the courtyard gate waving frantically for me to hurry. I dash across the dirt path and out the gate, and he pulls me around the corner just as another group of soldiers appears on the road. The guard has reached the top of the tower and spots Viznir and me ducking into a hedge, but the sight of his fellow soldiers seems to concern him more and he quickly vanishes back inside.

"Well that was fun." I grin at Viznir.

"I thought that guy was going to spear us. How'd you get past him?" he asks.

I explain my tactic to him and his eyes get a little wider. "You see, that's what they should have been teaching us how to do in guide school, instead of so much theory. How'd you learn to do that?"

"I had a friend who taught me a few things. He helped me to think more creatively."

Viznir shakes his head. "The time I come from is so regulated, they don't let you use time travel like that. They only want it used for official purposes."

"Who? ASCOTT?"

"Yeah. They regulate misuse of time travel and can fine you or put you in jail for misconduct. They can use the grid to track your jumps if you've had a violation."

"That sucks. Remind me to skip over that era."

"A lot of people feel that way. That's why you see more and more time travelers trying to escape to the fringes, or come farther back. Its more dangerous operating off Grid, but I can see how it might be more fun. That's also why a lot of people try to be chronothon competitors or guides. It's a good way to have ASCOTT-sanctioned activities off Grid and not get into trouble."

"Is that why you signed up?"

Viznir's brow furrows before he responds. "No. Not exactly. I had other reasons." He straightens his pack. "Come on, we need to get to our objective."

The map points to a district of the city inside the walls labeled "Quirinal." We attract more than a few curious looks from the citizens as we walk the streets of Rome's outlying suburbs. Most of the people here are wearing tunics, not terribly dissimilar to the Ancient Egyptians, but they seem to come in more varieties and almost all use belts around them. I think at first it is merely a fashion statement, as the tunic doesn't need any help staying on, but then notice bulges in some citizens' stomach areas that give away that they've been stuffing things down the front of their tunics in lieu of pockets.

When we near the city gates, we opt to bypass the inspection most citizens are getting by hopping onto the back of an enclosed produce cart and blinking ahead to when the cart is already inside the walls. It's a moderately risky move in public, but other than a man who drops his armload of bread at our sudden reappearance, no one seems to notice. Viznir and I hop off the cart and make our way uphill toward the Quirinal district.

The Quirinal Hill seems to be a middle class neighborhood of sorts with a great deal of shopping options available and blocks of apartments. The main thoroughfares are packed with shops and vendors, usually at the base of the apartment buildings. Viznir and I get our share of curious looks, but people are polite and no one accosts us. Even the soldiers we pass don't trouble us, as we're no longer gallivanting around on aqueducts. The most significant impressions I get from the streets are the sounds and the smells. The noise is the babble of voices, the creaking of carts, braying of mules or horses, and the laughter of children. The smells are mostly lingering smoke from cooking fires, food roasting, warm bodies and animals, and varying degrees of feces. The fecal smell gets worse at street corners where I discover there are receptacles for human waste. I quickly learn to steer well clear of those. The people themselves look fairly clean, but the streets are highly suspect, and I'm happy to be wearing shoes.

Viznir pulls his tablet out again and brings up the image of the ring we're after.

"The seal on this has multiple hits in the database. In seventy-eight percent of the timestreams on file, it belonged to Gaius Linus Flavian, a descendant of the former emperor, Domitian Flavius. The emperor got assassinated in sixty-six percent of the timestreams, usually between 94 to 98 AD."

"Well liked, I guess."

"The Flavians lost power after the assassination, and they fell out of favor for quite a while, but I'd guess any of his descendants will still be at least upper middle class. I'm betting we'll find the place farther up the hill."

"What year are we in now?"

"Based on what we're seeing for architecture, I'm guessing around 200AD. These buildings are all built to a post-Nero standard. He changed requirements for buildings after the great fire."

"So this guy we're looking for, his ancestor was emperor over a hundred years ago?"

"It just remains to be seen how close of a relative he was. That will factor into his social class."

"How are we going to get his ring off him?"

"You're the racer. I'll let you figure that out."

The map leads us to a home at the upper side of the Quirinal Hill. We can make out the Forum only a short distance away. I can also see the Colosseum, and various other aqueducts looming over the other buildings. Structures on the hill are built closely together and, while the home of Linus Flavius is stately, it shares the hill with a variety of homes of equal or greater proportions. A stone wall has been erected around the front of the house to keep out the riffraff, but a metal gate allows a view of the small garden leading to the entrance of the house. The main door is open, as are the windows, to allow the breeze to circulate inside.

"So now what?" Viznir looks at me. "You have a plan?"

"I guess we need to figure out if he's home." My mind wrestles with how we can get to our objective without being detected. The walls are tall and solid. It might be possible to get over them from a neighboring house, but that would mean getting inside one of those. "It's gonna be pretty hard to ninja our way in there without being seen."

Viznir pulls out his pistol and checks the ammo clip. "We could bust our way in and make him give it up once we show him what these weapons can do."

I frown at him. "What's with you and wanting to shoot everybody today?" I swing my pack off my back and open it.

"Well, you don't seem to have a better idea."

"Sure I do." I keep rummaging around in the pack, considering what

I have to work with.

"You have something in there that's going to convince him better?"

"We're from the future. We have to have something he'd want." I consider my flashlight, but decide I don't want to part with it. The fishing line and hooks are too mundane. Finally I grasp the black plastic compass Abraham gave me. I pull Charlie's compass out of my jeans pocket and compare the two. I put Charlie's back and hold up the plastic one. "How about this. They don't have these yet, right?"

Viznir enters something into his tablet and scans through the information he finds. "No. The Chinese invented a compass around 200 BC, but Western Europe won't have them for another thousand years."

"Good. There we go then. Priceless technology from the future. No batteries required. How can he pass that up?"

"It's his gold ring. Might be an heirloom."

"Gold, schmold. He probably has four or five more just like it. Look at this place. Think how many more he can make when he's rich from showing off his fancy future compass. You gotta sell it, Vizzy. Use some salesmanship."

"Me?"

I smile. "Yep. You're the only one who knows Latin. I can tell him to 'carpe diem' or 'deus ex machina' something, but then I'm out."

Viznir shakes his head but follows me to the house. I rattle the gate to get someone's attention. After a moment, a servant comes out to see what we're up to.

"Bene candidi." He bows politely, but doesn't open the gate. Viznir rambles off a stream of Latin that I can't follow, but it sounds professional. The servant cocks his head slightly, as if having trouble with the accent, but then bows again and opens the gate for us.

"What did you tell him?" I ask.

"I told him we're traveling merchants and we have wares his master requested we deliver personally."

"He bought it?"

"So far."

A child yells something from an upstairs window and I look up to see him pointing at us. Other members of the household begin to take notice as well as we are guided into a waiting area just off the main foyer. The home is beautiful. Elegant stonework on the façade is also maintained indoors. The house smells significantly better than the street. Another servant offers to take our packs, but I decline while trying to seem apologetic. We are also expected to take our shoes off, but after seeing the filth in the street, I can understand the need for that one. We dutifully remove our shoes and attach them to our packs. Seeing that we don't have our own sandals, a servant provides us with some. Mine are entirely too small, but I manage as best I can.

The master of the house is evidently home and willing to receive us because we are ushered up the marble stairs to a back patio on the second floor that commands a breathtaking view of the city. A well-fed man in a bleached white tunic is reclining on a couch enjoying the view. A servant is standing at attention to his side and whispers to him as we approach. The man shifts on his couch and rises. His curiosity at our attire is evident by his expression, but he does a good job of remaining polite and welcomes us with a litany of Latin that Viznir does his best to respond to. I merely smile when I feel like it's appropriate.

Linus is a gracious host and welcomes us toward a stone table to enjoy some refreshments. We put our packs down and take seats opposite him. Servants appear with fruit and nuts and set them out for our convenience. My stomach seems to know instantly and I snag as many as I can without seeming impolite. After a particularly rapid discourse during which Linus has repeatedly looked at me, Viznir finally turns and fills me in.

"He seems to be under the impression that you're the one in charge and I'm your servant."

"Why?"

Viznir lifts his dark forearm. "Probably because he's a racist. Also because you just sit there, nonchalantly stuffing your face. Apparently that's a masterly thing to do."

"Oh." I swallow and conceal my latest handful of dates. "What did he say about the ring?"

"We haven't gotten that far. So far he's just been asking where we're from and how we like Rome. He's very polite."

"Did you tell him we're from China?"

"No. Of course not. Do we look Chinese?" He pinches my elbow.

"It's not like he's gonna know the difference. It's 200 AD. I highly doubt he's been to China. If we said we were from there, it could make sense that we'd have a compass."

Viznir goes back to the conversation, and after a few minutes, gestures for me to get out the compass. I make a show of gently removing it from my pocket and present it to Linus. I open the plastic cover before handing it to him so he can see the needle bobbing around the compass rose. Linus accepts the compass respectfully and his brow furrows as he studies it. He turns it over and considers the writing on the bottom.

I elbow Viznir. "See, it even says 'Made in China' right on it! That could have added authenticity."

Viznir frowns and ignores me, then tries to assist Linus with orienting the compass, explaining how it works. Linus turns it with rapt curiosity. After a few moments, a smile breaks across the big man's face and he even shows it to his servant. It's clear that to him, the needle's persistent pointing to north is nothing short of magical. Once it's clear he wants to keep it, Viznir brings the conversation around to payment. Linus seems confused when Viznir points to his ring. He looks from Viznir to me and I nod. He considers the compass for a while longer and fidgets with the ring on his finger. It occurs to me that he may be worried about a primitive form of identity fraud if he uses the ring to verify his correspondence. It must not be a major concern; either that or the draw of the compass proves too great, because he slides the ring off his finger and drops it into my outstretched palm.

No sooner have my fingers wrapped around it, than we're startled by the sound of automatic gunfire from somewhere down the hill. The servant and Linus cast suspicious glances at us, but upon seeing that we're equally surprised, they join us by the railing of the porch.

"That doesn't sound good." I watch the people in the street below react to the unusual sound as more pops and bursts of the guns echo from somewhere near the Forum.

"Time for us to leave." Viznir turns back to our host and bows apologetically. He rambles off a bit more Latin, and it seems to do the trick.

"What did you tell him?"

"I told him we may have friends in need of help and that he and his family should stay indoors till the noises stop."

"Good idea."

We make our way back through the house, and Linus sees us as far as the front steps, still holding the compass in his hand. We make our exit as politely as we can with Viznir's vocabulary and find our way back down the street.

Once we're out of sight of the house, I break into a run. "I think that went pretty well, don't you?"

"He was very accommodating," Viznir agrees, his pack jostling on his back as he keeps pace beside me.

"And you didn't even have to shoot anybody."

"Doesn't sound like our competition had that luck," Viznir mutters. "Where's the next gate?"

I try to read the map as I run. "It doesn't show a gate symbol, but it shows the repository. It has to be near that, right?"

"Should be. Let's just get there quickly before whoever was shooting draws the Praetorians."

Roman citizens stop to stare as we careen through the streets, but no one attempts to slow us down. When we reach the location on the map noted as the repository, we're standing outside a shop nestled among at least two dozen others, on a lower terrace of the Quirinal Hill. I double-check the map and turn toward the shop. It's less busy than its counterparts to either side, which sell woven goods and bread respectively. The shop we want is selling sundials. The shopkeeper is a wizened old man, one of the only legitimately old people I've seen in Rome. He wears his age with a distinct air of satisfaction. As we approach, he bows and gestures us inside.

The shop is narrow, perhaps twelve feet wide, but deep. The interior is cool and a little stuffy. More than a few of the items on the shelves are layered in dust. A second room is barely visible through a curtained doorway. Not having a particular need for a sundial, I step into this second room and look around. A centurion is standing guard near a heavy wooden trunk. To his right, a wooden table is laden with metal trinkets of varying shapes and sizes. Unsure of what to do next, I turn to Viznir, relying on his Latin again. It turns out I don't need to, however, because the words that come out of the centurion's mouth are in modern English.

"Welcome, gentlemen. The repository is just here." He gestures to the wooden trunk and goes so far as to open the lid for us.

I step forward and remove Linus's ring from my pocket. I spot my name in a small cubby inside the chest. As I lean to place the ring inside, I note that two other receptacles are filled. Tad Masterson and Jonah Sprocket.

Wow. The kid with the dog beat us here? How did he manage that?

I get a flush of satisfaction looking at the empty space labeled Horacio Amadeus. When I place the ring into the receptacle, my bracelet beeps. The display showing my time flashes, and the stopwatch function is replaced by the number three. I show it to Viznir. "Good thing we crossed the river, huh?"

A clatter comes from the front of the store, and before Viznir has a chance to respond, the curtain is thrown aside by Marco Thomas. He has his assault rifle to his shoulder and does a rapid sweep of the room with the barrel, hesitating for a fraction of a second on me, then aiming the gun at the centurion. Andre backs into the room, keeping the curtain open and his weapon aimed toward the entrance of the shop. Marco scowls at the centurion and pulls the stock of his weapon closer to his cheek. I notice he has blood splattered on his face and collar.

"Whoa, dude. He's cool," I say, taking a step toward the centurion.

The centurion doesn't even flinch at the sight of the rifle. He merely gestures to the wooden chest in the same manner he did for me.

"Welcome, gentlemen. The repository is just here."

Marco reaches into a pack on Andre's back and extracts some type of medallion. He shoves it into the repository while still keeping his gun raised in our direction. His bracelet beeps.

"Where's the gate?" he barks.

The centurion gestures toward the table of assorted items to his right. "Your exit will be by anchor. Please select the item labeled with your place number and follow the attached jump coordinates."

Marco finally raises the barrel of his gun toward the ceiling and steps to the table. His fingers hesitate briefly over the pendant labeled #3, but after catching me watching him, he instead touches the bronze bust of a Caesar next to it. He swings his gun onto his back.

"Dre, we're out."

Andre abandons his post by the door and joins Marco by the table, shouldering his own weapon. Marco picks up the scrap of parchment with the jump coordinates and enters them into a Temprovibe around his bicep. He and Andre clasp forearms, and while Marco presses his hand to the anchor, Andre activates the Temprovibe. The actions appear well rehearsed. A moment later they've vanished.

"What a cheery bunch those two are," I say.

The centurion cracks a smile. He gestures me toward the table. I pick up the scrap of parchment with our jump coordinates and enter them into my chronometer, then hand the slip to Viznir. I'm considering the Latin inscription on the pendant when the curtain is flung open again, this time by Jettison and Cliff.

"Hey." I smile. Viznir steps back and gives the two men some room.

"Travers!" Cliff exclaims. "Didn't expect to see you here. We'd heard you were trailing the pack this round."

"We made up some time."

"I can see that. Who's this?" He looks Viznir over critically.

"Oh, right. Viznir Najjar, meet Cliff Sutherland and Jettison Marsh."

Viznir extends a hand. "I've seen your name on the lists of past chronothons, Mr. Sutherland. You have an impressive record."

Cliff accepts the handshake and grunts. "This race is about the kid here." He gestures toward Jettison. Jet gives Viznir's hand a perfunctory handshake, nods to me, and steps past us to the centurion.

"Welcome, gentlemen. The repository is just here."

Jettison places a black-handled dagger into the chest and watches his bracelet blink his position.

"Where's Genesis?" I ask.

"She's not far behind, but we can't wait for her," he says. "She's going to have to play it careful getting in. There's an army of Praetorians marching up the hill searching door to door."

"Some idiot shot up the barracks on his way through." Cliff scowls and turns to me. "Wasn't you, was it?"

"No. I think it was Thomas and Watts. They were through a minute ago."

Cliff nods. "I figured you'd have a bit more sense than that. You better get moving if you don't want to meet the Praetorians. They're some ornery bastards when they're angry, and those two riled 'em up good."

"We were just leaving," I reply. "We'll see you on the other side." I gesture to Viznir, and he places his fingertips on the pendant next to mine. I grip my chronometer with my free hand and count off.

The centurion nods to me. "Fortunum, gentlemen."

"E pluribus unum," I reply.

The centurion laughs.

We blink.

"Some people dislike other people. Some people dislike themselves. Time travelers have the unique opportunity to dislike other selves." —Journal of Dr. Harold Quickly, 1967

Chapter 13

We've only moved a couple of days, but we've relocated out of the city. The pendant at my fingertips is now resting on a table on a flagstone patio. I straighten the pendant and read the inscription. *Tempus Fugit.*

I can relate to that one.

The view beyond the patio is rolling green hills, vineyards, and a spectacular orange and pink sunset. I'm still marveling at it when someone addresses us from behind. I turn to find a jovial-looking, bald man in a toga walking toward me with his arms wide.

"Welcome, Benjamin Travers. You are, of course, right on time!" He stops a few feet away and beams at me. "Third place at the moment. A place of honor, to be sure. I am Octavius Theophilus Gracchus, but you can call me Phil."

"Nice to meet you, Phil."

"Welcome to my home. Come. Let your guide take your things, and I'll see you both get settled."

He turns and marches back the way he came, up a set of marble steps that lead to the main building of the villa. I look at Viznir and shrug, then follow.

The stairs lead to the main landing and a dining area of couches that looks out over the impressive view of the valley. The couches are arranged in a U shape, converging at the center of the back wall. The floor of the dining area is a mosaic, and I note with curiosity that the tile work includes pictures of food and other images scattered throughout. Phil gestures to some servants and directs them to Viznir. "These men will see you to your place in the guides' quarters." He turns to me and frowns. "Don't you want to have your man here take your things?"

I catch Viznir's look of irritation as I respond. "No, that's fine. I have some things in here I'd like to hang on to, so I'm good."

"Okay. Your choice. Come, I'll see you to your room and you can get yourself cleaned up for the feast."

"Feast?"

"Of course, my boy. You've reached your first rendezvous with an extremely good ranking. It's time to celebrate."

I turn to Viznir. "Okay, I guess we'll have to catch up later."

"Yeah. Got it." He frowns and follows the servants.

I turn back to Phil. "Hey, before I forget, I promised another racer I would get a message to an official. Are you considered a race official?"

Phil grips the chest of his toga and smiles. "As official as you'll find in ancient Rome."

"Okay. This guy from round one, Dennis, was having a problem with the time gate. He said it wouldn't open for him, even though he put his objective in the repository. Does that sort of thing happen often?"

Phil purses his lips before speaking. "Oh, I imagine it was a mix-up on the part of the racer. This Dennis you speak of probably had the wrong item or is confused somehow. He also could have been too slow to get through. These gates open on a timer, you know. You can't be dilly dallying around when you're supposed to be moving through."

"Yeah, I gathered that. But what's going to happen to Dennis?"

"I'll pass a message along to the committee. I'm sure they'll sort the situation out. If he legitimately did what he was supposed to, they'll let him keep racing. I imagine he'll be pretty far behind, but don't worry; you'll probably see him at the next rendezvous. Now come along. I'll show you to your room."

Phil leads me down a covered hallway to a room the size of a small studio. He opens the door and gestures for me to enter. Two women are waiting inside and smile graciously at me.

"Fausta and Lucinia will help you dress for the feast. It's a formal affair, and the toga can be a bit tricky for first timers. Have you worn a toga virilis before?"

I shake my head.

"I had my house attendant assign you women servants. Fausta can do wonders with a toga, but if you prefer boys . . ."

"Nope." I raise my hand. "No, no. This is going to be plenty awkward enough. No need to overkill it."

Phil grins and gives me a conspiratorial wink. "This is ancient Rome, my boy. You can loosen up those scruples." He claps me on the back and disappears out the door.

I cringe and brush my shoulder off reflexively. *Don't need my scruples loosened by the likes of you.*

Fausta and Lucinia smile at me pleasantly, and I bow my head in resignation. An uncomfortable half hour later, I emerge from my room, garbed like a Roman citizen with the exception of the athletic shorts I've snuck on below my toga. The women have also wrapped the toga around me in such a way that I have a sort of pocket around my left arm, into which I've stashed my pen and Dr. Quickly's journal, not wanting to leave it in the room unattended. The women direct me back to the main dining area where I find a couple of the couches occupied. Tad Masterson is lounging on the couch nearest Phil, smiling at the two women servants feeding him morsels of food. On the opposite side of Phil, Jonah Sprocket is an unusual sight in a special children's toga, while still wearing his oversized snail helmet. He's sitting straight up with his legs dangling over the edge of his couch. A servant has brought him appetizers and is stooping respectfully with a platter for the boy to choose from. There's no sign of the dog. It makes me wonder if, somewhere on the premises, Viznir has been seated next to Barley.

Phil gestures me toward the couch on the far side of Tad. I nod to Tad as I pass, and he grins at me with a mouthful of raisins. "I couldn't believe it when Phil here said I'd be sharing the patio with you, Travers." He sits up and shoos the servants away. "Heard you were dead last coming out of Egypt. Fainted was it?"

I gather up the folds of my toga as best I can and take a seat. "Not last. Dennis was last. Have you heard anything about him?"

"Dennis? No, that old windbag will be hours behind us if he made it through. Unless he pulled the same stunt you did somehow. What'd you do, Travers, pack a hang glider in that satchel of yours? No one even saw you on the road from what I heard."

"You have contact with the others?"

"Preston and Deanna fell behind, but we have a radio. They keep me apprised of things. Nobody saw you, though."

"I took a shortcut. Not short enough, I guess. You two must have had a nice head start." I gesture toward Jonah.

Tad frowns. "I don't know how that little punk did it. He was well behind in Egypt, but he was right on me in Rome. I know he had to have ditched that dune buggy. No way that was fitting through the gate."

I watch the boy patiently selecting appetizers from the man in front of him. "I guess he's just more clever than we are."

"That little shit's going down next round."

I'm startled by the anger in Tad's voice. "Hey man, he's just a kid."

"The hell he is. You don't know him like I do." Tad goes back to reclining on his couch and gestures for more wine.

I retreat to the opposite corner of my couch and try to get comfortable. Phil leans close to Tad and begins joyfully discussing the diversions available in Rome. I accept a cup of wine from a servant and pull Dr. Quickly's journal from the sleeve of my toga. I flip to the back where I've been logging my jumps with Mym and work on catching up on my entries. I've gotten as far as Ireland when Marco appears. I have to stifle a laugh at the look of mortification on his face about being seen in a toga. His discomfort is obvious as he makes his way to the couch next to Jonah. Being seated next to a nine year-old does nothing to improve his disposition, and he looks about the room with an expression of boiling hostility.

Jettison appears next, but he seems every bit as comfortable in his new attire as he did in his tracksuit. He bows graciously to our host and then takes the couch next to me. A servant materializes from the wings to offer him wine. Another approaches me with a platter, and I set the journal down to see what he's brought. The platter is loaded with breads and nuts, so I take a handful of each and deposit them in my napkin. Jettison leans over to see what I've got. "Ah, that's a safe bet. Just watch out when they bring the fish sauce."

"No good?"

"Not unless you like your fish putrefied for a couple months before you eat it."

"Ew. Yeah, I'll probably pass on that one."

I set my napkin on the table and go back to my journal.

"What do you have there?" Jettison asks.

"Just keeping a log. I'm bad at getting behind on my entries."

"Oh, right. Forgot you were an analog. Not sure I'd have the patience for that myself. Cliff's usually an analog, too. Seems tedious to me."

"You aren't scared someone will get ahold of your trace and track you?"

"That's less scary than getting fused into myself somewhere because I forgot to log an entry."

I consider the journal in my hands. "Yeah, I see your point."

The next servant arrives with a platter of what looks to be small rodents. The servant explains as best he can in broken English that they are roasted dormice. Jettison and I both shrug and take one. By the time the snails arrive, my taste buds know they are braving foreign territory, but then Phil unleashes his main entrée, stuffed cows udders, and I balk a little. I let Jettison bite into his first. When he doesn't immediately start gagging, I take a cautious bite. *It's not bad.*

"Hey, Ben." Jettison is looking at me while still holding a handful of the udder. "I'm sorry about Charlie. That had to be horrible, finding him like that."

I set my food down and wipe my fingers off. "Yeah. Thanks. But I should probably be consoling you. You and Genesis knew him much longer than I did. I really only met him yesterday. Seemed like an awesome guy. I was really looking forward to having him as a guide."

"Charlie was great." Jettison nods. "We only saw him occasionally as kids when he'd visit our dad for business, but he was always good to us. Can't imagine why anyone would want to kill him."

"How was Cliff today?"

"Not great. It definitely threw him off. In some ways I'm glad we had the race to concentrate on. Not sure what he would have been like otherwise."

"I felt that way, too. Anything to keep from thinking about it too long."

Phil has apparently been tuning in to our conversation because he slaps the table. "Benjamin, I almost forgot. I've been given a message to give you." He snaps his fingers and a servant steps forward from the wall behind him. "Get me the package for Benjamin Travers." The servant bows and disappears around the corner.

"I trust you'll be happy to know the results of the inquiry about you."

"About me?" I sit up straighter on the couch.

"Of course. The accusations against you regarding the murder of your guide. It's my understanding that all charges against you have been dropped."

"When were there charges against me?"

"Oh, you must have been considered unreachable by the representatives from ASCOTT. Formal accusations were lodged against you in Ireland by a group of fans that claimed they had seen you murder your guide. The inquiry sorted the mess out in short order, but they wanted me to deliver the official paperwork to you."

The servant reappears with a brown packet, and Phil instructs him to give it to me.

"I didn't look inside of course, but official word has gone out regarding your innocence."

I accept the packet from the servant, and after considering the outside briefly, stuff it into my sleeve. My curiosity makes me want to rip into it now, but Tad and Phil's eyes on me make me rethink the idea.

"Thank you."

Phil smiles. "Nothing like a bit of intrigue to keep a chronothon exciting."

I ignore him and go back to my food. *My guide being murdered was not amusing, asshole.*

"And speaking of the mysterious, how about you, young man?" He turns to Jonah. "Youngest competitor in chronothon history, I hear, and nearly leading the race. What's your secret? Hmm?"

Jonah merely bobs his head and keeps eating his bread. After a moment, a few words come out. "I have a good guide."

Phil laughs. "Indeed you do. If I could breed a dog like that, I'd take an army of them. Once in my younger days, I had these pups . . ."

Phil launches into a tale about his childhood, and I lean back toward Jettison. "What do you know about this little kid?"

Jettison frowns and moves closer. "Weird story. Genesis could tell you better than I could. She knew him better. They were in the same class once."

"Her and the kid?"

"Well, sort of. It's a little complicated. It wasn't this kid. He was older."

"Like an older version of him?"

"Yeah, but not exactly. Gen and I visited the academy a few times. We were never full-time, but Dad wanted us to attend some of the courses to round out our education. Jonah was a full-time student, but you could tell he didn't fit in well. He was lanky and awkward. Got picked on a lot. His dad is this eccentric inventor type. I don't know what happened to his mom. I don't think he was very well-adjusted for a place like the Academy. The kids there can be ultra-competitive and harsh. It must have gotten pretty bad because he dropped out. He was probably sixteen at the time. But that's where things got weird. When he dropped out, he didn't just go home to his dad. He went back in time."

"Why?"

"He didn't just want to escape the academy. Apparently he wanted some kind of revenge. He went back to when he was younger and started living there with his dad and the younger version of himself. He started calling himself Jay and acting the big brother to Jonah. God knows what he was telling this poor boy. Can't have been the most rational things because now the kid wears a snail on his head."

"How did he end up in a chronothon?" I watch Jonah picking at food on the table across from us and try to keep my voice low so he won't hear us.

"I'm not sure about that. Maybe Jay thought having his younger self beat these Academy kids in a chronothon would be a way to redeem himself. You can take one guess who his main tormentors were."

I glance at the couch beside me, where Tad is grabbing at one of the slave girls. I frown and look back to Jonah. "Seems like he should have done it himself, not send the younger version of him to do it."

"Yeah, I agree." Jettison says. "I don't think a chronothon is any place for a kid. If his dad had any kind of sense, he wouldn't have let it happen. The committee didn't stop it, though. I just worry how he'll hold up against all this adult competition."

I nod as I remember Marco and Andre storming through Rome with assault rifles. *How is this kid supposed to compete with that?* Jonah is smiling as a servant brings him a tray of fruit. *He beat you here, Ben. He must be doing something right.*

During our conversation, a couple more racers have arrived. The alien, Bozzlestitch, has somehow bypassed the toga requirement. He arrives adorned in his own loose-fitting clothing that is significantly more colorful than the white of our togas. His pants and shirt are earth tone linens, but his dark green arms are bare, and I notice they're covered with tattoos. The servants approach him with trepidation, but he samples their platters eagerly. They seat him in a chair at the table as they've run out of couches.

When Genesis arrives, I get up and offer her my spot. She tries to decline, but I convince her by telling her I'm needing some rest. Phil seems displeased that I'm leaving, and I get the impression that I may have committed some sort of etiquette faux pas by giving my seat of honor to someone else, but I don't care. I want to see what's in the packet in my sleeve, and I don't want to do it with an audience. I thank Phil for the meal and slip out the door, doing my best to navigate back to my room on my own. I find it unoccupied upon entering and am grateful that the servants haven't anticipated my return yet. I slide the bolt closed on the door and retreat to the bed, shedding the toga as fast as I can get out of it.

I climb onto the bed and sit cross-legged with my back to the wall as I tear into the sealed packet. It contains a letter. A quick glance at the signature reveals it's from Chairman Schnyder. I skim rapidly through the formal salutation and get to the heart of it.

" . . . your name has been cleared of suspicion . . . investigators to be thanked for their diligence in the matter . . . while it may come as small relief considering the enormity of your loss, you may rest assured that the true assassin is being sought for punishment . . . the marshals of ASCOTTs law enforcement division have assured us that she will not escape justice."

She?

" . . . While it came as a shock to the entire community, considering her heritage and the enormous contributions of her father to the realm of science, ASCOTT wishes to ensure all involved that neither will delay them from ensuring swift justice be done in the matter of Mym Quickly."

I have to read the line three times to make sure I haven't mistaken the meaning somehow. *They're hunting Mym for this?* I fly through the rest of the letter, searching for more detail, but all of it is maddeningly vague. The only other item in the packet is an official form of acquittal from ASCOTT. *Have they already found her? Is she on trial? Why do they think it was her?* My mind flashes back to the chairman's words in Charlie's tent. "We've already dispatched an investigator." It seems so long ago, but it was only my morning. My morning two thousand years from now. The gulf of time suddenly seems enormous. *That could mean the blonde hair I thought I saw in the woods really was hers. Mym. I can't even warn her.* I think about how much difficulty I had trying to contact her, even in my own time. *What hope do I have of contacting her from here?* My fist clenches the bedding in frustration. *Maybe they won't be able to find her either.* The thought gives me a moment of relief until I ponder the letter in my hand. They obviously have some way to communicate through time. They're more advanced than any analog traveler. *What chance does Mym have to avoid them?*

I'm tempted to throw the letter into the fireplace, but I fold it and the acquittal form and stuff them into the journal instead. I fall back onto the bed and stare at the ceiling, trying to wrap my head around this new information. *How could anyone think Mym was out to kill Charlie? She was the one who got him to help me. A friend of her father's. It would be like killing family, wouldn't it? Could Mym be capable of something like that?* I shake the thought away, remembering the look on her face the moment after I kissed her: the curiosity and the hope. *Maybe that's just what you wanted to see. How well do you really know her?*

I fold my arms and tell myself to snap out of it. I know who the real enemy is. If I think about it, I can still feel the man's fingers around my throat as he shoved my head into the tent pole. The black eyes staring into mine. *He'd almost admitted it, hadn't he?* I try to recall his exact words, but my mind won't let them come. I breathe out slowly, trying to expel my tension and anger. *I just need to get through this. Just survive and you can find Mym after.* I try not to think about what might happen if I'm too late. If the one person I trusted enough to guide me into this world was taken away from me . . .

I don't notice when I fall asleep, but I wake to a persistent knocking. I shake away the lingering cobwebs from unpleasant dreams and shuffle my way to the door. When I open it, I find Viznir in the hallway, wearing his pack.

"Hurry and get dressed. It will be our time at the gate soon."

I rub my eyes. "What time is it?"

"Just shy of dawn. Romans like to get an early start. Most of the teams are already gone."

"They got to go ahead? How does that work?"

Viznir follows me into the room. "They've had to go, but not ahead. The ones who placed highest get to linger longest and have the most rest. We'll still have a head start on the other side. That's how the time gates are programmed."

"I guess that works out well."

"For the ones in the lead. I think the last place team got maybe an hour's rest before they had to go on. We're the fortunate ones."

I get my jeans on, find a clean T-shirt, and stuff Quickly's journal into my pack. My shoulders ache under the weight of the pack again. I follow Viznir outside. A servant in the dining area helps us fill our canteens, then guides us downhill to the gardens.

The sky has lightened and birds have begun their chirping in the branches in anticipation of the sun. We find Phil chatting with a couple of guards who have been assigned to positions on either side of a stone archway. The arch is covered in flowering vines, but the yellow blooms have closed themselves for the night and have yet to awaken. Phil smiles at our approach and opens his arms in the same welcoming gesture as when I first laid eyes on him.

"Our time has been short, Benjamin." He reaches out to clasp my hand with both of his. "But it has been a pleasure."

"Thanks for the hospitality."

"It's nothing, nothing at all. It's me who should thank you. Who knows if I'll ever entertain a group like this again? It was a gift."

"What's next for you now?" I ask. "Once all of us have left."

"Blissful relaxation, one would hope. It's not a bad place to retire, eh? A fair trade for punching a few buttons and opening a time gate or two."

"So you'll stay here?"

"Someone has to, my boy. ASCOTT has spent a fortune on this technology and has to have it dismantled by someone."

"There's no way to get you back to the future? What year are you from?"

"I was born in 2112. I was an engineer most of my life. Would have been retiring soon anyway had ASCOTT not recruited me. They offered me a villa and a staff of servants and more money than I can ever hope to spend here. The perks won me over, I won't deny it. Certainly takes the edge off saying goodbye to the twenty-second century."

"Well, thanks. I appreciate you being here. You'll pass the message on about Dennis and his guide, right?"

"Of course, of course. It will be my first priority." Phil smiles. "I hope to get word of the race results eventually. Looks like a competitive bunch! Perhaps you'll tell me who won when you find a way back to visit me someday, eh?" His face has a tinge of desperation to it, and it makes me wonder how much he's not saying about his views on retirement.

I watch with interest as he steps to a control pad near the arch and inputs an activation code. The guards on either side of the arch step back as colored light shimmers between the columns. My bracelet beeps and the number three begins flashing.

"It's ready for you, gentlemen." Phil steps back and clasps his arms behind him. "Good luck!"

Viznir strides immediately through the arch. I take one last look at the gardens and nod to Phil before I follow.

I'm happy to find the passage this time doesn't involve falling. I step from Phil's predawn garden, directly into dappled sunlight. There's a chill in the air, and I get an involuntary shiver from the temperature change, but it's still mild. Can't be lower than the mid-fifties. Viznir is a few feet away, looking past me. I turn around when I'm through the gate and see that we've just stepped through the front door of a derelict cottage. The mud-daubed walls have chunks broken away, and the thatched roof is allowing sizeable amounts of sunlight through its many gaps. The cottage sits in a former clearing that's being reclaimed by nature.

"You find the objective box yet?" I take a few steps toward Viznir. He motions with his head for me to look right. I turn and see the silver objective boxes dangling by chains from a nearby pine tree like so many Christmas ornaments. I walk under the boughs and locate the one with my name on it. It releases into my hands with a wave of my bracelet just like the others did. I open it to find my map. This one is drawn on a piece of tanned animal hide. The names are in English this time, or something close. I study the writing and the drawings for a minute, then pass it to Vizir. "What do you think? Old-time English? Maybe somewhere medieval?"

"This writing could be from a variety of timestreams or eras," Viznir says.

"Yeah, but this plus Cinderella's pre-pumpkin digs over there, seems pretty medieval, wouldn't you say?"

"It's one possibility. There *is* a castle noted on this map. Our objective is inside."

"How far?"

"If this notation is in leagues, like it seems to be, we're looking at about six miles."

"Oh damn. Seriously?"

"Well it says two leagues. A league is about five and a half kilometers. Five kilometers is—"

"A little over three miles. Gotcha." I start parting the weeds around me with my feet. *Like hell if I'm going to schlep this pack six miles.* I can feel Viznir's eyes on me.

"What are you doing?"

I lean over and pick up a smooth stone that looks like it spent at least some of its life in a river but has one distinctly jagged edge. "I have an idea. Come on." I lead the way back toward the cottage. I avoid the front door since it's being used as the time gate and I'm not sure when the next team will be appearing. Instead, I forge through the weeds at the side of the cottage and make my way around back until I find a hole in the wall big enough to step through.

The inside of the cottage is only three rooms, a main room at the front by the door, a kitchen area, and a bedroom. The thatching on the bedroom ceiling is still mostly intact and has kept out the rain and sunlight. As a result, the hard-packed earthen floor is still relatively level and free of weeds. I lay my stone in the middle of the floor, then swing my pack off my back and set it down next to it. I debate taking the pistol out of it, but decide to leave it. I retrieve my canteen from the side of my pack and clip that to my belt before turning to Viznir. "Anything you don't feel like carrying?"

Viznir stares at my pile of belongings next to the rock. "We need these things."

"Yeah, but we don't need them all right this second. I'm sending my stuff ahead."

"To where?"

"To when I need it." I smile. "Anything you want to ditch? Last chance."

Viznir shakes his head. "I'm keeping my things."

"Me too," I reply. "I just don't want to carry them." I pull Quickly's journal out of my pack, then lead the way out of the room to the kitchen. Viznir follows me. I flip open the journal to my log entry page in the back and note the time on my bracelet. "We've been in this level just under eight minutes. We left the room at about 0:07:43 or so." I scribble the digits in the book. "Let's say it takes a minute or so to come back, pick up the gear, set my chronometer and bug out. Probably less, but we'll call it a minute. I just have to make sure I keep the orientation of the stone the right direction." I check the heading on Charlie's compass. "Right now the stone is aimed east. If I keep the orientation the same and make sure it's on level ground for the jump, should be a piece of cake."

"You're talking about coming back for it in the future?" Viznir frowns. "What happens if someone takes it?"

"I'm talking about coming back for it right now. If this works—" I wait for the timer on my bracelet to tick past 0:08:45. "—then it's already happened." I gesture for Viznir to look around the corner. I join him in the doorway. The floor of the bedroom is empty except for the jagged-edged stone.

Viznir lets out an audible gasp. "It's gone!"

"See? Told you it would work."

"But I didn't even hear anything."

"That's because I'm capable of being a sneaky bastard when I want to be." I walk to the center of the room and pick up the stone. I double-check that I can differentiate the top from the bottom and then slip it into my pocket. "Weighs a lot less than all that gear."

A sudden clatter comes from the front of the cottage. Heavy footsteps are followed by voices. I glance at my timer and see it reads 0:10:04. I put my finger to my lips and whisper at Viznir. "Marco and Andre are through." He joins me by the bedroom wall and we listen as the men tromp their way over to the objective tree and detach their box. I sneak a peek around the corner and see the pair studying their map. Marco points north and stuffs the map into a pocket of his cargo pants, then the two break into a trot, stomping their way through the weeds with their rifles at the ready. I wait till they've disappeared, then turn to Viznir.

"If the intervals are ten minutes for each racer this round, that means Tad and Blaine had a twenty minute head start on us. We've been here ten minutes, so their lead is almost half an hour now. We'll need to keep a good pace if we're going to catch up."

Viznir nods and cinches his pack tighter. "Then let's get going."

We climb back out the hole in the wall and jog north, following the same path Marco and Andre took through the weeds. The clearing is quickly absorbed by woods, and I have to make frequent use of my compass to keep us heading north. A few times I think I can hear Marco's voice up ahead somewhere, but neither of the men ever come into view. After the first few hills, I realize six miles through the woods won't be like any run I've done back home. It's significantly harder.

After just a few minutes, Viznir is sweating profusely. His pack is slightly smaller than mine was, but I have no idea how heavy it is for him. He stubbornly pushes ahead and doesn't complain. Even without my pack, I still get winded after about twenty minutes of hills and stop to catch my breath.

"This is why we don't have hills in Florida," I mutter.

Viznir tilts his head back and takes a drink from his canteen. Much of it runs down his chin. He stops and wipes his face with his sleeve. "I guess we can work off that dinner last night."

"Did you guys eat well? Where did all the guides end up eating?"

"We had tables in the garden."

"So not bad then?"

"No. It was well prepared, and most of the servants and slaves ate with us. Romans seem to treat their servants pretty well."

"Sorry it was so segregated."

"It's not your fault. Phil must get some thrill from the class system there."

"How did Cliff handle it?" I try to imagine how Cliff might respond to being marginalized.

"He actually didn't say anything about it. He was pretty quiet all night. He did ask about you. Wanted to know how you are doing."

"What did you tell him?"

"Not much. He's the competition."

"Cliff's all right. I trust him." I take a sip from my canteen.

"You shouldn't put your trust in your competitors. They're trying to defeat you."

"That doesn't necessarily make them untrustworthy. I guess I like to give people the benefit of the doubt." *Unless they're named Geo or Ariella.*

"That's a risk I wouldn't take." Viznir plunges ahead into the brush.

Around mile five of steadily climbing terrain, the woods begin to clear. Our view expands to include the downward slope of a mountainside and a wide valley. In the distance is a river, and perched on a hillside on the near bank, a white-stone castle commands a view of the entire valley. Tents and other more permanent structures have been erected at safe distances from the walls, and a collection of wooden ships is at anchor on the river side of the castle. One of the ships has an elaborate bridge structure extending from its rigging onto the outer wooden wall of the castle. I squint to try to make out the flags on the ships, but they're too far. I pull out my map and study it. Viznir scans the scene with his tablet and starts researching his databank.

"That river is on the map. What big rivers do they have in England?" I ask.

"This isn't England," Viznir replies.

"The map is English," I counter.

"The men in that castle are English, too. But that river is the Seine. We're in France. If this image scan is correct, that's the Castle Gaillard, and it's under siege by the French."

"Seige?" I study the landscape in front of me. "They're not causing much of a ruckus for having a siege. If they hadn't been downhill, we probably would have walked right into them before we heard them."

"That's because they aren't trying to take the castle by force yet. Depending on the timestream, this siege takes the French anywhere from eight months to a year. In most cases, they'll finally take it in March of 1204. Based on the temperature, we could be close to then. We'll have to see when we get closer."

"Castle siege, huh? This could be fun." I begin plodding down the hill still looking at our map. "Our object is a book of something religious I think. It's got crosses on it." I turn the image sideways to look at it. "Would they have us steal a Bible?"

Viznir consults his scan of the image. "It does look like one."

"Oh, man. We're going straight to Hell."

"Think of it as preserving it for posterity. You're doing them a favor."

I put the map back in my pocket and concentrate on the terrain. The hill begins to level out, and we see more and more evidence of the siege around us. Trees have been felled for lumber and there are occasional scorch marks from fires. We approach a berm of dirt and grass and crouch behind it to take in the view beyond.

The French encampment is sprawled around the castle in all directions, but most of the activity seems to be happening inside a wooden perimeter of the castle. The attackers have breached the wooden exterior wall and torn down sections of it to gain access to the stone walls inside. Gashes and a few indents on the walls show previous impacts from the siege engines and trebuchets, but the rounded exterior of the castle seems to have withstood them well.

Viznir pulls a pair of binoculars from his pack and scans the area. After a minute he hands them to me. "If thousands of French soldiers can't find their way in, I'm not sure how we're going to." He frowns and goes back to his tablet.

I observe the scene with curiosity through the binoculars. With the added magnification I can make out some of the defenders through the arrow slits in the towers and along the battlements. The south side of the castle we're looking at tapers to a point toward us and is guarded by three rounded towers. The towers occasionally open hatches at the top and drop things on the attackers below. I realize that our quiet descent downhill was coincidence as we'd merely arrived at a lull in the action. A creaking trebuchet launches a projectile into one of the upper walls with a tremendous crash, and bits of rock and debris tumble down the wall. I track the action at the base of the wall around to the right, scanning the other surfaces, and suddenly have to jerk back at what I see.

"Holy shit!"

"What?" Viznir looks up from his tablet.

I focus the lenses on my binoculars. "I see Jonah's dog!"

"Really? Where?"

I pass the binoculars to Viznir and point toward the right side of the castle. "It's along the far side, away from the action. Right near the base

of the wall." Even without the binoculars I can make out the Labrador pacing back and forth and looking up the face of the castle wall.

"Well look at that. I wonder where the kid is?" Viznir lowers the binoculars again and looks around. A rustling from the woods behind us makes me turn. At the sight of two figures approaching, my hand automatically reaches for my non-existent gun, but then I see who it is. Cliff's face is red from exertion. Jettison waves as they emerge from the trees and crouches as he jogs the rest of the way to our position.

"How's it looking, Travers?" He swings his pack off his shoulders and lies on the slope next to me, then pops his head up to have a look over the berm.

"We get to storm a castle." I smile.

"Yeah, I noticed." Jettison grins back. "They're ratcheting up the danger level on us."

Cliff is breathing hard when he collapses onto the berm next to Jettison. He nods to me, then gives another nod to Viznir. Viznir frowns and goes back to his binoculars.

"What are you guys after?" I ask, curious to hear about another team's adventures.

"Banner from a throne room." He shows me his map and I compare it to mine. His has a detailed drawing of the central keep labeled "Inner Bailey."

"Special banner?" I ask.

"Apparently it belonged to Richard the Lionheart," Jettison replies. "He's the one who built this castle."

"Sweet! The Robin Hood king? Are we going to get to meet him?"

"Nah." Jettison shakes his head. "According to the data, he died a decade ago. John's king now."

"Ah, bummer." I frown. "That's too bad. Although I always picture him as Patrick Stewart from *Robin Hood: Men in Tights*, anyway. Maybe I can just visit *him* sometime instead. You ever see that movie?"

Jettison shakes his head. "No. But I've seen the one called *Prince of Thieves*. We watched it in film studies class."

"A Kevin Costner movie makes it to the twenty-second century? Good for him." I turn back to the task at hand. "So what's our play here? You have any ideas on how to get over those walls?"

Viznir holds up his tablet. "We could go under. The French are tunneling under the outer wall. Depending on how far they've gotten, we might make it through."

"If you can convince the French to let you through and avoid the cave-ins," Jettison says. "The English are apparently counter-tunneling and collapsing tunnels all over the place."

"You sure know your history. I'm impressed," I say.

Jettison taps his jacket pocket, where the corner of an electronic tablet is peeking out. "I cheat. Just like everyone else past the middle of the twenty-first century." He gestures toward the woods. "I don't know about you guys, but there's my way over."

Genesis and Mayra are emerging from the trees. Viznir looks even more annoyed as our group expands, but I welcome Genesis with a high five. "Hey. How's it going?"

Genesis is breathing heavily but she smiles. "Not bad. Gonna be a tough level though."

"Yeah," I reply. "Storming a castle. Fun for the whole family." I nod to Genesis' guide, Mayra.

"Well, not the whole family," Genesis says. "The Ivans came through right behind me. They were after an objective in the French camp."

"The alien went that way, too," Mayra adds.

Jettison points to Genesis' pack. "You have the ascension gun?"

Genesis nods. "Can we get to the wall?"

"Let's find out." Jettison takes another look over the berm, then clambers over and sprints toward a pile of timber fifty feet ahead. Cliff pulls a pistol from his belt and follows him.

Genesis looks to me. "You guys coming?"

I turn to Viznir and shrug. He looks unhappy, but he doesn't say anything. "Yeah. I guess so."

We climb over the berm and try to catch up to Jettison, who is dodging from one hiding place to another and working his way closer to the castle's wooden perimeter. By heading east we're able to steer clear of the main attack on the castle. To our side, the walls are smooth and the rock cliff below offers little coverage from the battlements. The attackers have chosen to assault the other side, where they've filled in a portion of the dry moat and constructed a covered bridge that allows them to access the base of the wall.

I watch the castle's arrow slits and wonder if at any moment we'll be getting fired upon. I hope that the fact that we're not carrying ladders or anything remotely offensive might make defenders think twice about wasting their arrows on us. We reach an area that's protected by a rise in terrain about twenty yards from the wall. Jonah's dog is still trotting back and forth along the base of the wall, stopping to occasionally look up at the battlements and whine. I hear a periodic beeping coming from somewhere in his doggie saddlebags.

"You think Jonah already made it up somehow?" I ask.

"I can't imagine how," Viznir says.

"Maybe he has an ascension gun, too." Jettison says. "But he'd need

help using it."

"Is it like a grappling hook?" I ask.

Jettison smiles and begins unloading something from the back of Gen's pack. "Better. Time travelers scoff at grappling hooks."

The device he pulls out sets up like a tripod. He arranges a rail along the top that has a scope attached to it and a grip like a rifle. He crouches and aims the rail toward the top of the battlements, using the scope to make minor adjustments. Genesis opens a gray box from her pack and extracts a lightweight ball with what looks like little wings sticking out the sides.

"What is that thing?" I ask.

"Flying anchor," Genesis replies. She flips a switch on the bottom and tosses it to me. I cup my hands to catch it, but instead of falling, when it reaches the top of its arc, the little wings deploy and spin around like helicopter blades, making the ball stop its descent in mid-air.

"Wow. That's awesome!" I watch it hovering a few inches from my face.

Genesis reaches up and taps a button on the bottom and it falls into her hand. She smiles at me. "You ain't seen nothin' yet."

Jettison takes one last look through the scope and stands up. "You ready, Gen?"

Genesis tightens the straps on her pack and pulls her taser from her hip. "Any defenders up there waiting for me?"

"Not that I saw, but be ready." Jettison takes the winged ball from her, and folding the wings out of the way, holds it up for her. Genesis configures her Temprovibe and something she does makes the flying ball and her Temprovibe beep at the same time.

"Okay, I'm synched." She reaches out and touches the top of the ball. The next moment she disappears.

I stand there with my mouth open as Jettison sets the ball on the rail of the ascension gun and presses its activation switch. He squats and puts his hand to the gun grip, then after one last check of the scope, squeezes the trigger. The ball launches through the air, wings tucked behind it as it arcs its way up and over the wall. The arc of the trajectory tops out just at the apex of the wall and I see the ball deploy its wings and hover. To my astonishment, Genesis reappears next to it, her hand still touching the top, and drops to her feet onto one of the battlements. She immediately hops down behind the wall and disappears.

I let out a low whistle and turn to Viznir. "Now *these guys* are good!"

Viznir has been watching with rapt attention and only nods silently, but I can tell from his wide eyes that he's impressed, too.

Jettison has kept his eyes fixed on the battlements. He's watching, but doesn't seem concerned when Genesis doesn't immediately reappear. He merely mutters to himself, "She must have had to take care of a few guards."

I look up to the wall and watch as Genesis pokes her head back up. She takes a quick glance at the ground, then opens one of the hatches that overhang the wall that are used to drop things on attackers. Instead of rocks or boiling oil, she lets a nylon rope ladder tumble out.

"Ah, there we go." Jettison quickly disassembles the ascension gun and begins trotting toward the wall. Cliff and Mayra follow.

Viznir slowly moves toward them also. He pauses to look back at me. "You coming?"

My awe has changed to dread at the sight of the rope ladder. "I'm starting to think we should have used the tunnels."

As I walk toward the ladder, Barley the Labrador comes trotting over. He's still letting out periodic whines and is searching the top of the wall apprehensively. Seeing Jettison scaling the ladder, he lets out a bark.

"Hey, buddy. You all right?" I move toward the dog, but he backs away and growls at me. I stop moving. He goes back to whining and looking at the wall. I can still hear the beeping coming from his collar. The beeps are getting closer together.

Jettison has rapidly gained the wall. Mayra and Cliff are on the ladder next. I marvel at the fact that the synthetic ropes can support both of them simultaneously. Viznir starts climbing once Mayra reaches the top. I step over to the base of the ladder and gaze apprehensively up the height of the wall. *Why do I get myself into these things?* I touch the jagged stone in my pocket through my jeans. *My pack vanished, so I must survive long enough to go back and get it. That must mean I don't die falling off a wall.* The thought gives me some relief, but I'm still leery of setting foot on the ladder. I look up and see that Viznir is almost to the top. Cliff and Jettison reach through the hatch to help him climb through to the battlements. Jettison gestures for me to follow.

The dog's whining distracts me. Barley is pacing back and forth and the beeping from his collar is getting faster. *Is it some kind of bomb?* I'm suddenly worried. *Who would fix a bomb to a dog?* I look up the ladder and my companions have all disappeared. I hear shouting. *Shit! I wonder if more guards showed up. I need to get up there.* I'm beginning to regret not bringing my gun. The beeping suddenly turns into a solid tone, and I look back at the dog. Barley straightens up and stands rigidly still. For a moment he looks like he could be a taxidermy specimen. Not even his eyes move. The next moment Jonah appears next to him, gripping the handle of the dog's saddlebags. He slowly looks up from where he's landed and finds me staring at him. His face falls.

"Did you see me?" he asks.

"I see you now," I reply. It's slowly dawning on me how he's been getting places so fast. "I think your dog was having trouble with the wall."

Jonah considers the battlements and frowns. "Will you help me get him up there? I can't lift him."

I consider the Labrador and his saddlebags. I was already dreading the climb. I'm not sure it would even be possible toting a dog. *He's got to weigh a good sixty pounds.*

"What if we tie him to the bottom of the ladder and pull him up once we get to the top? Do you think he would tolerate that?"

"Yeah. I think so. He's really good."

The dog has calmed down completely now that the beeping has stopped. It pads over and nuzzles me in the hand. Jonah roots through the saddlebags and removes two carabineer clips and attaches them to the dog's harness. I help him check the tension of the harness and clip the carabineers to the slack at the bottom of the ladder. I point to the rungs. "You first."

I glance up the ladder in time to see Jettison poke his head over the wall. He stares at us and then shouts. "Where did he come from?"

I shrug. Jonah starts up the first few rungs. I climb onto the ladder after him. Something about having a nine-year old bravely scaling the wall ahead of me makes me get over my fear. Even so, I make a point to not look down as I climb. When I finally reach the top, Jettison helps pull me over. The interior of the battlements is a mess. The bodies of five defenders are lying unconscious on the stones. Myra and Genesis are guarding the approach from one tower, while Cliff is watching the other.

I tap Jettison on the shoulder. "Help me pull the ladder up. We've gotta haul up the dog."

Jettison looks over the wall at the dog and then back to me, but doesn't ask questions. He merely starts hoisting one side of the ladder while I take the other. Other than the dog's saddlebags scraping the wall a bit as we pull, the dog gets up without incident. Barley licks me in the face as I pull him over the battlements. He immediately begins sniffing the unconscious soldiers. I look around at the bodies, then turn to Jettison.

"So who are we pulling for in this battle? The English or the French?"

Jettison finishes coiling the ladder and stuffs it back into Genesis's pack. "Well, King Phillip II of France was a rabid anti-Semite who robbed Jewish synagogues and eventually expelled all Jewish people from France. King John of England was a usurper who murdered his own cousin to secure his claim to the throne. You can choose your poison."

I pick up a sword from one of the fallen soldiers. "Okay, I guess I'm rooting for team us."

Genesis pushes through the door to the tower on her side and gestures for us to follow. I hear a couple of zapping noises and climb over more bodies once I get inside the door. Mayra and Genesis are resetting the charges on their Tasers before pushing through the next door. Genesis looks up at me. "Where are you headed, Travers?"

"I have to find the chapel."

"Okay. Jet and I have to make it inside the main keep. We'll have to split up soon. You good?"

"Yeah. I'm good." I take a tighter grip on my sword as she gets ready to push the door open. Cliff is behind me holding his shotgun. Viznir has his pistol out. Even Jonah has something in his hand, though it doesn't look like any weapon I've ever seen. It looks like a miniature satellite dish attached to a power pack at his waist. I nudge him with my elbow. "What does that do?"

He looks up at me from under his snail helmet and smiles. "You'll see."

Genesis shoves the door open and sunlight floods through the doorway. She steps forward and a gray-feathered arrow strikes her in the neck.

"Free-jumping is making a jump without prior knowledge of the time and space you're arriving. It can be employed using walls, floors, or other stable objects as anchors. It should be used only in emergencies. Unfortunately, emergencies tend to happen quite often with time travel."–Journal of Dr. Harold Quickly, 1868

Chapter 14

"Get her back inside!" Cliff yells, as Jettison and Mayra reach for Genesis. The arrow is still quivering in the door and Genesis has her fingers to her neck in shock. She teeters sideways and Jettison and Mayra catch her and drag her back inside. Cliff lunges for the door handle and yanks it closed before more arrows can find their mark.

"Those sons of bitches!" Genesis curses as she pulls her hand away from her neck and looks at the blood. Mayra grabs her pack and starts tossing things out to get to her med kit. Jettison keeps pressure on Gen's neck with his palm until Mayra can replace it with a gauze pad. Genesis's steady stream of curses at her attackers reassures us that the injury is not grave.

When Jettison is relieved by Mayra, he steps to an arrow slit in the tower wall and tries to make out the source of the attack. "Looks like they fired on us from the main keep. That's where we're heading anyway." He gestures to me. "Ben, you're going to shoot this thing for me." He starts setting up the tripod for the ascension gun and aims the rail out the arrow slit to the top of the inner keep.

"Me?"

"Yeah. It's easy enough. I'll get it set. Just pull the trigger."

I look back to Genesis who is still seething but allowing Mayra to wrap her neck in bandages. She nods to me.

"Okay. Sure. I'll give it a shot."

Jettison pulls another gun type device from his pocket and stuffs it into the waist of his pants. "I'll set up the anchor on the other side, then shoot it back through here with the coordinates. The others will follow me over. We'll see if we can't take out some of those archers for you and give you an easier path to the chapel." He looks to Jonah. "Where are you headed?"

"I'm going to the chapel, too," Jonah replies.

"Okay, then you can stick with Ben." He programs his Temprovibe to the flying anchor and they both beep again. He checks the scope and then sets the flying anchor on the track.

Cliff steps over to Jettison and rests his hand on his shoulder. "Set that thing for two. I'm coming with you to sort out those defenders."

Jettison resets his Temprovibe. He slaps me on the shoulder before placing his hand on the anchor. "See you next level, Travers!" Then the two men vanish.

I look nervously to Genesis, but she just points me to the gun. "Just don't shake it too much."

I crouch and look through the scope, gently wrapping my hand around the grip. The trajectory looks clear, so I exhale and squeeze the trigger. The anchor zips off the rail and arcs over the inner bailey wall. I can't see where it lands. I study the battlements, then look back to Genesis. She gestures toward the ascension gun.

"Fold that thing up and get out of the way. Once they scout a good anchor location, they'll shoot the anchor back through for us."

I fumble with the legs of the tripod and drag the device over to the two women. Mayra has finished taping the last of the wraps around Genesis' neck. Genesis stretches a hand toward me. "Help me up." I pull her gently to her feet and she probes the bandages with her fingertips.

Jonah is consulting his map while Viznir fidgets with his gun. A sudden buzzing makes me turn around. The flying anchor has whizzed back through the arrow slit and hovers a few feet off the ground. Genesis taps the bottom and catches it as its rotary wings stop spinning. She presses another button on the anchor and consults her Temprovibe before turning to Mayra. "He sent us coordinates." She sets the anchor on the ground, and Mayra helps her gather the rest of their things. Mayra takes more than her share of the load so Genesis can keep her neck straight, and they both crouch low around the anchor.

After setting their respective devices, Genesis salutes me with her free hand. "Later, boys."

The pair of them vanishes, leaving only the anchor rocking gently on the floor. I wait a few seconds, then step forward and pick it up. It's lighter than the blown glass anchors I learned on, and its construction is far more complex. I consider the blade-like wings protruding from the side.

"Can I have that?" Viznir steps up next to me. "I might be able to program it to my unit."

I hand it to him. "Sure. If that fails, we'll find ourselves some brooms and have a killer game of quidditch."

Jonah perks up. "I can play that. I was in wizard club at my school."

THE CHRONOTHON

I pat Jonah on his snail helmet. "That doesn't surprise me one bit." I push past Barley and open the door a crack. The noise from the far side of the castle has increased. Shouting and the clang of steel are coming from the battlements past the next tower. I shut the door and consult my map. "We need to get to the ground and across to the other side of the castle." I point out the chapel on the map. "It's bound to be a mess on the way, but it sounds like the French are attacking for real now on the outer wall. If we move fast during the distraction, we might make it."

Viznir calculates the distance on his tablet and his brow furrows. "We'll never make it waiting on the kid."

Jonah is punching coordinates into the dog's collar.

"I have a feeling he'll keep up okay."

The metal skullcap of a dazed soldier scrapes against the floor, and the man wearing it lets out a moan.

"It's time for us to go." I pick up my sword and crack the door again. "Stay with me, Vizzy. We got this." I push the door wide and dash onto the wall.

Here we go.

The volume of the outside world has changed rapidly. The ring of metal on metal is inside the walls now. A French contingent has appeared from the chapel and is engaging the defenders around the moat of the inner keep. Arrows rain from the battlements on that side also. Wall defenders rush down from the outer battlements to engage the French. Viznir and I run along the wall behind a pair of defenders who haven't noticed us yet. They reach the stone stairs and we follow them down. On the lower landing, the trailing soldier turns his head and spots us. He looks immediately confused as I point my sword toward the chapel and shout "For England!" The man continues to run after his compatriots but looks back again twice before having to concentrate on the French attack.

Trailing the other English soldiers gives us a little added safety, as the archers on the wall of the inner keep are not firing at us. The feeling of safety is only momentary, however, as we are running headlong into the fray around the chapel. The French soldiers have used the element of surprise to their advantage and are fanning out into the courtyard. None of the French are carrying shields, but most have pikes and swords. The English fall on them in force, initially with deadly effect, but the French men-at-arms keep multiplying from the chapel.

Viznir snatches up the shield of a fallen Englishman and narrowly misses being stuck by a spear. One of the Frenchmen charges me with a pike and I dodge to the side, parrying it with my sword. The man's momentum carries him too far forward and he is struck down by an

English knight. I cringe as the sword cleaves through the man's shoulder. The knight wielding the sword pauses to look at me in curiosity, and for a moment I think he's going to attack me next, but he rushes forward to engage more of the French men-at-arms. The French have knocked a window out of the top of the chapel and are pouring onto the walls. The tide of the skirmish turns quickly and the knight yells for the English men-at-arms to fall back. I signal Viznir to follow me and we dash to the wall of the chapel and press ourselves against it near one of the broken windows. A couple more Frenchmen jump through and dash toward the gate before I poke my head around the corner.

"These guys smell pretty funky." I scrunch my face up as I get a whiff of body odor and feces. Viznir tosses his shield aside and we clamber through the remains of the window. Shouting and scuffling reverberate across the roof as fighting continues outside. The interior of the small room we've entered takes me aback because it looks nothing like a church. The stone walls are broken up by two wooden doors. The one to the outside is shut, but another stands slightly ajar and shows a route to a larger chamber. The wall to the exterior side of the castle has a wide slab of stone set horizontally with a series of holes cut out of it. It dawns on me that they are used for toilets. I hear voices coming from the latrine holes and inch my way closer out of curiosity. There is a smattering of French I don't understand, but then I hear a voice I recognize. I inspect the nearest hole and see a collection of ropes dangling down the chute. At the bottom, where the hole exits to the cliff face, a handful of French soldiers are rigging a makeshift harness around a frazzled looking Horacio. Donny is standing next to him holding their packs.

I can't help but laugh. A couple Frenchmen look up, and Horacio does as well. He scowls when he recognizes me.

"Hey, man. Having fun down there?" I grin.

Donny sees me and flips me off. Horacio scowls and pushes one of the Frenchmen away. He grabs the rope and starts climbing.

"Can you hurry up, man? Cause I kind of have to go."

Donny shouts up the shaft, "We're gonna beat your ass, Travers!"

"Oh. Hey Donny. Didn't see you back there. I guess it's cause you're number two." I grin at Viznir, but he merely rolls his eyes.

"We don't have time for this. We need to get our objective."

"Not even a chuckle? I know it's not my best stuff, but I'm still warming up. I've never been given this much ammo all at once." I gesture to the latrine. "This is a comedic goldmine."

"Laugh later. This place is dangerous."

As if on cue, the wooden door swings open and a snarling bearded man in chain mail takes only a moment to decide he doesn't like us. He swings his sword left-handed, slicing through the air toward my head.

Holy shit! I barely get my own sword raised in time to keep from being cut in half. Even so, the blow knocks me off balance and I stagger backward toward the latrine. His next swing requires Viznir to leap into the corner. I straighten up and slash at him before he can strike again. He deflects my blow with ease and starts hacking back at me, swords clanging as he drives me backward with brute strength. I stumble and land on my backside at the base of the stone latrine. He swings for my head, but impacts the top of the stone slab when I duck. He aims his next blow more carefully, but doesn't get to take it. He shudders as the room echoes with gunshots. He slumps over me in a heap and I scramble to get out from under him. Viznir is in the corner with the gun still smoking in his hands.

I get out a winded "Thanks."

I flinch as something furry leaps through the broken window. Barley skids on the landing, then immediately darts through the door into the chapel area. The beeps from his collar have gotten rapid again. I climb to my feet and look down at the body of the soldier. He's slumped over the latrine, staring vacantly into one of the holes. I brush myself off and look to Viznir. He's staring at the dead man, and his hand holding the gun is shaking.

"I owe you one, man."

"You should bring your own gun next time." Viznir holsters his pistol.

"Yeah." I nod and lead the way into the chapel.

Jonah has arrived and is searching the sanctuary at the far side of the room. Viznir stops in surprise when he sees him. "How'd he get past us?"

I gesture toward Barley. "Jonah's been using the dog as an anchor stand to get around. Saves all kinds of time."

Viznir scowls. "That's cheating!"

Jonah pauses in his search. "No it isn't. I asked the committee. They said no one has ever done it before so there's no rule against it."

The dog is panting happily. "That makes sense," I say. "I don't know how many other guides would be willing to run most of the racecourse without their racers. They'd probably want more of the winnings."

"I wouldn't do it," Viznir says. "The guide would be doing all the work. Why should the racer get any winnings in that scenario?"

I smile at the dog and pat him on the head. "And Barley here probably does it for milk bones." The dog wags his tail.

"He likes belly rubs," Jonah says.

I scratch behind the dog's ears. "I'll bet he does."

"There's the Bible." Viznir points to the altar and I climb the raised platform. I lay my sword against the altar and step over to the book. Its leather cover is embossed with metal, and when I flip it open, I realize the entire copy has been hand written. The beginnings of chapters are illuminated with elaborate colored illustrations.

"This thing is beautiful." I hold it carefully. "And heavy. What do you think the committee is going to do with it?"

"Probably preserve it," Viznir says.

I notice the smell of smoke getting worse, and it makes me wonder if the Bible originally survived the siege. A clatter comes from the doorway and two French men-at-arms are followed into the room by Horacio and Donny. I take a step toward my sword.

The soldiers stand at attention as Horacio says something to them in French. Jonah has found the object he was searching for and takes up a position near the dog, depositing the little wooden statue into the saddlebags. Viznir puts a hand to his gun holster. Cradling the Bible under one arm, I pick up my sword and step down from the altar. *What do these clowns want?* Horacio takes another step into the room while Donny shoots me dirty looks from behind.

"We can't stay and chat, boys, but we've arranged for you to have a little company so you won't get lonely." Horacio gestures behind him and a few more soldiers enter the room looking exceptionally unfriendly. "Good luck getting to the next gate in one piece." He smirks and disappears back through the doorway. He and Donny are replaced by three more soldiers. All of them have their weapons in hand. Viznir draws his pistol. The motion makes Jonah look up from his saddlebags and he finally notices the half dozen soldiers menacing us from the doorway. As they begin to approach, he pulls the unusual dish-ended weapon from his belt and aims it at them. He squeezes the trigger and each of the men's faces silently relax in turn. The men crumple to the floor like so many limp fish. One of the men slumps against the wall with his mouth in a sloppy grin. His eyes roll back in his head, his eyelashes flutter a few times and then his head droops forward on his shoulders.

I stare at Jonah in disbelief. "Holy crap, kid! What is that thing?"

Jonah calmly secures the weapon back to his belt. "It's my dad's organism gun. He invented it."

"Organism gun?"

"Yeah. He made it at his job, but they made it illegal so he couldn't sell it. He says it makes people feel like they're having organisms in their brains. He says it's not really bad though. People think it feels good."

I look at the goofy expressions on the soldiers' faces as they lay dazed on the floor. "Uh-huh. Are you sure the word he said was 'organisms?'"

"Yeah. He says they have thirty-minute organisms in their minds. He says I shouldn't shoot people too much, though, because they will try to steal my gun. I guess they really like the organisms."

I laugh and look at Viznir. "Kid's dad sounds like a unique guy. He'd be a zillionaire in my century."

Viznir doesn't smile. "We need to get to the repository. The French army will be all over this place soon. They were raising the gate from the inside. I don't know how we're going to get out through that mess."

"Barley can take us," Jonah offers. "You guys helped us over the wall. We could help you get back out."

I consider the handle on the back of the dog. Jonah has simply strapped a wooden stick from the woods onto the handle to use as an anchor. "Isn't that dangerous? What if someone stops him or tries to shoot him?"

Jonah shakes his head. "Barley is really fast."

Viznir looks skeptical, but after he takes a look out the window at the massing French troops in the courtyard, he seems to reconsider. "They're less likely to shoot a random dog. They're definitely going to have an issue with the three of us walking out of here."

"Do you think your dog can carry the Bible? There're no gravitites in it."

Jonah rearranges some things in the packs before looking up to Viznir. "Can you carry some things? These things can make the jump."

"Oh, that reminds me, I still need to grab my pack. I can fit stuff in there." I pull the stone from my pocket and set it on the floor away from the others. I check my compass so I'm standing on the proper side and then consult my bracelet. I aim for the next even minute to make the math easier in my head and set my chronometer. "Hold off the guards for another couple minutes. I'll be right back."

Jonah dutifully takes his weapon from his belt and faces the doorway as I crouch to my anchor and watch the last few seconds count down. I smile at Viznir and push the pin. The next moment I'm back in the little cottage in the woods.

My pack is just beyond the stone at my fingertips. I recognize the sound of my own voice from the next room. "Let's say it takes a minute or so to come back, pick up the gear, set my chronometer and bug out. Probably less, but we'll call it a minute . . ."

I gently pick up the pack and sling it over my shoulder. I crouch slowly back to my anchor, careful to not let anything clatter. I leave my time increment on my chronometer set the same, but merely flip the slider on the side from back to forward. I can't help but grin at the sound of Viznir's voice asking questions in the other room. I push the pin and reappear in the castle chapel. I straighten up from the stone and toss it to

Viznir. "Told you it would work."

Jonah reattaches his weapon to his belt. I notice a couple more prone bodies have been added to the pile by the door.

Viznir considers the stone, then tosses it aside. "How is this dog thing going to work?"

"It's easy," Jonah replies. He hands me a bag of dog food to put in my pack and puts the Bible in its place. "Just hold onto me. Barley knows the way from his collar."

"Like some kind of doggie GPS?" I ask.

"It makes noises only he can hear to tell him which way to go. Then, when the time comes for me to show up, it beeps a sound everybody can hear. If there are any people around, Dad says they are more likely to stand clear if they can hear the noise."

"That makes sense."

"Barley knows what to do. He wouldn't let anything hurt me."

The dog's clearly ecstatic expression in the proximity of its master makes me not doubt it.

Jonah takes up his position on the anchor and sets his instruments. Viznir and I stand behind him. When Jonah is ready, I rest my hand on top of his colorful snail helmet. The jump is instant, and I drop a few inches on the landing because the dog has wisely stood atop a stump in a clearing for our arrival. We all land in the grass. I straighten up and consider our surroundings. Just to our right, a dirt path leads into woods that resemble those around the cottage. The dog has accumulated a few leaves in his coat and is panting from the run to wherever we are, but otherwise seems fine. I appreciate that he didn't have us reappear in the forest where we might have been imbedded into a tree branch.

Jonah points to where the path enters the woods. "The drop off is in there."

I lead the way along the narrow path and find it passes through a channel of stone made by two boulders. Once we squeeze through the narrow opening, we find an empty space encircled by rock with no way to continue. I search fruitlessly for the repository. "It has to be here somewhere." I consult my map. It shows the stone ring we're in with a mark on one side for the repository. I look the direction it indicates but see only blank stone. I step up to the imposing wall and run my hand across the rough surface. As I do, the bracelet on my arm triggers a clunk somewhere inside the rock. I study the wall, then place both hands against the boulder and push. The face of the rock slides smoothly inward to reveal a chamber about six feet deep. A shelf has been carved into the rock along the right side, and I locate my name over a space just big enough for the Bible. "Found it."

THE CHRONOTHON

I step back into the sunlight and smile at Jonah. "You want to go first? You got us here."

Jonah grins. "Okay. Thanks." He tugs at the dog's saddlebags and removes the wooden saint statue and I trade him the dog food back for my Bible. He disappears into the alcove in the rock and I can tell when he deposits the statue because the narrow path behind us shimmers with light. Jonah reemerges and grins at me. "We got here first. There're no other anchors in there."

"Nice!" I give him a high five.

Jonah steps toward the shimmering light between the rocks. "Thanks for getting Barley into the castle."

"No problem, bud. We'll see you in a few."

Jonah waves and then orders Barley to enter the gate. The dog barks and happily bounds through. Jonah disappears after him and the shimmer fades.

"You know, at some point you're going to have to actually compete against him." Viznir says. "You just let the kid have first place."

"Second is nothing to be ashamed of, Vizzy. He just saved our asses." I step into the alcove and shove the Bible into the spot under my name. My bracelet beeps #2. The rock door closes automatically behind me as I exit. I tighten the straps on my pack and gesture toward the gate. "Let's see what level four has for us, huh?" Viznir draws his pistol this time as he steps through. I take a deep breath and follow.

"Knowing where you've been is easy, so pay attention to when you've been. We have spatial memories—that can't be helped, it's just the way our brains work. Train it to remember the 'when' of your experiences and then you'll begin to have the mind of a true time traveler."–Journal of Dr. Harold Quickly, 2006

Chapter 15

The air is humid and carries the scent of saltwater and bird droppings. We've emerged into twilight under a canopy of trees. Some are palms. I also recognize the swooping drapery of "old man's beard" lichen in the crooks of conifer branches. It reminds me of Florida and home. The coming night is being heralded by the sounds of insects, and a gap in the trees shows the last light of the sun on some high cirrus clouds.

"The boy didn't wait," Viznir says, holstering his pistol. "He'll have a five or ten minute head start on us if the timing on the gates stays consistent."

I ignore his observation and search for our objective box. Dog tracks dot the dirt near the rotted half of a fallen tree trunk, and the wood is eaten away by termites, so it's easy to lift. Our objective boxes are anchored to hooks in the ground underneath. I retrieve mine and let the log fall back over the others. When I get the box open, I smile at the contents. "It's a treasure map!"

I flash the document at Viznir. The parchment has rough edges and looks as though it's been aged. The cursive scripts across it are written in both Spanish and English in varying inks. The location of our object is marked with an X and has an illustration of an elaborate pistol next to it. According to the mark on the map, the pistol is located in the middle of a cove. I scan the rest of the map quickly. "Oh, man. This could be a problem."

"What?"

I show the map to Viznir. "The objective might be underwater. It points out here to this cove." I poke my finger at the mark for our objective. "But that's not the only issue. We're on an island, but it's not the same island as our repository. We're going to need a boat."

As Viznir takes the map from my hands, his face suddenly goes fuzzy. I blink and try to clear my head. I start to lose my balance.

"What's wrong with you?" Viznir reaches out to steady me but misses my arm as I stagger backward.

"Ben." The voice isn't Viznir's this time. *Oh God. Not again.* I tumble onto my back as my vision starts to go black. I fight for consciousness, but the tunnel of light narrows to a point and is gone. The light of reality is replaced with color and sound. Men in black are chasing people I recognize—Milo and Kara, Cliff and Genesis. One of the men with the glowing eyes stops to stare at me. *Who is that?* The scene tumbles on, and I try to make sense of my surroundings. I need to get somewhere, but I'm not sure why. Milo and Kara yell for me to follow them, and we plunge into a labyrinth of pipes and alleyways. We're rushing through some kind of subterranean city. My stomach is knotted, anticipating the approach of some impending doom, but then I'm past it. Mym is smiling at me from my bed in my apartment, looking up from a book. I try to smile back but something is still pulling at my mind, trying to turn my attention away. *No! Let me have a chance to talk to her. I just found her.* I finally turn my head to the right. I'm looking at a landscape like I've never seen before. Rivers of color climb out of a desert and into the sky. A man is a few yards ahead of me looking up. He turns and smiles. It's me. The other me stops smiling and looks me directly in the eyes. "You'll have to find me. When this is over. Find me, Ben."

"How?" I stammer back. "Where are you?"

"It's important. You have to find me. Your future depends on it."

I try to speak again, but the dream is fading. I'm sucked away from the desert and the rivers of color, and back into blackness.

"What's wrong with him?" This new voice is curious, but compassionate.

"I don't know. This has happened twice now." Viznir's voice sounds tired.

I pry open an eyelid and see a face staring at me. I recognize the wrinkles around the eyes of Harrison Wabash.

"Ah. He's coming around."

I blink and notice that I've been propped against a tree. The Admiral is a few feet away reading a compass and consulting his map.

Wabash puts a hand to my forehead. "You feeling all right, sport?"

I nod and clear my throat. "Yeah, must have gotten a little dizzy there."

Viznir shakes his head. I attempt to get up but Wabash holds my shoulder and presses me back. "Just sit there a minute. Your guide here says you're having some trouble staying conscious."

"Yeah. Something like that." I squirm a little under his direct gaze.

"What are you seeing?"

"What do you mean?"

"When you're unconscious. What do you see?"

"Oh. Different things. Dreams."

Wabash narrows his eyes. "Do they feel like dreams or do they feel like memories?"

"They're nowhere I've ever been before. So dreams, I guess." I rub my face and then remember the vision I had about Charlie. "Well, I had one that I recognized later."

"Later?"

"Yeah. It's just dreams, though." I look to the left and jolt away. "Whoa! Sorry. Didn't see you there." The forest-green figure of the alien is looming over me. His tattooed skin blends with the backdrop of woods beyond him. This is the closest I've ever been to him and I try my best not to stare.

"Hello, Benjamin Travers." The alien's voice is deep with a slightly gravelly quality. "My name is Mooruvio Jasoon Bozzlestitch, but you may call me Bozzle."

"Hey . . . Bozzle."

He inclines his head politely and crosses his arms. The tattoos on his arms involve what look like dragon or fish scales, but I can't be sure if those aren't just part of his skin. A figure of a tiger/demon creature wraps one forearm while another monstrous looking deity adorns his right. The angry looking figures are offset by what appear to be flowers. It makes me wonder if they are creatures or plants from his home world.

I turn my attention back to Wabash. He's still staring at me intently. "Benjamin, based on the symptoms Viznir has described, you may want to consider the possibility that your dreams are trying to tell you something."

"How? Is that normal?"

Wabash frowns. "Normal is a tricky word, but I'll say it's not unheard of. I spent a fair amount of time as a field medic and there have been instances where I've run across other time travelers who suffered from something similar. The consciousness of a time traveler can be a little different than that of regular people. It's not as linear. Not as confined in its memory."

"What does that mean for me?"

"I suppose you'll have to learn that for yourself. You need to figure out if you're dreaming or if you're remembering. And if you're remembering the future, it might not hurt to pay attention."

"Does this happen to you? Can you dream the future?"

Wabash frowns. "I think we all can. There are theories out there that suggest everyone does. Not just time travelers. Most people just don't pay much attention to their dreams." He scratches at his chin. "But yours seem to be demanding your attention more aggressively if they are coming on while you're awake."

"Why am I blacking out from them?"

"Not sure. But you'll want to be careful. A chronothon's not a safe place to be losing consciousness." Wabash pushes off his knees and stands as the Admiral walks over.

"Let's get moving, Harrison. We've finally reached a world where our skills will be paramount." The Admiral gives me a curt nod. "Better health to you, Mr. Travers. And good luck." The duo continues down the path. The alien moves in front of me and seems to be considering my face.

"If you would like markings of a better quality, I have some skill at my disposal. I have never marked a human face, but I have done other parts with success." He bows gravely and follows the Admiral and Wabash.

I look at Viznir. "What is he talking about?"

Viznir rummages in his pack, then tosses me a round hand mirror.

It takes me a few seconds to realize what I'm looking at because it's backwards, but then I make out the slurs and insults that have been written across my forehead. There is also a drawing of something indecent on my cheek. "Damn it, Viznir! You let them draw on me?"

Viznir is unapologetic. "I kept the big blonde guy from urinating on you. So, you're welcome."

I get to my feet and try to wipe my face with my shirtsleeve. I frown at the lack of results in the mirror and then try using my chronometer. I do a two second jump using a tree branch, but when I reappear, Viznir shakes his head. I check the mirror and the markings are still there. *They must have used a pen they brought with them.* The idea of Horacio and Donny gloating over my unconscious body makes my blood boil, but there's nothing to be done about it. I pick up my pack from next to the tree where I'd been lying, then start down the path.

"Who else saw me like this?"

"The two black guys who shot up Rome came through after us. They didn't pay much attention. Then you got drawn on by your friends from the latrine. The women we saw in Egypt came after that."

"Ariella? What did she say?"

"She didn't say anything. She just laughed."

Damn it.

"Anybody else?"

"Yeah. The Ivans and the two Academy guys."

"Tad and Blaine."

"Yeah, them. Then the four you just saw."

"How four?"

"The Admiral and the alien plus their guides."

"I've never seen a guide with the alien. I thought he was going solo."

"Just because you didn't see him, doesn't mean he wasn't there."

I ponder this while we walk. "Is his guide invisible?"

"No. I think he's just really small. Could be a she actually. Or maybe an it. I'm not really sure. He has a guide, though. The name is on the list. Sooka something. Or something Sooka. I can't remember."

"Weird. No sign of Jettison or Genesis?"

"No, not yet."

Viznir and I step out from under the shade of the trees and onto a narrow, rocky beach. I make straight for the water's edge, dropping my pack into the sand just prior to the high waterline. I scoop up water and a little sand and scrub at my face. The gentle waves lap over my shoes, but I ignore them, as I plan to dry off by time travel again anyway. After a minute of diligent scrubbing, I consult Viznir's mirror again to see if I've erased the graffiti. It takes a couple more attempts before I'm satisfied that I've gotten it all.

Viznir has uploaded our treasure map and is running a translation program on the cursive script when I get back to him. I pull Charlie's compass from my pocket and orient us to the compass rose on the map. After a moment's consultation, I look up and point across the water. "The island we need to get to for the repository is out there, but our objective is somewhere north around the point. Once we get it, we'll have to get over there somehow."

The water is turning from purples to black as it gets farther from the shore. The sky is showing a few planets and bright stars as the last light of the day drains from the atmosphere. Off in the distance I can just make out a dark mass on the horizon.

"It doesn't look too terribly far, but much farther than we can swim. Unless we train some sea birds to drop anchors over there, we'll definitely need a boat."

"The game designers will have something in mind. I'm guessing we'll find a method if we search long enough."

"All right. This way then." I trudge through the sand toward a rocky outcropping that's jutting out at the north end of the beach. A couple different sets of footprints in the sand have gone the same direction. When we get to the rocks, I immediately climb onto one and use it as an anchor to dry off. Next, I rummage through my pack and retrieve my flashlight and shine it at the pile of boulders, searching for the best path through.

We scramble up and gain the top without incident. I click my flashlight off and take in the view on the far side. The land falls away beyond the rocks as the waves flow into a sheltered cove. Two hundred yards to the right, the beach resumes in a half moon curve. This beach is occupied. A bonfire is burning in a ring halfway to the tree line. Dark figures are silhouetted against it. Another figure is standing near the bow of a wooden dinghy that's been dragged beyond the high waterline. The figure is staring out at the three-masted wooden ship lying at anchor in the cove. The ship's sails are furled, and it rocks gently in the waves.

"Oh good. That makes more sense. Our objective isn't underwater. It must be on that ship." I watch the waves gliding past the ship's stern. Even in the fading light, it's a thing of beauty. "That's a sweet ride. That's either a corvette or a little sloop of some kind. Looks like something from the 1700s."

Viznir holds up his tablet to capture an image. I find my way along the rocks toward the beach, trying to stay out of sight of the men on the beach.

Viznir scrambles to stay with me. "How did you know that?"

I pause to let him catch up. "You know those people who assemble little ships in glass bottles?"

"Yeah. Always seemed like a silly way to build something to me."

"Me too. But my dad loved that stuff. He probably has a dozen of them around his den back home. He had me build a couple with him when I was a kid. He loved sailing." I smile at the memory. "Once he graduated from the ones in bottles, he bought this beat up cabin cruiser off one of our neighbors and I had to spend a lot of my weekends helping him sand the deck. It was a piece of junk, but you couldn't tell him that. He glowed every time we went for a sail as a family. Of course once I was a teenager, I just wanted to go fast. I wanted a powerboat. I couldn't afford one myself, but that's how I ended up working at marinas and fixing boat engines." I turn to look at Viznir. "You ever learn to sail?"

"No. My family never lived near the water. We've always been in the city."

"What do your folks do?"

"My mom did a lot of serving and bartending to get herself through school. That's how she met my dad, working at a casino. He gambles."

"Oh, like those guys who do the *World Series of Poker*?"

"Something like that."

"Is he any good?"

"No."

Viznir forges ahead with extra energy as if to get away from the conversation. I flick my flashlight on here and there when the footing looks tricky, but resign myself to following him in silence.

As we get closer to the beach, I get a better view of what's happening. The men have erected a barrier made of palm fronds and driftwood between the bonfire and the water to keep the light from shining toward the open sea. I notice for the first time that there are no lights lit aboard the ship. *They're hiding from someone.*

I hold my finger to my lips and signal for Viznir to crouch lower as we slip around some shorter boulders and make for the tree line at the edge of the beach. Before we reach it, we run into competition. One of the Ivans is crouched near a rock watching something in the woods. He turns at our approach and surveys us cautiously.

"Hey," I whisper as I take a position behind the adjacent boulder.

Ivan nods at me and looks back to the woods. I slip quickly past the gap between our two boulders and join him at his. "What's going on?"

He looks irritated at my presence but consents to respond. "We look for way to ship." He jerks his thumb toward the water. "Must get past buccaneers."

His accent is heavy. I'm guessing Russian, but could be somewhere else in the vicinity. His use of "buccaneers" makes me smile. "Pirates? Really?" I poke my head up to see over the boulders. Ivan grabs my arm and tugs me back down.

"No! They see you!"

"Hey, it's okay. Those guys have got to be totally fire-blind right now, sitting around that thing. They won't have any kind of night vision this far."

Ivan seems to consider this, then nods. "Okay. We go." He gets to a crouch and dashes across the few feet of sand for the cover of the trees. I gesture for Viznir to join us and I follow Ivan. The bit of Viznir's face I can make out in the darkness looks miffed as he catches up to us in the trees. The other Ivan is a little farther into the woods trying to make out his map in the darkness.

"What are you doing?" Viznir asks.

"They're trying to find a way onto the boat. They said the guys on the beach are pirates."

"How do you know they're pirates?"

"I don't know." I walk over to the nearest Ivan. "How did you know they're buccaneers?

Ivan's face scowls a little as he responds. "They look like it."

I look back to Viznir and curl my fingers like a hook and make a clawing motion at him. He doesn't seem amused.

The other Ivan walks over but doesn't speak to Viznir or me. He converses with the other him in a slur of words I don't understand and gestures toward the beach.

The Ivan closest to me reaches into his jacket and removes a pistol from his shoulder holster. He follows his duplicate forward.

"So what's your plan, dude?" I sneak along behind.

"We take little boat."

"Good plan. Have you seen the others? Because that ship is going to be a challenge to sail with just four guys."

"The Italian and his guide went south at the beach. I saw him follow the pretty woman. No one else."

"Yeah, well we can do without that guy anyway. Did you see the dog?"

"No. No dog."

Viznir is close on my heels. "How do they think they'll get past the group on the beach?"

"I don't know. I'm just going along till we figure something out. We're going to need help from someone. There's no way we're figuring out that corvette in a hurry. Just getting the anchor up will be a project. We would probably be better off getting the pirates to join us."

"How do you plan to do that?"

"I don't know." I try to formulate a feasible plan as we walk. "Sailors are superstitious. Maybe we can convince them with a little magic."

Our progress through the palms is slow in the darkness as we're trying to not make too much racket. Finally, we're able to get a clear view of the men around the bonfire. Ivan was right. They don't look much like legitimate sailors. There are no parrots in attendance or obvious hook-hands in sight, but it's definitely a menacing crew.

A big man with a stained, sleeveless shirt is poking at the fire with a branch, while a half dozen others convene on logs they've dragged onto the beach. A few of the men have clearly been drinking, but not all. A wiry man with a pair of pistols tucked into the front of his trousers is pacing around the circle casting frequent glances northward along the beach.

"I tell ya, he'll find a way sure enough." The voice of one of the men on the logs carries to our position. "Cap'n Hew ain't never steered us wrong when it come to gettin our hands on what belongs to us. Once he's scouted the position of those frigates, he'll have a plan."

The grizzled man slumped next to him lets out a grunt. "The Spanish will be on us before we can get it clear. Marquez was there when Tanners dragged it off the wreck. Buried it deep, he said."

"There's more of us now than he had with him. More hands to dig it up." The first man scratches at his beard. "We get it quick and the Spanish'll never know the difference."

"The cap'n has the bearing, sure enough, but getting that swag aboard will be slow to—"

"Hey! Hold your tongues!" The man with the pistols holds up a hand and draws one of his guns with the other. "There's something moving in the woods."

I look at the Ivans to see if one of them made some commotion. The Ivan farthest from me is trying to back away from the beach. He's frozen in place as if he's stepped on something. One of the men from the logs rises with a cutlass in his hand and peers into the darkness. The other man snatches a burning branch from the fire and holds it aloft as a torch.

"Who goes there?" The man with the pistols asks. He's drawn his second pistol as well. I look right, and both the Ivans have their guns drawn. Viznir does too.

It's no good if we shoot them all.

"We're the spirits of the future!" I call out.

The pirates flinch at the sudden yell. Viznir looks at me in surprise. "What are you doing?" he whispers.

"Improvising." I drop my pack and slide sideways past a couple of trees. The heads and weapons of the pirates turn to follow the sound. "Listen and take heed!" I shout at them. "Strange spirits haunt these woods tonight."

The other pirates from around the fire have all risen and drawn their various weapons. I slip as quietly as I can onto a sandy path that heads out to the beach. I step over a piece of driftwood in the path but then have an idea and pick it up. I note the time on my bracelet. *Wouldn't hurt to have an escape plan.*

I pause behind a tree and flick my flashlight once in the direction of the pirates. A couple of them turn and point my way.

"Over there!"

I rush through the darkness and stop just before I lose all cover and take a breath. Then I step as dramatically as possible onto the beach. No one shoots at me immediately and my panic eases slightly. A few of the men still glance at the woods, but most now have their attention fixed on me.

"Who are you?" The biggest of the men steps forward to challenge me.

"I'm the ghost of the future," I shoot back. "Here to change your miserable fates."

"You look more of man than spirit," the one with the pistols says.

I toss my piece of driftwood onto the sand in front of me and step onto it to have more solid footing. I dial my chronometer for a two second forward jump as I speak. "You see me as your minds believe, but mortal minds are weak." I press the pin and blink. When I reappear, their faces are comically distraught.

"He come outta thin air!" A man is pointing his stump of a forearm at me while holding his cutlass with his left.

The man with the pistols scowls. "Just a trick o' the light." But he's lost his skeptical expression and now looks authentically worried.

"I may look of man, but this is merely the image you see. We spirits take the form of man at will." I gesture toward the tree line. "The woods be full of the lights of spirits tonight. So take care!" Nothing happens, so I try speaking a little louder. "LIGHTS OF THE SPIRITS SHOW THEY'RE LISTENING." This time Viznir and the Ivans catch on and their flashlights blink in the woods. It has the desired effect and the pirates nearest the woods back away a few steps. I watch the lights blinking in the woods and realize there are four of them. *We must've had another arrival.*

"Your wretched lives are forfeit this night, but we spirits are willing to strike you a bargain."

The pirates begin muttering among themselves. The red-bearded one finally answers. "What kind of bargain?"

"We will spare your depraved lives and keep the boatman from carrying your souls to the underworld, but you must agree to ferry our mortal forms off this island. The spirits here wish to journey to the island on yonder horizon." I point to the darkness where the horizon ought to be.

There is more muttering. I catch one who must be hard of hearing whispering too loudly. "They want the island with our reward. I told you that island had a curse!"

The big man with the burning branch finally steps forward. "Our Captain took a scouting party to the south point. We have orders to hold this beach till he returns."

I frown at this news. "Your loyalty is admirable, but you can return for your captain once you've seen us to the other side. You'll be of no use to him dead, so either prepare to make the journey for us, or prepare to cross to the afterlife. I will join the other spirits as you decide." I dial my chronometer and straighten up dramatically as I press the pin.

I reappear on the piece of driftwood back on the path just a minute prior to having picked it up. I step off gently and pick my way over a dune and behind a tree to wait, staying concealed in the darkness. The earlier me emerges from the woods on the other side. He steps over the driftwood, then changes his mind and reaches for it. I wait till he has taken the path out onto the beach before leaving my hiding place. I try to be as quiet as I can and retrace my steps through the woods to where Viznir and the Ivans are hiding. I sneak up behind them, looking to see who our other arrival might be, and frown when I don't see anyone. Through a break in the trees I can see my earlier self out on the driftwood addressing the pirates. They gasp as I disappear.

I whisper from behind Viznir. "Who else is here?"

Vilznir jumps and holds his hand to his chest. The Ivans are likewise startled by my sudden appearance. They do a double take of the version of me out on the beach. The other me is staring toward us in frustration.

"LIGHTS OF THE SPIRITS SHOW THEY'RE LISTENING!"

The situation finally dawns on me. "Guys, flashlights!" I pull my flashlight from my pocket and start blinking it. The others scramble to do the same with theirs. The other me on the beach looks satisfied and returns to addressing the pirates.

"What are you doing?" Viznir whispers.

"In a minute, I'm going to vanish again. The pirates should be pretty convinced after seeing me do it twice. They should agree to help us. We all come out of the woods and make a show of meaning business."

One of the Ivans smiles. "I like this."

I pick up my pack and watch for the other me to disappear. It's fun being able to watch the response of the pirates as it happens. A few of them actually stagger backward in fear. I have to force myself not to laugh. We wait a few minutes for them to mutter and converse before doing anything. The pirate with the pistols walks cautiously over to the piece of driftwood where I disappeared and pokes it with his foot.

"I don't like running afoul of no spirits," the loud one says.

"We would be running afoul of the captain's orders," the big man replies. "But the spirit said it true. We ain't no good to him dead."

"How do we know we can trust that spirit to not murder us all anyway?" A skinny pirate with a braid speaks up for the first time.

I switch my flashlight on and off a couple times. One of the pirates sees it.

"Shhh! The spirits be listening. Don't be speaking ill of them."

I smile at this and turn to Ivan. "You ready to be mysterious?"

Ivan gives me a smirk. "We can be mysterious." He turns and nods to his other self. The other Ivan smiles back.

I step through the foliage followed closely by Viznir. As we emerge onto the beach, the pirates back away cautiously.

We stare at each other in silence before one of the pirates finally speaks. "Is it only the two of you, m'lord?"

I stare at him with as stern an expression as I can manage, not wanting to have to turn and look behind me. *Why hasn't Ivan come with us?*

"More will come," I say. "Our numbers should not concern you."

The pirate with the braid looks at his companions quickly before deciding to speak. "Pardon m'lord, but we only ask as to see that we have enough space in the crew boat."

I glance toward the waterline where the wooden boat has been beached. It's invisible in the darkness, but I recall its general size from before we lost the light. "There will be room enough."

One of the Ivans steps through the trees. He's carrying a walking stick he's made from a branch. He flanks Viznir and me and holds the walking stick at a slight angle to his far side. He glares dramatically around at the pirates, as if daring them to speak to him. With his rough beard and stern expression he looks intimidating even to me. He stretches his free hand toward the sky as if to summon down lightning from the heavens. At that moment, the other Ivan appears at the other end of the walking stick. He drops a couple inches to the sand amid the startled cries of the pirates. The newly arrived Ivan scowls menacingly at the group.

If there had been any doubt left in the pirates' minds about the supernatural nature of our business, Ivan's arrival has smothered it. The pirates scramble to get out of the way as we stride forward, herding them toward the crew boat. One of the pirates goes so far as to walk backward the entire way so that he can keep up his obsequious bowing. I pick up my piece of driftwood and toss it into the bow of the boat in case I need it again. A few of the pirates push the boat into the shallows and wait as we climb aboard. Once they have the boat turned around, the rest of them pile into the stern, as far from us as possible. I watch them clambering over the side, but then the last man, the skinny one with the braid, turns at the last moment and sprints out of the water and onto the beach. The other pirates freeze and look at me to see what I will do. I keep my face impassive as the man vanishes into the trees.

"Row like your lives depend on it. Because make no mistake, they do. Failing at your duty will not bode well for your souls."

The men set the oars and begin rowing. It only takes a few minutes to reach the side of the ship. A silhouette of a man appears against the night sky and drops a ladder over the gunwale.

"Is the captain with you?" the voice from the darkness above inquires.

The man with the pistols eyes me cautiously, then calls up. "The captain's ashore, but we have orders."

One of the Ivans grabs the ladder and scales it rapidly. I hear a surprised exclamation when he reaches the top, but after a moment he calls back down. "Clear up here." The other Ivan has his pistol out but gestures for me to take the ladder next. I toss my piece of driftwood to one of the pirates to carry for me. "Don't lose that." The man holds the piece of wood gingerly, as if expecting it to spontaneously combust at any moment.

I pause with my hand on the rope ladder, then screw up my courage. Once I start up the ladder, I shut my eyes and climb until I feel like I must be close to the top. Ivan helps me over the gunwale.

The ship is rocking gently but I quickly adjust to the footing and look around. The ship isn't large by modern standards, but it's impressive nonetheless. The wood deck is divided into three levels. Two of the masts are amidships, but the third and smallest protrudes through the rear deck. The crewmember that tossed the ladder down is likely only in his thirties but is bald on top with frantic tufts of hair sticking out from behind his ears. He's fidgeting with a bit of wood he's been whittling. The other pirates climb over the gunwale, followed by the other Ivan. One of the pirates secures the dingy to the ship, then lets the tide pull it away to the end of its tether. The man who brought up my driftwood lays it at my feet and backs away.

I turn to the man with the pistols who seems to have some amount of authority. "How many other men aboard?"

"Just this one, sir. Kessler was left aboard to mind the ship."

"Very well. Heave the anchor and get us some sail. I want to be moving."

"Aye, sir, but it will take all the lads getting to the rigging. We're short handed and Edgars has naught but one hand."

"Then get to it. I won't take excuses." I keep my voice firm but realize he's right. *This won't be quick.*

I turn to the nearest Ivan. "You gentlemen have any sailing know-how?"

Ivan shakes his head.

"Okay. Then you two just concentrate on keeping the fear of God in them. We'll make do the best we can."

Ivan nods and speaks quickly to the other him in his own language. The two split up and take positions on the fore and aft decks like menacing bookends, facing each other and giving all the pirates ominous glares. Viznir is carrying my pack as well as his own and is looking less than amused by the whole situation. I invite him toward the back of the ship. "Let's find the captain's quarters and see if we can find our objective. We can see what else we can learn about this ship."

Viznir follows me through the doorway that leads aft. Two sets of steps run below from either side of a small hallway that leads to an ornate door for the captain's cabin. I try the handle, but it's locked.

"Dang it. I was hoping we'd at least get a few more charts of the area to see what we're dealing with out there. It's going to be tough to know where we're going in the dark." I shoulder the door but it doesn't budge. "Maybe we can find another way in."

Viznir hands me my pack. "Here. You may want your gun in case this plan of yours turns out to be as dangerous as it seems."

I sling the pack over my shoulder and walk back out to the weather deck. I climb the aft stairs to the poop deck, and stand next to Ivan as he surveys the men in the rigging. He has his most intimidating expression on his face but he whispers out the side of his mouth, "I don't know how to tell if they do it right."

I smile and pat him on the shoulder as I look at the men untying things above us. "Me either. But we'll know soon enough." I walk to the back of the ship and lean over the rail to see if there is another way into the captain's cabin. The bits of the windows I can see are closed and hard to access. I frown and look out at the beach. I let my pack slide to the deck. A three-quarter moon is rising over the island. I'm staring at the darkness of the trees where the skinny pirate had disappeared when I see movement. To my surprise, I recognize the shape of the man emerging from the tree line. The imposing dimensions and slightly bow-legged swagger are both distinctly Cliff. Jettison follows him. A moment later, I spy the dog. *Friends.*

I rummage in my pack and pull out my binoculars. Training them on the figures on the beach, I realize Cliff is doing the same thing looking my direction. I wave. He doesn't seem to see me so I blink my flashlight a few times. A flash blinks back, but it comes from behind him. I move my binoculars to focus on the man with the flashlight. I finally get him into focus and he's giving me a thumbs up. "What the hell?"

Viznir steps up next to me and squints toward the beach. "What do you see? Who's over there?"

I frown and toss my binoculars back into my pack. "It's me. Again."

Viznir peers harder at the shore. "How'd you get back over there? And why?"

I pick up my pack and walk back to the steps. "I guess that's what I have to figure out."

Stupid time travel.

"Think four-dimensionally. Double-check your math. If you fail at either of these, your experience as a time traveler is going to be brief. And for heaven's sake, if you do make it unscathed, be nice. Time travelers have a shaky reputation at best. Let's try not to make it worse."–Journal of Dr. Harold Quickly, 1941

Chapter 16

A mess of scribbles clutters the back few pages of Dr. Quickly's journal. I add a few more as I jot down all the times I have to calculate.

"Hey,Viznir, do you know how long we've been in this level?"

Viznir consults his tablet and shows me the digital readout the tablet has been keeping. "Your bracelet should say it, too."

"Really?" I press the button next to the display on my bracelet and sure enough, it cycles through a couple other modes, including a time-in-level clock. "Cool. Thanks."

"They did teach us a few useful things in guide school."

"Okay. So I need a way to get those guys onto the ship, and just rowing back over there and picking them up is clearly not an option."

"Why not?" Viznir asks.

"Because then there would be two of me." I frown at my scribbles and try to process through the puzzle. I'm reminded of word problems from math class. *Six time travelers need to cross a body of water. Two of them can't be in the same place at the same time . . .* I look around the ship. If I'm going to transport a bunch of people, I'll need a place that won't be disturbed. An idea strikes me and I take the journal and pick up my piece of driftwood. I then turn the corner toward the captain's cabin to stare at the locked door. Viznir has followed me. "What are you doing? We already tried that."

I get on my hands and knees and press my face to the deck, peering through the gap under the door. "I need something flat to use as an anchor." I pop back up and look around the alcove outside the door.

"Would this work?" Viznir tosses me a rag from a peg.

"No. It needs to be rigid. Something that will keep its shape when I slide it under the door." I scour the alcoves near the stairs to the lower decks. I spot a portable candleholder that has a flat wooden base. The receptacle for the candle is crusted with wax that crumbles away as I twist at it. Holding the flat plate portion steady and, with a little effort, the candle receptacle snaps off. I'm left with a round wooden plate about six inches in diameter. I brush the remaining fragments of wax from it and drop back to the floor. I test it to make sure that it will slide under the door, then set it down a few feet away in the open part of the hallway.

I straighten up and gesture for Viznir to follow me down the stairs. The lower deck is dark and smells of brine and unwashed sailors. I flick on my flashlight and look around. The structure of the ship has been reinforced with a variety of mismatched wood. It makes me wonder how much cannon fire it has withstood in its day.

Viznir clicks his flashlight on also and scans it around the narrow space leading to the main deck. His beam rests momentarily on the butt end of a cannon before he speaks. "So what are we doing now?"

I check my bracelet. "Nothing. We're just making a window of opportunity." I let the timer tick off another thirty seconds and scribble the time into my journal entry, then slap the book shut. "Okay. Let's go back up."

The wooden disk is as I left it. I lie back down on the deck and peer under the door. A rug lies approximately six feet away on the other side, but the area just inside the door seems clear. "Hey, give me your mirror." Viznir passes it to me and I angle it under the door to look for any more potential hazards. I take my best guess at the force needed to have the wooden plate land shy of the rug, then shove it under. It clatters and wobbles as it slides over the deck, but stays upright and skids to a stop midway between the door and the rug. I try to gauge how much space it has around it and then stand back up.

Viznir is frowning at the door. "How are you going to use it now if it's in there?"

"I'm going to use my window of opportunity." I flip my journal open and dial the time into my chronometer. "If this works, I should open this door for you in a just a minute. Stay right here." I stuff the journal into my back pocket and place my chronometer hand against the door. "I'll be right back." I push the pin and Viznir vanishes. I look down and the wooden plate is back where I left it in the middle of the hallway. I squat next to it and flip the switch on my chronometer from back to forward. Gently resting my fingertips to the plate's lip, I press the pin again and blink forward.

The captain's cabin is dimly lit with moonlight shining through the aft windows. I straighten up, flick on my flashlight and browse around. The captain has outfitted the room nicely with rugs and ornamentation. Sabers and muskets are mounted to the walls alongside rigid taper holders and a few framed nautical charts. I spot the pistol I have for an objective mounted to the wall. Loose charts are strewn on an open table in the center of the room, weighed down by what appear to be pieces of a fractured cannonball. I survey the space and smile. "This'll work." I walk to the door and find a key still in the lock. The cabin door swings open on well-oiled hinges. I bow deeply as I gesture for Viznir to enter. "Entrez, monsieur."

Viznir lets a faint smile curl his lips and enters the cabin to look around. I step past him to collect my piece of driftwood. Next I yank the rug from the floor and bundle it into a corner. I set the driftwood in the center of the open space and take a few measurements, jotting the notes on a fresh page in the journal.

"All right, if you can keep this room clear, I'll go get the others and bring them back. I'm not sure how long it will take me, but I'll aim to bring them here in a few minutes." I take a couple more last minute measurements and wedge a few of the broken cannonball pieces from the table around my driftwood. "Whatever you do, just don't let anybody move this thing." I jiggle myself around on top of the driftwood, making sure it stays in place, then set my chronometer. "It shouldn't move on its own with these light waves, but I hope we'll be back before we really get underway. If these guys are ready to go before I'm back, let 'em get moving."

"You know you could just leave them there," Viznir says. "This is a race after all. You're eventually going to have to stop helping your competition."

"Eventually. But I already did this, remember? I'm over there, so I can't very well back down now." I recite the young Mym's quote from Harry. "Creating temporal paradoxes is universally irresponsible." I grin at Viznir and push the pin.

I'm back on the sandy path that exits the woods. I've given myself a few minutes of space from when the other versions of me will first make use of the driftwood. I move south into the woods, past the spot where the second me will hide, and continue onward through the brush, headed in the general direction of the time gate. I use my map and compass to keep my bearings, but I'm cautious to steer well clear of the route Viznir and I took along the beach. Instead I make my way over the more difficult path inland, but close enough to the beach to keep an eye out for Cliff and Jettison.

I'm struggling through a particularly stubborn patch of vines when I hear a dog bark. I finally free myself from the mess of creepers as Barley comes bounding to me through the darkness. He jumps up and licks me before turning and racing back the way he came. Cliff, Jettison, and

Jonah emerge from the trees fifty yards ahead of me, followed closely by Genesis and Mayra. They all look ragged.

"Hey, guys." I brush the leaves off my jeans and stride over to meet them. When I get closer, I spot a cut above Cliff's eye and a gash in his forearm. "Whoa. What happened?"

Jettison has a rip in the jacket of his tracksuit and his hair is a mess. He runs a hand through it before responding. "France was hell. We made it into the keep, but the fighting was bad. We barely made it out of there once the French attack started."

"Is everybody okay?" I look to Mayra and Genesis. Neither appears hurt, but they both look exhausted.

"We are," Jettison says. "But not everybody was as lucky. The French got one of the teams that was trailing us."

"Oh God. Who?"

"Sam Tulley and his son Trent. You know them?"

I think back on all the faces from the dinner and the start of the race. "No, I don't think so. What happened?"

"Bloody mess is what it was," Cliff says. "French ran the son through with a pike and Tulley went berserk on them. Started shooting men right and left till they peppered him with their crossbows. It was a nightmare. We dragged the kid outta there, but he didn't make it to the gate. He died in the woods on the way."

I stare at their faces, unsure of what to say.

"It was tragic. And obviously, situation being what it was, that slowed us down plenty," Jettison says. "And this level hasn't been much easier. We went south from the gate because the map noted a fishing village that way, but by the time we got there it was too late. The teams ahead of us had taken all the boats, or trashed them. We found a couple that had been burned and sunk. The villagers described the arsonists as young and wearing matching shirts. We're guessing it was the academy teams. We found Jonah here on the way back north. He said he went east but there's nothing over there except cliffs."

"And rabbits," Jonah adds.

"How have you gotten on?" Cliff asks. He peers past me. "You lose your guide?"

"No. He's okay. We found a ship on the north end of the island. It's manned by pirates but we got some of the crew to let us aboard."

Genesis looks surprised. "How'd you manage that?"

"We conned them into thinking we were otherworldly spirits intent on their souls. Worked okay so far. I've got a way to get you guys on board, too, but we need to get a move on. The captain and the rest of the crew are around somewhere. I'd like to get the ship under way before they find us."

I do my best to explain the circumstances as I lead the way back to the beach. Genesis agrees to cover her bandaged neck with a scarf so as not to tarnish our already shaky reputation as invincible spirits. We take care to arrive after my previous departure and exit the tree line around the time I suspect the earlier me will be ascending to the ship's aft deck. Cliff pulls out his binoculars and scans the ship without even needing a prompt from me, and I wait for my cue. The light flashes from the deck and I flash mine back before holding my thumb up. I can't help but smile, knowing that the other me is staring back in confusion. *Now to solve the rest of this problem.*

"What now, Travers?" Cliff lowers his binoculars and looks to me.

"Now we have to make a jump back in time to find my anchor." I lead the way around to the sandy path and find the spot my piece of driftwood once occupied. "We need to go far enough back to find the anchor, then we'll use it to jump forward again to when it's onboard the ship. Piece of cake."

Jettison nods his approval and starts tapping his Temprovibe. "How far back are we going?"

I consult my journal entries. "An hour ought to be plenty. We'll still be a good fifteen minutes ahead of when I first find it."

The others dial in their respective time devices and I set my chronometer. We use local anchors like tree branches and rocks that won't have changed position in the last hour, and blink. We arrive within a few seconds of each other and reconvene on the path. To my surprise, the driftwood isn't there. "What the hell?" I consult my journal entries. *The math is right. What happened?*

Cliff fidgets with his gun. "You sure this is the spot?"

"Yeah, definitely. I used it twice, right here." I point to the spot in the sand where the log ought to be.

"What does it look like?" Mayra asks.

"I don't know, kind of wide and flat on top. It's maybe this big . . ." I hold out my hands.

"Like that?" Genesis points into the weeds.

Sure enough, my driftwood is a couple yards off the path, partially buried in the grass. I pick it up and examine it, brushing a spider from the bark. "Yep. This is it." I walk it over to the path and it finally dawns on me. *No wonder it was right where I would see it. I'm the one who put it there.* I plop the driftwood onto the sand. *Time travel.*

Jettison lifts the dog for Jonah and still manages to get a hand on my shoulder. The others gather around and grab various parts of me, making sure to keep their feet elevated higher than the bottom of the anchor. No one wants to end up embedded in the deck of the ship. I dial in my settings, and once everyone is set, push the pin.

Viznir actually gasps when the seven of us appear in the cabin. The pirates are even more astonished when I lead the group onto the weather deck. The man with the pistols approaches me and eyes the new arrivals cautiously.

"Sir, we're ready to make way."

"Excellent. What's your name, sailor?"

"Pims, sir."

"Get us out of this cove and head northwest."

"Aye sir."

After a minute, I hear the splash of oars as the handful of sailors work to get the ship turned into the wind. I man the wheel to keep the rudder in position for the turn. The wind is light till we're clear of the rocky outcropping to our left, but once we hit open water, the sails billow out to full and the men stow the oars. Pims shouts orders to the others as the ship gains speed. The moonlight illuminates the view enough that I can just make out the dark mass of our target island on the horizon. Cliff and Jettison wander the deck and consult with the other Ivan on the bow.

I'm enjoying the sea breeze and the sight of the stars and have just begun to relax when a boom and a flash of light jerks my attention to starboard.

"What was that?" Genesis asks.

There's a whistling above us, followed by a splash to our port side. Three more booms and flashes follow from the right.

"That's cannons!" Jonah exclaims. He points to the darkness to our right. I can't tell if he's scared or excited.

I instinctively begin steering to port to put distance between us and the new threat. Viznir fumbles for his binoculars and peers off the starboard side. Another cannonball sails overhead, but the accompanying splash is significantly closer.

"Pims!"

The sailor dashes up the poop deck stairs. "Yes, sir!"

"Who's shooting at us?"

"The Spanish, sir. They've been hunting us for a week now."

"Bloody hell. Why?"

"They've been waiting to ambush us for raiding a shipwreck. One o' their frigates ran aground and most of the crew died of disease. Mutiny done for the rest, but not before they got the cargo ashore and stashed it away. One of our crew was with 'em and survived. We come back for the cargo but the Spanish caught wind of us off Cook's Cay. We've been dodging them ever since."

"Why haven't they just gone after the wreck themselves?"

"It's sunk. And most of these islands look the same. They've been waiting for us to show our hand."

And now I just forced it.

"All right. Do you know what their ship is like?"

"Aye, sir. Thirty-two guns if it's one. Long guns, and carronades on the weather deck. They peppered us off Andros a week ago before we lost them in the shallows between the islands."

"They must have a deeper draft with all those guns. How many have we got?"

"Just twelve sir."

"Fair enough. We'll outrun them. Man the longest guns you have and move whatever artillery possible to starboard. If you get a shot, feel free to fire while we're in range, just to give them something to think about. We might get lucky and hit their rigging, but we're gonna do our best to not be in range for long."

"Aye, sir."

As Pims dashes off, Cliff and Jettison climb back to the poop deck, followed closely by the Ivans.

"What's your plan, Travers?" Cliff barks. "Got us into a bit of a mess it seems."

"We need to outrun that ship. I think we can beat them to our island."

"And then what?"

"We get off this ship and run like hell for the time gate."

"Gen and I still have objectives to find. They're on the island," Jettison says.

"Me too," Jonah pipes in.

I keep a firm grip on the wheel as we plow across the channel. "The way I see it, we can run this thing aground on the island and run for it, or we can hope to draw this other ship out far enough that we lose it in the open ocean, then find a way to sneak back. These sailors are screwed in option one, because the Spanish will definitely take the ship. I hate to do that to them, but the alternative is running around out in the ocean for God knows how long and hoping we'll get a chance to return."

"There's another option," Jettison says. "We can pull a Wittgenstein maneuver."

"What's that?"

"It's basically just the reverse of how you got us aboard. If we can get close enough to the island for one of us to swim ashore without running aground, we can jump back and take the rest of the group off by anchor. It's a whole lot easier to sneak one person ashore than ten."

I consider what he's saying. "I'd have to be one of the ones to go. My objective was here on the ship. There're no gravitites in it, so it won't make the jump."

"Mine either," Ivan says. He holds up a small wooden box of the sort that might hold tobacco or a handful of cigars. He must have found time to search it out below decks.

"Okay," Jettison explains. "So a few of us go overboard as we near the shore, taking the objectives and an anchor for getting back to the ship. We find a good spot for the anchor and bring the others over in a group. The ship can keep sailing and the Spanish never have to be the wiser. You can get to the gate, and the rest of us will be able to find our objectives without getting shot."

I work it through in my head. "Yeah, makes sense. Is that okay with the rest of you guys?"

Genesis and Mayra both nod immediately. Genesis still has her neck bandaged so I can see why she wouldn't want to be diving into the Caribbean, even under less violent circumstances. Jonah and Viznir agree as well. Jettison volunteers to be the one to take Ivan's objective ashore, but one of the Ivans shakes his head. "I'll trust myself with this." He throws an arm around his other self and grins.

I call for Pims and hand off the wheel duties. "Steer us just close enough to the shore that you won't run aground, then take the ship out to sea. From there we'll consider your obligation met."

"Aye, sir. And the other ones?" He looks to where Cliff and Jettison are piling our belongings.

"They'll be gone, too."

The relief on Pims' face is immediately evident. He takes a firm grip on the wheel and I leave him alone on the poop deck. The cannons from the Spanish ship still flash periodically in the darkness, but the balls are splashing farther and farther behind us. The ship can only fire at us with guns mounted to its bow as it gives chase. With all of our lights doused and only moonlight to aim by, they're having a hard time landing anything close. I duck into the captain's cabin and change from my jeans into my athletic shorts and stuff my shoes and other belongings into my pack. The one exception is a bit of rope that I use to secure the captain's prized pistol around my neck. It seems almost a crime to be diving into the saltwater with such an elaborate piece of workmanship, but my qualms are easily quelled by the sound of the cannons booming in the distance. *Ready to be off this ship as soon as possible.*

Jettison and one of the Ivans have stripped down to what they are able to swim in. Ivan has his cigarette box strapped to his waist. He's ditched his other gear and is standing in his boxers and a tank top. While Jettison and I are bare-chested, he still has his pistol latched into its shoulder holster, giving an air of seriousness to his otherwise humorous outfit. The other Ivan slaps him on the ass and winks before joining the others gathered around a wooden batten that Jettison has chosen for an anchor. Viznir looks unhappy about being separated from me, but I notice he's been careful to avoid any suggestion that he should swim too. He quietly joins the others near the main mast and prepares for departure.

Jettison puts a hand to my shoulder and faces us aft so we can't see the circle of our friends. Ivan lines up next to us with his arms crossed and faces the captain's quarters also. They both are clearly familiar with this simple method of avoiding paradoxes. I even do my best not to listen for the arrival of one of us from the future, but the sudden swearing of one of the sailors in the rigging cues me to the fact that someone has likely arrived. I can see Jettison's grin out of the corner of my eye. He is clearly enjoying the theatrics and the reactions of our audience. The gasping and swearing suddenly becomes universal throughout the deck and I finally turn around. Sure enough, the area around the wooden batten has been vacated.

A couple pirates near the bow are gaping open-mouthed and unabashed, but when I catch their stares, they quickly scramble to look busy. Jettison secures the piece of batten with a bit of cord around his neck and follows me up to the poop deck.

"That ought to give them enough tales for the pub for life, eh?" He smiles at me. "It's one of my favorite parts of being a time traveler. Every once in a while you get to totally blow people's minds."

Pims guides the ship between a pair of smaller islands with much more ease than I would have done. He clearly knows the waters and our hull depth well. As we round the western end of our island, he points to a bit of beach. "This is as close as I can come, but it's mild currents between here and the shore."

"Thank you, Pims. You've been a great service." I start to reach my hand toward him, but he flinches, reminding me that I'm still something otherworldly in his mind. I merely nod at him instead. "All right, keep her steady and we'll go over the side."

Jettison and I rejoin Ivan near the starboard gunwale.

"You guys ready for this?

Jettison is smiling. "Absolutely." As soon as we get abeam the beach, he swings his legs over the edge of the gunwale, pushes off the side of the ship, and dives cleanly into the water. Ivan and I both climb onto the gunwale next. I'm about to jump, when I get distracted by a man walking out of the hallway near the captain's cabin. He's dressed like a sailor but I don't remember him being on the beach. He's carrying a cutlass, letting it swing idly beside his right leg, but walking briskly toward us. There is something familiar about his sharp features. I pause to see if he has something to say to us. Ivan, seated on the gunwale with his face toward me, pauses and turns to see what I'm looking at. The man says nothing, but raises his cutlass and drives it directly through Ivan's ribs.

I'm too stunned to speak. Ivan grimaces and lets out a surprised curse. The man thrusts the cutlass forward and Ivan falls, plummeting overboard into the waves. The man merely stares at me with cold gray eyes, the cutlass shiny with blood. My brain finally registers the danger and I dive, crashing face first into the water with my heart pounding. I surface only a few yards away from Ivan's prone form. I swim to him and roll him over, getting an arm under his head and keeping his face clear of the waves. He's unconscious. The moonlight glints on his wet gun. I yank the pistol free from its holster and fire wildly at the gunwale where I last saw the attacker. I sink beneath the waves and have to kick hard to get Ivan and myself back to the surface.

"You son of a bitch!" I fire a couple more shots, but the ship has moved on in the darkness and, even if the man were still there, I can't see him. I hear splashing behind me and then Jettison is there.

"What happened?"

I don't have any words, so Jettison helps me keep Ivan afloat and we work together to pull him toward shore. I abandon the gun to the waves, but let the anger drive my muscles, kicking and reaching farther and harder with each breath. It's at least three hundred meters to shore, and when we finally drag Ivan onto the beach, Jettison and I are both spent and breathing hard. Ivan isn't breathing.

Jettison checks for a pulse, but shakes his head. I start chest compressions while Jettison does mouth to mouth. We work for ten minutes with no result. I finally accept the hopelessness of our situation. We're on a deserted island a thousand miles and three hundred years away from anyone who could save him. I collapse onto my back in the sand.

Jettison rolls Ivan's body onto its side and examines the wound. "How did this happen? Who did this?"

"I don't know who he is. But I've seen him before."

"A pirate?"

"He wasn't a pirate. I recognized his face. I saw him in New York. He was a homeless man."

"A time traveler." Jettison lets Ivan's body rest back in the sand.

"Yes."

Jettison gets to his feet and fingers the wooden batten around his neck. "We have to get the others." He stumbles briefly then steadies himself and walks toward the tree line. "I'll find an open space. Stay with Ivan."

Ivan's eyes are partially open, staring at the stars. I let my head roll back in the sand and stare at them too.

Only a few moments later, I hear voices. They are cheerful and chatty at first, but then I hear Jettison's voice among them. The babble stops and there is only the thudding of footsteps on sand as Ivan runs to his own dead body. His stoic expression cracks and his body shudders. He scoops the fallen corpse into his arms and sobs. I get to my feet and walk toward the trees. I can't take it. Genesis puts her hand out and grazes my arm with her fingertips as I pass by.

I stare at the trees in silence for a few moments, then begin brushing the sand from my hair and body and neck with increasing ferocity. I stop when Cliff lays a hand on my shoulder.

"Travers. What happened?"

"He was murdered." I picture the man's cold expression as he stared at me, the cutlass dripping. "Same as Charlie." The connection isn't made in my mind until the words are out of my mouth, but as soon as I speak them, I recognize them to be true. "Someone is murdering racers."

"Someone is murdering guides," Cliff says.

I look back to the Ivans and see the race bracelet around the wrist of the man cradling his fallen lover. As much as the relationship still seems bizarre in my mind, the pain is raw and primal on Ivan's face. The expression of catastrophic loss is universal.

In the moonlight on that unknown shore, I witness my first time traveler funeral. We gather at the water's edge and Ivan's body is laid in the waves, the most inconstant of anchors. Ivan gently kisses the lips of his lover before activating the timepiece around the other Ivan's wrist. The body vanishes, transported to who-knows-where, gravitites connecting with an unknowable number of water droplets and scattering bits of him to any of a million destinations. It's a harsh but vaguely poetic fate. I stare at the vacant waves and think of Mym.

As the eight of us follow the dog into the woods, my mind still lingers with thoughts of her. *Is she running? Has she been caught by whoever is hunting her? Does she even know she's in danger?* I try not to let the doubts overwhelm me. I console myself with the reality that time is irrelevant now. If ever I get the chance to tell her, I can warn her in time. If ever I get the opportunity to save her from this farce of an accusation, it could already be done. She may already be exonerated. It's just a matter of time. And surviving.

"Chronometers are electric. Sure, they can polarize gravitites and plunge you through a wormhole—but not without juice. Bring the charger."–Journal of Dr. Harold Quickly, 1967

Chapter 17

A subtle silence builds during the walk to the time gate. Ivan, Viznir and I part ways with the others as they go in search of their objectives. I keep up the silence out of respect for Ivan's grief, but when we reach the repository, it's he who breaks it.

"I think I stay for now."

"You're not coming through?" I pause with my hand on the lid of the repository. The committee has seen fit to model it after a decrepit treasure chest.

"I will come." Ivan is staring into the woods with his fingers resting on the cigar box tied to his waistband. "But not yet."

The hint of anger in his eyes makes me wonder if there's a motive of revenge to his lingering.

"Ivan, I don't know that you'll find him. I think he was a time traveler. I don't know who he is, but I'm almost positive I've seen him before."

Ivan's eyes drift back to my face and he blinks as if waking from a daydream. "It is not matter. I think I stay a little longer." He reaches out a hand to shake mine. "I will meet you later, Benjamin."

"Okay. It was good getting to know you. I'm so sorry for your loss."

"Thank you."

I wrestle with the urge to ask the next question, then finally my curiosity gets the best of me. "Ivan, I don't mean any offense by asking, and I'm sorry I'm not more knowledgeable about things like this, but Ivan—the other Ivan I mean—he was you. So . . . couldn't you go back and, I don't know, find yourself again? Will you do that?"

Ivan smiles wanly but shakes his head. "Ivan has been with me since we were boys. He was my friend. We saw world together, but different. He was him. I am me. There can be no other him."

"I guess that makes sense."

"Goodbye, Ben. I will see you again soon." Ivan turns and wanders into the woods, his movements quiet and slow, as though he has no destination. I watch his silhouette disappear between the trees before turning back to the task at hand.

I take time to change back into my jeans and my last clean T-shirt. This one has a picture of Gizmo from *Gremlins* on it, one of my acquisitions from the 1980s. I can't imagine it will be appropriate in any other era, but it will have to do. I straighten the pack on my shoulders and deposit the pistol in the repository. My bracelet blinks the number five.

Not bad.

Viznir leads the way through the shimmering doorway that springs up between a pair of pines. I step from humid Caribbean darkness into lightly overcast sun. I squint from the change of light and scan the world around me. An expansive prairie of withered grasses stretches to dusty and distant rock ridges. Viznir is standing at the edge of a wooden platform. My first few steps bring the rails into view beyond him. The platform belongs to a wooden train station which consists of little more than a ramp for unloading goods and a stark room with a few mismatched benches. A wind chime made of tin cans dangles from the overhang at the extreme end of the platform, patiently awaiting the first hint of a breeze.

"I was hoping we'd get another rendezvous." I frown at the barren landscape. "We finished two levels." I have no idea how many hours our day has been, but the vacant feeling in my stomach reminds me it's been a long time since a meal.

"The rendezvous will get farther apart," Viznir says. "We're not even officially guaranteed to get them. I think it's more of a tradition."

I take a long drink from my canteen to appease my stomach, then walk to the end of the platform and drop the few feet into the weeds. I poke my head around the corner of the ticket office. The room is empty, but a slate has been hung in the window advertising the next train's arrival time. The train station belongs to a ramshackle village that is eerily desolate. As Viznir and I stare down the empty dirt road between the clapboard buildings, I half expect a tumbleweed to roll by.

It takes a few minutes to find our objective boxes. Some diligent searching reveals that they've been hung under the raised train platform. I'm obligated to get on my hands and knees and crawl behind a bit of lattice that's precariously held together by desiccated vines. When I reemerge from the darkness under the platform, I've been adorned with several spider webs. I blow the dust off the top of my objective box and pop it open. My map shows a town called Pucketsville situated near a rail line that terminates at a mining camp in the hills. The mine lies to the north, but my objective is in the valley west of town. There is an illustration of a clown and the description reads "Barnaby McSweeny's Traveling Circus." I spit a bit of cobweb out of my mouth and hand the map to Viznir. He starts to scan it, then pauses. "Oh God. Clowns? I hate clowns."

An old man is seated in a rocking chair on a porch midway down the main street. Other than a pair of stray dogs, he's the only living creature we've seen.

"Excuse me, sir? Can you tell us what happened to everybody?" I pause with a hand on his shabby picket fence.

The man rouses from the edge of sleep and clears his throat. "Oh, you won't find many folk in town today. The ones that aren't working the mines are all out at the fairground. Circus is in town!" His grin is toothless but exuberant. "I'd be there myself, but I've got the gout." He reaches for his cane and thumps the porch with it for emphasis. He squints at the street, and I realize he's mostly blind. "What are you fellows doing in town today? I don't think I've seen you round here before."

"Just passing through, but we may check out the circus."

"Oh, you must do that. Yes, sir. They've got a man who eats fire, and I hear tell they have a woman who does that eastern dancing from the O-ri-ant."

"We'll be sure to check that out."

"You have to see the monster, too."

"Monster?"

"Oh yes! Eight arms and six legs, and half a dozen heads from what I hear. A regular demon of Hell itself. It'll cost you a half dollar to see it, though. They say they found him in the deepest jungles of Australia. Or maybe it was Asia. I can't recall. You check the handbill posted outside the market. You'll see I'm not telling tales."

"Thank you, sir. We'll be sure to do that."

On the way out of town we pass several flyers advertising the circus. All of them promise amazing sights, from exotic animals to tattooed women. One even advertises a werewolf, though the prized citizen of the "Freak Show" is clearly "The Monster." It's advertised as part man, part demon, and the drawing on the posters gives me pause. It indeed shows a multi-headed beast, with too many arms and legs to be believed.

Viznir and I follow the road out of town, but cut across an open field once we get the circus tents in sight. I pause and consider the view. Viznir walks past me a few steps before stopping.

"What is it?"

I weigh my possible answers a moment before responding with the truth. "I dreamed about this place. It wasn't exactly the same, but I dreamed this."

Viznir considers the waving flags and distant bustling crowds. "What happened when we got there?"

I sigh and step past him. "No idea. I didn't get to see that part." I'm walking past what must be the fiftieth shriveled up shrub when a sharp pain in my shin makes me stagger. "What the—"

"Son of a bitch!" Viznir fumbles for his pistol.

The diamond patterned snake retreats from us with impressive haste. I just spot the end of the rattle disappearing between some rocks when Viznir finally gets his pistol aimed.

"Whoa, Viznir, it's fine. Don't waste your bullets. It's not the snake's fault we barged in on its nap."

"But it's a rattlesnake! Did it get you?"

I step onto a reddish boulder and turn the seconds dial on my chronometer. "Yeah, he got me. I'll be right back." I blink past the next three seconds just to be sure, then step off the rock and admire the tiny splatter of poison I've left behind. *Amazing that such a tiny wet spot could kill a man.*

Viznir is still staring nervously at the shrubs around us. I pull up the leg of my jeans and note the pair of holes in my calf muscle. They've just started to bleed. I take off my pack and find my first-aid kit. I look at Viznir's pale face and pause. "It's okay, Viznir. I'll be fine."

He finally holsters his pistol. He watches me clean the wound with an antiseptic wipe and his shoulders droop a little. "I would have died. I wouldn't even have thought of that. I swear they never taught me the useful stuff. This makes sense." He gestures vaguely to my leg.

I Band-Aid my bite wounds and stand. "Viznir, I hope you don't mind me saying this, but it doesn't seem like time travel is really your thing. How did you even end up doing this?"

Viznir shuffles his feet. "I needed the money." He kicks a rock out of his way and starts walking again. I readjust my pant leg, and as I do, I notice a faint red glow around the bezel of my chronometer. *The low power annunciator. Jumping seven people onto that ship must have really drained the power supply.* I stand and fiddle with the dials. I'm stuck till I can charge it again. I trot to catch up with Viznir.

"Hey, man. Did you happen to bring any external power?"

Viznir stops and looks in his pack. "Yeah. I have a backup battery for the Temprovibe." He holds up a black box.

"Does it have an outlet to plug into?" I grab my charger out of a side pocket and hold out the two-pronged end. "Like a wall outlet?"

"Oh. No. This charges wirelessly." He touches the Temprovibe with his fingers. "Thanks for reminding me, though. I should probably check it." He taps a few things and a green light on the box lights up.

"Damn it. Well it looks like you'll have to do the next few jumps for us. My chronometer's drained till I can find some power." I frown and wad my charger into my front pants pocket.

Viznir puts his power supply back into his pack and keeps walking. I pick up on his new habit and we kick whatever loose stones we find ahead of us in an attempt to warn any more fanged reptiles of our approach.

Despite the barren landscape and the horrid end to our Caribbean adventure, I feel a little more optimistic about this level of the race. I don't know exactly what state or year I'm in, but it's clearly the United States. The red rock buttes in the distance could easily be in Utah or Arizona. *Almost home.* Florida and the twenty-first century are both a long way away, but I'm a little closer. Maybe even close enough to get a message to Mym. She told me once that Dr. Quickly had taken her to witness the Gettysburg Address as a child, so the 1800s are definitely in range of her abilities.

"Hey, Viznir, what timestream are we in?"

Viznir consults his Temprovibe. "Kilo Oscar Seven."

"Does the Kilo ever connect with the Lima stream?"

Viznir switches to his tablet and consults a timestream chart. "Yeah, it does, but not until 1903 at the earliest. Why?"

"I need to get a message to somebody."

"Communications with non-competitor time travelers while on the racecourse is grounds for disqualification. Didn't you read the rulebook?"

"I skimmed it." I frown at this news. "What if I'm not contacting a time traveler?"

"Why would you need to do that?"

"What if I just need to say something to somebody. Is it against the rules?"

Viznir works his tablet again and his eyes scan through the text of his digital rulebook. "It doesn't specify anything about contacting non-time-travelers." He flips through a few more pages. "I'd be careful though. The committee might read what you write and find it suspicious."

I try to puzzle my way around this new obstacle as we walk.

The "fairground" is little more than a dried lakebed, but the circus that has taken up residence there is lively and colorful. It has absorbed the population of the town and then some. The pathways between circus tents are jammed with curious patrons, farmers and townsfolk alike, listening to the various circus barkers shouting enticements from their platforms. The first crowd we reach is huddled around a man advertising the seven wonders of the sea brought to land. The painting on a banner behind him depicts a voluptuous mermaid, her breasts scantily covered by the tentacles of an octopus in her arms. There are eels and even a shark depicted, but it's clear what the main attraction will be.

Someone taps me on the shoulder and I turn to find a mustached man in a black hat giving me a stern glare. He has a silver star pinned to his vest and a hand resting on a gun at his hip. He points toward Viznir's holster. "You gentlemen will have to check your guns at the entrance." He doesn't wait for a response but merely leads us toward a small tent near the start of the midway. I trail slightly behind and scoop up an eligible pocket-sized stone. The tent we're brought to is guarded by another armed man perhaps a decade younger than the sheriff. He is sporting a badge as well. The sheriff throws the flap open and gestures me inside.

"Put your guns with the others. You can claim them when you leave."

I unpack my gunbelt and hang it on the corner of a wooden gun rack. Two rifles are in attendance. I drop my pack next to the rack and casually toss my stone to the open space next to them. When we exit the tent I make a show of chatting up the sheriff and the deputy about their favorite attractions. The deputy has clearly been bored and jumps at the opportunity to have a conversation. A couple minutes into his description of the werewolf, I excuse myself, leaving Viznir to listen to their banter. "Just forgot one thing in my pack. Be right back." I check my timer and duck into the tent to snag my stone. I smile at the absence of our packs and guns. I wipe the grin off my face before rejoining the conversation outside. We make our goodbyes and I idly take the stone from my pocket and show it to Viznir as we walk away.

"Did it work?" Viznir asks when we get out of earshot of the lawmen.

"Yep. Our stuff is safely in the future." I consult my map again. Our objective is shown as a jar of liquid. I hold the drawing closer to my face and recognize the shapes in the jar as eyeballs. *That's disgusting. Those better not be human.* I pocket the map again and look around for a tent that might be a likely candidate.

We pass a popcorn vendor and I'm immediately distracted. I pause and stare at the cart where the man is handing out paper bags of the heavenly-smelling snack, then turn to Viznir. "You think they'd take American money from the future? I'm in the right country at least."

"Good luck. I doubt money here even vaguely resembles what you've got."

"I really need something to eat. Racing on an empty stomach is making me grouchy."

"Then you should have planned better."

I look around and consider my options. A kid of perhaps ten is standing outside a magician's tent listening to the barker describe the magical feats the audience will witness inside. A girl a couple years younger is at the boy's elbow. The paintings on the banner shows the standard woman sawn in half and a manacled man in a box filling with water. The kid watching the barker is holding a pickle in one hand and nibbling from an ear of corn in the other. Periodically he lets his sister have a bite of one or the other. I watch him chew off another section of corn, then take a position next to him, pretending to be interested in the show.

"I bet this guy doesn't know a thing about *real* magic."

The boy chews a chunk of the pickle and glances sideways at me. The little girl pokes her head around her brother and stares at me unabashedly. One of the blue ribbons in her hair has come untied, but she hasn't noticed.

"How much are they charging for this nonsense?" I ask.

"You gotta have twenty cents to get in." The boy looks disappointed.

"You can probably buy a lot of food for twenty cents. How much did that pickle cost?"

"A penny."

"Yeah, see? This guy is a rip-off. I've seen magic ten times better than what he does."

"What's a rip-off?" the little girl asks.

"Something you shouldn't have to pay for," I say. "What if I told you kids that I could show you some real magic, honest to goodness magic, and it wouldn't cost you a thing?"

The boy looks at me suspiciously. "There's no free magic. All the shows cost money."

"Well, they cost money for some people. But it wouldn't have to cost money for you. In fact, I bet you could make money. You interested?"

"What would we have to do?"

Viznir is eying me suspiciously, too. "Yeah, Ben. What do they have to do?"

I wave him off. "Calm down. Just a little advertising. Come on kids. I'm gonna show you something amazing." I walk between the two tents to an empty area out back. The kids and Viznir follow cautiously. Viznir looks as uncomfortable as I've ever seen him.

When we get clear of people's view I stoop to the kids' level. "You see this guy right here? I'm gonna make him disappear."

Viznir stares at me. "You're what?"

"You're going to disappear, Viznir. A couple seconds ought to do it." I jerk my head toward his Temprovibe, then point to the nearest tent stake. "I am going to use this magical tent stake right here and make you vanish.

You kids ready?"

Viznir frowns but sets his Temprovibe and squats to place his fingertips on the metal tent stake.

I wave my hands in the air and then wiggle my fingers at Viznir. "Abracadabra, zippity pow!" I thrust my hands toward Viznir and he vanishes. The little girl gasps. The boy immediately tosses his corncob at the spot where Viznir was just squatting.

"Whoa! Don't do that!" I step between the boy and the tent stake. "You'll hurt somebody."

Viznir reappears and the little girl gasps again. The boy's mouth drops open too.

"Do it again!" the little girl shrieks.

I shake my head. "Nope. That was the free one. If you want to see it again we need to get a bigger audience. You two go round up a few of your friends and tell them what you saw, but let them know it will be ten cents to see the show. If you get us a good audience we'll give you half the profits."

"Half?" the boy says. "Honest?"

"Honest. See what you can do. Just don't take too long." I point to a solitary pine. "Bring whoever you can find over to that tree in ten minutes."

The boy grins and rushes off, towing his sister along behind.

Viznir shakes his head.

"What?"

"You'd make a good drug dealer."

"Whatever." I frown. "I can't help it if drug dealers use a practical system of doing business that also happens to work for scoring lunch money."

I walk to the tree and wait. A few minutes later our audience starts to arrive. Most are young kids or teenagers, but more than a few adults wander over too. I'm given a good deal of suspicious looks and a lot of attention is given to my Gizmo T-shirt, but I simply smile and try to look welcoming. When our recruiters return, I gesture for the boy to join me. "What's your name, kid?"

"Noah."

"I'm Hanna," the little girl chimes in.

"Those are good names. Okay, Noah, you and your sister are going to collect our fees." I straighten up. "Ladies and gentlemen, boys and girls, you are about to witness the most astounding magic that has ever been performed. Real magic needs no fancy tents or mirrors. It requires only that you believe. For a mere ten cents, you are about to witness the complete and utter disappearance of a human being. If you would like to gather in a circle around this tree, you will be able to see this amazing feat from any angle you choose."

The audience complies, but based on the expressions of some of the adults, it may be so I don't have a route to run off with their dimes before they get their money's worth.

Viznir rolls his eyes but takes a position near the tree. I add a lot more theatrics and hand gestures to this performance while Noah and Hanna gather the money. When Noah finally brings the hatful of change to me, I make Viznir disappear again. Kids and adults react with equal surprise. When Viznir reappears he's met with enthusiastic applause. The cheering immediately improves his disposition. He even takes a bow and shakes people's hands before the crowd disperses.

I start to divide the spoils into two parts until the little girl pipes up. "Which one is mine?"

"I was assuming your brother was going to share . . ." I take one look at the girl's dubious expression and count out a new pile. I've just gotten them even when Viznir clears his throat from behind me. I look up at his expectant face. "Oh come on. You too?" I rearrange the change into a fourth pile.

The kids are elated with our success and tag along with us as we reenter the midway. The duo takes turns tugging at our hands and pointing out the best items to eat. Before long I've got an armful of carnival food and a pair of inseparable shadows. I remove my map from my pocket and show the drawing of the jar of eyeballs to Noah. "Have you or any of your friends seen this anywhere?"

Noah stops gnawing on his candied apple and puts his hand to the map. It leaves a caramel thumbprint when he pulls it away. "That's the House of Horrors. That's where the monster is."

I wad the map up again. "Okay. Let's go see this thing."

The barker has finished his most recent spiel and is guiding his latest acquisitions through the entrance of the House of Horrors. This attraction is not merely a tent. It has an actual wood façade that's been painted to look like a creepy Victorian house. Depictions of ghoulish creatures leer from shadows and from behind window curtains. The upper story shows the multi-headed monster silhouetted against the drapes.

The fifty-cent fee stumps me momentarily, as my munching spree has left me slightly short, but Hanna and Noah generously spot me the difference since they get in half price. Viznir and I file inside after paying our half dollars, mostly in nickels. The ticket vendor doesn't look nearly as annoyed at this as I suspect someone from my century would. We take seats on wooden benches before a stage. The show begins with a curator who tells us of his daring exploits into the far reaches of dark and mysterious places. He promises amazing sights and wonders and then begins presenting us with specimens. Most of the supposed wonders, like dragons teeth and unicorn horns are obvious fakes, but a few of the items are authentically interesting. One of the supposed dragon skulls appears to be a fossilized carnivorous dinosaur of some kind. I pause my popcorn consumption and lean forward on the bench to see a little closer. He next presents a stack of cabinets on wheels and opens each cupboard in turn to display its exciting contents. The third one reveals my jar of eyeballs. He claims they are leftovers from human sacrifices in the amazon jungle, but I suspect their true origins might be a butcher shop closer to home.

The curator next brings out a live boa constrictor that evokes some screams from the ladies in the audience, and he makes a show of letting it coil around him. He also presents a "Giant Crocodile of the Nile." Having seen one recently, I know it isn't, but I keep my mouth shut. His "Giant Croc" is actually an average-sized alligator that could easily have called Florida home. There must be at least a few other southerners in the audience because the curator's boasting garnishes a few boos and some heckling from the back.

The curator appears undaunted by the crowd's criticism because his next item to be revealed is in a crate big enough to hold a horse. As he pulls the curtain back to display it, the crate begins to shake and thump.

"Ladies and Gentlemen, it is my privilege to exhibit the star of McSweeney's Traveling Circus. A beast so vicious, so foul, that no other captive specimen exists. I present to you, the mighty, the ferocious, GARGANTURON!"

The sides of the crate fall away to reveal a steel cage. The creature inside is a tangle of striped legs and arms, and four heads. It's ricocheting from one side of the cage to another, its arms gyrating and horned heads snarling.

The reaction of the crowd is total awe. One lady up front promptly faints into the lap of the man seated behind her, and her friends attempt to buoy her back up. There is a fair amount of shrieking and wonderment from the kids in the audience. I smile as the creature climbs the bars of its cage and dangles from the top. I work to puzzle out how it's being done. Two of the heads are static dummies, open mouths fixed in anger, but the other two lively shrieking faces do a good job of drawing attention. The arms and legs are likewise a mix. I notice that a few of the furry striped legs are linked together by what are supposed to be manacles, but upon closer inspection are in fact a clever way for the moving legs to actuate the dummy ones. But even understanding the dummy system, I can still make out at least four real arms and legs. *Two men in a suit working together?*

The creature rattles the bars of its cage and the curator steps forward to calm it. One of the beast's arms lashes out and clamps onto the curator's throat. The creature lifts the man off his feet and hurls him backward. The curator's limp form tumbles off the side of the stage and disappears. More screams erupt from the audience and they only increase as the beast grasps the gate to its cage and wrenches it from its hinges. It hurls the door aside and steps onto the stage. The audience panics and flees. Ladies lift their skirts away from their ankles and men abandon hats and carnival prizes in their haste to escape the tent. Viznir and I rise to let people get around us. A few onlookers are still frozen to their seats, not sure if this is part of the act or a real danger. As the crowd thins, I notice Ariella and her guide among the spectators. Unlike the surprised citizens around her, Ariella's gaze is almost amused. Beside her, her usually stone-faced guide, Dagmar Sensaborria, looks less than sure of herself.

To my surprise, the monster points an arm directly at Ariella and shouts. "I know who you are, mercenary whore! I won't be going back. Not today, not ever!"

I look down to find Hanna clinging to my leg in fear.

"Viznir, I think you should take the kids outside. I'll handle getting the objective."

Viznir is staring transfixed at the interaction between Ariella and the monster, but snaps out of it when I put Hanna's hand in his. He nods and grabs Noah's hand, guiding them hastily toward the exit.

Ariella rises from her seat and steps over the bench in front of her. "I'm not here on assignment, Ajax. But Geo will be fascinated to know I've run across you. You've got yourself quite the home here."

"You tell your Journeymen cohort not to bother coming for me. I'll be long gone."

"And leave all this?" Ariella gestures to encompass the tent. "Such a shame. It suits you so well."

Ajax twists one of the dummy heads off his costume and hurls it at Ariella's feet. He next rips the rest of the costume's appendages off in a single motion using all four arms. As the contraption crumples to a heap beside him, I can finally make out his real shape. The monster costume was merely an exaggeration of his actual body—or bodies—as there are two men joined together at the shoulder blades of their respective sides. At first I think they are conjoined identical twins, but the similarities between them go beyond even nature's gift for duplication. They are the same man.

I marvel at the way he's been fused together. He has somehow survived experiencing the fate every time traveler fears the most—accidentally occupying the same space with someone at the same time. His muscular frame has been stooped from the angle he joins with himself, but he moves forward with a surprisingly fluid gait considering his impediment. The two versions of him have developed a system of walking where one walks forward and the other steps sideways in a sort of skipping motion. He flips a bench out of his way, his four arms heaving it aside with ease. Ariella stands her ground.

"I'm not here for the bounty on you, but if you really want to suffer the embarrassment—" Her voice is cut off as Ajax vanishes then reappears directly in front of her. One of his arms shoots out and seizes Ariella's neck. He hoists her into the air, his other arms simultaneously pinning her wrists. She kicks at him but connects only with one of his knees. He slams her to the ground. I'm stunned by the sudden violence.

Dagmar reaches for her weapon, but she's too slow. One half of Ajax swings a bench and smashes her backward into the bandstand. Her body dislodges half a dozen wooden chairs as she crumples to the platform, limp and silent. The other half of Ajax contends with Ariella's flailing fists. She only manages to graze one of his chins with a punch before his other half seizes her arm and flattens it to the ground. She cries out as he pins her hips to the floor with a knee.

Don't just stand here. Do something.

I've dashed closer to the fight, but lacking any weapons, I hurl the only thing available to me—my half eaten bag of popcorn. The crumbled bag strikes the nearest of Ajax's faces and explodes with a shower of buttery, puffed kernels. Ajax pauses with his fist raised to strike Ariella.

"Get off her, asshole."

Both of his heads stare at me. The expression on one face is cautious, sizing me up. The other is merely angry. Unfortunately, the angry one is in control of the fist. It swings and connects with Ariella's face with a meaty thump.

Anger drives me forward. I launch myself into the midsection of the body closest to me. Either half of Ajax would be heavier than me on its own; his frame is dense muscle. But while I lack his bulk, my height translates to weight, and the momentum of my almost two hundred pounds is enough to unbalance him and topple him sideways. I land on top of him in a mess of arms and legs. He immediately uses them against me. Fists strike my ribs and face while another arm tries to wrap around my neck.

I lash out with my elbows and knees, squirming about and punching everything within reach. My right elbow connects solidly with one of Ajax's noses, eliciting a howl, but the other half of him shoves me away and I sprawl in the dirt. I spit out a few grains of sand and turn around. Ariella is getting to her feet, one hand reaching behind her back. Ajax springs up and clamps her in a bear hug with one half of him while the other half wrenches a gun out of her hands and tosses it away.

"No, no, little wench. It won't be that easy."

Ariella twists in his arms and lands a punch on the side of his right head. "You're dead, bastard!"

Ajax merely laughs at the attack and viciously head butts her, causing her to cry out in pain. I get my feet under me and spring onto his back, wrapping my arms around his right neck and squeezing. His other half attempts to pull me off, but latched onto his broad, fused-together back, I'm in the spot he's least able to access. *Let's see you fight without a windpipe.* With two of his arms wrapped around Ariella, and the other two angled away from me, Ajax is unable to land any effective blows. He careens around the tent, knocking over benches, and I let myself hope that I might choke him into releasing her, but then he stops at one of the cabinets. He reaches inside for something and the tent around us vanishes.

We've relocated to a rocky hillside. The anchor Ajax used is the head of a pickaxe that's sticking out of a stony embankment. Ariella narrowly misses having her head fused into the handle on our arrival, and the way Ajax is cursing, I suspect he may have been hoping it was going to skewer her. I'm still squeezing hard on one of his necks, and finally the half of him I'm choking starts to panic. He releases Ariella and throws his hands up to grab at me. Latching onto my arms just above my biceps, he heaves me over his head and I crash onto my back in the dirt. Ariella scrambles to her feet and starts tapping her Temprovibe. As Ajax lumbers toward her, she takes only a microsecond to look at me, then vanishes.

I have no idea if Ariella has jumped forward or backward to that spot elsewhere in time, I only know I'm suddenly very alone. Ajax pivots and scowls at me with both heads. Getting to my feet, I glance at my chronometer. The bezel is still glowing a solid red. *No skipping out of this for me.*

I clench my fists and check my surroundings. The dirt road we're on winds its way up the hillside to a cluster of dilapidated buildings. Below us, a couple hundred yards beyond Ajax, train tracks terminate abruptly into the hill. The deep ruts in the road tell of many trips by wheels carting something heavy. Broken shovels and rusted rail parts also give away that we're near the mine. The air is brisk and the shrouded sun is low, making me wonder if it's even the same day. *If he jumped us too far back I could be disqualified.* I check my bracelet. Nothing seems amiss. The counter is still ticking off seconds I've been in the level.

Ajax extracts the pickaxe from the side of the hill and moves toward me. "You gonna keep up this fight or have you had enough?"

I nod toward the pickaxe. "You make a very compelling argument for quitting. And since my reason for getting into this fight seems to have disappeared, I'm rapidly losing motivation."

"If you're caught up with that witch, you're in for a world of hurt worse than I'd give you. You should let me put you out of your misery before she stabs you in the back."

I back away slowly. "It's not like that. We're not exactly friends. I have a few scores to settle with her myself."

"That so? Then you should have let me get rid of her for you."

"Didn't look like a fair fight. And I'm not much for letting guys beat up on women."

"Ha! Hero type, huh?" His laugh is harsh and guttural. "You'll learn. Some women need a beating worse than men."

"That one needs a dozen," his other head chimes in. He lowers the pickaxe. "So why don't you vanish along now, too?"

"I'm not sure when we are. How far did you jump us?"

"Just popped back to this morning. Passed this pickaxe here on the way out of the mine." He considers the point of the tool in his hands. "Liked the way it looked and thought it might save me a walk back later. In fact, I'll be out of the mine in a few minutes to pick it up." He swings the pickaxe and buries one end into the embankment where he found it. Next he pulls a couple of items from his pocket. I recognize them as a degravitizer and some sort of round anchor. When he gets done working with them, he pockets the degravitizer and holds his palm out. The anchor is a tiny shrunken head. "You want to *head* back to the circus?" He laughs at his own joke.

"You're offering to help me?" I ask.

"Sure. You fought well, and the enemy of my enemy is . . . something or other. No hard feelings."

I think about how difficult it will be to get back to my own flow of time with no working chronometer and no way to charge it. Even if I were to walk back myself, I would be hours behind. I take a step forward. Ajax smiles with both of his faces and elevates his palm. His lips are smiling, but his eyes are still cold. My hand wavers, and I take a step back.

"Not today."

The smiles on Ajax's faces fade in unison, but one of his mouths turns up again at the corner. "Good decision."

"You wouldn't have helped me?"

"I would have buried you in the ground quick as breathing." He casually rotates the anchor in his hand. "And I wouldn't have wasted a single synapse on your memory."

I put my hands in my pockets. "Thanks for the belated honesty."

"Ha." Both heads grin. "Good luck finding any more around here. Time travelers are a bunch of cutthroat assassins. They're not getting me, not this time. I have connections now. Tell that bitch not to come near me again. Next time she won't walk away." He puts a hand to his belt buckle and vanishes. The shrunken head falls to the dirt with a plop. I stare at the little pinched face; its squinty eyes and tight-mouthed grimace mocking me from the ground. Almost without thinking, my foot lashes out to kick it. The tiny head flies over the embankment at the edge of the road and sails into the bushes below.

I breathe the tension out of my body and pull the map from my pocket. I stare at it blankly for a few seconds, then trace the line of the train tracks from Pucketsville to the mine. I get my bearings and start walking uphill to the dilapidated buildings. *Somebody has to know when the train comes.*

Birds are chirping in the underbrush despite the overcast sky, and the morning air is pleasant. It could be that the rest of the world is going to have a beautiful day. I'm reminded that my chronological future is less bright when Ajax comes striding down the hill ahead. His unusual gait seems even more out of place here against the backdrop of peaceful nature. He isn't wearing his striped costume pants yet. Instead he's dressed in custom-made denim suspenders that strap over opposite halves of his broad four-legged body. He looks clean and downright cheerful.

"Morning."

I'm startled by the pleasant ease in his voice. The expressions on his faces are something akin to satisfaction and make me wonder what he's been up to in the mine.

"Good morning." I try not to stare.

Ajax merely looks amused at my discomfort and continues on. I hear one of his heads whistling softly as he walks away. I plod up the hill, only glancing back once to see Ajax pull the pickaxe from the hillside and lean it over his shoulder. He saunters down the hill as if he hasn't a care in the world.

"See you in your future, Ajax," I mutter. I turn and head for the mine.

"It's surprisingly easy to get lost in time. Makes you realize whom you really value in your life. Would you navigate across a millennium to be with someone? That's the sign of a keeper."—Journal of Dr. Harold Quickly, 1996

Chapter 18

The mining camp is mostly quiet with the exception of two Chinese men who mutter indecipherable greetings as they pass with a wheelbarrow. After a little diligent searching, I find a white-bearded man in an apron scrubbing pots behind what appears to be the camp's mess hall. There's a fire burning in a pit dug behind the building with a massive pot perched above it. I smell what I guess to be chili simmering and wander closer to investigate.

"Excuse me, sir. Do you happen to know when the train comes through?"

The man doesn't look up, but keeps wiping out a pot with determined strokes. "Cars are loaded overnight. The train'll be by to pick 'em up round noon. I reckon you'll hear the whistle."

"Do you happen to know the time now?"

"Time when men ought to be workin' and not yappin'." The man stands and takes his pot indoors without looking at me.

"Thanks," I say to the back door as it slams shut.

I ignore the alluring scent of the chili and wander back through the camp. A sign labels the outpost as 'Ever Winding Silver Mine,' belonging to the D. Ambrose Mining Corporation.

"Ben?"

Milo and Kara are tromping up the hill, a sheen of sweat on both of their faces. "Hey, guys."

"What are you doing here?" Milo's expression is a mix of curiosity and annoyance. "Did you get lost? The first teams aren't supposed to be through the gate for at least a couple hours."

"Yeah, it's a long story. Got in a fight with a time traveling circus star."

"There are penalties for crossing the restricted time line," Kara says. "You're not supposed to be back before your arrival time."

"Yeah, I figured I'm probably in trouble for that." I fidget with the bracelet. "What's the penalty?"

"If you get caught, they tack thirty minutes onto your time or drop you a place ranking for every hour you stray outside the limits," Milo says.

"Dang. Okay. Do you know how many hours early we are right now?"

"Three hours twenty minutes." Milo doesn't even check his bracelet.

"So wait, why are you guys here so early then? I haven't seen much of you all race."

Milo shifts his pack and looks to Kara. She shakes her head at him.

"We're doing a bit of a side project," Milo says. "We had to investigate something on this side of the restricted line."

"Oh. What?"

Kara is tight-lipped and glaring at me, but Milo is thoughtful. "Look, Ben. We need you to not tell anybody you saw us here. Can you do that?"

"Yeah, I suppose so. Why? What are you guys investigating?"

Kara turns toward Milo and angles her back to me. "You can't tell him. He's bound to rat us out. This is already going to be a problem."

"I'm not going to rat out anybody, it'd just be nice to be in the loop for once if I'm keeping secrets." I rub at my jaw where I suspect I'm developing a bruise from my fight.

"He's already seen us." Milo gestures toward my Gizmo shirt. "And he's not one of them. Look at him. There's no way."

I don't know who "them" is, so I'm not sure if I should be offended.

"He could be," Kara counters. "Why is he even here if he's not involved? You don't think that him being here is suspicious, considering the circumstances?"

Milo seems to ponder what she's saying as he looks from her to me. His eyes range past me and linger on the mouth of the mine before coming back to my face. "Look, Ben. It's probably best if you got back. You're already facing a penalty. You don't want the committee to come down on you any harder and risk losing more positions."

"I don't get the impression that the committee necessarily expects me to finish," I say. "So I'm not super concerned about where I place. I do want to get back to my guide, but my chronometer is out of juice, so I'm stuck waiting on time the old fashioned way."

Milo's gaze has wandered to the mine entrance again, but his attention swings back to me as I finish speaking. "Why do you think the committee doesn't want you to succeed? What happened?"

"Let's just say I've had some interesting conversations with some less than pleasant individuals about my prospects."

Kara locks her eyes to mine. "Who? Who talked to you?"

"I actually don't know his name. He dresses in all black, has a nice scar on his face that really accents his lovely personality. We've met twice now."

My description of the man from my apartment seems to have had an impact. Milo's interest is completely with me now. He inclines his head closer and speaks just above a whisper. "Ben. It's important that you don't tell anyone we were here, but I do want to find out more about your side of this. If I help you out with some power for that chronometer, will you promise to keep this conversation under wraps?"

"Your secret side project has to do with the committee?"

"Keep your damn voice down," Kara says and waves her bizarre looking pistol at my face. I take a step back.

Milo puts a hand on my shoulder and addresses Kara. "It's okay, I swept the hill for microphones on the way up. I don't think they wired this road with any cameras, but we'll find somewhere more private anyway." He turns back to me. "Your unit is probably AC right? Wall outlet charger?"

"Yeah."

"I've got an adapter for that." He pulls his shoulder bag free and roots through it. He passes me a white device about the size of a deck of cards with different styles of outlets on its surface. "Here's the American size. Plug your charger into that. The micro-batteries are internal. Should give you plenty of power."

"Thanks." I palm the device and slip it into my pocket with my charger cord.

Milo gestures for me to follow him off the road behind one of the miner's shacks. A quick check of the windows tells us it's empty. Satisfied we won't be overheard by any locals, Milo finally addresses me. "We have reason to believe this race is not what it seems on the surface. Racers are being eliminated faster than any prior chronothon."

"They've made the race more dangerous?"

"More than dangerous. They're making it impossible. We were at the exit gate a few hours from now. We thought everyone else had gone through, so we figured we had a little time to play with the system."

"What system?"

"The time gate data link. It's encrypted, but I have a few tools at my disposal." Milo taps the frame of his glasses.

"You can hack into the time gate?"

"It's a port for the engineers, but there's tons of data in there. Opening and closing sequences, video files, relayed messages from upstream and downstream, all kinds of stuff. We weren't looking for it, but we ran across a video of this mine. One of the teams is going to get trapped by a cave-in here in a couple of hours. Marco Thomas and Andre

Watts. The video makes it look like they fired their weapons in the mine and caused the collapse themselves."

"That doesn't seem too unlikely. From what I've seen of them so far, they're a little trigger happy."

"Yeah. It looks plausible on the video, too, but we found the time gate sequences for the exit, and Marco and Andre aren't on it."

"They wouldn't be if they got trapped though, right?" I say.

"That's not how the gates are programmed. Each racer has a distinct ID number that's encoded into the design of the gate so the program will recognize their bracelets. As long as you're within the time parameters set for the level, the gate should still open when you arrive. The two guys involved in the cave-in might eventually tunnel their way out or get rescued by the other miners, but they'll be too late to continue the race. That's not the kicker, though. We compared the list of access codes to the last level's program. Thomas and Watts's number were never encoded on this new gate. Even if they hadn't been caved in, they still wouldn't have advanced."

I consider what he's saying. "How do you know the program isn't listing the codes based on later information? If Marco and Andre never make the gate, it never needs their code, so it doesn't include it. I'm not a time gate programmer obviously but this is time travel, and it seems like it could be sort of a chicken-egg situation. Maybe the gate knew not to include the data because it already had the video of the cave-in."

"I thought of that." Milo pulls a tablet from Kara's pack and it shuffles through pages with mere gestures from his fingertip. "Here. Check this out." He turns the tablet so I can see it. "This is the code for the gates. That sequence right there? That's Andre's base number. It shows up in all the levels prior to this but none after. But if you look at the origin code of this program, you can see it was written by someone who had access to the information before these gates were even built, way before the video ever got uploaded. It's in the root code, the stuff they originally programmed the gates with. Andre was never going to get through this gate. No chance."

"Do you have the list from Egypt?"

"I think so. I'll need to find it. Why?"

"This guy Dennis and his guide couldn't get through the gate. They said they put their objective in the repository and it disappeared. Then the gate wouldn't open."

"Disappeared? That's different. We were through by then. Did you see what their objective was?"

"No. I never saw it, but Dennis said it was a rock he found in a quarry."

Kara pulls her cap from her head and her auburn hair tumbles around her face as she smacks the wall with the cap. "This is all useless if we don't know why. They have all of our numbers. They're picking us off one by one. This has to be something big. Too many people are getting taken out on that list for this to ever blow over. The race committee won't be able to run another chronothon ever again. It's terrible for the sponsors, for ratings, for everybody. Why are they rigging it?"

Milo and I stand mute after her outburst. Kara runs her hand through her hair and puts her cap back on, then kicks a rock out of the way. As it tumbles along the ground she draws her weapon and blasts the rock into oblivion. I flinch initially, expecting a bang from the gun, but the only sound is the rock breaking apart into hundreds of pieces. The weapon seems even more deadly in its silence.

"Kara was the first one to find the discrepancy in the code," Milo says. "We just started hacking the gate for the last couple of levels, but we knew something was wrong since the Middle-Ages."

"How?" I ask.

"We had a warning message come through from one of our contacts back home. Part of it got damaged in the transfer, but we got enough of it to suspect the danger."

"Will you stop telling him everything?" Kara's expression toward me is still hard. "You're going to get all of us caught if he can't keep his yap shut."

"It's okay," I say. "I don't need to know what it said, but do you mean you have a way to send messages somehow? I actually really need to get a message to someone, but Viznir told me it could disqualify me."

"It could if you use channels that the committee monitors," Milo replies. "Our method is a bit more discreet."

"Can I use it? It's really important."

Milo looks to Kara. Instead of immediately shooting down the decision, her expression actually lightens a little. "We can do it. But only because it means if you turn on us, we'll have something that will get you disqualified just as fast."

I hold up my hands. "That's fair. I just need to send the message soon."

Milo tucks the tablet back into Kara's bag, then straightens his own. "Write down what you want to say and where and when it needs to go. We'll send it from the rendezvous. We've already spent too much time here. We need to see what they rigged in that mine and how."

"Thank you. That's the best news I've had all race." I can feel some of my tension lift. "And I think I know who planted your device, or at least a good suspect. The time traveler who brought me here was with the circus.

THE CHRONOTHON

He came out of that mine just a bit before you arrived and looked pretty pleased with himself about something. I can't prove anything, but I'd bet he's involved somehow. I didn't get the impression he was the type to worry over harming racers. He's the six legged monster in the show but he goes by Ajax."

Milo nods. "We'll look into that. We'll catch up more at the rendezvous. Just keep this all between us." He and Kara check for activity on the street before sprinting toward the mine entrance. I'm left alone beside the vacant miner's shack with just my thoughts.

As Milo and Kara vanish into the darkness of the mine, I turn south and walk downhill to the train tracks. I pull the power pack and charger cord from my pocket and plug in my chronometer. The red glow immediately disappears from the bezel and the chronometer begins its telltale humming while it charges. I make my way to where the train cars are waiting for pickup. This area is busier than the camp. Another group of Chinese men and a few guys who look like Native Americans are loading cars with ore. A couple of white men with rifles are guarding the operation. I keep out of sight and sneak around a stand of pine trees to some of the already loaded cars.

Searching for something on the train that might make a good anchor, I finally settle on a steel coupler between train cars. I suspect the area shouldn't be in use when the train stops in town, and it provides me some cover from the guards while I dial my chronometer settings. I realize I'm guessing at what time it is now, but the slate in the window of the train station listed the train's arrival as two in the afternoon. I mentally work my way backward from then and use Milo's statement about us being three hours and twenty minutes shy of the first racer's arrival to estimate the rest. I scratch out the math in the dirt next to the tracks with my finger and, once I have my best guess, set my chronometer. I settle myself on the coupler in a position that will be secure even if I misjudge and wind up on the train while it's moving. I double-check my settings one last time and press the pin.

Shit!

The rocking and swaying of the coupler is the immediate sign that I've indeed missed my target. I steady myself as the tracks whip beneath me in a blur of dry dirt and occasional tufts of withered grass. I grip the side of the train car and cautiously get to my feet on the coupler. I poke my head into the wind and search for my destination. Pucketsville is a slowly diminishing blob on the horizon behind me. I curse and reset my chronometer. I overshoot my next jump the other direction and arrive back on the coupler prior to reaching the town. Instead of recalculating, I just ride the train the last half-mile into the station.

The conductor stops the engine with the passenger car parallel to the platform. My ore car is a dozen car-lengths back, so I hop off into the weeds and steer clear of the crowd waiting to board. It takes me the better part of half an hour to walk back to the circus and locate Viznir. I find him staring dejectedly at a poster of a man with two noses.

"What are you doing?"

Viznir jumps. "God! Where did you come from? I've been looking all over for you."

I give him an abbreviated account of the fight with Ajax, but leave out the part about encountering Milo and Kara.

"You went past the restricted time line?" Viznir's forehead wrinkles in frustration. "We're going to be penalized for that."

"I know. What happened to the kids?"

"Their parents found them. Another happy conversation you missed. I thought the dad was going to level me." The withering glare he gives me suggests it's my fault.

"If you wanted to tangle with Ajax instead, speak up next time and I'll take the kids."

Viznir appears somewhat mollified by that. I notice he has the jar of eyeballs in his hand. I point to it. "You got the objective? Sorry I didn't get around to that."

"Yeah." Viznir passes me the jar. "You can carry it now. It's revolting."

"Did you happen to find a stone lying around near the bleachers? I lost the anchor to go back for our stuff when Ajax displaced us."

"Are you kidding? That place was a disaster after you guys started fighting. I barely had time to get in and grab the objective before the sheriff showed up."

"I guess we'll have to find another way to get our stuff back."

We make our way to the sheriff's tent, and luckily only the deputy is in attendance. Unfortunately he follows Viznir and me into the tent to retrieve our belongings. He surveys the racks. "We've had an interesting day today. People been coming in with some things I've never seen before."

I notice a few modern rifles and handguns hung on racks, making me wonder which other time travelers are still walking around the circus.

The deputy rubs his chin. "I can't say I remember which ones were yours."

"It's okay. I hid them." I smile at the deputy.

"You did? Where?" He looks around the scant furnishings of the tent for something he could be missing.

"Would you mind facing the other way for just a moment. I don't want to give away my secrets." I hand the jar of eyeballs back to Viznir and dial in my chronometer settings.

The deputy seems confused, but his curiosity gets the best of him and he agrees to face the other way with Viznir. I double-check my time coordinates and use the center tent pole as an anchor. When I arrive a couple of hours before, I can hear my own voice and the deputy outside discussing the fangs on the werewolf. It only takes me a few seconds to retrieve our belongings and blink back.

I clear my throat when I return and the two men turn around to face me. The deputy's eyes widen at the sight of all our stuff on my shoulders, and he nods in approval. Viznir takes his pack and gun belt and immediately returns the jar of eyeballs to me. I stuff the jar in with my other things and straighten up.

"You fellas ought to be in the magic show yourselves!" The deputy looks around the tent and even goes so far as to poke his head behind the gun rack. "You rig up some kind of trap door or something?"

"A magician never tells his secrets."

The deputy removes his hat to scratch his head then pats the top of the hat as he puts it back on. "All in good fun then, I reckon." He smiles. "I'm getting pretty good at the one with the coin from your ear. My kid loves it. You want to see it?"

"Um, sure."

The deputy fishes out a coin from his pocket and makes fair attempt at making it disappear. One edge of the coin is still visible between his knuckles as he shows us his "empty" hands, but I just smile and let him make it reappear from behind my ear with a flourish.

"Ta da!"

"That's pretty good. Any more back there? We can use some beer money."

The man grins at his success. "Yeah, the kids love that one. I'm working my way through a few playing card tricks, too. I didn't bring any with me or I'd show you."

"No worries. We really have to be on our way." After we exit the tent, I pull the map from my pocket and turn to our new friend one more time. "Do you happen to know where this is?" I point to the repository symbol on the map.

"Hmm. Looks like Pike's canyon. Just a bit north along the tracks."

"Walking distance?"

"It's a fair piece of walkin'. Train goes past, but there're no stops till Seaver's Junction. I've never seen anything other than jackrabbits out there. No reason for folks to stop that I know of. What are you looking for?"

"Meeting a few friends. Hopefully for some dinner."

Viznir and I cut across the open prairie heading north, and it takes about thirty minutes to intersect the tracks. We're both sweaty by the time we reach them and neither of us wants to hike the remainder of the way to the repository. We have a heated debate about the best way to get to the train since it's already departed and finally settle on using a red rock boulder as an anchor to jump back to when we expect it to pass. As we're standing there setting our respective time devices, I curse when it dawns on me that I'm still carrying the eyeballs and we have no way to get the jar back with us. Viznir seems to contemplate ditching me for the sake of the ride, but after a few moments of staring at each other in silence, we resign ourselves to the walk.

My muscles are starting to stiffen from the exertion of the fight and my calf is throbbing slightly from the snakebite, but despite the physical discomfort, the walk is relatively pleasant. The sun dips and settles behind a red rock butte on the horizon, decorating the sky in pink and orange.

As we near the canyon and veer away from the rails, we find other sets of tracks. Barley's paw prints are easy to identify. The others are tougher to decipher, but I pick out a few sets of feminine shoe prints in the mix, making me wonder if Ariella and Dagmar are ahead of us or whether they belong to Genesis or one of the other women. The light is growing dim by the time we enter the box canyon. It appears to lead nowhere, but after diligently following the tracks of our predecessors, we discover a narrow cave mouth leading into the rock. I follow my flashlight beam down a claustrophobic path that dead ends at an underground stream. When it seems we can go no farther, I scan the cave walls and discover they've been decorated in Native American drawings. The drawings depict deer and coyotes, wheels and figures with spears. Among them I'm surprised to find the wavy lined symbol for the repository. Stepping closer, I find a rock ledge that has been carved out with small divots. Resting in some of the divots are miniature wooden canoes that range in size from a few inches to a couple feet long. One of them has my name on it. Curious, I extract my jar of eyeballs and set it into the hollowed space in the canoe. Nothing happens. I double-check my bracelet then consider the spaces between the remaining canoes. No other objectives are in attendance, but there aren't many canoes left. I pick mine up and walk with it to the edge of the stream.

"I guess we send it floating down the river?"

Viznir flicks his flashlight beam to the cave wall where the little stream is disappearing into darkness. The sound of splashing beyond the wall suggests the stream must drop off somewhere beyond it.

THE CHRONOTHON

"We're never getting it back if you're wrong."

I search the cave for any other options, but seeing none, I squat and set the little canoe in the water. I test the weight of the jar of eyeballs in it, then give it a push, letting the current tug it along toward the wall. The little canoe picks up speed and vanishes into the hole. Time seems to slow down as I wait for a result. Viznir's foot is tapping as he stares into the darkness of the hole. Finally my bracelet beeps. The number on the display blinks the number ten but then beeps again to show a fourteen. I imagine the penalty will affect me later, but for now I'm just happy to be advancing.

The time gate opens against the far wall of the cave, so Viznir and I are obligated to wade through the stream to get to it. I let Viznir lead the way and follow him through the gate. We emerge into a marble hallway half a world away. The two women who greet us are Indian with telltale red dots between dark eyes and are dressed in simple robes with more elaborate red sashes thrown over one shoulder.

"Welcome to Hotel Shanat, gentlemen," the taller woman says. "Dinner has already begun. I will show you to your rooms so you may dress." She smiles. Both women bow and lead the way right along the hall. One wall of the hallway is open to expose a lush garden one floor below. The sky is shaded in twilight, but birds are still making music in the handful of trees that stretch above the roof. The building we're in wraps around the garden with more exposed hallways. A couple of children scamper across the garden laughing, then disappear below us.

The hallway turns right, and we pass a dozen doorways decorated with various animal reliefs before stopping before a door with an elephant on it. The elephant's trunk extends from the door and forms a handle. The tall woman opens it and hands me the key before gesturing me inside. "You will find all of your dinner attire has been set out for you. Dinner is in the main dining hall, and your attendance is most desired." She bows again and leads Viznir farther down the hall.

I'm elated at the prospect of a bed for the night and a bathroom with plumbing. The claw foot tub in the bathroom has hot water, and I immediately begin running a bath. I'm already late for dinner, so I move quickly, but I take the time to get scrubbed clean. The razor provided is a straight blade that I determine I'm bound to cut myself with, so I opt to show up scruffy rather than bloody. The clothing that has been left for me is a lightweight linen suit complete with suspenders, brown patent leather shoes, and argyle socks. A bowtie is provided as well, but since I haven't the foggiest idea how to tie it, I stuff that in the pocket of my jacket and head out the door.

I pause in the hall, remembering Milo's instructions. Going back inside, I search the writing desk near the window for paper. The pen at the desk is an elaborate fountain pen with a brass nib. I opt for my own and try to formulate what to say. *How do you tell a time traveler she's in danger without anyone else knowing?* I frown at the blank page for the better part of a minute, then finally start scribbling.

Dear Malcolm,

I hope you are well and the topic of our last conversation has been dealt with. Please add this to my last message instructions:

The sidewalk incident was just the start. CB is lost. Our New York friends are looking for you.

The language seems off, but I don't know how much scrutiny it might receive if it's intercepted. "Hunting for you" would be more accurate but probably a giveaway.

I pause, wondering how to get any personal message across, then add the last line.

I'm looking forward to seeing you again.—B

I add the date and time I need the message sent to for Milo, then stare at the words, hating them for how inadequate they are compared to how I really feel. Thinking of the possibility of the committee members reading them helps me resist adding more. *I'll just have to tell her how I feel in person.*

The hotel hallways traverse two more lush gardens on my way to the main dining hall. I follow the sound of instrumental music to the first floor and through an elaborate lobby. An usher in a swallowtail coat and tight vest bows stiffly before opening the door for me.

Dining room is too modest a description for the space I enter. *Banquet hall* might be more fitting, but even that sounds humble compared to the opulence in view. Waiters bearing silver trays weave in and out of marble columns that flank the parallel banquet tables and direct attention toward the far end of the room. A massive tapestry is hung behind the head table and its occupants, a heavyset Indian man and his equally rotund wife. The man is standing and has the attention of the room but pauses his speech as I enter. I bow and follow the usher toward a vacant seat between Viznir and Mayra Summers. Genesis smiles as I pass, and once I'm seated, the man at the front continues.

"The mettle of a chronothon racer has always been superior. These racers who have lost their lives did so in the act of achieving greatness. Their legacy will endure in the annals of chronothon history. The chronothon committee takes great pride in honoring our racers, regardless of their ranking at the outcome. Their families will likewise be honored at the closing ceremony." The man spreads his arms and smiles at us. "We are committed to providing you with the ultimate in racing adventure and to ensuring the course meets safety standards. These tragic losses will not daunt our enthusiasm for providing you with the best experience of your lives."

The man grins and looks around the room to a smattering of applause, but I notice most of it is coming from the hotel staff. The academy teams and the Admiral give brief claps, but the applause dies quickly. Our host seems satisfied, however, and eases himself back into an elegant oversized armchair.

I turn to Viznir. "What did I miss?"

"You missed the soup and the lentils, and most of the speech."

"Who is that guy? What did he say?"

"He's an undersecretary to the viceroy. Vikash Manavi. He said the committee is investigating the deaths but doesn't suspect foul play."

"Ivan got stabbed through the chest. How can that not be foul play?"

Viznir puts his hand up to hush me. "Not so loud."

"Why?" I whisper. "What's the—" I stop speaking as a pair of British soldiers walk behind us. Viznir concentrates on his soup. Once the soldiers are past I lean closer. "What's going on?" Viznir just shakes his head and ignores me. A woman with a serving tray passes and sets a plate of pita and various dipping sauces between Mayra and me. I nod at her and help myself.

The feel of this rendezvous dinner is far less jovial than Rome. Tad and Blaine are still laughing with one another at a position closest to the host, but the rest of the room is subdued. The few racers that are involved in conversations are doing so in hushed tones. I turn to Mayra on my left. "How did you make out in the last level?"

Mayra leans back and lets Genesis field the question.

"We did pretty well, considering the obstacles. We had to get aboard the train twice and find a car carrying our objective. It turns out the passenger car we needed didn't get loaded till a few stops after we found the train, so that slowed us down. We spent a bunch of time searching the wrong compartments."

"Were you with Jet and Cliff during it? How'd they do?"

"They did great. They had an objective on a ranch out in the middle of nowhere, but they found it right away. Where did you end up?"

"The circus."

"Aw, man. I heard there was a circus. That would have been more fun. Was it cool?"

"Yeah, I guess so. Its employees weren't the nicest, but it definitely wasn't dull." I flex my sore knuckles and go back to my bits of pita. Servers are beginning to pass out more steaming dishes from trays, and I'm anticipating their arrival at my end of the table when I catch Milo's eye from across the room. He and Kara are seated between Jonah and a team of men I haven't met yet. Milo inclines his head toward the door then gets up from the table. He slips out amid the chaos of the dozen busy servers, and no one seems to pay attention. I excuse myself and skirt around the columns to the door. Outside in the hall, Milo gestures for me to follow him up a servants' stairway cleverly hidden in the wall paneling. As I climb the narrow steps behind him, I can't help but voice my curiosity. "How'd you know about this?"

He waits till we reach the roof of the hotel to respond. "You're going to find there are lots of tech advantages to being from the future. Architectural analysis apps are the tip of the iceberg." He pulls his glasses off and cleans the lenses with his sleeve. Like me, he's been outfitted in a light-colored suit. The linen contrasts with his coffee colored skin and in the darkness of the rooftop gives the illusion that his clothes are glowing. "I don't know if you realize what these other teams are going to be capable of, but once we hit an era with the Grid in place, there's going to be a major shift in strategy. Teams have been conserving power and having to operate off Grid, but once we're past the dawn of the internet and the gadgets start coming out, it'll be game on." He puts his glasses back on. "Assuming we make it that far." Milo steps to the edge of the building. "Do you know where we are?"

I stare at the darkness beyond the hotel's walls. A few lamps flicker through the swaying trees, blinking at me in the warm breeze.

"We're in India, right?"

"Yes. Ajmer-Merwara province. You know when?"

"Not exactly."

"It's the beginning of 1900. Out there, out past those trees, six million people are starving to death from drought and famine."

"Why are we here?"

"I think we're being sent a message. I think someone thinks it's funny to have us attend a banquet in the middle of a country that's starving. Like it makes us complicit with this somehow."

"That's awful. Who thinks like that?"

Milo frowns at the horizon and then turns to me. "You have your message?"

I fish the folded paper out of my pocket and hand it to him. He scans the words quickly. "This is it?"

"All I could come up with on short notice."

He passes the paper back to me. I stare at it, confused. "Don't you need to copy it or something?"

"I already did." He taps the frames of his glasses. "I'll encrypt the info, send it through the etherweb via the timegate link disguised as some kind of backup maintenance code, and once it hits an eligible courier system, it will route to your receiver as you wrote it."

I nod as if I understand. "Who else is going to see it?"

"Nobody. The courier system only decrypts it in the presence of the recipient. You haven't used the courier system before?"

"Nope."

"Well you will." Milo turns back to the horizon. In the distance, a woman is wailing. Her voice wavers in the breeze, a cry of total despair. Milo's glare hardens. "The British mismanaged the food supplies here and exported so much that when the draught struck and the livestock started dying, the people weren't far behind. The child mortality rate was ... horrible. The fact that time travelers are participating in this makes me sick."

I stare at the darkness in the direction of the wailing. "What can we do?"

"Nothing. What happened here already happened, but we can figure out who would want to capitalize on it. Someone put us here for a reason."

"What did you find out in the mine?"

"We found the device. Definitely future tech, somewhere in the twenty-second century if I had to guess. It was subtle. We also found more info about your suspect. Ajax, as you called him, had an exit programmed in the time gate. Whoever gave him the job to blow up the mine also gave him an escape route."

"Then the committee is rigging this for sure. They're the ones who programmed the gates. They have to be in on it." This revelation makes my own predicament seem even more hopeless. I was aware Geo had a fix in somehow, and that was bad enough, but having the entire chronothon rigged is another layer of danger I wasn't prepared for.

"It may not be the whole committee," Milo says. "I doubt the whole organization has been corrupted, but certain members have to be in on it. At least one of the gate design engineers or programmers and whoever is recruiting saboteurs."

"Who gains from this? Kara said the chronothon will lose tons of money and credibility as a result. Why would the committee sabotage its own source of income?"

Milo checks the watch on his wrist, then slips his sleeve back over it. "People are already talking about forfeiting because of the danger. Titus and Leonard were next to me at dinner. They were deciding whether or not to continue. Another team, Carlos Palo and his guide, quit as soon as they arrived tonight. Whatever the saboteur is up to, my guess is it will happen soon. Otherwise there won't be a race left to tamper with."

"Ivan was murdered. There was no question. The same murderer was part of me getting signed up for this race."

"Was it the man dressed in black you mentioned? The one with the scar?"

"No. Another guy. He has these creepy gray eyes and sort of a mean look to him, like he enjoys hurting people."

"Was he wearing black, too?"

"No."

"What about the four-legged man? Ajax."

"No. He wore overalls. Is the black clothing significant?"

"It might be. I'll need to see if I can research the data we've got and check if either of these guys show up. I'll see what I can come up with. Any pieces of this puzzle are useful right now."

When Milo and I slip back into the dining hall, I find my place setting has been loaded with two more courses of food. The knowledge of the outside world and the memory of the woman wailing through the trees has robbed me of my appetite, but I do my best to not let the food I've already been given go to waste. I turn down the dessert course and attempt to get up and make my way back to my room as soon as it's socially acceptable. Cliff grabs my arm as I pass him and stops me. He's holding a glass of something dark in his other hand and thrusts it at me.

"Travers. You're in on this, too." He puts the glass in my hand and pours another for himself. He gets unsteadily to his feet and gestures for Jettison to rise, too. Jet catches my eye and shrugs apologetically as he stands. Cliff's words are slurred, but he has an air of gravity to his speech. "To Charlie Barnes. A good racer and a great man. He deserved better." He clinks his glass against mine and Jettison's and downs his shot in one gulp. I throw mine back as well, grimacing as the alcohol burns its way down my throat. Cliff tilts the bottle into his glass again, sloshing a bit of the dark liquor onto the tablecloth in the process. He next aims the bottle for my glass.

I shield the top with my free hand. "I think I'm good."

Cliff glares at me and knocks my hand aside with the bottle. "For Tulley and his boy."

I sigh and let him fill my glass. Cliff fills Jettison's and then raises his glass again. "Tulleys."

I down my drink and begin to count the others we've lost. *This is going to be a rough night.*

"We are all someone's past, but we are also someone's future. Try to give them both something to be inspired by."–Journal of Dr. Harold Quickly, 1903

Chapter 19

The banging won't stop. I stumble through the darkness and jerk the door open to find Viznir reading a note that's been tied to the elephant trunk on my door.

"Oh good. You already got the message." Viznir steps past me into the room while I squint at the note, trying to make out the writing in the light from the hallway gas lamp.

"Which message?" I pull the slip of paper from the door and blink a few times to get my eyes to focus. My head aches and my mouth is dry.

"That one. About wearing your suit again this morning. They must have something special in store for us this level."

I look down at my wrinkled clothing that I never took off after dinner. "Oh. Totally on top of that."

Viznir is lighting a lamp on the desk. He looks tired. He surveys the room, taking in my scattered clothing and the dented bed covers where I collapsed.

"What time is it? It's still so dark." I pick up my canteen and swish some water around my mouth.

Viznir frowns at me. "It's 3:30. Perks of coming in fourteenth. Any hope of sleep is for people who at least make the top ten. Get your stuff, we've got to go."

The departure time gate is in a courtyard filled with the sound of running water. Five separate fountains feed a common shallow pool at the center before being channeled off to some other part of the hotel. Vikash Manavi is standing in an illuminated archway at the far side of the courtyard, dressed in a jacket with no lapels that is buttoned up to his thick neck. He's having a discussion with Ariella and Dagmar when we arrive. The women are no longer dressed in the fashion of Indian women; this morning they are both wearing skirts that taper at the knees, and jackets. Both ladies are also wearing hats. Viznir and I round the pool and join them. As Vikash welcomes us, Ariella turns her face toward us also. She has angled the rake of her hat to her left side in an attempt to conceal the bruise on her face that has emerged in violet hues. While she doesn't seem any happier to be up at this hour than we are, her expression toward me has lost some of its usual mockery. Dagmar inclines her head toward me and I wave.

"Good morning, gentlemen," Vikash says, also giving the slightest of bows.

I bow back. "Good morning."

"The ladies will precede you through the gate. I've just finished telling them that you will leave your belongings here for this round. They will be forwarded ahead for collection at the next gate. Please place all your accouterments in this repository." He gestures toward a crate that's been set near a decorative archway.

This request takes me aback, and I can see Viznir grow concerned too. I open my pack and stare at the contents, trying to determine what I might need and won't want to leave behind. I settle for my pocketknife, Charlie's compass, Dr. Quickly's journal, and the little tin of chronometer tools and instructions from Abraham. The last two are less from need and more to keep anyone else from looking through them. Dr. Quickly has never explicitly told me not to show his diagrams and sketches to anyone, but I get the feeling that the Quickly's habit of secrecy ought to extend to their possessions. I slip my chosen belongings into my suit's pockets and hope for the best.

By the time Viznir and I are ready to give up our packs, Ariella and Dagmar are lined up in front of the arch. The light shimmers, and a moment later they've passed through and vanished.

I set my pack in the crate and turn to our host. "Must be sending us somewhere fancy if we're going in suits."

Vikash gives me a magnanimous smile. "Seems only fitting, as your destination is the *height* of affluence in its era." He chortles at first and then breaks into big hearty laughs that leave him breathless.

I give a polite smile, wondering if he'll fill us in on the joke, but when he finally calms down and wipes the tear of laughter from his eye, he merely gestures toward the gate.

"Bon voyage, gentlemen. Or perhaps I should say, Schoene Reise." He erupts in laughter again, and Viznir and I can only wonder at his mirth as we step through the gate.

Upon passing through the translucent archway, I find myself in a room so tiny that I could almost touch both walls with my arms extended should I choose. I am alone, which is fortunate as there is very little extra space to maneuver. To my immediate right is a metal-framed bunk bed that has been secured to the wall. On the opposite wall is a foldable sink, also metal and designed for efficient use in the narrow space. For a moment I fear I could be in some type of prison cell, since there are no windows, but the lack of a toilet and a distinct humming vibration in my body tells me I'm more likely aboard some type of ship. Pivoting where I stand, I can see that the time gate has somehow been rigged to exit me out of a solid door. The door's proportions are small, but when I turn the handle it opens easily, doing away with my fear of sudden imprisonment.

I peek my head out and see that my cabin is one of several along both sides of the brief hallway. One end of the hall is a dead end, but the other leads to a stairwell. Seeing no sign of Viznir, I shut my door again and examine my cabin. Searching the room doesn't take long, and I discover my objective box secured under the top berth. I extract it and am about to open it when I hear voices outside my door. I recognize one as Jettison's. I swing the door open and find him conversing with Genesis just outside. They both stop at my intrusion.

"Hey, guys."

Jettison looks at the objective box in my hand. "You open yours yet?" Something about his voice tells me he doesn't expect me to find good news.

"What's up? Where are we?"

Genesis looks more anxious than I've ever seen her. Her voice is low as she speaks. "The rules of the game are changing on us. We're not just after objectives this round."

I pop open my objective box. It contains blueprints to an airship. Along with the diagram, I've been given a list of people's names and accompanying black and white photographs. I look at the description in the schematic's title block and read the name: LZ-129 Hindenburg.

"Ho lee shit. Are they serious?"

"It's May 6th, 1937. It's the ship's last flight." Jettison holds up his list of people's names. "We have to get the crew and passengers off."

"All of them? Don't some people get out by themselves anyway?"

"Some. But most suffer injuries or burns in the process. A lot of people die in the hospital from the burns. We're supposed to get our group on the ground safely in order to pass the level. Who'd you get?"

I consult my list. "Birger Brinck, Wilhelm Dimmler, and Walter Banholzer."

Genesis is checking a tablet for information. "Brinck is a passenger, the other two are crew. In most timestreams where the Hindenburg crashed, those men all died, either in the crash or in the hospital."

"What about this timestream?"

"We're in a new one. No data. I'm guessing us being here for the race changed the prior stream we were sent to. The way it pans out is up to us now." Genesis lowers the tablet. "Anything can happen."

"Where are our guides?"

"Not here. Cliff and Mayra never showed up."

I jab a thumb toward my cabin door. "No Viznir either. You think they are on the ground?"

"Only one way to find out, I guess," Jettison says. "Let's go find our people."

We walk toward the stairway and turn right near a pile of stacked luggage, then emerge into an open dining area populated with more than a dozen people. Most are seated at tables inboard of a railing that divides the dining room from a walkway or leaning along a set of angled windows that give a view of a somewhat dim twilight sky. A tall, sandy-haired steward in a white coat is handing out sandwiches from a tray and pauses in the act as he catches sight of us. A few others notice our arrival as well and begin to chatter.

A passenger seated at a table close to us addresses us in surprise. "Hello, where'd you chaps come from?" The thin man with a brown-and-gray mustache stands and walks toward us. "Have you been hiding in your cabins all flight?"

A woman joins in his inquiry. Dark-haired and in her fifties, she leaves the company of another woman to investigate us. "There's no way a body could stay in those cabins three days, George. What would they eat?" She looks Jettison and me up and down, then turns her attention to Genesis. "I would have known if this young lady was anywhere to be seen." She extends Genesis her hands. "Margaret Mather, how do you do?"

"Ma'am, it's nice to meet you, but we have to get you to safety," Genesis replies.

I address the thin man. "George was it? We're here because we need to evacuate this airship. We'll need everyone's assistance in making it happen. Can we count on your help?"

"Evacuate?" George replies. "Is there something wrong?"

Jettison responds. "Not at the moment, but there is going to be an incident. Gather everyone you can and get them close to the exit stairs or windows. No one should go back to their cabins. Mrs. Mather, you too. You all need to be ready to jump if necessary."

"We're at least five hundred feet up!" A short, wiry man who has been listening in from behind Margaret pipes up. "There's no jumping out."

"What we're saying is that when we get this ship on the ground you'll need to move fast," I say. "Where do we find the captain?"

"What's going on here?" A mustached older man in a dark uniform and glasses breaks away from a conversation with a passenger and addresses us. "Where did you people come from?"

Before I have time to respond, Tad Masterson comes bounding up the stairwell from the lower deck, followed closely by Preston Marquez. He brushes past a pair of curious passengers and shouts at the group of people gathered by the windows. "All right, which one of you guys is Dooner? I need a Herman Dooner."

A woman seated with two blonde boys and a teenage girl gets to her feet. "I am Mrs. Doehner. Hermann is my husband. What do you want with him?"

"Where is he, lady? I've got to get him out."

"Calm down, Tad," Genesis says. "We're getting them all out." She turns to the woman with the children, eyeing one of the photos from the dossier in her hand. "Mrs. Doehner, is this young lady your daughter Irene?"

Mrs. Doehner is about to speak when the mustached man interrupts. "No one is going anywhere until we get an explanation of who you are and where you came from. How did you get aboard?" He looks to the white-jacketed stewards still holding sandwich trays. "Deeg, Balla, where did these people come from?"

The sandy-haired steward and his shorter compatriot look at each other and then reply in a string of German I can make nothing of. The result seems to be the older man dispatching the shorter steward downstairs on an errand. The man turns his attention back to us and his voice is scolding. "As chief steward of this ship, I am familiar with each of the passengers and crew members aboard. You are neither. Where have you come from and how did you get on this ship?"

"This is a story we only have time to tell once," Jettison says. "Can you get us to the captain?"

"The captain is busy landing the ship. We've been delayed over six hours and have a tight schedule to keep." The chief steward consults a pocket watch. I manage to note the time before he flips it shut and stuffs it into his jacket pocket. "The Hindenburg will be departing again as soon as it is provisioned. We don't have time for any more delays."

"Your schedule's about to go up in flames, buddy," Tad says.

More passengers have crowded around to better hear the conversation. I scan the faces for one who looks like the photos in my dossier, but none of the men in the dining room seem to match the balding passenger in my first photo. I tap Jettison on the shoulder. "It's almost seven. Any idea how much time we've got?"

Jettison walks us away from the curious passengers and discretely refers to his tablet. "The fire starts on landing around 7:25pm. We need to be ready by then. I've got a Captain Ernst Lehmann on my list. I'll head for the control car and see what I can do to get this thing on the ground faster."

"Who are your other objectives? It would make sense if we work together on this, team up based on location. If we've all got a mix of crew and passengers, we could take it by zones."

Tad has followed us to hear our conversation and grunts in derision. "Forget that. I'm not doing your work for you." He strides away to look for his man. Preston trails behind him.

We watch him go, then Jettison turns to me. "We don't need them anyway." He consults his tablet, then gestures to the blueprint in my hand and I open it up. "When the explosion happens, the first people to be affected are up in the nose. The fire shoots along this upper axial walkway and comes out the front. First priority is to keep everybody away from that walkway."

I stare at the blueprint. "This ship is pretty huge. Lots of people to locate. Wouldn't it be easier to just keep the fire from starting in the first place?"

"Maybe, but nobody knows exactly what caused it," Jettison says. "The best theories seemed to be static igniting leaking gas in the tail, but even that is conjecture. How do we stop it if we don't know why it started?"

Genesis chimes in. "If the race committee put us here, they'll have a way to keep the action going. I don't think we should count on them putting us on a version of the Hindenburg that isn't going to burn."

I think about what I know of the committee's methods so far and have to admit she's right. They could have any number of ways to ensure its ignition. "Okay, so we get the thing on the ground ASAP and make sure the people get clear."

Jettison nods, then turns to his sister. "You okay staying here, Gen, and trying to get the passengers out?"

Genesis has been consulting her information tablet and looks up. "Shouldn't be too bad. In most timestreams people were able to jump out the portside windows. I'll need to get the people from the starboard side over here, but after that it's just a matter of getting low enough to jump. I think I can handle it. Give me the photos of your passengers."

I hand her the dossier of Birger Brinck, and she passes me one of a radio operator named Franz Eichelmann. She trades one with Jettison also, then turns around and walks over to the cluster of passengers gathered around the chief steward. Jettison heads for the stairwell, and I follow him to the lower deck.

The "B Deck," as it's labeled on the diagram, is divided up into crew dining and kitchen areas and, aft of the stairs, the hallway continues to more passenger cabins. We turn left toward the crew areas and traverse the narrow hallway to the kitchen, passing what appears to be a bar. A dark-haired bartender is securing bottles behind the bar and pauses as we pass. His expression is curious but kind. Rounding the corner to the center hallway we are met by more stares and exclamations of surprise, but we aren't the first visitors. We find Milo and the man named Titus who had been next to him at dinner. They are trying to convince the kitchen staff to bust out the cellophane windows. Titus apparently speaks German, because he is bickering back and forth with a dark-haired man about my age wearing a white chef hat. Two other white-coated chefs are in attendance, but the one in the hat seems to be doing all the talking. I peek my head around the corner into a dining area full of comfortable looking booths and find a few more off duty crew members seated at tables. Some are in mechanic's jumpsuits, others appear to be serving staff. One pair are playing chess on a foldable wooden chessboard. I immediately recognize one young, wavy-haired player as a man from my list. I double-check the photo and then approach him. "Excuse me, are you Walter Banholzer?"

Banholzer looks up from the board, surprised, and rises from the booth. I extend my hand to him. "I'm Benjamin Travers."

He shakes my hand and replies in accented English. "Pleased to meet you." He looks behind me, perhaps wondering where I've come from. The other men in the dining area appraise me with curiosity and begin to take an interest in the conversation.

I stare at Banholzer awkwardly, then try to breach the subject. "So I guess we're going to change history together." Banholzer seems unsure, as if he didn't quite understand me. I turn to the other men. "You guys are going to want to get ready. We need to get you off this ship."

Jettison and I do our best to inform the crew of the impending disaster. A few of the men retrieve fire extinguishers and one of the mechanics dons his gloves but all seem hesitant to start busting windows or taking other precautions without orders from their superiors.

I reconvene with Milo and Titus. "We need to get to the control car. We've warned these guys. At least they know what's coming. If we can convince the captain, he can give them orders to evacuate that they'll really obey."

According to the diagram, the control car is forward along a keel walkway that runs the length of the ship. We pass another dining area on the way that is occupied by an adolescent boy stacking dishes in a cupboard. His hair is cut short on the sides and slicked back with the exception of one stray cowlick. The hairstyle instantly reminds me of the character Alfalfa from *Little Rascals* episodes that my dad would laugh along to in his den. The boy gawks at us as we pass and I can't help but wonder how someone so young is employed on a transatlantic airship.

We are forced to walk single file through the narrow keel toward the control car. To either side of the walkway are large drums of water and, as I get out from under the passenger deck above, I can now look up into the interior of the airship. Having grudgingly ridden in a hot air balloon on an occasion prior, my only experience of a lighter-than-air craft has involved voluminous open space. I had always imagined the interior of an airship to be similar, but to the contrary, it seems that every direction is taken up with aluminum girders and tensioned cables zigzagging their way through the structure. The gas bags of the airship above me have a vaguely translucent quality to them. The sight only increases my unease as I consider their flammable contents.

The path to the control car becomes suddenly blocked as two men exit a room off the side of the keel corridor. One is a crewmember but the other is an irritated Horacio Amadeus. He turns and shouts down a ladder into what I assume is the control gondola. "The others are coming. Let's get this show on the road."

The crewmember who has been forced into the walkway by Horacio seems to be contemplating socking the Italian in the face, but as we approach from the other end of the corridor he unfortunately seems to reconsider.

"What are you doing up here, Horacio? Anything useful?" I ask.

Horacio flips me off and climbs down the ladder into the gondola. I give the crewman a nod, and he seems to understand that we don't want trouble.

"Sorry about that guy. He's not really with us." I slip past the man and peek into the room he exited. A number of desks loaded with radios line the walls. Their analog gauges and big knobs look simplistic compared to modern standards, and there is even a typewriter mounted to one table. A clock on the wall reads just past seven. *Twenty minutes to go.* There is a commotion in the control car, so I ease myself over to the ladder to hear what's going on. I hear voices of men I don't recognize and then one I do. Admiral McGovern strides into view, still wearing his silver cape and gesturing toward the back of the ship.

"It'll be in the back. You'll have been losing lift already. You have, haven't you?"

A man with graying temples that seems to be in charge is a step behind him. Dressed in a dark jacket with four stripes on each sleeve to signify his rank and a flat-topped white hat, the man cuts a hand though the air to silence the admiral. "You are not in command of this vessel. We will land as planned and you will be prepared to explain your intrusion to the American customs agents when they come aboard. Get out of my control car!" The man's expression is hard and his mannerisms exude frustration.

"For God's sake, Admiral, just show him the footage already."

I recognize Ariella's voice coming from somewhere out of view. She must have pulled the video up on some type of device because the next moment I hear audio from the famous radio newscast. "Get this, Charlie; get this, Charlie! It's fire . . . and it's crashing! It's crashing terrible! Oh, my! Get out of the way, please! It's burning and bursting into flames and the . . . and it's falling on the mooring mast—" The captain turns at the sound and his face darkens as he takes in what he's seeing. " . . . it's a terrific crash, ladies and gentlemen. It's smoke, and it's in flames now; and the frame is crashing to the ground, not quite to the mooring mast. Oh, the humanity!"

The captain strides forward out of view and the Admiral looks up to see me watching him. "Travers! Who else is up there?"

"I've got Jettison, and Milo, and Titus," I reply.

"Good," the Admiral replies. "This lunk won't listen to reason and already sounded the signal for landing positions. You need to get the crew out of the nose. The men in the bow don't stand a chance once this thing goes. They'll be too high to jump and the flames get to them first."

"Where do we send them?"

"Anywhere with an escape path, preferably upwind."

"Which way is the wind blowing now?"

"Port to starboard."

"Okay, got it." I stand and gesture to Jettison. "You coming with me?"

Jettison glances from me to the ladder. "Hey, Admiral, is there a Captain Ernst Lehmann down there?"

The Admiral looks around and then gives Jettison a thumbs up. "He's here. They've got six captains aboard this thing. You believe that? Leave it to the Germans."

"Can you get him out?" Jettison asks.

"I'll put him by a window right now. Leave the control car to me. Get to the rest of the crew!"

"What's the plan for the landing?" I ask.

"Getting on the ground immediately," the Admiral replies. "I'll handle it. Get moving before we run out of time."

Forward of the control gondola we pass more bunks that appear to be crew quarters and a larger single cabin that I assume belongs to an officer. Beyond that the walkway begins to curve upward more steeply. Water and fuel tanks mounted along the walkway slosh gently as the three of us walk by. We locate more crew members in the bow of the ship near coils of rope. They are viewing the ground through observation windows in the hull. Jettison begins speaking to the men with the ropes in halting German and, as we approach, I get my first good look at the ground through the observation windows. The airship has moved into position over the airfield and dozens of men are lined up to assist with the landing ropes. The ground still looks alarmingly far, and I back up a step from the flimsy cellophane window.

The forward momentum of the ship slows even more and nearly stops. A man from farther up in the bow descends through the walkway and calls for the crewmen near the landing ropes to begin deploying them. I notice men on the ground are running toward the ship.

Jettison turns to me. "Sounds like the Admiral must have talked them into landing sooner. They're deploying the spider lines to get us on the ground. We still might beat the clock." He and Milo begin to help the men deploy the huge coils of rope.

A sudden shout comes from above us and the crewman from the bow dashes forward again to investigate. I follow him cautiously up a ladder to a platform in the bow where another crewmember is cradling a young man who has collapsed and is bleeding profusely from his head. I don't understand what they're shouting, but the bleeding man's voice is faltering. He points aft. The crewman assisting him is holding a rag to his friend's forehead to stop the blood. The man I've followed passes them and enters the axial walkway that runs from the nose to the tail. I'm met with suspicious glances from the men on the platform and try to look sympathetic. I gesture toward the walkway. "I'll go check it out. You guys need to get to a place where you can jump." The freckle-faced bleeding man still looks frightened, but I get the impression he's understood me. I can't imagine who would have attacked him, but I suspect it's one of our people. *Tad and Horacio are accounted for. Did he have a run-in with the alien?*

The crewman I'm following blocks most of the view down the walkway. Like the keel passage, there is barely room to walk single file through a triangularly structured frame. I'm obliged to duck at each of the ribs we pass and hold onto the cables to keep from slipping off the narrow footing. We pass directly through the center of the first two donut-shaped gas bags and then encounter a vertical passage with a ladder that runs up to the top of the ship. The man pauses and considers the vertical passage before looking back to me.

"Anybody up there?"

He shakes his head.

Thank God.

"Hey, I'm Ben by the way. Ben Travers."

"Alfred Bernhardt," he replies.

"Good to meet you, man."

"Someone attacked Spehl in the corridor. He said it was just one man."

"Let's go get him then."

Alfred nods and turns his attention back to the walkway. We navigate the passage through the gas bags in a sort of shrouded silence. I can still feel a tiny vibration from the engines in the wires, but all sounds seem distant and muffled. Occasional hisses emanate from the connections between the gas cells as gas is transferred forward or aft. Somewhere ahead and below us, a dog barks. *Did Jonah somehow manage to get Barley on board? What are they up to?*

We've gone hundreds of feet through the center of the ship and just passed into a new gas cell when we reach another vertical passage. Alfred looks up and immediately shouts. I scramble to join him and peer up the ladder shaft at a man who is affixing something to the rigging between the cells. I instantly recognize him as the same hawk-faced man who stabbed Ivan.

Alfred immediately sets a foot on the first rung of the ladder but I grab his shoulder and pull him back. "This guy's bad news. Let me handle it. Get below and get to a window. You're going to need to jump as soon as we're near the ground. Tell whoever you see that we don't have much time."

Alfred hesitates and casts another glance up the ladder, but finally relents. He transfers to the ladder that descends to the lower deck and gives me one last look. "Stop that man."

"I'm on it."

As Alfred vanishes down the ladder, I turn my attention to the saboteur above me. He finishes securing the device to the cable in front of him, then looks down and smiles. He drops the socket wrench in his hand, and I have to dodge out of the way as it clatters to the walkway at my feet. When I look back up, he has removed something else from the pocket of his jacket. He wags the cylindrical device at me. A button on top looks to be a detonator switch. "You want to know what brought down the Hindenburg, Travers? Here you go." He lets go of the device and I flinch, but he catches it again and laughs.

"Why don't you come down here and talk to me about it." I clench my fists and take a step back from the foot of the ladder.

"You'd like that, wouldn't you?" The man gives me an oily grin. "But I think I could use some fresh air." He slips the detonator back into his pocket and begins climbing farther up the ladder.

Son of a bitch.

I hesitate, then climb after him. About halfway up the ladder, I reach the device he has planted. It's a crude box that has been clamped to the cables with steel rings not unlike the ones used for our objective boxes. I examine the clamps to see if there is a way of removing the box quickly. The bolt heads have been intentionally stripped, so even if I were to retrieve the socket wrench, there would be little chance of getting them loose.

Ivan's killer has reached the apex of the ladder and flings open the hatch at the top of the ship. I grit my teeth and follow him, keeping my eyes on his pocket with the detonator. He exits out into the overcast sky above but leaves the hatch open for me. The wind whistles down the hatch and brings droplets of rain.

When I reach the top of the ladder and peek my head out, I'm daunted by the view. The ship stretches ahead in a gradual upward slope that blocks the horizon. Behind me the ship declines another few hundred feet with the exception of the enormous tail fin rising from the structure just a dozen or so yards aft of me. The man ahead of me is walking forward along the top ridge of the airship with casual, arrogant strides. He stops and looks back as he fishes a cigarette from a pack in his jacket, appraising me as he taps the cigarette on the box.

My arms are shaking slightly as I climb out of the hatch and push myself to my feet. I try to disguise my fear as I take a few cautious steps toward him. The man smirks and continues walking. I keep my eyes locked on his angular back and don't look down as the wind pelts me with periodic drizzle and threatens to push me to starboard. The sky beyond the man is full of ominous clouds, and I try not to think about how much static could be building in them, waiting to surge down and electrify the top of the ship. When my quarry reaches the highest point on the airship's back, he turns again and lights his cigarette. I wrestle with options in my mind. *Can I rush him and somehow come up with the detonator?* I glance at the ticking clock on my bracelet and note that I only have minutes left.

"It's about to get real hot up here, Travers. You picked a poor escape route." He gestures toward the massive airship hangar and the rest of the airfield. "Though I'll admit it's quite a view."

"Who are you? What's your game here?" I have to yell over the sound of the wind and the idling engines.

"You signed up for this chronothon. You should know what it's about."

"I didn't sign up for shit and you know it. YOU got me into this. And don't try to tell me this is an ordinary race. I watched you stab a man in the chest!"

"You should mind your business, Ben. It'll be healthier for you." He looks me over and exhales a puff of smoke, shielding his cigarette from the wind with his palm. "Though it doesn't seem like you're going to be the type to do as you're told. Geo seemed to think you'd be smart enough to know when you're out of your league and wouldn't give us trouble. Maybe he underestimated your stupidity."

"You don't have to be a genius to see this game is rigged. I knew I was conned from the start, but how long till the rest of the racers catch on? You going to strong arm all of us into staying? Why? What are you getting from this? You're betting on me to lose, I expect. No surprise there, but you have to kill people to do it?"

There's a yell from somewhere below and I notice we've finally descended low enough to hear the ground crew. Vehicles have deployed more men to aid in securing us to the ground. The tail rises under me from some action by the crew and I stagger to keep my footing. When I get my balance, my enemy has walked closer. His ashen eyes are cold as he appraises me. *I hate that condescending, colorless stare.*

"If you thought your being here was ever about a race, then you're even dumber than I thought. You advance because we say you do. Why is irrelevant. There's no getting out. So do as you're told and maybe, just maybe, we won't kill you. Capish?" He flicks his cigarette at me and pulls the detonator and his lighter from his pocket. "But you don't even die till we say you do, so stop putting yourself on top of pending infernos and making it so goddamn tempting." With his lighter between his fingers, he pushes the sleeve of his jacket up past his wrist to expose a Temprovibe. He depresses the button on the detonator with his free hand. A boom resonates from behind me and hydrogen in the cell aft of the ladder illuminates. I look forward and the man has already vanished. I barely have time to spin the dial on my chronometer and get my hand to the surface of the airship before the cell below mc lights up a terrifying orange. I squeeze the pin and immediately fall backward onto the rain-dappled skin of the airship with my hand still searing from the heat.

"You can cross to other timestreams if you have an anchor from there. If not, you'll have to back up and find the origin of that timestream somewhere in the past before you can follow it forward. I can't promise that time travel won't also be time consuming."–Journal of Dr. Harold Quickly, 2001

Chapter 20

The engine noise is louder again and the ship is moving under the overcast sky. I've only managed to jump back fifteen minutes, but I hope it's enough. I get unsteadily to my feet and stagger back toward the hatch. Besides my scalded hand, I have sharp pains in my legs and abdomen. As the wind continues to fling drizzle from the clouds down around me, I clench my stomach and try not to lose my balance. I've broken one of the cardinal rules of time travel—never make a jump into rain.

The little stinging pains in my body are my reminders of why two objects can't occupy the same space at the same time. I'm lucky that the droplets have been tiny—closer to mist than rain. I don't want to imagine what would have happened had I been fused with heavy drops. I could have them in my eyes or my spine. I mentally flog myself for my stupidity. *But what option did I really have? There are other cardinal rules to time travel. Not getting torched atop the Hindenburg has to fall under one of them, right?*

The hatch is harder to open with my injured hand, but I have too much adrenaline pumping through me to let that slow me down. I close my eyes as I throw my leg into the ladder shaft and feel for the rungs so I won't have to look at the deck below. I open them again as I descend, pausing momentarily at the spot where I know the gray-eyed man will be planting the bomb. *Is there anything I can do to stop him?* I consider my options but realize there is nothing I can do now that won't result in a new timestream or some type of paradox. The original stream would go on and I would accomplish nothing but get myself disqualified in the process.

Under normal circumstances disqualification might sound like a good idea, but after my talk with Ivan's killer, I'm less optimistic of lasting long after. If I'm going to have any hope of figuring out what I'm being used for, I have to stay in the race. As my feet hit the surface of the axial walkway, my other mission occupies my mind. *At least I'm saving people's lives this round. Whatever the committee has in store for me, there will be a few people that will benefit from my being here.* The thought helps dissipate my anger.

I climb down the next ladder, working my way to the keel walkway again. As I drop the last couple of rungs, I survey my surroundings. Just forward of my position are more cabins that I take to be crew quarters. Aft of me the walkway travels another twenty yards and terminates at a ladder that descends even farther. I try to think what could be lower than the keel and, as I walk toward it to investigate, I realize it's the lower tail fin. Voices are coming from the ladder well, and I recognize one as Bozzle. When I lean over the edge of the hole, I find the alien squatting on a platform gesturing to three rather terrified looking crewmembers. A fourth is farther into the fin manning one of the landing lines and casting nervous glances back to his crewmates. I clear my throat and Bozzle stops his dissertation and looks up at me. He's dressed in a sort of burka and has his head wrapped to conceal his horns. His face is exposed below his brow, however, and there is no disguising his dark green skin.

"Hey, man. You doing okay back here?"

Bozzle nods and points to a slightly overweight man in his thirties in an officer's uniform. "This man is a Nazi. I was explaining the effects of his doctrine on this century and how they parallel the attacks of Goosoon Hesperon and his invasion of the Currine Solar System."

The terrified expressions on the crewmen's faces are inadvertently comical, especially the overweight officer, and I can't help but smile at the thought of a devout Nazi suddenly having to explain his worldview to a green-skinned alien from another galaxy.

"How is the lesson going so far?"

Bozzle considers the men before responding. "I think they are very good listeners."

I lean down and smack him on the shoulder with my good hand. "Well, just make sure you all have a way out when we hit the ground so you can continue the lesson after. It's any minute now."

Bozzle points to a hatch at the starboard side of the tail fin. "We have already planned our exit."

"Excellent." I grimace as a twinge of pain stabs my abdomen, but try to ignore it. "Hey, have you seen Jonah yet this round?"

Bozzle gestures toward the front of the airship. "I saw him in the cargo area. Ahead of the sleeping quarters."

"Okay. I'm going to check on him. I'll see you guys outside."

I rub my aching stomach and follow the keel walkway forward again. As I'm passing the crew bunks I feel the momentum of the airship change as it slows and stops. Somewhere up in the bow, another me is watching the crew deploying the landing lines. In a few moments I'll be climbing up the axial walkway to work my way aft. *I don't have much time.* I consider the windowless walkway around me and quicken my pace. Once the gas ignites, the last place I'll want to be is here in the bowels of the ship with no path of escape.

I pass more water ballast and fuel tanks and then find the rear cargo area. My clomping footsteps draw attention and I suddenly find myself being barked at by a German Shepherd in a crate. A familiar snail-shaped helmet pops up from behind a second crate and Jonah appraises me quickly with his bright blue eyes.

"I need your help!"

I join him and watch as he struggles to lift a stuck latch on the second dog's crate. He moves aside for me. "It won't open."

"I'll bet it just needs a little persuading." I position myself squarely in front of the latch and use my non-singed hand to grip the handle. It takes two tries, but the pin finally pops loose. The brindle-coated dog in the crate bounces side to side and barks as I lift the handle. As I swing the door open, the dog bolts for the opening, but I manage to get a grip on its collar and restrain it.

"Nobody was coming to get them," Jonah explains. "They aren't on anybody's list, so I had to save them." He steps over to the German Shepherd's cage and pets the dog's head through the bars.

"Who did you have on your list, Jonah? Did you find them already?"

"Yeah. They were in the engines. That one and that one." He points to opposite sides of the ship. I look the direction he's indicating and notice the lateral passage that splits off the main keel walkway.

"How are they getting out?"

"They said they'd stop the propellers and climb out the hole with a ladder. Then they said thank you for telling them and I said I had to go save the dogs. This one's named Ulla." Jonah pulls the crate door open and the dog lunges forward.

"Wait! Grab its col—"

My warning comes too late and the dog shoots past Jonah's outstretched arms and into the walkway. I stretch to snag its collar as it bounds by, but my fingertips merely graze its fur. The dog vanishes up the corridor heading toward the bow.

"Damn it," I mutter. I lead the other dog over to the walkway.

"We have to go get her!" Jonah exclaims. He begins to pursue the German Shepherd but I grab the back of his shirt.

"No. Whoa, buddy."

He struggles and gestures toward the narrow hallway. "She's going to get lost! We have to save her!"

I turn the boy toward the dog in my hand. "Here. You get a good grip on this one. Get him to your friends in the engine bay. Hold tight to his collar and don't let go. I'll go get Ulla."

"You promise?"

"I promise. We just need to get out of this hallway." I lead the brindle dog and Jonah to the intersection of the lateral walkways and point them toward the port side engine. I make sure Jonah has a good grip on the dog's collar before letting go. "This thing is going to catch fire any minute now. You get down that hallway and, no matter what, you make sure you get clear. Once the fire starts we only have seconds to get out."

"I think it's thirty-six."

"What?"

"Seconds. It takes thirty-six seconds to crash. I looked it up."

"Oh, good. That makes my point then." I step around the boy and dog and let them start working their way toward the engine. "Hurry. I'll see you outside."

"Okay." The boy concentrates on guiding the dog, who seems plenty eager to get out. I watch them reach the upward slope of the walkway and then turn my attention to my own task. I scramble along the corridor past more fuel and water tanks and into another cargo area searching for any sign of the missing dog. This larger cargo area is in the heart of the airship with nothing but aluminum girders and cables in view around it. There are a hundred places a dog could wriggle through if it left the walkway, but no windows or escape routes out of the ship. *Damn dog could be anywhere.* I glance at my chronometer. *Unless I never give it a chance.* I step off the main walkway so I'm out of sight of where Jonah found the crates, and I set my chronometer for a three-minute backward jump. I double-check my setting and push the pin. The jump is barely noticeable. I peek my head around the corner and, along the passage I can just make out the earlier Jonah speaking toward the other me. I only have to wait a few seconds for the German Shepherd to come shooting down the walkway. I stay out of sight till the dog is almost to me, then lunge out and seize it by the scruff of the neck. The dog lets out a surprised little yelp but lets me pull her off the walkway and out of sight without much struggle. I keep my arm around the dog's neck to keep her calm and she licks my face in response.

I lean cautiously toward the walkway and peek at my earlier self trying to get Jonah to take the other dog. "All right, Ulla. That's our cue." The dog licks me again and lets me lead her into the walkway and rapidly toward the bow. Thankfully, the constant curve of the airship's hull reduces the visibility beyond short distances and we are quickly out of potential view from my other self.

We pass a dozen more fluid tanks and a second lateral walkway that leads to the forward engine bays. Beyond that we encounter more spaces that are used by the crew for engineering purposes of some kind. A variety of electrical equipment shares space with some generators, as well as more cargo storage. Beyond that are more crew bunks. I'm grateful to find the spaces vacant, making me believe that the message has been delivered for everybody to get out of the hull.

I'm making my way back into the B deck when a boom resonates through the ship and the walkway rigging shudders. My stomach sinks as the back of the airship plummets and the bow pitches up, forcing me to hang onto the handle of the gangway stairs door.

Holy shit. Here we go!

Screaming erupts from the other side of the door. The tail hits the ground and the ship shudders. I swing the door open and climb forward toward the gangway stairs which have already been lowered. Genesis has pairs of passengers lined up on the stairs ready to run as soon as the ship nears the ground. Ahead in the corridor, the boy I saw putting away dishes in the crew mess has emerged into the hallway. He is gaping back in my direction, and I turn to see what he's looking at and nearly fall over as a thundering ball of fire shoots through the axial walkway and starts consuming the gasbags above us. Ulla bolts out of my hands and leaps between a pair of passengers on the stairs, wriggling her way toward the freedom of the open gangway. She plunges the dozen feet off the end of the stairs and lands in the sandy dirt. The dog crumples to the ground on the landing, but the next moment she's back up and running. Some of the more limber passengers start to follow her example and jump. I scramble forward past the kitchen where more cooks and passengers are leaping from windows and I get suddenly splashed by water from somewhere ahead of me.

Wow that's cold.

One of the water tanks in the bow has come loose and is lying partially in view in the walkway beyond the B deck. The surprise drenching helps me focus on the task at hand. The young boy from the galley has pried open some sort of access hatch in the floor and gestures for me to follow him as he jumps down the hole. The airship is moaning and screeching, and as the bow levels out, I sprint the last couple of yards and leap after him. I land hard in the sand and start to turn to the right, but the boy has just turned around from that way—recognizing that the wind is hurling fire that direction. The bow of the ship bounces on its massive nose tire under the control car, giving us a few extra moments to flee. The boy grabs my arm and helps me to my feet, and we sprint out from under the collapsing hull as it crashes back down, raining melting metal and canvas around us.

I'm in good company as I race out from under the wreck. The officers and the Admiral have fled the control car ahead of me, while thirty-odd passengers and another dozen crew have made it out the main deck windows. Jettison, Milo, and a handful of crew must have found a way out of the bow even before the ship caught fire because they are teaming with ground crew from the air station to help get people free of the wreck. Genesis has cleverly fashioned ropes out of the dining room tablecloths to help people escape the windows. I rush to the aid of a limping elderly couple that she is guiding away from the gangway stairs, throwing the old man's arm over my shoulders and pulling him out from under the massive blaze. As we hustle through the sand, I spot Tad Masterson with a woman hefted over his shoulder moving toward a group of naval sailors. He sets her down in front of them and then turns to look for more. Once I am a safe distance from the blaze, I hand the elderly man in my charge off to some naval crewmen and go back looking for anyone else in need of assistance. Thankfully, there is no one left to save.

Despite the enormity of the hydrogen fire, most of the flames have shot upward with the gas and not outward, giving us enough time to get all the personnel free. The aircraft of course is a total loss. The metal shell of the airship is melting and collapsing from the heat and the fuel tanks have caught fire, sending thick black smoke billowing into the night sky.

As I stand in awe of the sight, a hand rests on my shoulder and I turn to find Jettison standing next to me.

"Not bad, huh Travers?" Jettison's face is smeared with soot and there are burn marks on his suit, but his expression is joyous. "See, this sort of mission I can get with—saving lives and keeping people safe. As soon as we had the bow lines out I had the crew start sliding down them. I think they had a few rope burns, but we were on the ground before the ship was." He slaps my shoulder, then lifts up my wrist and checks my bracelet. "What did you get for a placement?"

The display on my bracelet is blinking an eleven.

"Our objectives registered as soon as our people hit the ground, apparently," Jettison explains. "Total hodgepodge since we were all getting each others' people free, but we passed the level. I figure that's the main thing."

I nod along, but my attention is suddenly distracted by someone in the crowd.

Jettison keeps talking. "All we have to do now is get to the gate and we're good. I think it's near the infirmary. . ."

It's him.

Past a pair of naval sailors and a concerned group of crew is a cluster of other civilians and, standing among them, seemingly without interest in the proceedings, is Ivan's killer. He's staring at the smoking wreck with his hands in his jacket pockets.

Taking in your handiwork, bastard?

I slip away from Jettison without bothering with an explanation and edge my way into the crowd of onlookers. My fists are clenched at my sides and I ignore the pain in my scalded left hand as the anger boils up in me. I keep my eyes locked on my target and work my way past rain-soaked men and women who are conversing in excited tones or staring in shock at the sight of the burning wreck. Just as I'm nearing the man's position, he turns away from the view of the airship and begins walking toward the rest of the airbase. I curse inwardly and follow him, weaving my way among more onlookers who are now crowding onto the airfield.

It's a few hundred yards to the nearest buildings. I hustle over the now muddy terrain at a brisk walk, trying to close the gap between myself and my target. If he has an anchor handy, he can jump clear even with the rain, provided he's arriving somewhere dry, but I hope he won't risk the exposure of making a jump in public. I suspect he's making for a more secluded jump location.

My fingers find my Swiss Army knife in my pocket. It's not much of a weapon, but I palm it in my good hand as I walk, flipping the pointed leather punch open and letting it protrude between the middle fingers of my fist. I try to visualize what I'll do when I catch up to my quarry. *Can I subdue him somehow? Then what? Will anyone on the committee even care that he killed someone?* I consider Milo's suspicion that not all of the committee members can be in on what ever is being rigged in this race. *But how will I know the good ones from the bad?*

As my quarry approaches the buildings next to the airship hangar, I break into a jog. I close some of the ground between us but then have to duck to one side behind a fuel truck when the man suddenly stops and looks around. He seems to be deciding whether to head for the main hangar or one of the smaller outbuildings to the left. I'm peering around the hose reel of the fuel truck and contemplating rushing him, when a hand suddenly closes on my mouth. I jolt and spin around, ready to strike with my makeshift weapon, when I recognize the bright blue eyes and stray blonde curls peeking out from under a mechanic's cap.

"Mym?"

"Shh." She holds a finger to her lips and smiles. "Keep it down."

"What are you—"

She shushes me again and I lower my voice further. "What are you doing here?"

She leans past me and gestures toward the man now walking toward the open airship hangar. "Following him."

"How did you find him? How did—"

She puts her fingers to my lips this time and the sudden touch shuts me up. Despite the fact that she's disguised herself in men's clothing, I'm suddenly aware of her body so close to mine.

Mym smiles and retracts her hand but rests it on my arm. "Geo's not the only one who can play this game. If he wants to track my friends, then I'll track his."

"Did you get my message?"

Her eyes brighten. "Yes. Both of them."

Both? My mind is only on Charlie's murder and the blonde hair in the woods and I don't register what she's talking about until she speaks again.

"So you want to pick up where we left off?" Her smile is playful now and I struggle for a response.

"Oh, yeah. I mean, yeah, do you?"

She grins again. "I guess we'll see." She turns back to the view of the airship hangar. The man we're chasing has just reached the hangar door and vanishes inside.

"Come on. We need to hurry." She dashes out from behind the fuel truck and runs for the hangar.

Despite not making even five and a half feet in height, Mym moves fast. I race to catch up, and I am almost to her, when a pain shoots up my left leg and causes me to lose my footing. I crash to the ground in a heap, smearing mud all over the knees and forearms of my suit. Mym turns around, hurrying back to me. "Are you okay? What happened?"

"Nothing. I just slipped." The pain must still be registering on my face because Mym looks unconvinced. She gives me a hand up and eyes me skeptically. "Are you injured? Did you get hurt getting off the airship?"

I shake my head. "No. I'm just—I had to make a jump in the rain. I think it might have messed me up a little."

Mym's face goes white and she puts both hands on my chest. "Oh my God! How long ago was it? Was it out here?" She looks up at the rain falling from the clouds as if measuring its capacity for injury, then continues to probe my body and face with her hands.

"It was maybe thirty minutes ago, on top of the ship. It wasn't raining this bad though. Just mist really."

"Ben, you should never do that! Don't you know what that could do?"

"Yeah, I—"

"You could burst an artery or cause brain damage or—are you dizzy or anything? Does your head hurt?"

"No just a couple pains in my legs and stomach."

She puts an arm around me and points toward one of the buildings next to the hangar. "Come on. Let's get you out of here."

"Mym, you shouldn't be near me. They're hunting you for Charlie's murder. If they find out you're here—"

"They won't. I've been tracking Traus and keeping an eye on him. He's the one in charge of finding me."

"Who's Traus?"

Mym points toward the main hangar. "Traus. The guy you were following? His name's Traus Gillian."

"I never knew his name. So wait, *you're* following *him*?"

Mym smiles, "Last place they'd expect me to be. Plus it's turning out pretty well, right?" She squeezes my hand. "He led me to you."

"Yeah, that part's good. The part where he's killing people is less awesome. Mym, I'm not sure you should be anywhere near this guy. He's bad news. How did you even find him?" I limp my way forward as fast as I can manage.

"When you ended up in this race, I was mad, but I wanted to find out why. I went back to New York and found the homeless guy you saw. Only of course he wasn't homeless. It was Traus. I ended up following him to Ireland and saw him kill Charlie. That was before I got your messages, so I didn't know they were going to blame me yet, but I figured it out pretty quick. One of the committee members had tried to track me through the woods, and when I got your message, it all made sense."

"I saw you. In the woods."

"I know. I saw you, too."

I recall the image of the blonde hair disappearing into the woods and the bloody body at my feet. "I'm so sorry about Charlie. I know he was close to your dad."

"I'm sorry, too," Mym replies. "But not as sorry as Traus is going to be."

We make it under the awning of one of the air station buildings. The door is unlocked and we enter to get out of the damp. The block building contains offices and has been emptied of personnel by the sudden disaster. We duck into a room that contains a bank of filing cabinets, a broad oak desk, and a handful of chairs. Mym clears a space on the corner of the desk and places an item from her pocket gently on the wood. The knob wobbles briefly as she lets go. It's a tarnished brass piece that might be from a drawer or cabinet. It seems to match the era we're in rather well. Mym draws her chronometer pendant from her shirt and dials in a destination from the back of a photo of the knob.

"Don't move. I'll be right back." She places a finger to the knob and vanishes. She's back within seconds carrying a satchel. The anchor clatters to the floor at my feet as she slides the satchel onto the desk.

I bend and pick up the displaced hardware, setting it back. "Where does this take you?"

Mym is rummaging through the satchel and pulls a device out that looks like a remote control. "Dad has a place here in the thirties. It's in Massachusetts, but that's not far, considering." The next item she extracts looks like a shower curtain, but as she unfolds it I notice it's a much thinner, translucent material.

"You need to put this on," she says.

"What is it?"

"It's going to help us scan you."

I fumble with the transparent sheet. "What, just throw it over myself?"

"Yeah, make sure it goes all the way to the floor."

I slip out of my muddy jacket and toss it to the floor, then do as she asks and arrange the material over me. When I have it situated, I feel like a kid in a homemade ghost costume. Mym points the remote at me and the material illuminates.

"Try not to move."

"Is this like some kind of MRI?"

"Stop talking."

I shut my mouth and stand still for the next ten seconds.

"Okay. We're done. Fold that back up."

I slip the sheet off my head and do my best to refold it. "What's the prognosis, doctor?"

Mym is studying data on a tablet like Jettison's and her mouth turns down while a crinkle of concern appears between her eyebrows. I'm suddenly worried. "Is it bad?"

Finally Mym looks up. "It's not so bad. Definitely not great, but it could have been a lot worse." She flips the screen around and steps closer so I can see what she's looking at. The image is an outline of my body with the tissue highlighted in different colors ranging from greens to yellows and a few pixels worth of orange. She zooms in on one of the orange areas and narrows down to a tiny spot of red. "This looks like the worst in your leg. You had a pretty big droplet fused into the tissue of your calf right near this nerve cluster. Those cells look destroyed. That's probably where you felt the pain. Is there something wrong with your hand? It's showing damage to your surface tissue."

"I got a little burned, but I don't think it's bad."

Mym eyes my hand before checking it again on the screen. She zooms back out and runs her finger around the rest of the image. "You have a couple specs in your shoulder blades, a few in your abdominal tissue and looks like another one in your right femur."

I can't help but notice that the scan shows all areas of my anatomy, but as it's displaying only the insides, it's slightly less embarrassing. Even so, I'm grateful when she closes the image and turns her attention back to the real me.

"You got lucky."

"So I'm gonna be okay?"

"I didn't see anything that would cause hemorrhaging, or anything in your brain. That's good news. Though the decision to jump in the rain in the first place may suggest something else wrong with you."

I'm again aware of our close proximity. Mym seems to notice, too, but she doesn't move away. She lays the tablet on the desk and puts her hand on my arm.

"It would be easier to not worry about you if I could trust you to not do stuff like this."

"So you worry about me?"

Mym narrows her eyes, but her lips still hint at a smile. "Somebody has to. Look what happens when you go off on your own."

"Then don't leave me alone." I slip my hand to her waist, watching to see how she'll react. She eases closer to me.

"How many days has it been for you? Since . . ." her voice trails off softly.

"Five. They've been long days though. How long has it been for you?"

"Two weeks."

"Too long." I incline my head closer to hers.

"It was." She lifts her face toward mine and we linger there with our lips centimeters apart. The tip of her nose grazes mine. "Ben, I'm—"

I press my lips to hers and the rest of her words are lost in the kiss. Mym's other hand finds my stomach and my arms encircle her, one hand tracing up her back to the softness of her neck. She leans into me and her cap drops to the floor, her hair falling over my hand at the back of her head. Her lips part around mine and I breathe in the subtle scent of her. She smells like orange blossoms and a little like rain. I pull her to me till there is no space left between us. Her hands find my face and, as our lips separate from one another's, she keeps her hands there, staring into my eyes as if trying to read my thoughts. One of her fingertips touches my bottom lip.

"I thought about this."

"Just once?"

She laughs and strokes the side of my face, brushing over the week's worth of stubble, then tracing a finger around my ear and up into my hair. "Maybe more than once." Our lips find each other again and I let my hands glide down the outline of her. I lean and scoop her up onto the edge of the desk. Her eyes open and watch mine as I set her down, and her lips are smiling while still kissing me. Her eyelids settle back over the radiant blue of her gaze and we go back to our other senses, letting our bodies find their own way around one another. When I finally pull my face away from hers, she has her legs wrapped around the backs of mine, and her hands tarrying on my chest. She leans her head back, letting her arms drop to the desk behind her. She settles back on them but keeps her legs locked around mine.

"You're full of surprises, Benjamin Travers."

"As long as they're good ones." I reach my right hand out and she lifts one of hers to it, letting our fingers intertwine. We stay that way, relishing the newness of the moment and the anticipation of whatever is to come.

There is a clatter from the hallway as someone rushes past the door to one of the other offices. Mym glances at the door then slowly untangles her legs from around me, sliding off the desk to her feet.

"We shouldn't stay here." She packs her belongings into the satchel and hoists it over her shoulder. She slips past me to the door, so I scoop up my jacket and her fallen cap and follow. She pauses before opening it and extracts another device from her pocket. This one is only the size of a mobile phone, but I recognize it as the multi-function device she uses to calculate her jumps. "Traus looks like he's already gone. I wanted to see if he met anyone here, but I don't want to blink back and check now." She speaks toward the MFD as if thinking aloud. "There's no way of knowing who was where before the crash. It's too dangerous to free-jump something without a photo here, and I'll find him anyway."

"You have a way of tracking Traus?"

Mym looks back to me. "Yeah. Dad helped me with it. He figured out a way to find a person's timestream signature in the data used by the Temprovibes. I had to get close enough to Traus to get a reading from a temporal spectrometer on him, and I had to match that to the serial number of his specific Temprovibe. That wasn't easy, but once I did, we had enough to go on. Every Temprovibe transmits info through the Grid to a central data processor owned by Digi-Com. I couldn't pick up any of his signals farther back than the Grid satellite system has transmitters, but now I can track him anywhere from 1800 on in most timestreams."

"There have been satellites in orbit since 1800?" I follow Mym out the door into the hall.

"No. Well, some actually. Time travelers have launched satellites for personal use in a lot of times, but the actual Grid system doesn't start functioning till the late twenty-first century. Digi-Com uses transmitters that can relay data forward in time to keep their customers safe. Takes power though, and the lack of reliable electricity is a problem in earlier centuries. Dad tuned our tachyon pulse transmitter to intercept the company's Temprovibe frequencies and track Traus. He was too far out of range of my chronometer to chase till now, but from here I know where he's going."

"Where?"

"According to the data from his Temprovibe, he jumps to 2156 and visits the Academy of Temporal Sciences."

"I'd bet that's where the next gate will take me." I fish the paperwork from my objective box out of my pocket and look through it. On the back of the schematic of the airship I find a small map of the airfield. The time gate symbol is behind the airship hangar and has a note next to it that reads, PROXIMITY TRIGGER. I cycle through the modes of my race bracelet's display till I find my ranking number. It still shows an eleven, but the number isn't flashing. *It must open when I get close.*

Mym pauses by the front door of the office building, glances outside briefly, then shuts the door again. "It's probably best if we split up from here." She rummages in her bag and pulls out another anchor. This one is a golf-ball-sized geode that's been split in half to reveal the violet crystals inside. She shows me a matching photo of it and places both in my hand. "This is how you can find me at the Academy. We'll meet in the minerals wing of the science center. Do you still have your degravitizer?"

"Not on me, but it's with the rest of my stuff."

"Get it back and come find me." She puts her hand to my chest and rises up on her toes. Our lips meet again and she lingers there, clenching the front of my shirt in her fingers. When she drops back down she's smiling. "You'd better miss me when I'm gone."

I flop her cap back onto her head. "I'm starting right now."

Her fingers find mine and we grasp them together one last time before our hands slip reluctantly apart. Mym tucks her hair up under the cap and slides out the door. I wait thirty seconds before following. Outside there's no sign of her, but I can't help glancing around as I make my way toward the back of Hangar One. A grin breaks out on my face, and I have to concentrate in order to force a more appropriate expression. A few other pedestrians pass me. Most are Americans from the naval base, but I spot some of the survivors from the airship too. A few are wearing bandages on their hands or their heads, but even so, the atmosphere around the base seems lighthearted and even cheery. The news that everyone has survived the disaster seems to have spread.

THE CHRONOTHON

I locate the time gate at the back of the airship hangar and find that it's simply a plain doorway leading into the interior. *This must be where Traus was heading.*

I open the door and a beep comes from my bracelet. The air in the doorway shimmers and, despite the fact that I can still see the interior of a hangar in 1937, I know I'm headed somewhere completely unknown. I hesitate with my hand still on the doorknob, and consider the fact that I'm about to step beyond everything I've ever known.

Despite all the dangers I've faced traversing the past, there was something familiar about traveling through history. Now I'm facing a total question mark, the realm of my competitors, and at least one enemy who has been clear that he'll not hesitate to kill me. Options flit through my brain. I could still slam this door and make a run for it. They would find me eventually, but I could put up a fight.

I watch the colors shift and change in the light and my bracelet begins to beep faster. My mind finally settles on one clear thought. *It's not all unknown. She'll be there.*

I step into the doorway and let the future swallow me up.

"Once the invention of time travel became public knowledge, I feared an eruption of timestreams as everyone rushed to be a part of it. It didn't quite happen that way. Lots of people doing it wrong and dying of stupidity probably helped with that. It's the only time I've been grateful for idiots."–Journal of Dr. Harold Quickly, 2130

Chapter 21

A small, freckled man is beaming at me. He's young, not more than nineteen or twenty from the look of him. His giddy smile makes him seem even younger. He bobs forward from behind a control panel and bounces up a couple steps to seize my hand.

"You made it!" He energetically pumps my arm before spreading his other hand out to the space around us. "Welcome to platform thirty-seven! I'm Tucket."

I glance around the glass-enclosed room. Natural light is streaming from clear panes above us and from the circumference of the room. Viznir is behind the bank of controls that the young man came from, but his expression is far less joyful. He looks annoyed about something.

"Hi, Tucket. I'm Ben—"

"Ben Travers. I know!" Tucket interjects. "Such an honor to meet you. I've been waiting for you—I mean, we've been waiting for you." He gestures to Viznir and possibly the entire outdoors.

He straightens up and concentrates. "Are you . . . DOG TIRED . . . or um WIPED OUT from your trip?" He watches my face intently.

"Um. I'm okay, I think." I extract my hand from his grasp and look toward Viznir for some explanation of who this person is. Viznir merely clenches his jaw and shakes his head.

Tucket sallies onward unabashedly. "I've been assigned by the academy as your acclimation host. It's school policy to meet new temporal travelers on arrival and make sure they're adjusted. You being part of a chronothon is a special case, yeah? But we still wanted to do it. I put in an application last year and I'm a third year trainee, so I got to pick my favorite racer, so of course I picked you." Tucket grins again. "Cause I'm studying twenty-first century timestreams for my thesis, you know?"

"That sounds great, Tucket." I step around him toward Viznir. "I really appreciate that."

"Yes. It was a NO BRAINER, right? A no brainer? You say that where you're from, right? I've been excited to use my language training with a real life Jehitles."

I pause on the steps. "A what?"

"A Jehitles, like you." Tucket blinks at me, then smacks himself in the side of the head. "Oh sorry. You wouldn't say that. That's just the name we have here for your timestreams. You've got Jewish Jesus, right?"

"Were there other options?"

"Oh yeah. There was Chinese Jesus and Detroit Jesus, well actually his name was Jamal then, but messiahs are big for a culture's development, and you had that guy Hitler, right? He was a sort of bad guy, I guess."

"Bit of an understatement, but yeah. I guess you could classify—"

"See that's what I thought. I told my alternate history professor that and she said—"

"Wait, you guys didn't have Hitler?"

"No, not usually. A lot of early time travelers thought it was good to kill him. They seem to take him out right away for some reason, or sometimes they made it so he was never born, but it made some big changes. It started the Soviet States of Eurasia. That lasted a long time, but you never get the other defining characteristic of your time. You guys had The Beatles."

"The Beatles altered history that much?"

"Maximum alterations. They were the biggest influence on my favorite band, Avocado Problems."

"Ha. That's funny. You know I actually just saw them the other day."

"You saw Avocado Problems?"

"No, The Beatles."

"Oh wow. Yeah, they were cool, but I really think AP's new album does some—"

Viznir clears his throat.

"Yeah, we should probably get going here, Tucket," I say. "We do have a race to compete in."

Tucket bobs his head. "Oh, right. I bet you guys want your objective. The race officials said I should give it to you right away." He looks back and forth between Viznir and me. Finally Viznir speaks.

"So where is it?"

Tucket blinks again, then jumps. "Right! Mine bad, guys." He marches between us and out the glass doors onto the rooftop balcony of what I now realize is a very tall building. The clear blue sky around us does in fact contain clouds but they are lower than the top of the building.

As I cautiously approach Tucket's position, I get a better sense of where we are. Our arrival gate is in the penthouse of an enormous skyscraper. Its elevation is significantly higher than even my sojourn atop the Hindenburg.

"Doesn't anyone on this race committee believe in doing things on the ground?"

Viznir ignores my outburst and follows Tucket to a table that holds our packs and begins putting his on. I join him and rummage through mine, pushing items out of the way until I find Mym's degravitizer. I feel immediately relieved when my fingertips brush the cool metal and I have to resist the impulse to start degravitizing Mym's anchor right away.

"Here is your objective. That box is pretty GROOVY, huh?" He hands me the container.

"Sure. Thanks, man." I wave my bracelet over the box till I hear it click open. Viznir is watching intently. "So how long were you here waiting for me?"

Viznir frowns. "Not long. Just long enough for the committee to tell me they bumped the guides forward a level."

"Did you hear where they sent us?"

"The Hindenburg, right?"

"Yeah. It was pretty crazy. We had to get the people—"

"We should probably concentrate on this level," he says.

We stare at each other for a moment and his eyes drop back to our objective box.

"Yeah, sure. Whatever." I yank the lid open and extract a tablet like I've seen Gen and Jettison use.

"Oh wow. Haven't seen one of those in a long time!" Tucket is at my shoulder in an instant. "I guess that makes sense since you don't have a meta-space ID. That's cool, though. My cousin had to have his Third Eye removed because of a medical condition and he uses something like this now. It's a pretty common disability. Nothing to be ashamed of or anything." He smiles reassuringly and glances back to the tablet. He points toward the single irregular bump on the face of the screen. "Even has a button. Nice antique touch."

I press the button and the screen illuminates with three-dimensional depth. Tucket's head is immediately in my way, ogling the screen. "So historical. I can see why people like the chronothons. All this nostalgia and—"

I side-step the view of his cranium. "Hey Tucket, you mind if we have a minute here? It's kind of a confidential thing, race stuff, you know?"

Tucket bobs back in front of me and laughs. "Got carried away there! No BIGGIE guys. Right? NO WORRIES! I'm gonna be over here and I'll

CHILLAX while you guys get all jiggle with that stuff."

Viznir stares straight ahead with an expression that I now recognize as suppressed violence.

"Thanks, Tucket."

I skim through the information on the 3D display. Despite my lack of familiarity with the technology, I'm able to navigate through the data quickly. The image seems to intuitively know where I'm looking and brings up information I want to see without effort. The rest I can specify with simple movements of my hand or taps of the screen. A virtual envelope with my name on it opens and displays a 3D blueprint of a machine containing multiple vials of fluid. I scrutinize it briefly, then show it to Viznir. "What am I looking at here?"

Viznir takes the tablet and is able to pull up a text description of the device. "It's a medical containment unit. Looks like it disperses something, too." He zooms in farther on one side of the blueprint. "This is what we have to get, right here." I lean in and study the component. It's a ball of perhaps five inches in diameter. I have no idea what it does, but the description reads "Gravitan stabilizer."

What is a gravitan?

Viznir pulls up a location for the object and it's listed as a particle physics lab, Building 1701. According to the map on the screen, we're miles away.

"Hey Tucket, you know a quick way to the particle physics lab?"

Tucket grins. "Sure. Do you need the meta-lab or the physical lab?"

"Physical lab," Viznir replies.

My curiosity gets the better of me. "What's a meta-lab?"

"It's in the meta-space," Tucket replies. "It's enhanced, like in your century when technology first became able to link with other technology. 'Smart technology,' I think you called it. It's like that, but the whole environment."

"So virtual reality?"

"It's more than that," Viznir says.

"You've seen it?"

Viznir nods. "All the testing for guides now happens in the meta-space. It's less dangerous. The students here all learn in meta environments, too."

"So where are the actual classrooms?" I ask.

"We don't have physical classrooms," Tucket says. "You can enter the meta-space from anywhere and attend a class from wherever you are."

"So what about this lab? That's still a real place, right?" I gesture toward the tablet.

"Oh sure. It's on the other side of the channel though. We'll need to take the tunnel." Tucket leads the way around the side of the glass-paneled control room and we follow him into an elevator. He doesn't speak or press any buttons when we enter, but we are suddenly plummeting down the side of the building. I back against the interior wall and stare at my feet because the view out the elevator's window shows us dropping hundreds, if not thousands of feet. I sneak occasional peeks at the view as we descend. As we sink below the puffs of cumulus clouds, the view opens up to water in the distance and a cityscape below us.

"Where are we? What city is this?"

"This is London. 2156." Tucket smiles at the view. "But we'll be in France in a few minutes, that's where the physics lab is."

I manage to keep my eyes on the view a little longer now and check out the landscape of the twenty-second century. The buildings of London are immense and towering but elegant and beautiful at the same time. The architecture seems to favor windows and I see terraces full of plants on many of them. "Are those gardens?" I point to one particularly green building.

"That's an urban farm. The city is fully self-sustaining in its agricultural production and consumption. We harvest eighty percent of food for the local population and the other twenty gets exported or put back into the ground for next year's crops."

"That sounds fantastic."

"It is. We've been able to reduce the waste of food to under two percent. Almost everything gets recycled back through the system. One of these urban farm towers could be self-sufficient and feed five thousand people for a hundred years with produce to spare."

I marvel at the outside of the building as we continue our descent. "I notice there are no flying cars. That's a bit of a let-down."

"Oh. They exist. You could use one if you really wanted, but not many people do. Most people work through the meta-space now and do most of their traveling that way, too. Getting to actual places in the physical world stopped being as big of a priority. You can see and experience eighty-five percent of the planet on the meta-space now. I've been climbing Mt. Everest in my health program this month. Feels great."

"I could see looking at stuff in a virtual reality, but what about actually touching and smelling things? Physical touch. Don't people get lazy and fat, interacting by computer all day?"

I know Tucket is trying not to be condescending, but I can't help feeling talked down to as he slowly tries to explain himself. I can tell he's trying to simplify his vocabulary and make things easy on me.

"You see, all the things you smell and taste and hear are processed through your brain. Once scientists mapped the human brain in detail, they were able to trigger corresponding senses for the experience of the metaspace. So now you can smell flowers, eat dinner, even—what is it you say in your day? Get your freak on?"

I cringe. "Tucket, I appreciate you trying to use the vernacular from my time, but you can just use regular English if you want. It's cool how into slang phrases you are but—"

"Did I say it wrong?" Tucket's face falls. "I always get that one confused with just getting it on? And there's 'doing the nasty,' and something about a horizontal mambo . . ."

"Tucket! It's fine." I laugh. "You can just skip that bit. I get it."

"Okay. Right, so people don't feel like they're missing out by not going as many places." The elevator doors open and we exit into a spacious lobby, teaming with citizens. "But we can still get around fast if we need to." We follow Tucket to a turnaround for vehicles at the side of the lobby. People are coming and going from aerodynamic driverless vehicles that pull up to the curb and vanish smoothly back into traffic once they've dropped their passengers. A few seem designated to certain persons, but many drop off passengers only to take on different ones. I judge them to be the equivalent of cabs. I find I'm only partly correct. As we pile inside the plush interior of a shiny blue one, Tucket explains that they are actually owned by the city and are a form of free mass transit. Tucket sits facing backward and spends a brief moment with a control panel in the car, but I never see him touch anything before we speed off into the flow of other traffic.

"How are you doing that?" I lean forward to look at the screen. "I get that you guys don't need tablets or computers now, but how are you accessing this meta-space? You said something about a third eye?"

"That's just the name of one company, but the label stuck. Third Eye came up with the most common type of perceptor."

"What's a perceptor?"

"It's the unit in here." Tucket points to his forehead. "It's tiny. Just a means of receiving data and transmitting it to your brain."

"Like some kind of chip? Everybody gets computers in their brains? How did anyone ever agree to that?" The world outside begins to whip past at increasingly rapid speed.

"It's not a computer. It's hardly even hardware at all. The preceptor is just a key to access the meta-space slipped under your skin. Most kids get them put in as toddlers so they can have access to educational data. Parents can control what type of setting the perceptor uses and kids graduate to an adult version once they hit sixteen. Some parents authorize it earlier, but most wait till then. Keeps them out of trouble a little longer. Not that kids these days haven't found ways around that."

Tucket smiles at me. "I can see how the idea would seem foreign to you, but here it makes perfect sense. It's not just about work or travel. You can use your perceptor to check your health, know exactly what is going on inside your body, even optimize your diet. Since the global acceptance of the perceptor, average life expectancy has gone up to one hundred and twenty. Actually, our world's oldest citizen is from around your time. I want to say she was born in 2006. That's just local citizens on official record. There are time travelers who have lived longer."

The car rockets along the elevated highway in a chain of other vehicles all likewise driverless and moving at incredible speeds. The walls of the highway block the view almost completely, but the bit of scenery I can make out is a blur anyway. The only landscape I can see is the green of some fields and the distant hint of coastline. After a few more minutes of rocketing along, the cluster of cars we're with shifts lanes in formation and takes an exit, dropping below the highway and plunging into a tunnel. The vehicles tighten up till we're almost touching and the group picks up speed again. The lights on the tunnel walls blend into a solid streak as the speed indicator on the control screen creeps past 400kph. My good hand is tightly clenched to my armrest and I force myself to loosen my grip. *Holding on won't help you at this speed, Ben.*

Viznir is fiddling with his tablet. "The academy teams will have their own anchors to use here. They'll know their way around, too. We're not likely to catch them in this level."

"Do they have perceptors in their heads?" I ask.

"Definitely," Viznir replies. "Most of the racers from this century do."

I consider this new information. "Does that mean you have one? You're from this century, aren't you?"

Viznir looks me in the eye, then drops his gaze back to his tablet. "It's a requirement for new guides."

Since no more information seems forthcoming, I drop the topic and watch the blur of tunnel outside. I can't help but wonder where Mym is at this moment. *How long did it take her to make it to the 2150s? Days? Weeks?* The thought of Traus Gillian hunting her makes me fidget in my seat.

"How long till we reach this lab?"

Just as I finish speaking, the car emerges into sunlight. The cars ahead of us pull away and our car shears off to an exit, decelerating as we round a bend into another densely urban landscape.

"Have you ever been to Northern France?" Tucket asks.

"Actually, yeah. A couple days ago, but it looked a bit different."

The car stops in a central square bustling with pedestrians. The air is warm and the locals are dressed in light fabrics that suit the heat. A hundred and thirty years has had its effect on fashion. While I still see a few men and women in business suits, ties seem to have gone out of style and most of the passersby are minimal in their clothing and accessories, though sun hats seem to have revived in popularity. A few women are carrying small bags, but most people seem entirely unencumbered. Many don't even seem to have pockets. It makes me wonder how out of touch I must look, standing on the sidewalk in my suit from the 1930s. I shrug out of my jacket and roll it up, squatting to stuff it into my pack, and roll my sleeves up to my elbows. In the sunlight, my left hand looks decidedly red. I flex my fingers and attempt to make a fist. The skin of my palm is tender, but the damage doesn't appear to be deep, more in the nature of a sunburn. As I straighten up and turn around, I almost collide with a man in a blue skin-tight uniform. He dodges me deftly and steps around me without pausing.

"Whoa, sorr—"

I watch the man breeze along his way with a liquid gait that seems to emphasize that he doesn't have a care in the world. Then I notice the back of his bald skull has a logo stamped on it. I nudge Tucket and point toward the man's retreating form. "Was that—"

"A synthetic person? You bet." Tucket grins.

"We need access to that building." Viznir points across the plaza to another lofty structure that's sparkling with colored glass built on the edge of some type of channel or river. He leads the way and I hurry to catch up, looking side to side to try to spot more of the 'synthetic people.'

"So they're what? Like A.I. or robots?"

Tucket raises a finger. "They actually prefer to be called synthetic persons. The name 'Artificial Intelligence' has a negative connotation suggesting that it is of less quality as non-artificial things. The synths prefer to be treated as equals."

"So they're obviously self-aware. That didn't create problems? There was no robot uprising or anything like people worried about?" My mind is full of images from *The Terminator,* but this immaculate environment with its well-dressed citizens couldn't be farther from the skull-crushing tanks rolling rampant in that film.

"There actually has been quite a fight, socially speaking. Lots of organics had trouble recognizing synths as people. The trans-humans have a bit easier of a time because they are mostly organic, but there is a fair amount of tension there also, especially in less urban areas of the world."

"What's a trans-human?" I keep my voice low, not sure if any of the people walking by can hear me.

"Humans who have had their natural functions augmented with synthetic parts."

"Like cyborgs?"

Tucket titters a little at this and wags his finger again. "That's another word you don't really want to use these days."

I study more of the pedestrians. The bald one with the logo on his skull had been fairly obvious, but I now notice more subtle variation in certain people's skin textures and it makes me wonder if they are also synths. To my surprise, a pair of completely chrome-bodied figures cuts through the crowd ahead of me, holding hands and laughing. Despite the human gesture of affection, they are otherwise not making any attempts to disguise themselves.

"Do you have synthetic friends, Tucket?"

"Most of my coworkers in the Academy Acclimation Division are synthetic. I'm friends with lots of them. My girlfriend is synthetic, too."

I stop walking at this one, but Tucket breezes onward without noticing and I have to trot to catch up again. My mind is still trying to process the concept of dating a robot when Viznir brings us to a halt. He leans back and points toward the sky. "This whole building is it."

The glittering spire of the Academy Physical Sciences Lab has only one visible entrance. A spacious multi-story lobby can be viewed through the plate glass wall. From there it climbs hundreds of feet past the scattered clouds and terminates in a peak I can't make out.

"I don't suppose there's any chance they keep this machine in the lobby?"

Viznir starts walking toward the entrance while I retrieve the tablet I was given and look for more details on my objective. The entrance doors open automatically for us, and we cross a textured metallic floor that's broken up by four live trees in sunlit patches of earth. We pass between the trees to a bank of elevators. Just before the doors, a woman is seated at a guard stand. She's wearing a uniform with a badge but doesn't appear to be armed.

As we approach the guard stand, the woman rises to greet us. She smiles and addresses Tucket. "Good afternoon, Tucket Morris. Good afternoon, Viznir Najjar. Welcome to the Academy of Temporal Sciences Physical Science Center. Access to this building requires authorization from the ATS physical sciences faculty." Her white teeth and porcelain skin are flawless. She beams at the other guys but doesn't look in my direction.

"We're looking to visit the particle physics department," Viznir says.

"Access to the particle physics department requires authorization from the ATS physical sciences faculty. Visitors are permitted to enjoy the lobby and may schedule tours of approved lab spaces via our meta-space facility."

Noting that the woman still has not addressed my presence, I take a casual step to the side and ease toward the elevator. The guard doesn't make any move to stop me.

"How does a visitor view the physical lab space?" Viznir asks.

"Access to the particle physics department requires authorization from the ATS physical sciences faculty . . ." I tune her out and continue to the elevators. The doors of the center elevator stand open, so I poke my head inside and look around. Checking the walls, I notice a distinct lack of buttons. I can't locate a way to activate the elevator, so I wander back out and look around. There are entrances to a men's, ladies', and some other option's restrooms, and a ring of couches around a fountain. Otherwise, the lobby is lacking in features. I meander back to Tucket and nudge Viznir, who is still attempting to get information from the guard.

I jerk my head toward the door and they follow me back outside. Viznir is scowling, but Tucket seems pleased with the whole process, or possibly just life in general.

"So what was that all about in there?" I ask, when we're clear of the automatic doors and I'm fairly certain the guard can no longer hear us. "No access available."

Tucket is still smiling. "Oh no. They don't allow visitors into the facility. It's for faculty and scientists and a few select students who earn access through their studies."

"And you're not far enough along in your studies by chance—"

"No. I'm part of the temporal sciences department. They do control some floors in this building, but I won't get access. Maybe someday if I decide to come back to teach or do a doctorate . . ."

"So you have any idea how we're supposed to get in?"

Tucket's smile fades a little. "Don't you guys have a plan? I figured you would have a strategy since you're chronothon racers and everything."

He waits expectantly as I scan the outside of the building and then look back into the lobby at the lady guard. She's gone back to her desk and is staring off beyond the pair of trees to her left.

"I do have a plan, actually."

"Which is?" Viznir asks.

"She was a synthetic, right?"

Tucket nods.

"Did you notice how she only spoke to the two of you? What was that about? What do I look like to a synth? Do I look different in the meta-space?"

Tucket blinks once and his eyes take on a slightly distant stare. "Oh. You're right. You show up as a living entity, but you're not highlighted as a person. You could be a pet or a tree."

"If the security guard is constantly viewing the world through the meta-space, does that mean I may be able to bypass other security measures as well?"

Viznir frowns. "But without you having a perceptor to view the meta-space, they don't even need security to keep you out. All they need to do is shut the door and hide the handle in the digital ether. You're about the same threat as a tree or a dog at that point anyway."

"That's true, but I can find my way past a few doors. It worked on the pirate ship, right?"

"How will you even get past the elevator?"

"There have to be fire stairs somewhere. Building this size ought to have multiple, unless your fire safety measures are massively different this century."

Tucket tilts his head. "Our fire protection devices are nearly flawless, but you're right. We do still have stairs." He leans back and looks up the massive building. "I don't know many people who use them though."

"Good. Probably less security then." I root through my pack to find my sneakers and a change of clothes. "You guys stay here. I'll be right back."

I breeze through the lobby toward the men's room and the guard never looks up. I ditch my suit in one of the bathroom stalls to lighten my pack and unroll the smaller shoulder bag Abraham gave me. I stuff it with Quickly's journal and Abe's tools, followed by Mym's anchor and degravitizer. Milo's power supply and my charger make the cut, and I place the tablet with my objective info inside also. I bundle the stuff I don't need back into my pack and heft it onto my shoulder.

I reemerge into the heat of the outdoors more comfortably outfitted in jeans and a t-shirt and hand my pack to Viznir. "Hold onto that for me." I bend down and tighten the laces on my sneakers.

Tucket seems genuinely in awe of the plan. "You're really going to try to take the stairs? I looked it up. The particle physics lab is on the 118th floor."

"Unless you've got some jet-pack available that you haven't told me about yet. Do you guys have any better options right now?"

Viznir stares up the side of the building. "That's going to take a while. What do you want us to do while we're waiting for you?"

"If I can, I'll travel back to a little after now once I get to where the objective is, that way you won't have to wait as long. See if you can figure out which side of the building I'll be on. The objective won't have any gravitites in it so I won't be able to jump it out by anchor, but maybe I can drop it out to you somehow. We'll have to figure that part out." I pull the tablet out of my satchel and hand it to Tucket. "Show me how to work this thing. With all this fancy stuff on here, it has to have a phone somewhere, right?"

Tucket walks me through how to access the tablet's different functions. He locates his own I.D. and Viznir's and puts them in the corner of the screen so I only have to tap them, then shows me the camera and the 3D map. He is about to go into more advanced functions, but I stop him. "That should be enough to get me through."

I reach for the device, but he pulls away. "Wait. This is different . . . I wonder . . ." He gestures to something on the screen and grins. "It is! It's a meta-space window." He turns the tablet back to me and holds it up so I can see it. "They did give you a way to view the meta-space. You'll just have to look through this."

I take the tablet and scan it around the plaza. People and synths are highlighted with tags above their heads like a video game. I use the zoom functions at the side of the screen and can navigate in and out of the three dimensional space. Messages and art adorn the ground and walls. Even the sky is full of information. I play with some of the symbols and one de-clutters the screen, eliminating ads and highlighting new objects. Another symbol causes velocities and trajectories to appear around all the moving objects and people, predicting their paths and even recommending a route for me to take if I should like to navigate the plaza.

A child flings a toy into the air and it sprays a fan of light, whirling in brilliant colors through the sky. The spinning disk leaves a rainbow in its wake as it arcs away from the child, but the item is suddenly highlighted in orange and then red as it nears me. The disk skips off the ground a few yards away and skids to a stop at my feet. I stoop to pick it up. In reality, it's merely a flat, blue ring made of plastic or nylon, nearly identical to the long range Frisbees of the twenty-first century.

I study the disk briefly before tossing it back to the little girl, who shrieks joyfully and catches it. Her mother waves to me and guides her daughter back toward a less populated area of the plaza. Beyond the mother and daughter, I spot the vendor selling more of the Frisbees as well as dozens of other toys and doodads. The cart looks tame to the naked eye, even boring, but when I hold the tablet up I see the full onslaught of the man's marketing. The air above his cart is flashing different colors like the Frisbee and his name hovers over him. Firell's Fireworks and Toys. Every few seconds a colorful firework launches out of his stand and explodes. I lower the tablet and observe the undisturbed sky above him.

"So you guys can see this stuff all the time?" I turn back to Viznir and Tucket.

"I turn most of it off," Viznir replies. "You can view just the necessities if you want."

I look through the screen and press the de-clutter symbol a few more times and much of Firell's marketing fanfare disappears, leaving only his business name hanging over his cart. I lower the tablet and turn to Viznir. "You have any money from this century? I want one of those Frisbees."

"Why?"

"Did you see how thin it is? It will make a great anchor to slip under doors. And it flies."

Viznir agrees to get me a Frisbee while I play with more of the functions of the meta-space.

"Hey, Tucket, will the guard be able to see me with this thing on? It must have some kind of perceptor in it, too, right?"

Tucket's eyes train on the device and he tries to focus. "I can't see it. It won't highlight at all in the meta-space. It must be shielded."

"So I can get past the guard. What other security measures will they have in place? I can't be the first non-perceptor-wearer to try this."

"I don't know. They might have more security, but I've never been inside. It's a science center, so I'm not sure how tight the security is."

"Okay. At least it's not a bank."

Viznir reappears next to me and hands me the Frisbee. "There are no banks here. Money is all digital."

I slide the tablet back into my shoulder bag. "Then where do you keep all your tiny portraits of presidents?" Tucket laughs and I toss him the Frisbee. I back up a couple paces and we toss it a few times so I can get the feel of it. I deliberately toss it to the ground twice to make sure it keeps the same side up. As I hoped, it doesn't flip over, even when it skips off the pavement.

Viznir crosses his arms. "You gonna do this sometime today? This is a race, you know."

I grab Tucket's final toss and slide the Frisbee disk into my bag. "Yeah. I'm good." I start walking toward the lobby doors. "I'll call you when I've got it. Be ready."

My return through the lobby is uneventful, and as I approach the guard, I veer left, trying to look casual. She doesn't look at me at all, but stares straight ahead, like someone lost in a daydream. *Do robots dream?*

On a whim I enter the elevator again and move out of sight of the guard while I extract my tablet. This time I can see the controls. I try actuating the up button, but am met with a buzz and a message on the screen asking me to log in to the system. I frown and delete the warning. I fiddle with a couple other controls but receive the same response. I am about to exit to go look for the stairs when two women step into the elevator. Both are jovial and relaxed. Their age is hard to pin down, but I'd guess at mid-thirties. I notice a tiny spot of sauce on the darker-haired woman's mouth before she turns away. I do my best to look absorbed in my tablet as the doors close.

"Which floor?" The fair-haired woman asks.

"Oh, sorry." I jolt from my tablet and smile. "Same one, actually." I gesture toward the nothingness on the wall where the buttons were and nod. "That's lucky."

The woman surveys me once from head to toe, then goes back to the conversation with her friend. As I browse through more of the information on my tablet, the women discuss one of their boss's new policies on turning in project results and I do my best to look insignificant. When the doors open, I search for some indication of what floor we're on but see nothing. I smile and let the two women exit ahead of me, then use my tablet to scan the walls. As suspected, the floor number is highlighted on the wall in two large digits. 86. *Getting closer.*

The two women vanish through a door to the left that clicks solidly behind them. I scan the hallway. Another closed door to my right is also locked when I try the handle, but when I test the third door, just left of the elevator, the handle turns easily, revealing the stairwell. Thankfully, the stairs are walled in and I don't have to deal with a view of eighty-six floors below me. The walls are barren and sterile, but when I view the stairwell through the meta-space, it's tastefully decorated with colored walls and some framed art. The far wall of the next landing, a half dozen steps up, shows a window to the outside with an expansive view of the city below. I climb the steps and cautiously press my hand to the wall before daring to look back through the tablet. I feel like I'm looking through a magic portal that I could slip through and tumble into the sky. I back away from the wall and slide the tablet back into my bag, concentrating on the solid stairs instead.

I bound up the stairs two at a time at first, but after a dozen flights I slow as beads of sweat begin to dot the front of my t-shirt. I trot up the next five before I hear the noise above me. I freeze and listen as voices echo down the stairs. Without being able to see the stairs above me, I'm limited to the view of the half dozen steps above and below. I descend to the landing I've just come from, halfway between floors 102 and 103. I dial my chronometer for a twenty second jump and wait, hoping I can pull the same disappearing act I used on the aqueduct guard in Rome.

Another minute goes by and I realize the footsteps have stopped. The voices are arguing back and forth, a man and a woman from the sound of it, their conversation echoing down the stairs. The woman is chastising the man for something he's said to one of her friends, and his responses get repeatedly cut short by her admonishments. Their voices are raised and carry in the stairwell, so I can't tell exactly how far up they are. I eavesdrop on the conversation until it's clear that the woman is breaking up with him.

God. This could take a while.

I creep upward till I can try the handle for the door to the 103rd floor. It's locked from this direction. I pull out my tablet to see if there is a way to unlock the door, but when I attempt it, I'm again met with the request to log in. Frustrated and trapped, I realize that if the people keep descending I'll have no choice but to retreat downward. I decide to make myself an anchor point as a fallback position.

I extract my Frisbee from my messenger bag and lay it on the landing of the 103rd floor then descend to the 102nd, leaving it alone for a few minutes and writing the time in the journal. I repeat the process with the Frisbee on the 102nd, this time climbing a floor above it and writing the time, thus giving myself an option of climbing or descending away from my present self should I have to use it. I make a point of not listening for retreating footsteps while I wait, even going so far as sticking my fingers in my ears so I won't hear a future version of myself vacating the vicinity and accidentally cause some kind of paradox. Despite my efforts, when I pick the Frisbee up from the lower landing, I do hear something. Footsteps are thumping on stairs and not making a particular effort to be quiet. Furthermore, they are not retreating away from me, the way a future version of me ought to be. Instead they are climbing toward me, and they are close. I curse inwardly and climb away from them. I can't hear the couple above me anymore, making it hard to know if they are still there or if they have left the stairwell. Two floors farther up, I round a corner and almost collide with the man, who is sitting on the stairs holding his head in his hands.

"Whoa! Sorry, dude." I dodge to the side and skirt around him. The man looks up, teary-eyed, but merely makes a weak gesture with his hand to wave off the intrusion. I leap up the next few stairs and put him behind me as quickly as possible. A floor later, more voices trickle from above. I continue on and keep my eyes averted as I pass a group of gray-haired scientists on their way down. I am just even with them and trying to squeeze past their group when one of them breaks off his conversation and addresses me.

"Excuse me there. You need proper I.D. in this facility."

I wave at him and keep climbing. "Yeah, getting that sorted out with the—" I mumble something unintelligible—"department." I take the next few stairs in pairs and disappear around the corner, but his voice follows me.

"This is a secure facility, young man. You need to stop—"

I don't stop. I break into an all out run, as fast as I can climb. I've made it to the 117th floor, just one floor shy of my destination, when the guards appear. There are three of them. Two are synths from the look of their smooth skin and glowing eyes, but the third is mostly human. He's big. An easy fifty pounds heavier than me, and his arms bulge with muscles that could be straight from a comic book. The single inhuman feature that I can't help but notice is a distinctly metallic gleam from his knuckles.

"Halt. You are not authorized."

The man pulls a weapon from his belt that looks like zero fun to be shot with, so I hold my hands up. I have the Frisbee in my left hand, so I let it drop to the floor, making sure it lands right side up.

"Sorry guys, my mistake." I take a step to the side and stand directly atop the Frisbee. The two synths move to my sides and the first one is reaching for me when I get my hand on my chronometer. His fingers close on my right wrist.

"You will be detained for question—"

I press the pin.

I'm alone again. I look down at the Frisbee at my feet, back on the 103rd floor, but mere minutes before.

"Shit, shit, shit." I mutter under my breath as I climb up and away from my earlier self. In a few moments he'll complete his anchor point on the floor below and start his climb. The scientists will be above me momentarily. I'm trapped again. Mentally I scramble for options. I could jump any amount of time forward or backward just using the wall or the stairwell floor, but without any known safe time to arrive, I could collide with someone and end up fused together like Ajax, or die instantly. The odds of colliding with someone are low, but still more significant than I'm willing to risk. I only have one good option I can think of. Getting help.

I pull Mym's geode from my bag and use the silver degravitizer on it, scanning the cupped end over it as fast as I dare. When the green light on the degravitizer finally illuminates, I know I only have seconds till the earlier me will be climbing past. *Where can I put this thing where I won't see it? Didn't see it.* I spin around in the barren hallway. There's nowhere to hide it where it wouldn't be noticeable to the earlier version of me. There's nothing at all between the scientists and me—except a disconsolate man on the stairs. I look at the orientation of the geode in Mym's photo. *It could work.* I wrestle with the idea for only a moment before I start climbing. I only let the toes of my sneakers touch the edge of the steps as I work my way silently to the spot where I almost collided with the man on the stairs. When I am just below the landing he's on, I inch my way upward on my hands and knees till I can just see the toe of his left foot sticking out beyond the corner of the wall. I can hear his muffled sobbing. I ease the geode forward and nestle it into the space along the wall just outside of his black leather shoe. I double-check the photo and dial in the time coordinates on my chronometer. I'm lying on my side on the stairs at an awkward angle to the anchor, but the geode in the photo is on a shelf at least five feet off the ground. It's doable. I quietly tuck my feet up to the highest step I can to give myself clearance from the ground when I arrive. Footsteps echo on stairs below me. My footsteps. That's my cue. I take a breath and push the pin.

My chronometer hand glances off a shelf and I crash to the floor in a heap. A handful of geodes I've dislodged from the shelves rain down around me. I protect my face, and when the commotion has stopped, I open my eyes and roll over. A pair of legs in black boots are directly in front of me. I look up the legs to the hooded figure they belong to. The rest of her clothing is also black and a semi-transparent veil shrouds her face. Her arms are crossed at her chest but through the mesh of the veil I can make out a pair of smiling blue eyes.

"Hi, Mym."

"Some people go on spiritual journeys to 'find themselves.' Time travelers find themselves all the time. We usually take journeys to get away from ourselves."–Journal of Dr. Harold Quickly, 2010

Chapter 22

Mym surveys the fragments of mineral on me as I get to my feet.

"Anything else you want to break now that you're here, or do you think you got it all?" Her voice is playful. I can see the corners of her mouth turned up through the mesh over her face.

"I think I'm good." I smile back and dust myself off. "What's with the ninja outfit?"

"Precautions." She extracts the mineral I used as an anchor from the rubble I've created, and moves slowly toward a dusty glass door. I study the room, taking in the catalogued shelves of rocks before following her. The door opens automatically and we step onto a covered wooden walkway.

The environment couldn't be more removed from the urban skyscraper I just left. Beyond the walkway, a scraggly lawn has a tenuous foothold on the red sandy earth before it blends with sparse woods and brush. To the left, the ground tapers downhill to a pond, and an earthen trail winds it's way into the trees.

"Where are we?" I crane my neck upward. Even the sky looks different. The puffy cumulus clouds of England and Northern France have been replaced by wisps of cirrus clouds in the upper atmosphere.

"Mungkan Kandju."

I lower my gaze to the woods. "God bless you."

Mym laughs. It's a sweet sound that springs out of her, and despite her somber appearance, I can tell she's happy. "It's the name of this place. It's a forest."

"Is it Africa?" The lean trees stretching toward the sky around us look as though they've been wanting and needing their whole lives, never getting quite enough.

"No. Queensland, Australia. This used to be a national park. Now it's owned by the Academy of Sciences."

"Students of this school really get around, don't they?"

Mym leads us along the plank walkway and around the corner. More single story buildings are scattered in a loose rectangle. A colorful flock of parakeets is chirping away atop the roof of the building nearest to us. "You figured out how this school works, right?"

"You mean the meta-space? Yeah. It's pretty fancy."

"Take a look at this place." Mym gestures to the ramshackle buildings around us. It takes me a moment to realize what she's suggesting, but then I reach for my tablet and hold it up. Through the screen, the area is completely transformed. The wooden one-story buildings are now a series of interconnected towers with catwalks and bridges. The scraggly grass is lush and green and, to my surprise, the place is bustling with people. I have to lower the tablet and double-check my surroundings to make sure they are not really walking past me.

"Wait, so they're—"

"They call it commuting." Mym plucks a wildflower from one of the weeds and twirls it in her gloved fingers. "They used to maintain this campus as a real site in addition to the meta-space version, but people stopped coming. They preferred the illusion."

I scan the tablet around again. "So how come we can see it all? If it's all fake, why build it on the real site?"

"That's how the meta-space works. They mapped the surface of the earth and put it into a digital skin. Then designers started augmenting the spaces with meta-features that you could interact with. In some cases, like here, it worked so well that they basically stopped using the physical spaces. Most of the students here were commuters anyway, so it wasn't hard for them to let it go."

"So these people I see walking around, where are their physical bodies right now?"

"Home. Wherever home is for them. Or in a class, maybe. They're in what they call 'ranging mode,' where the mind is able to range free of the body. That way their bodies aren't walking around bumping into things while they are experiencing this place."

"That's so bizarre. It's pretty cool but—hey. Wait a minute—" I scan the tablet past where Mym is standing. The view through the screen shows nothing where she ought to be. "Where are you?" I lower the tablet again and she holds up a hand and waves her gloved fingers at me.

"Right here."

"But you don't show up!"

Mym steps closer and runs her fingers down my chest. "You miss me?"

I get a chill up my neck and smile. "So you really are a ninja."

Mym is smiling again from under her hooded veil. Up close, the black material has a slight shimmering quality. "Sometimes I don't feel like being looked at." She turns and starts walking toward the woods. "Like anytime in this century."

I follow her shadowy figure under the trees, and she guides me down a dirt path. I'm reminded of our trek through the Amazon where all of this started. This time she leads me to a building that is even more dilapidated than the others, but today there is no sign of Dr. Quickly. The building is constructed into a hillside and has only one entrance; a wide, rolling gate on rusty rails.

I help Mym roll the door open and close it again once we enter. We are blanketed in darkness as soon as it's closed. I can barely see my own body and Mym has completely vanished. I've just begun regretting not bringing my flashlight when a dim light flickers on above us. Mym is standing by a switch along the left wall. She's pulled her hood back and I finally have an unobstructed view of her face.

"Batteries are getting low. Come on. I've got to start the generators."

I follow her through a metal doorframe and we make a right into a workshop of some kind. The generators are old but seem to be well maintained because they both fire right up. She double-checks that the vent tubes are properly secured to the exhaust ports and directs me back to the hallway. "The rest of our equipment is this way."

The room she leads me to appears to be a type of control center with digital screens on the walls. A large one dominates the center of the room. She flips a switch at a master console and the screen buzzes to life. The image that appears is a rotating view of the earth. The planet has a green glow around it that I guess signifies the grid.

"Where do they have you going?" Mym asks.

"It's a particle physics lab in Northern France." I reach into my bag for my tablet to get the details. "What is this place?"

"It was a mineral mine for a while. But it was depleted quickly, so when the Academy bought it, they closed it up. Dad and I debugged it and took it off the grid. Now it just shows up like a hill in a forest. He wanted a place where he could show up in this century without being tracked, and since most of the Academy campuses are in Europe or the U.S., Australia turned out to be just the spot for it."

"How come?"

"Oh, you know us. We're shy." Mym punches a few more buttons on the console. "Dad's always been big on privacy. He has good reason, though. Lots of people want to meet the father of time travel. Problem is, they're not all people he wants to meet, and I think he'd be happier if nobody even knew I existed."

"Over-protective?"

"He just wants to keep me safe. So, protective. 'Over' would be a matter for debate." She pulls up a map of Northern France and zooms in on the city of Calais. After a quick survey of the city, she narrows the search to one building. "Is that it?"

I study the image on the screen. "Yeah. The particle physics lab is on the 118th floor."

She zooms in on the windows of the lab. "How close did you get?"

"I was on the 117th floor briefly." I get out my journal and consult my jump times. "The last point I was in the building was around 12:35 local time. I had some security on me though, so it wasn't going great."

"Okay. We can figure something out." She unlocks a cabinet and returns to the center table with a large fishing tackle box. When she flips open the lid I see a bunch of electronic devices and what I guess to be anchors. "What do you have to work with?"

I open my bag and lay Dr. Quickly's journal on the table, followed by Abe's tool kit and the degravitizer. I also extract Milo's power supply and use the opportunity to plug in my chronometer. "I have this stuff, and I did have a Frisbee, but I lost it."

"A Frisbee?"

"Yeah, it was one of those long-range ones with the hole in the middle. I was going to use it to slide under doors and maybe throw it if I had to get past any kind of laser beams or anything like that."

Mym is watching me with an amused smile on her face. "That's why I like you, Ben. You're so optimistic."

I smile back. "You like that idea?"

"No. I think it's a terrible idea, but I like that you *thought* it would work. Having a positive attitude is important." She smirks and goes back to her box of accessories.

"You've clearly never seen me throw a Frisbee. It's one of my many talents." I slide over next to her and brush my hand across the small of her back. "*Many* talents."

Mym turns to face me and is trying hard to keep her face serious, but her eyes are laughing. "I'm sure you do have lots of talents, but right now we're trying to get you into this building."

I slip my other hand to her waist. "Yeah, but we're time travelers. It's not like we have to go right this second." I incline my head closer to hers, moving slowly toward her lips. She laces the fingers of her left hand through my right and raises our hands up. She inclines her head toward my wrist and the metal bracelet. "You forgetting about this little thing, sweetie?"

I look at the bracelet and frown at its oppressive counting as the seconds tick by on the timer. "Well there is that. But let's talk more about the fact that you just called me sweetie. That seems interesting." I lean toward her again.

"You are impossible." Mym shakes her head but she doesn't shrink away. Our lips are only centimeters apart now. Her voice comes out softer. "I'm trying to help you."

"You are helping me." I close the gap and our lips meet, softly at first and then firmer. Mym's right hand moves to the back of my head and gently entwines in my hair. I wrap my arms around her, lifting her up to her tiptoes and then up onto the table. She slides back on the smooth surface and pulls me closer to her, wrapping her legs around me again.

"You seem to like putting me on top of things."

"That's what happens when short people try to kiss regular-sized people."

"Hey!" She holds up a finger. "I'm not short, I'm—"

"Perfect," I finish the sentence for her.

She smiles. "Okay, I was going to say petite, but I'm not going to argue with perfect, if that's the word you really want to use."

The compliment buys me another few minutes of kissing, but eventually she pulls away. "Seriously. We have work to do."

"Fine." I release her from my arms and slide my hands back to her knees.

"When you finish this stupid race of yours, we can take a break. We'll go somewhere nicer than this." Mym gestures to the dim control center.

"You picked it. I figured this was just your idea of a romantic make-out spot. I think it's pretty cool."

"If this is your idea of romantic, we may have more work to do than I thought." Mym slides off the table.

"If you want to go practice some romance in Hawaii or something, I'm all for it."

"First things first." She points to the image of the building on the screen. "Tell me the situation."

I recount my attempt to make it up the staircase and describe the guards who accosted me in as much detail as I can remember. Using the grid, she's able to locate the room we're trying to get to. She zooms around the room, looking at all the scientists and suddenly freezes on one. "Wait, I know that guy."

"The one with the hairy ears?"

"Yeah. That's Dr. Franklin. He could be our way in." She moves to the tackle box and rifles through the various compartments, finally selecting a tiny round device about the size of a dime. She walks away and I follow her down the hallway to a locked metal door. She unlocks it and walks to the center of what I recognize as a jump room. Like the initial classrooms I used in training with Dr. Quickly, this room is empty with the exception of a waist-high anchor stand to allow for a level surface for a jump. Mym foregoes the stand and sets the tiny anchor on the floor. When she straightens up she motions me back to the hall. We close the door and wait.

"What is that thing?"

"It's a magnetic anchor that I can remotely control to attach or detach from things. They come in handy." Mym records the time into her handheld multi-function device. Unlike my tablet, hers is only the size of a phone.

When enough time has elapsed, she reenters the jump room and retrieves the anchor, then guides me back to the control room. She draws her pendant chronometer from the front of her shirt and dials in a time. "Just stay here. I'll be right back."

"Where are you going?"

"Paying Dr. Franklin a house call."

The next moment, she's gone. I study the image of the laboratory, noting the locations of the different machines till I spot the one I want. A moment later, Mym is back.

She returns to the view of Dr. Franklin walking around the lab. She watches his every move until finally she smiles. "Ah, here we go." Dr. Franklin has walked into a supply closet of some kind and is rummaging around on the shelf between crates of supplies. Mym is holding a button about the size of an automatic car key and waits till the doctor turns to leave the closet before pressing it. I don't see anything happen but Mym seems pleased with the results.

"What did you do?"

She gestures to the screen and zooms in on the floor where the scientist had been standing. "It's right . . . there." The magnetic anchor is now lying on the floor near the leg of the stainless steel shelving. She makes a couple more movements with the button in her hand and the anchor rolls over a few times, hiding it from any passing viewers.

"That's awesome. How did you get it on the scientist?"

"Since I already knew what he was wearing, I broke into his bedroom this morning and clipped it inside his pant leg. He was nice enough to carry it to the 118th floor for us. He snores, in case you were wondering." She sets the button down and goes back to the control panel. "And here's where we can get really fancy."

She flips a few switches and checks a readout on the display, then moves a dial on the console. The image on the screen starts to move in fast forward. The scientists are bustling around at super speed, having rapid conversations and whizzing about the room.

"Whoa, what is that? Are you fast forwarding through time?"

"Yep." Mym smiles. "Not even the academy can do this, but Dad and Abraham figured out a way to hotwire the meta-space with the TPT. It actually relays it's own recorded images from the future. Saves the trouble of waiting around to see what happens."

I watch with fascination as the sun moves shadows across the desks in the lab and finally people start leaving. We watch until the last person has cleared out of the space. Mym slows the image back to normal speed. "That's our spot. I'm going to jump forward to that time so I can move the anchor into the open. Don't move." She places her hand on the side of the console, dials her chronometer and disappears. I observe the screen and marvel as the little anchor begins to roll itself back into the center of the closet. It sits undisturbed for a few seconds then a brown-haired man in jeans suddenly appears squatting above it, his fingertip pressed to its top.

Mym reappears in the control room next to me.

"Hey is that—"

"Oops." She smacks a button on the console and the image freezes. "You shouldn't watch that." She backs the image up until the image of me disappears and notes the time.

"That was me in the future?

"That was us in the future. Or will be soon."

"Should we watch more and see what happens?"

"You wanted to stay paradox free, didn't you? You think you could watch us do everything we're going to do and then duplicate it exactly, without overthinking it and screwing it up?"

"Oh. Right. That would be tough."

"Impossible tough. Come on, we've got work to do." Mym leads us back into the jump room and we set our chronometers to the window of time we allowed for ourselves before. When we arrive, the magnetic anchor is sitting on the floor, just where Mym left it. She tells me the time to set and I dial it into my chronometer.

"We're going to use the same chronometer?"

"Yeah, wrist mounted chronometers get a little better contact for this sort of thing. Just get a finger on it."

I squat and place my fingertip on the anchor. Mym squats next to me and laces the fingers of her left hand through my right. She pulls her hood back over her head then leans into me and I get a lingering scent of her hair as she activates my chronometer. The jump room vanishes and is replaced by the physics lab closet. Mym points to the anchor. "Take this with you and take it apart later. We need to destroy the evidence." She stands slowly, still holding my hand, then lets it go as she moves to the door. "Will you recognize this thing when you see it?"

"Yeah, I think so."

"Good, let's make this quick and get out. Remember, I'm not here." She swings the door open and lets me lead the way. I scan the laboratory and work from memory of the diagrams.

"It's this way," I whisper.

I work my way to the corner of the room and point out the machine with the odd little ball mounted to the side. Now that I see it in person, it has a green tint to it and I can make out fluid inside. It has two fittings attached to it that resemble quick-disconnects from an air compressor line. *Good. It won't leak all over when I take it off.* I get one of the lines off and am working on the second, when I notice Mym has gone oddly rigid. She's staring at the machine intently, and even though I can barely make out her features under her hood, her body is tense.

"Ben, what is this?" Her voice quivers.

I pause with my hands still on the fitting. "The description called it a gravitan stabilizer."

"Gravitan? You're sure it said gravitan?" She scans the room and starts reading the labels on other machines, moving between them and running her gloved fingertips over their controls.

"Yeah. You know what they are?"

"Shh. Get it off there and let's go." She gestures toward the door. I quickly remove the second fitting and stuff the gravitan stabilizer into my bag. It's heavier than I expected. I adjust the strap on my shoulder and lead the way out the door. I can see a dull glow of Mym's MFD through her pocket as she does something to summon the elevator. Instead of going down, once we're in, the elevator starts to climb. When we reach the top floor, she guides me through a doorway onto the roof. I shiver in the chill of the sudden blast of air. The stars are out, but occasional wisps of cloud are blackening them in intervals as they flee in the wind.

"There shouldn't be any audio up here. We can talk."

I nod and wrap my arms across my chest. "So what happened down there? You know what this thing is? The gravitan stabilizer?"

"Gravitans are what my dad was searching for. The naturally occurring gravitite particles." The rush of the wind almost carries her words away.

"What he and Abe were trying to find in the river. That's good then, right? This must mean he succeeds, doesn't it?" I avert my eyes from her when I realize I've been staring. If there are cameras up here, I ought to be pretending she's not here.

Mym crosses her arms. The motion is idle, her mind clearly somewhere else.

"Dad wouldn't have given his research to the Academy of Temporal Sciences. They've always wanted his original research but he didn't trust them with it. He said there are too many variables. Too many people he thought were unethical."

"So maybe someone else did the same research, or maybe made a deal with him later after we last saw him? He does have some kind of relationship with the Academy, right? They all seem to know about him."

"He's done talks here via telecommunications links. He did a debate once, early in his career, but some of the professors he debated didn't take well to losing. One in particular. He made enemies. I can't see him ever making a deal with them for this. This was his dream. Gravitans are the evidence that he has always searched for."

"Evidence of what?"

"That time travel was natural? That he didn't necessarily cause the rifts in the universe when he synthesized the gravitite particles."

"He worried he damaged the universe?"

Mym looks up at me and I can see the concern in her face. "Wouldn't you? He turned the laws of physics on their head, just because he theorized that the particle could exist. But when he made it, it caused paradoxes and alternate timestreams and God knows how many realities. Some time travelers have used his research to commit atrocities and change the whole order of the universe. How could he not feel responsible for that?"

"But if the gravitans already existed, then he didn't necessarily cause the rifts, he just discovered them?"

Mym turns away and brushes something from her arm. "Maybe. I don't know what he really feels. He doesn't like to talk about that very much. I just know that this research is important to him. It's personal. He's been working on it ever since I was born. Obsessing even. It's not something he would hand over to the academy without good reason." I pull the globe of green fluid out of my bag and balance it on my outstretched hand. She touches it tentatively. "Now it's part of a chronothon."

"What do you want me to do?" I ask. "I don't have to give this to them. We can make a new plan. You've been evading Traus and the committee so far. I could go with you. We could—"

"No. I shouldn't even be near you right now. We've already gotten too close. I don't know what I was thinking." She walks toward the edge of the building where she stares at the illuminated skyline around us. She removes her degravitizer and a cube shaped anchor from her pocket and sets to work with them. When she's finished she stands back up, but lets the little cube roll around her fingers.

I step closer to the edge than I want to. "Mym. I don't want to lose you."

She looks back, her silhouette outlined against the bright lights of the city. She watches me, reading my face. "I don't want to lose you either."

I slip the gravitan stabilizer back into my bag, take another step until I'm even with her, and stare out over the depths of the city below us. I let my fingertips find hers in the darkness, and we stay that way for a little, letting the wind blow between us.

When Mym finally speaks, it's barely audible. "I don't know where they're sending you next."

"You can't track Traus?"

She shakes her head. "Wherever he went after this, it's not on the Grid or any timestream chart I've seen. It could be a fringe stream somewhere or a new stream that hasn't been documented. Wherever it is, it's too far for me to follow you."

"Will you be safe? Will Traus be able to sneak up on you when he comes back?"

"Unless he found a way to remove the trace, he doesn't come back from wherever he went. I don't know what's going to happen, but I have this feeling like it's something big. Something awful. I have this fear that I'm not going to see you again and I can't shake it."

"So I don't go. We make a run for it."

Mym looks at the bag hanging across my shoulder and then up to me. "I wouldn't know how to run from this. Whatever that thing is they're having you bring them, it has something to do with Dad, and if they have something planned concerning him, it involves me, too. We can't run without knowing what that is."

I shift my feet and put my hands into my pockets. "So it's on me then."

Mym studies me from under her hood. "Do you think I'm selfish? Asking you to go through with this? I was the one who told you not to, and now I'm the one who needs you to finish it."

I look at the stars blinking and fading with the passing clouds. "No. It's not selfish to fight for the people you love. Sometimes you have to make sacrifices."

Mym rests her hand on my arm. "Come back to me. Don't let them win this." She slides her hand down my forearm till she can lace her fingers around mine. "We still have a lunch date in New York remember? You promised me calzones and roller disco."

I smile at this. "I was kind of hoping you forgot about that last part."

"A promise is a promise."

"I'll make it back then." I reach up and lift the veil from her face till just her chin and the tip of her nose are showing. I press my lips to hers and hold her against me. When she lets go and steps back, she's smiling. I reach out and tug the veil back into place. "How will I find you?"

Mym has her chronometer in her hand. She reaches into her pocket with her free hand and holds something out to me. I take the metallic disk from her and study the string of numbers imprinted on one side. "If you find anyone with a tachyon pulse transmitter, use those time coordinates to try to call me. I'm going to see what else I can find out about why the academy is dealing with gravitans. Try to reach me with the TPT. If that doesn't work, just come home. I'll be waiting for you."

A particularly strong gust of wind makes me squint, and when I reopen my eyes, Mym is gone.

"There are reasons we were born when we were. I won't cite cosmic significance or divine reasoning, because I'm a scientist and I shy away from the abstract, but I won't deny that a time traveler can only cease to be a traveler in their home time. The essence of us knows to when we belong."–Journal of Dr. Harold Quickly, 2008

Chapter 23

I curse the wind that threatens to abscond with Abe's chronometer schematics when I open his tool kit. I stuff the instructions into my pocket to keep them safe and locate the tiny screwdriver I need to get Mym's magnetic anchor apart. Once the anchor is in a dozen tiny pieces, I walk the perimeter of the roof, flinging them over the edge. I leave the last piece in a bird's nest I find under the eaves of the stairwell exit for good measure.

If anyone catches up with Mym, it won't be because of me.

Once I'm sure Mym's evidence is disposed of, I search for a place to hide the objective while I go back for Viznir. An air vent on the side of the stairwell is roughly the same size, so I stuff the gravitan stabilizer inside and take care to screw the vent cover back down. I do a few calculations in the back of Dr. Quickly's journal, then set my chronometer for 12:36 local time. Tucket answers my call immediately once I'm back.

"Let me talk to Viznir," I stare into the tablet and Tucket does something that causes Viznir to show up too.

Viznir wastes no time. "Did you get it?"

"Yeah, but it's on the roof later tonight. We need to get it down somehow."

Viznir frowns. "Is it fragile?"

"I think a hundred and fifty story fall would probably put a good dent in it. I can find something else to throw down if you want an anchor to get up here."

"You're on top now?"

"Unfortunately."

"How did you get up there?" Tucket asks.

"I'll explain later. Let's just concentrate on getting this thing down."

The process takes longer than I had hoped. It takes Tucket and

Viznir six attempts to locate and retrieve any of the things I attempt to lob off the roof to use as anchors, as most of them either drift into the river or land on some indiscernible balcony below. Finally a piece of air conditioner tubing lands in the plaza where they can see it and Viznir makes it up to the roof. I lie about when I first climbed to the roof and take Viznir to a time of night after Mym has departed. Tucket, not having achieved time traveler status, is obligated to wait the ten hours for our return but makes excellent use of the time to locate us a sort of anti-gravity jacket that is for use on toddlers who fall down a lot, and it turns out to be the perfect means of slowing the descent of the gravitan stabilizer.

The transfer of the jacket to the top of the roof is managed by creative use of a helium party balloon and some high-test fishing line. Getting the helium balloon all the way up the building in the wind is a feat that requires Tucket to navigate most of the plaza at the far end of the string, but since it is by now the middle of the night, hardly anyone is around to notice. Those who do, fail to comment on the man and his balloon, though from Tucket's account, one woman does attempt to record him while laughing.

Once I have the balloon, I reel up the anti-grav jacket and use it on the objective. By the time the three of us are safely on the ground and back in a car, it's well after midnight.

"I think it's safe to say we won't be in the top ten this round," I say, noting the time on my bracelet. "But at least we're done. Next stop: time gate." I lean my head against the cushion in the rear seat of the cab and let my eyelids close.

Tucket is still full of energy. "I think it's great you guys came up with that. I mean, balloons. It's so creative. When I graduate from the ATS program I'm definitely going to look you guys up. Would that be groovy with you? We could see the twentieth century together, maybe visit your favorite hip places. I've always wanted to see Marilyn Monroe. You guys know her? She was pretty gnarly, right?"

I let Tucket continue his recounting of twentieth century highlights until we make it back to London. Viznir is quiet, even when Tucket takes the rare break for a breath. The time gate is in a dive bar five stories below street level. The bouncer at the door gets one look at my bracelet and lets us into the back room. The gate has been creatively wired into the perimeter of a pool table. When I deposit the gravitan stabilizer into a cubby behind the bar, the pool table lights up and my bracelet blinks an eleven.

Viznir pumps Tucket's hand once and climbs a chair to the top of the table. He disappears into the shimmering surface of the table without a word. I use my remaining seconds to consolidate my bags and give Tucket a high five. "Good luck with school, man. You'll do great. I really appreciate all your help. There's no way I could have done it without you."

Tucket beams at this. "I'll have the Academy Acclimation Division send you a service survey. If I get all good reviews I can graduate earlier and then I can come visit your century!"

"I know you'll like it. I'm from 2009, so when you get there, look me up."

"I definitely will." Tucket waves as I climb the chair to the edge of the pool table.

I give him a salute and jump into the time gate. The next moment I'm spinning end over end toward a white floor, but it feels like it's happening in slow motion. As I rotate through the air, I spot Viznir stuck to a corner of the ceiling like a spider. *That's not right.* The floor rushes up to meet me and I bounce, ricocheting off in a new direction. My pack collides with a wall and I'm rotating again until I land spread-eagled across a Plexiglas window, staring at a view of a million stars.

"You have got to be kidding me." I look up and locate Viznir in the corner above me. Only now do I realize the room is rotating slowly around a door in the wall. Or the door is rotating and we are sitting still. The sensation is odd either way. I drift weightlessly away from the wall toward the doorway.

"Dude. Where are we?"

Viznir is clinging to the handle of a storage cabinet. "Far."

I collide with the wall the door is in and wait till it rotates around to the proper orientation before trying the handle. The door swings open freely, but when I push myself through, I get an unpleasant tugging on my face and arms and finally my whole body as I crash to the floor, stuck once again by the force of gravity. After weightlessness, I feel like a walrus, struggling to push my heavy body off the hallway floor.

Viznir flings himself through the doorway at the next rotation and manages to only stumble to his knees before getting back up. There is a window in the hallway and I pull myself over to it, inching closer to the view of the universe outside. Only this time I don't just see stars. A red and green planet looms out the window, its atmosphere swirling with angry gray clouds.

"Viznir, that is definitely not earth, right? How far into the future are we?"

Viznir has his tablet out. "It's not earth. We're not in our solar system. The sun here is red."

As the hallway rotates, I see what he's talking about. Beyond the planet, a massive red star is lighting the side of what I now understand to be a space station. My bracelet is still flashing an eleven, but finally reverts back to its clock mode. I look around for our objective boxes. I find mine hanging on a hook at the far end of the hallway. It's the last one left.

"We must have lost a little competition somewhere. Only eleven teams still in it." I point the hooks out to Viznir, but he only grunts.

The box opens and at first I don't see anything inside. I trace my fingers along its interior but find nothing. It's only when I lower the box that I find the point of color hovering in midair. It's about the size of a pea and almost the same color, only translucent. Amazed, I touch it with a fingertip and it expands, enlarging itself to the size of a beachball. Now the three dimensional image shows a diagram of the space station. A title block at the corner of the image labels the station as "Terra Legatus" and has a date of May 13th, 2230. A path through the interior is highlighted and terminates at a row of bays in one branch of the six-armed station. The bays each contain a pod that I interpret to be a form of transportation.

"So I guess we need to go here." I reach out and touch the hallway with the pods, and the image suddenly expands again. "Crap. What did I do?" The image is now the size of a small car and occupying the entire hallway. "Do you know how to shrink this thing back down?"

Viznir steps over and reaches for the sphere, but nothing happens. He makes a few gestures with his arms and I try to imitate him, waving and compressing my hands and trying various combinations. Something I do makes the image expand farther and it engulfs both Viznir and me, and the entire corridor. "Son of a—" I mutter continued curses as I try to compress the image back to a manageable size. Finally I give up.

"Okay. I think I saw where we were going. Did you see anything about our objective in there?"

Viznir shakes his head.

"Dammit." I study the bits of diagram that I can see and try making a beckoning gesture with my hand. Surprisingly, it has an effect and the entire image shifts toward me. "Ooh. I'm onto something." I make more of the gesture till I can move around the image. I'm zoomed-in much too close, but eventually I'm able to scroll my way over to the surface of the planet, and after a lot of wandering around the trackless topography, finally alight on a bit of settlement. The outpost is partially subterranean, but the diagram still shows the features that are below the surface. I spot our objective symbol blinking in a corner of one of the lower silos. I try to zoom in closer, but now I can't. I curse at the image again and finally resort to pulling the tablet from the last level out and taking a picture of the image.

"I still can't see what we're after, but it's right here. Maybe we can figure it out when we get to it."

Viznir does not seem especially concerned about the problem. He's staring out the window at the planet's surface again.

"You okay, man? You've been a little quiet today."

The question shakes him from his reverie and he turns his attention back to the hallway. "I'm fine. I'm just ready to go home."

"I hear you on that one. This is pretty cool though, right? I never in my life thought I would see something like this." I stare at the green and red planet rising through the window again. "It's beautiful."

Viznir leads the way through the airlock doors at the end of the hallway. They open automatically with a pleasant whooshing sound and close the same way behind us. I smile, thinking about every sci-fi movie I've ever watched and how the doors all sounded just like that. *I wonder if they designed these that way on purpose?*

After the initial feeling of gravity returning I had felt heavy and sluggish, but now, having acclimated, I realize I'm lighter than I was on earth. The sense of lightness is enjoyable, almost as if the physical weight being lightened has lifted some of my stress. Viznir and I travel a series of catwalks and finally end up in our designated leg of the station. A long row of pod doors line the right wall. Ten pods have been deployed, leaving only one remaining.

Just off the main corridor is a second hallway with a row of lockers. I notice Jettison's name on one and go inside to investigate. I run my fingers past names on the nameplates till I find the one belonging to Viznir and me. Opening the locker, I jump back in fear at the figure inside, then laugh and calm myself. The space suit hanging in the locker has a round helmet with a shiny reflective dome. I reach in and pull the first one out. "I guess this one's yours." I hand the suit to Viznir and then reach in for the second one. I shrug out of my pack and let it fall to the floor.

The space suit is made up of seven parts. The baggy pants are roomy enough to go over my clothes, and the boots they lock into are made to go over shoes. I step into the whole assembly and let Viznir help me get the torso part over my head. The upper half is bulky with pockets and what I guess to be small canisters of compressed oxygen on the back, but I get it over my head and manage to fasten it to the waist of the pants without too much trouble. I assist Viznir with his torso piece, but he seems to be quicker at it than I am. He gets his helmet mounted, snatches up our packs, and deposits them in the escape pod while I'm still fumbling with the gloves. I kick my helmet gently out to the hallway where Viznir is looking at the controls for the pod.

"You think we'll be able to fly that thing?"

Viznir merely nods and continues to look at the controls.

I turn back to my task and, once I get my gloves attached, waddle my way over to my helmet. My fingers feel bulky and awkward inside the space suit's gloves. I grasp vainly at the slick glass twice before finally picking up the helmet by the base instead. *Viznir made it look so easy.* I place it over my head and try to lock it into place, fiddling ineffectually with the latches. I feel the first couple click into place after multiple attempts, but the third one is defeating me. I turn around to get some help.

"Hey Viznir can you get this—" I stop when I realize he can't hear me. He's closed the airlock door to the capsule and is facing me from the other side of the window. His face is stoic. "Hey!" I exaggerate the words so he can tell what I'm saying. "Can you come back out and help me with this?" I gesture to the latch at my neck. He shakes his head a fraction of an inch from side to side. I try the handle but can't move it. "Hey, c'mon, man. I need some help out here!" He doesn't move. I jiggle the handle harder this time. I hear him throw a latch on the other side and I step back, expecting the door to slide open. Instead, a hiss comes from around the door seal as the airlock pressurizes the capsule. Red warning lights illuminate around the door and a buzzer sounds. I step back just in time as the outer doors slam another barrier between us. *No. This can't be happening.* I pound on the new set of doors and yell. "VIZNIR!" The shout echoes around the inside of my helmet. The window to the capsule has fogged up from the sudden change in pressure and I can no longer see inside, but as I try fruitlessly to pry open the barrier door, a gloved finger begins tracing letters on the condensation of the capsule window with slow but deliberate movements. Transfixed in shock, I watch the successive appearance of each of the letters. THEY MADE ME. I'M SORRY. As the last line of the Y is completed, the fingertip disappears. I stare mutely as the locks release with loud clunks, and after one final flash of the warning lights, the capsule is ejected from the side of the station. It barrels into the darkness, arcing its way toward the planet's surface till it's just a glint of light entering the atmosphere.

I realize my mouth has been hanging open and shut it. The reality of the situation begins to set in. *That fucker just left me alone on a space station in the twenty-third century.* I look left down the corridor. The lights along the row of closed escape pod doors have all gone dark. The station knows there are no more departures today. *I'm going to die up here, you bastard.*

Anger rises inside me. I stare out the window at the vacant space where my escape pod ought to be. *I'm sorry? They made you? You have got to be kidding me. I'm going to kill you.*

The anger supplants my fear and I let it. I'm tired of being scared. Angry is better. I'm not going to die up here. Not now. Not when I've come this far. I turn away from the pod corridor and back toward the center of the station. *There have to be other controls to this station. Something else I can use.* I stomp my way over the catwalk to the station's core and enter the main bridge. A bank of monitors is aligned before a variety of control screens and a massive window. It reminds me a little bit of a Star Trek set, only without the blinking lights and the impossible amount of buttons and toggle switches. *There has to be some control I can use to fix this situation.* As I stare at the touchscreen dials on a display, the realization suddenly hits me. *Of course I can fix this! I don't need any of this. I just need to get back to before the pods were all released.* A sudden wave of relief passes over me and I can feel myself start to smile. I'm struggling to unlatch the glove of my chronometer hand with my other clumsy fingers when a shape rises from one of the swivel chairs near the window. I'm startled by the movement, and even more surprised when I recognize the silver flowing cape and the white hair of the Admiral. He's not wearing a pressure suit but rather his dress clothes from the night of the opening dinner. He steps to the window and holds his left arm behind his back in a way that makes me think of a soldier at ease. His right hand is cradled in his jacket out of sight.

I step toward him. "Excuse me, Admiral?"

He turns his head at the noise and smiles wanly when he recognizes me, then goes back to contemplating the view of the planet's surface.

"Hey, man. What are you doing up here? Where's Wabash?"

He doesn't turn toward me this time, but he answers. "I sent him on ahead."

"He went without you?" *What's wrong with these guides?*

"No. I asked him to. He understood."

"Understood what?"

"That I won't go down there. He's never been, but I know what that place is. I tried to warn him of course. I told him it's better up here. Infinitely better. There are places even brave men shouldn't go."

"How do you plan on getting out of here, then?"

"The only way left."

"So you have a way?" My outlook brightens at this. "Where are you going instead? Can I go with you?" *Ducking the rules and escaping the course will get me disqualified, but it's better than dying.*

He turns and looks at me. "You will have to. There is no other way." He considers me for a moment. "It's been good racing with you, Benjamin Travers. You've been an honorable competitor."

THE CHRONOTHON

"Um, thank you," I mumble into my helmet. "It's been nice racing with you, too." He moves his left hand from his back and I extend mine as well, expecting he might be reaching for a handshake, but his hand goes into his jacket pocket and removes a soda can sized canister. The dull, gray metal is broken up only by the red of the switch on top. Instead of moving toward me, he steps to the window and presses the object to the glass. Its base adheres to the window and his fingers linger on it, caressing the smooth metal.

"Wait, what is that thing?" I get a sudden sense of panic as his finger moves toward a button on top.

"It's the finest concussion grenade money can buy." The Admiral smiles. "The last of it's kind. Just like me."

"Wait! No!" I move a step toward him but I'm not in time. His finger reaches the button. The red light illuminates and begins to flash. I stare at it for half a second before doing the only thing I can think of. I turn and run. My feet fly up the sloped floor of the bridge toward the exit. I'm not fast enough. I've only made it to the door of the catwalk when the explosion rocks the bridge. My hands find the frame of the door just as the contents of the room evacuate themselves out the gaping hole where the window used to be. My lower half is pulled from the floor and I cling frantically to the wide lip of the doorframe, suddenly unable to inhale as air whistles from the neck of my improperly sealed helmet. The air in my lungs goes with it. *I'm going to asphyxiate.* I feel like every gas inside me is trying to expand and turn me inside out. My lungs refuse to function. *I can't last like this.* I release my hands from the doorframe and slam them both onto the latch on my neck, forcing it into place and sealing it shut. But that moment is all it takes. I hurtle backward through the void in the shredded hull and into the blackness of space.

There are things that float around my memory from my childhood. Sights and scents, the way my dad smelled of grass clippings on Saturday afternoons and my mother's purple apron smelled of flour and lemons. My first kiss is stored in there, clumsy and furtive, the warm breath of Ginny Finch on my upper lip. My first car always smelled of motor oil and on stifling hot summer days released an infernal lingering whiff of cat piss from some recess I could never locate. On those days, I'd overload the rearview mirror with piney air fresheners and leave the windows down. To all these memories I've added the recent scents of hot Egyptian gardens, musty Roman aqueducts and the smell of burning hydrogen.

Despite all these references, there are more scents in my memory than I recognize. In my mind I can smell things that I can't remember ever seeing. I smell corpses and putrefaction. I smell lavender clouds and, somehow, I feel like I can smell eternity. Some hint of a world just beyond the edge of my recognition. There is a memory of someone there, too, a man with my face, yelling at me, shouting for my attention and gesturing. *What is he saying?* I try to focus on the memory. *Where have I seen him before?* I try to listen. I need to hear him.

"Oxygen levels at forty percent."

No. That's not what he's saying. His mouth wasn't moving like that. And he doesn't have a woman's voice. He's pointing to something. What does he want me to see?

"Life support systems entering limited functions mode. Please return to your vessel."

Stop talking lady. I'm trying to remember what he wanted me to see. What was it he said before? Come find me. How am I supposed to find—

"Potential collision imminent."

What are you talking about? He's way over there. I can barely even see him anymore.

"Collision assured."

What are you—

"Brace for impact."

My eyes open just in time for me to get my arms up over my helmet as I collide with the girder. My breath is forced from my gut as I bounce off the rigid aluminum and begin to tumble away. The world around me is in chaos. Bits of machinery and wreckage from the space station are careening about me, glancing off one another and spraying toward the planet's surface.

Oh God.

The view of the planet is terrifying despite its inherent beauty. The pure enormity of it couldn't be appreciated from the narrow windows of the space station. I bounce through another patch of tiny debris and swat at the bits that get near my face. The eerie and absolute silence makes the scene all the more terrifying. The only sound is my ragged breath inside my helmet.

"Please refrain from aerobic exertion while in limited functions mode."

"Hello? Who is that?"

"You are speaking with Automated Systems Management Services. My name is Claire."

"Claire? Are you a person? Where are you?"

"I am your personal systems manager. I am located in your Digi-Com certified Extra-planetary Leisure Suit."

"Leisure? I don't think this qualifies as leisure!"

"Digi-com produces the finest lines of extra-planetary and subterranean outerwear. Your enjoyment is our priority."

My burst of hope sputters and fades. "You're a computer program? Not a person?"

"I am a synthetic intelligence housed in a non-organic form."

"Well I hate to tell you this, Claire, but both our forms are in deep shit right now. Can you contact the chronothon committee? Do you have any kind of communication abilities?"

"My communications are routed through the transmitters aboard the Terra Legatus. The system is currently offline."

I angrily swat another piece of debris out of my way. "That is bad news, Claire. Real bad." As I float in a slowly rotating line away from the girder I last impacted, I try to get a sense of where the space station was. The hull has splintered into hundreds of component parts, the largest of which is a sort of solar sail that is drifting toward the darkness away from the planet. The remainder is slowly sinking toward the planet's atmosphere. I watch a cargo pod begin to burn as it falls through the outer layers.

"Your heart rate is elevated. It is recommended that you relax and conserve oxygen while in limited functions mode."

"How much time have I got, Claire? How much air?"

"The Digi-Com certified Extra-planetary Leisure Suit is capable of holding a maximum capacity of five hours of breathing oxygen. In the current configuration you are equipped for a one-hour excursion. One of your three certified tanks has been damaged and is currently inoperable. You have approximately nineteen minutes remaining."

"How long was I out?"

"You were in a state of unresponsiveness for twenty-five minutes. Due to your efficient use of oxygen during that period, you extended the service capacity of the system beyond factory settings."

"Oh, good for me. Being passed out bought me more time to be terrified."

"At Digi-Com, your enjoyment is our priority. If you would like to return the defective or damaged system apparatus to our nearest retail location, you may be entitled to compensation."

"I don't suppose there's a retail location within twenty minutes of slow drifting from here by chance?"

"The nearest retail location is—"

I tune out Claire and search the void around me for any sign of help on the way. All I see is bits of space station and the massive giant of a planet slowly swallowing them up.

I concentrate on slowing my breathing and try to relax my body as I drift silently and slowly toward the planet. *I never thought I'd die like this.* I float aimlessly through the nothingness, incapable of doing anything but waiting for my oxygen to run out.

"You know what, Claire?"

"I am listening."

"It's kind of funny. I've been scared of heights my whole life. Thought I might fall to my death. Now, when it's happening, when I'm really dying, I'm not scared of it anymore. It's actually kind of peaceful."

Claire doesn't respond.

"What will happen to you when I'm gone, Claire? Will you burn up in the atmosphere? Are you scared?"

"My mind is stored on five redundant hardware components. One stored on the Terra Legatus is damaged. Three others remain at Digi-Com, and United Machine facilities."

"Ah. That's handy. So no worries then."

Claire is silent for a few moments before she speaks again. "I do not believe losing this component of my mind will be pleasant."

I watch more bits of debris igniting in the atmosphere. "No. I don't know that it will be. But maybe part of you will get to go to android heaven and the other parts of you will be that much happier." I spread my arms out and watch my fingers move in the bulky gloves, suddenly very attached to my life and my body and not at all ready to let it go. I move each of my fingers in turn, a silent goodbye to their services. As I'm flexing the stiff fingers of my left hand, I can feel the pressure of the chronometer against my wrist. *Even being a time traveler can't save you from asphyxiation.*

I notice another piece of debris moving toward me from my left. It's larger than the last few have been, and as it draws closer, I recognize it as one of the chairs from the bridge. I'm staring at the slowly rotating seat, thinking only of how I can avoid being hit by it, when the realization dawns on me. *I can use that!*

"Claire! Can you see what I see?"

"I am able to observe your current field of—"

"Where is that chair from? The one coming toward us."

"My data shows that item to be a Digi-Com part number DC18462-321 console chair-crewman—left bridge control."

"I need that chair, Claire."

"The current trajectory of that part will not intercept our present course."

"What? No! I need to get to that!"

The inside of my helmet lights up with a display of the trajectories of all the moving objects in sight. The path of the chair is highlighted and shows that my own course will take me across its path prior to its arrival. I'll miss it by mere seconds.

"No, no no!" I flail my arms and legs, trying to swim my way toward the chair's trajectory, but in the vacuum of space my efforts are useless. I continue on my path away from the girder I last impacted.

"We need to do some physics, Claire. How do I get back there? Can I change course somehow?"

Claire takes a moment to process this request. "Newton's third law of motion states that to every action there is an equal and opposite reaction. Should you exert a force in the opposite direction of that in which you intend to travel, the force will exert an equal reaction in the direction desired."

"Yes! I know that one. Okay. So I need forces to exert." I reach around me, searching for any one of the bits of debris that have been pelting me. To my consternation I only find the tiniest piece of aluminum foil within reach. I hurl it away anyway but see no appreciable change in my course. The chair is drawing closer and I begin to panic, feeling around my person for anything to throw. All my loose objects like my pen and Swiss Army knife are inside my space suit where they do me no good. My hand finds one of the oxygen canisters attached to my back and my fingers close around it. "Claire! Which one of these canisters is the defective one?"

"Canister Alpha is currently inoperative. Digi-Com part number DC89015, personal oxygen container-left."

I reach my left hand around my back and jerk on the bottle until it comes loose of its fabric attachment. A hose runs to a shared manifold with the other bottles, but I'm elated to see a quick-disconnect fitting at the end of the line. I tighten the valve on the bottle to make sure it's off, then pop it loose from the manifold. The bottle almost slips from my clumsy fingers but I bobble it and hug it to my body. I twist myself around till I can see the chair again and aim the fitting end of the bottle in the opposite direction of my planned trajectory. "Here we go, Claire." I twist the valve and a burst of oxygen escapes the bottle. The effect isn't quite as powerful as I'd hoped, but I see my course line move on the screen. I give a couple more bursts of the bottle and line myself up with the chair. "Ha ha! What do you think of that, Claire!"

"You are now on a collision course with part number DC18462-321 console chair-crewman—left bridge control."

"Damn straight I am." I tuck the oxygen bottle into my armpit and brace myself for the impact with the chair. It comes within seconds. I scramble to hold onto the cushioned seat with my bulky arms but manage to hook the armrest and rotate the seat around behind me. I snatch one of the floating seat restraints and then the other and buckle myself into the chair.

"Bridge console chairs are designated for crew use only. Digi-Com would like to recommend the furnishings in the visitors lounge for your viewing pleasure."

"I'll be sure to check those out, Claire." I cinch the buckle tighter and wedge the oxygen bottle under the strap next to my leg. Next I try to move my left arm up the sleeve of my space suit. My elbow won't cooperate, however, and I can't get my arm through the narrow shoulder opening. I grunt and curse as I try to see my chronometer.

"It is recommended that you refrain from exertion while in limited functions mode. Heavy breathing reduces the useful service life of your oxygen reservoir."

I stop struggling and let my hand go back down my sleeve into my glove. "Claire, I need some more information."

"I am at your service."

"How long can a human body survive in a depressurized space suit?"

"A variety of factors influence longevity in a vacuum environment. Speed of decompression and total quantity of gases within the lungs are vital factors, as is length of exposure. Exhalation immediately prior to decompression greatly reduces damage to lungs caused by introduction of oxygen into the blood stream due to rupturing lung tissue. Prolonged exposure may cause severe sunburn due to radiation, tissue bloating, and rupturing of blood vessels may cause blindness as gases expand from the surface of the skin and eyes. These symptoms are typically preceded by unconsciousness and followed by death."

"How long till the bad stuff happens? How long can I function?"

"Useful consciousness is approximately ten seconds in a total vacuum environment, though you may experience some discomfort."

"Okay. I'm going to be faster than that." I calm my mind and remember my last chronometer setting. I flex the fingers of my right hand, limbering them up for the job of turning my chronometer dial. I bunch up the sleeve of my left arm at my elbow and pull it as tight as I can before folding it over and pinning it down on the armrest. I unhook my safety belt and wrap the left side around my arm and the armrest for good measure, pulling it as tight as I can. The makeshift tourniquet won't be completely airtight, but I hope it will buy me a little time. I float out of the seat slightly, but that is to my advantage as I don't want to arrive embedded in the cushion. I wrack my brain for the proper time to set, double-checking the indication on the visor's display. "Claire, how long have I been out here?"

THE CHRONOTHON

"This excursion is currently at thirty-eight minutes. You have approximately six minutes of useful oxygen remaining. Please return to your vessel."

"I'm trying. Believe me, I'm trying." I take one last deep breath and take in the vista of the planet below me, then exhale all of the air I can out of my lungs and reach for the glove latch on my chronometer hand. It sticks at first and I hear air starting to escape out of the useless crack in the seal. I curse it mentally and force it the rest of the way open, then twist the glove loose, letting it tumble away into the blackness. My left hand immediately begins to tighten as the nitrogen and other gases in it begin to swell. I clamp it on the bare metal of the armrest, ignoring the cold, and dial my chronometer with my other hand as fast as I can. The bulky fingers of my glove lack the dexterity I need so I miss the hour mark and end up on two, but it's good enough. I jam the directional slider to the back position. The whole process has only taken seconds but feels like an eternity. As the air is sucked out of my helmet, my vision starts to darken. I close my eyes and press the pin.

I crash into the console chair from three inches above it. The back of my head bounces roughly off the headrest, but it's the happiest sensation of my life. My helmet is gone. My bulky space suit is gone. I'm sprawled out in the chair in my jeans and sneakers, gulping air. I lift my left hand to inspect it. It's swollen and still cold to the touch, but I can move it. The flesh of my palm that was red and beginning to blister from the Hindenburg fire is now an ashen white, but as I probe it gently with my other hand, color begins to return. I press it to my abdomen to try to warm it and rock myself up and out of the chair.

Still alive.

I've come back two hours. I'm perhaps an hour ahead of Viznir and myself, but I don't know who else has yet to arrive. The window chair where I last saw the Admiral is vacant, as is the catwalk. I check the pod corridor and find three escape pods still in position. I breath a sigh and stagger past the one designated for Viznir and me. I've lost much of my anger in the joy of my escape, but some of it returns when I look at the airlock window where Viznir will scribble his message. I don't tarry, however. I proceed to the next available pod and immediately climb inside.

The interior of the escape pod is roughly a sphere, with one bank of controls that has a pilot chair and two other cushioned benches that occupy space between tiny porthole windows. I crawl to the first cushioned bench and lie down, still cradling my injured left arm. I have no other plan in mind, but I'm determined that whomever this pod belongs to will not be leaving the station without me. I spot a first-aid sign on one of the cabinet doors and scrounge through the cabinet for something that will help me. I find a bunch of syringes and pills with names I don't recognize but also a tube of burn cream and some gauze and bandages. I shove the rest back into the cabinet and take my discoveries back to my bench. The burn cream stings on my now open blisters but once I have my hand treated and bandaged, the discomfort dulls to a subtle throbbing. I curl back up on the bench, pulling one knee onto the cushioned surface and letting my other foot dangle to the floor.

At first I'm alert for the sound of voices, but after a few minutes my body begins to come down from the adrenaline and exertion of my last hours. Staring out the miniscule window at the silent array of stars, my eyelids have almost drifted closed when footsteps clomp their way into the hallway. I open my eyes and listen to the locker being opened and closed and someone struggling their way into a space suit. A few minutes later the clomping is at the entrance to the pod. I let my head roll toward the doorway and the white, glass-domed figure of Harrison Wabash.

"Travers. What are you doing here?" His voice is amplified by the helmet's speaker system.

"I'm coming with you."

"Where is your guide? You should have your own pod assigned."

I shake my head. "Nope. I'm going. With you."

"You'll need a pressure suit."

"I'm not getting out of this capsule. Don't try to make me."

Wabash stares at me for a moment then disappears back into the hall. When he returns, he's bearing another space suit and helmet in his arms. He deposits it near my foot at the base of the bench. "Here. The Admiral decided he won't be using his." He turns back to the control panel and presses something. The pod door slides closed and he latches it. My body relaxes as the seal around the door inflates. I sit up and start to put my legs through the pants of the space suit. Wabash has strapped himself into the pilot's chair and actuated more of the systems. Through the pod door window I see the space station doors slam shut, and a moment later, the pod gives a shudder as the locks are released. We are jettisoned from the side of the station and I have to hold onto the wall to keep from being flung from my bench.

Our descent is basically a controlled plummet. I have the forethought to put my helmet on before my gloves this time and the whole process goes a lot smoother. The entry through the atmosphere is shaky and loud. After the silence of space, the noise is harsh and unwelcome, but it fades to a steady whistling after we penetrate the upper atmosphere. The display on my helmet lights up with the Digi-

Com logo that breaks apart into a hundred stars and sends a musical jingle around the helmet's speaker system.

"Claire?"

"What's that?" Wabash turns his head from the controls.

"Nothing. Just seeing if anyone else was in my helmet with me."

Wabash studies me. "Your eyes are red. Looks like you might have busted a capillary or two. You feeling okay?"

"I got a little more of the 'outer' part of outer space than I wanted."

Wabash's eyes are questioning so I explain how Viznir left me and the Admiral blew up the space station. At this Wabash's face hardens.

"He told me he would wait till the station had been vacated."

I study the guide's face. "What's your plan now? How will you get through the next gate without your racer?"

"Silas gave me his bracelet."

"He got it off? How?"

"He broke his hand. He said it wouldn't matter now anyway."

I recall the Admiral's right hand resting in his jacket. "Wow, that's hardcore." I look out the window at the gray clouds whipping past. "What's down here that he's so scared of?"

Wabash goes back to his controls. "Unpleasant realities."

I look out the window at the planet and wonder what could possibly be bad enough to make the Admiral opt for suicide rather than face it. I'm still on a high from my recent escape from death, but as the surface of the planet nears, my apprehension begins to return.

The capsule jolts and shakes but seems to be slowing. Another few seconds and I'm sure of it. I climb to my feet and peer out the porthole. Something is streaming from the top of the pod. *A parachute? I never even heard it deploy.*

We impact the ground with a thud and a cloud of dust, but I've had worse jolts from waves on boats. Wabash checks the monitor on his control panel one more time, then opens the door. The pressure in the capsule changes and my suit expands slightly. My first view of the alien world comes as Wabash clears the doorway.

The ground is dark and gritty, but loosely packed. Jagged rocky outcroppings ring the valley and there are eight other pods partially buried in the soft earth in a semicircle around us. Tracks from the nearest pod lead into the reddish-sunshine-lit archway of some type of monument. Beyond the arch are a man-made wall and a tower with a dozen other structures jutting from the ground at interesting angles. Beyond that, two enormous cooling stacks stab at the sky. The whole facility is silent and vacant. Even the stacks show no sign of steam or smoke. The landscape is as silent as a Cubs fan at the World Series. *Was the Admiral scared of being bored to death?*

"We'll need to head for the entrance to the mine." Wabash points to the archway. "The rest of the compound is underground."

"What do they mine here?"

"What *did* they mine here," Wabash says. "This place hasn't been operated in twenty years."

"Okay. What did they mine here?"

"Colmetracite. It was an element they discovered that could power starship engines better than any of our fusion technology."

"What then? Did it run out?"

"No. It had been claimed."

A whistling noise above us makes me look up to see the next pod making its descent to the surface. It impacts fifty yards from us, and when the door opens, an unusual looking creature leaps from the opening. The space suit has four bulky legs and a long tapered helmet fixed around the neck. The creature shakes once and then barks, the amplified sound echoing off the ridges around us. I smile and make my way over to the capsule in time to help Jonah hand out his pack and the dog's saddle bags. He has his snail helmet attached to the back of his space suit, so for the first time, I can get a look at his tumble of dirty-blonde hair.

"What's up, buddy? Haven't seen you in a while." I give him a hand out of his capsule, and the dog head-butts me with his helmet in his attempt to lick at my other hand.

"You didn't meet me after the airship," Jonah says.

"No. I'm sorry about that. I ran into a friend I had to say hi to."

Jonah nods and I get the sense that I'm forgiven. "Do you know what we have to get?" His voice is high and excited.

"Here? No, actually. I still need to figure mine out."

"I have to get ore." He holds out his hand and has one of the tiny pea-sized dots floating in it. He expands it and it immediately shows his objective, a black rock with an unusual strand of green running through it."

"You're good at that. I couldn't get mine to cooperate at all."

Jonah closes his ball of light back to pea size again and starts to slip it into his pocket, but freezes in the act and points to the sky with his other hand. "Look!"

I turn skyward as bits of orange start streaking through the atmosphere. The space station is coming apart. A green-and-white striped parachute appears in a patch of clear sky, then the last capsule bursts through the bottom of the gray scattered clouds below it.

Viznir.

THE CHRONOTHON

As the capsule sinks toward us, I turn to Wabash. "You should get Jonah indoors. I'll meet up with you in a minute."

Wabash studies the spacecraft briefly, then puts an arm out to help Jonah with his things. "What are you going to do?"

I clench my good hand into a fist and move toward the falling pod. "I have some business to attend to."

"People often worry about the effects of time travelers on the nature of time, but rarely ponder the reverse. Time changes a traveler. We can never stay what we were. Change is the price we all pay for our years."–Journal of Dr. Harold Quickly, 1980

Chapter 24

The cloud of dust has yet to settle when I reach the fallen pod. It's sunk at a tilt with its door angled upward toward the sky. The door seal hisses as it equalizes the pressure. Viznir is struggling to push it open because of the angle. I approach from the blind side of the door and he has only managed to get one leg out of the capsule when I step into view. His gaze is concentrated on the blackened earth, but he looks up when my shadow falls across him. He doesn't have time to register surprise because I kick him hard in the chest and send him flying back into the capsule.

Viznir's body hits the back of the pod with a satisfying thud. I swing into the doorway after him and straddle his body. He moves in surprise, but I kick the face of his helmet, bouncing it off the porthole window frame.

"Surprised to see me, asshole?" I kick his helmet again for emphasis and this time a crack radiates across the visor. My fists are clenched, ready to swing, but Viznir's face falls and he starts to curl up and whimper. It makes me pause.

"Please, just don't kill me—" the rest is swallowed up in a sob and his body shakes. "Or—or do it quick." His face is contorted in pain or sorrow or fear. I'm not certain which. Whatever he's doing, he's not fighting.

"Why did you try to kill me, you son of a bitch?" I reach for his chest and grasp the fabric of his suit.

Fight me, you coward. Give me an excuse.

Viznir flinches. I shake him but he's dead weight in my hands.

"They made me!" Viznir glances at me cautiously but then stares at the wall, still not ready to meet my eyes. "I didn't have a choice."

"The committee? They have something on you? Geo? Who?"

His face twitches at Geo's name and I follow that track. "What, they bet on me to die? Somebody put a fix in? You could have killed me a hundred times during this race. Why now?"

Viznir shifts under me and I take a step back. I snatch both of our packs and rummage around in his until I find the pistol. When I grab it, I also spot Dr. Quickly's journal. I yank it from the bag and wave it at Viznir's face. "And this? What did you plan to do with this?"

He flinches again and his eyes flit to the pistol in my other hand. I fling his pack out the door and send the journal and my pack out after it, still aiming the pistol with my awkward bandaged hand. With the bulky gloves on, my finger barely fits inside the trigger guard, but Viznir doesn't seem likely to make me test it.

"They have my sister." His voice is quiet, just loud enough for the microphone in the helmet to pick up. "They're going to kill her now."

"Who does?"

"I don't really know who they are. They're men my dad knows. He owes them a lot of money."

"The gambling."

Viznir finally looks me in the eyes. "They said if I want to keep her alive, I had to do a job for them."

"Getting rid of me."

"I couldn't say no. . . . They gave me the training. They rigged my profile in the guide pool. I never actually took the exam. I would have, but they just made it so I passed. They've got people inside the committee."

"Why? Why me?"

"I don't know. They just said it had to be here. After we finished at the Academy."

I look down at his pitiful posture, curled up in the bottom of the pod. "Well I'm not going to just let you kill me. That—that sucks about your sister. And your dad. But I don't plan on dying here."

Viznir shakes his head. "They're going to kill me now anyway. They're going to kill all of us."

I'm not sure if he's talking about just his family or all the racers. "What else do you know?"

Viznir merely shakes his head and goes back to staring at the wall. I climb out of the capsule and upend Viznir's pack onto the ground. As the contents scatter in the dirt, I spot Mym's degravitizer and my water bottle. He hasn't bothered with Abe's tool kit, but I'm grateful now for the wind that made me stuff the chronometer schematics into my pants pocket. I locate his extra ammunition for the pistol and stuff that into my pack along with the journal and the rest of my belongings. I toss Viznir's empty pack at him through the pod door and leave the rest of his belongings on the ground. "I'm taking your gun." He doesn't make any objection. I stare at him, curled up at the base of the pod and another thought occurs to me. "How were you going to get home once I was dead?"

Viznir doesn't look up. He merely talks toward the wall. "It doesn't matter. It won't work now."

I shoulder my pack and walk away from the pod, my oversized boots leaving oval prints in the soft dirt. I'm about halfway to the monument archway when I hear the gunshots. *What are they shooting at?* I run for the arch. The spacesuit inhibits me, especially loaded down by my pack, but I can still jog. I switch Viznir's pistol to my good hand and flip off the safety as I peer around the corner of the columns.

Beyond the monument, the wall of the compound is open at the center with a paved road exiting and disappearing under drifts of the soft black dirt. Inside the compound is a courtyard with various vehicles assembled in rows. A shadow moves beyond the dusty windows of a truck, but I can't tell who it is. Then I hear the barking.

I jog along the road, forced to turn with my whole torso so I can see past the narrow confines of my visor. Passing the first vehicles, I spot the first sign of trouble. Empty sections of a space suit are strewn on the ground. The sleeve of one arm is ripped and the face shield of the helmet has been shattered. The barking starts again from my left. I cross the open space between the vehicles and jog the length of the wall to that side. There's a narrow metal door at the end of the wall that has been wrenched from its hinges, and I find a handful of shell casings on the ground.

I peek around the corner into the adjoining courtyard and duck inside, keeping my gun at the ready. The buildings have been constructed with a combination of man-made materials and hunks of the black rock formations from around the valley. Narrow windows and odd angles make them seem disjointed like some underground force has wrenched them off their foundations. I follow the barking around the corner to an overturned six-wheeled truck. Barley is out of his space suit. He's barking and snarling toward a black door in the building next to me. There's blood smeared on the wall and the distinct impression of a hand.

"Where did they go, boy?"

Barley turns and snarls at me, but immediately returns to barking at the door. I search the courtyard for any sign of Jonah and Wabash, but see nothing.

"Damn it. Why didn't they wait?" I inch my way toward the door and reach for the handle. Barley stops barking and lets out a low sustained growl.

The door hisses as I unlatch it. I swing it open and peer inside. Clear-faced masks with thin hoses and little oxygen canisters dangle from a rack. Beyond them another sealed door blocks the entrance. Its single black window stares at me like a brooding Cyclops. I aim my gun into all corners of the room to make sure they're vacant before stepping inside. I peer through the glass porthole of the inside door but can see nothing more than a few inches into the darkness beyond. The door handle is slick with blood. I grasp it with my gloved left hand but it won't budge. A red light is dimly glowing to the right of the handle. I look back at the open door behind me, realizing that I'll have to shut it to continue.

I clomp my way back to the entrance and grasp the latch on the outer door. Barley is staring silently past me. "You coming?"

The dog steps over the doorjamb slowly and gives me a wide berth. I take my pack off and locate my flashlight before closing the door. The room is total blackness with the exception of the red light. I flick on my flashlight and throw the locking mechanism on the outer door. The red light on the inner door switches to green. I don my pack again and try the handle. This time the latch opens with a heavy clunk.

The inner door swings toward me and I aim the beam of my flashlight inside. A few heavy crates look as though they have only recently been shoved away from the door. There are lines in the layer of dust on the floor and black footprints from someone who tracked dirt in from outside. It's hard to tell how many people have been through. Some of the prints are oversized like my own, but there are others. One smaller set of prints looks like they could belong to Jonah. The others are haphazard and seem to indicate someone staggering or perhaps dragging something.

I shine my light farther down the hallway and something skitters away in the darkness.

Does this planet have rats?

A light appears in the upper corner of my visor and a voice comes out of my helmet speakers. "Environmental oxygen has achieved recommended safety standards. Would you like to begin supplemented ventilation?"

"Hey. Bout time you woke up, suit. Who am I talking to?"

"You are speaking with Automated Systems Management Services. My name is Cal."

"Cal, I need some information about where I am."

"Current satellite triangulation indicates that you are located at the Diamatra Colmetracite Mining Facility, Area 29B, Sector 2."

"What's with the air here? Explain about the oxygen levels."

"The atmosphere of the planet Diamatra contains oxygen levels that are lower than standard safety protocols. Exposure to substandard oxygen levels may cause hypoxia, decreased color vision, and loss of mental clarity. Symptoms vary by individual. Prolonged exposure may lead to more severe symptoms and possible incapacitation or death."

I look at the dog at my heels and then have a pang of guilt about the crack I made in Viznir's visor.

"How long is too long to be out there?"

"Symptoms vary by individual. Conditions in this facility currently meet safety protocols. I can activate outside ventilation to conserve onboard oxygen."

I slide past the containers in the hall and shine my light at the path of dusty footprints. "Okay, do it." There is a whirring from somewhere in the suit and I get a whiff of stagnant, foul-smelling air. "Argh, seriously? You're sure this is safe to breathe?"

"Current air samples contain a variety of biological contaminants, but none that will cause grievous harm to humans."

"That nasty funk is harming my ability to not yak in this helmet."

"I am unfamiliar with the term 'yak' in this context. Do you wish to equip a—wild or domesticated shaggy ox—from—Tibet, planet Earth—with this equipment?"

"No. Forget it. I'll deal with the smell."

Barley sneezes once from the dust but continues to investigate the tracks. He trots down the hallway.

"Hey, hold up, buddy." I hurry to follow him, not anxious to lose my only living companion in this dank and eerie building. I keep my flashlight pointed ahead of the dog as I jog to keep up. "Hey, Cal. You have a map of this place?"

My visor illuminates and a circular map appears in the upper left corner. It shows a set of perpendicular hallways and a blue dot that I take to be my location. I reach the crossing hallway and follow the dog to the right. He leads me past a pair of partially open elevator doors. I get a whiff of cooler, slightly less foul air from the shaft, but the car is missing and the control panel has been pulled from the wall. Wires from the back of the panel have been deliberately cut with no attempted repair, and it hangs from the few remaining strands. Barley stops at a set of double doors next to the elevator shaft and starts to whine.

"Hold on, bud." I shine my light through one of the door's reinforced glass windows but see only the empty stairwell beyond. I try the handle and it turns freely, but the door doesn't open. I put more force into it and the doors flex slightly, but something is keeping them closed. Barley barks and paces impatiently, jumping up on the right hand door with his front paws.

"I know, I know. I'm trying."

Something scrapes the floor in the hallway to my right. Barley drops back to four paws and stares into the darkness. I flick my flashlight beam down the hall, but an overturned storage cabinet blocks much of the view.

"HELLO?" My voice echoes in my helmet's microphone. Something falls to the floor and rolls for a few feet before impacting an obstacle that's solid and metallic. Disturbed dust floats across the beam of my flashlight.

"IS SOMEBODY THERE?"

Silence.

I take a few steps to the side in order to shine my light beyond the metal cabinet, but all I see are some scattered tools, and at the other end of the hallway, another set of closed double doors. I turn back to the doors in front of me and give them a kick. They stay closed, but I hear a splintering sound. I give the door two more hard kicks, then put my shoulder into it and shove as hard as I can. The splintering continues, and finally, with a last slam of my shoulder, the doors buckle inward. There's a clang of metal and I stagger as my momentum carries me through. Barley barks and bolts down the first flight of stairs, his claws clattering on the concrete steps.

"Wait! Barley!" But the dog turns on the landing and vanishes down the steps into the darkness below. I regain my balance and shine my flashlight down the center of the staircase. I see a brief flash of fur a couple floors below, but then the dog is gone.

"Damn it." I frown at the darkness. "Why didn't I put a leash on him?" I return to the doorway and inspect the splintered pieces of wood. It was formerly the handle of a fire axe. The axe head is rusted and the once smooth metal is pockmarked and pitted. The lower half of the splintered handle has a bloody handprint on it. I pick it up and look at the imprint. *Who were they running from?* I take one survey of the hallway I came from and shut the doors. The handle is now useless, but I wedge the metal axe head through the door handles as a shorter substitute before turning my attention to the stairs.

I support my gun hand with my arm that's holding the flashlight, the way I've seen cops do it on TV, and ease my way down the first set of stairs.

"What's down here, Cal?"

The presence of the A.I. in my helmet is abstract, but helps me feel a little less alone in the darkness.

"You are currently descending into Area 29B, Sector 2, sublevel 1."

"How many sublevels are there?"

"At the time my data on this facility was last updated, there were thirty-five sublevels."

"How long ago was the data updated?"

"Nineteen years, seven months, and five days."

I pass a single dusty boot on the stairs. It's still sitting upright, as if someone walked right out of it.

"What happened here, Cal? What happened to the people?"

"The citizens of the Diamatra Mining Colony were—"

Three flashes of light illuminate the staircase below, interspersed with the sound of gunshots.

"Shit!" I aim my gun and light down the center of the stairwell but back up until my pack collides with the wall. A yell echoes from below that sounds distinctly like Jonah. The yell is followed by snarling and the pounding of feet along a corridor. Something makes a wet thud and the stairwell goes silent.

"JONAH!" My own voice bounces hollowly off the walls.

What in the hell were they shooting at?

As the seconds pass without any more noises, I take a few cautious steps forward. I crane my neck and peer over the railing, but see nothing on the landings below me. I tread softly as I navigate a full rotation of the stairwell to the level below, keeping my gun always steady on my new horizon. Two flights down I come to a doorway that has been propped open with a piece of cinderblock. I ease myself around the door and shine my light into the hallway. Somewhere in the darkness I can hear ragged breathing.

"Jonah?"

I wait for a response but get none. The raspy breathing continues and I hear a cough. The cough sounds small and pitiful. I inch forward. A vehicle is parked in the hallway with its engine cover removed. Engine parts dot the fender over the knobby tires. A rolling industrial toolbox on the opposite side of the hallway has had all the drawers pulled out and the weight of the tools has tipped the box onto its drawers, bending the bottom two at an odd angle. Wrenches and sockets are spilled on the floor. I accidently kick one and send it spinning away into the wall. It clatters into the darkness and ricochets off something before rattling itself to a stop. That's when I spot the foot. The small leather boot is toe-up beyond the toolbox, the leg stretched out to it from the shadows. I bring my light to the edge of the toolbox and the curve of multi-colored snail helmet protruding from beyond it.

"Jonah, are you okay?" I loop the lanyard of the flashlight over the bottom fingers of my gun hand and let the light swing as I reach for the boy's arm. His breathing is ragged and I expect him to turn toward me when I lay my hand on his shoulder, but he stays facing away. The flashlight beam swings like a pendulum from my fingers as I take a knee beside him.

"Hey, buddy. How are you feel—" The opening of the helmet finally turns toward me and the face inside lets out an ear-piercing shriek. Hands grasp my chest, yanking and tearing as I try to pull away. The eyes in the helmet flicker in the bouncing light and the mouth hisses through gnashing teeth.

"Holy—" I fall backward onto my ass in the middle of the hallway, but the creature is still clenching the fabric over my chest. The body is bony and small, and the weight of the helmet causes the creature's head to tilt. The bony fingers scrabble at the face shield of my helmet as the creature falls on top of me. I swing my free arm across my body and wedge my elbow between it and my torso, pushing as hard as I can to get it off me. The creature has its fingers on the metal collar at the base of my helmet and is chomping its mouth at me and drooling. I frantically shove the thing away from me, but not before it gets its teeth on the fabric of my shoulder. The suit rips as I fling the creature back against the toolbox.

Holy shitting shit.

I scramble to my feet and aim the gun and flashlight at it. The creature is wearing coveralls and its abdomen is soaked with blood. Multiple bullet holes punctuate the fabric and my guess is that one of the bullets must have struck its spine. The creature's legs lie limp and motionless even as the arms flail at me. Upon closer inspection, I realize that the diminutive monster is not a child, but rather a petite woman. The name on the coveralls over her heart reads *Eileen*. My finger wavers on the trigger.

Something tugs on my pack. Before I can turn around, I'm yanked backward into the doorway behind me. An emaciated hand scratches its fingernails across the bottom of my facemask. I shove the hand away and spin around to face the new threat. He's big. My height and broader in the shoulders, even though his face is gaunt, he must easily weigh 250 pounds. Before I can get my gun up, he clenches me in a bear hug, staring at me with hazy yellow eyes. His jaw drops open and his mouth gapes at the sight of me. He lets out a guttural moan and his teeth clunk against the visor.

Oh God.

Something is moving in the back of his throat. At first I think it's his tongue, but it's yellow and has spiny appendages protruding from its sides. Antennae and a beak precede a body like a centipede, thick enough that it takes up the whole width of the mouth. The yellow centipede scrabbles at the glass of my visor and has started to attach its front legs when I get the gun around the big man's arm.

I can only reach his shoulder with the muzzle but the first bullet rips through the muscle and causes his grip to relax. He roars from the pain and releases me. *Die die die*! I squeeze the trigger three more times before he takes another step. The noise from the gun is deafening inside my helmet, but the shots are effective. Two of the bullets rip into his upper chest and the third goes through his throat. Blood sprays from the last wound and spritzes the darkness behind him. He staggers and falls to his knees, one hand reaching for his throat while the other is still stretched out toward me.

As he collapses forward onto the floor, oozing darkness onto the concrete, the yellow centipede wriggles from his mouth. I stomp on it with my boot, sending green ooze across the floor and up the side of my other leg. I retch once and have to swallow down the bile that threatens to erupt from my throat. My hands are shaking with adrenaline. I notice the shadows shifting behind the body. Two more pairs of eyes reflect in the glow of my flashlight, and when I shine the beam directly at them, I realize they're not alone. At least half a dozen figures are crowded near the doorway and all of them now have their attention on me. *Shit*. I lower my flashlight and flee.

The thudding of my boots can't keep up with the pounding of my heartbeat in my ears. Shapes lunge at me in the darkness only to be defined in my flashlight beam as mattresses or overturned waste bins. The glowing map display in the visor rotates with each of my turns, but I lack the wherewithal to use it. I just run. When I've put the length of a half dozen corridors between myself and the site of the encounter, I finally slow to a walk and assess my options.

"Cal," I pant. "What the hell were those things?"

"The entities you encountered are the inhabitants of this facility."

"What happened to them? They looked human, but . . . what was wrong with them?"

"The Diamatra Colmetracite Mining Facility is home to approximately three-thousand human colonists who have been adapted by indigenous citizens as hosts."

"Adapted?"

"The primary sentient species on the planet Diamatra is the Soma Djinn. Soma Djinn, or 'Soma,' are a class of parasitic invertebrates that thrive in oxygen rich environments."

"Like mines that have been pressurized by humans?" I lift my light and continue to scan the corridor ahead of me.

"Indeed. This colony's automated environmental system is self-sustaining and produces a prime habitat for oxygen dependent species such as the Soma."

"What did they do to those people?"

"Soma Djinn require a host to maximize the intake of oxygen. They utilize a host's motor functions and respiratory tract for increased efficiency."

"So those people are still alive?"

"The host body's primary systems are kept intact while a chemical is secreted in the brain to assure responsive reception of the dominant species' inputs."

"They're like puppets, then. What was it trying to do to me?"

"In the presence of a healthier host body, a Soma Djinn will frequently attempt to relocate and consume the previous host body for fuel."

"Consume?"

"Conditions in the Diamatra Colmetracite Mining Facility have deteriorated due to discontinuation of food transport vessels and the depletion of previously stockpiled supplies. The current population of the colony is starving and has been observed to practice cannibalism."

"This place sucks, Cal. Get me out of here. Can you locate any of the others?"

The heads-up display on my visor illuminates and shows a path through an open section of floor plan and three distant blips of light on the far side. "The shortest path to other members of your party is through the hangar bay."

"Do you know which racers those blips belong to?"

"Negative, that information has been deemed unsearchable during chronothon competition."

"Okay." I watch the little dots moving along a corridor. *I don't care who they are. I'd even take Horacio and Donny over more of those creatures.*

I shove through a pair of double doors and get a chill from the cooler air on the other side. The blackness in the room is vast and my flashlight beam refracts off moisture in the air, limiting my view to a few dozen yards. The floor is flat concrete stretching out in three directions. The slam of the door behind me echoes faintly in the dark. I aim my flashlight upward but can't see the ceiling. A dim light from somewhere above is illuminating the mist overhead but doesn't reach the floor directly. I get another chill up my neck and shake it off, raising my gun and stepping forward into the haze.

"You have any kind of schematics on this room, Cal? How far to the other side?"

"Your destination is 185 meters northwest. Hangar bay corridor Foxtrot Seven Alpha."

"What did they keep in here?" I sweep my light side to side as I walk, noting cast off wheel chocks and drums labeled for fuel and hydraulic fluid.

"Hangar F7 houses air transport craft and subsurface—"

Shuffling from my left makes me spin and aim at the darkness beyond a decrepit tow vehicle. The winch on the vehicle has been left deployed and a dozen feet of cable is coiled haphazardly on the floor with a heavy tow hook at the end. A moan emanates from the darkness and a figure appears, moving slowly. Dark-skinned with shaggy, tight curls, he's wearing coveralls that match the creature I found in Jonah's helmet. He likewise has a name badge on his chest. *Terrance.*

I back away slowly as Terrance drags a hand along the back fender of the tow vehicle. His yellowed eyes are fixed on me as he shuffles his way directly into the coil of loose cable. He doesn't look down when his legs meet the resistance. His arms extend toward me, and his mouth drops open, then he falls. He tries to rise but has become even more entangled in the metal cable and begins to thrash. The heavy, metal hook on the end of the cable clunks and clatters against the floor with each attempt to get up. I put another ten yards between us to get away from the noise, but when I look back again, he has gained his feet and is staggering after me. The winch handle rotates on the vehicle as he walks, the ratcheting mechanism clunking solidly with each advance of the cable.

The noise seems amplified in the open space. I curse at the racket and turn to run, but almost collide with a woman in a flight helmet. She's trailing tubing from a detached oxygen mask and her mouth is drooling.

"Shit!" I veer right and hurdle a bundle of electrical conduits running along the floor. The pilot's hand reaches for me belatedly as I pass. I keep my gun and light raised, scanning the path ahead of me. I begin to jog, but have to stop after a few yards when I meet a cluster of another half dozen figures crouched around a fallen corpse. My heart jolts in my chest at the sight, but the body on the floor isn't recently deceased. Its bones have been picked at and its organs stripped away. One of the men facing me rises with a bit of the corpse's finger still protruding from its mouth. Another figure lunges at me from my right and I spin and fire at it in surprise. My first shot misses wildly, but the next two find their mark in the bearded man's forehead and face. The body teeters and falls backward with a soggy thud.

I start to run past him, but more shadows move in the haze, attracted by the sudden noise and flashes of light.

"How far to the door, Cal?" I shout into my helmet microphone, spinning in place and looking for a clear path.

"Corridor Foxtrot Seven Alpha is 79 meters northwest."

I follow the heads-up display on my visor and make it about ten more yards before encountering the wing of some kind of aircraft. A woman is staring idly at the vertical fin of the tail until my flashlight beam flickers across her face, then she turns and shrieks at me. I can still hear the distant clunking of Terrance and the winch when the pilot, trailing her oxygen mask hose, staggers out of the haze behind me. *Keep away from me, freaks . . .* I aim carefully and put a bullet through her left eye. She reels and collapses and is replaced almost instantly by three more figures that loom from the darkness. The woman at the tail of the aircraft takes a bullet in the chest but stays standing. She takes a couple of steps toward me, her expression curious. I aim more carefully and put the next bullet through her forehead. Two of the three men behind me lose parts of their heads and crash to the floor, but when I aim the gun at the third man and squeeze the trigger, the gun clicks on an empty chamber.

"Shit. Shit. Shit." I swing my pack off my back and squat down to fight with the latches, yanking dirty T-shirts and my water bottle out as I search for more ammunition. My hand closes on the handle of Charlie's revolver, and the man behind me gets a sizeable hole in his chest just as he's reaching for me. The gun has more kick than I expected and I lose my balance and end up on my backside as the body of my attacker hits the floor next to me. There is a rasping from his throat followed by a gurgling cough. Two long yellow antennae wriggle out his open mouth, followed by the thick, segmented body of the Soma Djinn.

I roll away from the creature in disgust and collide with the legs of another host body. The heavy man falls over me, flattening me to the concrete. I lose my grip on the flashlight and it spins away, rotating to a stop with its beam aimed at the aircraft's landing gear. I shove the man's legs off me, but he has turned to face me. His beard retains bits of rotting things and his teeth are brown. He clutches at my head, big meaty hands fumbling at my helmet. He hisses as he frantically scratches and flails at me. Something is pulling on my left foot. I shove the barrel of Charlie's gun directly into the mouth of the man attempting to eat me and squeeze the trigger. Chunks of skull, brains, and Soma Djinn spray into the air and rain back down with wet spattering sounds.

My boots are being clawed and chewed on by two more hangar workers. I can barely see them in the indirect glow of the flashlight, but I can feel the tugging and hear the tearing as they claw at my space suit. I aim at the head closest to me but someone falls on me before I can fire. I barely get my finger off the trigger in time to keep from shooting myself in the gut as the heavy body drives a knee into my abdomen and then knocks my arms aside.

This host is better fed than the others and his arm is heavy as he presses my elbow into the concrete. He leers at me with only one good eye, cocking it at me with eager intensity, a predator staring down prey. I can do nothing with the gun now and struggle to get my breath back as the man uses uncut fingernails to try to claw his way into my chest. I swing at the man's face with my left hand and barely manage to divert his attention with the punch. He snarls at me and knocks my arm away, still keeping his weight on my other elbow. I can feel my right boot being tugged loose from the space suit, and the panic in my mind reaches a new level of terror. *I'm being eaten alive.*

The man sitting astride me seems intent on tearing into my chest, and as the pressure of his fingers threatens to rip into me, I do the only thing I can think of. I grasp his collar, yanking on his neck and bringing my head up forcefully at the same time. His nose crunches into the top of my helmet and a crack radiates across my visor. It's enough to disorient him, and I shove hard to unseat him. He falls onto my right arm and I yank it free reflexively, losing my grip on the revolver but clearing my upper body from his oppressive weight.

I kick one of the creatures at my feet squarely in the jaw, and the resultant chaos gives me enough freedom to roll over onto my stomach. More hands and mouths arrive to claw and bite at my back and shoulders, but I concentrate on my left hand in front of me, working furiously to free the space suit glove. The yellow centipede legs of the loose Soma Djinn work in harmony to propel the creature over my left elbow and toward my face. Someone above me is wrenching at my helmet, trying to rip it from my body, but I can't focus on anything except my wrist. I throw my glove away and concentrate on the dials on my chronometer, moving them mostly from memory since I can barely see past the mustard yellow creature boring its way through the crack in my visor. The fingertips of my bandaged hand are pressed hard to the concrete as I use my other hand to reach for my chronometer. *Fifteen minutes. Be clear. Please, God, let it be clear.* I close my eyes and press the pin.

"Most time travelers are escapists at heart, constantly seeking the next adventure. With the inherent dangers we face, it's worth considering that the next jump could always be our last, and rushing onward may only hasten our untimely end."–Journal of Dr. Harold Quickly, 2019

Chapter 25

The concrete is cool and smooth below me. A draft is blowing from some unseen vent and has mercifully kept the hangar floor dust-free. My space suit is gone. My flashlight, pack, and weapons are gone. All I have is the darkness, and somewhere to my right, the ragged breathing of a creature that would like to eat me. I can't see even the floor below me, but I can remember the face of the woman who had been staring at the tail of the aircraft, the woman who was so curious until I shot her in the head. Will shoot her in the head.

Fifteen minutes.

For now, I lie still and do my best not to exist. Somewhere behind me and a little to the right is the aircraft. I try to focus and remember my bearings. It was another seventy meters to the wall: a terrifying distance in the dark. I stretch my blistered chronometer hand. My bandage is gone, left behind in the near future with my other belongings. I shift slightly and a sudden blue glow emanates from my right wrist. I clamp my burned hand over it, smothering it, hiding the oppressive ticking display on my race bracelet. It's funny that I never noticed the faint light before. Here, in this void, it seems to burn with the intensity of a searchlight.

I stare into the blackness and try to imagine the space. In a few minutes this place will be swarming with half-dead host bodies anxious to devour me. Without my suit to protect me, those sharp nails and eager jaws will have no difficulty separating flesh from bone. I need to be gone. The second danger lies in being discovered by myself. No paradoxes—the hard-and-fast rule of the chronothon and the sure ticket to disqualification. I have little confidence in the committee's willingness to let me continue the race under normal circumstances, let alone as a violator of the rules. My mind goes back to Dennis and the Asian woman, hiding in their Humvee. *Were they left behind in Egypt?* The thought makes me envious. Egypt was a vacation compared to this.

I tuck my right wrist into my armpit to cover up the light, and ease myself sideways, crawling as slowly as I can toward the place I remember seeing the landing gear of the aircraft. I get to my knees and then to a crouch, and finally I stand, stretching my left arm above me, feeling for the wing. My knee thuds into something solid and I freeze. I listen for the telltale signs of doom, footsteps or snarling, something to tell me that I'm now a target. For a moment I wonder if the creatures are all doing the same thing, standing and listening, trying to home in on the source of the sound.

I drop my hand to my knee and feel for my obstacle. My fingers brush the edge of the rigid panel, a flat vertical plane with occasional bumps of rivets. I probe the darkness beyond it and touch rubber, my fingertips tracing the lines of tread in the tire. I've found my landing gear. I run my hand upward along the vertical gear door until its apex at the bottom of the wing and then step forward again, feeling for the side of the fuselage. My hand encounters a tube of some kind protruding from the leading edge, then it travels onward to the crook of the wing where it angles away from the fuselage. *It must be here somewhere. Somehow they must climb this thing.* My hand searches the side of the aircraft in slow, methodical sweeping arcs, searching for the foothold, a step or a ladder.

I smell the creature even before I hear it. Without my helmet on, the sour stench of unwashed body and the fetid decay of its breath gives it away. The shuffling steps come next. Close. *An arms length? Two?* I let my fingers continue their silent search. I almost miss it, but then my hand sinks into the void, my fingertips brush the rough horizontal plane of the step, gritty and built for traction. With one step located, I have an idea where the next should be. *Is this for a right or left foot? Where is the handle?* My fingers find the handle at the same time I feel the creature's rasping breath waft across me. *It's designed for a right hand. Right hand, left foot.*

Releasing my right wrist from its hiding place, tucked against my body, I reach for the handle. The dull blue light of the bracelet illuminates the yellow eyes and ragged hair of the curious woman mere inches from my face. Her eyes widen in the glow of the light and her mouth opens in desire. I snatch the hair on the top of her scalp, forcing her head back at an angle as her jaw works open and shut. I keep her at a distance as she flails like a child in the grip of a schoolyard bully. I stretch my injured hand upward for the handle, obligated to reach across my body to grip it. My left foot inches upward for the step, while I press on the curious woman's head to keep my balance. Her fingers scrabble at my T-shirt, and the belt loops of my jeans, but I hold her at bay until I can pull myself onto the step, shoving her away at the last moment and using the few seconds where she's teetering to climb. The handholds come fast now and I draw my foot up and away just as her fingers scrape my calf. I kick her and send her staggering, then climb the rest of the way up to the cockpit.

The canopy is locked, or it uses some latch that is invisible to me in the darkness. In either case, entrance is lost to me. I slide sideways and flop myself onto the aircraft's wing instead. The surface is slick but I find a handhold in some crevice or flight control. I stabilize myself and lie prone atop the wing. There's nothing to see beyond the tiny orb of light around my wrist and I tuck that away again as I hear distant, muffled gunshots.

The next few minutes are surreal. First comes the banging of the doors, followed by the sweeping beam of the flashlight, hazy in the misty air. Then footsteps, clomping sounds that echo in the darkness. *How did I not realize how loud I was?* I lie still and listen to the approach of my earlier self, space boots thudding in the darkness, the flashlight a beacon to guide the creatures toward me. Terrance collides with the tow cable again and ratchets his way through the darkness. The woman pilot lurches from the void. When the flashlight illuminates the group eating the corpse, I'm close enough to view the scene clearly. Then the gunshots come, blinding, deafening flashes as each attacker's death draws more from the darkness. My predecessor ends up only a few yards from my perch on the wing. The flashlight twirls its way across the floor and I'm forced to squint as it lights up the landing gear below me. As the earlier me uses Charlie's gun to perforate the skull of the last doomed host, bits of gore rain down around me, one warm hunk landing atop my outstretched hand. I shudder, but stay silent.

It's almost painful to listen to the noises of the host bodies tearing and biting at the man in the suit below me. The terror is back and my heart pounds as I close my eyes, clench my fists, and wait out the horror. Finally, the earlier me makes his escape. The host bodies flail and rage, ripping and clawing at the space suit. I watch in fascination as the one-eyed man holds the empty suit aloft by its helmet and the other creatures tear it limb from limb. A wave of déjà vu washes over me and I close my eyes. *Wabash was right. My nightmares are coming true.*

The commotion over the space suit attracts more of the host bodies from around the hangar. Soon, the area underneath the wing is packed thick with them. I'm despairing of ever getting down when a door opens from the far wall and a voice calls out from the glow. "TRAVERS! YOU OKAY?"

The gruff tone of Cliff's shout is the sweetest melody now.

"HEY! I'M HERE!"

The hungry bodies below look up at my shout and start pawing at the wing.

"WHAT'S YOUR SITUATION?"

A few of the creatures turn their attention toward the light and the shouting and begin to stagger for the doorway.

"BAD!"

The door closes and I'm left alone with the monsters and the dull glow of my flashlight through their teeming legs. When the door opens again, an arm lobs something into the room, away from my position, and I hear it bounce a few times into the center of the hangar. The door slams shut again and I crouch low on the wing in case it's some kind of explosive. But once the object comes to a stop, a light begins to emanate from it, and soon a holographic projection of Jettison takes shape. He looks around the room and locates the horde of creatures near the plane, then starts waving his arms and shouting. The distraction has the desired effect. I watch one of the host bodies drop the boot she was chewing on and stumble off toward the light.

I crawl to the end of the wing and search for my belongings. The space suit is in tatters. The Soma Djinn successfully penetrated the face shield of the helmet and there is a sizeable hole where the crack had started. I don't see the creature anymore, but it could have fallen into the suit when the one-eyed man held it aloft. Bits of the rest of the suit are scattered all over.

My pack appears to be mostly intact, and I spot the silver gleam of Charlie's revolver, but can't make out Viznir's pistol through the darkness and shifting feet. One of the creatures kicks the flashlight and sends it spinning again, but I know the general orientation of things.

Jettison's decoy is getting swarmed, and I'm just considering jumping down for the gun and making a run for it when the door opens again. Cliff and Jettison are followed by Bozzle and Genesis. They have all shed their bulky space suits. The three humans have guns, but Bozzle is carrying a long metal pike with a blade on the end. They move in unison toward my position and, as they encounter their first resistance, a man in a tattered jumpsuit, Bozzle steps forward and jabs the creature cleanly through the eye. The next three attackers meet the same fate, Bozzle's long arms and extended reach with the pike ensuring that they never even get close. The host bodies below me shift and moan and their jaws drop open in hunger as they turn their attention toward the new arrivals. As the creatures begin to swarm, Cliff and the Marsh siblings begin to unload on them, blasting anything that threatens to get close. *Come on, guys. You can make it. Get me the hell out of here.*

THE CHRONOTHON

The area around the plane has vacated sufficiently for me to have a clear path to Charlie's gun, so I slide off the wing and drop the eight feet to the hangar floor. I land in a crouch but am up and moving immediately. The gun still has four rounds left in the cylinder chambers, but as soon as I reach my pack I locate more. I stuff a handful of the spare rounds into my back pocket and snatch up the flashlight. I do a sweep of the hangar floor, but there's no sign of Viznir's pistol. A short, bald man staggers out of the darkness in a zigzagging jog. Charlie's handgun bores a hole directly though the creature's chest and drops him on his back. The wriggling Soma's antennae have just felt their way to the floor when I stomp on its head.

Suck on that.

I retreat from the mess and dash to join the others.

"You okay? You get bit up?" Genesis asks.

"I'm okay. Just freaking out."

Bozzle steps past me and cleaves one of the creatures' heads off its body with the end of his pike. Cliff fires another blast of his shotgun at something I can't see, then signals the retreat. We fall back to the door and I fire the rest of my rounds in the process. As soon as we're closed off in the hallway, I stop to reload.

"We've located the security system control center," Jettison says. "The others are holed up in there."

"Did you find Jonah?"

"Yeah, he's there. And Harrison."

Cliff puts his hand on my shoulder. "Wabash took some heavy hits getting that kid through. He's in a bad state. But try not to scare the kid too much. He's pretty shaken up as it is."

"Is Wabash going to be okay?"

"We're not sure. He got stung by a Soma and those things are toxic as hell. They get some kind of neurotoxin in you before they head for your brain. He managed to kill it, but not till after he was jabbed."

"Did he make another jump to try to get the poison out?"

"Yeah, eventually he did, but he was in the thick of it and had to get the kid to safety. By the time he made the jump to get it out, it was pretty late. Some likely got absorbed and gravitized by his body. It's hard to say."

I fall back with Genesis and Bozzle as Cliff and Jettison lead the way to the control center. We descend another level in silence, only probing the darkness with our lights as necessary, trying to attract as little attention as possible. Jettison raps on the metal sliding door and it rolls open for us. Kara is on the other side, her gun at the ready.

We file into the control center. It's an octagonal room fitted with windows that look out over a massive abyss. Milo is fiddling with the controls at a bank of computers. The displays are fancier than anything from my time, but they seem antiquated compared to some of the technology I saw in the Academy lab.

Kara gives me a nod and Milo shakes my hand. "It's good you're here, Ben. I think we're going to need all the help we can get. How are you?"

"Tired, but still alive. That's saying something."

Milo nods soberly and gestures to one display in particular that is showing a constantly changing stream of numbers. "I'm trying to get us through the mine bay doors. The primary doors to the other sublevels have been sealed and the code-breaking program needs a little time to decrypt it. Rest a minute if you need to."

"Where's Wabash?"

Milo points through a second doorway into an attached conference room. "We set him up in there as best we could."

I step through the doorway into the dimly lit room. The floor is carpeted and Harrison Wabash is propped against one wall in a corner. The others seem to have built him a sort of cushion with their packs. His face is pale, but he smiles when I enter. Jonah is sitting on the floor beside him, also leaning against the wall, and Barley has his head and front paws draped protectively over the boy's lap. The dog's golden eyes follow me as I cross the room, but he doesn't lift his head. All three of them look exhausted.

"Good to see you made it, Ben." Harrison's voice is raspy. He gestures toward the space along the wall next to Jonah. "Come join us." He coughs twice, and the effort seems to drain him. I let my pack slump to the floor and lay the gun and flashlight next to it before sliding down the wall next to Jonah. The boy looks shaken.

"Looks like Barley found his way back to you. That dog was determined, let me tell you. That's one loyal friend you have there."

Jonah toys with the dog's ears and then wraps his arms around Barley's neck and leaves them there. "I thought I lost him."

I stretch my hand slowly to the dog's snout, and he licks my fingers before I scratch his head.

The boy's face is downcast. "I lost my helmet."

"That's okay. Your head probably feels lighter now, right?"

Jonah shakes his head. "I wasn't supposed to take it off. Jay says I have to keep it on or the brain invaders will get me."

"Jay is your brother?"

Jonah nods. "He says if you don't watch out, your self from the future can come back and steal your body. You won't know it's coming till it's too late and then you lose, and then the other you gets to have your brain."

THE CHRONOTHON

I put an arm around Jonah. "You know, Jonah, sometimes older brothers like to give their younger siblings a hard time, tell them things that aren't true just to scare them."

"Jay's not lying. He says he learned about it at school. The brain invaders are real. They make you one of them and then you start invading your own brain."

I look to Wabash to see if he will dismiss the account. To my surprise, he gives me a nod of confirmation.

Jonah leans into my chest. His face is dirty and his hair is a mess and, despite all his knowledge of the future, he still seems like just a little kid. I brush some of the loose hair away from his face. "You know what, Jonah? All that might be true, but you shouldn't worry about it, you know why?"

He looks up at me. "Why?"

"Because you're a good kid. And you'll always be one of the good guys. That means no future version of you is ever going to be anything except awesome. And awesome good guys don't invade people's brains."

"What about the other brain invaders?"

"You are going to beat the brain invaders. Hey, you can just zap 'em with your organism gun. It works on brains, right?"

Jonah frowns. "It didn't work. It didn't work on the . . . aliens." He fidgets with the fur around the dog's neck. "I couldn't help."

I pull Jonah a little closer and pat his shoulder. "Don't worry about that. We're getting out of here as fast as we can. And once we're gone, we're never coming back to this place."

Jonah eyes the gun lying next to my pack. "Did you beat the aliens?"

"We all did. And we're gonna stick together now. You just get some rest."

Jonah doesn't speak again. We just stay like that for a while. I listen to the muffled voices of Jettison and the others talking in the next room and Harrison's labored breathing. After a few minutes, Jonah's breathing becomes more even and his head droops a little on my shoulder. I notice Harrison is watching me.

"That boy looks up to you."

"He's a good kid." I study the bandages on Harrison's arms and hands. "You did a great thing getting him here. I know what it cost you."

He winces and adjusts his position. "It's all we can do in situations like this. Jonah shouldn't be here. None of us should." He turns to me. "Did you dream this? Is this what you saw?"

"Some of it. Bits and pieces."

"It's true then. You are dreaming the future. You should pay attention."

"What is it? What's happening to cause it?"

"I couldn't say. Traveling through time does strange things to a mind. We get disjointed. I think sometimes all the disconnecting and reconnecting from normal time does something to break us."

"Have you had trouble?"

"Not me personally, but there are others out there who have. Some even try to use it to their advantage. The 'brain invaders' the kid was talking about? They might sound like the boogey man, but they're real enough. Call themselves 'The Eternals.' They say they can live forever. It's a scary concept. They try to latch their consciousness onto their own younger bodies, subverting their younger minds."

"And it works?"

"Sometimes, I guess. Other times they end up with a multiple personality disorder, with all their minds fighting for control. Lots of them go insane. It's a creepy cult at best, and not one many people are eager to join."

"Why would his brother be concerned about them?"

"Jay is an older version of Jonah from what I hear, so if he's had contact with The Eternals, maybe he was scared that he might try to use the power on his younger self someday. Power does crazy things to people."

"But he's the one who gave him the helmet, right? So Jay can't be all bad. He's at least looking out to protect Jonah. Even if it's from himself."

"Let's hope that's the trait that wins out." Harrison rubs a hand across his brow and shifts a little. "What are your dreams about? Is it yourself you're talking to, or someone else?"

I think about my latest vision. "It's me."

"And what is your other self doing? Do you get the sense he's trying to take over your mind?"

"No, not really. He's trying to show me something. It's just hard to tell what he's saying. He said I need to come find him. When this is over."

"Where is he?"

"That's the scary part. I think he's dead."

Harrison studies me for a moment, then starts coughing again. When the fit passes, he raises his eyes back to me. "That sounds like a challenging search." He opens his hand and notices blood on his palm. "Though maybe I'll be seeing him before you do." He lets his head fall back against the wall.

"Do you need anything? Do you want some of my water?" I shift Jonah off my chest and prop him up against the wall in an effort to get to my pack. His mouth has dropped open and his head slumps onto his shoulder.

Harrison waves his hand weakly. "I'm okay. I just need a little rest."

Jettison pokes his head into the doorway and calls to me. "Ben, you might want to take a look at this."

I pat Harrison's hand and give it a brief squeeze before joining the others. Milo and Genesis are staring at a screen in the center of the control panel. Genesis moves aside so I can see. Jettison points to the figure in a space suit navigating a dark hallway. "I don't know what you want to do about this situation."

"Where is that?" I ask. The camera footage is dim, but I can make out the crack in the visor.

"One level up. He seems to be headed for the Level One domiciles," Milo replies. He pans through a few other camera feeds and stops on another image. "That's this one."

The camera shows a hallway teeming with Soma Djinn hosts. They are milling around the doorway and in and out of the personnel quarters. One appears to have a pillowcase stuck to its head. The image would be humorous if I didn't know what the creatures were capable of.

"He hasn't encountered much resistance, luckily, because he doesn't seem to be armed." Milo flips back to the shot of Viznir.

I frown at the screen. "He isn't. I took his gun."

"Wabash told us what he did to you," Jettison says. "It's your call."

"Damn it." I stride back into the conference room and snatch up my things. Wabash has fallen asleep against the wall. I carry my pack to the main room and set it on the desk behind the monitors. I pull Charlie's leather gun belt out of my pack and check the chambers before securing the holster to my thigh. "He's a bastard for what he did, but I can't let him just walk into that mess. Nobody deserves to die like that."

Cliff gives me a nod and cocks his shotgun. Bozzle slides away from the wall where he's been leaning and likewise picks up his weapon. "It is the right decision."

Milo points to a timer on a second screen. "We have a second issue. We've broken through the lock on the primary mine doors, but it's triggered a countdown on the time gate."

I check the display on my race bracelet, and a new clock has replaced the counting on the indicator screen. This one is ticking down and has just less than two hours remaining.

"We all need to get our objectives and be at that gate before this thing stops or we're getting stuck here."

"Do the others know?" I ask. "Where are the other racers?"

Milo flips through a few more images on the security screens and shows me a shot of a massive tunnel. Thick steel doors have parted, leaving a gap about ten feet wide. "Tad and Blaine were at the primary mine doors a few minutes ago. The academy teams were running their own code-breaking algorithm against the lock from there, but my program hacked it first. They'll be ahead of us."

"Who was with them?"

"Horacio and Donny, Ariella and Dagmar. Preston and Deanna came through a minute or two later. That's it for teams. Titus and his guide quit at the Academy, so we're all that's left."

I look around the room. "Wait, where's Mayra?"

Genesis's mouth hardens in a line and Cliff shakes his head.

"Oh. I'm sorry, Gen. I didn't mean to—I should have noticed earlier—"

"Forget it." Genesis' voice is firm. "Let's just get out of here."

Jettison steps forward. "Okay, here's the plan. Wabash and the kid are going to need help, and they'll be moving slow, so somebody has to guard them. Cliff, I'll be fine on my own. You and Gen can help Milo and Kara get the others to the gate, while Ben, Bozzle, and I round up the objectives for the rest of the team."

"That's a good idea. I can feed you info through the meta-space," Milo adds. "And if I get to the gate, I might be able to run interference on the countdown and buy us more time."

"So we meet you at the gate?" I ask.

"Yeah. Find your wayward guide and I'll lead you to the objectives via Jettison."

I pull the tablet from my pack and show Milo the photo I managed to take of my objective. "I had a hard time with the technology this round, but that's where my objective is."

Milo studies the photo briefly, then puts the tablet into one of his cargo pockets. "No problem. I'll add it to the list."

Genesis and Cliff step into the conference room, and a few moments later, Jonah and Barley walk out. Wabash follows them, leaning heavily on Cliff, but he has a determined scowl on his pale face when the pair joins the rest of us. Genesis hands back the rest of the team's belongings.

"Okay. We ready for this?" Milo doesn't wait for an answer but mashes a button on the console and the metal security room door slides open. Kara is the first one through. An emaciated Soma host has suffered the misfortune of finding its way into the hallway and Kara's blaster disintegrates the creature's entire upper body in one shot. The rest of us trail behind her and exit the double doors at the far end of the hall. Kara decimates what little resistance we meet, and I'm not required to even draw my gun until we reach the stairwell.

"We're up from here," Jettison says and leads the way up the stairs. Our party splits and I climb after Jettison while Bozzle takes the rear. Jonah waves to me just before I gain the first landing.

"I'll be back soon, buddy. I'll see you at the gate."

The rest of the group takes the stairs headed down and vanishes into the darkness below.

"We need to move quick; your guide is almost at the domiciles," Jettison says. His eyes have the same hazy look Tucket got when using the meta-space, but Jettison snaps out of it quickly and focuses on the task ahead. We emerge on the next floor in a cafeteria kitchen. The store cupboards have been ransacked long ago and bits of plastic wrappers and empty containers scatter in our wake as we jog through. A few Soma hosts stumble from the corners of the room but we are gone before they have time to get near.

The entrance to the domiciles involves a trek across a catwalk that spans the abyssal hole into the planet. The blackness yawns out in every direction around us, but for once it doesn't bother me. I focus on the beam of my flashlight and the glow of occasional emergency lights along the ceiling. Jettison suddenly stops walking and I can tell he's off in the meta-space again.

"Shit. They've seen him." He breaks into a run and we hurry to follow. We burst through a double door into the corridor where we last spotted Viznir. A throng of Soma are pushing and clawing at one another in an attempt to enter one of the narrow domicile doorways off the corridor. The room is overflowing with them already and my heart sinks. *How will Viznir survive that?*

The fringe of the horde turns its attention toward us and Jettison and I drop the first wave in a hail of gunfire. As we stop to reload, Bozzle steps past us and twists the handle of his pike until the tip sizzles with electricity. He lowers the pike toward the horde and fries the next group of attackers with a bolt of bright-white energy.

The hallway immediately takes on the odor of burnt flesh. Jettison and I come up firing and level the next row of host bodies. We repeat the process a few more times. I get faster with the reloading, and we've cleared a path almost to the crowded doorway when Bozzle's pike fails to fire. He doesn't hesitate however. He steps forward and begins cleaving his way through the mob with the still-glowing blade. His swings leave trails of light in the darkness. He reaches a container on the wall that holds an emergency fire axe and shatters the glass with the butt of his pike. He snatches the axe from its receptacle and tosses it back to me. I follow his lead and proceed to hack my way through the few Soma hosts that make it past his pike.

Jettison tips me off to a new danger by shining his light at one of the host body's decapitated heads. A yellow Soma Djinn has wriggled its way clear of the teeth and is waving its antennae in our direction. I look down and realize many of the fallen bodies are now leaking alien parasites. I put the blunt end of the axe to good use and start smashing them into the floor.

Jettison reaches into the domicile doorway and yanks a host body out of his way with his bare hands. The snarling man lands face up in front of me and gets only a second to growl about it before my axe finds his skull.

"VIZNIR! YOU IN THERE?" Jettison shouts into the room. One of the Soma hosts is holding an empty, cracked space helmet above his head and shaking it, as if hoping something good will tumble out. I begin to despair about finding Viznir alive, but then a muffled cry comes from somewhere beyond the snarling mob.

Jettison wrangles a woman wearing a scarf out of his way. "HANG ON. WE'RE COMING FOR YOU!"

It takes Jettison and me another five minutes to clear our way to Viznir. The last few Soma hosts are on their bellies, trying to reach under the frame of the metal bunk where he has hidden himself. He's managed to kill one of the creatures with his knife, and the fallen body has kept the others from crawling under the bed after him. The space is narrow, and I can understand why he had to lose his helmet before having any chance of squeezing under. We have a difficult time extracting him from the constricted space even without the host bodies. Viznir is covered in blood and green slime from the Soma Djinn he has stabbed with his knife, but he seems otherwise unharmed. He doesn't hold eye contact with me long, but it's long enough to get out a mumbled thank you.

I hold my hand out for Viznir's knife. He hesitates briefly, but then hands it over. I wipe the blade off on the shirt of one of the fallen bodies, then tuck it into my belt. "Come on. We've got work to do." I jerk my head toward the doorway, and we return to the corridor, where Bozzle has used the time to add another layer of bodies to the sizeable stack around the door.

Viznir climbs out of the torn and bloody wreckage of his space suit and tosses it to the floor. "Where are we going?"

"We're collecting the objectives for the group and getting out of here. We've got less than two hours to get it done, so we've got to hurry."

"It's not going to help," Viznir says. His face is solemn, but I detect no deceit in it, only quiet resignation.

"Why? Why wouldn't it?"

Jettison and Bozzle look back and listen.

"The others might make it, but we never will. Our objective was a lie."

"For a lot of years, people thought wormholes would require massive amounts of power to open. They failed to factor in a fundamental aspect of spacetime—its stretchiness. Want to squeeze a full-sized man through a microscopic hole? Yep, it's possible, because that's one stretchy time hole."–Journal of Dr. Harold Quickly, 1997

Chapter 26

"Explain yourself. What's the lie?" I stare into Viznir's eyes, trying to draw the truth out of him.

"You're not authorized to get through the gate. It was their backup plan in case I failed to kill you."

I remember the conversation with Milo and Kara in the old west and their theory about Marco and Andre. "Someone told you this? You know for sure?"

"It wasn't to me directly, but I overheard the conversation. The day they recruited me, there was someone from the committee there, too. They talked about rigging the time gates."

"Chairman Schnyder?"

"No, it wasn't the chairman. I don't think he knew. It was a woman. An Indian woman. She was a doctor or a scientist."

"Pia Chopra," Jettison says. "She was at the opening dinner."

"So you knew the thing was rigged the whole time. You knew I'd never make it off this planet either way." My temper is rising again. "And now I'm stuck here. Is that what you're saying?"

"We both are," Viznir replies.

Jettison interrupts. "We don't have time for a pow-wow right now. Let's figure this out at the gate. We've got to move."

I'm angry and I want to pry more information out of Viznir, but Jettison has a valid point. If we don't make the gate in time, nobody will have a chance at leaving.

Beyond the double doors at the end of the hall, snarling and banging indicate more of the Soma hosts arriving. Bozzle moves left and leads the way down another dark corridor with confident strides. Viznir ducks past me to follow him, and I say nothing else, but I'm careful to keep him in view.

Milo has mapped out the locations of the objectives for the rest of the team, and the first one is only one level below us. The Admiral's objective is a precision rock-cutting tool that is no bigger than my flashlight. Jettison helps me ensure it's off and won't accidently laser me through my bag before I pack it away. From the tool supply room we head downward toward the primary mine doors. Along the way, we pick up another objective intended for Genesis. Hers is a pair of night vision goggles that Jettison stows around his neck in case we might have to use them. We also locate Milo's objective, an ornate porcelain cigar case we find stuffed in a miner's closet. It's full of handwritten recipes for crab Rangoon, eggs benedict, and honey-barbeque wings, among other dishes I've never heard of.

We encounter a few of the Soma hosts along the way, but only individuals or small clusters, none like the dense horde from the hallway, and we are able to dispatch them as necessary. Some we merely block off by jamming doors shut behind us as we travel.

Below sublevel two, our path leaves the familiar confines of hallways and residential spaces and opens up onto an underground road. It's paved and wide enough for four vehicles abreast, but sections of the road have cracked and become disjointed over time. The road leads us ever downhill into the blackness. After perhaps a quarter mile, the road joins the edge of the hole I crossed via the catwalk. The abyss is bridged here by thick steel grating. The welded joints leave openings that a person could easily fall through, but block the hole from passage by anything larger.

The primary mine doors are massive metal slabs at least three feet thick. Crossing the road ahead of us, they stretch approximately thirty feet up and are wide enough that the ten-foot gap Milo managed to open in them seems a narrow space. As we pass through, I can't help but wonder why they were needed. *Were they keeping something out or in?* Descending farther, the air grows warmer and pipes along the walls hiss with vented steam. It is not a welcoming sound.

A few Soma Djinn host bodies dot the path in various states of dismemberment. The mostly disintegrated forms show evidence of Kara's passing. The sight gives me comfort that Jonah and Wabash are in good hands.

"The others will be headed straight for the time gate, but we need to grab the rest of the objectives along the way." Jettison points to a diverging road that angles away from the main thoroughfare. "Jonah's is this way."

We veer down a secondary road and pass through the center of an underground village. The main passage is rounded, as if bored out by a massive drill, and housing has been carved out of the earth to either side.

Rounded doorways and windows echo the shape of the tunnel and give the impression of hollow eyes and mouths gaping at us as we pass. The rocks are a deep black, a compressed and hardened version of the somber soil on the surface of the planet. Occasionally, I catch the glint of other minerals in the rock, threads of colored or white crystals. A band of silver arcs its way through the ceiling above us.

Our target lies in a structure at the end of the tunnel. A sign reading "Mineral Testing Lab" is mounted above a gate made of beige synthetic material. The lock only slows us down for the amount of time it takes Bozzle to bore an arm-sized hole through the gate with his electrically heated pike. He barely waits for the material to cool before thrusting a tattooed arm through the opening and fishing around for the latch. Smoke drifts off the seared edges of the hole and across my flashlight beam. Bozzle seems unconcerned with the heat, making me wonder just how tough his green skin is. When the gate swings open, we enter a narrower tunnel that is walled with plastic or fiberglass panels. Strips of emergency lighting illuminate along the floor as we walk, casting the hallway in hues of red. Bozzle is forced to stoop slightly to get his tall frame through the passage.

Jettison is navigating to our prize via the meta-space, and I merely follow along, keeping a wary eye on the curving hallway for signs of trouble, and keeping Viznir where I can see him. I holster Charlie's pistol but keep the axe over my left shoulder. We meet no resistance, and he leads us into a specimen room full of plastic bins and neatly labeled shelves. I'm immediately reminded of the mineral lab in Australia where I met Mym. This room is better organized and remarkably cleaner despite its underground location and twenty years of disuse. Air is circulating freely through the vents overhead, and when I pass a fingertip over the metal cabinet next to me, it barely lifts any dust.

Various glass display cases around the room house brightly colored minerals and crystals. A brilliant purple one catches my eye, and I pause to admire the nautilus spiral of color in its center.

"This is what we want." Jettison is two cases over, unlatching the door in front of a pitch-black rock on a silver stand. I wander over as he's pulling it from the case, and he tosses it to me to stow with the other objectives. I catch the rock one-handed and turn it over, noting a thin green streak from its core that meanders across its surface. The color is faint in the dim lighting, but there is no mistaking that it's green, a deep forest green. I hold it up to Bozzle's face. "This one should have been your anchor. You match."

Bozzle considers the stone with his ink-black eyes and pokes the surface with a pointed finger. "We have this on my planet. We call it, *meshtoon.*"

"Let's move," Jettison says. "Clock's ticking."

We rejoin the main road and have made it another quarter mile when we hear the screaming. It's high-pitched and female and echoes off the stone walls from somewhere below us. We race down the road and follow it around a hairpin turn that cuts back below us in the direction we came. A light from a turn of the road below us illuminates shapes moving in the glow. *Oh God, who's down there?* I lean over the edge to try to identify the source of the screaming and see a streak of blonde hair fleeing a pack of Soma hosts. I get an irrational fear for Mym, but then recognize the taller girl as Deanna. She's climbing the road away from the horde below her. There is a commotion near the light. Creatures are fighting for position over a fallen figure. My throat tightens as I realize someone else is down there. Someone human.

The mass of teeming bodies on the road is frenzied. The pack chasing Deanna is moving faster than the ones we encountered on the higher levels and consists almost exclusively of athletic looking men, but one six-foot tall, red-haired woman breaks away from them and starts scaling the side of the cliff to cut Deanna off. We round the corner at the upper curve of the road as Deanna turns the lower one. She is ahead of the main pack, but the red-haired woman clears the side of the cliff and intercepts her before we reach her. Deanna's eyes are wide and she's unarmed. Her forearms are scratched and bleeding, her hair a tangled mess.

I draw my gun, but the woman is in a direct line with Deanna, making a shot too dangerous. Deanna screams again as the woman lunges for her. The two tumble to the road and begin to roll downhill toward the group of men now rounding the corner. Their faces are hard, and their yellow eyes gleam with a hint of intelligence, unlike the hazy, distant stares of the host bodies we've dispatched so far. Some of these men are even carrying clubs and tools as weapons.

Jettison shoots first. A few of the creatures at the front of the pack go down, but the others break into a run. Bozzle's pike sizzles and sends a blast of electricity over Deanna, hitting the leader of the group in the chest. He twitches and falls under the feet of the others. The single shot must be all Bozzle has power for, because he doesn't attempt a second. Instead, he races forward and leaps cleanly over Deanna and the red-haired woman and plunges into the horde beyond. His attack knocks three of the men off their feet.

Viznir has stopped in the road with his fists clenched and looks like he might turn to run, but I race past him. I reach Deanna and drop the axe in order to yank back on her attacker's hair. The woman hisses and spins, faster than I was expecting. Her fingers stretch for my eyes. *Oh shit.* I duck back, narrowly avoiding her dirty, jagged nails. One of her hands wraps around the barrel of my gun and I struggle to catch her other flailing wrist, barely keeping it from my face. She's strong and quick, squirming and twisting while attempting to wrench the gun from my grasp. She knees me in the groin and I stagger. She goes for my throat with her bared teeth and I fall backward to avoid being bitten. The barrel of the gun is oscillating erratically between us in her grip. I keep my finger away from the trigger to keep from being shot with my own weapon, muttering curses and holding onto the gun with both hands now as she fights me for possession. She attempts to bite my hand and I knock her head away once with my elbow, but she comes at me again. Her teeth have just touched the skin of my hand when the axe blade caves in the side of her skull.

I reopen my eyes after the initial spray of blood and roll the body off me to find Deanna standing over me. Her face is scratched and bleeding and she is breathing hard. She yanks the axe from the dead woman's head with a grunt. "Bitch."

Deanna's red ATS shirt is torn to shreds. The black tank top she's wearing underneath is stuck to her in dark wet patches. As she straightens back up, her white-knuckled grip on the axe relaxes and her body shakes.

"You okay?" I ask as I climb back to my feet.

Deanna doesn't reply. She keeps her gaze on the wreck of the woman at our feet. I look beyond her. Bozzle and Jettison are being overwhelmed by a dozen men, Jettison's gun has fallen and he and Bozzle are both fighting hand to hand with their attackers. I raise my gun and fire at the first target I can get in my sights. I turn around and look for Viznir. He's still frozen in place on the road but watching the fighting. I pull his knife from my belt and toss it to his feet. "Come on. Stay with me." I step past Deanna and empty my gun into the pack. As I'm reloading, I watch Deanna out of the corner of my eye. She's clearly in shock, but it doesn't stop her from swinging at a rabid-looking Asian man who lunges at us. Viznir follows us into the melee too. From there it's all fighting for the next frantic minutes. When it's done, nearly twenty bodies litter the ground around us. The last couple of attackers have enough intelligence to run, but they don't make it out of range of Charlie's pistol.

Jettison is bleeding from a bite wound on his arm and cradles it gingerly as I stomp on the Soma Djinn that come wriggling out of the bodies. These Soma are darker than the ones I'd seen in the levels above. Instead of only yellow, their segmented bodies have hardened scales with dark patches of green and gray. They are larger, and I suspect they're a more mature variety of the species, giving their hosts an added touch of intelligence. They still squish the same under my heel.

Deanna is clutching the axe to her chest as we descend the next stretch of road. She stops completely as we near the glow of the dropped electric lantern. A few feet away, a pair of Soma hosts are chewing on the body of someone in a red uniform. Jettison shoots them before they can turn their attention to us. They fall next to the young man who is barely recognizable as Preston Marquez.

"He saved me." Deanna is staring at Preston's feet. His boots are the only part of him that seem to be untouched. "He held them off while I ran."

Jettison scans the ground around the body with his flashlight.

Preston's shaggy black hair seems to blend with the dark soil around his head. "What are we going to do?" I pull my eyes away from his vacant stare and turn to Bozzle. "It doesn't seem right to leave him here."

"We won't," Jettison replies. He stoops and snatches up a loose stone, then moves to Preston's side. He presses the stone into the dead man's open palm and pushes his tattered sleeve up beyond his Temprovibe, tapping a command on the device before stepping away. The body vanishes and the stone falls soundlessly to the dirt. Jettison picks it up and hands it to Deanna. "We'll find somewhere to bury him."

Deanna is shaking, but she clutches the stone and nods. We're quiet as we continue down the road. Viznir offers me his knife back but I wave it off and let him walk ahead of me. I don't suspect he'll try to stab me with others around. After two more turns, the road veers away from the abyss and begins to traverse some natural caverns. Bulbous stalactites drip some type of fluid into puddles alongside the road. It doesn't appear to be water, it sparkles too much. It makes me thirsty anyway. I fish around my pack for my canteen and find it nearly empty. I take a sip of what's left.

"Here." Deanna has paused near one of the shimmering pools. "Let's bury him here."

Bozzle steps forward and uses the end of his pike to bore a hole in a soft patch of dirt along the edge of the rocky pool. He gets the pike about a foot down before he contacts something solid and has to stop. Jettison nods, seeming to indicate that it will be enough, and Deanna drops the axe in order to cup the stone in both hands. She kneels slowly next to the hole and, after pressing the stone to her lips, sets it inside. She climbs back to her feet and Bozzle gently scrapes the earth back over the hole. When it's done, we stand there in silence. I can't help but wonder what it will be like when Preston's body reappears. He'll be fused permanently to this place, a very part of its rocks and soil. Viznir's comment about my objective surfaces in my mind and I wonder if I have a similar fate in store for me in this wretched place. *Or something worse.* I shake off the thought.

"Preston, I'm sorry." Deanna's voice quivers. "It wasn't supposed to be like this. It was supposed to be fun. It was going to be a story to tell our friends—" Her composure breaks and she begins to cry. She covers her face with her hands and sobs. I put a hand on her shoulder and she straightens a little, still crying but trying hard to hold it back. "I'm . . ." She wipes the back of her knuckles across her nose and sniffs hard. "I'm not going to forget what you did."

Bozzle speaks next, but it's a language I don't understand. His voice is soft and mellow as he speaks gently to his departed competitor. He ends his personal eulogy with a bow before lapsing back to silence. I don't think Deanna understands what Bozzle has said either but she seems consoled nonetheless. She brushes his arm with her hand and wipes the tears away from her eyes before picking the axe back up. Bozzle steps aside and lets her lead the way onward. Viznir follows them.

Jettison falls into step beside me and hangs back a little to give us some space from the others. He keeps his voice low. "We're running low on time. We're going to need to split up if we're going to make it to the gate with all the objectives."

"How will we find the rest?"

"Yours is directly below us. According to the data you gave Milo, there is a storage silo staircase just ahead and your objective is at the bottom."

"Viznir says it won't be there, but I'd like to look."

Jettison nods. "I would, too. If you want to go check it out, I'll take the others and get the rest. Take Deanna with you. When you get back up, it's a straight shot from here to the gate. Down this road and around the corner. I'll meet you there."

"You okay taking Viznir with you to find the other objectives?"

Jettison pulls the night vision goggles off his neck and hands them to me. "Yeah. Give the objectives we have to the others so they can get out of here. I'll be right behind you."

When we reach the entrance to the stairwell, Jettison explains the plan to the others. Viznir doesn't voice any objection to splitting up, but Deanna seems initially skeptical. Once Jettison explains that she and I will have a shorter distance to the time gate, she agrees and follows me into the silo stairwell. I scan my light down the center and count about ten flights of stairs.

"What is your objective?" Deanna asks as we begin the descent.

"I don't know. I didn't get a description."

"Where is your data sphere?"

"Is that what that's called?" I gesture toward the ceiling. "Mine got left behind on a disintegrating space station."

Deanna stops her descent. "So you don't even know what you're looking for? How do you expect to find it?"

I keep my eyes fixed on the steps below me and continue on. "I have a location. It's all I have to go on, so I just have to make the best of it and hope my objective stands out." As I round the next corner, Deanna resumes her descent and her footsteps fall into rhythm with mine. Doors yawn open in the corridors we pass on each landing, but the blackness holds only silence. I keep my gun ready just in case, but we make the bottom of the staircase without incident. The door at the bottom is locked. As I look around for something to open it with, Deanna breaks the silence.

"I just realized this is pointless. I won't get through the gate."

I pause my search. "Why?"

"Preston had the bracelet."

I think about the burial we just witnessed and the realization sinks in. *We buried both of them.*

"Damn it. We should have taken his bracelet off him. Why didn't we think of that?" I mutter more curses but stop when I look back to the girl beside me.

Deanna looks like her resolve is crumbling away with each passing second. Her shoulders droop and she backs against the wall before slumping to the floor. From there she merely stares into the blackness.

"We'll figure something out." I get on the floor beside her and shine my light through the thin space under the door. The area on the other side is clear. I pop the lens off my flashlight and use Mym's degravitizer to remove the gravitite particles from it.

"Hang tight. I'll be right back." I set my pack next to Deanna and tromp up the stairs to the next landing to set myself an anchor point. Once I've found a clear location, I return to Deanna and hand her the night vision goggles. "This won't take long, but you might want these." I give myself what I think to be a fair amount of time, then retrieve the plastic flashlight lens from the upper landing and slide it under the door before climbing the steps again to make the jump back. The process feels almost routine now, but I double-check my settings anyway, studying their position so I will be able to find my next setting in the dark. I get myself into position along the wall and flick off my flashlight. When I arrive the few minutes before, I feel around for my anchor using my fingertips. Once I touch it, I don't let it go. I have to spin the dials on my chronometer blindly but I'm confident about it. I flip the directional slider to forward, press the pin, and straighten up.

When I turn on the flashlight, I'm inside the room with my objective. Or I would be if there was anything in the room at all. One sweep of my flashlight reveals all I need to know. Bare concrete walls meet the floor in every direction. Viznir was right. My objective was a lie. *I'm stuck here.*

I don't know if it's the fact that I've been so close to death already or whether I'm just not processing the reality of the situation, but the empty room doesn't bring on the despair it was likely meant to.

I heave the heavy metal latch aside and swing the door open. Deanna is curled up with the axe in the corner of the stairwell and barely looks up when I exit.

"Did you find it?" Her voice is emotionless.

"No." I snatch up my pack and the night vision goggles and extend her my hand. "Come on. We've got to go."

"There's no point. We're not getting out."

"Bullshit. We'll figure something out." I don't feel nearly as confident as I'm trying to sound, but Deanna takes my hand and lets me pull her to her feet anyway. We've made it up about half the stairs when I feel the tremor.

At first it's just a slight vibration in the railing as my fingertips slide along it. Then there is a noise to accompany it, a deep, dull, grating sound, the friction of something rigid scraping earth. Tiny bits of debris begin to rain down the stairwell.

"What is that?" Deanna's eyes have widened at the cascading dust that crosses the beam of my flashlight.

"I don't know, but I don't think we should stay here." I pick up the pace and start taking steps three at a time. I only slow when Deanna is in danger of lagging behind. I burst back into the main road a few paces ahead of her and look around. The entire tunnel has begun to shake. Three host bodies stagger their way across the road to my left, but they pay me and my flashlight no attention. They seem fixated on getting out of the road and I watch them vanish down the first corridor they reach.

Deanna emerges from the doorway behind me with her axe raised. "I swear to God, if I get out of this place I am going straight home, last level or not. They can give me any penalty they want. I'm going home."

"You think we're close to the end?" I head toward the time gate and start to jog. Deanna follows.

"My dad has a friend on the committee. They said we only have nine levels in this chronothon. That means there's only one left. Not that I could finish now anyway."

"What happens to guides when the racer is lost?"

"You're on your own. That's part of the danger. It's supposed to make teams more bonded."

"Why did you sign up for this?" I scan the walls for the source of the trembling but see nothing.

Deanna lets out a bitter laugh. "Chronothons are glamorous. It makes you famous if you win. It's not supposed to be like this. No one ever had to go *here* before. They went places like Ancient Greece and Alexandria. Nice places. I don't understand why they're doing this to us."

The tremors seem to be lessening in the walls, and the grating noise fades away to nothing. We are left with an oppressive silence and the sound of our own breathing. "Whatever that was, I want to be gone before it comes back. The others should be close."

I follow Jettison's instructions and continue down the road. A few other tunnels diverge from the main passage, but I stay the course, and when we round the bend, I can finally see the repository. A cavernous chamber has opened up ahead that is at least fifty feet high and punctuated with stalactites. The walls are echoing with the familiar barking of a time traveling dog. I zero in on the sound and spot its source. The repository is ensconced in a tunnel opening halfway up an earthen wall on the far side of the cavern, above a set of steep stone stairs. Below the wall is a ditch teeming with Soma hosts.

The narrow stone steps only allow passage by one or two abreast, and at the top of the steps, Kara is seated with her gun, making sure none make it up at all. As I watch, she takes careful aim and obliterates the top half of a host, allowing the remains of the corpse to tumble backward down the stairs into a pile that is acting as a morbid dam at the base of the stairs. Other Soma hosts scratch and scrabble at the pile in an effort to climb over it.

Even at a distance, I catch the glow of Milo's digital glasses at the side of the tunnel opening. He is fiddling with something on the wall. Cliff is holding a lantern aloft, lighting the steps for Kara's gruesome chore. I hear Jonah before I see him. He gives a shout and Cliff looks up to see us on the far side of the cavern. Between him and us at least a hundred densely packed Soma hosts block the path.

"How are we going to make it through all those?" Deanna's voice trembles.

I check the chambers on my gun and scrounge around in the pockets of my pack for more bullets. "We'll figure something out."

Cliff sets the lantern down and it gets hard to see what he's doing, but a moment later he is aiming something at me. I try to make out what it is, but I get my answer when a flying anchor whizzes to a stop next to me and hovers a few feet off the ground. Genesis materializes next to it and drops to the ground. She's holding a machete in one hand and letting a second dangle from her wrist from a lanyard. "You have the anchors?"

"Most of them. I have yours."

Genesis retrieves the flying anchor and frowns. "Who are we short?"

"Mine and Viznir's and whatever Preston had. Preston didn't make it."

Genesis turns to Deanna. "I'm so sorry." Deanna nods slightly but doesn't reply. Genesis considers the bracelet on her wrist, then looks back to Deanna. "I lost my guide. But if you want to come with me, I can get you through."

Deanna looks up in surprise. "You'd do that?"

"It's what Mayra would have wanted."

Deanna looks at me. "What about Ben?"

Genesis hands me one of the machetes. "We think we have a plan for that. Milo's working out the details."

I take the offered machete and look up to the opening of the tunnel where Kara and Cliff are guarding the steps. "Was he able to slow the countdown at all?"

"No. We need to hurry." She turns and hacks down a Soma host that has wandered over to us.

As she's extracting her blade from the corpse's skull, the ground beneath our feet begins to tremble again. The shaking grows more violent and the Soma hosts nearest to us begin to jitter and turn away from their assault of the stairs. More notice our presence but they seem distracted by the shaking. They moan and start to part from one another. A yell from behind us makes me turn. Jettison and Viznir race out of a side tunnel and make the turn onto the road at a dead sprint. Bozzle emerges behind them, his face a mask of determination.

"GO! GO!" Jettison is flailing an arm at us, seemingly oblivious to the dense horde of host bodies behind us. A burst of rock and earth from the opening of the tunnel behind him shows his real concern. A jagged ring of fangs thrusts out from the darkness, propelled by a dark, shifting mass of tissue. The horrifying apparition heaves itself forward and into the light of the cavern, revealing its segmented form and massive proportions. The ground is shaking with the movements of its scaled body as it writhes forward at alarming speed, a gigantic thrashing worm. Once in the open, it turns its eyeless head side to side, tasting or smelling the air with hairy appendages that fan out from around its mouth. It takes only a second to orient itself before it hurls itself onward in pursuit of its prey.

"What the hell is that?" Genesis exclaims as her brother races up to us.

"GO!" Jettison flings himself at Genesis and forcibly points her toward the back wall of the cavern by her shoulders. "No time to explain." His hands are empty with the exception of a piece of shiny chain. As soon as Bozzle and Viznir reach our position, I raise my pistol and fire at the heaving worm. The bullet ricochets uselessly off the beast's scaly skin.

"It won't work!" Viznir shouts. "We tried that."

I fire another shot directly into the worm's fleshy mouth, but the creature pays it no notice. It merely heaves itself closer, its mouth gaping wide and exposing more rings of teeth inside.

I spin and follow the others toward the mass of Soma hosts. The host bodies on the fringes are starting to scatter in every direction at the approach of the worm. Jettison races ahead, shoving bodies out of the way while Bozzle dispatches others with his pike. His weapon has lost its glow and the blade is slick with blood. He uses the handle as much as the blade, knocking opposition aside to make way. Even with all our aggression and the fact that the Soma are more intent on escape than eating us, we are forced to slow when we get into the dense mass. The host bodies have begun to thrash into one another in a chaotic mosh pit of confusion. Even though I recognize a few of the more mature, well-fed Soma hosts in the crowd, none seem capable of making an organized exit and are flailing about with shrieks and grunts.

I look behind me and watch the worm suck one of the unfortunate stragglers into its mouth with a single, efficient slurp. Its rows of teeth keep the victim from wriggling loose as it is sucked headfirst into the beast's fleshy gullet. The worm arches its back in a wave of scales till its midsection almost reaches the top of the cavern, then uses the height to make a tremendous lunge forward. The ground trembles as the weighty body shoves the head across the cavern floor. Bits of rock and dirt are flung out around it from the force of its assault. Soma hosts are knocked headlong into the air, and the yawning orifice of its mouth stops mere inches behind me. That's when I smell the stench.

The force of the worm's movement has propelled a wave of air from its gaping throat. It brings the pungent odor of wet corpses and what I can only describe as sweaty, unwashed crotch. I flee the stench as much as the rows of teeth, shoving aside opposition with renewed vigor. I almost collide with Bozzle. He has turned around and is facing the worm. He raises his pike over his head with both arms and I briefly think he is going to hurl it at the beast, but instead of throwing the pike, he brings the tip down and buries it forcefully into the ground, leaving the long handle protruding up toward the ceiling of the cavern. I dodge around him just as he does something that makes the pike disappear. A moment later, he's next to me, using his bare hands to knock Soma hosts out of our way.

A crunching and grating accompanies the movements of the worm as it extends its feelers again to smell for us. It must like the scent of human and Anya Morey better than the funk of the Soma infested miners because it slithers directly toward Bozzle and me. Despite Kara and Cliff blasting away from the top of the stairs to try to clear us a path, the press of bodies ahead of us is still too thick, and I come to the sickening realization that we aren't going to make the stairs in time. Another big lunge of the worm will carry it to our position and beyond. Kara takes a shot at the worm, but the energy from her gun merely crackles around the hard scales before dissipating into an acrid smoke. My arms are exhausted from hacking and shoving through the cluster of bodies, but to my surprise, Bozzle stops and turns around. He glances once at a device in his hand and then stares down the worm's fang-filled throat. The creature lunges forward again, its mouth opening wide to swallow us, when its motion is suddenly and violently arrested. The bottom of its jaw slams into the floor of the cavern and it lets out a shrieking hiss. It thrashes once and then again as a spurt of dark green ooze gushes from its throat. It begins to choke on its own fluids and flail its head and tail back and forth. That's when I realize its midsection is pinned to the floor of the cavern by Bozzle's pike. The weapon has reappeared and is now fused to the creature's insides, anchoring the worm to the earth and no doubt causing damage with every jolt and twist of the segmented body. The worm continues to flail but can come no closer.

The tattooed alien says nothing about his victory. He merely spits once and turns back to the task of clearing the Soma.

We catch up to the others, working together to batter our way through the mess. Deanna is running out of energy and is having trouble swinging the axe, so I trade weapons with her, letting her take the lighter machete. I join Genesis at the front of the group to help bore a path through the crowd. Cliff and Kara have cleared an area around the foot of the stairs and are there to help pull us over the mass of fallen bodies.

I scale the stairs behind Genesis, dripping guts and gore. Barley stops barking when I reach the top step but doesn't approach me. I don't blame him. My hands are red and my clothes are soaked. I toss the axe and my pack to the ground and dial my chronometer while looking for a slightly elevated place to stand. I settle for a flat bit of rock and make the two-second jump while holding onto the wall, then step away from the puddle of muck I leave behind on the floor. I feel instantly better about myself. I hastily remove the objectives we've acquired from my pack, laying them gently on the floor of the tunnel, then repeat the jump process while holding the pack to get it clean, too. The others follow my example, using the same place to deposit their accumulated filth.

Once I'm clean, I get a lick on the hand from Barley and a hug from Jonah. Milo is busy working over a pile of wiring he has extracted from a conduit on the wall, but Cliff gives me a hearty handshake.

"You did good, kid." He gestures to the pile of objectives.

"Yeah, except I'm short one. There was nothing for me this round."

"Our boy Milo figured as much." Cliff lifts his stubbly jaw to indicate the wall where Milo is working. "He says they've got this gate wired against you."

"Any way around it?"

"We only know of one, but you'll have to talk to Wabash about that."

I step past Cliff and locate Harrison propped up against the tunnel wall. He has a small lantern nestled near his leg that is casting an eerie light upward at his face. He looks pale and drained. He watches my approach and I squat beside him.

"Hey, man. How are you feeling?"

"I've had better races. I don't think this place is going to make my list of highlights."

"We made the gate at least. Almost out of here."

"Some of us." He fumbles weakly at his shirt and tugs at a bit of string around his neck. He pulls it over his head and lets the attached bracelet dangle between us. "You need this more than I do."

The Admiral's race band. I watch it swing back and forth under his outstretched hand. "I can't ask you to do that for me. You barely know me."

"I know you well enough. And I know myself enough to know that even if I get to wherever this gate is taking us, I've got hours at most to enjoy it. What that creature did to me, it's not getting undone."

"You don't know where we're headed. There could be a hospital—"

"Just take it already." He thrusts his hand out. "And don't feel guilty. You owe me this. And you owe it to the kid. See this thing through for me and keep him safe the rest of the way. Make this shit count for something."

I take the bracelet and he lets the string drop.

"Thank you."

He coughs and leans his head back against the wall. "Silas was right about this place. There are some places you shouldn't go to die. But at least I didn't turn into one of those things down there."

I glance back to the tunnel opening. Kara has resumed her post at the top of the stairs and has her gun resting casually on her knee. Cliff has knelt behind her and is counting shotgun shells on the ground while

Jonah watches. Milo still hasn't looked up from his efforts with the conduit. He has three tablets spread around him and is fidgeting with all of them in intervals. I don't know what he's up to, but he's the most concentrated I've ever seen him.

"What's he doing over there? We don't need to slow the timer down now that we're all here. Can't we just use the objectives?"

"He's reading the gate's internal code. Says he needs to find something. He figured out your problem from looking in there. Not sure what he's finding now."

A few feet from the tunnel opening, Genesis is wrapping a bandage around Jettison's arm while Deanna waits to cut it with a pair of scissors. I turn back to Harrison. "Did you see any sign of the others? Tad and Horacio and them?"

He points to a row of cubbyholes carved into the wall. Three of them have objectives stored already. "They were through just ahead of us. They're what caused that horde down there. Got 'em all riled up and hungry. We only made it because of Cliff and Kara. Tough as nails, those two."

"I'm surprised Tad and Blaine left Deanna behind."

"I'm not surprised at all." Harrison coughs again. "Those two are out for themselves. Not sure about the other ones. There's some teamwork between the girl and the hairy Italian."

"Ariella and Horacio? Yeah, I think they're vaguely related or something. I met them together when this all started."

"Related? I guess that could make sense. Not a close bond obviously, but I got the impression they were working together." Harrison lets his eyes drift close.

"Their benefactor is how I got suckered into this, so if there are any racers in on the fix I'd bet—"

"Kara!" Milo's voice is sudden and everyone stops their conversations. Milo gestures hurriedly and Kara leaves her perch on the steps to investigate. She leans over Milo's array of tablets as he points to something on the screens. I try to listen, but Milo's voice drops to barely a whisper. The only part of the conversation I hear is when Kara straightens back up.

"I'm sure. That's the one."

Milo nods, accepting her confirmation, but whatever it was they've decided doesn't seem like good news. Milo gets to his feet and faces the rest of us, brushing the dirt off his knees before he speaks.

"We have a problem." His tone is factual and lacking emotion. "I've just confirmed something Kara and I have suspected for a while now." He scratches his head, then gestures to Kara. "You may know Kara is from farther ahead than most of us. We've all come from the twenty-one, or twenty-two hundreds." He pauses and looks at me. "Well, some of you are from earlier. But, we're all from more or less near the central primes. None of us have come from the area of timestreams Kara has, that's Negative Epsilon Vega. And she's from 2420."

The reactions on the faces of the other racers are a mix of incredulity and confusion. Genesis stares at Kara as if she's suddenly sprouted wings.

"We know you've heard stories and read the warnings. What you won't know is that Kara signed up for this race as a guide because she suspected the chronothon committee was up to something unusual in her home world, and now we have proof she's right. The committee set up two time gates there. The first is the other side of this doorway."

Cliff practically spits out his rebuttal. "There's no way in hell the committee could get away with sending us to a blacklisted stream. They're prohibited by ASCOTT." He steps away from his post by the stairs and points to the conduit. "Hell, they're prohibited by anyone with half a brain. They rounded up the anchors and cut off all the paths they could find to keep people from getting back from there." He eyes Kara with something akin to suspicion.

"That's true, but it doesn't change our situation."

"How could they set up a gate there?" Jettison asks. "That's why we don't go there. No one can. It's . . . it's impossible."

"Not impossible," Kara says. "Just . . . dangerous."

"We've got fifteen minutes left to decide." Milo gestures to his bracelet. "It's there or we stay here."

Genesis makes a choking sound and shakes her head. Deanna has gone ashen white.

I raise my hand. "Hey, not to sound like a dumbass, because I'm clearly the odd man out here, but nothing could be worse than this place, right?" I point to the cavern beyond the cave mouth. "I'm not up on all the timestreams, but where Kara's from, what could they have that's worse than giant worms and alien, body-snatching zombies?"

The faces of my companions are all serious. Finally it's Jettison who answers.

"They have the Zealots."

"One of the sweetest blessings of time travel is getting to see people who have passed away and also meet those not yet born. Treasure those moments, but use them sparingly. There is a reason we learn to let go, and a reason we let live. Sometimes love thrives most in our absence." – Journal of Dr. Harold Quickly, 1983

Chapter 27

A small square of fabric under the woman's right breast is still clean. Lavender. She's wearing a lavender sundress. The rest of the dress is covered in filth and tattered, but that one patch of color has survived her years of wandering in this forsaken place. As she stands at the top of the stairs with gaunt cheeks and knotted hair, her mouth opening and closing below hazy, yellowed eyes, I can't help but wonder what she was doing on her last day as a human being that caused her to put on such an outfit. *Did she have a date?*

Jettison and Cliff both notice the intruder at the same time, but it's Cliff who steps over to deal with it. He raises his shotgun and shoves the barrel into her face. The creature opens its mouth at his approach, her eyes widening, and gets the muzzle shoved between her teeth for her efforts. Cliff's movements are angry: sharp and forceful. I drop my eyes back to that single clean patch of color on her chest and wait for the blast of the gun. It doesn't come. As Cliff watches her chew on the gun muzzle like a teething child, his angry expression softens a little. His rage seems to melt into resignation and maybe a bit of sadness. He yanks the gun muzzle out of the woman's mouth, leans back and kicks her. His heavy boot connects with the tiny square of lavender and the woman flies backward. Her fingers and toes, reluctant to follow, hang in front of her as she's launched free of the earth and out into the void. For one distinct moment, tangled hair, yellowed eyes, and the once-lavender sundress dangle in midair before they succumb to darkness and gravity.

Cliff stares over the edge for only a second, then turns back to the rest of us, clustered around the time gate. "They can have this goddamn hellhole, and they can have the next one. Once we get back to the proper planet, we're out." He slings his shotgun over his shoulder and looks from Jettison to Genesis. "I told your dad I'd do my best to keep you two safe out here, but none of us ever thought that meant putting you through this. He'd want us to pull the plug."

Jettison's jaw works a little, but he doesn't argue. He hands Genesis her pack and shoulders his own, then he turns to Milo. "Where we're headed, facing the Zealots, what's the situation going to be like?"

Milo consults one of his tablets. "We're looking at a sector seven district, Northwest America . . ."

The dog lets out a whine and my eyes fall on Harrison, slumped against the wall. Barley is standing next to him. Harrison's head has fallen to his shoulder and his lips are slightly parted. The muscles of his face have relaxed, and in the light of his miniature lantern his face glows a pale white. His chest isn't moving. I put a hand to his wrist and feel for a pulse.

"Mr. Harrison?" Jonah grabs his other hand. The boy gives it a shake, but the arm is limp in his grasp. I feel no pulse.

"He's gone, Jonah."

Jonah keeps his grip on Harrison's hand as he looks up at me. "But he saved me. He can't be gone."

"He saved me, too." I lay Harrison's arm back at his side. "We both owe him for that."

The group lapses into silence as we circle around the body of our fallen friend. We stay there with our own thoughts until Bozzle speaks. "We cannot leave his body here for the creatures to befoul. It would be dishonorable."

Genesis reaches into her pocket and extracts the winged anchor. Jettison takes it from her and repeats the process he used on Preston's body, setting Harrison's Temprovibe for him with the anchor pressed firmly into his hand. The body vanishes.

Jettison collects the anchor and Cliff hands him the ascension gun. "Get him somewhere out of reach."

As Jettison secures the anchor to the rail of the gun, Genesis scans her flashlight across the ceiling of the main cavern. Her light stops on a dark alcove above a row of stalactites. "How about up there?"

Jettison raises the ascension gun and takes aim. When he squeezes the trigger, the metal ball launches off the end and makes a shallow arc into the darkness of the alcove. I see the wings deploy on the anchor just before it disappears into the hole and out of sight.

"So long, Wabash," Cliff mutters. He picks up his pack from the tunnel floor. "That man was a legend. He deserved better."

I stare at the hole where the anchor disappeared then drop my eyes to the Admiral's bracelet in my hand. "Thank you, Harrison." It's as much a prayer now as a thank you. "Hope you're someplace better."

The blinking display on the Admiral's bracelet matches the one on my own wrist. Both are flashing twelve minutes. I turn to Milo. "So how will this work? I have two bracelets now."

Milo stands up and reaches for my wrist. "We'll have to ditch yours. You're supposed to be dead anyway, so it shouldn't matter." He pulls a tool out of his bag that resembles a pair of pliers. He slips the jaws around my bracelet and squeezes, but instead of tightening, the jaws emit a flash of energy that neatly slices through the metal. The display screen instantly goes dead, and the metal ends of the bracelet smoke where they've been separated. He rotates the bracelet on my wrist and zaps it again on the other side. The two halves drop to the soft dirt at my feet.

"The Admiral's bracelet will open the gate once you install his objective. The bracelet may have recorded some irregularities in the transition from the Admiral, to Wabash, to you, but it's still functioning, and as far as I can tell, the time gate hasn't recognized either of them as deceased. Viznir can take Wabash's spot and you follow him through as the Admiral. I'll wait till you're through to make sure it works."

"Thanks. I appreciate that."

"Should we expect trouble on the other side?" Jettison has finished reloading his gun and holsters it.

Milo glances over to Kara. She's lacing herself into an armored leather jacket. "Yeah. I think so."

I take the opportunity to retrieve my own jacket from my pack and slip my arms through. The leather is scuffed and a few patches look like they've gotten wet during the race, but I feel better having an extra layer of protection between me and whatever is coming. I stuff Dr. Quickly's journal and Abe's tool tin into the inside pocket and slip Mym's degravitizer into my back pants pocket where it's handy. Lightening the pack seems like a good idea, so I take the opportunity to dump out the now uscless bullets for Viznir's gun. I leave the boxes in the dirt and straighten up to find Viznir watching me. He doesn't say anything, but his eyes travel from my face to the little pile of ammo before looking away. Kara has finished attaching her goggles to a military-style riot helmet and secures it to her head. Milo points to the alcoves in the wall. "Let's get going. We're almost out of time."

Cliff addresses the entire group. "Okay, here's the deal. We rally on the other side of this thing, and assuming we're back on the right damn planet, we make a plan to head for home. Wherever that might be." Cliff looks up to Bozzle, but the alien merely nods. Cliff addresses me next. "I'm going to head for the race start. If you want to come with me, you're welcome. Someone on the committee designed this course and at least a few yahoos approved it. It's time we pay them a visit."

Jettison and Cliff line up first, followed by Genesis and Deanna. Bozzle takes his place behind the girls and, from my spot behind him, I search over his body for where his guide could be located. Viznir had been sure the alien has one, but as I look over his tattooed arms and neck and down the streamlined silver compartments of his cargo pack, I see no evidence of it. *Is it hiding in his pack?* Viznir slides into position in front of me, blocking my view, and I have to discontinue my search.

Jonah and the dog line up behind me, and Kara takes the spot at the rear. Milo is positioned by the repository holes and has each of the objectives laid out in order in front of them. The decorative chain that Jettison found goes into its receptacle first and the circumference of the tunnel shimmers with its multicolored light.

I've been loath to bring down the barrier of tension between Viznir and me. I'm still angry about his betrayal, but at the moment, my concern about what we're walking into takes precedence.

"Hey, Viznir. What do you know about this? Who are the Zealots?"

Viznir shakes his head and keeps his eyes fixed on the gate. "I don't know. I've just heard rumors, but they're a religious group that hates time travelers. I know that much. Their religion teaches that time travel is an abomination. Nobody goes to their timestreams."

I keep my voice low to keep from worrying Jonah behind me. "Why? Are they that dangerous? What do they do to time travelers?"

"People don't talk about it much. Like I said, nobody goes there, or at least nobody comes back. That's why your friend means to get us out of there fast."

"Shit." I loosen the revolver in my holster and keep my palm on the handle. Jettison and Cliff vanish into the gate and Milo loads the night vision goggles into the next repository hole. Genesis checks her bracelet and gives Deanna the signal. I watch intently as her blonde hair vanishes into the swirl of color. The gate doesn't close or reject her and I exhale. Genesis follows Deanna through. *The plan is working so far.* I glance back at Jonah who has his hand on Barley's neck. *Wherever we're going, at least we're headed there together.* The gate shimmers again for Bozzle and his mystery guide, and I step forward. Viznir is gripping the knife in his belt and I consider whether I should be worried. There will be a time lapse on the other side of the gate. I could be on my own with him once we're through. Milo inserts the Admiral's rock-cutting tool into its spot in the repository and the bracelet around my neck beeps. Viznir doesn't look at me but simply walks through. I watch his back disappear into the ether and pull my pistol from its holster.

I feel a hand on my other arm and find Jonah beside me.

"Are you scared?" Jonah has his eyes fixed on the lights of the gate.

"A little. But we'll be okay."

"Will you wait for me?" He looks up and his blue eyes find mine.

"Absolutely." I muss the boy's hair and hold my fist out for him. He studies it for a moment and I suddenly wonder if the fist-bump has vanished from use by the time he's from. He looks unsure but finally holds his fist up. I bump it and make my fist explode back with added sound effects. Jonah smiles. "I'll see you on the other side."

I face the gate and steel my nerves. *Okay. Last level. Let's see what you've got.*

I stride forward and let the brilliance swallow me up.

The sound reaches my brain first—shouting, and scraping, and the whir of electric motors. The visuals are chaotic. I'm in a hallway that's been blasted open on both sides, and through the holes in the left wall, moonlight reveals a dark city skyline. Shapes move in the darkness beyond the wall to my right. The hallway flickers from damaged lights and a cable is sparking from an opening in the wall that's been torn by something large. Viznir is nowhere in sight, but flashes of light accompany booms from a shotgun. I hear voices to my right and creep toward the damaged wall, peering through the hole into the gutted interior of the building. Figures are appearing and disappearing around the shell of a room, occasionally trading fire. I recognize Jettison and Genesis. They are dodging around the room, avoiding the attacks of a man dressed in all black. His trench coat flows around him like a wave, and for a moment I think he's the man from my apartment, but when he turns toward me, I see a pallid complexion and a hint of gray to his hair. His irises glow with a pale light, and he has a weapon in his hand that resembles the one Kara carries. His shots are taking out sections of ceiling and support beams with every miss. Genesis has somehow reappeared with her back to him at the far side of the room and doesn't see him raising his gun behind her.

"LOOK OUT!" The cry is out of my mouth before I can think and Genesis blinks away without even turning. The man in black looks my direction and his lips curl into a scowl. He's immediately blocked from view by the metal torso of a robotic figure that steps in front of the hole from my right. I'm only staring at the torso because the entire height of the machine is imperceptible from my position. What is visible is the right arm that's carrying a six-barreled, belt-fed, Gatling gun. The barrels swing toward me with the now recognizable whir of an electric motor, and I hit the floor an instant before they unleash their bullets. The deafening pops and bursts of the gun accompany the hail of lead that tears a horizontal line through the wall. The gun whirs to a stop and I scramble away, flailing backward and landing on my pack with a thud. The wall bursts apart even further as the machine crashes its way through and steps into the hallway.

The time gate has been rigged to the perimeter of the hallway, and the section of the wall I'm now leaning against is the only part of the corridor that is undamaged. Considering the wreckage around it, it seems miraculous—until the reality of the situation dawns on me. *It was intentional. They were waiting for us.* I gape at the figure that has stepped into the hall, trying to recover from my shock. It's not simply a machine. The mechanized body rises at least eight feet from the ground but culminates in a head that is distinctly human. The man's face is visible through a transparent helmet faceplate, and while his glaring eyes and hard line of a mouth are anything but friendly, his expression of hate is clearly of my species. The mechanical body is porous at parts where a human body shouldn't be, so I rule out him being a man in a metal suit. I don't have a chance to contemplate him further because he aims his gun arm at me. I instinctually grab for my chronometer and only have time to press the pin before the bullets scream from the gun.

The two-second jump I had my chronometer set on is enough to skip his first burst of gunfire, but when I reappear, I'm right back where I started. Luckily, I'm fast with my dials and, before he can squeeze off another burst, I've flipped my slider to back and set myself another jump. This time I go back ten minutes. It's careless and dangerous, but luck is on my side. I reappear in the hallway without managing to fuse myself into anyone or anything that was there then. *Thank God.*

The cyborg is gone and the hallway is in somewhat better shape. When I try to get to my feet, I find my backpack is stuck to the floor. I shrug out of it and look to see what happened. The front pocket has been fused into the concrete and laminate flooring. I must have landed in a divot or bit of damage from the fight and jumped back to a time before the damage to the floor happened. I yank on the pack and it rips along the bottom seam, leaving a scrap of fabric protruding from the floor and ruining the bag in the process.

I don't have time to mourn the loss of the pack. My heart is too busy hammering away in my chest and it doesn't help when I think how that bit of pack, now made a permanent part of the floor, could easily have been my ass. I grab the smaller shoulder bag out of the pack and stuff it with what I can, then toss the pack into a corner of the hallway.

I straighten up and have only just begun to try to formulate a plan when Genesis appears in the hallway behind me. She's breathing hard and working to reload a weapon. She looks up from her gun and sees me. "Ben! You're alive! Come on!" She holsters her gun, grabs my arm and activates her Temprovibe before I can say a word. The next moment we've jumped again, and I have no idea whether it was forward or backward or remotely how far, but we're still in the hallway. "This way!" Gen pulls her gun again and leads us behind the time gate.

"What's going on? Who's shooting at us?"

"Members of The Order. They brought a couple of cryo-heads with them." Genesis checks her gun and I do the same. She consults her Temprovibe and taps in some coordinates. "Jonah is the next one through. We need to get that cryo out of the hallway before he shows up or he won't stand a chance." She pokes her head around a hole in the wall, then throws a leg through. "Come on."

I follow her through the hole and we enter the empty space on the other side. "What is a cryo-head? More body enhancement? Who would want to live like that?"

Genesis shakes her head. "They didn't choose it. The cryos were created by the Zealots from people who'd frozen themselves. They raided cryogenics labs early on in their strike against time travelers. They consider it punishment for trying to cheat death. The cryos are given the option to fight for The Order or be left to thaw without a body."

"Some choice," I say, scanning our surroundings.

We're in a skyscraper and high up, judging from the sky beyond the windows at the far end of the room. The entire floor has been gutted. A couple of elevator shafts and staircases punctuate the space in the center, and the hallway we've just come from runs the width of the building behind us. Otherwise, the space is comprised of structural support columns, electrical wiring and the remnants of an air conditioning ventilation system. Bits of insulation and broken concrete litter the floor. Genesis scans the area, then positions us in view of the wall where I last saw the cyborg crashing through to shoot me. We're behind his position now, or will be I suspect, when we jump back to whatever time that was.

"Okay, listen up. Jet and I have run this drill before. He's planning to meet us at the gate when Jonah arrives, too, so don't shoot him."

"Where is he now?"

"He and Cliff are taking out the other cryo."

"Where are the others?"

"I don't know. I lost track of Bozzle. He was alive when I saw him, but he disappeared. One of The Order was after him. Deanna is with Tad. Blaine didn't make it."

"He's dead?"

"Come on. We need the others if we're going to make it out of here. You ready?"

I don't feel ready for anything, but I nod anyway. Genesis grabs my arm and we blink.

We're back in the noise. My mind goes silent with adrenaline. Gunshots echo from the hallway and, through the gaping hole in the wall, I spot the cyborg's metallic body. Genesis seems to be aiming for its head, so I follow her example. She's fired at least three shots before I have the composure to fire my first. As best I can tell, I miss my target completely. I try to focus. Genesis's shots have landed and the cyborg turns, leaking a gas from a juncture at the back of his helmet. I squeeze the trigger and see a spark of contact near its neck. The right arm rises and we move. Genesis yanks me sideways and we sprint behind the concrete columns of the elevator shafts before the Gatling gun can cut us down. Bullets rip concrete as the cryo tries to track us.

"How are we supposed to kill that?" I exclaim when we've reached cover.

"We can't. We need Kara and Milo. We just need to distract that thing long enough to get them through. Jonah first, though. If you want that kid to live we've got thirty seconds to make it happen."

I'm about to speak when a man in black materializes to our right. He lifts his gun, but Genesis is faster. Her shot hits him in the chest and he staggers back. Surprisingly, he doesn't go down. He struggles to recover, but Genesis hits his gun arm with her next shot then puts two more into his chest. This time he yells in pain, dropping his weapon a moment before he disappears.

As soon as the gun hits the floor I'm running for it. I'm vaguely aware of Genesis shouting something I can't make out. The booming of the Gatling gun registers through the slow motion haze of my mind and bits of concrete explode from a column to my left as I go into my best softball slide and scoop up the gun. The rounds from the Gatling gun kick up debris around me and I turn in time to see Genesis step from the corner of the elevator to unload on the cyborg. I don't know whether her cover fire is distracting enough or if I'm just experiencing the kind of luck only stupid people enjoy, but the cyborg's bullets go high, screaming over me, and I'm allowed a brief second in which to aim. The weapon has levers and knobs and God-knows what any of them are for, but I ignore everything except the trigger, hoping that in however many centuries have elapsed, that one piece of firearm technology will have stayed the same. My faith is rewarded with a silent blast of raw power that explodes from the barrel and catches the metal torso of the cyborg where its non-existent heart ought to be. The metal body jolts and shudders as its chest fragments into oblivion. The head and shoulders twist and topple forward, bending the remaining strands of metal on the right side. The arm holding the Gatling gun crashes to the floor and is followed by the rest of the body.

I'm prone on the floor still staring at the heap of metal when Genesis sprints for the hallway. "Come on!"

I scramble to my feet, holstering Charlie's revolver but keeping my new weapon ready. The doorway ahead has been blasted from its hinges and leans precariously into the room on splintered chunks of doorframe. I follow Genesis through and almost collide with Bozzle as he reappears in the hallway. I jump aside and hit the wall. "Holy shit!" I grab at the wall to steady myself.

Bozzle's eyes are intent on me. I've never seen him anything but calm before, but now his brow is furrowed and it makes the horns on his head more prominent. They seem to have extended slightly. Everything about him is bristling and his eyes are an impossible shade of black. His body is tensed and, as he reaches out a hand to steady me, my heart skips. He's terrifying like this and I have to force myself to relax and remember he's a friend.

"More are coming. We must flee." Bozzle's voice is firm and forceful. From down the hallway I hear voices as Jettison and a ragged looking Cliff step around the time gate. Jettison kicks debris away from the arrival area and waves to Genesis.

"Jonah is almost here." Genesis checks her bracelet and dashes toward the time gate. The gate illuminates ahead of her and Barley bounds through. He skids to a stop and immediately begins to growl. The dog looks quickly from Jettison to Cliff but is addressing his aggression elsewhere. Barley's neck bristles and his nose twitches as he seems to smell something he doesn't like. I don't blame him. The hallway reeks of smoke and dust and something oily. Particles of insulation linger in the air around the flickering hallway lights. Jonah steps through the time gate and immediately smiles when he sees me.

What happens next occurs so quickly that my brain almost can't process it. My view of Jonah is mostly blocked by a figure that appears in the hallway just behind Genesis. She doesn't see him as she continues running for the gate. The man is facing away from me, but even from behind I recognize the shape of him, the hard angular lines of his shoulders and the haughty way he holds his head. The peppering of gray hair around his ears would match the color of his eyes if he was facing me, but he isn't. He's raising an arm holding a revolver that he levels directly at Jonah's head. From my angle I can see down the barrel to Jonah's face and his smile that is fading in confusion. There's no time to act and I'm barely able to get my empty left hand up in a useless gesture toward Traus Gillian's back. I can't reach him. He's too far. How can I explain to him about this boy and that there must be some terrible mistake. Something must be broken with the world if anyone has sent him to shoot this innocent kid who should never have ended up anywhere near such an awful place.

Traus doesn't hear my anguished protestation because it only exists inside my head as he's squeezing the trigger. His hand seems to be moving in slow motion and I hear the explosion of the gun before I see what has changed beyond it. It's Jettison now, stepping in front of Jonah and taking the bullet in the chest. The force of his intervention keeps him moving sideways and the bullet vanishes into his body as he knocks Jonah away behind him.

My gun arm finally responds and lifts my weapon toward Traus's back. Cliff raises his shotgun, too, but Traus vanishes as fast as he appeared, leaving us pointing our guns at one another. I immediately aim mine to the ceiling as Genesis screams. She rushes to Jettison, trying to catch his collapsing body as he tumbles to the floor. Bozzle pulls a knife from his belt and spins in the hallway, holding it by its blade and set to throw at any new attacker. I dash toward Jettison and Genesis, casting glances through the holes in the walls, wary of more threats. Jonah is standing shell-shocked behind Jettison's fallen form. The dog snarls as Genesis runs up, and it snaps at her, but she only has eyes for her brother. She drops to her knees and reaches for him.

Jettison is still alive, but his chest has started to bleed. He's grimacing in determination, trying to keep himself propped up on one elbow, and has the wherewithal to grip Gen's hand when she reaches for him. I move to Jonah's side and crouch next to the siblings. I'm no doctor, but I can tell it's bad. The bleeding wound is almost directly in the center of Jettison's chest. Blood is soaking his T-shirt and a little red mist sprays out of his mouth as he tries to speak. He coughs and more dribbles from the side of his mouth. He must realize his danger because, when he looks at me, his eyes have an edge of fear. He reaches his other hand out for me and I take it as Genesis cradles his head and shoulders in her lap. Jettison uses some of his fading strength to pull me closer as Genesis tries to put pressure on the wound in his chest. Jettison stares into my eyes and chokes out the words. "Tell the kid it's not his fault."

I don't know what to say, so I merely squeeze his hand. "I will."

Jettison's eyes start to grow hazy and he looks from me to Genesis. For a moment he seems almost surprised to see her there. "Hey, Gen." His mouth curls into a smile and the light in his eyes fades away. Genesis is frantic. She presses harder into his chest and screams his name. Her face is streaked with tears and her mouth keeps forming the word 'please' even after all the sound is choked from her voice. Cliff steps to her side and crouches next to her to console her. He looks at me and jerks his head toward the hallway. I understand what he means and I stand to take over guarding us. Jettison's fingers fall from mine as I rise, and his hand lands limply in his lap.

Bozzle continues to scan the area as I step over Jettison's feet to join him. The dog has gone to Jonah and positioned itself in front of his legs. I gesture for Jonah to join me and he does so hesitantly. He looks from my face to my gun and fumbles at his belt for his own weapon. He holds it up with both hands and points it down the hallway toward the spot where Traus appeared. I nod to him and use my free hand to squeeze his shoulder. I have no idea what to say to the kid that could make any of this any better, but he holds his arms up steadily and concentrates on the hallway. It's fortunate that he does because, mere seconds later, an armed man in all black appears a few feet from where Traus had been. Jonah instantly squeezes the trigger of his weapon and the man's expression goes limp just before Bozzle's knife thuds into his forehead. The man crumples backward onto his back, his muscles flaccid.

The alien stalks forward and keeps his back between the fallen body and us as he extracts his knife. The colored lights of the time gate dapple the ceiling and I turn to witness Kara stepping through. She takes one glance at Jettison's fallen body in Gen's arms, then sees Bozzle crouched over the man in black and strides immediately past me, gun at the ready.

"How many were there?"

"A couple of these guys and some robots with human heads," I reply.

"Cryos." She almost spits the word. "Before or later?"

I point through a hole in the wall toward the heap of metal that was the cyborg. "Just a few minutes ago. The guys in black keep popping around and there was another. The man who shot Jet. It's the same guy who killed Ivan."

Kara's eyes narrow. "Was he one of The Order?"

"I don't know what The Order is. I just know it's been the same guy since the islands. I ran into him in New York and the Hindenburg, too."

Milo's voice comes from behind me and I turn to find him at the edge of the time gate looking down at Jettison. He raises his eyes to Bozzle next, and the prone body in black. "That is a Zealot of The Order of Zsa. They won't stop hunting us out here in the open. We need to get to safety." He looks from Genesis to me. "How many did we lose?"

Cliff answers him. "The boy from the academy is outside, pretty banged up. His guide didn't make it."

"Where's Viznir?" I haven't had time to fret over my own guide's absence until now, but his disappearance is starting to make me wonder.

"He must've lit out as soon as he arrived because I never saw him," Cliff says. He stoops and grips Genesis's shoulders. "Come on, Gen.

We've got to let him go."

"NO!" Genesis clutches her brother's body tighter, but her anger instantly crumbles back to grief and the emotion breaks across her face like a wave, her lip quivering and tears flowing freely down her face. Cliff lifts her bodily to her feet and she shrieks once like a wild animal, but he presses her to his chest till she buries her face in his shirt. He keeps his arms around Genesis as she weeps, but looks at me, gesturing toward Jettison with his head.

I swallow hard and nod, stepping over to Jettison's body. I study the Temprovibe on his arm, not sure how to turn it on but not wanting to disturb Cliff. "Where do we send him?"

Kara glides past the others and squats over Jettison's body. She doesn't ask me to move, but I get out of her way anyway. She brushes through a bit of rubble on the floor and selects a smooth black stone. She taps the Temprovibe and selects time coordinates faster than I can follow. Then, in the only moment of sensitivity I've seen from her, she gently takes Jettison's hand and places it palm up on his lap. She sets the stone in his upturned palm and holds her finger over the Temprovibe. It wavers there for only a moment. In that moment she looks sad, but the moment passes and the hardness returns to her eyes. She taps the Temprovibe and Jettison's body disappears. The stone clatters to the floor and she scoops it up in one fluid motion and hands it to Cliff.

Genesis has stopped sobbing but is still pressed against Cliff's chest. Her one visible eye follows Kara's movements as the stone is passed to Cliff, then closes again.

Kara yanks her pack loose and searches one of the side pockets before extracting a plain metal length of pipe. She has a photograph attached to it and I recognize it as an anchor. Milo helps her degravitize it as she pulls a nearly identical pipe from the other side of the pack and explains the plan. "We need to relocate quickly. I have somewhere we can go that will be safe for now."

"You've been here before?" I ask.

Kara merely glares at me in response. She notices the gun I've picked up and points to it. "You know how to use that?"

I study the side of the gun. "Squeeze the trigger and blow big holes in stuff?"

Kara steps over and yanks the gun from my hand. She flips a toggle back and forth on the side. "This turns it off. This is low power. This is high. The rest of the features will be beyond you." She flips the switch to off and shoves it back into my hands. "Don't obliterate yourself with it." This last statement is uttered without condescension, making me acknowledge the fact that I really could obliterate myself somehow. I double-check the off switch.

I follow the others outside onto the wrecked roof of the larger floor below us. The building is tiered and we've arrived near the apex. The holes on our level are repeated elsewhere in the shell of the building below. The skyline is bleak under dark patches of gray shifting clouds. Moonlight illuminates a few neighboring structures from somewhere above but doesn't penetrate near us. Mountains define the eastern horizon, but the air has the distinctive scent of the sea. I take a few steps toward the edge and am surprised to find the bases of the buildings are not anchored in dry land, but climb directly out of turbulent water below. Looking east in new fascination I try to orient myself to the nature of this strange city. In that direction the skeletal buildings gradually run to ground, and in the distance I make out a familiar lighted shape. "Is that the Space Needle?"

I've addressed my query to no one in particular and when I turn toward the others it's clear that no one has heard me. Bozzle is helping Deanna to her feet from her hiding place behind a wreck of an air conditioner. Deanna in turn reaches into the darkness behind the machine and she and Bozzle both work to lift a battered-looking Tad Masterson. Tad staggers forward a step, then nearly collapses again, Bozzle catches him just in time and props him back up. Deanna gives me a semblance of a smile as she tries to assist her friend over to where Kara has stopped.

Kara and Milo have measured out a space for the anchors and are discussing the proper spacing of the pipes. Ultimately they lay the pipes across a few stacked cinder blocks and when they seem satisfied with them, instruct me to join them. Cliff and Genesis linger near the edge of the building. I catch just a snippet of Cliff's speech. "He would like the ocean well enough. Seems our best option . . ."

I can't make out what Genesis says in reply, but Cliff offers her the stone anchor. She shakes her head and her shoulders shudder as she tries to contain her emotions. Cliff nods, rubs his thumb across the top of the stone once, and then hurls the anchor toward the darkness of the sea in the west. The black stone vanishes immediately in the night and I wouldn't be able to see it hit the water from where I'm standing anyway, but I imagine it plunging into the waves and sinking its way to the floor of the bay.

I can think of worse places to be buried, but the thought stirs anger in me, too. I'm tired of watching friends get buried. I'm tired of this race and the future, and I'm tired of feeling overwhelmed by it all. I turn back to Kara and Milo and take my place at one of the anchors with the others. Kara gives us the time to set and we each adjust our respective devices.

Deanna helps Genesis with her Temprovibe when Cliff and Gen join us.

Jonah has the dog's leash secured tightly around his arm and the dog is pressed flush against the boy's legs for better contact. Jonah's messy hair is blowing in the breeze and he meets my eyes as Kara counts off. I try to give the kid a reassuring smile, but I doubt it's convincing. I feel anything but sure about our prospects. Kara finishes the countdown and I activate my chronometer, trading the dim rooftop for an even darker tunnel. I drop a couple of feet onto cement steps as the piece of pipe has now become a railing.

"Where are we?" Deanna asks. She and Bozzle help Tad stay upright as he descends the steps.

"We're in the Seattle Underground," Kara replies.

The floor below me is an old sidewalk, and despite scraps of plywood and bits of debris, the tunnel walls look as if they were once well kept. "Is this some type of subway access?"

Kara secures her riot helmet. "No." She stomps forward with her gun at the ready. Milo lets Cliff and Genesis follow her next before falling into step beside me.

"This was part of the old city," Milo explains. "It was actually here in your time. It's been here since the beginning of the twentieth century. The original city of Seattle was built on a tidal plain, and after a fire around 1890 they decided to raise the level of the streets. The old ground floors of the buildings were still down here even though the main street is now up above us." He points to some ancient looking glass blocks that penetrate the concrete over our heads. Dim light is filtering from a streetlight somewhere above, refracting on the walls like sunlight through a beer bottle. "The city grew out over the water in the next few centuries and this old part of town stopped being used much, but that works well for us."

"Have you been here before?" I study Milo in the half-light. "You said you were from the 2140's didn't you?"

Milo flicks on his flashlight to light the sidewalk ahead of us. The beam illuminates the concrete beyond Bozzle and Deanna's feet as they help Tad along. Kara is somewhere ahead on the fringe of darkness while the others trail closely behind us.

"Ben, there are some things I didn't tell you before about why I'm in this race. In fact, I told you a couple of lies."

"You aren't the first." I keep my voice light but my grip on my gun tightens a little. "So you're not from the twenty-second century?"

"I am actually. I didn't lie about that, though I haven't lived there in quite some time." He keeps his eyes fixed ahead as he continues. "I lied about Kara. I didn't get assigned her from the guide pool. We arranged to be in this race together. In fact we've been working hard to be in this race for a long time."

"Why? Did you think it was going to be something else?" I recall Deanna's shattered expectations of celebrity and wealth.

"No. We knew that this wasn't a normal chronothon. I think we were the only ones who knew the truth. But we needed to come anyway."

"What truth?" My curiosity increases at the thought of getting real answers. "What's really going on here?"

"I'm going to explain it, but everyone deserves to hear it together. We're almost there." Milo shines his light farther down the passage to where Kara has stopped in front of a brick archway. She pounds on the thick metal door beneath it and waits until something heavy is thrown clear on the other side. I hear the clunk as we near the door. In the corner of the archway, a small red light next to a camera lens flashes to green.

Kara turns the handle and the door swings open smoothly. Someone speaks to her from the other side, then shuts the door again. Kara strides back to us and heads for Milo.

"We need to check in first, then we can bring the others."

Milo nods and addresses the rest of us. "Take a rest here. It will be safe in these tunnels. Kara and I need to get you clearance for the rest of the way but it won't take long."

"Where are you taking us?" Bozzle's voice is firm, and indicates none of the shakiness I feel.

"We have contacts here," Milo explains. "Friends who will be able to keep us safe from the Zealots."

My stomach growls audibly and I get the sudden hope that whomever we're meeting will have some food. Genesis slumps to the floor against the corner of a stone wall. Cliff sets his gear next to her and walks over to stand near me.

"You have a way out of this place?" Cliff growls. "That's what we need right now."

Milo reaches a hand out and places it on Cliff's shoulder, suddenly the leader. "Just stay put. We'll get you out of this. I promise."

It seems there is nothing else to be said. Kara raps on the door again, and this time she and Milo are admitted. Deanna helps Tad to a sitting position near the archway, then checks on Genesis. I get the sense that she has found a purpose in helping the others—her own grief no longer shows as prominently in her eyes. Cliff watches Deanna wet a bandana and run it across Gen's forehead, then seeming satisfied enough with the current situation, eases himself to the floor. I let my own satchel slip from my shoulder and find a place next to him.

We sit in silence for a few minutes, watching Bozzle slowly patrolling the passage. Jonah and Barley follow the alien, the dog sniffing the ancient timbers and crumbling mortar of the buried walkway.

Slumped against the wall next to Cliff, I'm drained of energy. Cliff looks exhausted, too, but his hands are still fiddling with the stock of his shotgun. From down the passage I hear wet, muffled sobbing from Genesis. Cliff hears it, too, but says nothing.

"So what are you going to do now?" I ask, not sure if I should broach the subject.

Cliff grunts and flips the safety back and forth on the gun, but then noticing me still waiting for an answer, he lays the gun down. "I'll help Gen get back on her feet. She has to get home."

I fidget with the top of my canteen. "So, I know she's really upset obviously, but I was thinking . . . she's a time traveler, right? So once this is over and we've got these bands off, couldn't she just go back to a time before Jet was killed, and save him?"

Cliff stares at some imaginary horizon. "She'll probably go back and see him, at least from a distance. Most people do in the beginning, when the pain is still fresh. It won't be so awful since she's a sister. But they're close, and that makes it harder."

"How so?"

"You have to remember, any time she returns to in one of her own timestreams, Jet will still be alive, but she'll be there, too."

"Oh yeah."

"Makes things complicated."

"So there will be two of her and only one of him," I say. "What would happen then?"

"How would you feel if one day you're spending time with the person closest to you, and another you shows up, saying they've lost everyone and everything and they want to spend some time with your loved one?"

"I guess I would try to be understanding."

"Yeah, you would. And if it's just that this other you lost his mother, and now he wants to come take your dear old mum out for lunch and hear the sound of her sweet voice one more time, maybe that's okay, and she's none the wiser. Maybe you even feel good about yourself for helping him out, considering he's you and all.

"But then, maybe sad, distraught other you decides that he wants to make himself feel better by sleeping with your girlfriend. You still gonna feel understanding?"

"No. I guess not."

"No. Things start to get complicated real fast. You start layering your life with multiple versions of yourself, it can get a little crowded. Maybe you think you've got it all worked out, and everything with your other self is copacetic. Then you wake up one morning to a knife through your gut, and your mirror image looking down at you, saying, 'Sorry bud, I just don't want to share anymore.' Happens more often than you'd think. It's hard for authorities to solve a murder when the supposed victim is standing there smiling at them." Cliff picks his shotgun back up and rests it across his knee. "No. Most time travelers learn to leave themselves alone. Best to clear off before things get stabby."

"I guess that makes sense." I sip the last drops from my canteen.

"Genesis will do what everyone else does. Grieve her brother, then find a way to move on. Knowing her, I wouldn't be surprised if that means some revenge. I've got a bit of my own grief to work through, and it may take finding whoever's responsible for this cock-up of a chronothon, getting my hands around their throat, and giving it a good squeeze."

We lapse back to silence as we wait for Kara and Milo's return. It's perhaps ten minutes before we hear the clunk of the door being unlatched. When it swings open, Milo gestures for us to join him. He's holding a device in his hand that he scans across each racer's bracelet as they pass. For a moment he reminds me of a bouncer, although a bookish sort. He explains the device to Cliff ahead of me. "We're putting a data freeze on your race bracelets. We don't want the committee to be able to track where we're going."

I pull the Admiral's bracelet from my pocket and he scans the electronic wand over that as well. I follow the others through the archway and into an open, brick-lined basement. At least it was a basement once. Now the lower floors have been ripped out, creating a new ceiling a couple of stories up. The old façade rises above the street level, but the windows are bricked over. The room is lit from industrial light fixtures that hang from vestigial copper plumbing pipes. A few support columns have been left alone, stretching to the building overhead and giving the place a feeling of stability despite the gutted interior.

Kara leads the way up a set of steel steps to a raised platform surrounded by a railing. Two burly guards watch our assent with weapons at the ready. The two men are dressed in durable clothing of canvas and leather and are laden with knickknacks like binoculars and knives. The gear looks surprisingly low tech for the twenty-fifth century, but the stern looks on the men's faces leave no room for doubt about their ability to use it. I try not to stare at the guard on the right as we pass, despite the detailed tattoo of eagle talons that stretches across one side of his face. It's an elaborate image and skillfully drawn, but my admiration of the artistry doesn't override my instinct to stay well clear of him.

Kara crosses the concrete platform and stops at a pair of rusty elevator doors. The elevator bank is old even by my standards but must be positively ancient for the others. An analog brass needle is attached to a spindle over each door, designed to point to the appropriate floor. The needle on the right is dangling loosely toward the floor, but the indicator on the left currently reads seven. The tarnished brass backsplash could very well be original to the building. If so, it is about all that remains. The space above the elevator is vacant. Perhaps twelve feet above the basement floor, the shaft of the elevator has been dismantled. Bricks and mortar have been smashed and the shaft is missing completely, leaving a spacious void of perhaps forty feet and then a gaping square hole in the ceiling that may once have been the third or fourth floor.

Admiring the old brass indicator hands, it occurs to me that the elevator is as out of its own time as I am and I get a brief sentimental attachment to it just before Kara presses the up button. That irregular action jars me back to the present.

I glance at Milo, but he doesn't seem to have a problem with his guide waiting for a non-existent elevator. I fidget with my gun, wondering for the first time whether the secret Milo needs to share with me could involve any type of mental illness. I take a step back and ease my way toward Bozzle. At the moment, with Cliff involved with consoling Genesis and Deanna back attending to Tad, the alien seems the likeliest of allies if Milo and Kara turn out to be crazy people. I've just found the safety of my gun with my fingertips when I notice the needle above the elevator doors moving. I stare incredulously as the indicator counts its way down the missing floors and stops at the capital B.

The doors still ding when they open.

My curiosity replaces my nervousness, and I take a step closer to peer inside the doors. The interior of the elevator is well lit. Bozzle has his head tilted slightly to the side, considering the device, and I'm happy to know I'm not the only one ill at ease with the situation. No one makes a comment about the elevator's miraculous appearance. The others merely file inside. I follow cautiously, surmising that perhaps the elevator descends to subterranean levels and I'm mistaking the numbers on the indicator for stories above us. It's a tight fit to get all of us into the wood and polished brass interior. Unlike the outside of the elevator, the interior has been carefully maintained and gives a feeling of nostalgic opulence. A neatly lettered nameplate to the left side of the door reads "Tempus Mobilus- Fine Elevators since 1882." Kara extracts a brass key on a chain from around her neck and inserts it into a keyhole under the inscription. She turns it clockwise three full revolutions and the doors close, and to my complete consternation, the elevator begins moving upward.

The interior of the elevator has a matching brass floor indicator, and this shinier needle begins to tick off floors with regular consistency. Our ascent seems in no way impeded by the complete lack of an elevator shaft above us. When we reach the seventh floor, the doors ding open again, and seemingly just to solidify my complete and utter shock, the windows of the room beyond are streaming with sunlight.

The dog's tail begins to wag as it wriggles past me onto the polished floor of the seventh story. I follow Bozzle out of the elevator and into the spacious, elegantly furnished penthouse. Kara steams past me and we follow her down a marbled hallway and through a doorway into a sunlit library. Along the window side of the room, a broad-shouldered man rises from behind a mahogany desk and appraises us with a tight-lipped sternness reinforced by his thick, bristly beard. His intense gaze sweeps over the seven of us, pauses briefly on the dog, then returns to rest on Kara. Beyond the man, in the radiant blue sky, sunshine glints off the side of an airship moored to the top of the Space Needle. Two more silver-sided airships hover offshore, lingering with their noses pointed toward the city.

The man behind the desk straightens his military-style jacket. "All right, Lieutenant LaCuesta, you've got them here. We may as well get them some chairs." He snaps his fingers at a man along the far wall who is standing at attention near a second doorway. He then points to Tad. "Corporal, see that this man gets medical attention immediately, and get our other guests something to sit on before they fall over." He settles back into his own chair. "They're going to need a seat once they hear what we've got to say."

"Most people think of time as linear. It would be more accurate to describe it as a web or a snowflake. Its nature is fractal and complex. Getting around in a universe that complicated is bound to cause confusion. Don't forget where you parked your car."–Journal of Dr. Harold Quickly, 2180

Chapter 28

"I'm frankly happy to see so many of you alive." The man behind the desk has waited for us to get settled before speaking. Tad has been helped from the room by Deanna and two male nurses, while the corporal and a couple of his contemporaries have found armchairs for the rest of us to sit in—with the exception of Kara. She has chosen to remain standing between us and the man at the desk. If I didn't know better I'd find her positioning something akin to protective. She's shed some of her riot gear, but kept her leather jacket on. Her posture is rigid, hands clasped behind her back. A strand of hair has fallen from the bandana around her head and is partially obscuring a portion of tattoo that points upward from her collar. The blue and red spike that traces its way up the skin of her neck could be anything really. *Point of a star?*

I drag my eyes from Kara's back and let them survey the man in front of us. He's clearly in a position of authority, but I don't recognize any of the insignia on his uniform. The nameplate on his desk reads Major Troy McClure. I suppose he could be Scottish, but he more closely resembles a bear. There was a time when this situation might seem intimidating. A few months ago, being confined in a room with a group of military types who clearly own some type of fantastical time elevator would have set off every mental alarm I had. Now, after all I've been through, the pleasantly air-conditioned room and cushioned armchair are making me the most comfortable I've been in innumerable hours, and I'm struggling to keep my body from putting me right to sleep. Luckily, Kara's voice cuts through my mental lethargy.

"The mission got results. We still don't have all the pieces, but we at least know we were correct about the time gates. The race was a cover-up from day one. They used the gates for transportation, but the racers were just pack mules."

"Carrying what?" The major keeps his intense gaze on Kara's face.

THE CHRONOTHON

"Were you able to isolate the cargo?"

"The time gate data wasn't conclusive. Milo can explain that better." Kara angles her body to the side and signals for Milo to stand.

"Ah yes, our new recruit." The major looks Milo over. "Lieutenant LaCuesta gave you a high commendation for your technical know-how, Mr. Kalani."

Milo nods to Kara and gives her a quick smile before addressing the major. "I'm honored to have been selected for the mission. As Lieutenant La Cuesta said, we were able to use the time gate data to gain a great deal of information on the transportation system disguised in the race. It was encoded, but we found it."

The major leans back in his chair. "And what was your conclusion?"

"The committee's gates were rigged for use by specific racers. Instead of allowing all racers through every gate, it was coded to isolate certain individuals for elimination from the race. They were also set to allow passage to a couple of select additional individuals."

"What kind of individuals?"

"It would be easier to show you visually. Do you have a display screen I can interface with?"

The major taps something on the surface of his desk. I see nothing there, but the wall behind him responds. The entire brick wall, including the view of the airships out the windows, disappears. The wall is replaced by solid black, and I realize that the surface is a digital skin. The major lifts his palm toward Milo. "It's all yours."

Milo taps the side of his glasses, and the wall lights up with a photo image of Traus Gillian. I hear Jonah gasp behind me at the appearance of the oversized face. I glance over my shoulder and Genesis is wearing an expression of pure hate. Cliff, sitting between the two, places a hand on Jonah's shoulder.

"This man is a known assassin," Milo explains to the major. "He appeared multiple times during the race and eliminated two racers, though we suspect he intended to eliminate more." He acknowledges Jonah briefly before turning his attention back to the wall. "But he wasn't the only assassin employed. There was this man, or *men* to be technically accurate." A full body shot of Ajax covers the wall, followed by a shot of Viznir at the time gate at the start of the race. "As well as this guide who also turned out to be employed or coerced into their scheme. I suspect these last two were used to terminate players in levels out of range of Mr. Gillian. This man, Viznir Najjar, attempted to eliminate one of our companions on the planet Diamatra."

"For what purpose?" the major asks.

"To cover up the fact that they'd been used to transport contraband."

Milo turns to look at us. "It is my belief that these racers were engaged, without their knowledge, in smuggling unauthorized materials through time."

The major runs a hand over his beard. "It makes sense. No one had built time gates anywhere near these locations before—especially not Diamatra. God, that had to have been in the works for ages just to get a crew there." He looks us over thoughtfully. "But we still need to prove why." His eyes land on me and he seems to be sizing me up. "I know you all have questions about why you're here. You've been traumatized by this experience and are no doubt still concerned for your safety. I don't blame you. You've been through more than anyone should ever be subjected to."

I raise my hand, not sure if I should speak.

"Mr. Travers, isn't it?"

"Ben is fine," I reply. "I don't think we were really introduced officially. Pardon my asking, but who are you people? And where are we?"

The major stretches both palms to the desk. "A valid question." He gestures to the digital wall while looking at Milo. "Do you mind?"

Milo taps his glasses and the image of Viznir vanishes. Milo sits back down.

The major stands and the brick walls and window views return to the screen. "You are looking at an image of the last year of peace here in the Northwest. We've brought you here because this is the front line, the last stronghold of relative safety before the time of The Order of Zsa."

The image on the wall changes and becomes a massive web of lines in a three dimensional format. I recognize it as a timestream chart. I've seen a few of the digital maps of time in my experience as a time traveler, but this is the most densely filled image yet. The major zooms in on one particular corner of the multi-layered web.

"Most of you are from near the Primes from what Kara tells me, and I know most of you haven't come this far into the mid-millennial streams before. If you have, you almost certainly didn't come to our corner of the map." He zooms in farther. "This is negative territory, Epsilon stream. Negative Epsilon Vega to be precise." He highlights a particular strand of the map. "And as many of you know, there is a damn good reason why time travelers don't come out this way. Out here we've got the godddamn Order of Zsa. The most fucked-up religion ever to spawn a following on this planet, and the leading cause of death for time travelers in the twenty-fifth century. I've been living out here for over fifteen years now, holding this front with my team, because for better or worse, this is our home and we'll be buggered if we're gonna let a bunch of blacked-out Zealot nutcases take our home streams from us."

THE CHRONOTHON

Major McClure scans the group and steps out from behind his desk, pacing the front of the room. "I know what you might be thinking. You might feel the need to mention that we lost this fight already, or part of it. And you'd be right. We did concede the future of this timestream to the Zealots. We were outgunned and outmanned and we got hunted down like rabbits. We ran. It was not a proud time for any of us, but we survived, and we only fled back far enough in time till we could hold the line again." He indicates a glowing point on the map. "And hold it we have."

The major stops pacing and puts his hands behind his back. "We aren't looking for a thank you. We figure it's our duty to keep these yahoos from overrunning the other streams. Do you all sleep safer at night in your homes as a result? Damn straight you do, but it comes at a cost. We've scoured the decades of this stream for any bit of Zealot activity before the treaty date line. For the most part, we've eradicated any links from this stream to the heart of our system. The primes have been kept almost completely free of this so-called prophet and his anti-time-travel rhetoric. A couple of Zealots have slipped by us, but we've found them, hunted them down one by one the way they once hunted us. We've held the line." The major looks at me. "That's who we are, son. And that's why we're here."

Cliff clears his throat. "Major, I'm sure the boy is adequately grateful for your sacrifices, if he understands any bit of this. We all appreciate what your men do out here, but you still didn't answer his question. What has this got to do with us? Why would a chronothon committee chart a race to this end of the universe? No one in their right mind would want to see racers go through what we've been through."

"They haven't." Milo interrupts the conversation. He stands up and taps his glasses. The map on the wall disappears again. "The time gates haven't been transmitting video from the race since the Hindenburg escape, and even that was altered. I'll show you the images." The wall flashes to life and we're shown a view of the Hindenburg wreckage followed by a shot of the exiting time gate. I see myself in one of the shots, hesitating before stepping through the hangar doorway.

"These were the last frames of actual footage from the race that we competed in. But that didn't stop them from broadcasting." The scene changes to a lush landscape around a lake. Racers are sprinting through the woods near the waterline. I spot Jettison there with Cliff and even the Ivans are in attendance. Jonah is preceded through the time gate by a clean and fluffy Barley who barks happily before bounding through.

Milo fast-forwards to a scene in a field back in Ireland. "There were three more levels after the Hindenburg according to the footage. There was even a pedestal ceremony where Tad Masterson took first place and Admiral Silas McGovern took second. Ben here was the surprise third-place finisher." The screen flashes to a shot of the three of us waving cheerfully to the crowd. An experience I obviously failed to ever have.

"Despite the fact that we are time travelers, there is one thing we are quite sure of. This event will never happen. Silas McGovern died on a space station above the planet Diamatra. The spectators of this chronothon will never know that, thanks to some excellent digital image duplication and what I suspect were synthetically fabricated clones.

"The reality we know, the race through the Academy, the tunnels of Diamatra, and finally our time here; none of that was ever transmitted. Not to the chronothon committee anyway. Kara and I made sure to freeze the data stream on these race bands before we got into the elevator to prevent anyone from tracking us, but now we know more about where the data is actually headed."

Bozzle is the next to speak. "If we've been used as smugglers, what have we been smuggling?"

Milo frowns. "That's what we aren't positive about, but we have a theory. We know that the time gates were set up to transport a few of the objectives we'd gathered onward through time. Unfortunately, the code wasn't specific enough for me to gather what each item was. We do have a clue, in that after each level where an objective was smuggled via the gate, we also lost racers, or almost did."

"Sam Tulley and his boy," Cliff grunts. "Were they part of this?"

Milo nods. "I believe so. That's where I need your help. Does anyone know what the Tulleys were carrying the round before they died? If we can pinpoint what their objective was that they smuggled, we may be able to figure out why they were eliminated."

"It was something from the tunnels under the castle, I think." It's Genesis who's speaking. The first words I've heard her utter since the shooting. Her eyes are red, but she is sitting up straighter, listening attentively to Milo's conversation.

Milo shakes his head. "They never made it to the time gate in medieval France, so it would have been something they had the round before. The only team we think got taken out in the same level where they found their objective, was all the way back in Egypt. Ben here is the only one who knew what they were carrying."

The major's eyes fall on me.

"It was a rock." The words are out of my mouth before the memory has even fully returned. "They said it was a rock anyway. I never actually saw it." I recall Dennis' puffy red face as he blustered about the repository taking his anchor.

"A rock?"

"Yeah. A black rock, from a quarry."

Milo brings an image on screen that I recognize. It's the black stone with the green vein through it that I found in the tunnels on Diamatra. "I suspect it would have been much like this one," he says.

"That's Jonah's anchor," I say, remembering the store room and the weight of the stone.

Milo nods. "Yes it is. And as soon as he got to the next level, Traus Gillian tried to kill him." Milo glances at Jonah and then over to Genesis. "Even though Jettison was the victim of that shooting, Jonah appeared to be the target, and we have one other racer who likewise survived an assassination attempt." He turns to me. "What were you carrying the round before Viznir Najjar tried to kill you?"

I think about Viznir's betrayal on the space station, then backtrack to the skyscraper in Northern France at the Academy of Sciences. "It was a metal ball full of fluid. The objective map called it a 'gravitan stabilizer.'"

Major McClure raises his eyebrows, then shares a glance with Milo. He runs his hand across his beard and sits back at his desk, proceeding to shuffle through something in his drawer.

Milo smiles at me. "That confirms our suspicions." He points to the wall and walks over to the image of the rock from Diamatra, tapping his finger on the wall. "This stone is a chunk of ore. It's not what they were mining for on Diamatra, but it's something very valuable to have found. This green vein running through the stone is made of gravitans—an organic form of gravitites—naturally occurring particles capable of escaping the bonds of time itself."

I think of Dr. Quickly and Abraham sitting ankle-deep in the stream with their sifting pans in the 1970s. *He was right. They do exist.*

"We're still missing a bit of information. We don't know what the Ivans were carrying before they were eliminated, but I suspect it was something they dug out of the tunnels under Castle Gaillard. Marco Thomas and Andre Watts got eliminated before I could figure out what they'd been carrying, but the scene of their elimination held more clues. The assassin, Ajax, buried them in a mine. A mine I believe at least one of the racers extracted more ore from. The gravitan-laced ore was the key to the location choices of this whole race." He posts up images of the objective maps from the various levels. I recognize Egypt, the Old West circus, even the island from the Caribbean. Each map has a section circled that involves a rock quarry or mine, or some other buried item. "And I believe that we have one more bit of evidence to corroborate our theory." Milo steps in front of Bozzle. "The data for the next time gate is coded to only allow three more racers to get through. Horacio Amadeus and his cousin, Ariella Cipriani, have already entered. We found it suspicious that only one other racer was allowed to pass. That last lucky bracelet belongs to our tallest, greenest friend here."

The tension in the room is palpable as Milo stares at Bozzle. I sit up straighter, wondering what he's talking about and if something confrontational is about to happen. My eyes flit to the major and I notice both of his hands are concealed beneath the desk. *Does he have a weapon?* Kara is still in the same position, facing the major's desk with her hands behind her back, attentive but unmoved.

Jonah springs from his chair and latches onto Bozzle's shoulders as he shouts at Milo. "You're wrong! Bozzle is one of the good guys!" He keeps his arms wrapped around the alien's neck, determined to protect him from whatever Milo has planned.

Milo merely smiles and crosses his arms. "You're right, Jonah. He is one of the good guys. But he's also an Anya Morey." He leans against the edge of the major's desk. "Would you mind telling your friends why that's relevant, Bozzle? Or do you want me to?"

"It's not his fault!" Jonah yells. "If you're mad because he doesn't do it like we do, you shouldn't be. He doesn't have to!"

Milo says nothing but remains smiling.

The alien gently unwraps Jonah's arms from his neck and rises from his chair. From my sitting position, his seven-foot height seems even bigger. His green, tattooed skin and pointed horns are a stark contrast to the brick walls and pale painted ceiling of the library.

The alien turns slowly to face us. "The boy is correct, as is Milo Kalani. I am an Anya Morey, and we do not need your time devices."

For the first time, I notice that the alien's elaborately tattooed arms lack the one thing I should definitely have noticed. He has no chronometer or Temprovibe to work with.

"We are born with the ability to travel in time. My species, my family, we have traveled for many centuries, but on my world we do not use this gift for adventure or for pleasure. We use it only with solemn purpose. Here, on this planet, you have used the gift for many things. Some things I have found to be frivolous. I once saw a human bend time so that he could catch a train. On my world such a thing would never happen. Only the children would be so foolish, and they would be punished if they were." Milo has set the wall screen back to the image of the windows and Bozzle points out one of them as he continues. "I was invited to this world for this race because I was told it will be an honor to compete with other travelers. I have been honored. I have found many good people here. I have also seen things that I never wish to see again." He turns to face Milo and the major. "If you believe that I wish to continue in this race, you are wrong. If there is a path away from this place, I intend to take it. I have no wish to finish this competition. Now that these companions of mine are safe, my wish is to return home."

The major moves his hands from under the desk and I see he's not holding a weapon after all, but rather a tablet. He stands and smiles at our group. The first smile I've seen from him.

"Mr. Bozzlestich is an eloquent speaker. He speaks the truth. The Anya Morey have always been an honorable race and careful caretakers of time. Our mission was to figure out why he was invited to participate in this race in the first place. Being able to solidify our theory about the gravitans, I think we now have enough information to go on. Whoever wants these ore samples, likely wants an Anya Morey for the same reason. We know something more as well. Lieutenant La Cuesta, Mr. Kalani, you'll both want to see this. We gained this information while you were on your mission, and I believe it holds the key to figuring out the mystery of why the race committee built a time gate in the middle of hostile territory." He selects something on the tablet and another image fills the wall screen. This time we see a shot of a time gate. Like the starting gate in Ireland, it is constructed between two stone pillars. These pillars aren't Celtic or ancient, however. They are a simple concrete structure inside an industrial warehouse.

"We lost three good soldiers getting this footage here, but I think the information was valuable to our cause." He begins the video and I watch as six figures move toward the gate. I recognize Ariella and her guide, Dagmar Sensaborria, followed by Horacio and Donny, but behind the groups of racers is a young girl. She's wearing an old-fashioned nightgown and appears to be around Jonah's age. Her long black hair reaches almost to her waist. The last figure to enter the scene is the man from my apartment. He's still dressed in all black, the uniform I now recognize to be the garb of a Zealot. The Zealot's presence seems of little concern to the others. Ariella activates the time gate, and as the colors swirl between the columns, she gestures for the little girl to enter. The Zealot takes her hand and guides her through the gate. The rest of the group follows them and the colors quickly vanish.

The major shuts the video off and turns his attention back to us. "What was important to show you there was that the people responsible for this operation have gone beyond merely smuggling gravitans. They've also smuggled at least one person." He flashes an image on the screen showing a gray-haired man in black robes and a girl next to him that I recognize from the video. The pair is standing near a podium at some large event and the man is stretching an arm toward the crowd.

"This is Corman Task, better known to his followers as The Prophet

Zsa. He is head of the entire Order. His daughter, Elenora, is the girl from the video. What we don't know is why she was transported by time travelers."

Kara speaks up. "Do you suspect kidnapping?"

"It would be believable. A hostage would be a valuable defense against an attack by The Order, but our investigators turned up more information. Corman Task has been meeting with members of a well-known organization from the central streams, and we believe he may have been bartering some kind of deal with them. If we're not completely wrong, we believe he *wanted* them to take his daughter."

"Why would the most well-known hater of time travel give his daughter to one of us?" Genesis is on the edge of her chair. "It doesn't make sense."

"It might make sense if you were dying." Major McClure crosses his arms. "Corman Task has stage five kidney disease. From what we know they've already attempted kidney donor transplants for him and they didn't go well. Zealot medicine is not like ours. They are a backward-thinking belief system and they won't perform many of the synthetic procedures we do in the central streams. I believe Task is getting his daughter out before something big happens. He's dying but he hasn't stopped working. If anything, the Zealots have been growing stronger than ever. They're recruiting faster, training harder, getting themselves all worked up for something. If I didn't know better, I'd think they were prepping for an all out war."

The major steps from behind his desk. "So you all know what we know. You've suspected you'd gotten involved in something bigger than your average chronothon. You have. I believe we're on the edge of something big. All of you have been through plenty getting this far, and I'm sure you're eager to get home, but you are welcome here as well. When whatever it is that's about to happen goes down, we're going to need all the help we can get right here. I'm sure of it."

Cliff is the one to respond. He pushes himself out of his armchair and stands to face the bearded officer. "Major McClure, I appreciate all you've done for us. Getting us clear of Zealot territory no doubt saved all of our lives. We owe Kara and Milo our lives, too, not just once, but several times. If we hadn't had them with us in the mines at Diamatra, I doubt any of us would have made it back." Cliff hitches his belt a little higher under his middle. He looks a bit thinner today and I realize he's likely been missing meals.

"I'm sure we all appreciate what it is you folks do out here. You keeping the likes of the Zealots away from the central streams is a thankless job, and I doubt near as many people realize that as they should. You deserve help, and if I can, I'll do my best to find you more, but this group—" He waves toward the rest of us. "—I don't believe we're it." He fixes his gaze on the major. "We're ragged here. We're cut up and hurting in more ways than we can count. We've lost good people. We fought hard all right. Nobody can question the bravery of this group. I've never seen anything like our green friend here cutting his way through that horde of Soma. The boy, the dog, Ben Travers, even the academy kids, I've never been prouder to compete with a group of racers than these right here. But we aren't soldiers. I promised Gen and Jet's father I'd see them home safe. I failed at that promise. I can't change what happened to Jet. He did what he did because he thought it was worth it. But it's up to me now to see that it was. I need to get his sister and this boy he gave his life for out of harm's way. I owe him that."

The major chews his lip and the bristles of his beard protrude farther as he listens. When Cliff is finished, he unclasps his arms. "We deeply appreciate the service your group has provided us. This information you gave us today could very well be the key to our survival." He gestures toward the soldiers near the far door. "My men will see that you have everything you need. Food, clothing, a place to sleep, and when you're rested up and ready, we can see you safely back to the central streams."

Cliff steps forward and shakes the major's hand. "Thank you. That would be very kind." He helps Genesis up and starts to collect their things. The soldiers at the far wall open the door and hold it for us. Jonah hands Bozzle his pack and the alien smiles. I'm about to follow the group through the doorway when the major calls to me. "Mr. Travers, would you mind if I have a word?"

I study the man by the desk. Milo is behind him, but his face gives away nothing. Kara is equally stoic, but that is the norm for her, so I have no way of knowing if she is expressing any particular new emotion.

"Yes?" I set my pack back down on one of the armchairs.

"If you don't mind, before you go, there's something I'd like to show you."

I walk cautiously closer to the front of the room and stop behind the first row of chairs, letting my hands rest on a leather seatback.

"Your group is going to get rested and head home. We'll get them all fed and cleaned up and we'll get them back on the elevator."

"I appreciate that." I hesitate to say more since I'm not sure where the conversation is heading. I try for a polite compliment. "It's a great elevator. Unique. Is it some kind of time gate technology?"

The major smiles and accepts the conversational tangent. "It is, yes. That elevator is one of the very first time gates ever invented. Marvelous history to it. It ran continuously from the 1880s all the way till the end of the twenty-fourth century. Zealot activists came back and destroyed it when they started their anti-time traveler campaign of course, but we were able to reconstruct one of the cars. It doesn't service all the times it once did, but it will get you back quite a few centuries into the past. And now, since our reconstruction project, it even provides a path back into Zealot occupied time. They'd go bat-shit crazy if they found out we rebuilt it, but I think I can trust you to keep our secret, can't I?"

I give what I hope is a reassuring smile. "I don't have much desire to meet any more Zealots. Your secret is safe with me."

"That's what I like to hear. No telling who might get to asking you questions, though, where you're headed."

"Home? I don't think any people I know would believe a word out of my mouth when I tried to talk about this."

The major chuckles. "I suppose you're right about that. Not much use for time elevators in the November Prime around . . . 2009 was it?" He looks to Milo for confirmation.

I glance at my friend's face and find it serious. He studies me with a penetrating stare that seems slightly unfriendly. That look unnerves me far more than the major's questioning.

"What is it you wanted to show me? As much as I appreciate your interest in me, I have to say that I feel the same as Cliff on this one. I admire what you guys do here, but I don't think staying to help would really be for me. I have someone I need to get home to." Saying the words out loud makes me want them to be true even more. I hope she's waiting for me at home, now that this race is over. *She said she would be, didn't she?* I have a promise to keep. Lunch date and roller disco.

"Ben, we aren't expecting you to stay here and fight with us." The major has an amused look in his eyes.

"Oh. Okay good. I mean . . . right. I'm glad we're on the same page then."

"But you aren't going home yet, either."

I stare at the man, trying to make sense of his words. "Pardon me?"

"You don't go home from here, Ben."

"Why not?"

The major reaches for his tablet and activates the screen behind him. "That was what I was hoping you could tell me."

The image on the screen is the time gate in the warehouse again. I stare blankly at the vacant space for a few moments, then suddenly a man walks into the frame. The worn blue jeans and leather jacket are unmistakable, as is my uncombed hair and Abraham's canvas messenger bag. The man in the video doesn't look at the camera, but I know without a doubt it's me. I watch in shock as the future me steps toward the time gate and checks his race bracelet. He watches it for what seems like a long time, but the monitor only ticks off about ten seconds. When he is satisfied with the time, he steps forward and waves the bracelet in front of a metal plate with a power symbol on it. The colors swirl between the pillars and, after only a moment's hesitation, the other me steps through. The colors fade as quickly as they've appeared and the warehouse is once again vacant.

The major sets the wall display back to bricks and windows and says nothing. He just looks at me.

"Why? Why am I going to do that?" The image of the other me, confidently stepping through the gate replays in my mind.

The major consults his wristwatch. "That's something you'll have to figure out for yourself, because I don't have the answer. What I do know is that tomorrow, a little over half an hour after we reactivate the race bracelets, you walk through that gate. And as far as we know, you don't come back out."

The major collects his hat from the desk and heads toward the door. "Think it over, Mr. Travers. And when you figure it out, do us a favor and let us know, will you?" He sets his hat on his head and strides out the door.

"I'm sure every timestream in the universe has something good to offer. That doesn't mean I need to visit them all. You say you've brought dinosaurs back from extinction in your twenty-first century? I'll pass. I've seen how that movie ends."–Journal of Dr. Harold Quickly, 2035

Chapter 29

"Where does that gate even go?" I'm seated at a cafeteria-style table across from Milo and Kara. I have a platter full of mashed potatoes, vegetables, cornbread, and a grilled bit of meat that may or may not be beef. It all smells delicious, but I seem to have lost my appetite.

"We do have a partial answer to that question," Milo says. Since we left the library, both he and Kara have shown more concern, Milo guiding me to the cafeteria and trying to look sympathetic. He showed me the room where I'll be staying, and had some soldiers take care of my things. Kara has acted more or less the same as always, but hasn't yelled at me for anything during the entire walk downstairs, so I take that as her being supportive, too.

Milo is searching something behind his glasses but has brought along a tablet for me to use. He holds the tablet up and shows me a timestream chart. "We call it a solitaire." The thin glowing line on the display doesn't branch off any of the timestreams around it but seems to exist all by itself. It doesn't have any offshoots of its own either but rather continues as a solid, unbroken line. "These are extremely rare. They only occur when all other timestreams leading to it have been eradicated. Someone went to a lot of trouble to isolate this spot. They didn't want anybody stumbling onto it accidentally. As far as we can tell, the time gate must be the only way left to get there. We've named it Epsilon Vega Solo."

I consider what he's saying, trying to reconcile what little I know about timestream navigation. "The way I always understood it, timestreams are like highways. If you want to take a parallel route, you just have to back up to the point where that path broke away from the main road, then you can just jump ahead again on the other stream using something from there."

"Right," Milo agrees. "But in this case, it's like they built the road, then went back and removed the exit. You can't get there anymore. Not by conventional navigation."

"Does that mean that whoever is over there is stuck now?"

"Possibly, unless they have an anchor from another nearby timestream to jump to." He zooms out a little from the thread on the map. "A well-charged device could probably make the leap over to Negative Epsilon Winter, but you would need an anchor from there before you went in. Like I said, once they built this thing, nobody has tried to come back."

I swirl my fork around my mashed potatoes and take a half-hearted bite. "So we know the chronothon committee, or at least some of the members, used their influence to get time gates built in specific places and times. Places where someone could get access to the gravitan ore. Have you guys tried interviewing committee members to see what they know? I can think of a pretty persuasive guy to have ask the questions." I recall what Cliff had told me in the tunnel. *It'd be hard to answer questions with Cliff's hands around their throats, but they might be able to choke something out.*

"We've done some research," Kara replies, "but the committee members we suspect were in on it have disappeared from their home streams."

"To where?"

Milo holds up the image of the solitaire. "One guess."

I take a sip from my water glass and make another attempt at my mashed potatoes. "And tomorrow, I go there myself for some stupid reason."

That part is driving me crazy. *What possible motivation would I have? Sheer curiosity? A death wish?* I consider what my strongest motivations are. Right now all I can come up with is Mym. I have other friends at home, too, family, and of course my new friends I've met recently, Abraham, Dr. Quickly ... I think about the two of them laughing their way through the tall grass toward the river. They seemed so carefree. None of this had affected them yet. *Why would Dr. Quickly's gravitan research one day become so important that people would go to this much trouble, even kill for it?*

I voice my next question out loud. "The items with the gravitans in them that we picked up; why get so many? Why not use one and just reproduce more? Gravitites replicate really fast, shouldn't gravitans, too?"

"That would make sense," Milo replies, "but these gravitans weren't all the same. They were different strains." He strokes his chin and studies his glasses. "In fact, now that you mention it, it could be ..." He trails off and we lose him inside the world of his lenses. It takes about thirty seconds till he pops back out to us. "There are!" He does something to make the image from his glasses appear on the tablet again. "We've identified six known strains of naturally occurring gravitans. The same number as attempted killings we had in this race. At least that's what we suspect anyway." He starts talking faster as he unravels something in his mind. "They wouldn't have wanted to make it obvious, so they scatter the gravitan pick-ups over nine levels, make sure there were plenty of other objectives to clutter up the mix. It's a brilliant plan. No one would look too closely at what happened to the objectives as long as everybody was intent on the race. Once they got the race going, they didn't need the façade anymore. They just made digital levels to fool the fans at home. Meanwhile they were really using the money to build gates in places like Diamatra and Negative Epsilon Vega, places no sponsor in their right mind would ever fund."

"But how would they actually get the gates built without anyone noticing?" I ask. "I know in the time travel world things might be different, but where I come from, if you're going to build some billion-dollar structure, someone would need a permit for it, insurance, probably a zillion lawyers to sign off on it. Corporations don't just drop that kind of cash to sponsor something without wanting to see the results. If you're going to slip that past a budget committee, at least somebody would have to be in on it."

Milo stares at me like I've either said something ridiculous or he's about to have a heart attack. "That's it! That has to be it. The sponsors are in on it, too!" He jumps up from the table and starts talking to himself as he speeds out of the cafeteria. I watch him disappear into the hallway before turning back to my tray of half-eaten food. Kara has polished hers off and is draining the last of her cup of water.

She clunks the empty cup down on her tray. "You just set him off on at least a couple hour research mission. Way to get him fired up." She swings her leg over the bench and stands up.

"Where are you going?"

"I'm going to get some sleep. You should, too. I have a feeling you're going to need to rest up for whatever you've got planned for tomorrow."

"I don't have a plan. That's the problem."

"You will, and being exhausted never helped any plan I ever heard of." She takes Milo's tray with her and dumps them both at the dish rack against the far wall where kitchen staff is collecting them, then heads back toward me. Without her riot gear and weapons, she just looks like a slender young woman. In my world she probably would have been a college student, not a battle-hardened soldier. I call out to her as she passes by.

"Hey, Kara, do you have a way to communicate from here? Like a tachyon pulse transmitter? I need to call somebody."

Kara studies me briefly, seeming surprised by the request. "You'll have to talk to the major. He clears all communications." She slips her hands into her pockets, then disappears out the door in the same direction as Milo.

I make a few more attempts at my food before finally giving up. I do gulp the rest of my water and snag an extra bottle from the kitchen before wandering back into the hallway. The building has turned out to be a hotel, and a rather nice one at that. One side boasts a view of the Space Needle, and just like I saw in the major's digital penthouse windows, there really are airships in the sky. There was a time when I thought the flying ships were elegant, but now I only picture the Hindenburg's gas cells glowing beneath my feet and the smell of smoke and burning fuel from the aftermath. I flex my stiff left hand and turn away from the windows.

In the center of the building I find the elevator bank. Both elevators are working here, running up and down the fully existent shafts with no sign of time travel involved. I inspect the keyhole in the left elevator as I press the button for the seventh floor and run my fingertip over the raised letters on the nameplate. "Tempus Mobilus." I whisper the name as if it could be a spell that could whisk me home. The doors merely ding open on the seventh floor and I make my way down the marbled hallway toward the major's office.

My progress is quickly halted by two burly soldiers who make me wait in the hall while one of them searches for the major. I use the time to stare out the windows at the sun setting over the city. The atmosphere is aglow with pinks and purples. The light reflects off the sides of buildings and makes it hard to believe that anywhere out there people are on the edge of war.

"Mr. Travers. Have you reached a decision?" The major is leaning against the doorframe of his office.

"Not yet, actually. I was hoping to talk to someone first. Kara seemed to think you might be able to help me with a TPT?"

The major frowns but straightens up. "And who would you be calling?"

"A friend."

"Does this friend have some information to offer that we can't?"

"She might."

"Ah. A she-friend. I see." He stands aside and invites me to enter the office. I step inside and he leads me behind his desk. The bookshelf along one side of the room swings open with seemingly no effort from the major and he gestures me through the new doorway into a ten by ten room lined with electronics. There are no windows here, digital or otherwise, only a table and chair with a bunch of cables running to them. A metal box on the table has a bunch of dials and gauges on it and looks like it belongs at NASA in the 1960s.

Major McClure throws a breaker switch on the wall and the room buzzes to life. He gestures me toward the chair and moves to the box controls. "You have the coordinates?"

I extract the coin-shaped disk from my pocket and read off the thirteen digits. The major uses the selector knobs and inputs them for me. When he's finished, he points to a glowing orange button. "Press this when you're ready. I'll give you some privacy." He waits till I'm seated, then steps back into his office and shuts the bookcase.

I survey the room briefly. Actual privacy seems unlikely. Any one of the machines around me could be broadcasting every movement I make, but right now I don't really care. I just want to hear her voice. I press the orange button and wait. Static emanates from speakers mounted to the table followed by a sharp buzzing. I'm looking around for some type of squelch knob to get rid of the irritating noise when it stops and is replaced by the most lovely sound in the world.

"Hello? Ben?"

"It's me. Can you hear me?" I lean forward, not sure what I'm supposed to be speaking into.

"Is this right? The I.D. says you're calling from the 2400s. Are you that far?"

"Yeah. I'm in Negative Epsilon Vega, just before the start of some war with Zealots. I'm in Seattle."

"What are you doing there?"

"It's a long story. Where are you? Are you okay?"

"I'm fine, but Ben, there is a lot I have to tell you. I've been researching what we talked about and it's worse than I thought. And this race you're in is a sham. Abraham was at the finish line. It was all fake. I don't know where they're sending you, but it's not back to Ireland."

"They're using us to smuggle gravitans. It wasn't just the stabilizer. Apparently there are like six different kinds. Your dad was right about them. I don't know why they want them, but they're moving them somewhere."

The room goes silent with the exception of the equipment buzzing and I worry that something has gone wrong. "Mym? Are you still there?"

"I'm here. Listen, I'm going to try to get to you. I've never been that far, so I'm not sure how long it will take me, but can you set that anchor up somewhere safe? There is an arrow on the up side. Point that toward the safe place to arrive. You know how tall I am. Just keep me out of the floor."

I pick up the metallic coin with the numbers on it. The other side does in fact have an arrow on it. "You're coming here?"

"I'll try. I can't promise I'll make it, but just keep me away from other people. I don't know who to trust there. Can you do that?"

"Yeah, definitely. What time?"

"Midnight? Will it be safe then?"

"Yes. I'll make sure."

"Okay. Be careful, Ben. These race people are awful. And listen, if I don't make it there tonight, just—be careful."

"I will. I promise."

"Okay. I'll see you soon."

The buzzing comes back and the connection is lost. I stare at the machine, then snatch up the metal coin from the table, suddenly my most precious possession.

I bang on the wall near the bookcase exit and the major reappears. "You get your sweet talking in?"

"Something like that."

"Good. You have an answer for me yet?"

"No. I still don't have any good reason to go through that gate tomorrow."

The major walks me to the elevator and looks at his watch. "You've got about twelve hours till we have to reactivate those race bands. I'd say you have about that much time to figure it out."

I step into the elevator and press the button for my floor. "You'll be the first to know."

The hotel rooms of the twenty-fifth century are not all that different from rooms at home. They still have four walls and a bed. A dresser in the corner seems like a candidate for Mym's anchor. I carefully position the coin on the edge so that when she arrives there will be nothing in her way. I shove the little writing desk farther away, just to be sure, but otherwise the space is satisfactory. One thing I do notice as I survey the room is that there are no visible light fixtures. Ambient light is coming from a window in the wall, but on closer inspection it's clear that window isn't real. The wall is covered in a digital film like the major's office. The light seems to emanate from everywhere at once. It's a cool bit of technology, but slightly irritating because I would like to try to get some rest. I search the wall for any type of switches, hoping they aren't tucked away in the meta-space again. Finally, when I've found nothing else, I simply speak to the room.

"Room, dim lights!" The command comes out a little harsh. "Please," I add as an afterthought, not sure how intelligent a hotel room might be in this century and not wanting to upset it. My request is silently granted. The light dims to a subtle glow and I retreat to the comfort of the bed. I can't find any clocks in the room and I'm not sure how I will know Mym's arrival time.

"Room, please set alarm for 11:30pm."

The room beeps and a mellow voice replies. "Alarm has been set. Have a restful sleep."

My body is exhausted and I expect to drop off right away but my mind won't seem to settle. I keep my eyes closed, trying to force sleep to come, but images keep processing through my mind. Jettison getting shot, the cryo-head blasting away at me with its Gatling gun—so close to tearing me apart. My brain feels disjointed, like all the time jumping has affected my way of sorting through memories. I get little snippets trying to force their way into my consciousness: my dad working on one of his glass bottle ships, my friends back home sitting around the bar after a softball game. Then I see Mym, her legs swinging in the sunshine on top of the radio tower, Apollo 11 racing into the sky beyond. It's all there, flowing around in my consciousness, contending with the stress I feel about that one video image that doesn't seem to fit: me walking calmly through the time gate headed to a place that no one has come back from. I puzzle the image around in my mind, but reach no new conclusions.

I drift off eventually but wake again, unsure of how much time has passed. I stare at the ceiling for a little, then shove off the bed and head for the bathroom. It takes me multiple requests and a much lengthier conversation with the shower than I had planned for, but I get myself washed. I could have made a time jump to get myself clean, but I opted to enjoy the soothing, old-fashioned method of soapsuds and warm pulsing water. The shower tries to impress me by spraying me from various angles, but I'm finally able to talk it into sticking to one conventional stream by using compliments and flattery.

I've just toweled off and gotten my pants on when someone knocks on my door. Milo is there when I open it and plows straight through to the bed without waiting for an invitation. He dumps an armful of items onto my bed including timestream charts, maps from our race, a couple of tablets, and a faceplate from a space helmet.

"You were right," he exclaims as he lays out his belongings. "I think I found the link. One of them anyway."

"Hey, man. What time is it?"

Milo doesn't answer but keeps laying out items. I step over to the bed to see what he's looking at.

"It wasn't all of the sponsors, but I suspect one for sure." He holds up the helmet faceplate. "United Machine made the extra-planetary suits for use on Diamatra, but that's like trying to implicate Coca-Cola because someone drank one of their drinks. United Machine is everywhere. But the fact that they were on Diamatra gave me an idea. That had to be the most difficult time gate to build, right? It was on a space station in another solar system. That's about as far away as you can get. The other gates were distant in time, but this one had geographic distance as well, and would have required some serious transportation to set up." He picks up one of the tablets. "That's when I started digging around records for who might have worked on that space station that could have been capable of constructing a time gate. There was only one person, a woman named Angela Tomlin, who had the engineering prowess to do it. Also, she was the only registered time traveler aboard." Milo effortlessly commandeers the hotel wall for a screen and, as my windows and, curtains disappear, he shows me an image of a middle-aged, pleasant looking woman with dark hair that has a single streak of gray in it.

"Angela Tomlin ended up on the crew of the Terra Legatus, but just prior she was an engineer for Ambrose Cybergenics."

"That's cool. Um, what time is it?"

Milo glances at his tablet. "It's 11:15." He points back to the wall. "Ambrose Cybergenics definitely has the money to fund something like this."

I glance at the space near the dresser, then settle onto the edge of the bed, keeping myself between it and Milo. "That was the sponsor we talked about the day I met you, the one who makes the traces for people to track their time traveling."

"Exactly. One of the company's prime objectives over the years has been regulating individual time travel. Some people protest that they're repressive of individual time travelers' rights, but of course their public relations statements are always angled to say that they're only looking out for user safety. They sponsor events like chronothons frequently, but some say it's just a way to improve their image despite an otherwise restrictive technology agenda."

"I know they make the traces for time travelers, but what else do they do? What's cybergenics?"

"Cybergenics is body augmentation. It's not just for time travelers. The majority of their customers are the general public. They help people with body modifications, implants, performance-enhancing customization. Might be purely cosmetic, or it could be utilitarian like the vision enhancing lenses most emergency responders use. They can do lighting, binocular vision, improved running, jumping, you name it really. They can turn people into super-men."

"Who runs it?"

"That's the Ambrose part of the company name. Dr. Ambrose himself. He was a scientist and professor. I want to say he started Ambrose Cybergenics after he left the Academy of Temporal Sciences."

"Doctor Ambrose." I repeat the name to myself. "Why does that name sound so familiar? I feel like I've heard it before."

"I'm sure you saw the Ambrose Cybergenics logo on all kinds of things from the race committee. Being a sponsor of the race gets you lots of product placement."

"Maybe. It wasn't the company logo, though, I know what that looks like. It was the name Dr. Ambrose—no! Actually it wasn't. I remember now, it was in the Old West, in Utah or wherever we were. It was 'D. Ambrose.' The D. Ambrose Mining Company, do you remember? It was on the sign where I ended up with Ajax. I ran into you and Kara right after. Is the cybergenics company also into mining?"

Milo studies his tablet then switches to his glasses. "I don't remember that, but hang on." He scans through something and projects an image onto the wall. It's a frame of video of the mining camp in Utah. I'm in the scene, as is Kara. The shot is from the perspective of Milo's glasses. He advances the video forward and freezes it when the mining sign comes into his frame of vision. He pauses there and zooms in on the sign. The lettering reads "Ever Winding Silver Mine" and below it the owner is listed as "D. Ambrose Mining Corporation." Milo smiles. "You have a great memory, Ben."

"For some things."

Milo searches the meta-space and pulls up something new. "You're right, there is a mining corporation under the umbrella of the business. And look what else they bought." He displays a contract for a purchase that appears to involve a land deed. The name of the property is listed as a colmetracite mining facility on the planet Diamatra.

"So they owned the mine that got run overrun by the Soma Djinn." I look at the buying price and it's into eleven figures. "Talk about a bad investment."

Milo shakes his head. "Actually, that's cheap. Really cheap." He skims to the final line of the contract and highlights the date line. "Ah. And there's the reason why."

"I don't get it. Was that a bad year in the mining market or something?"

"No." Milo is smiling. "That's fifteen years after the Soma took the mine over."

I stare at the image on the screen. "Wait, you're telling me the company paid seventy billion dollars for a mine *after* it had been taken over by body-snatching aliens?"

"The public records say that's exactly what they did."

"Why?"

"Maybe they wanted to build a time gate somewhere no one else would want to go." He's grinning now. "I think we've found our path to Epsilon Vega Solo."

I try to process what he's saying. "So they chart the race through an alien occupied mining colony, then they run it through a Zealot occupied timestream that I'm guessing even fewer people would try to pass. What for? Added security? One more layer of protection?"

"Maybe. Or maybe they needed something here." Milo changes the image on the screen to the shot of Ariella shepherding the prophet's daughter through the time gate. "Or more accurately, someone."

I stand up and walk around while I think aloud. "So Ambrose Cybergenics sponsors a chronothon to secretly collect samples of six different types of gravitans. It smuggles the ore samples though the gates, then chooses to route the whole operation through an era of time where everyone hates time travelers. Not only do they not get stopped by the Zealots, but the head prophet of the whole organization gives them his daughter? How the hell does any of that make sense?"

"There's one more piece of the puzzle you're forgetting." Milo brings another image up on screen; a racer profile. "They systematically eliminated specific racers, then attempted to leave the rest in Zealot occupied territory to get picked off. But then they leave the door open for one last racer." He points to the profile on the screen. "Mooruvio Bozzlestitch, the Anya Morey."

"Six different types of ore, a prophet's daughter, and a time traveling alien. What are they going to do with them?"

Milo leans back on his hands and studies the layers of images on the wall. "I think that's the big question."

"And for all this, I'm no closer to figuring out why I walk through that gate tomorrow." I run a hand through my messy hair then let my arm drop to my side.

The room suddenly starts buzzing. Milo looks at me. "What's that for?"

"Nothing." I address the wall. "Thanks, room. I'm awake." The buzzer stops and I turn to Milo. "I've actually got to cut this short."

Milo gets up from the bed. "You have something you have to do?"

"Uh, sort of. I have a visitor coming."

Milo gathers his things and makes for the door. "A visitor?" He fumbles a little trying to reach for the knob and I open it for him.

"Yeah."

"I didn't know the major lets us have 'visitors' to our rooms. I know it's not illegal in this timestream . . . How much did you pay for—"

"Nope. No, no. Not that kind of visitor."

"Oh. I didn't mean to seem judgmental—" Milo steps into the hall and turns to face me.

"Thank you for doing this, man." I go for a change of topic. "Thanks for trying to help me figure this out."

Milo considers me a moment and his face grows serious. "You don't have to thank me, Ben. You're somehow caught in the middle of this, so of course I'm going to help you, but that's not my main motivation. Whatever this is, whatever is going on behind this façade of a chronothon, I think it's just a fraction of the story.

"Something big is happening. Not good big either. I believe the major is right about that. When Kara first sought me out, told me what they do here, I didn't think I wanted to get involved, but she convinced me of the danger they're facing and I can feel it now, too. This Order of Zsa might be a crackpot religion, and they're definitely dangerous; they've been trying to kill time travelers their whole existence, but to be honest, if that's all it was, I probably wouldn't have come to help. Crazy people do crazy things and start stupid wars of ideology all over the place. You can find that in almost any timestream on this planet. That didn't scare me, but now, the crackpot religion suddenly lets one of the most influential and richest corporations in the time traveling world build a chronothon gate smack in the middle of their territory? Then I find they've given them their prophet's daughter? That kind of cooperation scares me worse than when they were trying to kill us. That means someone on our side of the fence found something in common with them and got them to talk. What could they have found common ground on? We have no idea what they talked about, and *that* really scares me."

Milo backs down the hallway. "I don't know why you walk through that gate tomorrow, but I hope it brings us answers. We desperately need them." With that he turns and walks away. I watch him round the corner toward the elevator before closing the door to my room.

I still don't have a clock, but I imagine I've only got minutes to wait. I move to the bathroom and run some water through my hands and try to get my hair to look less disorganized. I do a last minute mouth scrubbing with my toothbrush and try to push a wrinkle out of my t-shirt. I give up on that and step back into the room to wait. First I sit on the edge of the bed, then switch quickly to the chair. I try to get comfortable and look casual at the same time. *What's the proper way to wait for someone who is appearing in your bedroom? Should I stand up?* I stand up.

Mym arrives in midair and drops about a foot to the carpeted hotel floor. She takes her fingertips from the anchor and turns around. Her blue eyes find mine and she looks me over. We stand there like that, both of us in blue jeans. She's got two tank tops layered over one another and her chronometer pendant hanging around her neck. Her blonde hair is loose over her shoulders, but I notice it's curled. She's gotten prepared for this meeting too.

"Hey you." I can't help but smile.

"Hey, yourself."

I take a few steps closer. "You made it."

She takes in the room, pausing slightly on the bed and at the digital wall of windows. "I don't think you could find a farther away place."

"Long trip?" I take another step closer.

"Six weeks. And you don't even want to know how many people I had to talk to just to find anchors from this stream."

"If it makes you feel any better, the few hours I had to wait since I talked to you *felt* like a lot longer."

Mym shakes her head, but smiles. "At least you found us somewhere private."

I put my arms around her waist. "It's really good to see you." I kiss her then, not able to wait any longer. Her arms wrap around my back and she presses herself against me. Her hair smells like orange blossoms again. It smells like home. I let myself relish the electric feel of her skin against mine and it makes the rest of the world melt away.

She pulls away for a moment. "I missed you."

"But you found me."

"If you could try to make it less difficult to get to you next time, I would appreciate that."

"Said, the hardest girl to locate ever . . ."

Mym looks up and squeezes me tighter. Her expression is playful. "I'm here now. What are you going to do about it?"

"I'm going to make your trip worth it." I scoop her up and spin around, depositing her firmly in the center of the bed. She lets out a startled laugh, but when I land on the bed over her, she's smirking at me.

"It was a long trip, Ben."

I kiss her again and my fingers find the button on the front of her jeans. "Then I guess we'd better take our time."

The rest is just details. The absolute best kind of details. We get lost in the feel of each other's bare skin and the exhilarating newness of exploration. For the first time in days, I escape the chronothon. I don't think about Milo's research. I don't remember the danger I've been through or losses we've taken. The future me can have his time gate. I don't care about the Zealots or the major and his war. I only care about right now and this girl. We keep each other confined in the moment, taking it prisoner between our interlocked fingers and our intertwined bodies. We share it with our lips and press it tight until we've run out of strength to contain it. For the first time since I've been a time traveler, I can think of no place else I'd want to be.

Mym studies my face from the pillow next to me, relaxed now, but still holding my hand. Neither of us is ready to come back to the real world yet. There is a faint smile on her face and, as her eyes drift closed, she looks content. I watch her subtle breathing and just stay there listening as it turns into a more steady rhythm. I'd like to stay that way, ignore the world till the morning, but I know we can't. Despite our best efforts, the clock is still ticking.

I slip from bed and get dressed. Mym stirs slightly but settles back into sleep. I'll need to wake her soon, but I let her rest a little longer from whatever journey she's been through to get here.

The hotel corridors are quiet. I pass a beautiful grandfather clock at the end of the hall that reads 3:30. A little moon and stars are showing in a window of the clock face to clue me in that it's nighttime. I appreciate the help because my body is long past knowing what time it is. The frenetic pace of the last few days has destroyed whatever biological rhythm I may have had. Now I'm just physically tired and mentally lost.

I take the stairs down a couple floors and wander into the cafeteria. I find a coffee machine that's still backlit, and I select two cups from the dispenser. The machine hums to life when I press the power button and I hear the hopeful sound of something percolating. While I wait, I step to the windows.

Adjacent to the cafeteria, a set of doors leads onto a balcony. I push my way through and onto the patio, enjoying the freshness of the salt air. To my surprise, I'm not the only one out there. Reclined in one of the half dozen patio chairs, Bozzle has his face skyward and is studying the stars. The lights of the city and the starlight above reflect in the deep black pools of his eyes. I make my way toward him slowly so I don't startle him.

"Beautiful night out, isn't it?"

The alien keeps his face pointed skyward but he blinks slowly. "I enjoy the nights on this planet. It's a time of peace."

"Lack of other people usually helps with that. Sorry to disturb you."

"You do not disturb me," Bozzle replies. "Your company is welcome. Please. Join me."

I take a deck chair one spot away from where the alien is seated and settle myself. I admire the view of the night sky silently for a few moments, then turn to my companion. "I appreciate the hospitality.

Could you not sleep either? Need some time alone with the universe?"

Bozzle smiles. "I am never alone."

I don't immediately respond while I try to work out what he means. *Is he talking about his mysterious guide I've never seen?*

The alien seems to read my mind. "My wife is with me. I carry her, but *she's* the one who guides me." He reaches for the neck of his shirt and extracts a pendant on a chain. I expect that it might be a locket of some sort and he is going to show me a photo of his wife. Instead, he whispers to the shiny triangular shape and it begins to glow. The light is a blend of purples and blues and twists around the pendant like a living thing. He raises his other hand and the light transfers from the pendant to his palm. He holds it out in front of him and smiles, letting his hand fall and staring into the twisting threads of color with an expression of joyful calm. He seems in no way concerned that the light will fall or fade or drift away in the breeze, and while the swirling colors do rise and fall gently, they do not leave his eye line.

I'm not sure how to respond. I opt for an introduction. "What is your wife's name?"

"She is Sooka Moon."

"That's a pretty name. Very celestial."

Bozzle shakes his head. "No, in your language 'moon' is different, a word of the sky. In my world it is very small. It is a flower. It is this." He points to the tattoo on his bicep and indicates one of the flowers between the monsters that encircle his arm. The flower repeats frequently in the pattern, encircling the other elements and wrapping in and out of the elaborate illustrations. "This is our story."

He traces the artwork down his forearm. "When Sooka Moon was Anya Morey, her body told our story as well."

I consider the light just hovering in front of the alien. "So she wasn't always . . . like she is now?"

"Once, we were Anya Morey together. We grew a family, we spoke the language of the world with one another. Now we speak only in here." He taps the side of his head softly. "But she loves to speak to me. She tells me of the things that I cannot yet see, and I remind her what it feels like to be Anya Morey."

Bozzle smiles the broadest smile I have ever seen on his face. "She says you are full of questions. And she says you should not be afraid to ask them."

"She can see me?"

"She sees the essence of you."

"Like what? What do mean?"

"You might say she sees your spirit, the you that is not your body."

"Like my soul?"

"Yes. She sees your soul." Bozzle laughs. It's a carefree sound, deep and jovial. "Humans often wear the expression you wear now. You are surprised about your soul, like perhaps you forgot it was there."

I smile back at his amusement. "I guess I haven't spent much time thinking about it."

"That is like forgetting about your own mind." Bozzle goes back to contemplating his glowing wife. "I think it is unkind that the human essence is a color that human eyes cannot see. I wish I could tell you the color of a human soul, but you have no words for it. You do not have the ability to see such a color, so you have not named it."

"I've heard about that. Apparently even butterflies see more colors than we do." I grin. "Are Anya Morey related to butterflies?"

Bozzle doesn't seem to mind the association. "Who can say? The universe has been painting its creations with many of the same brushes."

"Do all of the Anya Morey tell their love stories on their bodies?"

Bozzle lifts a hand toward his wife's essence and she wraps herself around his fingers. "When you are born with the gift of moving in time, it is very easy to become lost. You can lose those whom you love, and miss the chance to find them again. Or you can find them at the wrong time. You may get mixed up about who is your love and who belongs to another you. When you share your stories on your bodies, you can compare. You can be sure you are experiencing the right time of your love. You share your stories and make them belong only to each other. Another you may tell a different story, but you will not be confused. You will always know your own story."

"That's a brilliant solution." I admire the elaborate artwork twisting up his arm. "And it looks like you two have had a wonderful story."

Sooka Moon works her way down Bozzle's arm and slips back into the pendant around his neck. Bozzle holds his hand protectively over his chest once she's inside, and returns to staring at the stars. "My story on this planet is nearing an end. I am happy to have met you, Benjamin Travers."

"So you don't have any intention of going on through the gate tomorrow?"

Bozzle looks down at the bracelet on his wrist and then over to me. "The men who want me to go through that gate do not know me. I will not finish their race." He presses on the knuckle of his right thumb by using his left and compresses his long fingers to a position where he can easily slide the bracelet from his wrist. "And they do not know much about my people." He holds the bracelet out to me. "I think you need this now more than me."

I hesitate but then sit up on the edge of the chair and reach for the bracelet. I turn the silver ring over in my palm. "I don't know why I should go through that gate, either. The only reason I have to go on is the fact that I've already done it in that video. Have you ever done something that you didn't want to, just because it would create a paradox if you didn't?"

"A paradox cannot make a man do what he will not, any more than it can keep a man from doing what he must. The decision will always be yours."

"That's what I'm worried about. I don't want to make the wrong choice." I stand up and put his bracelet into my pocket with the admiral's. "Thank you for the advice. I feel like I can use every bit I can get."

Bozzle nods and goes back to his contemplation of the stars. I make my way back into the cafeteria and find the coffee machine ready. I pour two cups and carry them gingerly back upstairs to my room. The bed is vacant when I walk in. I find Mym in the corner of the room pulling on her tank top.

"Where did you go? You left me—" She stops when she sees the cups of coffee in my hand. I stretch out my arm to offer her one and her voice changes from hurt to conciliatory. "I guess you might be forgiven."

I smile and settle into the room's only chair. "You looked like you needed the rest."

Mym tugs on her jeans and straightens her shirt over them. "We still have a lot to talk about."

"You found something out about your dad's gravitan research?"

She takes a sip of coffee before beginning. "I talked to Dad about it, but it was Abraham who found what I was looking for."

"What did he find?"

"Turns out it wasn't a what, it was a who." She sinks onto the edge of the bed. "Abraham went to the end of the chronothon to see you finish. Only you weren't there. None of the fans were allowed anywhere near the finisher's podium, but he could tell it wasn't you up there. Nobody else seemed to know the difference except one other fan. He met an inventor named Ebenezer Sprocket."

"Jonah's dad?"

"Yeah, apparently he's another racer? In any event, they got to talking, inventor to inventor, you know? Only they both knew the race was a sham. Ebenezer was in on it."

"Jonah's dad was part of the setup?" I try to wrap my brain around Jonah somehow being involved.

"These people are really bad news, Ben. Bad enough to put a guy's kid in a chronothon to keep him from talking. Abe says he was scared.

He freaked out when his boy wasn't back at the finish line and started ranting."

"What was he not supposed to talk about?"

"What they're doing with the gravitans. They're building a weapon. It's already built. They just haven't used it yet."

"What kind of weapon?"

"From what Abe got out of Ebenezer, it destroys gravitites. It's a weapon to use against time travelers. Ben, if they use this thing, it could affect everybody. I mean *everybody*. Every time traveler. Ever."

I try to fit this new information into what I already know. "That makes sense from a Zealot standpoint, they want to kill all the time travelers, but what about the ones who *are* time travelers themselves? The Order uses their own time travelers to fight, and the company sponsors are all time travelers. If this thing can affect everyone, are they going to wipe themselves out, too?"

"That's what I thought, but Dad has a theory about it. He thinks if Ebenezer was forced to design a weapon that will wipe out gravitites, they could be using the gravitans as a way to survive it. That could explain why they need them."

"How?"

"Gravitites are synthetic. They're the particle Dad invented. It's what ASCOTT and the Academy and every other time travel facility uses to infuse time travelers. If you could come up with an alternative strain, a natural variant of the particle, maybe you could find a replacement that will survive the weapon, or design the weapon specifically to work that way."

"Replace gravitites in your body with gravitans, and wipe the gravitites out?"

"Exactly."

"They still had to have the chronothon committee build the gates. They aren't Zealots, why would they do anything to help them? It's suicide."

Mym shakes her head. "I don't know. But if Ebenezer built what he says he did, every time traveler we know is in danger."

I lapse into silence. My coffee has grown cold and I've lost my taste for it. I stand up and pace the room. "Major McClure seems adamant that I go through that time gate. Hearing about the weapon is only going to make him insist on it more. He obviously thinks me going will make a difference."

"Do you trust him?"

"I trust Milo and Kara. They've helped me survive this far. The major definitely has an agenda, but he isn't trying to hide it. After fighting the

Zealots all these years I'd probably trust him less if he didn't have some scheme. I don't know what the future me in that video knows that I don't, but he seemed confident walking through there. He must think he's going to accomplish something."

"What do you think?" Mym studies me from the bed.

"I think I'm tired of being a pawn in everyone else's plans, but if there is going to be an end to this, I need to keep playing. Whatever the endgame is, it happens on the other side of that gate."

"Do you know anything about what the major expects you to do?"

"Not yet. But I think it's time I found out."

"War has scarred every timestream I've visited. If there is a world where mankind has learned to resolve conflict without aggression, it is a time I've yet to witness—but also one I have not ceased hoping for."–Journal of Dr. Harold Quickly, 1776

Chapter 30

"What is it?" I ask.

The major is standing over the open crate with an expression akin to a child showing off a new toy. I try to look appreciative of the contents, but to me it just looks like cans of lubricating oil. The gray metal cylinders nestled in the straw packing have a threaded top with slightly more complicated looking lids, but they could hold anything really.

"This is how we knock them out of this fight." He picks up one of the cans and models it appreciatively. "If your new information is right and they've got a weapon to use on us, we'll need to beat 'em to the punch."

Mym is beside me. Her surprise arrival has gone largely uncommented on with the exception of a creepy wink from the major when I arrived in his office with her. He seems unaware that she is something other than a female overnight guest and that my "new" information came from her. He addresses his explanation toward me, oblivious to the fact that he's just met the daughter of the greatest mind in the world of time travel. Mym seems disinclined to enlighten him, so I follow her lead.

The major has brought us to the basement to explain his new strategy, complete with visual aids. He practically beams at the device in his hand. "We confiscated the plans from a Zealot warehouse and used them for our own design. The black-clads never did figure out how to get them to work, but you have to give them credit for trying. Our engineers finished the job, and now we're going to give them back a dose of their own medicine."

The other men around the basement armory are silent and serious. Milo and Kara are nearby, but Milo is away in the meta-space and Kara has used the opportunity to clean the underside of her nails with one of her knives. She casts occasional glances at Mym and me, but her emotions are as invisible to me as ever.

Major McClure is on a roll. "With this baby, we can escalate your trip through the time gate from a recon mission to an offensive strike."

"So, they're some kind of grenade?" I'm just guessing now.

"No, no. Not that we didn't think of using explosives. That's still a decent plan B, but we need to hit all of them. Take 'em down and keep 'em down. You know what I'm saying?"

No. I most definitely do not.

"It's more what your generation would've called an EMP. Only this pulse is far more effective."

I stare into the crate at the dozen or so devices, then slowly detach my fingers from the side of the box. "Aren't EMPs a product of nuclear bombs?" I put my hands in my pockets and try to ease away without appearing obvious. Not that it would matter. If I'm stuck in a basement with a dozen nuclear weapons, a few feet won't make a sliver of difference if one goes off.

"That's the old way. Technology has advanced since your day, son. These EMPs are for electronics only. It'll mess up anything in a planet-wide range, though, sure as shootin.'"

I consider the canister in his hand and can't help but be skeptical. "The whole planet?"

"It's what they call 'redundant wave technology.' Can't say as I know all the engineering specifics, but it'll just keep looping around the atmosphere, knocking out anything electronic it hits, for what? Couple years?"

A man in a canvas jacket next to the major bobs his head. He seems pleased to be called on and gestures a lot while he speaks. "The pulses ricochet around the surface and hit any given spot at least once every hour. It could take a decade before the waves finally get absorbed, depending on the topography. The higher you are when you set it off, the better the results."

"Why am I supposed to use this?"

The major looks annoyed. He turns to where Milo is leaning against the brick wall of the elevator and shouts, "Kalani, I thought you said you explained to him about the solitaire."

Milo looks up and adjusts his glasses. "I did. We talked about it. Last night."

The major looks back to me with an expression that clearly says I must be the root of the trouble. He glances at Mym, perhaps wondering how such an attractive girl could be seen with anyone so dense.

"I get the bit about the solitaire," I explain, "it's a timestream all by itself with no other connections. But why the EMP?"

"To knock out the time gate, of course, and keep them from getting out!" The major's nostrils flare, and he thumps the top of the crate with a fist. "If they want to squirrel themselves into one timestream, well by God we'll let 'em. And we'll see to it they never come back."

I try to digest the plan. "But, we know where the time gate is. It's in the warehouse in the video. Why don't we just go take it apart there and shut them—"

"You think we haven't thought of that?" The major's beard seems to swell as he puffs up his cheeks with the exertion of his speaking. "We need to make sure we get any gates they might have on the *other* side, too. A gopher don't dig a hole with one exit. You gotta plug 'em all and be sure they can't go burrowing a new one. THAT'S what the EMP is for."

"Okay, so I EMP the planet. Then what? How will I get out?"

The major closes the lid on the weapon's crate. "That's where you have to talk to Kalani. He's got the exit plan."

I turn toward the elevator shaft. In this time period it's undamaged and the bricks blend seamlessly into the ceiling. Milo pushes off from the wall. "Well it's largely untested, of course, because we haven't been able to set off one of these devices in any modern timestreams. Even out here there aren't many places you can get away with zapping the technology of the entire planet. You have to go back a few centuries. But the farther back you go, the more durable the technology gets. That's why we think you'll be able to get back out."

"Why?"

Milo smiles and points to my wrist. "You're an analog. The electronics in your chronometer should be minimal. A pulse that would decimate a Temprovibe would probably leave your device unharmed."

"Probably? That's kind of taking a lot on faith, isn't it?" I glance at Mym. It's hard to read her expression but she doesn't seem to be dismissing the possibility outright.

"They won't see it coming. That's why we think it will work. They're expecting Bozzle to come through that gate, but you get through, jump away immediately till whenever you can, and set off the EMP. We'll give you an anchor to use for a jump to a parallel stream. You degravitize it and get out of there. Bam. Problem solved."

Everyone is looking at me now, the major and his engineer friend, the couple of guards behind me, even Kara has put her knife away and is waiting for a response.

"Won't they just rebuild the time gates once the EMP pulses wear off?"

"Not where they are," Major McClure snorts. "They don't have the technology. Did you show him where this stream is on the timeline, Kalani?"

Milo steps closer and puts his hands in his pockets. "It's 1996, and it's a timestream where Dr. Harold Quickly was never born." He casts a subtle glance at Mym. "No Dr. Quickly means no one is there to discover time travel. The farther into the future they get, the farther they'll be from a parallel timestream they can make a jump to even if they do rebuild the tech. The closest one is Negative Epsilon Winter. That's where we'll be waiting for you, and if they ever decide to try to follow you out, we'll be ready for them. I think Major McClure has that part of the plan covered."

Major McClure puffs up a little at this. "Damn right."

The idea of getting back to a century near my own is tempting. "1996, huh? Won't me setting off an EMP in 1996 have major repercussions?"

"Definitely," Milo replies. "But don't worry, this won't be a 1996 you'll have ever heard of. Whatever they did to make this solitaire, it's all brand new. It's like they wanted a fresh start, completely virgin territory when it comes to time travel. Whatever effects you cause there won't produce any repercussions in the central streams."

The major crosses his arms and smiles. "They'll have all their problems to themselves. And with this plan, we can make sure to keep it that way." He concentrates his stare on me. "So what do you say, kid?"

"Nobody else wanted to volunteer for this, huh?"

"Couldn't," the major replies. "You'd already done it."

Stupid time travel.

I frown at the crate of EMPs and pull my hands out of my pockets. More than anything I just want to go home, but I don't want to ever walk into my apartment and find Geo's goons waiting for me again. This could shut the door on them for good. No more looking over my shoulder. No more ambushes. *One more time gate, then home.*

I turn to Mym and keep my voice low. "What do you think?"

She angles herself toward me and away from the others. "It's not impossible. I'd like to see the schematics on that device to see what it would do to your chronometer, but it might work. It's your decision though. I'll support you either way."

I fiddle with the dials on my chronometer, studying the concentric rings that make up the dates. I realize I've absentmindedly set it for 2009. *Home.* Finally I look back up and address the major. "Okay. I'll try it. But I want breakfast first."

Breakfast is a jovial affair. The major is in a wonderful mood now that I've agreed to his plan of attack. His men are lighthearted also, sharing his good humor. I get clapped on the back and wished well by lots of people I don't know. Then I finally get to spend time with some people I do. Although Mym has opted to skip breakfast in the interest of enjoying a shower in my room, I'm not alone in the cafeteria for long.

Genesis has taken the bandage off her neck, and even though her wound is still red and noticeable, it seems to be healing well. She enters the cafeteria accompanied by Deanna, who is much more at ease now that the group is headed home. Deanna even laughs with one of the soldiers who makes a flattering comment as the girls walk by. Genesis is still reserved and doesn't even look at the soldiers, but she uses the distraction to escape Deanna and come sit next to me. She's wearing a baggy hoodie that I suspect belonged to Jettison. The sleeves have swallowed most of her hands, and the tips of her fingers are all that show while she braces herself against the table and climbs over the bench. They disappear again when she tucks her hands under her armpits and stares vacantly at the tabletop. I offer her some of my remaining breakfast items, but she shakes her head. She does agree to take my second paper cup of coffee that I haven't touched yet. She cradles it in her sweatshirt-padded palms and blows over the top. We don't talk, but we don't really need to. After what we've been through in the last few days, words have become superfluous.

Cliff shows up with Jonah, and the pair put a sizeable dent in the breakfast buffet. Morning has brought better moods for everyone, and Jonah laughs at Cliff's corny jokes. The gruff older man has lost a bit of his edginess, and while I know he's still mourning for Jettison, he puts on a good face for the kid. It makes me wonder if Cliff has ever had children of his own.

Our table slowly fills. Deanna detaches herself from her admirers and Bozzle arrives as well. Tad is still in the infirmary, but his prognosis is good. It turns out he had to have a bunch of shrapnel removed from our close encounter with the cryo-heads. Deanna informs us that he may get some synthetic organs during the surgery. She says it like it's a positive, so I try to seem appropriately excited. When she gets up to go talk to the major, Jonah slides down the bench to me.

"I heard what you're going to do."

"You did?"

"Yeah. They said you're going to finish the race."

"I don't think it's really a race anymore at this point, bud."

"My brother said someone not from the Academy should win the race. That's why he wanted me to do it, but he said if I can't be the one to win, then I should help someone else do it."

My thoughts stray to Jonah's father and I wonder just how deeply involved his family is. "You have helped, Jonah. You've been a big help. And when this is all over, maybe someday I'll meet your family. I can tell your brother how great you did."

"I don't think he'll believe you."

"That doesn't matter. It's true. No one can take that away from you. You've done amazing."

The boy is obviously pleased with the compliment. He plucks a dehydrated marshmallow from his cereal and puts it in his mouth. He chews slowly, then looks back up. "Will we still be friends when we get home? Can we still have breakfast with Cliff and Bozzle and Genesis in our time?"

"I don't see why not. We'll be able to visit each other."

The boy seems satisfied with that. "Okay."

Cliff pauses his breakfast to look at me. He seems to be debating what to say, but finally lets it out. "You don't have to do it, you know. Paradox or not. Nobody would blame you for not walking through there." He glances around the room at soldiers at nearby tables and only lowers his voice slightly. "Nobody who matters, anyway."

I finish buttering my blueberry muffin before responding. "I appreciate that. I know I don't have to. But something is going on there, and I think someone ought to know what it is, don't you?"

Cliff frowns but doesn't deny it. "I mean to get some answers from this chronothon committee once we're back. Someone is responsible for this mess."

"That's why I'm going on. From what Milo and Kara have said, they believe the answers are ahead, not back."

"Is anyone going with you? I've got the trip back to make, but if you need a hand . . ."

"It's okay. That's not what happened according to the video. I know you'd help if you could." He doesn't know that I wouldn't want him to come anyway. The idea that Cliff and the others will be safely away from this place is one of my biggest consolations. After all we've been through, if there is going to be more danger I'd rather it be far away from them.

"We'll see what we can do on this side of the gate anyway." Cliff goes back to his food. I have little doubt that he will be stirring up trouble when he gets back. Whatever members of the chronothon committee he encounters are in for a rough time.

It's not long before the major comes to collect me. He gives me a little privacy to make my goodbyes, but he lingers near the door and it's clear he's ready to get to work. My departure from the cafeteria is strained. I find myself staring at the table full of racers who have become my friends. I can't think of a way to express the respect I have for them. I'm wished luck by each of my friends, but there is a brief moment when I'm standing at the end of the table when no one says anything at all. It's that moment that says the most, and I'm grateful for it. Somehow in that silence I can feel the things that have gone unsaid. It's a silence of shared respect bred from common experience. Words could never adequately sum up what we've been through together, and everyone has the good sense not to try.

I walk away from that table without any logical expectation of seeing them again, but things have not been decided yet. For me the future is still an unscripted story, and I mean to write it myself.

The major allows me the detour to my room to collect my things. Mym is looking at my log entries in the back of her dad's journal when I enter the room. She looks up and smiles when she sees me.

"Will you hang onto that for me? Keep it safe?" I look over her shoulder at the book that contains so much of her father's hard work.

"You might need it." She closes the journal and holds it out to me.

I shake my head. "Hold onto it. I've got what I need." I gather up Abraham's satchel and my jacket. "I don't want it ending up in the wrong hands."

"Do you have an anchor to get back?"

"Milo said he'll have something for me. Something from the nearest timestream."

"And your chronometer charger?" Mym seems determined to make sure I'm prepared.

"Got it. I've got Abe's tool kit, I've got your degravitizer, this handy gun . . ." I pick up the weapon I stole from the Zealot and double-check the safety. I stuff it in my bag with my other belongings.

Mym's forehead is wrinkled in concern, but she nods. "Make sure you use it if you have to." I've never known Mym to suggest violence as a solution to anything before, but as she steps closer I can almost feel her anxiety. "Do what you have to do to come back to me."

I rest my forehead against hers and watch her run her hand across my chest. "I'll be back before you know it."

"You'd better be." She lifts her head and kisses me quickly then, after pulling away for a second, thinks better of it and kisses me again, this time longer and with more intensity. "You have promises to keep."

"I know I do." I brush the hair away from her face and tuck it behind one ear. "Come on. The major's waiting."

Major McClure seems surprised to see Mym with me when I meet him in the basement. Milo and Kara are waiting with him near the elevator.

"I thought you would've had time to say your goodbyes already, Mr. Travers."

Mym doesn't move from my side. "I'm seeing him to the gate."

The major straightens to his full height. "This is a critical mission deep inside Zealot occupied territory, it's not a place for tagalongs."

Mym's expression of determination is unfaltering, and while the major doesn't seem to realize that she was not asking permission, Kara picks up on the situation just fine. She pulls her gun from her holster and offers it handle-first to Mym.

"It's okay, major. She'll be all right."

Mym accepts the weapon and gives Kara a nod of thanks. Kara responds by walking over to the nearest guard and holding out her hand. The guard takes a furtive glance at the major, perhaps looking for a means of escape from Kara's stony glare but ultimately removes his own weapon from its holster and places it in Kara's upturned palm. She checks its condition briefly, shoves it into the holster at her thigh, and returns to join us by the elevator.

The major watches the whole scene but says nothing. He opts to concentrate on the EMP canister instead. He plucks the device from the crate beside him and hands it to me. "You'll have only a few seconds delay on this thing once you activate the switch. Ideally, get it as high up in the atmosphere as you can, but it will work on the ground in a pinch."

I accept the device and secure it into a pocket of my satchel. Milo hands me my anchor and I'm surprised to find it's an autographed baseball. He also hands me a photo of the baseball in a stand on a countertop. The signature is facing up. I try to read the scrawl then look to Milo. "Cal Ripken Junior?"

"I would've tried to find you one from your Tampa Bay Devil Rays, but 1996 was a little early for them. Epsilon Winter still has the Orioles though. We can get you back to your home stream after."

"No worries, man. This is awesome." I tuck the ball away in my bag.

Someone must have pressed the elevator button because the doors ding open beside us. Major McClure straightens up and addresses Kara sternly. "Lieutenant LaCuesta, you have command of this mission from here on out. It's on you to see them safely to the gate."

Kara salutes the major in return. "Understood, sir."

I follow Kara and Milo into the elevator. Mym squeezes in next to me and wraps her fingers through mine. The major looks at me just before the doors close. "Good luck, Mr. Travers. We'll see you on the other side." The polished brass doors slide closed and we're back on our own. Kara pulls her elevator key out of her shirt and inserts it into the keyhole. This time, after she turns it, she only has to press the B-button again and the doors slide back open.

We're back in the ruined basement. I assume it's only shortly after we left because the guard with the tattooed face is still standing sentry near the stairs. A third soldier is waiting expectantly for us. Milo turns to me as soon as I've exited the elevator. "You have the alien's race bracelet?"

I pull both my race bracelets from my pocket, the Admiral's, and the one I got from Bozzle. Milo takes the Admiral's and hands it to the soldier but scans the other with his electronic wand. The bracelet blinks back to life and continues counting as if nothing had happened.

"We'll reactivate the others too, but we're going to plant them on decoy agents around town. If we're lucky, if the Zealots or the chronothon committee are tracking them, they won't catch on till well after you're through the gate."

Milo extracts a pile of other bracelets from his cargo pockets and hands them to the soldier. The man closes them into a metal-sided briefcase and steps away.

Kara has reached the door to the tunnel and opened it. We follow her back into the Seattle underground, making our way through the darkness using only flashlights or the occasional glow of a streetlamp that finds its way through the gratings above. We keep a steady pace, jogging wherever possible and keeping a sharp eye out for any opposition. After what feels like a mile or more of underground tunnels, Milo directs us up a flight of stairs and through a sheet metal trapdoor that leads into an alley. Night has a tight grip on the corners and doorways, their blackness making the alley even more ominous than the confines of the tunnel.

We move quickly from shadow to shadow, skirting the bases of buildings and dodging the glare of occasional streetlights. I don't know who might be monitoring our progress or from where, so I merely trace Kara's footsteps as best I can. Milo stops us at an intersection of two alleys and, after peeking around the corner, turns back to address us. "From here it gets tricky. We have to cross through midtown and there's no way to hide. We won't be in the open for long, but do your best to be inconspicuous. If we're lucky, we can get through without attracting attention from The Order. The warehouse is in the arts district, just on the other side. We'll get you there, then we'll have to run." He holds a hand up, as if to steady me. "We've got the surveillance video that shows you've already done this, so be confident, but not cocky. We still have to make it happen on time. When we get you there and we say go, you go. No questions asked. Got it?"

I nod. "Got it. What happens if we mistime it?"

"Then we'll have a bit of a paradox on our hands. I doubt a few seconds would change much, but we definitely don't want to fracture the timestream. We only want to do this once. If we muck it up we'll have two timestreams to deal with and double the problems."

THE CHRONOTHON

Kara gives the signal and leads the way around the corner. The street at the end of the alley is not packed, but vehicles and pedestrians are passing by. As we exit onto the sidewalk, Kara steps directly off the curb. The street actually lights up with her footsteps, a path of green glowing below her, giving a warning to passing vehicles. The cars hardly slow—they merely weave around her automatically, the passengers not even bothering to look up. Kara keeps her eyes ahead, unconcerned about the traffic.

Milo urges me forward and I step off the curb, attempting to quell my fear of getting creamed by the oncoming vehicles. The pressure sensitive panels under my feet do their job, lighting green ahead of me and red behind. The red panels seem to pursue me as I cross, forcing me forward like a game of Frogger. I reach the center of the road but hesitate a moment too long between lanes and the red panels catch up to my heels. An audible tone buzzes beneath my feet and literally makes me jump. The car in the lane I'm about to cross automatically slows. This time the woman riding inside raises her head from whatever she was doing and scowls at me. "Come on!" Kara yells from the far curb.

I spring forward again, catching up to my green panels and the car behind me whizzes off down the lane with the woman shaking her head. The others fair better. Mym is the next to cross, with Milo right on her heels, both reaching the safety of our side of the street without incident. The pedestrians on the sidewalk are a mix of humans and synths, all modestly dressed for inclement weather. Despite the centuries of progress, I get the impression Seattle is still a rainy corner of the country. The sidewalks are damp as though we only recently missed the rain, but the atmosphere seems subdued by more than just poor weather. Expressions on people's face are serious, not looking too closely at one another and frequently disguised by sunglasses despite the overcast sky and the time of night. It's as if everyone is trying to avoid being noticed or singled out. Our own attempts at subtlety blend evenly into the dynamic of the crowd. It makes me wonder whom they're afraid of. *Is this time traveler war affecting the civilian population, too?*

We've made it across the main thoroughfare and are gliding through the crowd headed uphill when I spot the first Zealot. He's standing at the corner of a coffee shop at the intersection ahead, hands in the pockets of his black coat, scanning the crowd. His face is hard, and it's his eyes as much as his all black clothing that sets him apart—the eyes of a hunter. Milo spots him, too, and points out a second man farther along on our side of the street who has his back to us, searching the block ahead.

Milo hunches his shoulders and turns back toward me. "Stay sharp. Here's where things get hairy."

Kara has set the device on her glove and reaches for the wall. "I've got point." Without further explanation, she disappears. Milo gestures for Mym and me to follow him. Mym pulls the gun Kara gave her from under her jacket and holds it low, out of people's eye line but ready for whatever comes next. I reach a hand into my bag for my own weapon and keep it there, gripping the handle and doing my best to keep up with Milo's brisk pace. He heads straight for the Zealot in front of us, paying no attention to the one at the corner to our left. I hastily glance over there myself to keep tabs on him and make the mistake of making direct eye contact with the man. His eyes widen and he draws his wrist up toward his face to speak into some type of communicator on his arm. He never gets the chance. As his mouth is opening, Kara appears behind him, wrapping her arm around his throat and disappearing again just as quickly. Their sudden departure gets the attention of a couple of people on the far sidewalk, but no one screams or shouts. Pedestrians who were close by merely scurry that much faster to leave the scene.

The man ahead of us on the street corner is taller. Broad shouldered and blond, his hair is buzzed short and he has sunglasses on despite the darkness. As he continues to scan the street, his eyes fall on the corner where his companion had been. His hand goes to the side of his glasses, adjusting something, then he reaches for the communicator on his wrist. We are still twenty-five yards from him, but the crowd between us has thinned to only a handful of pedestrians. If he were to turn around he would see us plainly. Kara is there and gone again even quicker this time. She appears with her back to us. I barely have time to register the auburn hair and leather jacket before the pair has vanished. I catch a smile on Milo's face.

He notices me watching him and gestures toward the spot where Kara disappeared. "The best defense is a good offense."

"Where is she taking them?"

"She'll introduce them to friends of ours." He starts to jog. "Come on. We're almost there."

We run past a collection of art galleries and studios. A girl with dreadlocks is standing outside one of them flinging paint onto an oversized canvas. A few admirers are gathered around with drinks in their hands. The girl has just bent over to dip one of her brushes when the canvas bursts from the shot, splattering the group with flecks of blue paint and tiny bits of brick wall that have been impacted behind the canvas. This time people scream. Mym shoves me sideways toward the wall of the warehouse and already has her gun aimed behind us. A Zealot is walking directly down the center of the street, ignoring the red panels below his feet and the cars slowing around him. He's a tall, bald, black man wearing glasses like the blond one, but this man has his weapon drawn and is aiming for us.

Mym's gun hand wavers. Pedestrians are fleeing around us, and the cars around the Zealot all look occupied. The Zealot fires again and I pull Mym to the ground as the energy crackles over our heads. I yank my own gun out of my bag and peek up to look for our attacker, but he's disappeared. Somehow that is even more frightening. Milo is at my elbow a moment later. "We have to move!"

The awning of a building ahead of us erupts with sparks as a gaping hole is blown in it. I glimpse Kara sprinting between cars. A Zealot appears on the sidewalk and aims for her, but she slides onto the hood of the next car and vanishes. The man blasts the front of the car anyway, and I hope for Kara's sake that she's gone back in time and not forward. A man staggers from the ruined vehicle, takes one look at the Zealot, and flees. The Zealot turns toward us just as Milo grabs my arm. He's holding something in his other hand. "Hold on!" Mym grabs onto me immediately and the three of us blink away.

Milo has used a doorknob for an anchor and releases it once we arrive. We're inside a storeroom of some kind. Dusty windows look out onto another alley.

"I didn't want to take this route, but we'll have to now. If Kara can keep them distracted, we should be able to make it."

"How far to the gate?" I ask.

"We're close, but it's going to be a sprint from here. We're going to need cover. Mym, how good is your aim?"

"I'm okay, but these guns seem like they hit a large area."

Milo points to the side of her gun. "Set the precision dial down to one and you'll narrow the shot. Dial it back up to go wide. The narrow shot packs the same punch, but you'll be less likely to hit us. You can cover us from here or anywhere you think is safe. The doorway to the warehouse is at the end of this street." Milo roots in his bag and pulls out a screwdriver. "Degravitize this and use it as your anchor if I don't make it back to you before the Zealots do." He hands her the screwdriver and a photo. "Ben, you ready to run?"

I get a grip on my gun and look to Mym. "Ready as I'm going to be." I use my free hand to pull Mym closer to me and she wraps me in a hug.

"Be careful. I need you back."

"I will. You'd better be, too." I kiss her, give her hand a squeeze and reluctantly turn back to Milo. "So I sprint for this door and then what?"

"As far as we can tell, they never even bothered to set up objectives this round since the gate was rigged, but we have seen the video. Bozzle's bracelet will activate the gate. Get in, find a place to set off the EMP, and get back out. We'll be waiting for you in Epsilon Winter."

"You make it sound simple."

"Simple is best. If you get as high up as you can and set that off, whatever else they're up to won't matter."

"Any idea what kind of terrain I'm going to be walking into? There aren't going to be more alien zombies are there?"

"I doubt it, but I don't really know. It's approximately 1996 there. That's the best I can tell you."

"Planet Earth at least?"

Milo cracks the door and peers into the street. "Let's hope."

My heart is pounding and I barely hear Milo when he gives the signal. After one last glance at Mym, I follow him out and lock my eyes on the door he points to. We jump off the alley steps and land running. My sneakers slap the asphalt, and the contents of my bag jostle with each step. Milo is quick, but I stay with him. We cover half the block without incident, then two thirds. I'm about to get hopeful that we'll make it cleanly when bricks and mortar blow apart in the second story of a building to our left. We veer right and I keep my gun ready. The shot must have come from Mym, but I see no sign of her target.

The next shot is definitely meant for us. A blast of energy sizzles past my legs and craters the pavement beside me. Milo aims and shoots toward the building to our right, blowing a metal door to pieces in the process. "Just run! Don't stop for anything." With that exhortation, Milo falls behind and starts blasting things behind us. I look back momentarily and see Mym crouched by the doorway taking careful aim down the street beyond me. I concentrate my efforts forward again and put all my remaining energy into the sprint for my target. The warehouse has a rolling door for deliveries and a pedestrian entrance up a flight of three concrete steps. The pedestrian door bursts open and a heavyset man in black raises a weapon toward me. I aim mine at his chest, but I never squeeze the trigger. The man is hurled backward by a blast from behind me.

Thank you, Mym. I fly through the doorway and skid a little on the slick floor. I ignore the fallen form of my would-be attacker and locate the time gate standing on its own in the middle of the warehouse. I keep my gun ready for any more surprises and jog toward it. *One more gate, then home. One more gate, then home.*

The stone pillars are a dingy brown but have been outfitted with some power cables and various emitters. I'd normally be at a loss for what to do, but I've seen the video. I know I'm supposed to merely wave my wrist at the power symbol and look confident. It occurs to me that if I'm the man from the video now, the confidence was always a lie. I'm tempted to turn in the direction of the camera and say so, but only for a moment. *No paradoxes. I've come too far.* I check my bracelet and watch the count tick onward till the point I've been told to use, then step forward to the gate. The colors blaze across the opening after a single swipe. The unknown beckons. I set my weapon to high.

Time to end this.

"If you make a jump without contacting an anchor, you'll be untethering yourself from the physical world, and from time. I can't say for certain what would happen, but you shouldn't hope to end up anywhere pleasant." –Journal of Dr. Harold Quickly, 2090

Chapter 31

I thought I was mentally prepared for anything. Aliens. Zombies. Killer robots. I didn't count on what I'm seeing now. One thing is certain, my badass gun that can blast holes in solid walls will do me no good here. I lower it slowly to my side and face my next confounding obstacle, a dozen beautiful women holding pints of beer.

A congratulations banner is hanging from the ceiling behind the women. In my rapid assessment, the space vaguely reminds me of a classroom from grade school. A waist-high brick wall meets louvered windows to my left. The congratulations banner only partially obscures a chalkboard on the far wall. The scholastic nature of the scene ends there as the room has been converted for the celebration. A champagne fountain is bubbling on an hors d'oeuvres table, and the patrons around it are wearing dresses and suits.

The expressions of the provocatively dressed women in front of me are wavering. Their megawatt smiles begin to dim as confusion or perhaps disappointment registers in their minds. That is the only feature of this scene that feels normal. Milo's and Major McClure's exhortations seem distant memories. *Get in, EMP the planet, get out.* The mustached man to my left has a stuffed shrimp paused halfway to his mouth. *Stuffed shrimp.* The woman in the pencil skirt next to him has French manicured fingertips stretched around her crystal champagne flute. *Is that a mimosa?* The diamond ring on her finger must be four karats. *EMP the planet.*

"Benjamin Travers?" The voice cuts through the ambient murmurs and jazz music. Both guests and the female welcome committee part down the center of the room to reveal a man in a tailored gray suit. His black hair is silver at the temples, but his face is hard to put an age to. Something about his features is off but not readily apparent. The area around his eyes shows a few smile lines, but the skin itself practically glows. His teeth are likewise radiant, and they flash openly as he smiles.

THE CHRONOTHON

"Well aren't you the surprise."

I'm almost sure I've never seen the man before, but I suddenly doubt myself. *Do I know him?* As the man takes a step toward me, I get a glimpse of the people behind him. These I've seen before. Traus Gillian is beside the man in black from my apartment. Pia Chopra, the Indian woman from the race committee is at his elbow.

Get in. EMP the planet, get out.

The man with the mustache loses his shrimp as I plow through him. Two of the women with the beers shriek as the pints tumble from their hands and shatter on the floor. Suddenly I'm staring at Horacio's chest hair that's still trying to escape the collar of his dress shirt. The expression on his face is as confused as I feel. I veer left through an elderly couple that has the misfortune of being in my path. Arms reach out for the old woman as I bowl her over.

I'm into the hallway now and sprinting. I crash through a pair of double doors and find myself in a lobby I recognize. The fish tank on the wall is bubbling benignly and the receptionist rises from the desk at my sudden appearance. She starts to speak, but I don't give her a chance. I shove through the glass doors into late morning sun and spin around when I reach the sidewalk. The sign on the building hasn't changed. Saint Petersburg Temporal Studies Society. *It is. It's St. Pete. It's home. Of all places, why would they pick here?*

I run for the street. *Get in, EMP the planet, get out.* I scan the street for a safe jump location, Dr. Quickly's lessons flooding back into my mind. *Aim to arrive at night to avoid hazards . . . look for little used places like rooftops . . .* Three men come rushing out the glass doors. I don't know them and I don't want to. I jump onto the hood of the nearest parked car, spinning my chronometer as I go. One of the men is reaching into his jacket. I don't care what he has. He's too late. I press my chronometer hand to the roof of the car and blink.

I've switched locations and night has fallen. I'm still atop the car but in another neighborhood. Luckily, the car hasn't wound up inside a garage or traveling down a freeway. I've jumped back eighteen hours to arrive sometime the preceding night. I don't stay long. I'm off the car and over the fence of one of the houses in a matter of seconds. I hastily use a child's swing set as an anchor to jump forward a few hours. I run two blocks and dodge down an alley, trying to put a little physical distance between my jumps, then make a third one using the ladder on a parked RV. As I jump down from the RV, the sky is a pre-dawn blue to the east. I'm out of breath and my heart is pounding. "Let's see them follow me now." I try to organize my thoughts as I walk to the street corner. *I'm in St. Pete in 1996. Where can I go to set off an EMP? Tall building? How far am I from downtown?* I turn around to check the street signs and my legs suddenly turn to jelly. A stabbing pain lances through my brain and I collapse to the ground with uncontrollable spasms. When my twitching body finally calms itself, I'm staring at the sky, unable to move. I try to blink but even moving my eyelids is beyond me. A shadow moves across the streetlight, and at first I only see a silhouette. It's all I need, because I know who it is even before he comes into focus. I study the scar that crosses the left eyebrow of the nameless man from my apartment. I would look elsewhere, but I've lost that option. I'm focused on that nameless face and forced to fume in silence.

The man stands over me and watches my helplessness with amusement. He squats and holds up some type of weapon. Three separate coils protrude from the end of a black baton handle.

"Had it set for Anya Morey in case he decided to be uncooperative. That's some tough skin those green buggers have." He lifts the weapon and studies the handle. "Could have reset it for a human I suppose, but I didn't really feel like it." He looks down at me. "That'll explain the pain you'll be experiencing. Your body's still in shock at the moment, but the pain will come. If you're lucky you'll pass out and miss the worst of it." He flips something on the handle of the device and slips it back under his coat. "Figured you might've been a little more of a challenge. I haven't had a good hunt in a while. When you split out of that party and left all the mucky-mucks in a tizzy, I thought I was finally going to have some fun." He picks up my limp right arm. "But you decided to make it easy." He pushes the sleeve back on my jacket and checks my wrist, then drops my arm and starts rooting through my pockets. "Ah. Here we go." He holds up Bozzle's race bracelet. "And here I had you pegged for more brains." He taps the bracelet against my forehead a few times then idly tosses it away.

I'm angry, but it's a hazy sort of anger. Anger at myself for getting caught by this guy. More than anything, I'd like to punch him in the face, but even the desire seems hazy. I can hardly make out his face anymore. He's rummaging through my bag now and extracts the EMP canister. He lets out a low whistle. "Is this what I think it is?" His blurry face appears to be smiling. I wish I could blink because my eyes have started to water.

"Ope, leaving so soon, Ben? You don't want to stay conscious for the fun part? I thought you might have lasted longer. Pity really . . ." His words circle through my mind like so many bubbles around a drain. They move faster and faster till they're swallowed by deep, soundless darkness.

When I open my eyes, the sensation comes as a relief. I'm glad to be moving anything. But when I blink a few times and try to feel my limbs and other body parts, I get a weird feeling of weightlessness. I look down to find myself hovering above the floor by a couple feet. The sensation jolts me awake. There is a circular disk on the floor below me and, when I look up, I find an identical one on the ceiling above. I don't seem to be suspended by anything in particular. My jacket is gone, as is my shoulder bag. I'm relieved to see my chronometer still on my wrist, but I've been lightened of my other belongings. I feel the pockets of my jeans and find them empty. No degravitizer or pocket knife. Charlie's compass and anything else I had to work with have all disappeared. My heart sinks when I remember I've lost the EMP.

I inspect the room and realize I'm back in one of the labs at the Temporal Studies Society. This space hasn't been decorated for any festivities and has retained its scientific atmosphere of beakers and microscopes. These are mostly shoved aside for new items that don't look like they belong in 1996 at all, a digital projection screen and a gravitizer, as well as a device that vaguely resembles Jettison's ascension gun. A table has been cleared for the collection of ore samples gathered from the race. All of them have been labeled and little chunks of each are missing. Jonah's is there and others like it. I recognize my gravitan stabilizer attached to the microwave-shaped gravitizer.

I've just twisted to try to look behind me when the double doors to the hallway burst open and the host of the party leads an entourage of followers inside. He's ditched his suit jacket and has the sleeves of his shirt rolled up. His tie has been loosened, but he retains his swaggering confidence as he rounds the tables at the far end of the room. I spot Pia Chopra among his eager followers, and a couple faces I vaguely recognize from the race committee. Geo Amadeus casually trails the group, and more trickle in behind the initial swell. Traus Gillian enters alone, but a delayed following that includes Ariella and Horacio are not far behind. A half dozen people I don't know round out their group followed lastly by my nameless enemy in black who, to my surprise, is guiding the little girl from Major McClure's video.

"Ben Travers. It's so nice you could rejoin us." The man in the shirt-sleeves stops only a few feet from me and beams his bright-white smile at me. "It's a shame you missed the speech and the champagne." He shrugs. "Some think it was my best yet."

Pia Chopra bobs up and down next to him. "A beautiful speech for such an occasion. We'll be replaying it for years."

"Who are you?" My voice comes out raspier than usual and I wonder if my vocal chords are still feeling the effects of the stunning.

Shirt-sleeves laughs and claps his hands together. A few others smirk, too. "You're just fresh as wet paint, aren't you, Ben." He grins and gestures to the group around him. "I guess I should introduce myself, eh?"

His followers chuckle and he gives me a bow. "Declan Ambrose, at your service."

Pia Chopra pipes up immediately. "Don't forget the 'Doctor'."

Ambrose waves a hand to dismiss the title, but he seems pleased by the comment. "We won't trouble the young man with details. He looks like he has a lot to digest as it is." His cluster of friends laughs heartily this time, amused grins passing among them like so many inside jokes.

I search the group of faces, trying to gather some clue about what's happening to me. I catch Ariella looking at me from the back of the room and she's not smiling. Her mouth actually presses into a firmer line when we make eye contact, but she looks away before I can discern anything more from her reaction.

"Since you had to dash out before the speech, I suppose I should give you the highlights." Ambrose steps close enough to brush the toe of his leather dress shoe across the disc below my dangling feet. "It doesn't look like you'll be going anywhere this time." His hand reaches toward my chronometer and I reflexively jerk it away, tucking it under my other arm. Ambrose merely smiles. "Amazing bit of workmanship. Not to mention the lock you've got on the band." He places his arms behind his back. "Traus wanted to detach your hand to get it off, but I thought that might be a bit too ghastly an activity for a festive brunch. Today's about celebration after all, and it only makes sense to include you in the festivities now that you're here."

I keep my chronometer buried in my armpit. "What do you want from me?"

"Nothing at all, Ben. You have already performed fantastically for us. In fact, your knack for building new relationships is why we selected you for this race." He grins his bright-white smile again and looks toward Traus and the rest of his followers.

What is he talking about? What new relationships? I scan the crowd and note where Ariella and Horacio have moved toward the door. *Does he mean how I let them dupe me into this?* The thought just makes me angry.

"Why are you here then? Why are you in St. Pete?"

Ambrose crosses his arms and considers me with his still amused smile. "We're not in St. Petersburg because of you. We're here because of history." He gestures to the room around us, then glances at the others. "Forgive me, those of you are hearing this twice, but I think our friend Ben ought to hear at least this part of my speech." He addresses me again. "This is where it all began, Ben. This very lab is where Dr. Harold Quickly first sent himself through time. October 18th, 1996. The day time travel was made possible. It's only fitting that we use today to celebrate the rebirth of the time travel universe. It's true that the good Doctor Quickly declined to be a part of this new universe, but we will always owe him a debt of gratitude for what he began. Without his research we wouldn't have had gravitites, and without his theories, we never would have discovered the gateway to our new destiny, the gravitans." He pauses and gestures to Pia Chopra. "And yet another great mind has showed us the way onward."

Pia blushes at the compliment and bows to a few people around her, her floral dress stretching at her hips as she does so. She returns her gaze adoringly to Dr. Ambrose, and I get my first sense of her feelings toward him.

"Dr. Chopra brought us into the next stage of evolution as it were. And today we shall all embark on that journey together."

I scowl at him. "Your next stage of evolution involves building weapons to kill time travelers?" I'm not sure how much of my knowledge I should reveal to this man, but dangling helplessly above the floor, I have no better options.

"Once again your simple understanding of the situation shows your naiveté, Ben. This project has never been about killing people. It's about new beginnings!" He spins and gestures to one of the men near the projector screen. "But since you've provided me such a handy segue, we may as well continue with the second part of the celebration. The demonstrations!"

A cheer goes up from one of the more drunken members of the party and there is a smattering of applause that quickly fades. The man by the projector screen gets it activated, and the Ambrose Cybergenics logo springs to life on the display.

"Ladies and gentlemen, you all know the crisis that has brought us to this point. You've all seen the data and recognized the dangers or you wouldn't be standing here today. We all were once like Benjamin here, fresh and innocent. We didn't understand the effects that ungoverned time travel was having on the universe." He gestures toward the screen, and a timestream chart appears. A thin spider web of threads adorns the chart.

"When Dr. Harry Quickly first discovered that the true nature of time was a fractal and not a line, he himself charted the first fractures. His experiments became the basis for our system of primes. Since his day, other time travelers have carried on his work, delving farther into the reaches of time. Men and women in this very room were part of the research and development that became the foundation of our society." He points to a gray-haired man in the corner who looks like he's had too much to drink. "Dean Templeton was the first head of the Academy of Temporal Sciences. Karla Drummond—" he points to a middle-aged woman wearing a fur—"gave us the very first Temprovibe, the amazing technology that every one of us uses today." The woman gives a small wave to her contemporaries. Ambrose places both of his hands to his chest. "I myself have advanced time travel, albeit responsible, paradox-free time travel, via the trace system created by my company, Ambrose Cybergenics." A few more people applaud.

A pair of female drink servers glide into the room bearing trays of champagne and begin refilling glasses. Ambrose appears annoyed that they've chosen this moment to interrupt his speech, but he lifts his chin a little higher and opens his arms wide. "*We,*" he continues, "are responsible for the current shape of the universe. However well intentioned we all have been, we are responsible for this!" He points dramatically to the screen and it changes from the thin spider web of lines to a giant tangled knot. One woman actually gasps, but she also uses the feigned shock as an excuse to reach for more champagne.

Ambrose scans the room and finally his gaze lands on me. He takes a step closer, apparently about to make me the recipient of his magnanimity. "It is a responsibility, Benjamin, that drives us to this day. Time travelers have fractured the universe beyond comprehension." He zooms in on a particular section of the chart, then returns his attention to me. "We have fractured it to such extremes that one can get irretrievably lost in time. There are more timestreams now than could ever be explored in a lifetime. With that expansion we have lost our individuality, we have lost our uniqueness, we have lost our very purpose." Murmurs of agreement emanate from the crowd. Reading the audience, Ambrose raises his voice. "The time has come to right the wrongs of our generation. We will take responsibility for the recklessness we showed with our youthful yearnings for the unknown. In our quest for new horizons, we lost our way. The time has come to cleanse the map and take us back to a simpler time. One time. One system of operation that we can use to regulate responsible time travel and keep it out of the hands of those unable to use it properly." He changes the image on the screen to a single unbroken line. His audience applauds heavily at this.

"So you're going to kill the rest of us?" I clench my fists and shift a little in my prison of weightlessness. I don't want to move too much because I don't understand the physics behind whatever is holding me and I don't want to suddenly find myself ass-end up in front of all these people. I point to the wall where the nameless Zealot has a hand on the shoulder of the little girl. "You're what? Going to join a crazy religious cult and get them to do your dirty work?"

THE CHRONOTHON

Ambrose looks exasperated, but he smooths his hair back and lowers his voice as if speaking to a particularly difficult child. "Yet again you have missed the point, Benjamin. This weapon is the ultimate technology of the age. It doesn't *kill* time travelers. It makes it so they never even *were* time travelers. That is the sheer brilliance of it." He strides to the table and picks up the device that looks like the ascension gun. There is something familiar about it. The lines and shape of it remind me of Jonah's 'organism gun.' *That must be what Ebenezer Sprocket designed.*

"Phase One was a weapon like that." Ambrose continues. "Pia's research team discovered the way to target the gravitites in a person's body and remove them while still keeping the patient alive. A feat that even the great Harry Quickly could never accomplish." He sets the gun back down and walks toward me. My heart starts to accelerate as he approaches. Ambrose doesn't stop at me, however. He walks past me and I crane my neck to see what he's doing. That's when I notice the other two prisoners. Behind me, forming roughly a triangle with my own position, Donny and Viznir are each suspended in a stasis field of their own. Neither of them appears to be conscious.

Ambrose pauses in front of Viznir. "Gioachino, have you finished with Mr. Najjar's services?"

Geo is leaning against a set of sinks along the wall and crosses his arms at the question. "He's served his purpose."

Ambrose gestures to a wiry man in a paisley tie. "Wake him up. I want them both awake for this." The man with the tie rummages through a cabinet and extracts two syringes already primed with fluid. He pops the cap off the first syringe and sticks it in Viznir's arm. He uses the second syringe on Donny and both begin to wake.

Ambrose steps over to Donny, and I have to pivot the other direction to see what he's doing. "We've used Dr. Chopra's Phase One device on our friend Donny here. He had doubts, too. His reluctance in appreciating our research earned him a degravitization. He is no longer a time traveler." Ambrose signals the man who had the syringes and the man hands him a Temprovibe. "And we will prove it." Ambrose slides the device over Donny's arm and fastens it to his bicep. "You all can appreciate the position our friend Donny is in, suspended above the ground, free of any suitable anchors. Not a place to be traveling in time if you expect to make it back. Of course Karla Drummond was smart enough to include a safety in her design to avoid such a lapse in judgment, but we've bypassed that for the purposes of this demonstration."

A few murmurs go up from the enraptured audience. Donny is alert now and squirms a little. "Wait, what are you doing?"

"Have no fear, my boy. We've made some changes to your constitution. If Doctor Chopra's device has worked, you are no longer a time traveler and need not fear being flung into the ether of the Neverwhere." He says this last bit with all the showmanship of a magician on stage. A few members of his audience laugh, but nervously, as it's a circumstance I doubt they would volunteer for themselves.

Ambrose sets the Temprovibe and gets one of the audience members to check the settings are correct. When the woman nods in confirmation, Ambrose smiles and, with a flourish of his hand, presses the button.

Donny doesn't go anywhere.

"Ta da!" Ambrose gives another flourish and takes a bow. The audience claps and laughs, and Donny relaxes. Ambrose pats him on the shoulder and turns to his assistant. "Get him down, he's done his part."

Ambrose makes his way to me again.

Shit. Am I the other half of this demonstration? Is he planning to send me to the Neverwhere? I bury my chronometer under my arm again.

Ambrose merely smiles at me. "Each of you racers did your part in this competition. Some of you smuggled items for us, some of you were persuaded to perform specific tasks, and with the exception of the Anya Morey, all of you gave us blood samples." He motions to the man with the paisley tie again. "Dr. Emory, show our guests the materials." The man has lowered Donny from his imprisonment, and as Donny shrugs his way through the audience to stand near Horacio, Dr. Emory crosses the room to a locked refrigerator. He extracts a tray of vials and sets it on a stainless steel rolling cart, then wheels the cart in front of me where everyone can see it. One of the vials has my name on it. It contains only a tiny drop of blood at the bottom. I look up to find the Zealot staring at me from the far wall. *Vaccinations my ass.*

"We were very specific about the racers we selected for this chronothon." Ambrose gestures toward the clump of people near the door. "Montgomery McCandless of the chronothon committee was especially key in that role." A few people look behind them, but I don't see who McCandless is. "We needed to ensure our project was able to reach all corners of the time travel community. We already had a vast collection of project material collected as part of my company's tracing program. Each recipient of a trace volunteered for blood tests in advance. For this race, we selected persons connected to vital clusters of the time travel community who are not in the trace program. There are notable families, alumni of the Academy, and—" Ambrose makes his way around to me again. "—had Benjamin not surprised us with his presence instead, we would have had one member of the oldest family line of Anya Morey.

Why, you ask? Because these individuals are a path to others." Ambrose walks past me and stops at Viznir again. "Mr. Najjar here had a different task, one which he failed to accomplish. I hold him responsible for our current lack of an Anya Morey."

"I did what you told me," Viznir whispers. "You have him right here."

"That's not what we asked for, was it?" Ambrose's voice is silken, betraying no anger. "But you are correct. We will get what we want."

"What are you going to do with my family?"

Ambrose raises his eyebrows. "Well, I suppose that's a good question. Gioachino, do we still retain an interest in Mr. Najjar's family?"

Geo uncrosses his arms and puts his hands in his pockets. "I consider that debt settled. I don't plan to pursue it further."

Ambrose smiles. "You see, all settled. Nothing to worry about."

Viznir's shoulders relax. "Thank you, that means everything—"

Ambrose pulls a derringer from his pocket and shoots Viznir in the chest.

"No!" I shout. I squirm in my stasis field and try to reach for Viznir as his body slumps into limpness. His chin hits his chest and lists to one side. "What did you do!"

Ambrose studies the side of the tiny weapon in his hands, then tosses it onto a table behind him. "I'm showing you the past, Benjamin." He gestures toward his audience. "This is the *demonstration* part of the presentation." The crowd murmurs among themselves.

"You just—you just killed him!"

Ambrose slides his hands into his pockets. "In the present. But how do you really *kill* a time traveler? That's the big question isn't it? Viznir Najjar is dead enough *now*. I just put a bullet through his heart. Fine, but ten minutes ago he was alive. What's to stop someone from going back to a time when he was alive, making a new timestream and enjoying another version of the man? It's a problem our Zealot friends in The Order of Zsa have faced for years." Ambrose looks to the little girl standing next to the man in black. She has her face buried in the shirt of her protector. "To really kill a time traveler, you can't just eliminate them in one moment, you have to eliminate them in *every* moment. That's where our brilliant Dr. Pia Chopra comes in." He gestures toward the Indian woman and invites her to the front. "Why don't you take it from here, Doctor Chopra."

Pia Chopra smiles and the audience gives her some hesitant applause. She fidgets with her hands and takes a position near me and the tray of blood samples. "What we've discovered is that the gravitites that bond to our cells as time travelers actually exist outside of a standard sense of time. While our bodies are subject to the passage of time, aging and changing, a gravitite merely *is*. It's as if they are particles belonging to a different time: eternal, permanent, even god-like. When we interact with a gravitite particle in the present moment, we effectively interact with it in all of its moments simultaneously. What that led to was the discovery that destroying a gravitite particle destroys not only its present or its future, but its past as well. We have carefully researched a method of delivery, a synthetic virus if you will, that can do just that."

This gets another murmur from the audience. I'm trying hard to understand the implications of what she's saying.

"This is obviously very dangerous knowledge. One could use this virus to eliminate all the particles in a person's body and cause a ripple effect through time. You would eliminate that person or object from every moment of their lives when they had gravitites in their cells. This would cause irreparable damage to the timestreams we know." She raises a finger. "But the person's life before they became a time traveler would remain unharmed."

"How will you control it?" A man in a blazer asks. "Gravitites can be transferred sometimes from person to person, parents to children, and you know, bodily fluids . . ."

Pia blushes a little at the mention of bodily fluids. "Yes. The effects can be transferred. The gravitites you destroy that have been transferred to other people will be affected also. That is why this project will only be employed once all the parties we've selected have been administered the vaccine." She steps over to the table of ore samples. "This chronothon project provided us with multiple natural strains of gravitans that can be used to replace those gravitites we destroy. Our select group of individuals will continue to be capable of time travel under new selected guidelines. But we will only do so in a forward direction. We intend to remedy the mistakes of the past, remove the threats of universal complication, and return to a simpler system of paradox-free, scientifically sanctioned time travel. This will be the beginning of a new era."

Pia begins to fiddle with the screen and show more pictures of the timestream problem. I try to work through what I've just learned, considering everything I've experienced since becoming a time traveler. It's clear they mean to wipe that out and set all but a select few back to being regular people.

Mym.

The most significant part of my last few months would be gone.

"Dr. Chopra."

The woman stops gesturing at the screen and turns around, seeming surprised at my capability of speech. Ambrose has a flute of champagne in his hand and looks curious, too.

"You said the virus will effect people back to the point they became time travelers. What about people who were born time travelers? What happens to them?"

Dr. Chopra straightens up and I see the man who had mentioned children earlier take an acute interest.

"Assuming they are among the group selected to join us, they will receive the gravitan-based vaccine and be fine."

The man in the blazer nods and goes back to his hushed conversation with a companion.

"What if they're not on your list?" I already know the answer, but I don't intend to let her off the hook.

Pia Chopra merely shrugs. "They should have tried harder to get an invitation." She goes back to her presentation.

They'll kill Mym. I look at the vials of blood from the various racers on the cart in front of me. If they infect my blood with their virus, even if I did get the gravitan antidote, Mym would still be affected. How many kisses have we shared now? How many gravitites have transferred from one to the other? If gravitites really exist outside of the moment, I have bits of hers inside me right now. Infecting me will infect her, too. Does that mean it will affect Dr. Quickly also? She's his daughter, how many gravitites did she get from him? Dr. Quickly wasn't always a time traveler, so there would be versions of him that would survive, just an anonymous scientist who hasn't discovered anything yet, but his future will be gone. *I'm going to be his downfall.*

I study the other names on the vials. The Marsh siblings, the Ivans, Sam Tulley and his son. Ambrose said they were all chosen specifically. *Could infecting twenty racers and their guides really be enough to spread it to the whole time traveler world? How carefully did they research this?* I get a brief hope that they may have calculated wrong and there will still be plenty of survivors, but then I remember what Ambrose said about his trace system. He's been collecting samples from people for years. It was only the fringes he had left to access.

I'd been lost before, but the puzzle pieces are starting to fit now. ASCOTT's accusations against Mym were never about resolving Charlie's murder. She's just always been elusive—one time traveler they couldn't get their hands on. They needed an excuse to get her into custody—at least until I came along. I think about our furtive kiss atop the Academy building. Ambrose's comment about my knack for relationships wasn't to do with Geo or Ariella. *He knows about Mym and me.* They don't need to hunt Mym anymore because they have me.

No matter what research they've done, one thing is crystal clear.

Mym's fate is tied to mine. She may have eluded them on her own, but now I've dragged her into this with no way of getting out.

For the first time I can remember, I feel authentic despair. I feel exactly like what I have been reduced to, a limp puppet controlled by the real powers of the world. My ability to travel through time, my supposed successes in the race, even my inclusion in Major McClure's plot against the Zealots has all been reduced to nothing but the pitiful attempts of an amateur. I'm going to dangle like the useless pawn I am, while the people in this room literally reshape the course of the universe and kill most of the time travelers I know in the process. There is not a single thing I can do about it.

Pia Chopra has finished her presentation to polite applause from the group. Declan Ambrose makes his way back to the center of the room and draws the attention of his audience. He lets the silence build before he speaks, as if channeling the energy of the room into himself. He holds his hands out to his audience. "Now we have arrived at the moment you've all been waiting for. The beginning of our new life." He signals toward the door and they open to reveal the serving girls bearing trays of bourbon glasses. The liquid inside each of them is green and seems to glow. I suspect it's a trick from the glasses and not really the liquid itself, but the illusion is effective. The girls file into the lab and fan out beside Ambrose. He lifts the first glass from a tray and holds it aloft. "Today we drink to the future. Please come take your glass and take your place in this new world." The guests don't hesitate to gather for this. The girls don't pass the trays around this time however. Instead, Declan hands each drink out personally, requiring the recipients to line up in front of him like a priest distributing communion. The effect is the same, each recipient cradling the glass reverently and carrying it back untouched to their positions.

I drop my gaze to the tray of blood samples in front of me. I know I won't be on the list of the Kool-Aid drinkers. I stare at the little vials with racers' names on them: Jonah, Genesis, Cliff, Jettison . . . *He's gone now anyway. Will they still infect his blood to wipe out all trace of him? Elitist assholes.* I consider kicking over the tray. Then the idea occurs to me. *I can't do anything to stop them now, not really, but what if I could save some of them?* I stretch my toe out and catch the bottom of the rolling tray with my shoe. I glance up, but no one is paying attention; everyone is intent on Ambrose's glowing drink ceremony. I gingerly pull the tray closer. It's within range now. The labeled vials are close enough to reach out and take. *Should I throw them on the floor? How many could I break before they stopped me? Would it matter?* I imagine someone simply extracting all the blood and lumping it together. It wouldn't really matter whose was whose. Infecting the whole batch would kill them all just the same. *How can I destroy gravitites?*

The answer comes to me immediately and firmly, too simple to dismiss. There is really only one way to be sure. The only way I'm capable of. My fingertips touch the vial with my own name and I palm it quickly. *Mym has always been hard to find. If I get rid of my blood maybe they'll never be able to find her.* I slip the tube into my pocket.

When I look up, I notice the Zealot staring at me from the wall. He's studying me with a gaze of intense curiosity. For some reason he hasn't joined Declan's procession. The little girl must be somewhere in line because he's alone, just staring at me. I glare back hoping to show him that I don't care that I've lost. I'll make life difficult for them every step of the way. I have nothing left to lose.

I drop my gaze and reach for the other vials. I've already been seen. I don't know why he hasn't warned anyone but I don't have time to wonder about it. I snag the vials for Jonah, Genesis, Cliff, and Kara and stuff them into my back pockets. I check the wall again as I reach for more. The Zealot is still watching me. Still not saying anything. He breaks his gaze away and goes back to watching Declan distribute his gravitan juice with an air of casual disinterest, then moves over for the little girl as she returns with her glass.

The vials for Milo and Wabash end up in my front pocket. Ivan's and Mayra's follow them. I'm running out of room. My heart is pounding, but I like it. I feel alive. It's better to fight, right till the very end. I shove the remaining vials into the waistband of my boxers, covering them with my T-shirt.

"Oi! What do you think you're doing?" It's the scientist with the paisley tie, Dr. Emory, who has spotted me. He's standing stock still with his drink partially raised, glaring at me. Ambrose has finished handing out the glasses and was apparently about to propose his toast when Emory shouted. He turns around with glass likewise lifted and looks for the cause of the interruption.

"He's taken the samples!" Dr. Emory points to the rolling tray and the now empty vial rack.

Ambrose glances at the tray and back to my face. "Honestly, Benjamin, am I going to have to get you a babysitter?" He frowns in exasperation. "Where do you think you can hide them? Won't exactly be a long search."

"Don't let him drop them," Dr. Chopra interjects. "If he contaminates the samples, we'll have to collect new ones from the racers."

Dr. Ambrose scowls at this. "You might cause a very insignificant delay, Ben. A little more work for my collection agents, but you won't accomplish anything worthwhile. Only ensure yourself some very rough treatment." Traus Gillian steps through the crowd and looks very eager to assist. He takes a few steps toward me, and I kick the tray hard and in his direction. It topples over and sends the vial rack skidding across the floor toward his feet.

Ambrose raises his hands. "Ben! Really. Are you quite finished? Enough of this."

I consider Ambrose with his perfect skin and brilliant teeth. Traus looks like a scary troll beside him but he is fearsome. I spy Ariella in the crowd behind them. She's studying me intently, questioning. Horacio is next to her, confused by the activity. He looks totally lost in all of this. I realize now that, despite all his bravado, he was a pawn, too, just one more piece of his uncle's puzzle. Geo himself has a mask of impenetrable seriousness on his face. As I watch him, he sips from his glass, not willing to wait any longer for the reward he was promised. In that simple act of disobedience I learn all I've ever needed to know about him. Self-preservation first. In my current state I can't fault him. He's now part of the chosen few, while I dangle like a piñata waiting for the worst.

Ambrose takes a step closer. "You're not contributing very well to the celebration. How are we supposed to enjoy this moment with you kicking over the equipment Dr. Chopra needs to work?"

I try not to think of Viznir slowly dripping blood onto the floor behind me, or Kara and Milo waiting for me at a rendezvous I'll never make. I push them from my mind and concentrate only on what needs to be done. Mym will never get to see how badly I wanted to get home, but there is nothing to be done now. I clutch at my chronometer and try not to imagine all the adventures we've never gotten to have. My only consolation lies in the hope that she'll survive this somehow. If they never get my blood they may not be able to contaminate hers.

"We can just get more of your blood later, Ben." Ambrose finally seems to be catching on. "Even if you manage to smash those vials, we'll still have you. I promise we have syringes aplenty in this place. Getting another sample from you won't be a struggle."

My hand is shaking as I inch it toward my chronometer. *How is this my only option? Is it going to hurt?* I try hard to keep the fear out of my voice. Defiance is better.

"I know how you prioritize keeping the timeline pure, Declan. You won't go to the past to get another sample and risk your precious solitaire. You'll have to find me in the future."

Ambrose tilts his head and chuckles, and his mirth draws a little nervous laughter from his companions as well, but he looks concerned, as if puzzling out whether I could be holding some card he isn't aware of.

THE CHRONOTHON

I glance at the wall and see the Zealot watching me intently. He crouches and whispers something to the little girl.

"Benjamin, just how hard of a search do you think that will be?" He gestures toward my invisible prison. "Look where you are. You have nowhere to go."

I get a good grip on my chronometer with my fingertips.

"Then I guess that's where you'll need to look."

I spin the dial a final time. I don't need to see where it lands. There is no destination. I take a last breath and think of home. Then I press the pin.

"Time travel can't solve all of your problems. That girl who broke your heart in sixth grade? She could do it again. She probably would, too. Don't dwell on your losses and wonder what if: look to the future and wonder what's next."—Journal of Dr. Harold Quickly, 2055

Chapter 32

I thought I was mentally prepared for anything. Aliens. Zombies. Killer robots. I didn't count on what I'm seeing now. One thing is certain, my badass gun that can blast holes in solid walls will do me no good here. I lower it slowly to my side and face my next confounding obstacle; a dozen beautiful women holding pints of beer.

"Benjamin Travers?" The voice cuts through the ambient murmurs and jazz music. Both guests and the female welcome committee part down the center of the room to reveal a man in a tailored gray suit. "Well aren't you the surprise."

I'm almost sure I've never seen the man before, but I suddenly doubt myself. *Do I know him?* As the man takes a step forward, I get a glimpse of the people behind him. Traus Gillian is beside the Zealot from my apartment. Pia Chopra, the Indian woman from the race committee, is at his elbow.

Get in. EMP the planet, get out.

A man with a mustache loses his stuffed shrimp as I plow through him. Two of the women with the beers shriek as the pints tumble from their hands and shatter on the floor. I almost collide with Horacio but veer left through an elderly couple that has the misfortune of being in my path. Arms reach out for the old woman as I bowl her over.

I'm into the hallway now and sprinting. I crash through a pair of double doors and find myself in a lobby I recognize. The fish tank on the wall is bubbling benignly and the receptionist rises from the desk at my sudden appearance. She starts to speak, but I don't give her a chance. I shove through the glass doors into late morning sun and spin around when I reach the sidewalk. The sign on the building hasn't changed. Saint Petersburg Temporal Studies Society.

I run for the street, scanning for a safe jump location. *Get in, EMP the planet, get out.* Three men come rushing out the glass doors after me. I don't know them and I don't want to. I jump onto the hood of the nearest parked car, spinning my chronometer as I go. One of the men is reaching into his jacket. I don't care what he has. He's too late. I press my chronometer hand to the roof of the car and blink.

I've changed locations and arrived on top of the car the previous night. I scan the neighborhood for another safe place to make a jump. The backyards of houses appear to be the most secluded. I'm about to climb off the car when I hear the voice. "Don't run, Ben. We need to talk." My hand is back to my chronometer instantly, but I turn around. The Zealot from my apartment is standing in the middle of the street with his hands raised. The little girl from the video is with him. *Was it Ellen? Elenore?* I crouch low and touch the roof of the car, ready to flee. "I'm not trying to stop you this time," he says.

I study the man, and as he steps farther into the glow of the streetlight, I realize he's wearing my messenger bag and leather jacket. I glance at my chest and double-check that I still have mine. *Why does he have the same bag? Is he trying to copy my style now?*

"We need to help each other, Ben."

"Since when have you ever been interested in helping me? You've only gotten me into messes and harassed me."

"I'll help you right now. You were just thinking of climbing the fence into that backyard." He points to the house across the street. "From there you'll run down the alley to an RV and make another jump, after which you are going to be intercepted and tased because you forgot to get rid of the alien's race bracelet in your pocket. It's there now."

I mentally curse myself and know he's right. *Is this some ploy to get me to take my hand off my chronometer?* I watch him carefully as I pull the bracelet out of my pocket.

The Zealot continues to look me in the eye. "Would I have told you that if I wasn't trying to help?"

"Why are you helping me? What do you want?" I toss the bracelet away.

"We need to help each other. You need to avoid what's coming, and I need a way out of here." He lowers a hand to the satchel.

"Hey, watch it!" My hand goes back to the pin of my chronometer.

He pauses. "You know what's in this bag, Ben, because it's the same thing as what's in yours."

"Says you."

"Inside this bag you have a degravitizer, a dynamo-powered pulse cannon, and a canister-type redundant wave emitter. You also have a pen, a wrapper from a granola bar, and an autographed baseball from Cal Ripken Junior."

"You're a good guesser."

"You don't have to guess what you know. I'm from your future, Ben, and the only chance you have of making it out of this place alive. It just so happens you're my only chance, too. Shall we agree to a truce?"

The child at his side is staring at me.

"What's with the girl?"

"She's with me."

"Why?"

"Her father entrusted her to me. He wanted her to have a chance at this new world order they're creating, so he sent her here in trade for agreeing to dispense their virus."

"What virus?"

"The virus that Declan Ambrose and company came here to celebrate. They're going to vaccinate themselves against it and release it on the rest of the time traveler population."

"Why would you be telling *me* this? Isn't that what your religious order is all about? Wiping out time travelers?"

"Let's just say I've changed my mind. Elenora's father may think this new world will be a safe place for his daughter, but I don't. She may be his daughter, but she also happens to be my niece, and if her mother were alive to see what I've seen of this new world, she wouldn't want Elenora here, either. I'm getting her out. But I need your help."

"Why should I help you? You're the one who forced me into this."

"I think you'll help me for two reasons. One is that I just saved your life. You may not know it, but I have. The second reason you'll help is because it's in your nature. You're the type who does that sort of thing."

"What makes you think you know me?"

"Because I watched you die."

I hesitate, finger ready on the pin of my chronometer, considering my enemy. The girl beside him is wearing a blue shift dress. It's simple and looks almost Amish. It makes me wonder if the Zealots have something against modern clothing. *At least it's not black.*

The little girl is holding onto the back of her uncle's jacket. My jacket. It's obvious she's scared. Whether it's of me or something else, I can't really tell, but the situation is clearly not being faked.

"If I were willing to help you, what would you want?"

The Zealot reaches slowly toward the satchel. He gently lifts the flap and extracts the baseball. "I'm guessing this is an anchor that will get you out of this place, and I'm guessing there are a whole lot of people waiting for you on the other side who might not be happy to see a member of The Order."

"Your guessing streak continues."

"You can tell them not to kill me."

"You want to use my anchor?"

"Ambrose made everyone dispose of their anchors from other times. This is the only one left. We'll agree on a time, and I'll come through right after you, giving you enough time to tell them I'm not a threat."

"What do I get out of this?"

"Like I said, you get to not be dead, and I'll do half your job for you."

"Half of what job?"

The Zealot reaches back into the bag and trades the baseball for the EMP canister. "You plan to use this here, but you have a problem. Since I just came back in time to save you, I violated all of Ambrose's protocols and created a new timestream. Now we have double the targets. Two Ambroses, two crowds of drunk groupies. Two of just about everybody except you. Like I said, you're dead. Luckily we now have two of these as well. I'll rig this emitter to blow in this new timeline just after I depart, which will shut them down and solve your duplicate problem here. But you'll need to go back to the future I just left and do the same thing there."

"Where would I be going?"

"It was chaos after your death. I took Elenora back ten minutes beforehand and made the jump from an observation area above the lab. I can send you back there. You just need to get out before I show up with Elenora the first time.

"This is a confusing plan." I jump down from the top of the car and take a few steps toward him.

"It won't be. Just get back, avoid interrupting me from coming back to save you, and set off that device somewhere effective." He checks a wristwatch. "If we're going to do this we need to get a move on. We've been lingering here longer than you did before, and there's no telling what the other me from here will do. I don't want him to catch you. Have we got a deal?"

I think about the scenario he's just described. Part of me wants to dismiss it, but I can't argue with his logic. If I'm really dead in a parallel future, I don't have much choice. I look at the little girl cowering behind his back and stoop to speak to her. "I'm Ben." She shrinks away.

"This has all been a lot for her."

I straighten up. "Understandable."

The Zealot reaches into the satchel again and hands me an anchor. It's a stapler. There is a slip of paper with it containing jump coordinates. "That's the time I left. You'll have a few minutes after that until I show up with Elenora. Get out of the building fast. I plan to set off this device somewhere high up. You should do the same in your timestream. I'll expect to see you after, and without your friends shooting me."

"If I make it, it's a deal."

"Very good." He waits while I set my chronometer and degravitize the stapler. I set it on the hood of the parked car next to me to get the height right. After I get my settings correct, I hesitate, then look back to him.

"How did I die? The first time."

"You sacrificed yourself to keep Ambrose from using his virus on your friends. Deliberately sent yourself to the Neverwhere. It was stupid, but it was certainly effective. Now we just need to slam the door on them. If the engineers behind your pulse emitter are worth their salt, this will destroy the tech Ambrose brought with him. I'm not exporting their virus for them anymore, so they'll be on their own with no way to disperse it. You'll have your wish."

"I don't even know your name. Is that a Zealot thing?"

"In The Order, we never tell our names to those we find undeserving of knowing them."

"I see."

He holds out his hand. "My name is Lazarus Vane."

I take his offered hand. "Lazarus. Shouldn't you be the one coming back from the dead?"

"Who says I haven't? Good luck, Benjamin Travers."

I feel like I should have more to say to him, but I keep it simple. "Thank you." I double-check my settings, then pause. "Hey. If for some reason this plan of yours doesn't work and I die again, I need you to tell Mym that I love her."

"Who's Mym?"

"I imagine she'll be the one who's the most upset when you tell them I'm dead."

"If you're not there, they're going to kill me. The last words out of my mouth will not be telling some bawling girl that you love her. I'm not a goddamn Hallmark card. If you've got shit to say to people, suck it up and tell them yourself."

I study his dark eyes. "You're still an asshole, you know that?"

Lazarus cracks the first hint of a smile. I press the pin and blink.

It's an ugly office. Durable brown carpet and faux wood paneling is the backdrop for a few sailboat paintings that are dated even for 1996. The biggest feature of the office is a trio of windows that don't look outside but rather down into a laboratory space. I step forward to have a look and find the lab occupied by the same group of dressed up people I ditched earlier. The man who knew my name is standing front and center. He's taken off his jacket and rolled up his sleeves. *That must be*

THE CHRONOTHON

Ambrose.

I'm about to turn for the exit when I see myself. I'm suspended in space a few feet off the floor behind Ambrose. Viznir is there, too, but he isn't moving. When I look closer I see the dark red stain on his chest. *Oh God. Did they kill Viznir? Do they shoot me, too?*

I know I should run. I need to get out and detonate the EMP, but I'm riveted by the scene below me. *How do I die?* I'm not sure if the glass is one way or both, so I shift to the side of the windows and peek around the corner of the frame. I spot Lazarus and Elenora near the wall. She has a glass of green liquid in her hand. Everyone does, actually. Ambrose is handing out the last few from trays borne by attractive serving girls. *What are they up to?* My eyes find my other self again and I'm surprised to see him stuffing vials of something down his pants. *What the hell?*

Someone shouts and Ambrose turns. He's addressing the other me, but I can't make out the words. Pia Chopra is involved now, too, and Traus Gillian is edging his way through the crowd to join Ambrose. The other me kicks over a stainless steel tray and definitely has the attention of the entire room. I watch in fascination as Ambrose takes another step closer. I can't see his face, but I know he's speaking. The other me reaches for his chronometer. He's speaking, too, then suddenly he's gone.

I don't need to hear in order to recognize the shock from the crowd. One woman drops her champagne glass and it shatters on the floor. Ambrose is staring transfixed at the space the other me has vacated. Lazarus and Elenora are already moving for the exit. *I need to go.* I take one last look at the spot where the other me disappeared, and that's when I notice him. Traus Gillian has turned around and is staring right at me. *Shit.* I bolt for the door.

I've never been in the upper story of this building before but I find the stairs immediately. I plummet down them into a hallway that crosses the building laterally. The voices of the crowd are spilling into the hall around the corner. I sprint the other way and crash out a fire exit, triggering some sort of buzzer in the process. A chain link fence surrounds the parking lot about sixty yards from the edge of the building. I make it there faster than any of my high school track times. I'm up and over without pausing to look back. *I need somewhere high up.*

The Temporal Studies building is in a residential neighborhood, so my flight involves dashing through the side yards and alleyways of single story bungalows.

It's three blocks till I reach a main street. I'm winded and sweating when I stop at a corner. I need a ride. St. Petersburg is no Manhattan where taxis are a dime a dozen, but I keep my eyes open for one anyway as I jog south on Ninth Street. There is a droning noise above me, and I look up to spot a single engine airplane descending toward downtown. *Get somewhere high.* I'm shouted at by a pair of rollerbladers in neon who streak past me on the sidewalk. I check for any more potential hazards behind me and spot a taxi. I flag the driver down, elated to see the back seat unoccupied. The driver is a forty-something black man in a tracksuit who has the windows rolled down. I lean into the passenger side. "Hey, can you make it to the municipal airport downtown in fifteen minutes?"

"Albert Whitted Airport?"

"Yeah the one by the college."

"I could make it in ten."

"You're positive? This is important."

He swells a little. "I'm telling you, it's not a problem."

"Okay, your fare is going to be in the parking lot of the airport in fifteen minutes."

The man's eyebrows furrow. "Which lot?"

"Where you go to rent an airplane."

"You'll want the flight school."

"That's the one, then. This part's important. You need to make sure you park in a spot that has nothing around it, okay?"

"This fare is picky about where I park?"

"Just needs a little space around the car, can you do that?"

"Sure I can—"

"Great. See you there." I step into the driver's blind spot while dialing my chronometer and use the back corner of the cab as my anchor. I blink and I'm in the parking lot of the airport with the cab idling in front of me. I dash past the front of the cab and head for the flight school. "Great job, man!"

The cabby shouts in surprise. "Hey, where's the fare? How did you—"

I don't wait for the rest. The bell jingles on the door of the flight school. An advertisement in the window offers an introductory flight lesson for twenty-five dollars. I straighten myself up and walk in slowly. A tall man with a mustache is chatting with a receptionist behind the counter.

"Hello, welcome to Bayside Flyers," the girl says.

The man beside her looks up and smiles. "What can we do for you today?"

I check out the countertop racks of aviation headsets and charts, then scan the board advertising rental rates. "I saw a sign in the window offering intro flight lessons. What does that involve?"

"Yes, we let you go up in one of our planes with an instructor and get a feel for flying. You get to use the controls and see what it's like to be a pilot. See if it's something you might want to learn."

"Very cool. So how high up would we be going?"

"Oh we usually just fly out to the beach and back. It's about a twenty minute flight, so we don't go too high—maybe two or three thousand feet."

"Well that sounds pretty high. Is that higher than anything else around here?"

"Definitely. There are a couple of TV station antennas over in Tampa that might be close, but we'll definitely be the highest thing in the sky today, except other airplanes."

"Okay, fantastic. One other thing I was wondering about. Let's say the plane had, I don't know, some kind of electrical failure while flying, would that make it crash?" I watch his face, but he doesn't seem to find the question odd. I'm happy to be asking in a timestream before 9/11.

"Planes are actually very safe that way. The engine ignition system operates on something called magnetos. My mechanics could probably explain it better to you, but it basically makes it so the engine is completely separate from the electrical system."

"So it can stay flying without any electrical system at all?"

"Absolutely. We have some older aircraft here on the field that were even designed without electrical systems. But our planes are more modern, mostly from 1986 or so. They're all very safe."

"I think you guys answered all my questions. Where do I sign up?"

"Are you looking to go up now?" The girl consults a paper schedule on the counter then looks at the other man. "Dave is flying with maintenance still, and Bill is on a cross country with his student."

"I can take him up myself, I suppose," the man with the mustache replies. "I've got a little time. Set us up in seven five zulu."

The girl snatches a clipboard and keys from a basket and hands them to her boss. "Have a good flight!"

The man steps out from behind the counter, carrying the clipboard and two headsets. He shifts them to one hand and holds the other out to me. "I'm Don."

"Nice to meet you, Don." I glance at the door I came in, then follow Don out a different door to the tarmac. A handful of single engine planes are tied down on concrete pads in the asphalt. Don leads us toward a blue and white Cessna that has grass stains on its landing gear. He begins to discuss the plane's characteristics, and I nod along as he takes samples of the fuel and checks the oil. I keep my eye on the parking lot and one hand in my satchel on the EMP. Don directs me toward the pilot seat and tells me to strap in.

"Have you ever been in a small plane before?"

"I've actually had a fear of heights until recently, but I've been working on getting over it. I was in a hot air balloon before." I leave out the Hindenburg and the trip to the space station, as he might find those a bit tough to swallow.

Due to the tight quarters, I'm obligated to shove my satchel into the back seat. Don follows a checklist and chats amiably with ground control before taxiing toward the runway. "Do you want to try to steer?" He points to the pedals near my feet.

"No, I'm good. Maybe once we get in the air."

Don nods, and after another quick dialogue with the control tower, begins to taxi onto the runway.

I'm looking out the window toward the parking lot when I spot him. Traus Gillian has just entered the gate and is peering in the windows of the flight school. Don gets lined up with the center of the runway and shoves the throttle forward. I glance back at the flight school and find Traus staring at us. *How did he find me?* I watch in shock as he pulls a gun from his jacket. *Holy shit.*

"This makes it go faster, right?" I push on the throttle lever Don was using.

"That's as far as it goes," Don replies.

Traus's gun flashes, and I duck instinctively. I don't know where the bullet went, but we're not hit. We're rolling at a decent rate now and putting the flight school behind us. I catch sight of Traus running past a couple of parked planes to aim again, but Don lifts off and we're airborne. If Traus gets off any more shots, they don't hit us. I try to relax and go back to the task at hand.

Don hasn't noticed my little freak out, or perhaps he has chalked it up to nerves, but as we make a turn north over the pier he gives me his full attention. "You want to take the controls? You just use nice easy motions, make a left turn using the yoke here." He explains the basics of flying to me as I take the controls. I pay close attention when he starts describing the gauges.

"So that's the altimeter? How high are we now?"

"Just climbing through a thousand feet. We'll head up to twenty-five hundred or so on our way out to the beach."

I watch the needle slowly making its way around the gauge and pull back harder on the yoke.

"Whoa, not too much now. You don't want to aim too high or you'll start to lose lift. That can cause what we call a wing stall."

I lower the nose of the airplane and wait for him to finish his lesson on aerodynamics, but he stops midsentence. He puts one hand to his headset and looks back toward the airport. The tower had been speaking to someone else on the radio, but I had tuned out since Don didn't seem to be paying attention either. Now he's heard something to make him listen. From what I can make out on the radio, the air traffic controller is attempting to get a response from another aircraft. He doesn't sound happy.

"What's going on?" I crane my neck to try to see, while still doing my best to keep the plane level.

"Someone took off without a clearance. And they're in one of my planes." Don pivots farther in his seat. "Wow, they aren't even trying to use the pattern. They just cut right past the control tower. If I find out who's pulling that stunt they'll never rent here again. Better not be one of Dave's students . . ."

Don directs his attention back to me. "You're doing really great here. Just keep us aimed west. We'll go out over the gulf and do a couple maneuvers. You'll be able to get the feel for flying." He points toward the gulf shoreline, then turns to look backward again. He seems perfectly happy to leave the controls in my hands, and while my grip may be a bit tense, it's not just the new experience of flying making my heart race. I keep an eye on the altimeter needle, trying to ignore what I suspect about the pilot of the plane behind us. *He won't be able to catch us up here. Two thousand feet ought to be enough.*

As the altimeter needle climbs past eighteen hundred feet, I reach my hand into the back seat for my satchel.

"You need me to grab you something?" Don asks.

"Um, actually, can you take the controls a minute? I'd like to get my camera. Great view up here, you know?"

"Oh. Sure." Don rests a hand on the yoke. "Do you live around here? We can probably get a shot of your house on the way back in."

I fiddle with the latch on my bag, trying to get it open with one hand. "Um. I'm actually not sure where my place is from here." The bag finally opens, and I lift the flap enough to slide my hand in. The smooth metal finish of the canister is easy to locate. I slip it out of the bag but leave it on the seat momentarily while I try to remember how to work the controls. The top of the device looks a lot like the concussion grenade the Admiral set off on the Terra Legatus. A single red light adorns the top next to a safety guarded trigger switch.

I lift the canister into my lap and note the altimeter has passed twenty-three hundred feet. "Do these windows open? Like if I want a clearer shot?"

"Oh, sure. Gets a bit windy, so be careful not to lose your camera."

"Okay, thanks. I attempt to unlatch the window and Don reaches across me to help. The window pops open part way and the gusting wind makes the microphone on my headset crackle.

Don raises his voice to compensate for the extra noise. "What kind of camera is that?" He's looking at my lap. Something thuds into the aircraft and distracts him. "What the hell?" The noise came from the right side of the plane. After a brief survey, he curses and banks the airplane left. "There's a hole in our tank! It's like someone took a shot at us!" I peer past his head and see blue fluid leaking out a hole in the bottom of the wing. Don moves a lever on the floor labeled "Fuel Selector" to the left position.

I press the button on the top of the EMP and the light starts to blink. It increases in speed and lets out an audible tone. "Sorry, Don. I gotta do this." I drop the EMP out the window. It detonates just below the aircraft and all the electronics in the plane immediately blink off. One radio actually emits a puff of smoke. Don is staring at me wide-eyed.

"What did you do!" The headsets no longer amplify his voice, but I can still hear him over the engine noise. He looks at the dashboard and runs a hand over the circuit breaker panel. Almost all of them have popped out. He rips the headset off and starts resetting breakers. His nostrils are flared and he angrily switches knobs on the radios to no effect. I start to point out the smoke issuing from the top of the radio stack, but he slaps my hand. "Don't touch anything!"

I glance out the window and see the other Cessna gaining on us. "Don, we have another issue." I point toward the plane. "He's the one shooting at us." Don stares out the window at the other plane, and we are close enough to make out the hole that Traus has broken in the windshield. As we watch, he pushes his hand out the hole again and takes aim with his handgun. He seems to be taking no heed of the spinning propeller out front, or perhaps our height above him is allowing him to miss it.

Don banks the plane hard right and Traus's shot misses. "Is everybody losing their minds today?" Don shouts over the engine noise. He dives the plane below the level of Traus's Cessna and makes a turn back toward downtown. I get a temporary feeling of weightlessness during the dive, followed by the feeling of being pressed into my seat as he levels back out. "You'd better have a good lawyer, buddy, because I will be suing you for all the damages to my planes."

In the intersections of the city below, people are milling around on foot in the streets. The EMP has shut down traffic lights, and a lot of vehicles are now parked haphazardly where they stalled. I reach into the back seat for my satchel again and pull it into my lap. I find the baseball still inside, and the soft leather feels excellent in my hand. "As much as I would love to stick around for that, my work here is actually done." I use the photo of the baseball to set the coordinates on my chronometer. Don watches me use the degravitizer on the baseball while still trying to fly the plane. It's awkward trying to position the baseball in a way that will let me land on my feet even though I'm leaving from a sitting position, but once the gravitites are all extracted, I orient the ball in my hand in a way that will work.

"Who are you?" Don's expression makes him seem disgusted with my very existence.

I position my finger on my chronometer and grin at him. "I'm a time traveler." I press the pin.

Nothing happens.

I double-check my settings and make sure the slider is set in the right direction. "What the heck?"

Don goes back to concentrating on flying. "I get all the crazies. I swear I need to get out of this business."

The baseball in my hand confounds me. A bump of turbulence almost makes me lose my grip on it. I check my chronometer again. *Son of a bitch. Did the EMP break it? Damn you, Milo. You said it would still work.*

Don is concentrating on the control tower in the distance. "These guys need to be giving me light signals if we're going to get a clearance."

"I doubt their light signal is going to work. Is it plugged in or battery powered?"

"What? Why?"

"They've had a power outage down there."

Don looks out the window and starts to notice the chaos on the ground. "What did you—"

A sharp crack resounds through the aircraft as a bullet busts the back window and penetrates the aluminum floor between our seats. Don banks left and yells. "Stop putting holes in my plane!"

I reach into my satchel and yank out the Zealot gun. I pivot in my seat and try to get a look at the plane behind us. "Can you turn us so I can get a clear shot at him? I might be able to take him out."

Don looks from me to the gun. "What is that thing?"

"It's called a dynamo-powered pulse cannon. It's great for blasting through—" Don snatches the weapon out of my hand and chucks it out the window. "No!" I watch it plummet toward Lake Maggiore. "I was—he's trying to kill us—"

"STOP WRECKING MY PLANES!" Spit flies out of his mouth and he dives the aircraft, forcing me to hold on. "If he wants a fight, he can get in line when we're on the ground. I'll kick his ass right after I'm through beating yours." I keep a tight grip on the armrest until he levels out around eight hundred feet. He's approaching one of the runways at a diagonal and making adjustments to the controls with short, angry movements. "If I wasn't flying this plane right now, you would be in a world of hurt."

I shake my chronometer and start to fiddle with the lock on the band. *I need to get out of here.* I pull Abe's tool kit out of my jacket and get out one of the tiny screwdrivers.

"What are you doing now?" Don eyes me suspiciously.

"Nothing, don't worry about it."

"Is that another bomb?"

"No. It's just a . . . fancy watch." It's not even that at the moment. I get the lock loose using the technique Abe taught me, then slip the chronometer off my wrist. I start working on taking the backplate off.

"I swear to God, if you mess up one more thing on my airplane . . ."

"You just land the plane, Don. Don't worry about me."

"You're the one who should be worried you piece of . . ." He carries on into a description of me full of colorful adjectives. I check his progress toward the runway, then work to unscrew the backing on the chronometer. Luckily, Don's ranting doesn't seem to be affecting his flying skills. He drops us the remaining few hundred feet and lines us up with the runway with an efficiency I've never witnessed before. He puts the plane on the ground right on the runway numbers and is applying the brakes by the very first taxiway exit. I gather my belongings hastily and detach my seatbelt.

"I don't know where you think you're going, we've got business to attend to." Don brakes hard at the taxiway intersection and the airplane slows almost to a stop.

"Sorry I can't stay for that." I pop open the door and throw my legs out.

"Hey, get back here!" Don grabs at the back of my jacket, but my momentum is already pulling me out the door. I manage to avoid the landing gear and roll free of the aircraft before the tail can hit me. I'm back up in seconds, making sure I still have everything I need. I dash across the grass drainage ditch next to the runway and onto a parallel taxiway. Don is revving the engine again and making for the next taxiway exit, so I pause to look at my chronometer. I work the screws the rest of the way off and inspect the inside. The damage is readily apparent. While most of the pieces look fine, including the power supply, one diode just inside the bezel has blackened and come unattached at one end. The connection is burnt.

"Damn it." I fumble for Abe's tool tin and rummage around for more diodes. I find three of them tucked in brown wax paper, but I have no way to install them. I scan my surroundings. People are milling around the flight school pointing toward the aircraft on approach. I recognize the plane with the busted windshield trying to line up for the runway. It's clear that Traus is nowhere near the pilot Don is because he comes in high and is still fifty feet over the threshold where Don touched down. The plane porpoises its way to a landing a couple thousand feet beyond where Don made contact, but despite the difficulties, Traus does manage to put it on the ground. I hold out hope that he'll go off the end of the runway into the bay, but he brakes hard before he hits the seawall and comes to a stop amid a screeching of burning rubber. To my dismay, he guns the engine and starts turning the plane around. I sprint for the buildings near the flight school.

Where can I hide?

There are two big hangars next to the flight school. One is labeled maintenance, and the other has a plate glass door that reads Bayside Avionics. I head for that one since it's closest. While there had been a cluster of people outside the flight school, I find the front room of the avionics shop deserted. I ease through the office toward voices coming from the back shop.

"I'm telling you, I tried that. The power supply is shot, just like the others."

The lights are out in the shop, but daylight is still illuminating the back office where two men are bickering over some electronics. They both have their backs to me. "Did you check the breakers out back?" The bald, taller man flips open the breaker panel on the wall and shuts it again.

The shorter technician rotates on his stool. "I can walk over to the pilot shop and see if they have power. They're usually on a different transformer than us." It's clear the two men haven't left their workshop yet and are still unaware of the scope of the power outage.

"Did Trish over at the school have power?"

"Phone was dead, too, remember?"

"Figures this would happen on a day we were already busy." The bald man turns and notices me in the doorway holding my handful of chronometer parts. "Oh, hey there. Afraid we aren't accepting new work today." He steps over to have a look anyway. "What do you have there?"

"Hi. I actually just have a timepiece I need to solder a diode into. You guys happen to have a soldering iron?"

The shorter man slips off his stool and wanders over. "Got about four of 'em. Won't do you much good though, because the power is out."

"Damn. They're all electric?"

The bald man moves over to his toolbox. "Actually I do have a butane powered kit in here somewhere. If I've got enough butane in it we could try that." He slides open a drawer and starts shifting tools around.

A loud crash out front makes all three of us jump. The short man immediately squeezes past me and heads for the window. The bald man temporarily abandons his search and steps to the doorway, too. I want to encourage him to keep looking, but he seems intent on finding out the cause of the ruckus. The shorter technician shouts from the window. "Somebody just clipped the side of the fuel truck with the wing of one of Don's planes. He's gonna be ticked."

His compatriot joins him by the windows. "Oh, there's Don right there."

I slide over to the toolbox and hesitate momentarily. In the maintenance world, rummaging through a man's tools without permission is something akin to groping his wife, and I'm not used to violating that unwritten rule, but time is of the essence. I push the top drawer shut and pull out the next one. I shift a box of electrical connectors aside and find the soldering kit underneath. A loose roll of solder lies next to it. I toss my other things onto a stool and put my chronometer on the workbench. The butane soldering torch has plenty of fluid in the reservoir, so I flip it on and strike the igniter button. It blazes to life with a sound like a miniature jet engine. One of the men shouts from the window. "Oh shit, he's got a gun!"

There is scrambling for the door and the front room goes quiet. I poke my head around the corner and get a look out the window. To the men's credit, they haven't run away from the danger, but rather toward it. Traus is out of the plane and waving a gun around. Don seems to be facing the majority of his anger and I'm worried for the big man's safety, but I also imagine Traus is trying to save whatever bullets he has left for me. It doesn't keep him from pointing the gun in people's faces. Some of his threats must work because someone I don't recognize points toward the avionics shop. Traus looks my way, and while I doubt he can see me from his position, I curse inwardly and dash forward to lock the office door. I shut the door to the back shop as well. It's a flimsy plywood door and won't hold up long, but I need to buy all the time I can get.

I dart back to the soldering torch and find it plenty hot. I carefully burn away the solder holding the ruined diode and use a pair of needle-nose pliers to yank the part free. The new diode has a line on one end that means it's directional, but the old one is burnt too badly to decipher which side was which. I have a fifty-fifty chance of getting it to work. I try to imagine what getting something backward in a precision chronometer could mean. I hesitate just long enough to remember the diagrams. I plunge my hand into each of the pockets of my jacket and pants till I find

Abe's schematics. The sound of plate glass breaking heralds Traus's entry into the building. *Shit.*

I locate the blueprint, and the new diode slips into place after a little trimming. I drip solder onto the ends as quick as I can, blowing on the droplets to try to cool them into place. It looks messy, but I think it will hold. The shop door shakes as someone slams against it. *I need more time.* The door withstands the first few blows then starts to buckle. I scoop the loose parts from my chronometer into Abe's tool tin and gather up my things, then duck under the workbench next to the door. The door splinters in the center and the top half of Traus's body appears first before he kicks open the remnants of the door. As soon as he steps into the room, I sink the hot soldering iron into his thigh.

The smell of burning flesh and leg hair accompanies Traus's scream. I take a small delight in the sound as I sprint for the side door to the parking lot. I collide with a parked car as soon as I'm out the door, and I ricochet off it toward the maintenance shop. I fly across the parking lot as fast as I can. Traus still has the gun, even if he won't be moving very fast, and I don't intend to give him an opportunity to use it.

The maintenance hangar is cluttered with at least a dozen airplanes. Most are single-engine aircraft, but there is also a turbo prop commuter and a helicopter parked on a rolling wooden helipad. I check the door to the office but find it locked. The mechanics all seem to have left, drawn away by the crash. I dodge around the various protruding wings and tail surfaces, looking for a place to hide. *A couple minutes. That's all I need.* I make my way to the back wall of the hangar and I'm headed toward the big turboprop aircraft when I hear the yell.

"Come on out, Travers!"

Traus's voice echoes around the hangar. I duck behind the nearest airplane. I realize the landing gear tires will give very little cover if Traus decides to bend down to look under the planes. I can see his legs near the front of the hangar. I crouch low and move to the rolling helipad. The helicopter has no doors, but it's facing the back wall away from Traus. I wait till he limps around a plane in the front of the hangar before climbing into the pilot seat of the helicopter. I extract my tool kit as silently as I can and locate the tiny screws for the chronometer backplate. I work furiously as Traus starts his search of the hangar.

"I don't know how you did it, Travers, but you shouldn't have come back." I peek out of the cockpit and spot him peering behind some oil drums in the corner. He has his pistol ready. "Ambrose might have been fooled by that disappearing act of yours, but I knew better. You aren't the type to leave it alone. You had to come back."

I spin the second screw in as fast as I can and rummage around for the third. Abe had been specific about being sure everything was right before using the chronometer. I know the backplate functions as a ground for the user to the device and, it's possible I might not need every screw, but I'm not about to take the risk and accidentally mess this up. I only want to do this once. I get the third screw in but can't find the last one. I lift up my satchel to see if it fell out on the seat and something tumbles out the unlatched top of the bag. The object hits the wooden helipad and bounces off. I watch in dismay as the baseball rolls under the wing of the neighboring aircraft and finally stops over a metal drainage grate.

Son of a bitch. Are you TRYING to get yourself shot?

Traus's taunts have stopped, which I dislike immensely. Now I have no idea where he is. I spot the loose screw on the carpet of the passenger side foot well and snatch it up. I work the screwdriver as fast as I can, and once the backplate is secured, slide the chronometer onto my wrist. It latches into place and I get a wave of relief. I ditch the satchel and climb slowly over to the passenger side door. *All right, Traus. Where are you?*

The bullet rips a hole out the front of my jacket just below my armpit. I fall out of the helicopter and hit the epoxied hanger floor with a thud. The pain in my arm registers first, then the burning at my ribs. *He shot me. He actually shot me.* Traus laughs from the far side of the helicopter. Looking under the helipad from my position on the floor, I can see his feet walking casually around the front of the next aircraft over. I cringe from the burning in my side as I roll over and spy the baseball still well out of reach. *I need more time.*

I dial my chronometer for thirty minutes into the past. I get my hand to the floor just as Traus rounds the helicopter. He raises the gun. I blink.

Of all the jumps I've made, there have been few that have given me anywhere near the relief I now feel staring up at the ceiling of the airplane hangar. Warm blood is wicking into my T-shirt from my ribs and the inside of my bicep, but when I lift my jacket and look at the wounds, I can tell it's far from fatal. I've been fortunate, and the bullet just grazed my side and the inside of my arm on its way through. *Thank God.* My jacket is ruined, but I'm ready to take it off anyway. I live in Florida for God's sake. *I'm almost home.*

There's an Ace of Base song on the maintenance shop radio, *Don't Turn Around,* giving me an instant flashback to my teenage years. In the background is a steady buzzing that I realize is coming from the high intensity overhead lights hanging from the ceiling. The lights are on.

Shit! The lights are on! I scramble to my feet and stagger from the discomfort in my ribs. I try to remember how long ago I set off the EMP.

THE CHRONOTHON

I am not going to fix this chronometer again.

I spin the dial on the chronometer back to the time I left, not sure if I have minutes or even just seconds till the device detonates. I use the hangar wall so I'll arrive behind Traus and press the pin.

He's still aiming the gun at the floor when I arrive. I actually catch a glimpse of my other self disappearing in front of him as I show up. Traus doesn't have any time to react before I tackle him from behind. We both hit the floor and the gun skitters away across the slick epoxy, glancing off a tire and out of reach. Traus's surprise doesn't keep him from reacting quickly. He lashes at me with an elbow that just misses and rolls over to punch me. His fist strikes my shoulder and dislodges me from on top of him. He's spry for his age and moving astonishingly well. *All right, asshole. Let's do this.* I punch him hard in the thigh, right where I jabbed him with the soldering iron. I'm ready to fight dirty now. The chronothon has taught me that much at least. Traus bellows and shoves me away. I bounce off the front cowling of an airplane, denting the aluminum and narrowly missing the propeller as I topple over.

I spring to my feet again, not willing to give him a chance at the gun. Blood is running down my arm and into my palm. It makes a squishing sound as I clench my fist and swing at Traus's face. He blocks the blow and hits me hard in the ribs. It's the opposite side from where he shot me, but it still hurts like hell. I get one jab in with my left, striking his right temple before he lowers his shoulder and barrels into me. We both hit the edge of a low-wing airplane where the wing joins its fuselage, and our momentum carries us up and over. The wing must have been recently waxed because we both slide headfirst toward the floor on the other side without a hint of a stop. We land in a tangle of limbs and I struggle to get up, but Traus kicks my legs out from under me.

I'm winded and aching now, my energy starting to ebb. Traus flails at me and catches the top of my head with one punch and then another. *Come on, show a weakness somewhere.* I defend my head as best I can, but I'm taking a beating. I jam my heel hard into his groin. It pauses his attack long enough for me to crawl away. To my relief, Traus doesn't follow, but when I look back, I see why. He's spotted the gun underneath the airplane. *Shit.* He gets down on one knee to grab it. I try to get to my feet, but my bloody hand slips out from under me. When I start to try again, Traus is looming over me with the gun.

"About time somebody finally kills you, boy. Who would've thought it would be so goddamn hard—" The thud cuts his words short. His eyelids flutter and his eyes roll back in his head as he crumples to the floor.

Behind him, Don is holding a crescent wrench and is flanked by the two men from the avionics shop. He steps over Traus's prone body and picks up the gun. "I told you. STOP WRECKING MY AIRPLANES!"

I slump back to the hangar floor and let my arms fall open. It hurts too badly to laugh, but I laugh anyway.

"When I look at the tangled state of time in our universe, with its near infinite pathways to trod, it is intimidating. It also looks like a whole lot of fun."–Journal of Dr. Harold Quickly, 2210

Chapter 33

I'm happy to find that despite Don's blustering, he's not the type to hit a man while he's down. The sight of my bloody shirt may have evoked a little sympathy as well. While Traus ends up rather roughly handcuffed by means of some industrial strength zip ties, I manage to avoid that fate by explaining that I was trying to stop him. I make vague allusions to a non-specific government agency and hope that they buy my B.S. I suspect they don't, but with the whole world suddenly experiencing the effects of a planet-wide power loss, no one is too quick to call my bluff. The mechanics merely keep an eye on me while Don makes more attempts to phone the police.

The crew of the Bayside Flyers maintenance shop seem like they'd normally be amiable fellows, the kind I'd typically love to hang out with, at least on a day when I hadn't wrecked most of their planes. That's not today. I also have a recollection of Major McClure's scientist touting the recurring nature of his redundant wave technology. I don't know how long it will be till the next pulse makes its way through the atmosphere, and I'm not looking to do any more roadside repairs. Also, more importantly, one more jump is all that stands between me and freedom. *One more jump till I'm back to her.*

One of the mechanics is kind enough to help me retrieve my satchel and even picks up my baseball for me before I retreat to the bathroom under the premise of getting my wounds cleaned up. I do need medical attention but as soon as I get the door closed I'm entering chronometer coordinates from the back of Milo's baseball photo. I doubt Cal Ripken Jr. could ever have imagined how vital his autograph could be to saving the universe. Hopefully someone will enjoy it once I leave it behind. My hand is shaking with anticipation and adrenaline as I get a firm grip on the ball and hold it to the proper height. *So long Epsilon Solo.*

I'm going home.

In hindsight, getting the blood cleaned up and trying a little first-aid might have been smart to do before making the jump, as my gory appearance causes gasps of concern from Mym and Milo when I arrive in the memorabilia shop in Seattle. Major McClure and Kara are there also, as well as a handful of soldiers and a pair of full-size cardboard cutouts of Mark McGwire and Ken Griffy Jr.

Mym is at my side instantly, propping me up as I teeter from the landing. My head is fuzzy from the fight and possibly the blood loss. Major McClure can't contain his curiosity more than a few seconds. "Did it work? Did you set it off?"

I smile and nod while wrapping my arm around Mym. "Hey, you."

"Hey, yourself." She probes my bloodied shirt and finally smiles at me, resting slightly easier once she's seen my wounds aren't serious. "God you're a mess. Sit down."

McClure grabs the stool from in front of a '50s jukebox and shoves it toward me. Milo reaches for the baseball on the stand and I suddenly remember my deal. "WAIT! Don't touch that! There's another one coming through." I back away from the space I arrived in and shoo people out of the way.

McClure's expression hardens. "What are you talking about? Who did you—"

Lazarus arrives with Elenora right in the middle of his question. The soldiers and the major have guns drawn in an instant.

"NO! He's with me." I step in front of the major. "They're cool."

Major McClure doesn't lower his weapon.

"This Zealot is part of Ambrose's organization. We've got him on the surveillance."

I keep my hands up. "He saved my life. Don't shoot him." I turn around and find Lazarus has his hands raised, too. Elenora is clinging to the back of his jacket with her body pressed against him.

I give the group an abbreviated explanation of how the Zealot eliminated the parallel timestream. Thankfully, the major lowers his gun about halfway through my explanation. He finally holsters it when I tell him about the successful use of the EMP in both streams.

He steps forward and extends a meaty hand. "I guess we owe you a thank you, Mr. . . . ."

"Your gratitude isn't necessary," Lazarus replies. "I did what I did because I don't believe what Ambrose had planned will ever be the answer. I only want to get my niece back to her father."

McClure rests his hands on his hips. "Will you tell Zsa to stop this fighting?"

"I'll tell him what I experienced, and I'm sure he will respect that you've allowed his daughter safe passage. I can't speak to his plans beyond that."

Major McClure seems satisfied with that answer. As he straightens up and directs his men outside, I see the hint of a smile on his lips. I don't know if he's pleased that the prophet now owes him a favor or is pleased that there will be more of the war to come. I get the impression he's not ready for a life of peace just yet.

Lazarus gestures toward Mym. "Is this the girl you had the message for?"

"What message?" Mym looks up at me.

I squirm a little. "Nothing."

"What were you going to tell me?"

"I'll tell you later." I squeeze her closer. "We've got lots of time."

As much as Seattle in 1996 seems like an enjoyable city, I only linger with the major and his men long enough to get bandaged up and into some clean clothes. Lazarus has saved me the leather jacket he took from the version of me who died, and as I fold up my own bloodstained jacket, I can't help but think about the other me disappearing into the ether. The image is still lingering once I say goodbye to the major. I promise him a full debriefing in the future once I've had time to recover, but for now I've had enough of his strategies. Kara and Milo actually agree to get coffee with Mym and me before we say our goodbyes. I promise I'll keep in touch, and wish them well in their ongoing surveillance of the Epsilon Solo solitaire. Kara even gives me a hug in an unprecedented display of affection that leaves me grinning like an idiot. I wink at Milo and try to draw his attention to this new softer side of Kara, but he seems oblivious to my matchmaking. Mym has the sense to steer me out of the coffee shop before I can cause any more awkwardness.

Mym still has some of the anchors she used during her trip from the central streams, and we pick up a few more en route. She makes a call to Abraham via the TPT in her dad's Australian lab and gives him the news that I'm alive. It takes us a couple of days worth of traveling to get back to the heart of the central streams and finally to November Prime in 2009. Walking up the steps to my own apartment is a surreal experience. We've chosen to arrive on the same day I left. Everything looks exactly the same. It couldn't feel more different.

I survey the table where Lazarus first surprised me and spy my cell phone on the coffee table still blinking from missed calls. It seems like another lifetime when I set out for the start of the chronothon. Mym appears to recognize my struggle. She slips her fingers through mine and waits for me to process it.

"How do you do it? How do you go back to a normal life after an experience like this? Does it ever feel like you have your life back?" I realize as I'm speaking that Mym has been a time traveler since she was born, so she may not know anything other than the extraordinary. *Does having a life that involves jobs or friends who stay in the same place seem dull to her?*

She steps in front of me and wraps her arms around my waist. "How about we figure it out together?"

I lean down and kiss her and suddenly the problem doesn't seem nearly so important.

A knock on the door interrupts our moment, and when I open it, I'm surprised to find Abraham and Dr. Quickly on my steps.

"There's our chronothon champion!" Dr. Quickly grins. "Congratulations on your success."

"I don't know if you could really call it a successful chronothon," I reply.

Abraham smiles. "According to the chronothon committee you can." He hands me an envelope that has my name printed on the front. I invite them inside and stare at the envelope a moment before tearing into the back. "What's this?"

"Apparently a Mr. Cliff Sutherland had some words with the chronothon committee about their practices. They've launched a major investigation into many of their missing members and are conducting an overhaul of the chronothon guidelines. It turns out they were legally obligated to award the funds even though the race was corrupted and the ending was faked. According to the authenticated data provided by Milo Kalani, you were technically the third racer to complete all the time gates. And since the first two racers, Horacio and Ariella, have been inexplicably reported missing, they've decided to award you with the first-place prize."

I pull the paper check from the envelope and blink a few times at the absurd number of digits in the amount block. "Is this in dollars?"

"They had to fuss a bit to convert it into a 2009 value, but you can deposit that into any account you see fit," Abraham says.

Dr. Quickly claps me on the back and reads the check over my shoulder. "Ah, good. You'll have some funds to do some celebrating, just in case you want to have your victory party on a yacht . . . on your own private island." He cruises past me and pokes his head into my refrigerator. "Or you could buy some food."

"That's actually in my immediate plans," I say. "I've got a date with your daughter I need to keep."

"Annd . . ." Mym grins.

"I was going to talk to you about that. Roller disco—it's just—"

Mym narrows her eyes. "Yes . . ."

"I feel like it's one of those things we should invite a few friends along for. If I'm going to do something that embarrassing, we may as well get everyone there to see it."

"I bet you've got some people in mind."

"A few." I smile. I turn toward Abraham and Dr. Quickly. "How about you guys? You want to experience the glory of the 1970s with Mym and me?"

Abe holds his hands up. "I think I'll go experience the glory of my armchair and a nap while you young people have that one. You be sure to tell me about it after, though."

"A nap? Come on . . . well, actually, I have to give you that one. A nap sounds kind of awesome right now."

"Perhaps you can just dream of disco lights," Dr. Quickly says.

I pause and slip my hands into my pockets, stuffing the check in, too. "I have something I've been meaning to ask you about that. When I was racing, there was another racer who tried to help me with it, but I still have questions."

"Sure, what is it you're dealing with?" Dr. Quickly and Abraham are both attentive.

"During the race, I started to dream the future. I dreamt about things that happened later and I also had dreams of someone trying to contact me." I glance at the leather jacket draped on my couch. "Now I think I know who it was."

Dr. Quickly's brow furrows as he responds. "Are you having contact from someone from the future?"

"I don't think so. I think it's technically my past now, or an alternate future. I think I'm getting messages from the me who died."

Dr. Quickly and Abraham look at each other and Abraham murmurs something I don't catch. Dr. Quickly turns back to me. "What is this other version of you trying to tell you? You said it was a message?"

I recall the last image I had before Diamatra. "He said he wanted me to come find him when this was over. I don't know how to explain it, but I don't think the other me is dead."

The two men stay quiet and I notice Mym studying me as well. I feel like maybe I've said too much and she's going to think I'm a crazy person now for even bringing it up. She doesn't say anything at all. She just moves closer and puts her hand in mine again. That simple gesture makes me feel instantly better.

"You're ranging into territory that I'm afraid I have very little experience with," Dr. Quickly says. "It sounds like you may be right, but if there is a displaced version of you out there who needs to talk to you, that may be a journey you'll have to take on your own."

"But it doesn't mean we won't help," Abraham adds. "I'll do some research. It seems to me I've read a book or two that had something to say on this subject. I've heard rumors of some folks who do all sorts of communication with their minds, even through time. When you get done with your celebration, why don't you come look me up? I'll let you know what I find, and it will give me a chance to show you my workshop. From what Mym tells me, you have some promise as a chronometer repairman."

I shake my head but recognize the opportunity for assistance. "Thank you, but I have a long way to go to earn that title. I'll definitely come by your shop, though. I won't turn down any chance for help with research."

"Good. It's a plan then." Abraham smiles and claps Dr. Quickly on the shoulder. "Let's leave these two some privacy, Harry. I have a feeling they might have a bit of catching up to do themselves, and I doubt they want a couple of old farts like us around for it."

Dr. Quickly gets a hug from Mym, and Abraham does, too. I shake both their hands and see them to the door. Mym and I watch from the porch steps as the duo descends to the driveway and wanders down the street. I can still hear Abe's jovial laughter after they've turned the corner.

Walking through the front doors of The Empire roller rink in Brooklyn could easily be mistaken for entering a time gate. Only in this time, the swirl of multicolored lights is purely electric and is accented with the prismatic reflections of a disco ball. The place is already in full swing when I walk up to the skate rental kiosk. Jonah blazes by the padded wall at full speed and waves to me as he passes. He's being followed slowly around the rink by a man with unkempt white hair who must be Ebenezer. The old man is smiling at his boy and trying hard to keep up. Deanna is skating backwards and calls out a hello when she passes. I even spot Genesis over by the DJ booth sharing music suggestions. Her hair is longer and she looks more content than the last time I saw her. She gives me a wave from across the rink.

I order size thirteen skates and am issued a pair of brown leather rentals. I turn in my sneakers and make my way to the carpeted benches where I find Francesca lacing up her own brown skates.

"Hey Fresca, glad you made it!"

"Ben!" She jumps up and balances on one half-laced skate while she hugs me. "I was wondering when you were going to get here. Late to your own party, huh? I would have thought all your time traveling would have made you more punctual."

THE CHRONOTHON

"Mym and I took a little longer at dinner than we planned."

"She still beat you here. She said hi to me before she went out there," Francesca says. I survey the crowd of skaters and spot Mym rolling past Jonah and tagging him on the head. The boy laughs and starts to chase her. "Things going well with you two?" Francesca is smirking at me.

"Really well."

"You know I'm going to want specifics."

"I know you do." I finish lacing my skates and flex my ankles back and forth in the leather.

"So why did she beat you here?"

"I ran into my friend Bozzle in the parking lot. He decided to make an appearance but thought he might be a bit . . . tall, for this place."

"You mean he thought they wouldn't rent skates to a green, tattooed alien?" Francesca laughs. "Your friend Genesis told me about him. Is he scary looking?"

"No. Not at all. I'm so glad he came to say hi. I had actually been meaning to talk to him about something anyway. He's a really talented artist, and I have a project for him."

"You going to get some alien ink tattooed on your butt?" Francesca smiles.

I stand up and glide toward the wall of the rink. "It won't be on my butt."

I turn around and Francesca's mouth is still open. "Ben—I was joking. Are you serious? You're going to let an alien tattoo you? Why?"

I smile and move toward the opening of the rink. "I've got someone I don't want to lose track of."

"Where are you getting it? Ben, I need to know—"

I glide onto the hardwood and skate away. "I'm not telling!"

I meld into the flow of colorful skaters in bellbottoms and sparkly tops. I spot Mym in the center of the rink, and she starts skating backwards when she sees me. She smiles and motions for me to join her. The music changes to some type of Genesis-inspired remix and the DJ bobs his head in approval. All my past and future plans get wiped from my head with the new beat and I get lost in the rhythm of Mym's hips as they sway to the music. Somewhere out there is a vast universe of time and space just waiting to be discovered, but I've found the only moment I really need. The rest is just details.

ACKNOWLEDGEMENTS

Thank you for reading! The response from readers has been one of the most enjoyable aspects of this process. I could not have persevered without your support. If you enjoyed this book and would like to share the experience, please consider leaving a review on Amazon or Goodreads.

I am deeply grateful:

For all the beta readers who read my early drafts and kept me motivated. Paul Sherman and Amy Bell—two of the people who help make the Time Travel Goodreads group the best spot on the internet. Peter G Pollak, Dwight Young, Leslie Young, and especially my mom, Marilyn Bourdeau, who never flagged in both her support and her search for typos. All of you have made this book so much better.

For Rysa Walker, E.B. Brown, Geoff Jones, Mark Speed and April White for sharing their knowledge of this publishing frontier.

For Patrick Russell at Faces of the Hindenburg, whose amazing blog made researching the disaster so fascinating.

For Emily Young, who has been my editor, writer's group partner, and unfailing friend through this entire process. Thank you for encouraging me to get to the zombies.

For Stephanie Haines, whom I love more than anything, and who is always willing to go on more adventures.

This book is dedicated to all of you.

THE CHRONOTHON GLOSSARY

Academy of Temporal Sciences (ATS):

A branch of the Academy of Sciences specifically devoted to time travel. The Academy of Temporal Sciences operated for a little over a decade around the year 2150 before being shut down by civilian political forces opposed to time travel. Later time travelers began jumping back to the time when it was still open and created new timestreams in which to study, leading to a burst of timestreams around that decade. Subsequent regulations by ASCOTT have made acceptance to the Academy more difficult.

The Academy of Temporal Sciences frequently sponsors chronothon race teams.

Ambrose Cybergenics:

A corporate chronothon sponsor, Ambrose Cybergenics, founded by Dr. Declan Ambrose, specializes in body augmentation, including: synthetic parts, replacement organs, and heightened body performance.

Analog:

Slang term used to describe time travelers who do not use digital Temprovibe technology. Users of chronometers designed by Abraham Manembo are frequently referred to as analogs.

Anchor:

An object fixed in time that does not contain gravitites and cannot time travel. Used to relocate in time while still staying fixed to the earth. If an anchor is moved during the time period the time traveler is absent, the time traveler will reappear at the anchor's new location. Photos or video of the location are frequently used in conjunction with anchors to assure safe arrival.

Anya Morey:

A race of humanoid aliens capable of time travel. They are typically identified by their frequently tattooed, forest-green skin, prominent ridges of horns, and pitch-black eyes.

ASCOTT:

The Allied Scientific Coalition of Time Travelers. The dominant scientific organization in the time travel community. ASCOTT promotes time travel for scientific purposes only and supports strict regulation of non-scientific time travel. This position has been compromised by lack of adequate funding, causing the organization to align with the Chronothon Committee to gain resources to finance expensive time travel expeditions. While ASCOTT grudgingly endorses the Chronothon Committee's entertainment goals, it enforces penalties on racers who stray from the racecourse or create additional timestreams or paradoxes.

Chronometer:

A watch-like device that enables the wearer to travel in time. It was pioneered by Dr. Harold Quickly and designed by Abraham Manembo. The device activates gravitites in a time traveler's body and displaces the user in time while staying grounded to the nearest anchor. A chronometer will ground to an anchor through the shortest available distance, typically the wearer's fingertips.

Chronothon:

An entertainment race for time travelers. Typically containing 8-10 levels, a chronothon requires racers to achieve objectives in order to pass time gates. The race is won when a time traveler passes all time gates after achieving each of their objectives. Winners receive monetary prizes and significant fame.

Chronothon Committee:

A group of scientists and entertainment tycoons who fund and organize chronothons for the entertainment of the time travel community and for significant monetary gain. The organization receives funding from a variety of corporate sponsors and, while the committee disavows association with organized crime, it has been known to benefit from the generosity of a deep-pocketed "family" of investors.

Degravitizer:

A device for removing gravitites from anchors prior to time travel. Since an anchor must stay behind when a time traveler makes a jump, any anchors that have previously time traveled must be purged of gravitites prior to use.

THE CHRONOTHON

Digi-Com:
A corporate chronothon sponsor. Digi-Com is the company founded by Karla Drummond. While it markets everything from vehicles to spacesuits, its most profitable technology is the Temprovibe, a time travel device used almost exclusively by time travelers from the twenty-second century and beyond.

Gravitans:
A naturally occurring form of gravitites. Their existence was hypothesized by Dr. Harold Quickly and later discovered by scientists of the Academy of Temporal Sciences.

Gravitites:
Synthetic particles created by Dr. Harold Quickly that displace matter from the flow of time by creating anchor-based wormholes. The gravitites may be activated through electricity. A high concentration of gravitites in a body or object will "net" the entire mass of the object and transport it (in the same manner a fish net can effectively lift or displace a mass of fish without contacting each individual fish.) The netted mass of the gravitized object is relocated through time via the anchor-based wormhole to arrive at the same relative location in the new time.

Gravitizer:
Machine used to infuse gravitites into an object or person. While infusion of inanimate objects is common, infusion of persons can be highly dangerous and is heavily regulated. Time travelers infused after the turn of the twenty-second century must pass a rigorous training program and complete testing prior to being made time travelers.

The Grid:
Used in conjunction with a trace, the Grid is a global system of tracking time travel that prevents a user from arriving at a location at the same time and place as another time traveler.

The Meta-space:
Augmented reality. The meta-space is digital imagery layered over real world items that is visible through the use of a perceptor or chip that projects the images directly to the brain.

Neverwhere:

A space outside of time. Some time travelers believe that if you travel in time without being properly anchored, you end up in the Neverwhere. The existence of the Neverwhere has not been scientifically proven, but it persists as a belief among members of the time travel community.

Solitaire:

A timestream that cannot be reached by means of conventional timestream navigation. All paths to or from the timestream have been eliminated.

Temprovibe:

A digital version of a chronometer that links to the Grid and can also sync with anchors for special use. Designed by Karla Drummond, the Temprovibe offers safety features to protect a user from common dangers, such as fusing with other time travelers or accidental displacement to the Neverwhere due to improper grounding.

Time Gate:

(Also known as a transverse wormhole gate.) A fixed method of travel to or from a location in time. Time gates are programmed for single uses in given moments, and exits from gates are carefully timed to ensure safety of travelers. Time gates are the primary method of time travel employed in chronothons, but require advanced engineering to set up and are prohibitively expensive for an average time traveler to employ. Funding for time gates primarily comes from chronothon sponsors.

Timestream:

The flow of time in a given reality. The advent of time travel is believed to have created the fractal nature of the universe, wherein multiple timestreams can exist simultaneously. New timestreams can be created by significant changes or alterations to a given reality, though some paradoxical changes have been known to be absorbed or relegated to minor paradox bubbles.

Timestream Navigation:

The act of traveling from one timestream to another. This can be accomplished by using anchors from the destination timestream. If a traveler does not possess an anchor from the desired timestream, he/she must navigate to the point where the timestream split off and fabricate an anchor to travel forward again. The process can be complicated and dangerous, and is best accomplished by experienced travelers.

Trace:

A system of tracking designed by Ambrose Cybergenics to monitor and record time travel activity. The technology automatically logs a time traveler's jumps, and when used in conjunction with Grid technology, safeguards against involuntary fusing with other travelers.

United Machine:

A corporate chronothon sponsor. United Machine manufactures advanced hardware and software components including artificial or "synthetic" intelligence units. United machine is responsible for the genesis of synthetic individuals and also the intelligent systems integrated into space suits, vehicles, and many other components in the twenty-second century and beyond.

Made in the USA
Lexington, KY
11 June 2019